The Complete Dr. Thorndyke

Volume III:
Stories From
Dr. Thorndyke's Casebook
The Puzzle Lock
and
The Magic Casket

The Complete Dr. Thorndyke

Volume III:
Stories From
Dr. Thorndyke's Casebook
The Puzzle Lock
and
The Magic Casket

by

R. Austin Freeman

Edited by
David Marcum

ISBN Hardback 978-1-78705-532-2
ISBN Paperback 978-1-78705-533-9
AUK ePub ISBN 978-1-78705-534-6
AUK PDF ISBN 978-1-78705-535-3

These works are in the Public Domain in Great Britain
Portrait of Dr. Thorndyke by H.M. Brock (1908)

Published in the UK by
MX Publishing
335 Princess Park Manor, Royal Drive,
London, N11 3GX
www.mxpublishing.co.uk

David Marcum can be reached at:
thepapersofsherlockholmes@gmail.com

Cover design by Brian Belanger
www.belangerbooks.com and *www.redbubble.com/people/zhahadun*

CONTENTS

Introductions

Adventures

Dr. Thorndyke's Casebook

The Puzzle Lock

The Magic Casket

(Continued on the next page . . . .)

The Complete Dr. Thorndyke

Volume III:
Stories From
Dr. Thorndyke's Casebook
The Puzzle Lock
and
The Magic Casket

Dr. John Thorndyke

5A King's Bench Walk
in the late 1890's when
Thorndyke would have moved in

5A King's Bench Walk
Photographed by the Editor
during his
Sherlock Holmes Pilgrimage No. 3
(September 8th, 2016)

Meet Dr. Thorndyke
by R. Austin Freeman

My subject is Dr. John Thorndyke, the hero or central character of most of my detective stories. So I'll give you a short account of his real origin – of the way in which he did in fact come into existence.

To discover the origin of John Thorndyke I have to reach back into the past for at least fifty years, to the time when I was a medical student preparing for my final examination. For reasons which I need not go into I gave rather special attention to the legal aspects of medicine and the medical aspects of law. And as I read my text-books, and especially the illustrative cases, I was profoundly impressed by their dramatic quality. Medical jurisprudence deals with the human body in its relation to all kinds of legal problems. Thus its subject matter includes all sorts of crime against the person and all sorts of violent death and bodily injury: Hanging, drowning, poisons and their effects, problems of suicide and homicide, of personal identity and survivorship, and a host of other problems of the highest dramatic possibilities, though not always quite presentable for the purposes of fiction. And the reported cases which were given in illustration were often crime stories of the most thrilling interest. Cases of disputed identity such as the Tichbourne Case, famous poisoning cases such as the Rugeley Case and that of Madeline Smith, cases of mysterious disappearance or the detection of long-forgotten crimes such as that of Eugene Aram. All these, described and analysed with strict scientific accuracy, formed the matter of Medical Jurisprudence which thrilled me as I read and made an indelible impression.

But it produced no immediate results. I had to pass my examinations and get my diploma, and then look out for the means of earning my living. So all this curious lore was put away for the time being in the pigeon-holes of my mind – which Dr. Freud would call the *Unconscious* – not forgotten, but ready to come to the surface when the need for it should arise. And there it reposed for some twenty years, until failing health compelled me to abandon medical practice and take to literature as a profession.

It was then that my old studies recurred to my mind. A fellow doctor, Conan Doyle, had made a brilliant and well-deserved success by the creation of the immortal Sherlock Holmes. Considering that achievement, I asked myself whether it might not be possible to devise a

1

detective story of a slightly different kind – one based on the science of Medical Jurisprudence, in which, by the sacrifice of a certain amount of dramatic effect, one could keep entirely within the facts of real life, with nothing fictitious excepting the persons and the events. I came to the conclusion that it was, and began to turn the idea over in my mind.

But I think that the influence which finally determined the character of my detective stories, and incidentally the character of John Thorndyke, operated when I was working at the Westminster Ophthalmic Hospital. There I used to take the patients into the dark room, examine their eyes with the ophthalmoscope, estimate the errors of refraction, and construct an experimental pair of spectacles to correct those errors. When a perfect correction had been arrived at, the formula for it was embodied in a prescription which was sent to the optician who made the permanent spectacles.

Now when I was writing those prescriptions it was borne in on me that in many cases, especially the more complex, the formula for the spectacles, and consequently the spectacles themselves, furnished an infallible record of personal identity. If, for instance, such a pair of spectacles should have been found in a railway carriage, and the maker of those spectacles could be found, there would be practically conclusive evidence that a particular person had travelled by that train. About that time I drafted out a story based on a pair of spectacles, which was published some years later under the title of *The Mystery of 31 New Inn*, and the construction of that story determined, as I have said, not only the general character of my future work but of the hero around whom the plots were to be woven. But that story remained for some years in cold storage. My first published detective novel was *The Red Thumb-mark*, and in that book we may consider that John Thorndyke was born. And in passing on to describe him I may as well explain how and why he came to be the kind of person that he is.

I may begin by saying that he was not modelled after any real person. He was deliberately created to play a certain part, and the idea that was in my mind was that he should be such a person as would be likely and suitable to occupy such a position in real life. As he was to be a medico-legal expert, he had to be a doctor and a fully trained lawyer. On the physical side I endowed him with every kind of natural advantage. He is exceptionally tall, strong, and athletic because those qualities are useful in his vocation. For the same reason he has acute eyesight and hearing and considerable general manual skill, as every doctor ought to have. In appearance he is handsome and of an imposing presence, with a symmetrical face of the classical type and a Grecian nose. And here I may remark that his distinguished appearance is not merely a concession to my personal taste but is also a protest against the monsters of ugliness whom some detective writers have evolved.

These are quite opposed to natural truth. In real life a first-class man of any kind usually tends to be a good-looking man.

Mentally, Thorndyke is quite normal. He has no gifts of intuition or other supernormal mental qualities. He is just a highly intellectual man of great and varied knowledge with exceptionally acute reasoning powers and endowed with that invaluable asset, a scientific imagination (by a scientific imagination I mean that special faculty which marks the born investigator, the capacity to perceive the essential nature of a problem before the detailed evidence comes into sight). But he arrives at his conclusions by ordinary reasoning, which the reader can follow when he has been supplied with the facts, though the intricacy of the train of reasoning may at times call for an exposition at the end of the investigation.

Thorndyke has no eccentricities or oddities which might detract from the dignity of an eminent professional man, unless one excepts an unnatural liking for Trichinopoly cheroots. In manner he is quiet, reserved and self-contained, and rather markedly secretive, but of a kindly nature, though not sentimental, and addicted to occasional touches of dry humour. That is how Thorndyke appears to me.

As to his age. When he made his first bow to the reading public from the doorway of Number 4 King's Bench Walk he was between thirty-five and forty. As that was thirty years ago, he should now be over sixty-five. But he isn't. If I have to let him *"grow old along with me"* I need not saddle him with the infirmities of age, and I can (in his case) put the brake on the passing years. Probably he is not more than fifty after all!

Now a few words as to how Thorndyke goes to work. His methods are rather different from those of the detectives of the Sherlock Holmes school. They are more technical and more specialized. He is an investigator of crime but he is not a detective. The technique of Scotland Yard would be neither suitable nor possible to him. He is a medico-legal expert, and his methods are those of medico-legal science. In the investigation of a crime there are two entirely different methods of approach. One consists in the careful and laborious examination of a vast mass of small and commonplace detail: Inquiring into the movements of suspected and other persons, interrogating witnesses and checking their statements particularly as to times and places, tracing missing persons, and so forth – the aim being to accumulate a great body of circumstantial evidence which will ultimately disclose the solution of the problem. It is an admirable method, as the success of our police proves, and it is used with brilliant effect by at least one of our contemporary detective writers. But it is essentially a police method.

The other method consists in the search for some fact of high evidential value which can be demonstrated by physical methods and which constitutes conclusive proof of some important point. This method also is used by the police in suitable cases. Finger-prints are examples of this kind of evidence, and another instance is furnished by the Gutteridge murder. Here the microscopical examination of a cartridge-case proved conclusively that the murder had been committed with a particular revolver, a fact which incriminated the owner of that revolver and led to his conviction.

This is Thorndyke's procedure. It consists in the interrogation of things rather than persons, of the ascertainment of physical facts which can be made visible to eyes other than his own. And the facts which he seeks tend to be those which are apparent only to the trained eye of the medical practitioner.

I feel that I ought to say a few words about Thorndyke's two satellites, Jervis and Polton. As to the former, he is just the traditional narrator proper to this type of story. Some of my readers have complained that Dr. Jervis is rather slow in the uptake. But that is precisely his function. He is the expert misunderstander. His job is to observe and record all the facts, and to fail completely to perceive their significance. Thereby he gives the reader all the necessary information, and he affords Thorndyke the opportunity to expound its bearing on the case.

Polton is in a slightly different category. Although he is not drawn from any real person, he is associated in my mind with two actual individuals. One is a Mr. Pollard, who was the laboratory assistant in the hospital museum when I was a student, and who gave me many a valuable tip in matters of technique, and who, I hope, is still to the good. The other was a watch- and clock-maker of the name of Parsons – familiarly known as Uncle Parsons – who had premises in a basement near the Royal Exchange, and who was a man of boundless ingenuity and technical resource. Both of these I regard as collateral relatives, so to speak, of Nathaniel Polton. But his personality is not like either. His crinkly countenance is strictly his own copyright.

To return to Thorndyke, his rather technical methods have, for the purposes of fiction, advantages and disadvantages. The advantage is that his facts are demonstrably true, and often they are intrinsically interesting. The disadvantage is that they are frequently not matters of common knowledge, so that the reader may fail to recognize them or grasp their significance until they are explained. But this is the case with all classes of fiction. There is no type of character or story that can be made sympathetic and acceptable to every kind of reader. The personal equation affects the reading as well as the writing of a story.

R. Austin Freeman
(1862-1943)

5A King's Bench Walk
in the early 1900's when
Thorndyke was in practice

Dr. Thorndyke: In the Footsteps
of Sherlock Holmes
by David Marcum

When Sherlock Holmes began his practice as a "Consulting Detective", his ideas of scientific criminal investigations caused the London police to look upon him as a mere "theorist". He was perceived as an amateur to be tolerated, often with amusement – until, that is, his assistance was required. Then they were more than willing to come knocking upon his door, asking for whatever help that they could receive. And usually this help took the form of brilliant solutions to bizarre and otherwise insoluble problems.

Holmes espoused methods and ideas that were considered ludicrous in the late 1800's. For instance, his frustration knew no bounds when a crime scene was disturbed. Holmes realized that so much could be determined from the physical evidence – footprints, fibers, and spatters. The police were happy to trod into and disturb the evidence as if they were herds of field beasts, with the equivalent level of intelligence.

However, Holmes's methods, and the science behind catching criminals, eventually won out and became so important that it's hard to now imagine the world without them. Many of the exact same techniques and methods that he advocated are now standard practice. From being an amateur with unusual ideas, Holmes is now recognized around the world as The Great Detective. In 2002, Holmes received a posthumous Honorary Fellowship from the British Royal Society of Chemistry, based on the fact that he was beyond his time in using chemistry and chemical sciences as a means of solving crimes.

And before that, in 1985, Scotland Yard introduced *HOLMES* (*Home Office Large Major Enquiry System*), an elaborate computer system designed to process the masses of information collected and evaluated during a criminal investigation, in order to ensure that no vital clues are overlooked. This system, providing total compatibility and consistency between all the police forces of England, Scotland, Wales, and Northern Ireland, as well as the Royal Military Police, has since been upgraded by the improved *HOLMES 2* – and like the first version, there is absolutely no doubt as to who is being honored and memorialized for his work in dragging criminology out of the dark ages.

Many famous Great Detectives followed in Holmes's footsteps – Nero Wolfe and Ellery Queen, Hercule Poirot and Solar Pons – each with their own methods and techniques, but before they began their careers, and while Holmes was still in practice in Baker Street, another London consultant – Dr. John Thorndyke – opened his doors, using the scientific methods developed and perfected by Holmes and taking them to a whole new level of brilliance.

Meet Dr. Thorndyke

Dr. John Evelyn Thorndyke was born on July 4th, 1870. We don't know about where he was raised, or if he has any family. At no point will we be introduced to a more brilliant brother who sometimes *is* the British Government. He was educated at the medical school of St. Margaret's Hospital in London, and while there, he met fellow student Christopher Jervis. They became friends but, after completing school in 1895, they lost touch with one another. Over the next six years, Thorndyke remained at St. Margaret's, taking on various jobs, hanging "about the chemical and physical laboratories, the museum and *post mortem* room," and learning what he could. He obtained his M.D. and his Doctor of Sciences, and then was called to the bar in 1896.

He'd prepared himself with the hope of obtaining a position as a coroner, but he learned of the unexpected retirement of one of St. Margaret's lecturers in medical jurisprudence. He applied for the position and, rather to his own surprise, it was awarded to him. (He would continue to maintain his association with the hospital, going on to become the Medical Registrar, Pathologist, Curator of the Museum, and then Professor of Medical Jurisprudence, all while maintaining his own private consulting practice.)

It was when Thorndyke was named lecturer that he obtained his chambers at 5A King's Bench Walk, in the Inner Temple, that amazing and historic area between Fleet Street and the River. Founded over eight-hundred years ago by the Knights Templar, it is one of the four Inns of Court, (along with the Middle Temple, Lincoln's Inn, and Gray's Inn.) The buildings along King's Bench Walk, and particularly No.'s 4, 5, and 6, have a great deal of historical significance – and not just because Dr. John Thorndyke practiced at 5A for a number of years.

Thorndyke was quite fortunate to obtain a suite of rooms on multiple floors at this location, which leads to speculation about his influence and resources – a question which has no answer. In any case, it was there that he opened his practice and began to wait for clients and cases. He also made the acquaintance of elderly Nathaniel Polton, that man-of-all-work with the crinkly smile who ran the household, as well as Thorndyke's upstairs laboratory.

8

Like Sherlock Holmes during those early years in the 1870's when he had rooms in Montague Street next to the British Museum and spent his vast amounts of free time learning his craft, Thorndyke also found a way to make the empty hours more useful. He had the unique idea of imagining increasingly complex crimes – often a murder or series of them, for instance – and then, when he had planned every single aspect of the crime, he would turn around and work out the solution from the other side. While doing this, he made extensive notes of each of these theoretical exercises, and retained them for their later usefulness when encountering real-life crimes.

His first legal case was *Regina v Gummer* in 1897. Sadly, no further information about this affair is ever revealed to us, but we may be certain that Thorndyke used his considerable skills to bring it to a satisfactory conclusion, adding to his reputation as he did so.

In the meantime, Jervis had a more unfortunate story. As his time at school ended, his funds ran out rather unexpectedly, and after paying his various fees, he was left with earning his living as a medical assistant, or sometimes serving as a *locum tenens*, moving from one low-paying and temporary job to another, with no prospects of improvement.

Jervis is unemployed on the morning of March 22nd, 1901 when he encounters Thorndyke a few doors up from 5A King's Bench Walk. The two friends are happy to see one another, and before long, Jervis is involved in an investigation that will change his life in several ways, as recounted in *The Red Thumb Mark*.

But it should not be assumed that every Thorndyke adventure is narrated by Jervis in a typical Watsonian manner. In fact, the very next book, *The Eye of Osiris*, is instead told from the perspective of one of Thorndyke's students, Dr. Paul Berkeley. It is one of several that provide a look at Thorndyke – and Jervis – from a different perspective. But Jervis returns as narrator in the third novel, *The Mystery of 31 New Inn*, and we see Thorndyke through his eyes for a good many of both the novels and short stories.

Here a word might be mentioned about the Chronology of the Thorndyke stories. For some this is an irrelevant factor, but for others – like me – understanding the correct chronological placement of the stories is very important. Like the volumes that make up the Sherlock Holmes Canon, the Thorndyke stories aren't published in chronological order – a case set in 1907 (such as "Percival Bland's Proxy") might be collected before one that occurs in 1908, ("The Missing Mortgagee"), or it might not. For instance, *The Red Thumb Mark* (1907) is set in March and April 1901. (This chronological placement, by the way, is

9

determined by noticing that a specific date is given three times in the book – in the British fashion of day before month – *9.3.01* – or *March 9th, 1901*. The dates for the events of the rest of the book can be carefully worked out from this fixed point.)

The next book, *The Eye of Osiris* (1911) is primarily set in the summer of 1904 (with Chapter 1, something of a prologue, taking place in late 1902.) Then, the next book to follow, *The Mystery of 31 New Inn* (1912), jumps back to the spring of 1902, about a year after the events of *The Red Thumb Mark*, and before *The Eye of Osiris*. And one of the short stories, "The Man With the Nailed Shoes" occurs in September and October 1901, between the first two books. Clearly, there is a great deal of material for the chronologicist in the Thorndyke Chronicles.

As Jervis becomes a part of Thorndyke's world, following their reacquaintance in March 1901, he meets others in Thorndyke's circle, including policemen such as Superintendent Miller and Inspector Badger, lawyers like Robert Anstey, Marchmont, and Brodribb, and other physicians like Dr. Paul Berkeley and Dr. Humphrey Jardine. He also has more opportunity to learn from his friend as he begins his own studies in order to become a similar specialist in the medico-legal practice – although he'll never be another Thorndyke.

Through Jervis's eyes – as well as others along the way – we build up our knowledge of Dr. Thorndyke. In appearance, he is tall and athletic, just under six feet in height, slender, and weighing around one-hundred-and-eighty pounds. He is exceptionally handsome – and has been called the handsomest detective in literature. He has no vices, except – perhaps – that he enjoys a Trichinopoly cigar upon occasion when he is feeling especially triumphant – although there is one time when the criminal's knowledge of this fact leads to a clever attempt at Thorndyke's murder . . . .

There are several instances where Thorndyke displays a marked resemblance to Sherlock Holmes – and not just in his scientific approach to crime. The two men sometimes say similar things – such as when Holmes says "*It is quite a pretty little problem,*" (in "A Scandal in Bohemia") or ". . . *there are some pretty little problems among them*" (in "The Musgrave Ritual"). Thorndyke mimics this in *Felo de Se?* ("*There, Jervis,*" said he, "*is quite a pretty little problem for you to excogitate*") or "*Ah, there is a very pretty little problem for you to consider*" (in *The Eye of Osiris*).

And who can forget the many instances when Holmes refers to *data*:

- *"It is a capital mistake to theorize before one has data. Insensibly one begins to twist facts to suit theories, instead of theories to suit facts." – "A Scandal in Bohemia"*
- *"I had," said he, "come to an entirely erroneous conclusion which shows, my dear Watson, how dangerous it always is to reason from insufficient data." –* "The Speckled Band"
- *"No data yet," he answered. "It is a capital mistake to theorize before you have all the evidence. It biases the judgment." – A Study in Scarlet*
- *"The temptation to form premature theories upon insufficient data is the bane of our profession." –* The Valley of Fear
- *"Still, it is an error to argue in front of your data." –* "Wisteria Lodge"

Thorndyke's version? "*. . . believe me, it is a capital error to decide beforehand what data are to be sought for.*" – from *The Mystery of 31 New Inn*. There are others.

Then there is Holmes's quote from "The Man With the Twisted Lip":

"You have a grand gift of silence, Watson," said he. "It makes you quite invaluable as a companion."

Here's the Thorndyke equivalent:

"It has just been borne in upon me, Jervis," said he, "that you are the most companionable fellow in the world. You have the heaven-sent gift of silence."

And then there is the time, in "The Anthropologist at Large", that a client – expecting a Holmes-like performance as based on "The Blue Carbuncle" – presents Thorndyke with an object for examination:

"I understand," said he, "that by examining a hat it is possible to deduce from it, not only the bodily characteristics of the wearer, but also his mental and moral qualities, his state of health, his pecuniary position, his past history, and even his domestic relations and the peculiarities of his place of abode. Am I right in this supposition?"
The ghost of a smile flitted across Thorndyke's face as he laid the hat upon the remains of the newspaper. "We must

11

not expect too much," he observed. "Hats, as you know, have a way of changing owners . . . ."

Another area of intersection between Holmes and Thorndyke is the assembly of information. Recall Holmes's *"ponderous commonplace books in which he placed his cuttings"* as mentioned in "The Engineer's Thumb". We find, also in "The Anthropologist at Large", that Thorndyke does the same thing:

> [H]is method of dealing with [the morning newspaper] was characteristic. The paper was laid on the table after breakfast, together with a blue pencil and a pair of office shears. A preliminary glance through the sheets enabled him to mark with the pencil those paragraphs that were to be read, and these were presently cut out and looked through, after which they were either thrown away or set aside to be pasted in an indexed book.

No doubt and examination of Thorndyke's lodgings at 5A King's Bench Walk would reveal – in addition to a series of indexed commonplace books filled with clippings – a number of other items and aspects that would remind one of 221b Baker Street.

Like many locations where the detective's residence is almost a character in and of itself – Sherlock Holmes's London address at 221 Baker Street, and the New York homes of Ellery Queen on West 87th Street and Nero Wolfe's Brownstone on West 35th Street – Thorndyke's rooms at 5A King's Bench Walk are a living and vibrant place – from the entry way, where a heavy door known as "The Oak" leads visitors into a most comfortable wood-paneled sitting room, located on the (British) first floor, one flight up from the ground floor. On the next floor up, Polton has his laboratory and workshop, containing everything that is needed (or what might be manufactured) in order to solve the case.

On the next floor, underneath the attic, are bedrooms belonging to Thorndyke, Jervis, and Polton. Even after Jervis has married – and now you know that he does get married! – he continues to reside a good deal of the time in King's Bench Walk. As he explains in *When Rogues Fall Out* (1932, with the U.S. title of *Dr. Thorndyke's Discovery*):

> Here, perhaps, since my records of Thorndyke's practice have contained so little reference to my own personal affairs, I should say a few words concerning my domestic habits. As the circumstances of our practice often made it

12

desirable for me to stay late at our chambers, I had retained there the bedroom that I had occupied before my marriage; and, as these circumstances could not always be foreseen, I had arranged with my wife the simple rule that the house closed at eleven o'clock. If I was unable to get home by that time, it was to be understood that I was staying at the Temple. It may sound like a rather undomestic arrangement, but it worked quite smoothly, and it was not without its advantages. For the brief absence gave to my homecomings a certain festive quality, and helped to keep alive the romantic element in my married life. It is possible for the most devoted husbands and wives to see too much of one another.

Thorndyke's Other Appearances

Through the years, Thorndyke's reputation continues to grow, as presented through a number of adventures. Surprisingly, in light of the tens of thousands of Post-Canonical Sherlock Holmes that have come to light over the years, as discovered by latter-day Literary Agents taking over Watson's first Literary Agent, Sir Arthur Conan Doyle, stopped literary-agenting, there have been almost no additional Thorndyke cases brought to the public's attention. The few exceptions to this statement are *Goodbye, Dr. Thorndyke* (1972) by Norman Donaldson, and *Dr. Thorndyke's Dilemma* (1974) by John H. Dirckx. Both narratives deal with Thorndyke and Jervis in their latter years, and each is written by an expert in the field of Thorndyke scholarship.

Donaldson also wrote what might be the final scholarly word on the subject, *In Search of Dr. Thorndyke* (1971). In fact, he had intended his pastiche, *Goodbye, Dr. Thorndyke*, to be published as the conclusion to this book, but it ended up appearing separately.

To my knowledge, "The Great Fathomer", as Thorndyke is sometimes known, has rarely appeared in other locations. He is mentioned in the Solar Pons tale "The Adventure of the Proper Comma" by August Derleth, which finds Dr. Parker returning "from Thorndyke & Polton with an analysis of the capsules Mrs. Buxton had carried with her . . . ."

In my own book of authorized Solar Pons stories, *The Papers of Solar Pons* (2017), Thorndyke makes two appearances. "The Adventure of the Additional Heirs" has Pons and Parker visiting King's Bench Walk:

At 5A, we learned that our friend Thorndyke, the *medical juris-practitioner, was out on some investigation or other, but Pons handed the papers,* sans *photograph, into the care of Polton, his crinkly-faced laboratory technician, with a detailed explanation of what he wished to learn. The man nodded and smiled, and without any extraneous chit-chat, shut the door, freeing us to return to Fleet Street. We paused at the edge of the walk to look at the photograph, still in Pons's hand.*

Later Thorndyke sends Pons a detailed report that helps toward the solution of the problem. And in "The Affair of the Distasteful Society", set in July 1921, Pons and Parker attend the first meeting of a group gathered to honor Sherlock Holmes, where the following conversation occurs:

"I see that you invited Thorndyke, and that little Belgian over on Farraway Street," said Rath.
"And Sexton Blake as well," replied Sir Amory.
"Sexton Blake is a fictional character, Sir Amory," said Pons with a smile.

In my story, "The Adventure of the Two Sisters", included in *The New Adventures of Solar Pons*, Dr. Parker writes:

Pons was not the only detective who offered his services to the London populace, although he might have been the most well-known. We were friends with several others, including the former Belgian policeman who lived in Farraway Street, and another rather mysterious fellow in nearby Bottle Street. And of course, Pons went way back with Thorndyke, whose chambers were across town. It wasn't unusual for Pons and the others to regularly confer on investigations, or simply to sit down and share a few drinks and professional anecdotes.

Thorndyke doesn't just appear in some of my Solar Pons adventures. He's also been referenced off-stage in a couple of Sherlock Holmes adventures that I've pulled from Watson's Tin Dispatch Box – and it's more than likely that others will follow. In "The "London Wheel", contained in *The MX Book of New Sherlock Holmes Stories –*

Part IV: 2016 Annual (2016), Holmes, looking through some documents, states:

> *"I believe," said Holmes, "that I have enough amateur legal training that I can get a sense of the implications of the clauses in question in both of these documents." He pulled the folded pages from his pocket. "I thought about sending a message to my* protégé *Thorndyke in King's Bench Walk for his opinion, as he could have been here very quickly, should he be at home at all and not out on his own business. However, I don't believe that will be necessary."*

Perhaps it is a point of interest that Thorndyke is referred to Holmes's protégé. Possibly more information will be forthcoming, such as that which is hinted in my story, "The Coombs Contrivance" (in *The Irregular Adventures of Sherlock Holmes!*). Set in 1889, when Thorndyke was nineteen years old, Holmes and Watson are discussing a precocious Baker Street Irregular:

> *[Holmes] pinched the bridge of his nose. "Do you trust Levi's judgment, Watson?"*
> *I considered. "For an eight-year-old, he's remarkably perceptive – as much as any of the other Irregulars who have assisted you. The Wiggins family, or the Peakes, or Thorndyke, before he went away to university."*

So was Thorndyke, perhaps, a gifted Irregular who learned from The Master, and then went on to create his own successful practice, taking what he learned to a next very successful level? Possibly. In my forthcoming story "The Inner Temple Intruder", to be found in a volume of Great Detective cross-overs, such an origin story is posited. As Robert Downey, Jr. succinctly stated when playing Holmes in 2009's *Sherlock Holmes*: "Food for thought!"

Thorndyke is also mentioned in Bob Byrne's Holmes story, "The Adventure of the Parson's Son" (*The MX Book of New Sherlock Holmes Stories – Part III: 1896-1929*), wherein Holmes, examining a piece of evidence, cries:

> *"Ha! I believe we have discredited the coat entirely. Though I wish I could get Thorndyke to examine it. Would that we were back in London."*

And it isn't just Thorndyke who has appeared elsewhere. His lawyer friend Marchmont has assisted Holmes and Watson in a small way a couple of my own "The Coombs Contrivance" and the forthcoming adventure *Sherlock Holmes and The Eye of Heka.*

Although I have encouraged these Thorndyke cameos in my own stories or in Holmes and Pons books that I edit, his appearances elsewhere are much more fleeting. In the 2015 BBC radio series *The Rivals*, Inspector Lestrade, Holmes's most frequent associate at Scotland Yard, is placed into the events of the Thorndyke short story "The Moabite Cipher". And Thorndyke has only had a handful of other media appearances. In 1964, the BBC produced seven episodes (now lost) of *Thorndyke*, starring Peter Copley. The episodes were:

- "The Case of Oscar Brodski'
- "The Old Lag"
- "A Case of Premeditation"
- "The Mysterious Visitor"
- "The Case of Phyllis Annesley" – Adapted from "Phyllis Annesley's Peril"
- "Percival Bland's Brother" – Adapted from "Percival Bland's Proxy"
- "The Puzzle Lock"

From 1971 to 1973, Thames TV aired *The Rivals of Sherlock Holmes*, and two stories were adapted: "A Message from the Deep Sea" starring John Neville (who had also played Holmes in 1965's *A Study in Terror*), and "The Moabite Cipher" starring Barrie Ingram. Except for a 1963 BBC Radio adaption of *Mr. Pottermack's Oversight*, and a few on-air readings by a single performer, there have been no other Thorndyke adaptations – which is a terrible shame, as the stories certainly lend themselves to visual and audible interpretations. Perhaps a new generation will discover Thorndyke, Jervis, and the rest, and they will find popularity once again, as they did more than a century ago.

Copley, Neville, and Ingram as Thorndyke

A Few (Hundred) Words About R. Austin Freeman
Thorndyke's Chronicler

Richard Austin Freeman was born on April 11, 1862 in the Soho district of London. He was the son of a skilled tailor and the youngest of five children. As he grew, it was expected that he would become a tailor as well, but instead he had an interest in natural history and medicine, and so he obtained employment in a pharmacist's shop. While there, he qualified as an apothecary and could have gone on to manage the shop, but instead he began to study medicine at Middlesex Hospital.

Austin Freeman qualified as a physician in 1887, and in that same year he married. Faced with the twin facts of his new marital responsibilities and his very limited resources as a young doctor, he made the unusual decision to join the Colonial Service, spending the next seven years in Africa as an Assistant Colonial Surgeon. This continued until the early 1890's, when he contracted Blackwater Fever, an illness that eventually forced him to leave the service and return permanently to England.

For several years, he served as a *locum tenens* for various physicians, a bleak time in his life as he moved from job to job, his income low, and his health never quite recovered. (These experiences were reflected in the narratives of Doctors Jervis and Berkeley.) However, he supplemented his meager income and exercised his creativity during these years by beginning to write. His early publications included *Travels and Live in Ashanti and Jaman* (1898), recounting some of his African sojourns.

In 1900, Freeman obtained work as an assistant to Dr. John James Pitcairn (1860-1936) at Holloway Prison. Although he wasn't there for very long, the association between the two men was enough to turn Freeman's attention toward writing mysteries. Over the next few years, they co-wrote several under the pseudonym *Clifford Ashdown*, including *The Adventures of Romney Pringle* (1902), *The Further Adventures of Romney Pringle* (1903), *From a Surgeon's Diary* (1904-1905), and *The Queen's Treasure* (written around 1905-1906, and published posthumously in 1975.) The specifics of the two men's writing arrangement are unknown to the present day, although much research was carried out by Freeman scholar Percival Mason ("P.M.") Stone, who was actually able to confirm Pitcairn's involvement and influence. Following this association, which apparently helped to train Freeman to be a better writer and to focus on a recurring character, his luck changed,

17

and he was able, within just a few years, to abandon the practice of medicine, which had never been successful, and become a professional author.

In approximately 1904, Freeman began developing a mystery novella based on a short job that he had held at the Western Ophthalmic Hospital. This effort, "31 New Inn", was published in 1905, and it is the true first Dr. Thorndyke story. In it, we meet narrator Dr. Christopher Jervis, working as a *locum tenens*, moving from practice to practice in the same bleak existence that Freeman had experienced. Jervis becomes involved with a patient that may or may not be in danger. Unsure what to do, he recalls his former classmate, the brilliant Dr. John Thorndyke.

Curiously, this novella, (included in Volume II of this newly reissued collection *The Complete Dr. Thorndyke*), has numerous references to the events of the first Thorndyke novel, *The Red Thumb Mark*, which would not be published until 1907. Much of Freeman's life is obscure and unknown, including his writing processes and milestones, but clearly, with so much already clearly defined in this novella about Thorndyke and Jervis, he had firmly established not only fixed aspects of their histories, but the plot of *The Red Thumb Mark* as well, several years before the book's publication. One wonders why he chose to first publish "31 New Inn", since it occurs chronologically a whole year *after* the events of *The Red Thumb Mark*.

Interestingly – at least to a chronologicist such as myself – the original novella of "31 New Inn" is specifically set in April 1900, as indicated internally. However, when it was later revised to become the third Thorndyke novel, *The Mystery of 31 New Inn*, (1912, and included in Volume I of *The Complete Dr. Thorndyke*), the narrative's date is changed to 1902 – which fits, since the events definitely occur after *The Red Thumb Mark*, which takes place in March and April 1901.

Like Rex Stout's Nero Wolfe, who seemed to have sprung fully formed from his creator's brow, Thorndyke and his world are well-defined and immediately real. Although certain characters are added to the circle through the years, the basic layout – with Thorndyke, Jervis, and Polton (the man-of-all-work crinkly-smiled assistant) are always at 5A, ready to spring into action when Jervis – or one of the other varied narrators who show up throughout the series – arrive with a curious problem.

Freeman had found his voice with the Thorndyke books and short stories, and he was able to make use of his lifelong interest in medicine and natural science – often conducting extensive experiments to work out exactly how the solutions in his stories could be discovered. And in Thorndyke's early days, Freeman was able to turn the literary form inside out with the creation of the "Inverted Mystery Story", wherein the criminal is known from the beginning – the motive is explained, the planning and execution of the crime are observed, and the miscreant is left to believe that all is well and that he'll never be caught. And then, in the second part of the story, Thorndyke enters to inexorably follow the trail that is completely invisible to everyone else, scraping away, layer by layer and point by point, until the truth is inevitably revealed.

As Freeman explained:

> *Some years ago I devised, as an experiment, an inverted detective story in two parts. The first part was a minute and detailed description of a crime, setting forth the antecedents, motives, and all attendant circumstances. The reader had seen the crime committed, knew all about the criminal, and was in possession of all the facts. It would have seemed that there was nothing left to tell. But I calculated that the reader would be so occupied with the crime that he would overlook the evidence. And so it turned out. The second part, which described the investigation of the crime, had to most readers the effect of new matter.*

This format went on to be used by a great many authors through the years. For example several of the Lord Peter Wimsey narratives come close to being this type of story, and television's *Columbo* used this type of story-telling as its basis.

While these volumes are an attempt to reintroduce the modern reader to Thorndyke, and are a celebration of him and his world, it must be discussed at some point that Freeman held views that are unacceptable. Unlike Sir Arthur Conan Doyle, who spent his last decades championing spiritualism but never allowed it to creep into the Sherlock Holmes stories, Freeman sometimes did let his own prejudices make their way into the Thorndyke tales. In his book *Social Decay and Regeneration* (1921), he expressed his rather nationalistic view that England had become an "homogenized, restless, unionized working class". Worse, he inexcusably and detestably supported the eugenics movement, arguing that people with "undesirable" traits should not be allowed to reproduce by means such as "segregation, marriage restriction, and sterilization". He referred to immigrants as "Sub-Man", and argued that society needed to be protected from "degenerates of the destructive type."

Some have attempted to excuse his beliefs as being a product of his times. For instance, it has been written that he had a distrust of Jews because of the competition that his father, a tailor, had faced when Freeman was a boy. Later, he served in the Colonial Service in Africa during some of the worst years in terms of treatment of natives by the British, and as an older man, he existed in the Great Britain between the two wars when great upheavals disrupted much of what he had known and expected.

Sadly, there are occasional racial stereotypes and references in the Thorndyke books. As I explain in the *Editor's Caveat*, some of these stereotypes had to be unfortunately maintained within the story in order to accurately reflect the plot and the characters of those times. However, there are some words or phrases that were used in the original stories – vile racial epithets that have no business being repeated or perpetuated anywhere – that I have cheerfully and happily removed. (There weren't many of them, but any are too many.)

These books are intended to bring Dr. Thorndyke and his adventures to a new generation – and not to be an untouchable and sacred literary artifact, with every nasty stain preserved and archived for the historical record. As I warn in the *Caveat*, if readers find that they want to experience the original versions as they were first written, with those hateful words included, then they would be advised to go and seek out the original books, because you won't find that filth here. These versions celebrate Dr. Thorndyke and Dr. Jervis – who do not use the awful stereotyped language, I'm glad to say! – and as such, I felt no need whatsoever to include and perpetuate the objectionable and offensive material

From Thorndyke's creation until 1914, Freeman wrote four novels and two volumes of short stories. Then, with the commencement of the First World War, he entered military service. In February 1915, at the age of fifty-two, he joined the Royal Army Medical Corps. Due to his health, which had never entirely recovered from his time in Africa, he spent the duration of the war involved with various aspects of the ambulance corps, having been promoted very early to the rank of Captain. He wrote nothing about Thorndyke during this period, but he did publish one book concerning the adventures of a scoundrel, *The Exploits of Danby Croker* (1916).

Following the war, he resumed his previous life, writing approximately one Thorndyke novel per year, as well as three more volumes of Thorndyke short stories and a number of other unrelated items, until his death on September 28th, 1943 – likely related to Parkinson's Disease, which had plagued him in later years.

Upon learning the news, *Chicago Tribune* columnist Vincent Starrett wrote:

> *When all the bright young things have performed their appointed task of flatting the complexes of neurotic semi-literates, and have gone their way to oblivion, the best of the Thorndyke stories will live on – minor classics on the shelf that holds the good books the world.*

Raymond Chandler wrote in his famous essay, which initially appeared in a couple of magazines and then was published in the book of the same name, *The Simple Art of Murder* (1950):

> *This man Austin Freeman is a wonderful performer. He has no equal in his genre, and he is also a much better writer than you might think, if you were superficially inclined, because in spite of the immense leisure of his writing, he accomplishes an even suspense which is quite unexpected.. . There is even a gaslight charm about his Victorian love affairs, and those wonderful walks across London.*

In the introduction to *Great Stories of Detection, Mystery, and Horror* (1928), Dorothy L. Sayers, Chronicler of Lord Peter Wimsey, stated:

> *Thorndyke will cheerfully show you all the facts. You will be none the wiser . . . .*

Discovering Dr. Thorndyke

I first encountered Dr. Thorndyke in a rather backwards way – in passing only – and it took several decades to correct that mistake. In approximately 1980, my dad gave me Otto Penzler's *The Private Lives of Private Eyes, Spies, Crime Fighters, and Other Good Guys* (1977). This wonderful oversized book has biographies of twenty-five well-known heroes, along with lists of the original books featuring each one.

My dad bought it for me because it had a chapter about Sherlock Holmes. There were a few others in there that I recognized or had already read about– Ellery Queen and Perry Mason – and soon I would become fanatical about a few more – Nero Wolfe and Hercule Poirot.

Over the next few years I would also find the chapters on James Bond and Lew Archer indispensable, and later than that I would come to appreciate the entries about Philip Marlowe, Sam Spade, Miss Marple, Philo Vance, and Lord Peter Wimsey. But there were a few that, to this day, I've never bothered to read – such as Modesty Blaise or Mr. Moto – and a few others that I skimmed but otherwise ignored. And one of these was the biography of Dr. Thorndyke.

That fact was easily understandable, as throughout the entire time that I was growing up in eastern Tennessee – and in the years since as well – I've never come across a Thorndyke book for sale here in the wild, either in a new bookstore or in a used one. If I'd found one, I might have bought and read it, liked it, and then sought out others. Instead, I was bound to discover Thorndyke by way of Sherlock Holmes.

I've been collecting traditional Sherlock Holmes pastiches since the same time that I discovered the Sherlockian Canon, when I was ten years old in 1975. Since that time, I've collected, read, and chronologicized literally thousands of them. It never gets old, and I'm constantly looking for more – and that means checking Amazon to see what new releases are on the horizon.

In 2012, someone – and I've never determined who – began releasing a variety of Holmes stories for Kindle under the author name *Dr. John H. Watson.* This wasn't too unusual – there have been a number of pastiches that officially list Watson as the author, rather than putting the editor of Watson's papers first. Of course, after determining that these latest entries weren't going to be available as real books, I bought the e-versions, and then printed them on real paper. (I cannot stand e-books – ephemeral electronic blips that you lease instead of buy. I'll only buy those titles if they aren't going to be released as legitimate books – and in this case, it's a good thing that I did, as each of these Kindle stories that I found and paid for were soon withdrawn.)

As I read these latest "Holmes" stories, I noticed that each had a definite style that captured the writing from the late 1800's or early 1900's. (No matter how modern pasticheurs try to achieve that, they never quite pull it off.) But in one of the first two or three titles that I read, I caught a couple of mistakes. In one story, Holmes and Watson leave 221 Baker Street and are immediately in the area around The Temple and Fleet Street, rather than in Marylebone, where Baker Street is properly located. On another occasion, the story's policeman – who had been identified up to that point as Inspector Lestrade – was inexplicably named *Superintendent Miller* – but only in one instance. And in another place in one of the stories, Holmes's address was stated to be *5A King's Bench Walk.*

It was then that some vague memory triggered in my head, and I realized why these stories had captured the style of the late Victorian and early Edwardian eras: *It was because they had actually been written then.* I recalled – from reading Otto Penzler's book of biographies so long ago - that 5A King's Bench Walk belonged to Dr. Thorndyke, and not Sherlock Holmes. Someone was taking the original Thorndyke stories, which I had never before read, and simply changing names: Dr. Thorndyke, Dr. Jervis, and Superintendent Miller became Sherlock Holmes, Dr. Watson, and Inspector Lestrade, respectively.

Between 2012 and 2014, the anonymous author continued to load new Kindle editions on Amazon of Thorndyke-converted to-Holmes stories, and I continued to buy them. As soon as I had one, I would read it, and then try to figure out the original Thorndyke story from which it was taken. When I'd done so, I'd post a review, identifying what this editor was doing, from where he or she was taking the story, and urging that person, whoever it was, give credit to R. Austin Freeman instead of listing the author as Dr. John H. Watson.

Soon after each of my reviews would appear, the story would be withdrawn. I don't know if it was because the editor had made enough money from the initial sales, or if my reviews alerted him or her that they're game had been uncovered. In any case, I still have the printed copies of each of these converted stories – possibly the only copies that are still in existence.

For the record, over that two year period, this editor produced sixteen converted tales – four of the original Thorndyke novels, and twelve short stories. One of the original short stories, "The Mandarin's Pearl", was converted twice, with slight variations – initially published as "The Dragon Pearl", withdrawn, and later revised and reloaded as "The Oriental Pearl":

- "The Bloodied Thumbprint" – Originally the first Thorndyke novel, *The Red Thumb Mark*;
- "The Eye of Ra" – Originally the second Thorndyke novel, *The Eye of Osiris*;
- "The Cat's Eye Mystery" – Originally the sixth Thorndyke novel, *The Cat's Eye*;
- "The Julius Dalton Mystery" – Originally the ninth Thorndyke novel, *The D'Arblay Mystery*;
- "The Green Jacket Mystery" – Originally "The Green Check Jacket";
- "Mr. Crofton's Disappearance" – Originally "The Mysterious Visitor";

- "The Coded Lock" – Originally "The Puzzle Lock";
- "The Duplicated Letter" – Originally "The Stalking Horse";
- "The Bullion Robbery" – Originally "The Stolen Ingots";
- "The Talking Corpse" – Originally "The Contents of a Mare's Nest";
- "The Blue Diamond Mystery" – Originally "The Fisher of Men";
- "The Dragon Pearl" – Originally "The Mandarin's Pearl". (This story was also reworked and published again as a Holmes story under the title "The Oriental Pearl");
- "The Ingenious Murder" – Originally "The Aluminium Dagger";
- "The Bloodhound Superstition" – Originally "The Singing Bone"; *and*
- "The Magic Box" – Originally "The Magic Casket".

For quite a while, I was happy to have these as Holmes stories, and I even considered converting the rest of the Thorndyke adventures into additions to the extended Holmes Canon as well. (For at that time I cared nothing for Dr. Thorndyke.) It was partly with these converted stories in mind that I was motivated to go ahead and publish *Sherlock Holmes in Montague Street* (2014, 2016), which did the same thing to the Martin Hewitt stories, making them early adventures of Holmes before he met Watson and moved to Baker Street. I had long before decided to my own satisfaction that Martin Hewitt *was* a young Sherlock Holmes, with his identity changed through the preparations of a different literary agent than Sir Arthur Conan Doyle.

The taking of old public-domain stories featuring other detectives as the main protagonists and switching them so that Holmes is the main character has also been done by Alan Lance Andersen for his collection *The Affairs of Sherlock Holmes* (2015, 2016), wherein various non-series Sax Rohmer stories from nearly a hundred years ago were reworked as Holmes tales. Other non-Holmes authors have sometimes done the same thing. Raymond Chandler revised some of his early short stories so that the original characters' names were changed to Philip Marlowe. Ross MacDonald – (Kenneth Millar) also rewrote his old stories as well, making them into Lew Archer cases instead. More recently, the British ITV series *Marple* has taken non-Miss Marple Agatha Christie stories and converted them into episodes featuring that character.

So I had no problems with this type of change – and still don't. In fact, in my foreword to *Sherlock Holmes of Montague Street*, I wrote that I would rather have these converted Thorndyke stories as Holmes adventures, because I would rather read about Holmes than Thorndyke. But gradually my mind began to change, and I became more curious about Thorndyke, as presented in the proper fashion.

In 2013, I was able to go to London, as well as other places in England and Scotland, on the first (of three so far) Holmes Pilgrimages. For the most part, if a location wasn't related to Holmes, I didn't visit it. There were a few exceptions – I did intentionally visit Solar Pons's house at 7B Praed Street, Hercule Poirot's two residences, James Bond's flat in Chelsea – but everything else was pretty much pure Holmes.

One day, during my Holmesian rambles, I was making my way east down Fleet Street, and I visited both of the possible locations of "Pope's Court" (as featured in "The Red-Headed League"), Poppin's Court and Mitre Court. (The latter is also one of the locations where Denis Nayland Smith and Dr. Petrie had quarters in some of the Fu Manchu books.) I decided that Mitre Court was certainly the original of "Pope's Court", and I passed through it to find myself unexpectedly in The Temple.

That's the amazing thing about a Holmes Pilgrimage to London – one travels to a site and finds two more very close by. I had planned to visit The Temple, but hadn't realized that I was so close. And now here I was – and more interesting was the fact that I was walking along King's Bench Walk, which runs downhill from the Miter Court passage. I recalled that Thorndyke had lived at 5A, so I made my way there – but without too much awe on that day, because I hadn't actually read any Thorndyke adventures yet – just some converted Holmes stories.

After I returned home, the thought of that side-trip to Thorndyke's front door stuck in my mind, and I sought out and read the first novel in the series, *The Red Thumb Mark*. I was so impressed that I kept going, and discovered a wonderful series of books and stories – fascinating characters and mysteries, and very evocative descriptions of both the London and the countryside of those times.

When I returned on my second Holmes Pilgrimage in 2015, I took the second Thorndyke book with me, reading it while there – while also reading Holmes stories too, of course! This one, *The Eye of Osiris*, has a great deal of London atmosphere, and I spent part of one late afternoon tracking down locations in this book – or what's now left of them – in the area around Fetter Lane to the north of Thorndyke's home in The Temple. It was truly unforgettable.

And of course I made an intentional stop at King's Bench Walk on that 2015 trip, and again on Holmes Pilgrimage No. 3 in 2016. By that point I was a Thorndyke fan, and I took the trouble to write to the current occupiers of 5A before I traveled to see if I could step inside and perhaps spend a moment in Thorndyke's old quarters. Sadly, they did not respond – either because it was simply beneath them to do so, or possibly because they get too many people like me who want to make a literary pilgrimage to what is a functioning and thriving business location.

While making photographs at Thorndyke's old doorway, I had several chances to go inside when someone else would enter or leave – My ever-present deerstalker and I could have simply been bold enough to slip in and then talk my way onward. It worked at other places on my Holmes Pilgrimages – the laboratory at Barts where Holmes and Watson met, for instance, and the site of the (former?) Diogenes Club at No. 78 Pall Mall, where they acted just oddly enough to make me think that the club is still there. But for some reason, barging into Thorndyke's old chambers without proper permission didn't feel quite right. But if or when I make Holmes Pilgrimage No. 4, I'll definitely make an even greater effort to see the doctor's former rooms.

The Editor and his deerstalker at 5A King's Bench Walk
September 2016

With many thanks . . . .

These last few years have been an amazing ride, and I've been able to play in the Sherlockian sandbox more than I'd ever imagined. (And subsequently, the Solar Pons sandbox, and now Thorndyke, too! Along the way, I've been able to meet some incredible people, both in person and in the modern electronic way, and also I've been able to read several hundred new Holmes adventures, as well as to be able to share them with others.

Still, what is most important is my amazingly wonderful wife (of over thirty years!) Rebecca, and our truly awesome son and my friend, Dan. I love you both, and you are everything to me! I am the luckiest guy in the world.

I have all the gratitude in the world for everyone that I've encountered along the way – It's an undeniable fact that Sherlock Holmes authors are the *best* people! I'd like to thank those who offer support, encouragement, and friendship, sometimes patiently waiting on me to reply as my time is directed in many other directions. Many many thanks to (in alphabetical order): Brian Belanger, Derrick Belanger, Bob Byrne, Roger Johnson, Mark Mower, Denis Smith, Tom Turley, Dan Victor, and Marcia Wilson.

In particular, I'd also like to especially thank Steve Emecz, who is always supportive of every idea that I pitch. It's been my particular good fortune that he crossed my path – it changed my life in a way that would have never happened otherwise, and I'm grateful for every opportunity!

I hope that these books will provide pleasure to those discovering Dr. Thorndyke for the first time, and to others who have known him for a long time. As always, I approach these matters from a Sherlockian perspective, so of course these stories, to me, are a peripheral extension of Holmes's world, and as such they are just more tiny threads woven into the ongoing Great Holmes Tapestry. However, they are wonderful on their own, and however one reads them, I wish great joy upon the journey.

David Marcum
(Revised October 2019)

Questions, comments, and story submissions
may be addressed to David Marcum at
thepapersofsherlockholmes@gmail.com

5A King's Bench Walk
in the late 1890's when
Thorndyke was in residence

Editor's *Caveat*

These stories have been prepared using modern text-converting software, and as such, occasional deviations in punctuation have occurred. Those who absolutely must have the original version, down to each jot and dash, should understand that this version was created in order to present Dr. Thorndyke's adventures to a modern audience, and not to preserve an absolute pristine model for the historical archives.

Similarly, these stories were written in a time when racial prejudice and stereotypes were much more common than today. While some of these stereotypes must be unfortunately maintained within the story in order to accurately reflect the plot and the characters of those times, there are some words that were used in the original stories – vile racial epithets that have no business being repeated or perpetuated anywhere – that I have cheerfully removed. (There weren't many of them, but *any* are *too many*.)

If readers find that they want to experience the original versions as they were first written, with those hateful and ignorant words included, then they would be advised to seek out the original books. These versions celebrate Dr. Thorndyke and Dr. Jervis – who do *not* use the awful stereotyped language, I'm glad to say! – and as such, I felt no need whatsoever to include objectionable and offensive material simply for the sake of honoring or archiving the historical record.

David Marcum
Editor

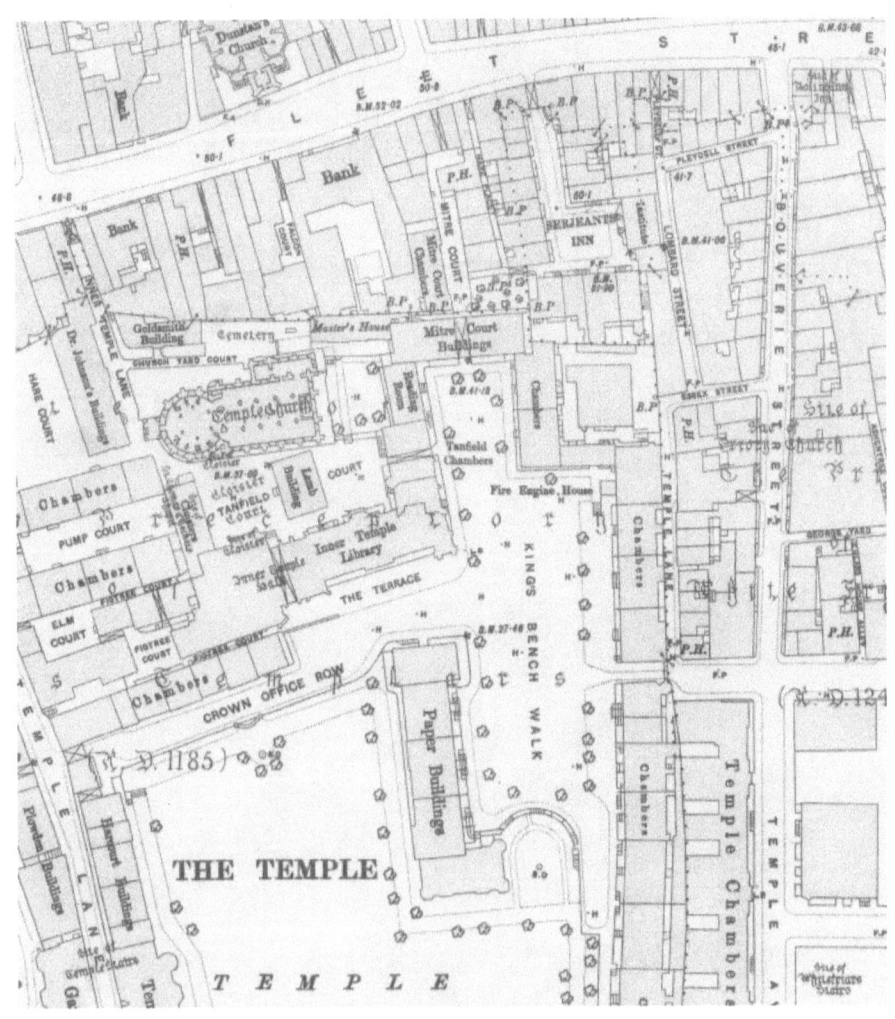

King's Bench Walk and the Temple, London
around 1900

Dr. Thorndyke's Case-Book

R. AUSTIN FREEMAN

H&S

1923 Hodder & Stoughton, London Cover

The Case of the
White Footprints

"Well," said my friend Foxton, pursuing a familiar and apparently inexhaustible topic, "I'd sooner have your job than my own."

"I've no doubt you would," was my unsympathetic reply. "I never met a man who wouldn't. We all tend to consider other men's jobs in terms of their advantages and our own in terms of their drawbacks. It is human nature."

"Oh, it's all very well for you to be so beastly philosophical," retorted Foxton. "You wouldn't be if you were in my place. Here, in Margate, it's measles, chicken-pox, and scarlatina all the summer, and bronchitis, colds, and rheumatism an the winter. A deadly monotony. Whereas you and Thorndyke sit there in your chambers and let your clients feed you up with the raw material of romance. Why, your life is a sort of everlasting Adelphi drama."

"You exaggerate, Foxton," said I. "We, like you, have our routine work, only it is never heard of outside the Law Courts, and you, like every other doctor, must run up against mystery and romance from time to time.

Foxton shook his head as he held out his hand for my cup. "I don't," said he. "My practice yields nothing but an endless round of dull routine."

And then, as if in commentary on this last statement, the housemaid burst into the room and, with hardly dissembled agitation, exclaimed "If you please, sir, the page from Beddingfield's Boarding House says that a lady has been found dead in her bed and would you go round there immediately.

"Very well, Jane," said Foxton, and as the maid retired, he deliberately helped himself to another fried egg and, looking across the table at me, exclaimed, "Isn't that always the way? Come immediately – now – this very instant, although the patient may have been considering for a day or two whether he'll send for you or not. But directly he decides you must spring out of bed, or jump up from your breakfast, and run."

"That's quite true," I agreed, "but this really does seem to be an urgent case."

"What's the urgency?" demanded Foxton. "The woman is already dead. Anyone would think she was in imminent danger of coming to life again and that my instant arrival the only thing that could prevent such a catastrophe."

"You've only a third-hand statement that she is dead," said I. "It is just possible that she isn't, and even if she is, as you will have to give evidence at the inquest, you do not want the police to get there first and turn out the room before you've made your inspection."

"Gad!" exclaimed Foxton. "I hadn't thought of that. Yes. You're right. I'll hop round at once."

He swallowed the remainder of the egg at a single gulp and rose from the table. Then he paused and stood for a few moments, looking down at me irresolutely

"I wonder, Jervis," he said, "if you would mind coming round with me. You know all the medico-legal ropes, and I don't. What do you say?"

I agreed instantly, having, in fact, been restrained only by delicacy from making the suggestion myself, and when I had fetched from my room my pocket camera and telescopic tripod, we set forth together without further delay

Beddingfield's Boarding House was but a few minutes' walk from Foxton's residence, being situated near the middle of Ethelred Road, Cliftonville, a quiet, suburban street which abounded in similar establishments, many of which, I noticed, were undergoing a spring-cleaning and renovation to prepare them for the approaching season.

"That's the house," said Foxton, "where that woman is standing at the front door. Look at the boarders, collected at the dining-room window. There's a rare commotion in that house, I'll warrant."

Here, arriving at the house, he ran up the steps and accosted in sympathetic tones the elderly woman who stood by the open street door.

"What a dreadful thing this is, Mrs. Beddingfield! Terrible! Most distressing for you!"

"Ah, you're right, Dr. Foxton," she replied. "It's an awful affair. Shocking. So bad for business, too. I do hope, and trust there won't be any scandal."

"I'm sure I hope not," said Foxton. "There shan't be if I can help it. And as my friend Dr. Jervis, who is staying with me for a few days, is a lawyer as well as a doctor, we shall have the best advice. When was the affair discovered?"

"Just before I sent for you, Dr. Foxton. The maid, noticed that Mrs. Toussaint – that is the poor creature's name – had not taken in her hot water, so she knocked at the door. As she couldn't get any answer, she tried the door and found it bolted on the inside, and then she came and told me. I went up and knocked loudly, and then, as I couldn't get any reply, I told our boy, James, to force the door open with a case-opener, which he did quite easily as the bolt was only a small one. Then I went in, all of a tremble, for I had a presentiment that there was something wrong, and there she was lying stone dead, with a most 'orrible stare on her face and an empty bottle in her hand."

"A bottle, eh!" said Foxton.

"Yes. She'd made away with herself, poor thing, and all on account of some silly love affair – and it was hardly even that.

"Ah," said Foxton. "The usual thing. You must tell us about that later. Now we'd better go up and see the patient – at least the – er – Perhaps you'll show us the room, Mrs. Beddingfield."

The landlady turned and preceded us up the stairs to the first-floor back, where she paused, and softly opening a door, peered nervously into the room. As we stepped past her and entered, she seemed inclined to follow, but, at a significant glance from me, Foxton persuasively ejected her and closed the door. Then we stood silent for a while and looked about us

In the aspect of the room there was something strangely incongruous with the tragedy that had been enacted within its walls, a mingling of the commonplace and the terrible that almost amounted to anticlimax. Through the wide-open window the bright spring sunshine streamed in on the garish wallpaper and cheap furniture. From the street below, the periodic shouts of a man selling "Sole and mack-ro!" broke into the brisk staccato of a barrel-organ and both sounds mingled with a raucous voice close at hand, cheerfully trolling a popular song, and accounted for by a linen-clad elbow that bobbed in front of the window and evidently appertained to a house-painter on an adjacent ladder.

It was all very commonplace and familiar and discordantly out of character with the stark figure that lay on the bed like a waxen effigy symbolic of tragedy. Here was none of that gracious somnolence in which death often presents itself with a suggestion of eternal repose. This woman was dead – horribly, aggressively dead. The thin, sallow face was rigid as stone, and the dark eyes stared into infinite space with a horrid fixity that was quite disturbing to look on. And yet the posture of the corpse was not uneasy, being, in fact, rather curiously symmetrical, with both arms outside the bedclothes and both hands closed, the right grasping, as Mrs. Beddingfield had said, an empty bottle.

"Well," said Foxton, as he stood looking down on the dead woman, "it seems a pretty clear case. She appears to have laid herself out and kept hold of the bottle so that there should be no mistake. How long do you suppose this woman has been dead, Jervis?"

I felt the rigid limbs and tested the temperature of the body surface

"Not less than six hours," I replied. "Probably more. I should say that she died about two o'clock this morning."

"And that is about all we can say," said Foxton, "until the *post mortem* has been made. Everything looks quite straightforward. No signs of a struggle or marks of violence. That blood on the mouth is probably due to her biting her lip when she drank from the bottle. Yes, here's a little cut on the inside of the lip, corresponding to the upper incisors. By the way, I wonder if there is anything left in the bottle."

As he spoke, he drew the small, unlabelled, green glass phial from the closed hand – out of which it slipped quite easily – and held it up to the light.

"Yes," he exclaimed, "there's more than a drachm left, quite enough for an analysis. But I don't recognize the smell. Do you?"

I sniffed at the bottle and was aware of a faint unfamiliar vegetable odour.

"No," I answered. "It appears to be a watery solution of some kind, but I can't give it a name. Where is the cork?"

"I haven't seen it," he replied. "Probably it is on the floor somewhere."

We both stooped to look for the missing cork and presently found it in the shadow, under the little bedside table. But, in the course of that brief search, I found something else, which had indeed been lying in full view all the time – a wax match. Now a wax match is a perfectly innocent and very commonplace object, but yet the presence of this one gave me pause. In the first place, women do not, as a rule, use wax matches, though there was not much in that. What was more to the point was that the candlestick by the bedside contained a box of safety matches, and that, as the burnt remains of one lay in the tray, it appeared to have been used to light the candle. Then why the wax match?

While I was turning over this problem, Foxton had corked the bottle, wrapped it carefully in a piece of paper which he took from the dressing-table, and bestowed it in his pocket

"Well, Jervis," said he, "I think we've seen everything. The analysis and the *post mortem* will complete the case. Shall we go down and hear what Mrs. Beddingfield has to say?"

But that wax match, slight as was its significance, taken alone, had presented itself to me as the last of a succession of phenomena each of which was susceptible of a sinister interpretation, and the cumulative effect of these slight suggestions began to impress me somewhat strongly

"One moment, Foxton," said I. "Don't let us take anything for granted. We are here to collect evidence, and we must go warily. There is such a thing as homicidal poisoning, you know."

"Yes, of course," he replied, "but there is nothing to suggest it in this case – at least, I see nothing. Do you?"

"Nothing very positive," said I, "but there are some facts that seem to call for consideration. Let us go over what we have seen. In the first place, there is a distinct discrepancy in the appearance of the body. The general easy, symmetrical posture, like that of a figure on a tomb, suggests the effect of a slow, painless poison. But look at the face. There is nothing reposeful about that. It is very strongly suggestive of pain or terror or both."

"Yes," said Foxton, "that is so. But you can't draw any satisfactory conclusions from the facial expression of dead bodies. Why, men who have been hanged, or even, stabbed, often look as peaceful as babes."

"Still," I urged, "it is a fact to be noted. Then there is that cut on the lip. It may have been produced in the way you suggest, but it may equally well be the result of pressure on the mouth."

Foxton made no comment on this beyond a slight shrug of the shoulders, and I continued, "Then there is the state of the hand. It was closed, but, it did not really grasp the object it contained. You drew the bottle out without any resistance. It simply lay in the closed hand. But that is not a normal state of affairs. As you know, when a person dies grasping any object, either the hand relaxes and lets it drop, or the muscular action passes into cadaveric spasm and grasps the object firmly. And lastly, there is this wax match. Where did it come from? The dead woman apparently lit her candle with a safety match from the box. It is a small matter, but it wants explaining."

Foxton raised his eyebrows protestingly. "You're like all specialists, Jervis," said he. "You see your speciality in everything. And while you are straining these flimsy suggestions to turn a simple suicide into murder, you ignore the really conclusive fact that the door was bolted and had to be broken open before anyone could get in."

"You are not forgetting, I suppose," said I, "that the window was wide open and that there were house-painters about and possibly a ladder left standing against the house."

"As to the ladder," said Foxton, "that is a pure assumption, but we can easily settle the question by asking that fellow out there if it was or was not left standing last night."

Simultaneously we moved towards the window, but halfway we both stopped short. For the question of the ladder had in a moment became negligible. Staring up at us from the dull red linoleum which covered the floor were the impressions of a pair of bare feet, imprinted in white paint with the distinctness of a woodcut. There was no need to ask if they had been made by the dead woman, they were unmistakably the

41

feet of a man, and large feet at that. Nor could there be any doubt as to whence those feet had come. Beginning with startling distinctness under the window, the tracks shed rapidly in intensity until they reached the carpeted portion of the room, where they vanished abruptly, and only by the closest scrutiny was it possible to detect the faint traces of the retiring tracks.

Foxton and I stood for some moments gazing in, silence at the sinister white shapes, then we looked at one another.

"You've saved me from a most horrible blunder, Jervis," said Foxton. "Ladder or no ladder, that fellow came in at the window, and he came in last night, for I saw them painting these window-sills yesterday afternoon. Which side did he come from, I wonder?"

We moved to the window and looked out on the sill. A set of distinct, though smeared impressions on the new paint gave unneeded confirmation and showed that the intruder had approached from the left side, close to which was a cast-iron stack-pipe, now covered with fresh green paint.

"So," said Foxton, "the presence or absence of the ladder is of no significance. The man got into the window somehow, and that's all that matters."

"On the contrary," said I, "the point may be of considerable importance in identification. It isn't everyone who could climb up a stack-pipe, whereas most people could make shift to climb a ladder, even if it were guarded by a plank. But the fact that the man took off his boots and socks suggests that he came up by the pipe. If he had merely aimed at silencing his footfalls, he would probably have removed his boots only."

From the window we turned to examine more closely the footprints on the floor, and while I took a series of measurements with my spring tape Foxton entered them in my notebook.

"Doesn't it strike you as rather odd, Jervis," said he, "that neither of the little toes has made any mark?"

"It does indeed," I replied. "The appearances suggest that the little toes were absent, but I have never met with such a condition. Have you?"

"Never. Of course one is acquainted with the supernumerary toe deformity, but I have never heard of congenitally deficient little toes."

Once more we scrutinized the footprints, and even examined those on the window-sill, obscurely marked on the fresh paint, but, exquisitely distinct as were those on the linoleum, showing every wrinkle and minute skin-marking, not the faintest hint of a little toe was to be seen on either foot.

"It's very extraordinary," said Foxton. "He has certainly lost his little toes, if he ever had any. They couldn't have failed to make some mark. But it's a queer affair. Quite a windfall for the police, by the way, I mean for purposes of identification.

"Yes," I agreed, "and having regard to the importance of the footprints, I think it would be wise to get a photograph of them."

"Oh, the police will see to that," said Foxton. "Besides, we haven't got a camera, unless you thought of using that little toy snap-shotter of yours."

As Foxton was no photographer I did not trouble to explain that my camera, though small, had been specially made for scientific purposes.

"Any photograph is better than none," I said, and with this I opened the tripod and set it over one of the most distinct of the footprints, screwed the camera to the goose-neck, carefully framed the footprint in the finder, and adjusted the focus, finally making the exposure by means of an Antinous release. This process I repeated four times, twice on a right footprint and twice on a left.

"Well," Foxton remarked, "with all those photographs the police ought to be able to pick up the scent."

"Yes, they've got something to go on, but they'll have to catch their hare before they can cook him. He won't be walking about barefooted, you know."

"No. It's a poor clue in that respect. And now we may as well be off, as we've seen all there is to see. I think we won't have much to say to Mrs. Beddingfield. This is a police case, and the less I'm mixed up in it the better it will be for my practice."

I was faintly amused at Foxton's caution when considered by the light of his utterances at the breakfast-table. Apparently his appetite for mystery and romance was easily satisfied. But that was no affair of mine. I waited on the doorstep while he said a few – probably evasive – words to the landlady and then, as we started off together in the direction of the police station, I began to turn over in my mind the salient features of the case. For some time we walked on in silence, and must have been pursuing a parallel train of thought for, when he at length spoke, he almost put my reflections into words.

"You know, Jervis," said he, "there ought to be a clue in those footprints. I realize that you can't tell how many toes a man has by looking at his booted feet. But those unusual footprints ought to give an expert a hint as to what sort of man to look for. Don't they convey any hint to you?"

I felt that Foxton was right, that if my brilliant colleague, Thorndyke, had been in my place he would have extracted from those footprints some leading fact that would have given the police a start along some definite line of inquiry, and that belief, coupled with Foxton's challenge, put me on my mettle.

"They offer no particular suggestions to me at this moment," said I, "but I think that, if we consider them systematically, we may be able to draw some useful deductions."

"Very well," said Foxton, "then let us consider them systematically. Fire away. I should like to hear how you work these things out."

Foxton's frankly spectatorial attitude was a little disconcerting, especially as it seemed to commit me to a result that I was by no means confident of attaining. I therefore began a little diffidently.

"We are assuming that both the feet that made those prints were from some cause devoid of little toes. That assumption – which is almost certainly correct – we treat as a fact and, taking it as our starting point, the first step in the inquiry is to find some explanation of it. Now there are three possibilities, and only three: Deformity, injury, and disease. The toes may have been absent from birth, they may have been lost as a result of mechanical injury, or they may have been lost by disease. Let us take those possibilities in order.

"Deformity we exclude since such a malformation is unknown to us.

"Mechanical injury seems to be excluded by the fact that the two little toes are on opposite sides of the body and could not conceivably be affected by any violence which left the intervening feet uninjured. This seems to narrow the possibilities down to disease, and the question that arises is: What diseases are there which might result in the loss of both little toes?"

I looked inquiringly at Foxton, but he merely nodded encouragingly. His rôle was that of listener.

"Well," I pursued, "the loss of both toes seems to exclude local disease, just as it excluded local injury, and as to general diseases, I can think only of three which might produce this condition – Raynaud's Disease, ergotism, and frost-bite."

"You don't call frost-bite a general disease, do you?" objected Foxton.

"For our present purpose, I do. The effects are local, but the cause – low external temperature – affects the whole body and is a general cause. Well, now, taking the diseases in order. I think we can exclude Raynaud's Disease. It does, it is true, occasionally cause the fingers or toes to die and drop off, and the little toes would be especially liable to be affected as being most remote from the heart. But in such a severe case the other toes would be affected. They would be shrivelled and tapered, whereas, if you remember, the toes of these feet were quite

44

plump and full, to judge by the large impressions they made. So I think we may safely reject Raynaud's Disease. There remain ergotism and frost-bite, and the choice between them is just a question of relative frequency. Frost-bite is more common – therefore frost-bite is more probable."

"Do they tend equally to affect the little toes?" asked Foxton

"As a matter of probability, yes. The poison of ergot acting from within, and intense cold acting from without, contract the small blood-vessels and arrest, the circulation. The feet, being the most distant parts of the body from the heart, are the first to feel the effects, and the little toes, which are the most distant parts of the feet, are the most susceptible of all."

Foxton reflected awhile, and then remarked, "This is all very well, Jervis, but I don't see that you are much forwarder. This man has lost both his little toes and on your showing, the probabilities are that the loss was due either to chronic ergot poisoning or to frost-bite, with a balance of probability in favour of frost-bite. That's all. No proof, no verification, just the law of probability applied to a particular case, which is always unsatisfactory. He may have lost his toes in some totally different way. But even if the probabilities work out correctly, I don't see what use your conclusions would be to the police. They wouldn't tell them what sort of man to look for."

There was a good deal of truth in Foxton's objection. A man who has suffered from ergotism or frost-bite is not externally different from any other man. Still, we had not exhausted the case, as I ventured to point out.

"Don't be premature, Foxton," said I. "Let us pursue our argument a little farther. We have established a probability that this unknown man has suffered either from ergotism or frost-bite. That, as you say, is of no use by itself, but supposing we can show that these conditions tend to affect a particular class of persons, we shall have established a fact that will indicate a line of investigation. And I think we can. Let us take the case of ergotism first.

"Now how is chronic ergot poisoning caused? Not by the medicinal use of the drug, but, by the consumption of the diseased rye in which ergot occurs. It is therefore peculiar to countries in which rye is used extensively as food. Those countries, broadly speaking, are the countries of North-Eastern Europe, and especially Russia and Poland.

"Then take the case of frost-bite. Obviously, the most likely person to get frost-bitten is the inhabitant of a country with a cold climate. The most rigorous climates inhabited by white people are North America and North-Eastern Europe, especially Russia and Poland. So you see, the areas associated with ergotism and frost-bite overlap to some extent. In fact they do more than overlap, for a person even slightly affected by ergot would be specially liable to frost-bite, owing to the impaired circulation. The conclusion is that, racially, in both ergotism and frost-bite, the balance of probability is in favour of a Russian, a Pole, or a Scandinavian.

"Then in the case of frost-bite there is the occupation factor. What class of men tend most to become frost-bitten? Well, beyond all doubt, the greatest sufferers from frost-bite are sailors, especially those on sailing ships and, naturally, on ships trading to Arctic and sub-Arctic countries. But the bulk of such sailing ships are those engaged in the Baltic and Archangel trade, and the crews of those ships are almost exclusively Scandinavians, Finns, Russians, and Poles. So that, again, the probabilities point to a native of North-Eastern Europe and, taken as a whole, by the over-lapping of factors, to a Russian, a Pole, or a Scandinavian."

Foxton smiled sardonically. "Very ingenious, Jervis," said he. "Most ingenious. As an academic statement of probabilities, quite excellent. But for practical purposes absolutely useless. However, here we are at the police station. I'll just run in and give them the facts and then go on to the coroner's office."

"I suppose I'd better not come in with you?" I said.

"Well, no," he replied. "You see, you have no official connection with the case, and they mightn't like it. You'd better go and amuse yourself while I get the morning's visits done. We can talk things over at lunch."

With this he disappeared into the police station, and I turned away with a smile of grim amusement. Experience is apt to make us a trifle uncharitable, and experience had taught me that those who are the most scornful of academic reasoning are often not above retailing it with some reticence as to its original authorship. I had a shrewd suspicion that Foxton was at this very moment disgorging my despised "academic statement of probabilities" to an admiring police inspector.

My way towards the sea lay through Ethelred Road, and I had traversed about half its length and was approaching the house of the tragedy when I observed Mrs. Beddingfield at the bay window. Evidently she recognized me, for a few moments later she appeared in outdoor clothes on the doorstep and advanced to meet me.

"Have you seen the police?" she asked, as we met.

I replied that Dr. Foxton was even now at the police station.

"Ah!" she said, "it's a dreadful affair, most unfortunate, too, just at the beginning of the season. A scandal is absolute ruin to a boarding house. What do you think of the case? Will it be possible to hush it up? Dr. Foxton said you were a lawyer, I think, Dr. Jervis?"

"Yes, I am a lawyer, but really I know nothing of the circumstances of this case. Did I understand that there had been something in the nature of a love affair?"

"Yes – at least – well, perhaps I oughtn't to have said that. But hadn't I better tell you the whole story? That is, if I am not taking up too much of your time."

"I should be interested to hear what led to the disaster," said I.

"Then," she said, "I will tell you all about it. Will you come indoors, or shall I walk a little way with you?"

As I suspected that the police were at that moment on their way to the house, I chose the latter alternative and led her away seawards at a pretty brisk pace.

"Was this poor lady a widow?" I asked, as we started up the street.

"No, she wasn't," replied Mrs. Beddingfield, "and that was the trouble. Her husband was abroad – at least, he had been, and he was just coming home. A pretty home-coming it will be for him, poor man. He is an officer in the Civil Police at Sierra Leone, but he hasn't been there long. He went there for his health."

"What! To Sierra Leone!" I exclaimed, for the "White Man's Grave" seemed a queer health resort.

"Yes. You see, Mr. Toussaint is a French Canadian, and it seems that he has always been somewhat of a rolling stone. For some time he was in the Klondyke, but he suffered so much from the cold that he had to come away. It injured his health very severely, I don't quite know in what way, but I do know that he was quite a cripple for a time. When he got better he looked out for a post in a warm climate and eventually obtained the appointment of Inspector of Civil Police at Sierra Leone. That was about ten months ago, and when he sailed for Africa his wife came to stay with me, and has been here ever since."

"And this love affair that you spoke of?"

"Yes, but I oughtn't to have called it that. Let me explain what happened. About three months ago a Swedish gentleman – a Mr. Bergson – came to stay here, and he seemed to be very much smitten with Mrs. Toussaint."

"And she?"

"Oh, she liked him well enough. He is a tall, good-looking man – though for that matter he is no taller than her husband, nor any better-looking. Both men are over six feet. But there was no harm so far as she was concerned, excepting that she didn't see the position quite soon enough. She wasn't very discreet, in fact I thought it necessary to give

47

her a little advice. However, Mr. Bergson left here and went to live at Ramsgate to superintend the unloading of the iceships (he came from Sweden in one), and I thought the trouble was at an end. But it wasn't, for he took to coming over to see Mrs. Toussaint, and of course I couldn't have that. So at last I had to tell him that he mustn't come to the house again. It was very unfortunate, for on that occasion I think he had been "tasting", as they say in Scotland. He wasn't drunk, but he was excitable and noisy, and when I told him he mustn't come again he made such a disturbance that two of the gentlemen boarders – Mr. Wardale and Mr. Macauley – had to interfere. And then he was most insulting to them, especially to Mr. Macauley, who is a black gentleman, calling him all sorts of offensive names."

"And how did the gentleman take it?"

"Not very well, I am sorry to say, considering that he is a gentleman – a law student with chambers in the Temple. In fact, his language was so objectionable that Mr. Wardale insisted on my giving him notice on the spot. But I managed to get him taken in next door but one. You see, Mr. Wardale had been a Commissioner at Sierra Leone – it was through him that Mr. Toussaint got his appointment – so I suppose he was rather on his dignity."

"And was that the last you heard of Mr. Bergson?"

"He never came here again, but he wrote several times to Mrs. Toussaint, asking her to meet him. At last, only a few days ago, she wrote to him and told him that the acquaintance must cease."

"And has it ceased?"

"As far as I know, it has."

"Then, Mrs. Beddingfield," said I, "what makes you connect the affair with – with what has happened?"

"Well, you see," she explained, "there is the husband. He was coming home, and is probably in England already."

"Indeed!" said I.

"Yes," she continued. "He went up into the bush to arrest some natives belonging to one of these gangs of murderers – Leopard Societies, I think they are called – and he got seriously wounded. He wrote to his wife from hospital saying that he would be sent home as soon as he was fit to travel, and about ten days ago she got a letter from him saying that he was coming by the next ship.

"I noticed that she seemed very nervous and upset when she got the letters from hospital, and still more so when the last letter came. Of course, I don't know what he said to her in those letters. It may be that he had heard something about Mr. Bergson, and threatened to take some action. Of course, I can't say. I only know that she was very nervous and restless, and when we saw in the paper four days ago that the ship he would be coming by had arrived in Liverpool, she seemed dreadfully upset. And she got worse and worse until – well, until last night."

"Has anything been heard of the husband since the ship arrived?" I asked.

"Nothing whatever," replied Mrs. Beddingfield, with a meaning look at me which I had no difficulty in interpreting. "No letter, no telegram, not a word. And you see, if he hadn't come by that ship, he would almost certainly have sent a letter to her. He must have arrived in England, but why hasn't he turned up, or at least sent a wire? What is he doing? Why is he staying away? Can he have heard something? And what does he mean to do? That's what kept the poor thing on wires, and that, I feel certain, is what drove her to make away with herself."

It was not my business to contest Mrs. Beddingfield's erroneous deductions. I was seeking information – it seemed that I had nearly exhausted the present source. But one point required amplifying.

"To return to Mr. Bergson, Mrs. Beddingfield," said I. "Do I understand that he is a seafaring man?"

"He was," she replied. "At present he is settled at Ramsgate as manager of a company in the ice trade, but formerly he was a sailor. I have heard him say that he was one of the crew of an exploring ship that went in search of the North Pole and that he was locked up in the ice for months and months. I should have thought he would have had enough of ice after that."

With this view I expressed warm agreement, and having now obtained all the information that appeared to be available, I proceeded to bring the interview to an end.

"Well, Mrs. Beddingfield," I said, "it is a rather mysterious affair. Perhaps more light may be thrown on it at the inquest. Meanwhile, I should think that it will be wise of you to keep your own counsel as far as outsiders are concerned."

The remainder of the morning I spent pacing the smooth stretch of sand that lies to the east of the jetty, and reflecting on the evidence that I had acquired in respect of this singular crime. Evidently there was no lack of clues in this case. On the contrary, there were two quite obvious lines of inquiry, for both the Swede and the missing husband presented the characters of the hypothetical murderer. Both had been exposed to the conditions which tend to produce frost-bite, one of them had probably been a consumer of rye meal, and both might be said to have a motive – though, to be sure, it was a very insufficient one – for committing the crime. Still, in both cases the evidence was merely speculative, it suggested a line of investigation but it did nothing more.

When I met Foxton at lunch I was sensible of a curious change in his manner. His previous expansiveness had given place to marked reticence and a certain official secretiveness.

"I don't think, you know, Jervis," he said, when I opened the subject, "that we had better discuss this affair. You see, I am the principal witness, and while the case is *sub judice* – well, in fact the police don't want the case talked about.

"But surely I am a witness, too, and an expert witness, moreover – "

"That isn't the view of the police. They look on you as more or less of an amateur, and as you have no official connection with the case, I don't think they propose to subpœna you. Superintendent Platt, who is in charge of the case, wasn't very pleased at my having taken you to the house. Said it was quite irregular. Oh, and by the way, he says you must hand over those photographs."

"But isn't Platt going to have the footprints photographed on his own account?" I objected.

"Of course he is. He is going to have a set of proper photographs taken by an expert photographer – he was mightily amused when he heard about your little snapshot affair. Oh, you can trust Platt. He is a great man. He has had a course of instruction at the Fingerprint Department in London."

"I don't see how that is going to help him, as there aren't any fingerprints in this case."

This was a mere fly-cast on my part, but Foxton rose at once at the rather clumsy bait.

"Oh, aren't there?" he exclaimed. "You didn't happen to spot them, but they were there. Platt has got the prints of a complete right hand. This is in strict confidence, you know," he added, with somewhat belated caution.

Foxton's sudden reticence restrained me from uttering the obvious comment on the superintendent's achievement. I returned to the subject of the photographs.

"Supposing I decline to hand over my film?" said I.

"But I hope you won't – and in fact you mustn't. I am officially connected with the case, and I've got to live with these people. As the Police Surgeon, I am responsible for the medical evidence, and Platt expects me to get those photographs from you. Obviously you can't keep them. It would be most irregular."

It was useless to argue. Evidently the police did not want me to be introduced into the case, and after all the superintendent was within his rights, if he chose to regard me as a private individual and to demand the surrender of the film.

50

Nevertheless I was loath to give up the photographs, at least until I had carefully studied them. The case was within my own speciality of practice, and was a strange and interesting one. Moreover, it appeared to be in unskilful hands, judging from the fingerprint episode, and then experience had taught me to treasure up small scraps of chance evidence, since one never knew when one might be drawn into a case in a professional capacity. In effect, I decided not to give up the photographs, though that decision committed me to a ruse that I was not very willing to adopt. I would rather have acted quite straightforwardly.

"Well if you insist, Foxton," I said, "I will hand over the film or, if you like, I will destroy it in your presence."

"I think Platt would rather have the film uninjured," said Foxton. "Then he'll know, you know," he added, with a sly grin.

In my heart, I thanked Foxton for that grin. It made my own guileful proceedings so much easier, for a suspicious man invites you to get the better of him if you can.

After lunch I went up to my room, locked the door, and took the little camera from my pocket. Having fully wound up the film, I extracted it, wrapped it up carefully and bestowed it in my inside breast-pocket. Then I inserted a fresh film, and going to the open window, took four successive snapshots of the sky. This done, I closed the camera, slipped it into my pocket, and went downstairs. Foxton was in the hall, brushing his hat as I descended, and at once renewed his demand.

"About those photographs, Jervis," said he, "I shall be looking in at the police station presently, so if you wouldn't mind – "

"To be sure," said I. "I will give you the film now if you like."

Taking the camera from my pocket, I solemnly wound up the remainder of the film, extracted it, stuck down the loose end with ostentatious care, and handed it to him.

"Better not expose it to the light," I said, going the whole hog of deception, "or you may fog the exposures."

Foxton took the spool from me as if it were hot – he was not a photographer – and thrust it into his handbag. He was still thanking me the quite profusely when the front-door bell rang.

The visitor who stood revealed when Foxton opened the door was a small, spare gentleman with a complexion of peculiar brown-papery quality that suggests long residence the tropics. He stepped in briskly and introduced himself and his business without preamble.

"My name is Wardale – boarder at Beddingfield's. I called with reference to the tragic event which – "

Here Foxton interposed in his frostiest official tone. "I am afraid, Mr. Wardale, I can't give you any information about the case at present.

51

"I saw you two gentlemen at the house this morning – " Mr. Wardale continued, but Foxton again cut him short.

"You did. We were there – or at least, *I* was – as representative of the Law, and while the case is *sub judice* – "

"It isn't yet," interrupted Wardale.

"Well, I can't enter into any discussion of it – "

"I am not asking you to," said Wardale a little impatiently. "But I understand that one of you is Dr. Jervis."

"I am," said I.

"I must really warn you – " Foxton began again, but Mr. Wardale interrupted testily.

"My dear sir, I am a lawyer and a magistrate and understand perfectly well what is and what is not permissible. I have come simply to make a professional engagement with Dr. Jervis."

"In what way can I be of service to you?" I asked.

"I will tell you," said Mr. Wardale. "This poor lady, whose death has occurred in so mysterious a manner, was the wife of a man who was, like myself, a servant of the Government of Sierra Leone. I was the friend of both of them, and in the absence of the husband I should like to have the inquiry into the circumstances of this lady's death watched by a competent lawyer with the necessary special knowledge of medical evidence. Will you or your colleague, Dr. Thorndyke, undertake to watch the case for me?"

Of course I was willing to undertake the case and said so.

"Then," said Mr. Wardale, "I will instruct my solicitor to write to you and formally retain you in the case. Here is my card. You will find my name in the Colonial Office List, and you know my address here."

He handed me his card, wished us both good afternoon, and then, with a stiff little bow, turned and took his departure.

"I think I had better run up to town and confer with Thorndyke," said I. "How do the trains run?"

"There is a good train in about three-quarters of an hour," replied Foxton.

"Then I will go by it, but I shall come down again to-morrow or the next day, and probably Thorndyke will come down with me."

"Very well," said Foxton. "Bring him in to lunch or dinner, but I can't put him up, I am afraid."

"It would be better not," said I. "Your friend Platt wouldn't like it. He won't want Thorndyke – or me either for that matter. And what about those photographs? Thorndyke will want them, you know."

"He can't have them," said Foxton doggedly, "unless Platt is willing to hand them back, which I don't suppose he will be."

I had private reasons for thinking otherwise, but I kept them to myself, and as Foxton went forth on his afternoon round, I returned upstairs to pack my suitcase and write the telegram to Thorndyke informing him of my movements.

It was only a quarter-past-five when I let myself into our chambers in King's Bench Walk. To my relief I found my colleague at home and our laboratory assistant, Polton, in the act of laying tea for two.

"I gather," said Thorndyke, as we shook hands, "that my learned brother brings grist to the mill?"

"Yes," I replied. "Nominally a watching brief, but I think you will agree with me that it is a case for independent investigation."

"Will there be anything in my line, sir?" inquired Polton, who was always agog at the word "investigation".

"There is a film to be developed. Four exposures of white footprints on a dark ground."

"Ah!" said Polton, "you'll want good strong negatives, and they ought to be enlarged if they are from the little camera. Can you give me the dimensions?"

I wrote out the measurements from my notebook and handed him the paper, together with the spool of film, with which he retired gleefully to the laboratory.

"And now, Jervis," said Thorndyke, "while Polton is operating on the film and we are discussing our tea, let us have a sketch of the case."

I gave him more than a sketch, for the events were recent and I had carefully sorted out the facts during my journey to town, making rough notes, which I now consulted. To my rather lengthy recital he listened in his usual attentive manner, without any comment, excepting in regard to my manœuvre to retain possession of the exposed film.

"It's almost a pity you didn't refuse." said he. "They could hardly have enforced their demand, and my feeling is that it is more convenient as well as more dignified to avoid direct deception unless one is driven to it. But perhaps you considered that you were."

As a matter of fact I had at the time, but I had since come to Thorndyke's opinion. My little manœuvre was going to be a source of inconvenience presently.

"Well," said Thorndyke, when I had finished my recital, "I think we may take it that the police theory is, in the main, your own theory derived from Foxton."

"I think so, excepting that I learned from Foxton that Superintendent Platt has obtained the complete fingerprints of a right hand."

Thorndyke raised his eyebrows. "Fingerprints!" he exclaimed. "Why, the fellow must be a mere simpleton. But there," he added, "everybody – police, lawyers, judges, even Galton himself – seems to lose every vestige of common sense as soon as the subject of fingerprints is raised. But it would be interesting to know how he got them and what they are like. We must try to find that out. However, to return to your case: Since your theory and the police theory are probably the same, we may as well consider the value of your inferences.

"At present we are dealing with the case in the abstract. Our data are largely assumptions, and our inferences are largely derived from an application of the mathematical laws of probability. Thus we assume that a murder has been committed, whereas it may turn out to have been suicide. We assume the murder to have been committed by the person who made the footprints, and we assume that that person has no little toes, whereas he may have retracted little toes which do not touch the ground and so leave no impression. Assuming the little toes to be absent, we account for their absence by considering known causes in the order of their probability. Excluding – quite properly, I think – Raynaud's disease, we arrive at frost-bite and ergotism.

"But two persons, both of whom are of a stature corresponding to the size of the footprints, may have had a motive – though a very inadequate one – for committing the crime, and both have been exposed to the conditions which tend to produce frost-bite, while one of them has, probably, been exposed to the conditions which tend to produce ergotism. The laws of probability point to both of these two men, and the chances in favour of the Swede being the murderer rather than the Canadian would be represented by the common factor – frost-bite – multiplied by the additional factor, ergotism. But this is purely speculative at present. There is no evidence that either man has ever been frost-bitten or has ever eaten spurred rye. Nevertheless, it is a perfectly sound method at this stage. It indicates a line of investigation. If it should transpire that either man has suffered from frost-bite or ergotism, a definite advance would have been made. But here is Polton with a couple of finished prints. How on earth did you manage it in the time, Polton?"

"Why, you see, sir, I just dried the film with spirit," replied Polton. "It saved a lot of time. I will let you have a pair of enlargements in about a quarter-of-an-hour."

Handing us the two wet prints, each stuck on a glass plate, he retired to the laboratory, and Thorndyke and I proceeded to scrutinize the photographs with the aid of our pocket lenses. The promised enlargements were really hardly necessary excepting for the purpose of comparative measurements, for the image of the white footprint, fully two inches long, was so microscopically sharp that, with the assistance of the lens, the minutest detail could be clearly seen.

54

"There is certainly not a vestige of little toe," remarked Thorndyke, "and the plump appearance of the other toes supports your rejection of Raynaud's disease. Does the character of the footprint convey any other suggestion to you, Jervis?"

"It gives me the impression that the man had been accustomed to go bare-footed in early life and had only taken to boots comparatively recently. The position of the great toe suggests this, and the presence of a number of small scars on the toes and ball of the foot seems to confirm it. A person walking bare-foot would sustain innumerable small wounds from treading on small, sharp objects."

Thorndyke looked dissatisfied. "I agree with you," he said, "as to the suggestion offered by the undeformed state of the great toes, but those little pits do not convey to me the impression of scars produced as you suggest. Still, you may be right."

Here our conversation was interrupted by a knock on the outer oak. Thorndyke stepped out through the lobby and I heard him open the door. A moment or two later he re-entered, accompanied by a short, brown-faced gentleman whom I instantly recognized as Mr. Wardale.

"I must have come up by the same train as you," he remarked, as we shook hands, "and to a certain extent, I suspect, on the same errand. I thought I would like to put our arrangement on a business footing, as I am a stranger to both of you."

"What do you want us to do?" asked Thorndyke.

"I want you to watch the case and, if necessary, to look into the facts independently."

"Can you give us any information that may help us?"

Mr. Wardale reflected. "I don't think I can," he said at length. "I have no facts that you have not, and any surmises of mine might be misleading. I had rather you kept an open mind. But perhaps we might go into the question of costs."

This, of course, was somewhat difficult, but Thorndyke contrived to indicate the probable liabilities involved, to Mr. Wardale's satisfaction.

"There is one other little matter," said Wardale, as he rose to depart. "I have got a suitcase here which Mrs. Beddingfield lent me to bring somethings up to town. It is one that Mr. Macauley left behind when he went away from the boarding house. Mrs. Beddingfield suggested that I might leave it at his chambers when I had finished with it, but I don't know his address, excepting that it is somewhere in the Temple, and I don't want to meet the fellow if he should happen to have come up to town."

"Is it empty?" asked Thorndyke.

"Excepting for a suit of pyjamas and a pair of shocking old slippers." He opened the suitcase as he spoke and exhibited its contents with a grin. "Pink silk pyjamas and slippers about three sizes too small."

"Very well," said Thorndyke. "I will get my man to find out the address and leave it there."

As Mr. Wardale went out, Polton entered with the enlarged photographs which showed the footprints the natural size. Thorndyke handed them to me, and as I sat down to examine them, he followed his assistant to the laboratory. He returned in a few minutes and, after a brief inspection of the photographs, remarked, "They show us nothing more than we have seen, though they may be useful later. So your stock of facts is all we have to go on at present. Are you going home to-night?"

"Yes, I shall go back to Margate to-morrow."

"Then, as I have to call at Scotland Yard, we may as well walk to Charing Cross together."

As we walked down the Strand we gossiped on general topics, but before we separated at Charing Cross, Thorndyke reverted to the case.

"Let me know the date of the inquest," said he, "and try to find out what the poison was – if it was really a poison."

"The liquid that was left in the bottle seemed to be a watery solution of some kind," said I, "as I think I mentioned."

"Yes," said Thorndyke. "Possibly a watery infusion of strophanthus."

"Why strophanthus?" I asked.

"Why not?" demanded Thorndyke. And with this and an inscrutable smile, he turned and walked down Whitehall.

Three days later I found myself at Margate – sitting beside Thorndyke in a room adjoining the Town Hall, in which the inquest on the death of Mrs. Toussaint was to be held. Already the coroner was in his chair, the jury were in their seats, and the witnesses assembled in a group of chairs apart. These included Foxton, a stranger who sat by him – presumably the other medical witness – Mrs. Beddingfield, Mr. Wardale, the police superintendent, and a well-dressed black man, whom I correctly assumed to be Mr. Macauley.

As I sat by my rather sphinx-like colleague, my mind recurred for the hundredth time to his extraordinary powers of mental synthesis. That parting remark of his as to the possible nature of the poison had brought home to me in a flash the fact that he already had a definite theory of this crime, and that his theory was not mine nor that of the police. True, the poison might not be strophanthus, after all, but that would not alter the position. He had a theory of the crime, but yet he was in possession of no facts excepting those with which I had supplied him. Therefore those

56

facts contained the material for a theory, whereas I had deduced from them nothing but the bald, ambiguous mathematical probabilities.

The first witness called was naturally Dr. Foxton, who described the circumstances already known to me. He further stated that he had been present at the autopsy, and that he had found on the throat and limbs of the deceased bruises that suggested a struggle and violent restraint. The immediate cause of death was heart failure, but whether that failure was due to shock, terror, or the action of a poison he could not positively say.

The next witness was a Dr. Prescott, an expert pathologist and toxicologist. He had made the autopsy and agreed with Dr. Foxton as to the cause of death. He had examined the liquid contained in the bottle taken from the hand of the deceased and found it to be a watery infusion or decoction of strophanthus seeds. He had analysed the fluid contained in the stomach and found it to consist largely of the same infusion.

"Is infusion of strophanthus seeds used in medicine?" the coroner asked.

"No," was the reply. "The tincture is the form in which strophanthus is administered unless it is given in the form of strophanthine."

"Do you consider that the strophanthus caused or contributed to death?"

"It is difficult to say," replied Dr. Prescott. "Strophanthus is a heart poison, and there was a very large poisonous dose. But very little had been absorbed, and the appearances were not inconsistent with death from shock.

"Could death have been self-produced by the voluntary taking of the poison?" asked the coroner.

"I should say, decidedly not. Dr. Foxton's evidence shows that the bottle was almost certainly placed in the hands of the deceased after death, and this is in complete agreement with the enormous dose and small absorption."

"Would you say that appearances point to suicidal or homicidal poisoning?"

"I should say that they point to homicidal poisoning, but that death was probably due mainly to shock."

This concluded the expert's evidence. It was followed by that of Mrs. Beddingfield, which brought out nothing new to me but the fact that a trunk had been broken open and a small attaché case belonging to the deceased abstracted and taken away.

"Do you know what the deceased kept in that case?" the coroner asked.

"I have seen her put her husband's letters into it. She had quite a number of them. I don't know what else she kept in it except, of course, her cheque-book."

"Had she any considerable balance at the bank?"

"I believe she had. Her husband used to send most of his pay home, and she used to pay it in and leave it with the bank. She might have two- or three-hundred pounds to her credit."

As Mrs. Beddingfield concluded, Mr. Wardale was called, and he was followed by Mr. Macauley. The evidence of both was quite brief and concerned entirely with the disturbance made by Bergson, whose absence from the court I had already noted.

The last witness was the police superintendent, and he, as I had expected, was decidedly reticent. He did refer to the footprints, but, like Foxton – who presumably had his instructions – he abstained from describing their peculiarities. Nor did he say anything about fingerprints. As to the identity of the criminal, that had to be further inquired into. Suspicion had at first fastened upon Bergson, but it had since transpired that the Swede sailed from Ramsgate on an ice-ship two days before the occurrence of the tragedy. Then suspicion had pointed to the husband, who was known to have landed at Liverpool four days before the death of his wife and who had mysteriously disappeared. But he (the superintendent) had only that morning received a telegram from the Liverpool police informing him that the body of Toussaint had been found floating in the Mersey, and that it bore a number of wounds of an apparently homicidal character. Apparently he had been murdered and his corpse thrown into the river.

"This is very terrible," said the coroner. "Does this second murder throw any light on the case which we are investigating?"

"I think it does," replied the officer, without any great conviction, however, "but it is not advisable to go into details."

"Quite so," agreed the coroner. "Most inexpedient. But are we to understand that you have a clue to the perpetrator of this crime – assuming a crime to have been committed?"

"Yes," replied Platt. "We have several important clues."

"And do they point to any particular individual?"

The superintendent hesitated. "Well . . . ." he began with some embarrassment, but the coroner interrupted him.

"Perhaps the question is indiscreet. We mustn't hamper the police, gentlemen, and the point is not really material to our inquiry. You would rather we waived that question, Superintendent?"

"If you please, sir," was the emphatic reply.

"Have any cheques from the deceased woman's cheque book been presented at the bank?"

"Not since her death. I inquired at the bank only this morning."

This concluded the evidence, and after a brief but capable summing-up by the coroner, the jury returned a verdict of "*Wilful murder against some person unknown*".

As the proceedings terminated, Thorndyke rose and turned round, and then to my surprise I perceived Superintendent Miller, of the Criminal Investigation Department, who had come in unperceived by me and was sitting immediately behind us."

"I have followed your instructions, sir," said he, addressing Thorndyke, "but before we take any definite action I should like to have a few words with you.

He led the way to an adjoining room and, as we entered we were followed by Superintendent Platt and Dr. Foxton.

"Now, Doctor," said Miller, carefully closing the door, "I have carried out your suggestions. Mr. Macauley is being detained, but before we commit ourselves to an arrest, we must have something to go upon. I shall want you to make out a *prima facie* case."

"Very well," said Thorndyke, laying upon the table the small green suitcase that was his almost invariable companion.

"I've seen that *prima facie* case before," Miller remarked with a grin, as Thorndyke unlocked it and drew out a large envelope. "Now, what have you got there?"

As Thorndyke extracted from the envelope Polton's enlargements of my small photographs, Platt's eyes appeared to bulge, while Foxton gave me a quick glance of reproach.

"These," said Thorndyke "are the full-sized photographs of the footprints of the suspected murderer. Superintendent Platt can probably verify them."

Rather reluctantly Platt produced from his pocket a pair of whole-plate photographs, which he laid beside the enlargements.

"Yes," said Miller, after comparing them, "they are the same footprints. But you say, Doctor, that they are Macauley's footprints. Now, what evidence have you?"

Thorndyke again had recourse to the green case, from which he produced two copper plates mounted on wood and coated with printing ink.

"I propose," said he, lifting the plates out of their protecting frame, "that we take prints of Macauley's feet and compare them with the photographs."

"Yes," said Platt. "And then there are the fingerprints that we've got. We can test those, too."

"You don't want fingerprints if you've got a set of toeprints," objected Miller.

"With regard to those fingerprints," said Thorndyke. "May I ask if they were obtained from the bottle?"

"They were," Platt admitted.

"And were there any other fingerprints?"

"No," replied Platt. "These were the only ones."

As he spoke he laid on the table a photograph showing the prints of the thumb and fingers of a right hand.

Thorndyke glanced at the photograph and, turning to Miller, said, "I suggest that those are Dr. Foxton's fingerprints.

"Impossible!" exclaimed Platt, and then suddenly fell silent.

"We can soon see," said Thorndyke, producing from the case a pad of white paper. "If Dr. Foxton will lay the finger-tips of his right hand first on this inked plate and then on the paper, we can compare the prints with the photograph.

Foxton placed his fingers on the blackened plate and then pressed them on the paper pad, leaving on the latter four beautifully clear, black fingerprints. These Superintendent Platt scrutinized eagerly, and as his glance travelled from the prints to the photographs he broke into a sheepish grin.

"Sold again!" he muttered. "They are the same prints."

"Well," said Miller, in a tone of disgust, "you must have been a mug not to have thought of that when you knew that Dr. Foxton had handled the bottle."

"The fact, however, is important," said Thorndyke. "The absence of any fingerprints but Dr. Foxton's not only suggests that the murderer took the precaution to wear gloves, but especially it proves that the bottle was not handled by the deceased during life. A suicide's hands will usually be pretty moist and would leave conspicuous, if not very clear, impressions."

"Yes," agreed Miller, "that is quite true. But with regard to these footprints – We can't compel this man to let us examine his feet without arresting him. Don't think, Dr. Thorndyke, that I suspect you of guessing. I've known you too long for that. You've got your facts all right, I don't doubt, but you must let us have enough to justify our arrest."

Thorndyke's answer was to plunge once more into the inexhaustible green case, from which he now produced two objects wrapped in tissue-

60

paper. The paper being removed, there was revealed what looked like a model of an excessively shabby pair of brown shoes."

"These," said Thorndyke, exhibiting the "models" to Superintendent Miller – who viewed them with an undisguised grin – "are plaster casts of the interiors of a pair of slippers – very old and much too tight – belonging to Mr. Macauley. His name was written inside them. The casts have been waxed and painted with raw umber, which has been lightly rubbed off, thus accentuating the prominences and depressions. You will notice that the impressions of the toes on the soles and of the "knuckles" on the uppers appear as prominences, in fact we have in these casts a sketchy reproduction of the actual feet.

"Now, first as to dimensions. Dr. Jervis's measurements of the footprints give us ten-inches-and-three-quarters as, the extreme length and four-inches-and-five-eighths as the extreme width at the heads of the metatarsus. On these casts, as you see, the extreme length is ten-inches-and-five-eighths – the loss of one-eighth being accounted for by the curve of the sole – and the extreme width is four-inches-and-a-quarter – three-eighths being accounted for by the lateral compression of a tight slipper. The agreement of the dimensions is remarkable, considering the unusual size. And now as to the peculiarities of the feet.

"You notice that each toe has made a perfectly distinct impression on the sole, excepting the little toe, of which there is no trace in either cast. And, turning to the uppers, you notice that the knuckles of the toes appear quite distinct and prominent – again excepting the little toes, which have made no impression at all. Thus it is not a case of retracted little toes, for they would appear as an extra prominence. Then, looking at the feet as a whole, it is evident that the little toes are absent, there is a distinct hollow, where there should be a prominence."

"M'yes," said Miller dubiously, "it's all very neat. But isn't it just a bit speculative?"

"Oh, come, Miller," protested Thorndyke, "just consider the facts. Here is a suspected murderer known to have feet of an unusual size and presenting a very rare deformity, and they are the feet of a man who had actually lived in the same house as the murdered woman, and who, at the date of the crime, was living only two doors away. What more would you have?"

"Well, there is the question of motive," objected Miller.

"That hardly belongs to a *prima facie* case," said Thorndyke. "But even if it did, is there not ample matter for suspicion? Remember who the murdered woman was, what her husband was, and who this Sierra Leone gentleman is."

"Yes, yes, that's true," said Miller somewhat hastily, either perceiving the drift of Thorndyke's argument (which I did not), or being unwilling to admit that he was still in the dark. "Yes, we'll have the fellow in and get his actual footprints."

He went to the door and, putting his head out, made some sign, which was almost immediately followed by a trampling of feet, and Macauley entered the room, followed by two large plain-clothes policemen. The black man was evidently alarmed, for he looked about him with the wild expression of a hunted animal. But his manner was aggressive and truculent.

"Why am I being interfered with in this impertinent manner?" he demanded in a deep buzzing voice.

"We want to have a look at your feet, Mr. Macauley," said Miller. "Will you kindly take off your shoes and socks?"

"No," roared Macauley. "I'll see you damned first!"

"Then," said Miller, "I arrest you on a charge of having murdered – "

The rest of the sentence was drowned in a sudden uproar. The tall, powerful man, bellowing like an angry bull, had whipped out a large, strangely-shaped knife and charged furiously at the Superintendent. But the two plain-clothes men had been watching him from behind and now sprang upon him, each seizing an arm. Two sharp, metallic clicks in quick succession, a thunderous crash, and an ear-splitting yell, and the formidable fellow lay prostrate on the floor with one massive constable sitting astride his chest and the other seated on his knees.

"Now's your chance, Doctor," said Miller. "I'll get his shoes and socks off."

As Thorndyke re-inked his plates, Miller and the local superintendent expertly removed the smart patent shoes and the green silk socks from the feet of the writhing, bellowing man. Then Thorndyke rapidly and skilfully applied the inked plates to the soles of the feet – which I steadied for the purpose – and followed up with a dexterous pressure of the paper pad, first to one foot and then – having torn off the printed sheet – to the other. In spite of the difficulties occasioned by Macauley's struggles, each sheet presented a perfectly clear and sharp print of the sole of the foot, even the ridge-patterns of the toes and ball of the foot being quite distinct. Thorndyke laid each of the new prints on the table beside the corresponding large photograph, and invited the two superintendents to compare them.

"Yes," said Miller – and Superintendent Platt nodded his acquiescence – "there can't be a shadow of a doubt. The ink-prints and the photographs are identical, to every line and skin-marking. You've made out your case, Doctor, as you always do."

"So you see," said Thorndyke, as we smoked our evening pipes on the old stone pier, "your method was a perfectly sound one, only you didn't apply it properly. Like too many mathematicians, you started on your calculations before you had secured your data. If you had applied the simple laws of probability to the real data, they would have pointed straight to Macauley."

"How do you suppose he lost his little toes?" I asked.

"I don't suppose at all. Obviously it was a clear case of double ainhum."

"Ainhum!" I exclaimed with a sudden flash of recollection.

"Yes, that was what you overlooked. You compared the probabilities of three diseases, either of which only very rarely causes the loss of even one little toe and infinitely rarely causes the loss of both, and none of which conditions is confined to any definite class of persons, and you ignored ainhum, a disease which attacks almost exclusively the little toe, causing it to drop off, and quite commonly destroys both little toes – a disease, moreover, which is confined to the black-skinned races. In European practice, ainhum is unknown, but in Africa, and to a less extent in India, it is quite common.

"If you were to assemble all the men in the world who have lost both little toes, more than nine-tenths of them would be suffering from ainhum, so that, by the laws of probability, your footprints were, by nine-chances-to-one, those of a man who had suffered from ainhum, and therefore a black-skinned man. But as soon as you had established a black man as the probable criminal, you opened up a new field of corroborative evidence. There was a black man on the spot. That man was a native of Sierra Leone and almost certainly a man of importance there. But the victim's husband had deadly enemies in the native secret societies of Sierra Leone. The letters of the husband to the wife probably contained matters incriminating certain natives of Sierra Leone. The evidence became cumulative, you see. Taken as a whole, it pointed plainly to Macauley – apart from the new fact of the murder of Toussaint in Liverpool, a city with a considerable floating population of West Africans."

"And I gather from your reference to the African poison, strophanthus, that you fixed on Macauley at once when I gave you my sketch of the case?"

"Yes, especially when I saw your photographs of the footprints with the absent little toes and those characteristic chigger-scars on the toes that remained. But it was sheer luck that enabled me to fit the keystone into its place and turn mere probability into virtual certainty. I could have embraced the magician Wardale when he brought us the magic slippers. Still, it isn't an absolute certainty, even now, though I expect it will be by to-morrow."

And Thorndyke was right. That very evening the police entered Macauley's chambers in Tanfield Court, where they discovered the dead woman's attaché case. It still contained Toussaint's letters to his wife, and one of those letters mentioned by name, as members of a dangerous secret society, several prominent Sierra Leone men, including the accused, David Macauley.

The Blue Scarab

Medico-legal practice is largely concerned with crimes against the person, the details of which are often sordid, gruesome, and unpleasant. Hence the curious and romantic case of the Blue Scarab (though really outside our speciality) came as somewhat of a relief. But to me it is of interest principally as illustrating two of the remarkable gifts which made my friend, Thorndyke, unique as an investigator: His uncanny power of picking out the one essential fact at a glance, and his capacity to produce, when required, inexhaustible stores of unexpected knowledge of the most out-of-the-way subjects.

It was late in the afternoon when Mr. James Blowgrave arrived, by appointment, at our chambers, accompanied by his daughter, a rather strikingly pretty girl of about twenty-two, and when we had mutually introduced ourselves, the consultation began without preamble.

"I didn't give any details in my letter to you," said Mr. Blowgrave. "I thought it better not to, for fear you might decline the case. It is really a matter of a robbery, but not quite an ordinary robbery. There are some unusual and rather mysterious features in the case. And as the police hold out very little hope, I have come to ask if you will give me your opinion on the case and perhaps look into it for me. But first I had better tell you how the affair happened.

"The robbery occurred just a fortnight ago, about half-past-nine o'clock in the evening. I was sitting in my study with my daughter, looking over some things that I had taken from a small deed-box, when a servant rushed in to tell us that one of the outbuildings was on fire. Now, my study opens by a French window on the garden at the back and, as the outbuilding was in a meadow at the side of the garden, I went out that way, leaving the French window open, but before going I hastily put the things back in the deed-box and locked it.

"The building – which I used partly as a lumber store and partly as a workshop – was well alight and the whole household was already on the spot, the boy working the pump and the two maids carrying the buckets and throwing water on the fire. My daughter and I joined the party and helped to carry the buckets and take out what goods we could reach from the burning building. But it was nearly half-an-hour before we got the fire completely extinguished, and then my daughter and I went to our rooms to wash and tidy ourselves up. We returned to the study together, and when I had shut the French window my daughter proposed that we should resume our interrupted occupation. Thereupon I took out of my pocket the key of the deed-box and turned to the cabinet on which the box always stood.

"But there was no deed-box there.

"For a moment I thought I must have moved it, and cast my eyes round the room in search of it. But it was nowhere to be seen, and a moment's reflection reminded me that I had left it in its usual place. The only possible conclusion was that during our absence at the fire, somebody must have come in by the window and taken it. And it looked as if that somebody had deliberately set fire to the outbuilding for the express purpose of luring us all out of the house."

"That is what the appearances suggest," Thorndyke agreed. "Is the study window furnished with a blind, or curtains?"

"Curtains," replied Mr. Blowgrave. "But they were not drawn. Anyone in the garden could have seen into the room, and the garden is easily accessible to an active person who could climb over a low wall."

"So far, then," said Thorndyke, "the robbery might be the work of a casual prowler who had got into the garden and watched you through the window, and assuming that the things you had taken from the box were of value, seized an easy opportunity to make off with them. Were the things of any considerable value?"

"To a thief they were of no value at all. There were a number of share certificates, a lease, one or two agreements, some family photographs, and a small box containing an old letter and a scarab. Nothing worth stealing, you see, for the certificates were made out in my name and were therefore unnegotiable."

"And the scarab?"

"That may have been lapis lazuli, but more probably it was a blue glass imitation. In any case, it was of no considerable value. It was about an inch-and-a-half long. But before you come to any conclusion, I had better finish the story. The robbery was on Tuesday, the 7th of June. I gave information to the police, with a description of the missing property, but nothing happened until Wednesday, the 15th, when I received a registered parcel bearing the Southampton postmark. On opening it I found, to my astonishment, the entire contents of the deed-box, with the exception of the scarab, and this rather mysterious communication."

He took from his pocket and handed to Thorndyke an ordinary envelope addressed in typewritten characters, and sealed with a large, elliptical seal, the face of which was covered with minute hieroglyphics.

"This," said Thorndyke, "I take to be an impression of the scarab, and an excellent impression it is."

"Yes," replied Mr. Blowgrave, "I have no doubt that it is the scarab. It is about the same size."

Thorndyke looked quickly at our client with an expression of surprise. "But," he asked, "don't you recognise the hieroglyphics on it?"

Mr. Blowgrave smiled deprecatingly. "The fact is," said he, "I don't know anything about hieroglyphics, but I should say, as far as I can judge, these look the same. What do you think, Nellie?"

Miss Blowgrave looked at the seal vaguely and replied, "I am in the same position. Hieroglyphics are to me just funny things that don't mean anything. But these look the same to me as those on our scarab, though I expect any other hieroglyphics would, for that matter."

Thorndyke made no comment on this statement, but examined the seal attentively through his lens. Then he drew out the contents of the envelope, consisting of two letters, one typewritten and the other in a faded brown handwriting. The former he read through and then inspected the paper closely, holding it up to the light to observe the watermark.

"The paper appears to be of Belgian manufacture," he remarked, passing it to me. I confirmed this observation and then read the letter, which was headed "*Southampton*" and ran thus,

Dear Old Pal,

I am sending you back some trifles removed in error. The ancient document is enclosed with this, but the curio is at present in the custody of my respected uncle. Hope its temporary loss will not inconvenience you, and that I may be able to return it to you later. Meanwhile, believe me,

Your ever affectionate,

Rudolpho

"Who is Rudolpho?" I asked.

"The Lord knows," replied Mr. Blowgrave. "A pseudonym of our absent friend, I presume. He seems to be a facetious sort of person."

"He does," agreed Thorndyke. "This letter and the seal appear to be what the schoolboys would call a leg-pull. But still, this is all quite normal. He has returned you the worthless things and has kept the one thing that has any sort of negotiable value. Are you quite clear that the scarab is not more valuable than you have assumed?"

"Well," said Mr. Blowgrave, "I have had an expert's opinion on it. I showed it to M. Fouquet, the Egyptologist, when he was over here from

Brussels a few months ago, and his opinion was that it was a worthless imitation. Not only was it not a genuine scarab, but the inscription was a sham, too, just a collection of hieroglyphic characters jumbled together without sense or meaning."

"Then," said Thorndyke, taking another look at the seal through his lens, "it would seem that Rudolpho, or Rudolpho's uncle, has got a bad bargain. Which doesn't throw much light on the affair."

At this point Miss Blowgrave intervened. "I think, Father," said she, "you have not given Dr. Thorndyke quite all the facts about the scarab. He ought to be told about its connection with Uncle Reuben."

As the girl spoke, Thorndyke looked at her with curious expression of suddenly awakened interest. Later I understood the meaning of that look, but at the time there seemed to me nothing particularly arresting in her words.

"It is just a family tradition," Mr. Blowgrave said deprecatingly. "Probably it is all nonsense."

"Well, let us have it, at any rate," said Thorndyke. "We may get some light from it."

Thus urged, Mr. Blowgrave hemmed a little shyly and began.

"The story concerns my great-grandfather, Silas Blowgrave, and his doings during the war with France. It seems that he commanded a privateer of which he and his brother Reuben were the joint owners, and that in the course of their last cruise they acquired a very remarkable and valuable collection of jewels. Goodness knows how they got them – not very honestly, I suspect, for they appear to have been a pair of precious rascals. Something has been said about the loot from a South American church or cathedral, but there is really nothing known about the affair. There are no documents. It is mere oral tradition and very vague and sketchy. The story goes that when they had sold off the ship, they came down to live at Shawstead in Hertfordshire, Silas occupying the manor house – in which I live at present – and Reuben a farm adjoining. The bulk of the loot they shared out at the end of the cruise, but the jewels were kept apart to be dealt with later – perhaps when the circumstances under which they had been acquired had been forgotten. However, both men were inveterate gamblers and it seems – according to the testimony of a servant of Reuben's who overheard them – that on a certain night when they had been playing heavily, they decided to finish up by playing for the whole collection of jewels as a single stake. Silas, who had the jewels in his custody, was seen to go to the manor house and return to Reuben's house carrying a small, iron chest.

"Apparently they played late into the night, after everyone else but the servant had gone to bed, and the luck was with Reuben, though it seems probable that he gave luck some assistance. At any rate, when the play was finished and the chest handed over, Silas roundly accused him of cheating, and we may assume that a pretty serious quarrel took place. Exactly what happened is not clear, for when the quarrel began Reuben dismissed the servant, who retired to her bedroom in a distant part of the house. But in the morning it was discovered that Reuben and the chest of jewels had both disappeared, and there were distinct traces of blood in the room in which the two men had been playing. Silas professed to know nothing about the disappearance, but a strong – and probably just – suspicion arose that he had murdered his brother and made away with the jewels. The result was that Silas also disappeared, and for a long time his whereabouts was not known, even by his wife.

"Later it transpired that he had taken up his abode under an assumed name, in Egypt, and that he had developed an enthusiastic interest in the then new science of Egyptology – the Rosetta Stone had been deciphered only a few years previously. After a time he resumed communication with his wife, but never made any statement as to the mystery of his brother's disappearance. A few months before his death he visited his home in disguise and he then handed to his wife a little sealed packet which was to be delivered to his only son, William, on his attaining the age of twenty-one. That packet contained the scarab and the letter which you have taken from the envelope."

"Am I to read it?" asked Thorndyke.

"Certainly, if you think it worth while," was the reply. Thorndyke opened the yellow sheet of paper and, glancing through the brown and faded writing, read aloud:

Cairo, 4 March, 1833.

My Dear Son,

I am sending you, as my last gift, a valuable scarab and a few words of counsel on which I would bid you meditate. Believe me, there is much wisdom in the lore of Old Egypt. Make it your own. Treasure the scarab as a precious inheritance. Handle it often but show it to none. Give your Uncle Reuben a Christian burial. It is your duty, and you will have your reward. He robbed your father, but he shall make restitution.

Farewell!

Your affectionate father,

Silas Blowgrave.

As Thorndyke laid down the letter he looked inquiringly at our client.

"Well," he said, "here are some plain instructions. How have they been carried out?"

"They haven't been carried out at all," replied Mr. Blowgrave. "As to his son William, my grandfather, he was not disposed to meddle in the matter. This seemed to be a frank admission that Silas killed his brother and concealed the body, and William didn't choose to reopen the scandal. Besides, the instructions are not so very plain. It is all very well to say, '*Give your Uncle Reuben Christian burial*', but where the deuce is Uncle Reuben?"

"It is plainly hinted," said Thorndyke, "that whoever gives the body Christian burial will stand to benefit, and the word 'restitution' seems to suggest a clue to the whereabouts of the jewels. Has no one thought it worth while to find out where the body is deposited?"

"But how could they?" demanded Blowgrave. "He doesn't give the faintest clue. He talks as if his son knew where the body was. And then, you know, even supposing Silas did not take the jewels with him, there was the question, whose property were they? To begin with, they were pretty certainly stolen property, though no one knows where they came from. Then Reuben apparently got them from Silas by fraud, and Silas got them back by robbery and murder. If William had discovered them, he would have had to give them up to Reuben's sons, and yet they weren't strictly Reuben's property. No one had an undeniable claim to them, even if they could have found them."

"But that is not the case now," said Miss Blowgrave.

"No," said Mr. Blowgrave, in answer to Thorndyke's look of inquiry. "The position is quite clear now. Reuben's grandson, my cousin Arthur, has died recently, and as he had no children, he has dispersed his property. The old farm-house and the bulk of his estate he has left to a nephew, but he made a small bequest to my daughter and named her as the residuary legatee, so that whatever rights Reuben had to the jewels are now vested in her, and on my death she will be Silas's heir, too. As a matter of fact," Mr. Blowgrave continued, "we were discussing this very question on the night of the robbery. I may as well tell you that my girl will be left pretty poorly off when I go, for there is a heavy mortgage on our property and mighty little capital. Uncle Reuben's jewels would have

70

made the old home secure for her if we could have laid our hands on them. However, I mustn't take up your time with our domestic affairs."

"Your domestic affairs are not entirely irrelevant," said Thorndyke. "But what is it that you want me to do in the matter?"

"Well," said Blowgrave, "my house has been robbed and my premises set fire to. The police can apparently do nothing. They say there is no clue at all unless the robbery was committed by somebody in the house, which is absurd, seeing that the servants were all engaged in putting out the fire. But I want the robber traced and punished, and I want to get the scarab back. It may be intrinsically valueless, as M. Fouquet said, but Silas's testamentary letter seems to indicate that it had some value. At any rate, it is an heirloom, and I am loath to lose it. It seems a presumptuous thing to ask you to investigate a trumpery robbery, but I should take it as a great kindness if you would look into the matter."

"Cases of robbery pure and simple," replied Thorndyke, "are rather alien to my ordinary practice, but in this one there are certain curious features that seem to make an investigation worthwhile. Yes, Mr. Blowgrave, I will look into the case, and I have some hope that we may be able to lay our hands on the robber, in spite of the apparent absence of clues. I will ask you to leave both these letters for me to examine more minutely, and I shall probably want to make an inspection of the premises – perhaps to-morrow."

"Whenever you like," said Blowgrave. "I am delighted that you are willing to undertake the inquiry. I have heard so much about you from my friend Stalker, of the Griffin Life Assurance Company, for whom you have acted on several occasions."

"Before you go," said Thorndyke, "there is one point that we must clear up. Who is there besides yourselves that knows of the existence of the scarab and this letter and the history attaching to them?"

"I really can't say," replied Blowgrave. "No one has seen them but my cousin Arthur. I once showed them to him, and he may have talked about them in the family. I didn't treat the matter as a secret."

When our visitors had gone, we discussed the bearings of the case.

"It is quite a romantic story," said I, "and the robbery has its points of interest, but I am rather inclined to agree with the police – there is mighty little to go on."

"There would have been less," said Thorndyke, "if our sporting friend hadn't been so pleased with himself. That typewritten letter was a piece of gratuitous impudence. Our gentleman overrated his security and crowed too loud."

"I don't see that there is much to be gleaned from the letter, all the same," said I.

"I am sorry to hear you say that, Jervis," he exclaimed, "because I was proposing to hand the letter over to you to examine and report on."

"I was only referring to the superficial appearances," I said hastily. "No doubt a detailed examination will bring something more distinctive into view."

"I have no doubt it will," he said, "and as there are reasons for pushing on the investigation as quickly as possible, I suggest that you get to work at once. I will occupy myself with the old letter and the envelope."

On this I began my examination without delay, and as a preliminary I proceeded to take a facsimile photograph of the letter by putting it in a large printing frame with a sensitive plate and a plate of clear glass. The resulting negative showed not only the typewritten lettering, but also the watermark and wire lines of the paper, and a faint grease spot. Next I turned my attention to the lettering itself, and here I soon began to accumulate quite a number of identifiable peculiarities. The machine was apparently a Corona, fitted with the small "Elite" type, and the alignment was markedly defective. The "lower case" – or small – "a" was well below the line, although the capital "A" appeared to be correctly placed, the "u" was slightly above the line, and the small "m" was partly clogged with dirt.

Up to this point I had been careful to manipulate the letter with forceps (although it had been handled by at least three persons, to my knowledge), and I now proceeded to examine it for finger-prints. As I could detect none by mere inspection, I dusted the back of the paper with finely powdered fuchsin, and distributed the powder by tapping the paper lightly. This brought into view quite a number of finger-prints, especially round the edges of the letter, and though most of them were very faint and shadowy, it was possible to make out the ridge pattern well enough for our purpose. Having blown off the excess of powder, I took the letter to the room where the large copying camera was set up, to photograph it before developing the finger-prints on the front. But here I found our laboratory assistant, Polton, in possession, with the sealed envelope fixed to the copying easel. "I shan't be a minute, sir," said he. "The Doctor wants an enlarged photograph of this seal. I've got the plate in."

I waited while he made his exposure and then proceeded to take the photograph of the letter, or rather of the finger-prints on the back of it. When I had developed the negative I powdered the front of the letter and brought out several more finger-prints – thumbs this time. They were a little difficult to see where they were imposed on the lettering, but, as the latter was bright blue and the fuchsin powder was red, this confusion disappeared in the photograph, in which the lettering was almost invisible while the finger-prints were more distinct than they had appeared to the eye. This completed my examination, and when I had verified the make of typewriter by reference to our album of specimens of typewriting, I left the negatives for Polton to dry and print and went down to the sitting-room to draw up my little report. I had just finished this and was speculating on what had become of Thorndyke when I heard his quick step on the stair and a few moments later he entered with a roll of paper in his hand. This he unrolled on the table, fixing it open with one or two lead paper-weights, and I came round to inspect it, when I found it to be a sheet of the Ordnance Map on the scale of twenty-five inches to the mile.

"Here is the Blowgraves' place," said Thorndyke, "nearly in the middle of the sheet. This is his house – Shawstead Manor – and that will probably be the out-building that was on fire. I take it that the house marked Dingle Farm is the one that Uncle Reuben occupied."

"Probably," I agreed. "But I don't see why you wanted this map if you are going down to the place itself to-morrow."

"The advantage of a map," said Thorndyke, "is that you can see all over it at once and get the lie of the land well into your mind, and you can measure all distances accurately and quickly with a scale and a pair of dividers. When we go down to-morrow, we shall know our way about as well as Blowgrave himself."

"And what use will that be?" I asked. "Where does the topography come into the case?"

"Well, Jervis," he replied, "there is the robber, for instance – he came from somewhere and he went somewhere. A study of the map may give us a hint as to his movements. But here comes Polton 'with the documents', as poor Miss Flite would say. What have you got for us, Polton?"

"They aren't quite dry, sir," said Polton, laying four large bromide prints on the table. "There's the enlargement of the seal – ten-by-eight, mounted – and three unmounted prints of Dr. Jervis's."

Thorndyke looked at my photographs critically. "They're excellent, Jervis," said he. "The finger-prints are perfectly legible, though faint. I only hope some of them are the right ones. That is my left thumb. I don't see yours. The small one is presumably Miss Blowgrave's. We must take her finger-prints to-morrow, and her father's, too. Then we shall know if we have got any of the robber's." He ran his eye over my report and nodded approvingly. "There is plenty there to enable us to identify the typewriter if we can get hold of it, and the paper is very distinctive. What do you think of the seal?" he added, laying the enlarged photograph before me.

"It is magnificent," I replied, with a grin. "Perfectly monumental."

"What are you grinning at?" he demanded.

"I was thinking that you seem to be counting your chickens in pretty good time," said I. "You are making elaborate preparations to identify the scarab, but you are rather disregarding the classical advice of the prudent Mrs. Glasse."

"I have a presentiment that we shall get that scarab," said he. "At any rate we ought to be in a position to identify it instantly and certainly if we are able to get a sight of it."

"We are not likely to," said I. "Still, there is no harm in providing for the improbable."

This was evidently Thorndyke's view, and he certainly made ample provision for this most improbable contingency, for, having furnished himself with a drawing-board and a sheet of tracing-paper, he pinned the latter over the photograph on the board and proceeded, with a fine pen and hectograph ink, to make a careful and minute tracing of the intricate and bewildering hieroglyphic inscription on the seal. When he had finished it he transferred it to a clay duplicator and took off half-a-dozen copies, one of which he handed to me. I looked at it dubiously and remarked, "You have said that the medical jurist must make all knowledge his province. Has he got to be an Egyptologist, too?"

"He will be the better medical jurist if he is," was the reply, of which I made a mental note for my future guidance. But meanwhile Thorndyke's proceedings were, to me, perfectly incomprehensible. What was his object in making this minute tracing? The seal itself was sufficient for identification. I lingered, awhile hoping that some fresh development might throw a light on the mystery. But his next proceeding was like to have reduced me to stupefaction. I saw him go to the book-shelves and take down a book. As he laid it on the table I glanced at the title, and when I saw that it was Raper's *Navigation Tables*, I stole softly out into the lobby, put on my hat, and went for a walk.

When I returned the investigation was apparently concluded, for Thorndyke was seated in his easy chair, placidly reading *The Compleat Angler*. On the table lay a large circular protractor, a straight-edge, an architect's scale, and a sheet of tracing-paper on which was a tracing in hectograph ink of Shawstead Manor.

"Why did you make this tracing?" I asked. "Why not take the map itself?"

"We don't want the whole of it," he replied, "and I dislike cutting up maps."

74

By taking an informal lunch in the train, we arrived at Shawstead Manor by half-past two. Our approach up the drive had evidently been observed, for Blowgrave and his daughter were waiting at the porch to receive us. The former came forward with outstretched hand, but a distinctly woebegone expression, and exclaimed, "It is most kind of you to come down, but alas! You are too late."

"Too late for what?" demanded Thorndyke,

"I will show you," replied Blowgrave, and seizing my colleague by the arm, he strode off excitedly to a little wicket at the side of the house and, passing through it, hurried along a narrow alley that skirted the garden wall and ended in a large meadow, at one end of which stood a dilapidated windmill. Across this meadow he bustled, dragging my colleague with him, until he reached a heap of freshly-turned earth, where he halted and pointed tragically to a spot where the turf had evidently been raised and untidily replaced,

"There!" he exclaimed, stooping to pull up the loose turfs and thereby exposing what was evidently a large hole, recently and hastily filled in. "That was done last night or early this morning, for I walked over this meadow only yesterday evening and there was no sign of disturbed ground then."

Thorndyke stood looking down at the hole with a faint smile. "And what do you infer from that?" he asked.

"Infer!" shrieked Blowgrave. "Why, I infer that whoever dug this hole was searching for Uncle Reuben and the lost jewels!"

"I am inclined to agree with you," Thorndyke said calmly. "He happened to search in the wrong place, but that is his affair."

"The wrong place!" Blowgrave and his daughter exclaimed in unison. "How do you know it is the wrong place?"

"Because," replied Thorndyke, "I believe I know the right place, and this is not it. But we can put the matter to the test, and we'd had better do so. Can you get a couple of men with picks and shovels? Or shall we handle the tools ourselves?

"I think that would be better," said Blowgrave, who was quivering with excitement. "We don't want to take anyone into our confidence if we can help it."

"No," Thorndyke agreed. "Then I suggest that you fetch the tools while I locate the spot."

Blowgrave assented eagerly and went off at a brisk trot, while the young lady remained with us and watched Thorndyke with intense curiosity.

"I mustn't interrupt you with questions," said she "but I can't imagine how you found out where Uncle Reuben was buried."

"We will go into that later," he replied, "but first we have got to find Uncle Reuben." He laid his research case down on the ground, and opening it, took out three sheets of paper, each bearing a duplicate of his tracing of the map, and on each was marked a spot on this meadow from which a number of lines radiated like the spokes of a wheel.

"You see, Jervis," he said, exhibiting them to me, "the advantage of a map. I have been able to rule off these sets of bearings regardless of obstructions, such as those young trees, which have arisen since Silas's day, and mark the spot in its correct place. If the recent obstructions prevent us from taking the bearings, we can still find the spot by measurements with the land-chain or tape."

"Why have you got three plans?" I asked.

"Because there are three imaginable places. No. 1 is the most likely, No. 2 less likely, but possible, and No. 3 is impossible. That is the one that our friend tried last night. No. 1 is among those young trees, and we will now see if we can pick up the bearings in spite of them."

We moved on to the clump of young trees, where Thorndyke took from the research-case a tall, folding camera-tripod and a large prismatic compass with an aluminium dial. With the latter he took one or two trial bearings and then, setting up the tripod, fixed the compass on it. For some minutes, Miss Blowgrave and I watched him as he shifted the tripod from spot to spot, peering through the sight-vane of the compass and glancing occasionally at the map. At length he turned to us and said, "We are in luck. None of these trees interferes with our bearings." He took from the research-case a surveyor's arrow, and sticking it in the ground under the tripod, added, "That is the spot. But we may have to dig a good way round it, for a compass is only a rough instrument."

At this moment Mr. Blowgrave staggered up, breathing hard, and flung down on the ground three picks, two shovels and a spade. "I won't hinder you, Doctor, by asking for explanations," said he, "but I am utterly mystified. You must tell us what it all means when we have finished our work."

This Thorndyke promised to do, but meanwhile he took off his coat, and rolling up his shirt sleeves, seized the spade and began cutting out a large square of turf. As the soil was uncovered, Blowgrave and I attacked it with picks and Miss Blowgrave shovelled away the loose earth.

"Do you know how far down we have to go?" I asked.

"The body lies six feet below the surface," Thorndyke replied, and as he spoke he laid down his spade, and taking a telescope from the research-case, swept it round the margin of the meadow and finally pointed it at a farm house some six-hundred yards distant, of which he made a somewhat prolonged inspection, after which he took the remaining pick and fell to work on the opposite corner of the exposed square of earth.

For nearly half-an-hour we worked on steadily, gradually eating our way downwards, plying pick and shovel alternately, while Miss Blowgrave cleared the loose earth away from the edges of the deepening pit. Then a halt was called and we came to the surface, wiping our faces.

"I think, Nellie," said Blowgrave, divesting himself of his waistcoat, "a jug of lemonade and four tumblers would be useful, unless our visitors would prefer beer."

We both gave our votes for lemonade, and Miss Nellie tripped away towards the house, while Thorndyke, taking up his telescope, once more inspected the farm house.

"You seem greatly interested in that house," I remarked.

"I am," he replied, handing me the telescope. "Just take a look at the window in the right-hand gable, but keep under the tree."

I pointed the telescope at the gable and there observed an open window at which a man was seated. He held a binocular glass to his eyes and the instrument appeared to be directed at us.

"We are being spied on, I fancy," said I, passing the telescope to Blowgrave, "but I suppose it doesn't matter. This is your land, isn't it?"

"Yes," replied Blowgrave, "but still, we didn't want any spectators. That is Harold Bowker," he added steadying the telescope against a tree, "my cousin Arthur's nephew, whom I told you about as having inherited the farm-house. He seems mighty interested in us, but small things interest one in the country."

Here the appearance of Miss Nellie, advancing across the meadow with an inviting-looking basket, diverted our attention from our inquisitive watcher. Six thirsty eyes were riveted on that basket until it drew near and presently disgorged a great glass jug and four tumblers, when we each took off a long and delicious draught and then jumped down into the pit to resume our labours.

Another half-hour passed. We had excavated in some places to nearly the full depth and were just discussing the advisability of another short rest when Blowgrave, who was working in one corner, uttered a loud cry and stood up suddenly, holding something in his fingers. A glance at the object showed it to be a bone, brown and earth-stained, but evidently a bone. Evidently, too, a human bone, as Thorndyke decided when Blowgrave handed it to him triumphantly.

"We have been very fortunate," said he, "to get so near at the first trial. This is from the right great toe, so we may assume that the skeleton

77

lies just outside this pit, but we had better excavate carefully in your corner and see exactly how the bones lie." This he proceeded to do himself, probing cautiously with the spade and clearing the earth away from the corner. Very soon the remaining bones of the right foot came into view and then the ends of the two leg-bones and a portion of the left foot.

"We can see now," said he, "how the skeleton lies, and all we have to do is to extend the excavation in that direction. But there is only room for one to work down here. I think you and Mr. Blowgrave had better dig down from the surface."

On this, I climbed out of the pit, followed reluctantly by Blowgrave, who still held the little brown bone in his hand and was in a state of wild excitement and exultation that somewhat scandalised his daughter.

"It seems rather ghoulish," she remarked, "to be gloating over poor Uncle Reuben's body in this way."

"I know," said Blowgrave, "it isn't reverent. But I didn't kill Uncle Reuben, you know, whereas – well, it was a long time ago." With this rather inconsequent conclusion he took a draught of lemonade, seized his pick, and fell to work with a will. I, too, indulged in a draught and passed a full tumbler down to Thorndyke. But before resuming my labours, I picked up the telescope and once more inspected the farm-house. The window was still open, but the watcher had apparently become bored with the not very thrilling spectacle. At any rate he had disappeared.

From this time onward, every few minutes brought some discovery. First, a pair of deeply rusted steel shoe buckles, then one or two buttons, and presently a fine gold watch with a fob-chain and a bunch of seals, looking uncannily new and fresh and seeming more fraught with tragedy than even the bones themselves. In his cautious digging, Thorndyke was careful not to disturb the skeleton, and looking down into the narrow trench that was growing from the corner of the pit, I could see both legs, with only the right foot missing, projecting from the miniature cliff. Meanwhile our of the trench was deepening rapidly, so that Thorndyke presently warned us to stop digging and bade us come down and shovel away the earth as he disengaged it.

At length the whole skeleton, excepting the head, was uncovered, though it lay undisturbed as it might have lain in its coffin. And now, as Thorndyke picked away the earth around the head, we could see that the skull was propped forward as if it rested on a high pillow. A little more careful probing with the pick-point served to explain this appearance. For as the earth fell away and disclosed the grinning skull, there came into view the edge and ironbound corners of a small chest.

It was an impressive spectacle – weird, solemn, and rather dreadful. There for over a century the ill-fated gambler had lain, his mouldering head pillowed on the booty of unrecorded villainy, booty that had been won by fraud, retrieved by violence, and hidden at last by the final winner with the witness of his crime.

"Here is a fine text for a moralist who would preach on the vanity of riches," said Thorndyke.

We all stood silent for a while, gazing, not without awe, at the stark figure that lay guarding the ill-gotten treasure. Miss Blowgrave – who had been helped down when we descended – crept closer to her father and murmured that it was "rather awful", while Blowgrave himself displayed a queer mixture of exultation and shuddering distaste.

Suddenly the silence was broken by a voice from above, and we all looked up with a start. A youngish man was standing on the brink of the pit, looking down on us with very evident disapproval.

"It seems that I have come just in the nick of time," observed the new-comer. "I shall have to take possession of that chest, you know, and of the remains, too, I suppose. That is my ancestor, Reuben Blowgrave.

"Well, Harold," said Blowgrave, "you can have Uncle Reuben if you want him. But the chest belongs to Nellie."

Here Mr. Harold Bowker – I recognised him now as the watcher from the window – dropped down into the pit and advanced with something of a swagger.

"I am Reuben's heir," said he, "through my Uncle Arthur, and I take possession of this property and the remains."

"Pardon me, Harold," said Blowgrave, "but Nellie is Arthur's residuary legatee, and this is the residue of the estate."

"Rubbish!" exclaimed Bowker. "By the way, how did you find out where he was buried?"

"Oh, that was quite simple," replied Thorndyke with unexpected geniality. "I'll show you the plan." He climbed up to the surface and returned in a few moments with the three tracings and his letter-case. "This is how we located the spot." He handed the plan numbered "3" to Bowker, who took it from him and stood looking at it with a puzzled frown.

"But this isn't the place," he said at length.

"Isn't it?" queried Thorndyke. "No, of course, I've given you the wrong one. This is the plan." He handed Bowker the plan marked No. 1, and took the other from him, laying it down on a heap of earth. Then, as Bowker pored gloomily over No. 1, he took a knife and a pencil from his pocket, and with his back to our visitor, scraped the lead of the pencil, letting the black powder fall on the plan that he had just laid down. I watched him with some curiosity, and when I observed that the black scrapings fell on two spots near the edges of the paper, a sudden suspicion flashed into my mind, which was confirmed when I saw him tap the paper lightly with his pencil, gently blow away the powder, and quickly producing my photograph of the typewritten letter from his case, hold it for a moment beside the plan.

"This is all very well," said Bowker, looking up from the plan, "but how did you find out about these bearings?

Thorndyke swiftly replaced the letter in his case, and turning round, replied, "I am afraid I can't give you any further information."

"Can't you, indeed!" Bowker exclaimed insolently. "Perhaps I shall compel you to. But, at any rate, I forbid any of you to lay hands on my property."

Thorndyke looked at him steadily and said in an ominously quiet tone, "Now, listen to me, Mr. Bowker. Let us have an end of this nonsense. You have played a risky game and you have lost. How much you have lost I can't say until I know whether Mr. Blowgrave intends to prosecute."

"To prosecute!" shouted Bowker. "What the deuce do you mean by prosecute?"

"I mean," said Thorndyke, "that on the 7th of June, after nine o'clock at night, you entered the dwelling-house of Mr. Blowgrave and stole and carried away certain of his goods and chattels. A part of them you have restored, but you are still in possession of some of the stolen property – to wit, a scarab and a deed-box."

As Thorndyke made this statement in his calm, level tones, Bowker's face blanched to a tallowy white, and he stood staring at my colleague, the very picture of astonishment and dismay. But he fired a last shot.

"This is sheer midsummer madness," he exclaimed huskily, "and you know it."

Thorndyke turned to our host. "It is for you to settle, Mr. Blowgrave," said he. "I hold conclusive evidence that Mr. Bowker stole your deed-box. If you decide to prosecute, I shall produce that evidence in court and he will certainly be convicted."

Blowgrave and his daughter looked at the accused man with an embarrassment almost equal to his own.

"I am astounded," the former said at length, "but I don't want to be vindictive. Look here, Harold, hand over the scarab and we'll say no more about it."

"You can't do that," said Thorndyke. "The law doesn't allow you to compound a robbery. He can return the property if he pleases and you can do as you think best about prosecuting. But you can't make conditions."

There was silence for some seconds. Then, without another word, the crestfallen adventurer turned, and scrambling up out of the pit, took a hasty departure.

It was nearly a couple of hours later that, after a leisurely wash and a hasty, nondescript meal, we carried the little chest from the dining-room to the study. Here, when he had closed the French window and drawn the curtains, Mr. Blowgrave produced a set of tools and we fell to work on the iron fastenings of the chest. It was no light task, though a century's rust had thinned the stout bands, but at length the lid yielded to the thrust of a long case-opener and rose with a protesting creak. The chest was lined with a double thickness of canvas, apparently part of a sail, and contained a number of small leathern bags, which, as we lifted them out, one by one, felt as if they were filled with pebbles. But when we untied the thongs of one and emptied its contents into a wooden bowl, Blowgrave heaved a sigh of ecstasy and Miss Nellie uttered a little scream of delight. They were all cut stones, and most of them of exceptional size: Rubies, emeralds, sapphires and a few diamonds. As to their value, we could form but the vaguest guess, but Thorndyke, who was a fair judge of gem-stones, gave it as his opinion that they were fine specimens of their kind, though roughly cut, and that they had probably formed the enrichment of some shrine.

"The question is," said Blowgrave, gazing gloatingly on the bowl of sparkling gems, "what are we to do with them?"

"I suggest," said Thorndyke, "that Dr. Jervis stay here to-night to help you to guard them, and that in the morning you take them up to London and deposit them at your bank."

Blowgrave fell in eagerly with this suggestion, which I seconded. "But," said he, "that chest is a queer-looking package to be carrying abroad. Now, if we only had that confounded deed-box – "

"There's a deed-box on the cabinet behind you," said Thorndyke.

Blowgrave turned round sharply. "God bless us!" he exclaimed. "It has come back the way it went. Harold must have slipped in at the window while we were at tea. Well, I'm glad he has made restitution. When I look at that bowl and think what he must have narrowly missed, I don't feel inclined to be hard on him. I suppose the scarab is inside – not that it matters much now."

The scarab was inside in an envelope, and as Thorndyke turned it over in his hand and examined the hieroglyphics on it through his lens, Miss Blowgrave asked, "Is it of any value, Dr. Thorndyke? It can't have any connection with the secret of the hiding-place, because you found the jewels without it."

"By the way, Doctor, I don't know whether it is permissible for me to ask, but how on earth did you find out where the jewels were hidden? To me it looks like black magic."

Thorndyke laughed in a quiet, inward fashion. "There is nothing magical about it," said he. "It was a perfectly simple, straightforward problem. But Miss Nellie is wrong. We had the scarab – that is to say we had the wax impression of it, which is the same thing. And the scarab was the key to the riddle. You see," he continued, "Silas's letter and the scarab formed together a sort of intelligence test."

"Did they?" said Blowgrave. "Then he drew a blank every time."

Thorndyke chuckled. "His descendants were certainly a little lacking in enterprise," he admitted. "Silas's instructions were perfectly plain and explicit. Whoever would find the treasure must first acquire some knowledge of Egyptian lore and must study the scarab attentively. It was the broadest of hints, but no one – excepting Harold Bowker, who must have heard about the scarab from his Uncle Arthur – seems to have paid any attention to it.

"Now it happens that I have just enough elementary knowledge of the hieroglyphic characters to enable me to spell them out when they are used alphabetically, and as soon as I saw the seal, I could see that these hieroglyphics formed English words. My attention was first attracted by the second group of signs, which spelled the word 'Reuben,' and then I saw that the first group spelled 'Uncle.' Of course, the instant I heard Miss Nellie speak of the connection between the scarab and Uncle Reuben, the murder was out. I saw at a glance that the scarab contained all the required information. Last night I made a careful tracing of the hieroglyphics and then rendered them into our own alphabet. This is the result."

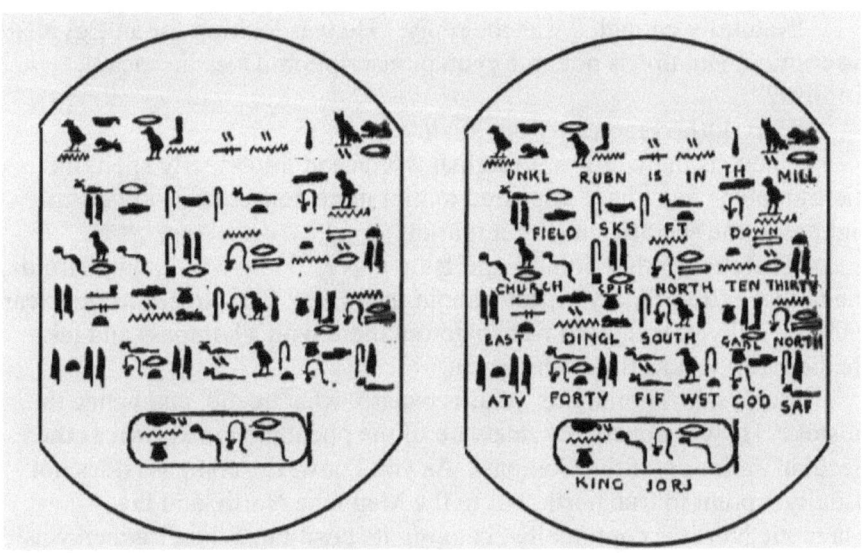

Thorndyke's Tracing of the Impression of the Scarab and
The Transliteration of the Heiroglyphics

He took from his letter-case and spread out on the table a duplicate of the tracing which I had seen him make, and of which he had given me a copy. But since I had last seen it, it had received an addition, under each group of signs the equivalents in modern Roman lettering had been written, and these made the following words.

> *unkl rubn is in th mill field sks ft down church spir north ten thirty east dingl south gabl north aty forty fif west god saf king jorj*

Our two friends gazed at Thorndyke's transliteration in blank astonishment. At length Blowgrave remarked, "But this translation must have demanded a very profound knowledge of the Egyptian writing."

"Not at all," replied Thorndyke. "Any intelligent person could master the Egyptian alphabet in an hour. The language, of course, is quite another matter. The spelling of this is a little crude, but it is quite intelligible and does Silas great credit, considering how little was known in his time."

"How do you suppose M. Fouquet came to overlook this?" Blowgrave asked.

"Naturally enough," was the reply. "He was looking for an Egyptian inscription. But this is not an Egyptian inscription. Does he speak English?"

"Very little. Practically not at all."

"Then, as the words are English words and imperfectly spelt, the hieroglyphics must have appeared to him mere nonsense. And he was right as to the scarab being an imitation."

"There is another point," said Blowgrave. "How was it that Harold made that extraordinary mistake about the place? The directions are clear enough. All you had to do was to go out there with a compass and take the bearings just as they were given."

"But," said Thorndyke, "that is exactly what he did, and hence the mistake. He was apparently unaware of the phenomenon known as the Secular Variation of the Compass. As you know, the compass does not – usually – point to true north, but to the Magnetic North, and the Magnetic North is continually changing its position. When Reuben was buried – about 1810 – it was twenty-four degrees, twenty-six minutes west of true north. At the present time, it is fourteen degrees, forty-eight minutes west of true north. So Harold's bearings would be no less than ten degrees out, which of course, gave him a totally wrong position. But Silas was a ship-master, a navigator, and of course knew all about the vagaries of the compass and, as his directions were intended for use at some date unknown to him, I assumed that the bearings that he gave were true bearings – that when he said 'north' he meant true north, which is always the same, and this turned out to be the case. But I also prepared a plan with magnetic bearings corrected up to date. Here are the three plans, No. 1 – the one we used – showing true bearings, No. 2, showing corrected magnetic bearings which might have given us the correct spot, and No. 3, with uncorrected magnetic bearings, giving us the spot where Harold dug, and which could not possibly have been the right spot."

On the following morning I escorted the deed-box, filled with the booty and tied up and sealed with the scarab, to Mr. Blowgrave's bank. And that ended our connection with the case, excepting that, a month or two later, we attended by request the unveiling in Shawstead churchyard of a fine monument to Reuben Blowgrave. This took the slightly inappropriate form of an obelisk, on which were cut the name and approximate dates, with the added inscription, "*Cast thy bread upon the waters and it shall return after many days*," concerning which Thorndyke remarked dryly that he supposed the exhortation applied equally even if the bread happened to belong to someone else.

The New Jersey Sphinx

"**A** rather curious neighbourhood this, Jervis," my friend Thorndyke remarked as we turned into Upper Bedford Place. "A sort of aviary for cosmopolitan birds of passage, especially those of the Oriental variety. The Asiatic and African faces that one sees at the windows of these Bloomsbury boarding houses almost suggest an overflow from the ethnographical galleries of the adjacent British Museum."

"Yes," I agreed, "there must be quite a considerable population of Africans, Japanese, and Hindus in Bloomsbury – particularly Hindus."

As I spoke, and as if in illustration of my statement, a dark-skinned man rushed out of one of the houses farther down the street and began to advance towards us in a rapid, bewildered fashion, stopping to look at each street door as he came to it. His hatless condition – though he was exceedingly well dressed – and his agitated manner immediately attracted my attention, and Thorndyke's too, for the latter remarked, "Our friend seems to be in trouble. An accident, perhaps, or a case of sudden illness."

Here the stranger, observing our approach, ran forward to meet us and asked in an agitated tone, "Can you tell me, please, where I can find a doctor?"

"I am a medical man," replied Thorndyke, "and so is my friend."

Our acquaintance grasped Thorndyke's sleeve and exclaimed eagerly, "Come with me, then, quickly, if you please. A most dreadful thing has happened."

He hurried us along at something between a trot and a quick walk, and as we proceeded he continued excitely, "I am quite confused and terrified – it is all so strange and sudden and terrible."

"Try," said Thorndyke, "to calm yourself a little and tell us what has happened."

"I will," was the agitated reply. "It is my cousin, Dinanath Byramji – his surname is the same as mine. Just now I went to his room and was horrified to find him lying on the floor, staring at the ceiling and blowing – like this," and he puffed out his cheeks with a soft blowing noise. "I spoke to him and shook his hand, but he was like a dead man. This is the house."

He darted up the steps to an open door at which a rather scared page-boy was on guard, and running along the hall, rapidly ascended the stairs. Following him closely, we reached a rather dark first-floor landing where, at a half-open door, a servant-maid stood listening with an expression of awe to a rhythmical snoring sound that issued from the room.

The unconscious man lay as Mr. Byramji had said, staring fixedly at the ceiling with wide-open, glazy eyes, puffing out his cheeks slightly at each breath. But the breathing was shallow and slow, and it grew perceptibly slower, with lengthening pauses. And even as I was timing it with my watch while Thorndyke examined the pupils with the aid of a wax match, it stopped. I laid my finger on the wrist and caught one or two slow, flickering beats. Then the pulse stopped too.

"He is gone," said I. "He must have burst one of the large arteries."

"Apparently," said Thorndyke, "though one would not have expected it at his age. But wait! What is this?"

He pointed to the right ear, in the hollow of which a few drops of blood had collected, and as he spoke he drew his hand gently over the dead man's head and moved it slightly from side to side.

"There is a fracture of the base of the skull," said he, "and quite distinct signs of contusion of the scalp." He turned to Mr. Byramji, who stood wringing his hand and gazing incredulously at the dead man, and asked, "Can you throw any light on this?"

The Indian looked at him vacantly. The sudden tragedy seemed to have paralysed his brain. "I don't understand," said he. "What does it mean?"

"It means," replied Thorndyke, "that he has received a heavy blow on the head."

For a few moments Mr. Byramji continued to stare vacantly at my colleague. Then he seemed suddenly to realise the import of Thorndyke's remark, for he started up excitedly and turned to the door, outside which the two servants were hovering.

"Where is the person gone who came in with my cousin?" he demanded.

"You saw him go out, Albert," said the maid. "Tell Mr. Byramji where he went to."

The page tiptoed into the room with a fearful eye fixed on the corpse, and replied falteringly, "I only see the back of him as he went out, and all I know is that he turned to the left. P'raps he's gone for a doctor."

"Can you give us any description of him?" asked Thorndyke.

"I only see the back of him," repeated the page. "He was a shortish gentleman and he had on a dark suit of clothes and a hard felt hat. That's all I know."

"Thank you," said Thorndyke. "We may want to ask you some more questions presently," and having conducted the page to the door, he shut it and turned to Mr. Byramji.

"Have you any idea who it was that was with your cousin?" he asked.

"None at all," was the reply. "I was sitting in my room opposite, writing, when I heard my cousin come up the stairs with another person, to whom he was talking. I could not hear what he was saying. They went into his room – this room – and I could occasionally catch the sound of their voices. In about a quarter-of-an-hour, I heard the door open and shut, and then someone went downstairs, softly and rather quickly. I finished the letter that I was writing, and when I had addressed, it I came in here to ask my cousin who the visitor was. I thought it might be someone who had come to negotiate for the ruby."

"The ruby!" exclaimed Thorndyke. "What ruby do you refer to?"

"The great ruby," replied Byramji. "But of course you have not – " He broke off suddenly and stood for a few moments staring at Thorndyke with parted lips and wide-open eyes, then abruptly he turned, and kneeling beside the dead man he began, in a curious, caressing, half-apologetic manner, first to pass his hands gently over the body at the waist and then to unfasten the clothes. This brought into view a handsome, soft leather belt, evidently of native workmanship, worn next to the skin and furnished with three pockets. Mr. Byramji unbuttoned and explored them in quick succession, and it was evident that they were all empty.

"It is gone!" he exclaimed in low, intense tones, "Gone! Ah! But how little would it signify! But thou, dear Dinanath, my brother, my friend, thou art gone, too!"

He lifted the dead man's hand and pressed it to his cheek, murmuring endearments in his own tongue. Presently he laid it down reverently, and sprang up, and I was startled at the change in his aspect. The delicate, gentle, refined face had suddenly become the face of a Fury – fierce, sinister, vindictive.

"This wretch must die!" he exclaimed huskily. "This sordid brute who, without compunction, has crushed out a precious life as one would carelessly crush a fly, for the sake of a paltry crystal – he must die, if I have to follow him and strangle him with my own hands!"

Thorndyke laid his hand on Byramji's shoulder. "I sympathise with you most cordially," said he. "If it is as you think, and appearances suggest, that your cousin has been murdered as a mere incident of robbery, the murderer's life is forfeit, and Justice cries aloud for retribution. The fact of murder will be determined, for or against, by a proper inquiry. Meanwhile we have to ascertain who this unknown man is and what happened while he was with your cousin."

Byramji made a gesture of despair. "But the man has disappeared, and nobody has seen him! What can we do?"

"Let us look around us," plied Thorndyke, "and see if we can judge what has happened in this room. What, for instance, is this?"

He picked up from a corner near the door a small leather object, which he handed to Mr. Byramji. The Indian seized it eagerly, exclaiming, "Ah! It is the little bag in which my cousin used to carry the ruby. So he had taken it from his belt."

"It hasn't been dropped, by any chance?" I suggested.

In an instant Mr. Byramji was down on his knees, peering and groping about the floor, and Thorndyke and I joined in the search. But, as might have been expected, there was no sign of the ruby – nor, indeed, of anything else, excepting a hat which I picked up from under the table.

"No," said Mr. Byramji, rising with a dejected air. "It is gone – of course it is gone, and the murderous villain – "

Here his glance fell on the hat, which I had laid on the table, and he bent forward to look at it.

"Whose hat is this?" he demanded, glancing at the chair on which Thorndyke's hat and mine had been placed.

"Is it not your cousin's?" asked Thorndyke"

"No, certainly not. His hat was like mine – we bought them both together. It had a white silk lining with his initials, *D. B.*, in gold. This has no lining and is a much older hat. It must be the murderer's hat."

"If it is," said Thorndyke, "that is a most important fact – important in two respects. Could you let us see your hat?"

"Certainly," replied Byramji, walking quickly, but with a soft tread, to the door. As he went out, shutting the door silently behind him, Thorndyke picked up the derelict hat and swiftly tried it on the head of the dead man. As far as I could judge, it appeared to fit, and this Thorndyke confirmed as he replaced it on the table.

"As you see," said he, "it is at least a practical fit, which is a fact of some significance."

Here Mr. Byramji returned with his own hat, which he placed on the table by the side of the other, and thus placed, crown uppermost, the two hats were closely similar. Both were black, hard felts of the prevalent "bowler" shape, and of good quality, and the difference in their age and state of preservation was not striking, but when Byramji turned them over and exhibited their interiors, it was seen that whereas the strange hat was unlined save for the leather head-band, Byramji's had a white silk lining and bore the owner's initials in embossed gilt letters.

"What happened," said Thorndyke, when he had carefully compared the two hats, "seems fairly obvious. The two men, on entering, placed their hats crown upwards on the table. In some way – perhaps during a struggle – the visitor's hat was knocked down and rolled under the table. Then the stranger, on leaving, picked up the only visible hat – almost identically similar to his own – and put it on."

"Is it not rather singular," I asked, "that he should not have noticed the different feel of a strange hat?"

"I think not," Thorndyke replied. "If he noticed anything unusual he would probably assume that he had put it on the wrong way round. Remember that he would be extremely hurried and agitated. And when once he had left the house, he would not dare to take the risk of returning, though he would doubtless realise the gravity of the mistake. And now," he continued, "would you mind giving us a few particulars? You have spoken of a great ruby which your cousin had, and which seems to be missing."

"Yes. You shall come to my room and I will tell you about it, but first let us lay my poor cousin decently on his bed."

"I think," said Thorndyke, "the body ought not to be moved until the police have seen it."

"Perhaps you are right," Byramji agreed reluctantly, "though it seems callous to leave him lying there." With a sigh he turned to the door, and Thorndyke followed, carrying the two hats.

"My cousin and I," said our host, when we were seated in his own large bed-sitting-room, "were both interested in gem-stones. I deal in all kinds of stones that are found in the East, but Dinanath dealt almost exclusively in rubies. He was a very fine judge of those beautiful gems, and he used to make periodical tours in Burma in search of uncut rubies of unusual size or quality. About four months ago he acquired at Mogok, in Upper Burma, a magnificent specimen over twenty-eight carats in weight, perfectly flawless and of the most gorgeous colour. It had been roughly cut, but my cousin was intending to have it recut, unless he should receive an advantageous offer for it in the meantime."

"What would be the value of such a stone?" I asked.

"It is impossible to say. A really fine large ruby of perfect colour is far, far more valuable than the finest diamond of the same size. It is the most precious of all gems, with the possible exception of the emerald. A fine ruby of five carats is worth about three-thousand pounds, but of course, the value rises out of all proportion with increasing size. Fifty-thousand pounds would be a moderate price for Dinanath's ruby."

During this recital I noticed that Thorndyke, while listening attentively, was turning the stranger's hat over in his hands, narrowly scrutinising it both inside and outside. As Byramji concluded, he remarked, "We shall have to let the police know what has happened, but, as my friend and I will be called as witnesses, I should like to examine this hat a little more closely before you hand it over to them. Could you let me have a small, hard brush? A dry nail-brush would do." Our host complied readily – in fact eagerly. Thorndyke's authoritative, purposeful manner had clearly impressed him, for he said as he handed my colleague a new nail-brush, "I thank you for your help and value it. We must not depend on the police only."

Accustomed as I was to Thorndyke's methods, his procedure was not unexpected, but Mr. Byramji watched him with breathless interest and no little surprise as, laying a sheet of notepaper on the table, he brought the hat close to it and brushed firmly but slowly, so that the dust dislodged should fall on it. As it was not a very well-kept hat, the yield was considerable, especially when the brush was drawn under the curl of the brim, and very soon the paper held quite a little heap. Then Thorndyke folded the paper into a small packet and having written "outside" on it, put it in his pocketbook.

"Why do you do that?" Mr. Byramji asked. "What will the dust tell you?"

"Probably nothing," Thorndyke replied. "But this hat is our only direct clue to the identity of the man who was with your cousin, and we must make the most of it. Dust, you know, is only a mass of fragments detached from surrounding objects. If the objects are unusual, the dust may be quite distinctive. You could easily identify the hat of a miller or a cement worker." As he was speaking he reversed the hat and turned down the leather head-lining, whereupon a number of strips of folded paper fell down into the crown.

"Ah!" exclaimed Byramji, "perhaps we shall learn something now."

He picked out the folded slips and began eagerly to open them out, and we examined them systematically – one by one. But they were singularly disappointing and uninforming. Mostly they consisted of strips of newspaper, with one or two circulars, a leaf from a price list of gas stoves, a portion of a large envelope on which were the remains of an address which read "   n   don, W.C.", and a piece of paper evidently cut down vertically and bearing the right-hand half of some kind of list. This read:

el 3 oz. 5 dwts
eep 9½ oz

"Can you make anything of this?" I asked, handing the paper to Thorndyke.

He looked at it reflectively, and answered, as he copied it into his notebook, "It has, at least, some character. If we consider it with the other data, we should get some sort of hint from it. But these scraps of paper don't tell us much. Perhaps their most suggestive feature is their quantity and the way in which, as you have no doubt noticed, they were arranged at the sides of the hat. We had better replace them as we found them for the benefit of the police.

The nature of the suggestion to which he referred was not very obvious to me, but the presence of Mr. Byramji rendered discussion inadvisable, nor was there any opportunity, for we had hardly reconstituted the hat when we became aware of a number of persons ascending the stairs, and then we heard the sound of rather peremptory rapping at the door of the dead man's room.

Mr. Byramji opened the door and went out on to the landing, where several persons had collected, including the two servants and a constable.

"I understand," said the policeman, "that there is something wrong here. Is that so?"

"A very terrible thing has happened," replied Byramji. "But the doctors can tell you better than I can." Here he looked appealingly at Thorndyke, and we both went out and joined him.

"A gentleman – Mr. Dinanath Byramji – has met with his death under somewhat suspicious circumstances," said Thorndyke, and glancing at the knot of naturally curious persons on the landing, he continued, "If you will come into the room where the death occurred, I will give you the facts so far as they are known to us."

With this he opened the door and entered the room with Mr. Byramji, the constable, and me. As the door opened, the bystanders craned forward and a middle-aged woman uttered a cry of horror and followed us into the room.

"This is dreadful!" she exclaimed, with a shuddering glance at the corpse. "The servants told me about it when I came in just now and I sent Albert for the police at once. But what does it mean? You don't think poor Mr. Dinanath has been murdered?"

"We had better get the facts, ma'am," said the constable, drawing out a large black notebook and laying his helmet on the table. He turned to Mr. Byramji, who had sunk into a chair and sat, the picture of grief, gazing at his dead cousin. "Would you kindly tell me what you know about how it happened?"

Byramji repeated the substance of what he had told us, and when the constable had taken down his statement, Thorndyke and I gave the few

91

medical particulars that we could furnish and handed the constable our cards. Then, having helped to lay the corpse on the bed and cover it with a sheet, we turned to take our leave.

"You have been very kind," Mr. Byramji said as he shook our hands warmly. "I am more than grateful. Perhaps I may be permitted to call on you and hear if – if you have learned anything fresh," he concluded discreetly.

"We shall be pleased to see you," Thorndyke replied, "and to give you any help that we can." And with this we took our departure, watched inquisitively down the stairs by the boarders and the servants who still lurked in the vicinity of the chamber of death.

"If the police have no more information than we have," I remarked as we walked homeward, "they won't have much to go on."

"No," said Thorndyke. "But you must remember that this crime – as we are justified in assuming it to be – is not an isolated one. It is the fourth of practically the same kind within the last six months. I understand that the police have some kind of information respecting the presumed criminal, though it can't be worth much, seeing that no arrest has been made. But there is some new evidence this time. The exchange of hats may help the police considerably."

"In what way? What evidence does it furnish?"

"In the first place, it suggests a hurried departure, which seems to connect the missing man with the crime. Then, he is wearing the dead man's hat, and though he is not likely to continue wearing it, it may be seen and furnish a clue. We know that that hat fits him fairly well and we know its size, so that we know the size of his head. Finally, we have the man's own hat."

"I don't fancy the police will get much information from that," said I"

"Probably not," he agreed. "Yet it offered one or two interesting suggestions, as you probably observed."

"It made no suggestions whatever to me," said I.

"Then," said Thorndyke, "I can only recommend you to recall our simple inspection and consider the significance of what we found."

This I had to accept as closing the discussion for the time being, and as I had to make a call at my bookseller's concerning some reports that I had left to be bound, I parted from Thorndyke at the corner of Chichester Rents and left him to pursue his way alone. My business with the bookseller took me longer than I had expected, for I had to wait while the lettering on the backs was completed, and when I arrived at our chambers in King's Bench Walk, I found Thorndyke apparently at the final stage of some experiment evidently connected with our late adventure. The microscope stood on the table with one slide on the stage and a second one beside it, but Thorndyke had apparently finished his microscopical researches, for as I entered he held in his hand a test-tube filled with a smoky-coloured fluid.

"I see that you have been examining the dust from the hat," said I. "Does it throw any fresh light on the case?

"Very little," he replied. "It is just common dust – assorted fibres and miscellaneous organic and mineral particles. But there are a couple of hairs from the inside of the hat – both lightish brown, and one of the atrophic, note-of-exclamation type that one finds at the margin of bald patches, and the outside dust shows minute traces of lead, apparently in the form of oxide. What do you make of that?"

"Perhaps the man is a plumber or a painter," I suggested.

"Either is possible and worth considering," he replied, but his tone made clear to me that this was not his own inference, and a row of five consecutive *Post Office Directories*, which I had already noticed ranged along the end of the table, told me that he had not only formed a hypothesis on the subject, but had probably either confirmed or disproved it. For the *Post Office Directory* was one of Thorndyke's favourite books of reference, and the amount of curious and recondite information that he succeeded in extracting from its matter-of-fact pages would have surprised no one more than it would the compilers of the work.

At this moment the sound of footsteps ascending our stairs became audible. It was late for business callers, but we were not unaccustomed to late visitors, and a familiar rat-tat of our little brass knocker seemed to explain the untimely visit.

"That sounds like Superintendent Miller's knock," said Thorndyke as he strode across the room to open the door. And the superintendent it turned out to be. But not alone.

As the door opened the officer entered with two gentlemen, both natives of India, and one of whom was our friend Mr. Byramji.

"Perhaps," said Miller, "I had better look in a little later."

"Not on my account," said Byramji. "I have only a few words to say and there is nothing secret about my business. May I introduce my kinsman, Mr. Khambata, a student of the Inner Temple?"

Byramji's companion bowed ceremoniously. "Byramji came to my chambers just now," he explained, "to consult me about this dreadful affair, and he chanced to show me your card. He had not heard of you, but supposed you to be an ordinary medical practitioner. He did not realise that he had entertained an angel unawares. But I, who knew of your great reputation, advised him to put his affairs in your hands –

93

without prejudice to the official investigations," Mr. Khambata added hastily, bowing to the superintendent.

"And I," said Mr. Byramji, "instantly decided to act on my kinsman's advice. I have come to beg you to leave no stone unturned to secure the punishment of my cousin's murderer. Spare no expense. I am a rich man and my poor cousin's property will come to me. As to the ruby, recover it if you can, but it is of no consequence. Vengeance – justice is what I seek. Deliver the wretch into my hands, or into the hands of justice, and I give you the ruby or its value, freely – gladly."

"There is no need," said Thorndyke, "of such extraordinary inducement. If you wish me to investigate this case, I will do so and will use every means at my disposal, without prejudice, as your friend says, to the proper claims of the officers of the law. But you understand that I can make no promises. I cannot guarantee success.

"We understand that," said Mr. Khambata. "But we know that if you undertake the case, everything that is possible will be done. And now we must leave you to your consultation."

As soon as our clients had gone, Miller rose from his chair with his hand in his breast pocket. "I dare say, Doctor," said he, "you can guess what I have come about. I was sent for to look into this Byramji case and I heard from Mr. Byramji that you had been there and that you had made a minute examination of the missing man's hat. So have I, and I don't mind telling you that I could learn nothing from it."

"I haven't learnt much myself," said Thorndyke.

"But you've picked up something," urged Miller, "if it is only a hint, and we have just a little clue. There is very small doubt that this is the same man – '*The New Jersey Sphinx*', as the papers call him – that committed those other robberies, and a very difficult type of criminal he is to get hold of. He is bold, he is wary, he plays a lone hand, and he sticks at nothing. He has no confederates, and he kills every time. The American police never got near him but once, and that once gives us the only clues we have."

"Finger-prints?" inquired Thorndyke.

"Yes, and very poor ones, too. So rough that you can hardly make out the pattern. And even those are not absolutely guaranteed to be his, but in any case, finger-prints are not much use until you've got the man. And there is a photograph of the fellow himself, But it is only a snapshot, and a poor one at that. All it shows is that he has a mop of hair and a pointed beard – or at least he had when the photograph was taken. But for identification purposes it is practically worthless. Still, there it is, and what I propose is this, we want this man and so do you. We've worked

94

together before and can trust one another. I am going to lay my cards on the table and ask you to do the same."

"But, my dear Miller," said Thorndyke, "I haven't any cards. I haven't a single solid fact."

The detective was visibly disappointed. Nevertheless, he laid two photographs on the table and pushed them towards Thorndyke, who inspected them through his lens and passed them to me.

"The pattern is very indistinct and broken up," he remarked.

"Yes," said Miller, "the prints must have been made on a very rough surface, though you get prints something like those from fitters or other men who use files and handle rough metal. And now, Doctor, can't you give us a lead of any kind?"

Thorndyke reflected a few moments. "I really have not a single real fact," said he, "and I am unwilling to make merely speculative suggestions."

"Oh, that's all right," Miller replied cheerfully. "Give us a start. I shan't complain if it comes to nothing."

"Well," Thorndyke said reluctantly, "I was thinking of getting a few particulars as to the various tenants of No. 51 Clifford's Inn. Perhaps you could do it more easily and it might be worth your while."

"Good!" Miller exclaimed gleefully. "He 'gives to airy nothing a local habitation and a name'."

"It is probably the wrong name," Thorndyke reminded him.

"I don't care," said Miller. "But why shouldn't we go together? It's too late to-night, and I can't manage to-morrow morning. But say to-morrow afternoon. Two heads are better than one, you know, especially when the second one is yours. Or perhaps," he added, with a glance at me, "three would be better still."

Thorndyke considered for a moment or two and then looked at me.

"What do you say, Jervis?" he asked.

As my afternoon was unoccupied, I agreed with enthusiasm, being as curious as the superintendent to know how Thorndyke had connected this particular locality with the vanished criminal, and Miller departed in high spirits with an appointment for the morrow three o'clock in the afternoon.

For some time after the superintendent's departure, I sat wrapped in profound meditation. In some mysterious way the address, 51 Clifford's Inn, had emerged from the formless data yielded by the derelict hat. But what had been the connection? Apparently the fragment of the addressed envelope had furnished the clue. But how had Thorndyke extended "*n*" into "*51, Clifford's Inn*"? It was to me a complete mystery."

Meanwhile, Thorndyke had seated himself at writing-table, and I noticed that of the two letters which he wrote, one was written on our headed paper and other on ordinary plain notepaper. I was speculating on the reason for this when he rose, and as he stuck on the stamps, said to me, "I am just going out to post these two letters. Do you care for a short stroll through the leafy shades of Fleet Street? The evening is still young."

"The rural solitudes of Fleet Street attract me at all hours," I replied, fetching my hat from the adjoining office, and we accordingly sallied forth together, strolling up King's Bench Walk and emerging into Fleet Street by way of Mitre Court. When Thorndyke had dropped his letters into the post office box, he stood awhile gazing up at the tower of St. Dunstan's Church.

"Have you ever been in Clifford's Inn, Jervis?" he inquired

"Never," I replied. (We passed through it together on an average a dozen times a week.) But it is not too late for an exploratory visit."

We crossed the road and, entering Clifford's Inn Passage, passed through the still half-open gate, crossed the outer court, and threaded the tunnel-like entry by the hall to the inner court, in the middle of which Thorndyke halted, and looked up at one of the ancient houses, remarked, "No. 51."

"So that is where our friend hangs out his flag," said I.

"Oh come, Jervis," he protested, "I am surprised at you. You are as bad as Miller. I have merely suggested a possible connection between these premises and the hat that was left at Bedford Place. As to the nature of that connection I have no idea, and there may be no connection at all. I assure you, Jervis, that I am on the thinnest possible ice. I am working on a hypothesis which is in the highest degree speculative, and I should not have given Miller a hint but that he was so eager and so willing to help — and also that I wanted his finger-prints. But we are really only at the beginning, and may never get any farther."

I looked up at the old house. It was all in darkness excepting the top floor, where a couple of lighted windows showed the shadow of a man moving rapidly about the room. We crossed to the entry and inspected the names painted on the door-posts. The ground floor was occupied by a firm of photo-engravers, the first floor by a Mr. Carrington, whose name stood out conspicuously on its oblong of comparatively fresh white paint, while the tenants of the second floor – old residents, to judge by the faded and discoloured paint in which their names were announced – were Messrs. Burt and Highley, Metallurgists.

"Burt has departed," said Thorndyke, as I read out the names, and he pointed to two red lines of erasure which I had not noticed in the dim light, "so the active gentleman above is presumably Mr. Highley, and we may take it that he has residential as well as business premises. I wonder who and what Mr. Carrington is – but I dare say we shall find out to-morrow."

With this he dismissed the professional aspects of Clifford's Inn and, changing the subject to its history and associations, chatted in his inimitable, picturesque manner until our leisurely perambulations brought us at length to the Inner Temple Gate.

On the following morning we bustled through our work in order to leave the afternoon free, making several joint visits to solicitors from whom we were taking instructions. Returning from the last of these – a City lawyer – Thorndyke turned into St. Helen's Place and halted at a doorway bearing the brass plate of a firm of assayists and refiners. I followed him into the outer office, where, on his mentioning his name, an elderly man came to the counter.

"Mr. Grayson has put out some specimens for you, sir," said he. "They are about thirty grains to the ton – you said that the content was of no importance. I am to tell you that you need not return them. They are not worth treating." He went to a large safe from which he took a canvas bag and, returning to the counter, turned out on it the contents of the bag, consisting of about a dozen good-sized lumps of quartz and a glittering yellow fragment, which Thorndyke picked out and dropped in his pocket.

"Will that collection do?" our friend inquired.

"It will answer my purpose perfectly," Thorndyke replied, and when the specimens had been replaced in the bag, and the latter deposited in Thorndyke's hand-bag, my colleague thanked the assistant and we went on our way.

"We extend our activities into the domain of mineralogy," I remarked.

Thorndyke smiled an inscrutable smile. "We also employ the suction pump as an instrument of research," he observed. "However, the strategic uses of chunks of quartz – otherwise than as missiles – will develop themselves in due course, and the interval may be used for reflection."

It was. But my reflection brought no solution. I noticed, however, that when at three o'clock we set forth in company with the superintendent, the bag went with us and, having offered to carry it and having had my offer accepted with a sly twinkle, its weight assured me that the quartz was still inside.

"'*Chambers and Offices to Let*'," Thorndyke read aloud as we approached the porter's lodge. "That lets us in, I think. And the porter knows Dr. Jervis and me by sight, so he will talk more freely."

"He doesn't know me," said the superintendent, "but I'll keep in the background, all the same."

A pull at the bell brought out a clerical-looking man in a tall hat and a frock coat, who regarded Thorndyke and me through his spectacles with an amiable air of recognition.

"Good afternoon, Mr. Larkin," said Thorndyke. "I am asked to get particulars of vacant chambers. What have you got to let?"

Mr. Larkin reflected. "Let me see. There's a ground floor at No. 5 – rather dark – and a small second-pair set at No. 12. And then there is – oh, yes, there is a good first-floor set at No. 51. They wouldn't have been vacant until Michaelmas, but Mr. Carrington, the tenant, has had to go abroad suddenly. I had a letter from him this morning, enclosing the key. Funny letter, too." He dived into his pocket, and hauling out a bundle of letters, selected one, and handed it to Thorndyke with a broad smile.

Thorndyke glanced at the postmark ("*London, E.*"), and having taken out the key, extracted the letter, which he opened and held so that Miller and I could see it. The paper bore the printed heading, "*Baltic Shipping Company, Wapping*", and the further written heading, "*S.S. Gothenburg*", and the letter was brief and to the point:

> *Dear Sir,*
>
> *I am giving up my chambers at No. 51, as I have been suddenly called abroad. I enclose the key, but am not troubling you with the rent. The sale of my costly furniture will more than cover it, and the surplus can be expended on painting the garden railings.*
>
> *Yours sincerely,*
>
> *A. Carrington.*

Thorndyke smilingly replaced the letter and the key in the envelope and asked, "What is the furniture like?"

"You'll see," chuckled the porter, "if you care to look at the rooms. And I think they might suit, They're a good set."

"Quiet?"

"Yes, pretty quiet. There's a metallurgist overhead – Highley, used to be Burt and Highley – but Burt has gone to the City, and I don't think Highley does much business now."

"Let me see," said Thorndyke, "I think I used to meet Highley sometimes – a tall, dark man, isn't he?"

"No, that would be Burt. Highley is a little, fairish man, rather bald."

"Hadn't we better have a look at the rooms?" Miller interrupted a little impatiently.

"Can we see them, Mr. Larkin?" asked Thorndyke.

"Certainly," was the reply. "You've got the key. Let me have it when you've seen the rooms, and whatever ever you do," he added with a broad grin, "be careful of the furniture."

"It looks," the superintendent remarked as we crossed the inner court, "as if Mr. Carrington had done a mizzle. That's hopeful. And I see," he continued, glancing at the fresh paint on the door-post as we passed through the entry, "that he hasn't been here long. That's hopeful, too."

We ascended to the first floor, and as Thorndyke unlocked and threw open the door, Miller laughed aloud. The "costly furniture" consisted of a small kitchen table, a Windsor chair, and a dilapidated deck-chair. The kitchen contained a gas ring, a small saucepan, and a frying-pan, and the bedroom was furnished with a camp-bed devoid of bed-clothes, a wash-hand basin on a packing-case, and a water can.

"Hallo!" exclaimed the superintendent. "He's left a hat behind. Quite a good hat, too." He took it down from the peg, glanced at its exterior and then, turning it over, looked inside. And then his mouth opened with a jerk.

"Great Solomon Eagle!" he gasped. "Do you see, Doctor? It's *the* hat."

He held it out to us, and sure enough on the white silk lining of the crown were the embossed, gilt letters, *D.B.*, just as Mr. Byramji had described them.

"Yes," Thorndyke agreed, as the superintendent snatched up a greengrocer's paper bag from the kitchen floor and persuaded the hat into it. "It is undoubtedly the missing link. But what are you going to do now?"

"Do!" exclaimed Miller. "Why, I am going to collar the man. These Baltic boats put in at Hull and Newcastle – perhaps he didn't know that – and they are pretty slow boats, too. I shall wire to Newcastle to have the ship detained and take Inspector Badger down to make the arrest. I'll leave you to explain to the porter, and I owe you a thousand thanks for your valuable tip."

With this he bustled away, clasping the precious hat and from the window we saw him hurry across the court and dart out through the postern into Fetter Lane.

"I think Miller was rather precipitate," said Thorndyke. "He should have got a description of the man and some further particulars."

"Yes," said I. "Miller had much better have waited until you had finished with Mr. Larkin. But you can get some more particulars when we take back the key."

"We shall get more information from the gentleman who lives on the floor above, and I think we will go up and interview him now. I wrote to him last night and made a metallurgical appointment, signing myself W. Polton. Your name, if he should ask, is Stevenson."

As we ascended the stairs to the next floor, I meditated on the rather tortuous proceedings of my usually straightforward colleague. The use of the lumps of quartz was now obvious, but why these mysterious tactics? And why, before knocking at the door, did Thorndyke carefully take the reading of the gas meter on the landing?

The door was opened in response to our knock – a shortish, alert-looking, clean-shaved man in a white overall, who looked at us keenly and rather forbiddingly. But Thorndyke was geniality personified.

"How do you do, Mr. Highley?" said he, holding out his hand, which the metallurgist shook coolly. "You got my letter, I suppose?"

"Yes. But I am not Mr. Highley. He's away and I am carrying on. I think of taking over his business if there is any to take over. My name is Sherwood. Have you got the samples?"

Thorndyke produced the canvas bag, which Mr. Sherwood took from him and emptied out on a bench, picking up the lumps of quartz one by one and examining them closely. Meanwhile Thorndyke took a rapid survey of the premises. Against the wall were two cupel furnaces and a third larger furnace like a small pottery kiln. On a set of narrow shelves were several rows of bone-ash cupels, looking like little white flower-pots, and near them was the cupel-press – an appliance into which powdered bone-ash was fed and compressed by a plunger to form the cupels – while by the side of the press was a tub of bone-ash – a good deal coarser, I noticed, than the usual fine powder. This coarseness was also observed by Thorndyke, who edged up to the tub and dipped his hand into the ash and then wiped his fingers on his handkerchief.

"This stuff doesn't seem to contain much gold," said Mr. Sherwood. "But we shall see when we make the assay."

100

"What do you think of this?" asked Thorndyke, taking from his pocket the small lump of glittering, golden-looking mineral that he had picked out at the assayist's. Mr. Sherwood took it from him and examined it closely. "This looks more hopeful," said he. "Rather rich, in fact."

Thorndyke received this statement with an unmoved countenance, but as for me, I stared at Mr. Sherwood in amazement. For this lump of glittering mineral was simply a fragment of common iron pyrites! It would not have deceived a schoolboy, much less a metallurgist.

Still holding the specimen, and taking a watchmaker's lens from a shelf, Mr. Sherwood moved over to the window. Simultaneously, Thorndyke stepped softly to the cupel shelves and quickly ran his eye along the rows of cupels. Presently he paused at one, examined it more closely, and then, taking it from the shelf, began to pick at it with his finger-nail.

At this moment Mr. Sherwood turned and observed him, and instantly there flashed into the metallurgist's face an expression of mingled anger and alarm.

"Put that down!" he commanded peremptorily, and then, as Thorndyke continued to scrape with his finger nail, he shouted furiously, "Do you hear? Drop it!"

Thorndyke took him literally at his word and let the cupel fall on the floor, when it shattered into innumerable fragments, of which one of the largest separated itself from the rest. Thorndyke pounced upon it, and in an instantaneous glance, as he picked it up, I recognised it as a calcined tooth.

Then followed a few moments of weird, dramatic silence. Thorndyke, holding the tooth between his finger and thumb, looked steadily into the eyes of the metallurgist, and the latter, pallid as a corpse, glared at Thorndyke and furtively unbuttoned his overall.

Suddenly the silence broke into a tumult as bewildering as the crash of a railway collision. Sherwood's right hand darted under his overall. Instantly, Thorndyke snatched up another cupel and hurled it with such truth of aim that it shattered on the metallurgist's forehead. And as he flung the missile, he sprang forward and delivered a swift upper-cut. There was a thunderous crash, a cloud of white dust, and an automatic pistol clattered along the floor.

I snatched up the pistol and rushed to my friend's assistance. But there was no need. With his great strength and his uncanny skill – to say nothing of the effects of the knock-out blow – Thorndyke had the man pinned down immovably.

"See if you can find some cord, Jervis," he said in a calm, quiet tone that seemed almost ridiculously out of character with the circumstances.

There was no difficulty about this, for several corded boxes stood in a corner of the laboratory. I cut off two lengths, with one of which I secured the prostrate man's arms, and with the other fastened his knees and ankles.

"Now," said Thorndyke, "if you will take charge of his hands, we will make a preliminary inspection. Let us first see if he wears a belt."

Unbuttoning the man's waistcoat, he drew up the shirt, disclosing a broad, webbing belt furnished with several leather pockets, the buttoned flaps of which he felt carefully, regardless of the stream of threats and imprecations that poured from our victim's swollen lips. From the front pockets he proceeded to the back, passing an exploratory hand under the writhing body.

"Ah!" he exclaimed suddenly, "just turn him over, and look out for his heels."

We rolled our captive over, and as Thorndyke "skinned the rabbit", a central pocket came into view, into which, when he had unbuttoned it, he inserted his fingers. "Yes," he continued, "I think this is what we are looking for." He withdrew his fingers, between which he held a small packet of Japanese paper, and with feverish excitement I watched him open out layer after layer of the soft wrapping. As he turned back the last fold a wonderful crimson sparkle told me that the "great ruby" was found.

"There, Jervis," said Thorndyke, holding the magnificent gem towards me in the palm of his hand, "look on this beautiful, sinister thing, charged with untold potentialities of evil – and thank the gods that it is not yours."

He wrapped it up again carefully and, having bestowed it in an inner pocket, said, "And now give me the pistol and run down to the telegraph office and see if you can stop Miller. I should like him to have the credit for this."

I handed him the pistol and made my way out into Fetter Lane and so down to Fleet Street, where at the post office my urgent message was sent off to Scotland Yard immediately. In a few minutes the reply came that Superintendent Miller had not yet left and that he was starting immediately for Clifford's Inn. A quarter-of-an-hour later he drove up in a hansom to the Fetters Lane gate and I conducted him up to the second floor, where Thorndyke introduced him to his prisoner and witnessed the official arrest.

"You don't see how I arrived at it," said Thorndyke as we walked homeward after returning the key. "Well, I am not surprised. The initial evidence was of the weakest. It acquired significance only by cumulative effect. Let us reconstruct it as it developed.

"The derelict hat was, of course, the starting-point. Now, the first thing one noticed was that it appeared to have had more than one owner. No man would buy a new hat that fitted so badly as to need all that packing, and the arrangement of the packing suggested a long-headed man wearing a hat that had belonged to a man with a short head. Then there were the suggestions offered by the slips of paper. The fragmentary address referred to a place the name of which ended in 'n' and the remainder was evidently 'London, W.C.' Now what West Central place names end in 'n'? It was not a street, a square or a court, and Barbican is not in the W.C. district. It was almost certainly one of the half-dozen surviving Inns of Court or Chancery. But, of course, it was not necessarily the address of the owner of the hat.

"The other slip of paper bore the end of a word ending in 'el,' and another word ending in 'eep,' and connected with these were quantities stated in ounces and pennyweights troy weight. But the only persons who use troy weight are those who deal in precious metals. I inferred therefore that the 'el' was part of 'lemel,' and that the 'eep' was part of 'floor-sweep,' an inference that was supported by the respective quantities, three-ounces-five pennyweights of lemel and nine-and-a-half ounces of floor-sweep."

"What is lemel?" I asked.

"It is the trade name for the gold or silver filings that collect in the 'skin' of a jeweller's bench. Floor-sweep is, of course, the dust swept up on the floor of a jeweller's or goldsmith's workshop. The lemel is actual metal, though not of uniform fineness, but the sweep is a mixture of dirt and metal. Both are saved and sent to the refiners to have the gold and silver extracted.

"This paper, then, was connected either with a gold smith or a gold refiner – who might call himself an assayist or a metallurgist. The connection was supported by the leaf of a price list of gas stoves. A metallurgist would be kept well supplied with lists of gas stoves and furnaces. The traces of lead in the dust from the hat gave us another straw blowing the same direction, for gold assayed by the dry process is fused in the cupel furnace with lead, and as the lead oxidises and the oxide is volatile, traces of lead would tend to appear in the dust deposited in the laboratory.

"The next thing to do was to consult the directory, and when I did so, I found that there were no goldsmiths in any of the Inns and only one assayist – Mr. Highley, of Clifford's Inn. The probabilities therefore, slender as they were, pointed to some connection between this stray hat

103

and Mr. Highley. And this was positively all the information that we had when we came out this afternoon.

"As soon as we got to Clifford's Inn, however, the evidence began to grow like a rolling snowball. First there was Larkin's contribution, and then there was the discovery of the missing hat. Now, as soon as I saw that hat my suspicions fell upon the man upstairs. I felt a conviction that the hat had been left there purposely and that the letter to Larkin was just a red herring to create a false trail. Nevertheless, the presence of that hat completely confirmed the other evidence. It showed that the apparent connection was a real connection."

"But," I asked, "what made you suspect the man upstairs?"

"My dear Jervis!" he exclaimed, "consider the facts. That hat was enough to hang the man who left it there. Can you imagine this astute, wary villain making such an idiot's mistake – going away and leaving the means of his conviction for anyone to find? But you are forgetting that whereas the missing hat was found on the first floor, the murderer's hat was connected with the second floor. The evidence suggested that it was Highley's hat. And now, before we go on to the next stage, let me remind you of those finger-prints. Miller thought that their rough appearance was due to the surface on which they had been made, But it was not. They were the prints of a person who was suffering from ichthyosis, palmar psoriasis, or sonic dry dermatitis.

"There is one other point. The man we were looking for was a murderer. His life was already forfeit. To such a man another murder more or less is of no consequence. If this man, having laid the false trail, had determined to take sanctuary in Highley's rooms, it was probable that he had already got rid of Highley. And remember that a metallurgist has unrivalled means disposing of a body, for not only is each of his muffle furnaces a miniature crematorium, but the very residue of a cremated body – bone-ash – is one of the materials of his trade.

"When we went upstairs, I first took the reading of the gas meter and ascertained that a large amount of gas had been used recently. Then, when we entered I took the opportunity to shake hands with Mr. Sherwood, and immediately I became aware that he suffered from a rather extreme form of ichthyosis. That was the first point of verification. Then we discovered that he actually could not distinguish between iron pyrites and auriferous quartz. He was not a metallurgist at all. He was a masquerader. Then the bone-ash in the tub was mixed with fragments of calcined bone, and the cupels all showed similar fragments. In one of them I could see part of the crown of a tooth. That was pure luck. But observe that by that time I had enough evidence to justify an arrest. The tooth served only to bring the affair to a crisis, and his response to my unspoken accusation saved us the trouble of further search for confirmatory evidence."

"What is not quite clear to me," said I, "is when and why he made away with Highley. As the body has been completely reduced to bone-ash, Highley must have been dead at least some days."

"Undoubtedly," Thorndyke agreed. "I take it that the course of events was like this, The police have been searching eagerly for this man, and every new crime must have made his position more unsafe – for a criminal can never be sure that he has not dropped some clue. It began to be necessary for him to make some arrangements for leaving the country and meanwhile to have a retreat in case his whereabouts should chance to be discovered. Highley's chambers were admirable for both purposes. Here was a solitary man who seldom had a visitor, and who would probably not be missed for some considerable time, and in those chambers were the means of rapidly and completely disposing of the body. The mere murder would be a negligible detail to this ruffian.

"I imagine that Highley was done to death at least a week ago, and that the murderer did not take up his new tenancy until the body was reduced to ash. With that large furnace in addition to the small ones, this would not take long. When the new premises were ready, he could make a sham disappearance to cover his actual flight later, and you must see how perfectly misleading that sham disappearance was. If the police had discovered that hat in the empty room only a week later, they would have been certain that he had escaped to one of the Baltic ports, and while they were following his supposed tracks, he could have gone off comfortably via Folkestone or Southampton.

"Then you think he had only just moved into Highley's rooms?"

"I should say he moved in last night. The murder of Byramji was probably planned on some information that the murderer had picked up, and as soon as it was accomplished, he began forthwith to lay down the false tracks. When he reached his rooms yesterday afternoon, he must have written the letter to Larkin and gone off at once to the East End to post it. Then he probably had his bushy hair cut short and shaved off his beard and moustache – which would render him quite unrecognisable by Larkin – and moved into Highley's chambers, from which he would have quietly sallied forth in a few days' time to take his passage to the Continent. It was quite a good plan, and but for the accident of taking the wrong hat, would almost certainly have succeeded."

Once every year, on the second of August, there is delivered with unfailing regularity at No. 5A King's Bench Walk a large box of carved sandal-wood filled with the choicest Trichinopoly cheroots and accompanied by an affectionate letter from our late client, Mr. Byramji.

For the second of August is the anniversary of the death (in the execution shed at Newgate) of Cornelius Barnett, otherwise known as *"The New Jersey Sphinx"*.

The Touchstone

It happened not uncommonly that the exigencies of practice committed my friend Thorndyke to investigations that lay more properly within the province of the police. For problems that had arisen as secondary consequences of a criminal act could usually not be solved until the circumstances of that act were fully elucidated and, incidentally, the identity of the actor established. Such a problem was that of the disappearance of James Harewood's will, a problem that was propounded to us by our old friend, Mr. Marchmont, when he called on us, by appointment, with the client of whom he had spoken in his note.

It was just four o'clock when the solicitor arrived at our chambers, and as I admitted him he ushered in a gentlemanly-looking man of about thirty-five, whom he introduced as Mr. William Crowhurst.

"I will just stay," said he with an approving glance at the tea-service on the table, "and have a cup of tea with you, and give you an outline of the case. Then I must run away and leave Mr. Crowhurst to fill in the details."

He seated himself in an easy chair within comfortable reach of the table, and as Thorndyke poured out the tea, he glanced over a few notes scribbled on a sheet of paper.

"I may say," he began, stirring his tea thoughtfully, "that this is a forlorn hope. I have brought the case to you, but I have not the slightest expectation that you will be able to help us."

"A very wholesome frame of mind," Thorndyke commented with a smile. "I hope it is that of your client also."

"It is indeed," said Mr. Crowhurst. "In fact, it seems to me a waste of your time to go into the matter. Probably you will think so too, when you have heard the particulars."

"Well, let us hear the particulars," said Thorndyke. "A forlorn hope has, at least, the stimulating quality of difficulty. Let us have your outline sketch, Marchmont."

The solicitor, having emptied his cup and pushed it towards the tray for replenishment, glanced at his notes and began, "The simplest way in which to present the problem is to give a brief recital of the events that have given rise to it, which are these, The day before yesterday – that is last Monday – at a quarter-to-two in the afternoon, Mr. James Harewood executed a will at his house at Merbridge, which is about two miles from Welsbury. There were present four persons: Two of his servants, who signed as witnesses, and the two principal beneficiaries – Mr. Arthur

Baxfield, a nephew of the testator, and our friend here, Mr. William Crowhurst. The will was a holograph written on the two pages of a sheet of letter-paper. When the witnesses signed, the will was covered by another sheet of paper so that only the space for the signatures was exposed. Neither of the witnesses read the will, nor did either of the beneficiaries, and so far as I am aware, no one but the testator knew what were its actual provisions, though, after the servants had left the room, Mr. Harewood explained its general purport to the beneficiaries."

"And what was its general purport?" Thorndyke asked.

"Broadly speaking," replied Marchmont, "it divided the estate in two very unequal portions between Mr. Baxfield and Mr. Crowhurst. There were certain small legacies of which neither the amounts nor the names of the legatees are known. Then, to Baxfield was given a thousand pounds to enable him either to buy a partnership or to start a small factory – he is a felt hat manufacturer by trade – and the remainder to Crowhurst, who was made executor and residuary legatee. But, of course, the residue of the estate is an unknown quantity, since we don't know either the number or the amounts of the legacies.

"Shortly after the signing of the will, the parties separated. Mr. Harewood folded up the will and put it in a leather wallet which he slipped into his pocket, stating his intention of taking the will forthwith to deposit with his lawyer at Welsbury. A few minutes after his guests had departed, he was seen by one of the servants to leave the house, and afterwards was seen by a neighbour walking along a footpath which, after passing through a small wood, joins the main road about a mile-and-a-quarter from Welsbury. From that time, he was never again seen alive. He never visited the lawyer, nor did anyone see him at or near Welsbury or elsewhere else.

"As he did not return home that night, his housekeeper (he was a widower and childless) became extremely alarmed, and in the morning she communicated with the police. A search-party was organised and, following the path on which he was last seen, explored the wood – which is known as Gilbert's Copse – and here, at the bottom of an old chalk-pit, they found him lying dead with a fractured skull and a dislocated neck. How he came by these injuries is not at present known, but as the body had been robbed of all valuables, including his watch, purse, diamond ring, and the wallet containing the will, there is naturally a strong suspicion that he has been murdered. That, however, is not our immediate concern – at least not mine. I am concerned with the will, which, as you see, has disappeared, and as it has presumably been carried away by a thief who is under suspicion of murder, it is not likely to be returned."

108

"It is almost certainly destroyed by this time," said Mr. Crowhurst.

"That certainly seems probable," Thorndyke agreed. "But what do you want me to do? You haven't come for counsel's opinion?"

"No," replied Marchmont. "I am pretty clear about the legal position. I shall claim, as the will has presumably been destroyed, to have the testator's wishes carried out in so far as they are known. But I am doubtful as to the view the court may take. It may decide that the testator's wishes are not known, that the provisions of the will are too uncertain to admit of administration."

"And what would be the effect of that decision?" asked Thorndyke.

"In that case," said Marchmont, "the entire estate would go to Baxfield, as he is the next of kin and there was no previous will."

"And what is it that you want me to do?"

Marchmont chuckled deprecatingly. "You have to pay the penalty of being a prodigy, Thorndyke. We are asking you to do an impossibility – but we don't really expect you to bring it off. We ask you to help us to recover the will."

"If the will has been completely destroyed, it can't be recovered," said Thorndyke. "But we don't know that it has been destroyed. The matter is, at least, worth investigating, and if you wish me to look into it, I will."

The solicitor rose with an air of evident relief.

"Thank you, Thorndyke," said he. "I expect nothing – at least, I tell myself that I do – but I can now feel that everything that is possible will be done. And now I must be off. Crowhurst can give you any details that you want.

When Marchmont had gone, Thorndyke turned to our client and asked, "What do you suppose Baxfield will do, if the will is irretrievably lost? Will he press his claim as next of kin?"

"I should say yes," replied Crowhurst. "He is a businessman and his natural claims are greater than mine. He is not likely to refuse what the law assigns to him as his right. As a matter of fact, I think he felt that his uncle had treated him unfairly in alienating the property."

"Was there any reason for this diversion of the estate?"

"Well," replied Crowhurst, "Harewood and I have been very good friends and he was under some obligations to me, and then Baxfield had not made himself very acceptable to his uncle. But the principal factor, I think, was a strong tendency of Baxfield's to gamble. He had lost quite a lot of money by backing horses, and a careful, thrifty man like James Harewood doesn't care to leave his savings to a gambler. The thousand pounds that he did leave to Baxfield was expressly for the purpose of investment in a business."

"Is Baxfield in business now?"

"Not on his own account. He is a sort of foreman or shop-manager in a factory just outside Welsbury, and I believe he is a good worker and knows his trade thoroughly."

"And now," said Thorndyke, "with regard to Mr. Harewood's death. The injuries might, apparently, have been either accidental or homicidal. What are the probabilities of accident – disregarding the robbery?"

"Very considerable, I should say. It is a most dangerous place. The footpath runs close beside the edge of a disused chalk-pit with perpendicular or overhanging sides, and the edge is masked by bushes and brambles. A careless walker might easily fall over – or be pushed over, for that matter."

"Do you know when the inquest is to take place?"

"Yes. The day after to-morrow. I had the subpoena this morning for Friday afternoon at 2:30, at the Welsbury Town Hall."

At this moment footsteps were heard hurriedly ascending the stairs and then came a loud and peremptory rat-tat at our door. I sprang across to see who our visitor was, and as I flung open the door, Mr. Marchmont rushed in, breathing heavily and flourishing a newspaper.

"Here is a new development," he exclaimed. "It doesn't seem to help us much, but I thought you had better know about it at once." He sat down, and putting on his spectacles, read aloud as follows:

> *A new and curious light has been thrown on the mystery of the death of Mr. James Harewood, whose body was found yesterday in a disused chalk-pit near Merbridge. It appears that on Monday – the day on which Mr. Harewood almost certainly was killed – a passenger alighting from a train at Barwood Junction before it had stopped, slipped, and fell between the train and the platform. He was quickly extricated, and as he had evidently sustained internal injuries, he was taken to the local hospital, where he was found to be suffering from a fractured pelvis. He gave his name as Thomas Fletcher, but refused to give any address, saying that he had no relatives. This morning he died, and on his clothes being searched for an address, a parcel, formed of two handkerchiefs tied up with string, was found in his pocket. When it was opened it was found to contain five watches, three watch-chains, a tie-pin, and a number of bank-notes. Other pockets contained a quantity of loose money – gold and silver mixed – and a card of the Welsbury Races, which were held on Monday. Of the five watches, one*

has been identified as the one taken from Mr. Harewood, and the bank-notes have been identified as a batch handed to him by the cashier of his bank at Welsbury last Thursday and presumably carried in the leather wallet which was stolen from his pocket. This wallet, by the way, has also been found. It was picked up – empty – last night on the railway embankment just outside Welsbury Station. Appearances thus suggest that the man, Fletcher, when on his way to the races, encountered Mr. Harewood in the lonely copse and murdered and robbed him, or perhaps found him dead in the chalk-pit and robbed the body – a question that is now never likely to be solved.

As Marchmont finished reading, he looked up at Thorndyke. "It doesn't help us much, does it?" said he. "As the wallet was found empty, it is pretty certain that the will has been destroyed."

"Or perhaps merely thrown away," said Thorndyke, "in which case an advertisement offering a substantial reward may bring it to light."

The solicitor shrugged his shoulders skeptically but agreed to publish the advertisement. Then, once more he turned to go, and as Mr. Crowhurst had no further information to give, he departed with his lawyer.

For some time after they had gone, Thorndyke sat with his brief notes before him, silent and deeply reflective. I, too, maintained a discreet silence, for I knew from long experience that the motionless pose and quiet, impassive face were the outward signs of a mind in swift and strenuous action. Instinctively, I gathered that this apparently chaotic case was being quietly sorted out and arranged in a logical order, that Thorndyke, like a skilful chess-player, was "trying over the moves" before he should lay his hand upon the pieces.

Presently he looked up. "Well?" he asked. "What do you think, Jervis? Is it worthwhile?"

"That," I replied, "depends on whether the will is or is not in existence. If it has been destroyed, an investigation would be a waste of our time and our client's money."

"Yes," he agreed. "But there is quite a good chance that it has not been destroyed. It was probably dropped loose into the wallet, and then might have been picked out and thrown away before the wallet was examined. But we mustn't concentrate too much on the will. If we take up the case – which I am inclined to do – we must ascertain the actual sequence of events. We have one clear day before the inquest. If we run down to Merbridge to-morrow and go thoroughly over the ground, and

111

then go on to Barwood and find out all we can about the man Fletcher, we may get some new light from the evidence at the inquest."

I agreed readily to Thorndyke's proposal – not that I could see any way into the case, but I felt a conviction that my colleague had isolated some leading fact and had a definite line of research in his mind. And this conviction deepened when, later in the evening, he laid his research-case on the table and rearranged its contents with evident purpose. I watched curiously the apparatus that he was packing in it and tried – not very successfully – to infer the nature of the proposed investigation. The box of powdered paraffin wax and the spirit blowpipe were obvious enough, but the "dust-aspirator" – a sort of miniature vacuum cleaner – the portable microscope, the coil of Manila line with an eye spliced into one end, and especially the abundance of blank-labelled microscope slides, all of which I saw him pack in the case with deliberate care, defeated me utterly.

About ten o'clock on the following morning we stepped from the train in Welsbury Station, and having recovered our bicycles from the luggage van, wheeled them through the barrier and mounted. During the train journey we had both studied the one-inch Ordnance Map to such purpose that we were virtually in familiar surroundings and immune from the necessity of seeking directions from the natives. As we cleared the town, we glanced up the broad by-road to the left which led to the race-course, then we rode on briskly for a mile, which brought us to the spot where the footpath to Merbridge joined the road. Here we dismounted and, lifting our bicycles over the stile, followed the path towards a small wood which we could see ahead, crowning a low hill.

"For such a good path," Thorndyke remarked as we approached the wood, "it is singularly unfrequented. I haven't seen a soul since we left the road." He glanced at the map as the path entered the wood, and when we had walked on a couple of hundred yards, he halted and stood his bicycle against a tree. "The chalk-pit should be about here," said he, "though it is impossible to see. He grasped a stem of one of the small bushes that crowded on to the path and pulled it aside. Then he uttered an exclamation.

"Just look at that, Jervis. It is a positive scandal that a public path should be left in this condition."

Certainly Mr. Crowhurst had not exaggerated. It was a most dangerous place. The parted branches revealed a chasm some thirty feet deep, the brink of which, masked by the bushes, was but a matter of inches from the edge of the path.

"We had better go back," said Thorndyke, "and find the entrance to the pit, which seems to be to the right. The first thing is to ascertain

112

exactly where Harewood fell. Then we can come back and examine the place from above.

We turned back, and presently found a faint track which we followed until, descending steeply, it brought us out into the middle of the pit. It was evidently an ancient pit, for the sides were blackened by age, and the floor was occupied by a trees of some of considerable size. Against one of these we leaned our bicycles and then walked slowly round at the foot of the frowning cliff.

"This seems to be below the path," said Thorndyke, glancing up at the grey wall which jutted out above in stages like an inverted flight of steps. "Somewhere hereabouts we should find some traces of the tragedy."

Even as he spoke my eye caught a spot of white on a block of chalk, and on the freshly fractured surface a significant brownish-red stain. The block lay opposite the mouth of an artificial cave – an old wagon-shelter but now empty and immediately under a markedly overhanging part of the cliff.

"This is undoubtedly the place where he fell," said Thorndyke. "You can see where the stretcher was placed – an old-pattern stretcher with wheel-runners – and there is a little spot of broken soil at the top where he came over. Well, apart from the robbery, a clear fall of over thirty feet is enough to account for a fractured skull. Will you stay here, Jervis, while I run up and look at the path?"

He went off towards the entrance, and presently I heard him above, pulling aside the bushes, and after one or two trials, he appeared directly overhead.

"There are plenty of footprints on the path," said he, "but nothing abnormal. No trampling or signs of a struggle. I am going on a little farther."

He withdrew behind the bushes, and I proceeded to inspect the interior of the cave, noting the smoke-blackened roof and the remains of a recent fire, which, with a number of rabbit bones and a discarded tea-boiler of the kind used by the professional tramp, seemed not without a possible bearing on our investigation. I was thus engaged when I heard Thorndyke hail me from above and coming out of the cave, I saw his head thrust between the branches. He seemed to be lying down, for his face was nearly on a level with the top of the cliff.

"I want to take an impression," he called out. "Will you bring up the paraffin and the blower? And you might bring the coil of line, too."

I hurried away to the place where our bicycles were standing, and opening the research-case, took out the coil of line, the tin of paraffin wax and the spirit blowpipe and, having ascertained that the container of the latter was full, I ran up the incline and made my way along the path. Some distance along, I found my colleague nearly hidden in the bushes, lying prone, with his head over the edge of the cliff.

"You see, Jervis," he said, as I crawled alongside and looked over, "this is a possible way down, and someone has used it quite recently. He climbed down with his face to the cliff – you can see the clear impression of the toe of a boot in the loam of that projection, and you can even make out the shape of an iron toe-tip. Now the problem is how to get down to take the impression without, dislodging the earth above it. I think I will secure myself with the line."

"It is hardly worth the risk of a broken neck," said I. "Probably the print is that of some schoolboy."

"It is a man's foot," he replied. "Most likely it has no connection with our case. But it may have, and as a shower of rain would obliterate it, we ought to secure it." As he spoke, he passed the end of the cord through eye and slipped the loop over his shoulders, drawing tight under his arms. Then, having made the line fast to the butt of a small tree, he cautiously lowered himself over the edge and climbed down to the projection. A soon as he had a secure footing, I passed the spare cord through the ring on the lid of the wax tin and lowered it to him, and when he had unfastened it, I drew up the cord and in the same way let down the blowpipe. Then I watched his neat, methodical procedure. First he took out a spoonful of the powdered, or grated, wax and very delicately sprinkled it on the toe-print until the latter was evenly but very thinly covered. Next he lit the blowlamp, and as soon as the blue flame began to roar from the pipe, he directed it on to the toe-print. Almost instantly the powder melted, glazing the impression like a coat of varnish. The flame was removed and the film of wax at once solidified and became dull and opaque. A second, heavier, sprinkling with the powder, followed by another application of the flame, thickened the film of wax, and this process, repeated four or five times, eventually produced a solid cake. Then Thorndyke extinguished the blowlamp and, securing it and the tin to the cord, directed me to pull them up. "And you might send me down the field-glasses," he added. "There is something farther down that I can't quite make out."

I slipped the glasses from my shoulder, and opening the case, tied the cord to the leather sling, and lowered it down the cliff, and then I watched with some curiosity as Thorndyke stood on his insecure perch, steadily gazing through the glasses (they were Zeiss 8-prismatics) at a clump of wallflowers that grew from a boss of chalk about half-way down. Presently he lowered the glasses and, slinging them round his neck by their lanyard, turned his attention to the cake of wax. It was by

114

this time quite solid, and when he had tested it, he lifted it carefully, and placed it in the empty binocular case, when I drew it up.

"I want you, Jervis," Thorndyke called up, "to steady the line. I am going down to that wallflower clump."

It looked extremely unsafe, but I knew it was useless to protest, so I hitched the line around a massive stump and took a firm grip of the "fall".

"Ready," I sang out, and forthwith Thorndyke began to creep across the face of the cliff with feet and hands clinging to almost invisible projections. Fortunately there was at this part no overhang, and though my heart was in my mouth as I watched, I saw him cross the perilous space in safety. Arriving at the clump, he drew an envelope from his pocket, stooped, and picked up some small object, which he placed in the envelope, returning the latter to his pocket. Then he gave me another bad five minutes while he recrossed the nearly vertical surface to his starting-point, but at length this, too, was safely accomplished, and when he finally climbed up over the edge and stood beside me on solid earth, I drew a deep breath and turned to revile him.

"Well?" I demanded sarcastically, "what have you gathered at the risk of your neck? Is it samphire or edelweiss?"

He drew the envelope from his pocket and, dipping into it, produced a cigarette-holder – a cheap bone affair, black and clammy with long service and still holding the butt of a hand-made cigarette – and handed it to me. I turned it over, smelled it, and hastily handed it back. "For my part," said I, "I wouldn't have risked the cervical vertebra of a yellow cat for it. What do you expect to learn from it?"

"Of course, I expect nothing. We are just collecting facts on the chance that they may turn out to be relevant. Here, for instance, we find that a man has descended, within a few yards of where Harewood fell, by this very inconvenient route, instead of going round to the entrance to the pit. He must have had some reason for adopting this undesirable mode of descent. Possibly he was in a hurry, and probably he belonged to the district, since a stranger would not know of the existence of this short cut. Then it seems likely that this was his cigarette tube. If you look over, you will see by those vertical scrapes on the chalk that he slipped and must have nearly fallen. At that moment he probably dropped the tube, for you notice that the wallflower clump is directly under the marks of his toes."

"Why do you suppose he did not recover the tube?"

"Because the descent slopes away from the position of the clump, and he had no trusty Jervis with a stout cord to help him to cross the space. And if he went down this way because he was hurried, he would not have time to search for the tube. But if the tube was not his, still it belonged to somebody who has been here recently."

"Is there anything that leads you to connect this man with the crime?"

"Nothing but time and place," he replied. "The man has been down into the pit close to where Harewood was robbed and possibly murdered, and as the traces are quite recent, he must have been there near about the time of the robbery. That is all. I am considering the traces of this man in particular because there are no traces of any other. But we may as well have a look at the path, which, as you see, yields good impressions."

We walked slowly along the path towards Merbridge, keeping at the edges and scrutinising the surface closely. In the shady hollows, the soft loam bore prints of many feet, and among them we could distinguish one with an iron toe-tip, but it was nearly obliterated by another studded with hob-nails.

"We shan't get much information here," said Thorndyke as he turned about. "The search-party have trodden out the important prints. Let us see if we can find out where the man with the toe-tips went to."

We searched the path on the Welsbury side of the chalk-pit, but found no trace of him. Then we went into the pit, and having located the place where he descended, sought for some other exit than the track leading to the path. Presently, half-way up the slope, we found a second track, bearing away in the direction of Merbridge. Following this for some distance, we came to a small hollow at the bottom of which was a muddy space. And here we both halted abruptly, for in the damp ground were the clear imprints of a pair of boots which we could see had, in addition to the toe-tips, half-tips to the heels.

"We had better have wax casts of these," said Thorndyke, "to compare with the boots of the man Fletcher. I will do them while you go back for the bicycles."

By the time that I returned with the machines, two of the footprints were covered with a cake each of wax, and Thorndyke had left the track, and was peering among the bushes. I inquired what he was looking for.

"It is a forlorn hope, as Marchmont would say," he replied, "but I am looking to see if the will has been thrown away here. It was quite probably jettisoned at once, and this is the most probable route for the robber to have taken, if he knew of it. You see by the map that it must lead nearly directly to the race-course, and it avoids both the path and the main road. While the wax is setting we might as well look round."

It seemed a hopeless enough proceeding and I agreed to it without enthusiasm. Leaving the track on the opposite side to that which Thorndyke was searching, I wandered among the bushes and the little

116

open spaces, peering about me and reminding myself of that "aged, aged man" who sometimes searched "the grassy knolls for wheels of hansom cabs".

I had worked my way nearly back to where I could see Thorndyke, also returning, when my glance fell on a small, brown object caught among the branches of a bush. It was a man's pigskin purse, and as I picked it out of the bush I saw that it was open and empty.

With my prize in my hand, I hastened to the spot where Thorndyke was lifting the wax casts. He looked up and asked, "No luck, I suppose?"

I held out the purse, on which he pounced eagerly. "But this is most important, Jervis," he exclaimed. "It is almost certainly Harewood's purse. You see the initials, 'J. H.', stamped on the flap. Then we were right as to the direction that the robber took. And it would pay to search this place exhaustively for the will, though we can't do that now, as we have to go to Barwood. I wrote to say we were coming. We had better get back to the path now and make for the road. Barwood is only half-an-hour's run."

We packed the casts in the research-case (which was strapped to Thorndyke's bicycle), and turning back, made our way to the path. As it was still deserted, we ventured to mount, and soon reached the road, along which we started at a good pace toward Barwood.

Half-an-hour's ride brought us into the main street of the little town, and when we dismounted at the police station we found the Chief Constable himself waiting to receive us, courteously eager to assist us, but possessed by a devouring curiosity which was somewhat inconvenient.

"I have done as you asked me in your letter, sir," he said. "Fletcher's body is, of course, in the mortuary, but I have had all his clothes and effects brought here, and I have had them put in my private office, so that you can look them over in comfort."

"It is exceedingly good of you," said Thorndyke, "and most helpful." He unstrapped the research-case and, following the officer into his sanctum, looked round with deep approval. A large table had been cleared for the examination, and the dead pickpocket's clothes and effects neatly arranged at one end.

Thorndyke's first proceeding was to pick up the dead man's boots – a smart but flimsy pair of light-brown leather, rather down at heel and in need of re-soling. Neither toes nor heels bore any tips or even nails excepting the small fastening brads. Having exhibited them to me without remark, Thorndyke placed them on a sheet of white paper and made a careful tracing of the soles, a proceeding that seemed to surprise the Chief Constable, for he remarked, "I should hardly have thought that the question of footprints would arise in this case. You can't charge a dead man."

Thorndyke agreed that this seemed to be true, and then he proceeded to an operation that fairly made the officer's eyes bulge. Opening the research-case – into which the officer cast an inquisitive glance – he took out the dust-aspirator, the nozzle of which he inserted into one after another of the dead thief's pockets while I worked the pump. When he had gone through them all, he opened the receiver and extracted quite a considerable ball of dusty fluff. Placing this on a glass slide, he tore it in halves with a pair of mounted needles and passing one half to me, when we both fell to work "teasing", it out into an open mesh, portions of which we separated and laid – each in a tiny pool of glycerine – on blank labelled glass slides, applying to each slide its cover-glass and writing on the label, "*Dust from Fletcher's Pockets*".

When the series was complete, Thorndyke brought out the microscope and, fitting on a one-inch objective, quickly examined the slides, one after another, and then pushed the microscope to me. So far as I could see, the dust was just ordinary dust – principally made up of broken cotton fibres with a few fibres of wool, linen, wood, jute, and others that I could not name, and some undistinguishable mineral particles. But I made no comment, and resigning the microscope to the Chief Constable – who glared through it, breathing hard, and remarked that the dust was "rummy-looking stuff" – watched Thorndyke's further proceedings. And very odd proceedings they were

First he laid the five stolen watches in a row, and with a Coddington lens minutely examined the dial of each, Then he opened the back of each in turn and copied into his notebook the watch-repairers' scratched inscriptions. Next he produced from the case a number of little vulcanite rods, and laying out five labelled slides, dropped a tiny drop of glycerine on each, covering it at once with a watch-glass to protect it from falling dust. Then he stuck a little label on each watch, wrote a number on it, and similarly numbered the five slides. His next proceeding was to take out the glass of watch No. 1 and pick up one of the vulcanite rods, which he rubbed briskly on a silk handkerchief and passed across and around the dial of the watch, after which he held the rod close to the glycerine on slide No. 1 and tapped it sharply with the blade of his pocket-knife. Then he dropped a cover-glass on to the glycerine and made a rapid inspection of the specimen through the microscope.

This operation he repeated on the other four watches, using a fresh rod for each, and when he had finished he turned to the open-mouthed officer. "I take it," said he, "that the watch which has the chain attached to it is Mr. Harewood's watch?"

"Yes, sir. That helped us to identify it." Thorndyke looked at the watch reflectively. Attached to the bow by a short length of green tape was a small, rather elaborate key. This my friend picked up, and taking a fresh mounted needle, inserted it into the barrel of the key, from which he then withdrew it with a tiny ball of fluff on its point. I hastily prepared a slide and handed it to him, when, with a pair of dissecting scissors, he cut off a piece of the fluff and let it fall into the glycerine. He repeated this manoeuvre with two more slides and then labelled the three "*Key, Outside*", "*Middle*", and "*Inside*", and in that order examined them under the microscope.

My own examination of the specimens yielded very little. They all seemed to be common dust, though that from the face of watch No. 3 contained a few broken fragments of what looked like animal hairs – possibly cat's – as also did the key-fluff marked "*Outside*". But if this had any significance, I could not guess what it was. As to the Chief Constable, he clearly looked on the whole proceeding as a sort of legerdemain with no obvious purpose, for he remarked, as we were packing up to go, "I am glad I've seen how you do it, sir. But all the same, I think you are flogging a dead horse. We know who committed the crime and we know he's beyond the reach of the law."

"Well," said Thorndyke, "one must earn one's fee, you know. I shall put Fletcher's boots and the five watches in evidence at the inquest to-morrow, and I will ask you to leave the labels on the watches." With renewed thanks and a hearty handshake he bade the courteous officer *adieu*, and we rode off to catch the train to London.

That evening, after dinner, we brought out the specimens and went over them at our leisure, and Thorndyke added a further specimen by drawing a knotted piece of twine through the cigarette-holder that he had salved from the chalk-pit, and teasing out the unsavoury, black substance that came out on the string in glycerine on a slide. When he had examined it, he passed it to me, The dark, tarry liquid somewhat obscured the detail, but I could make out fragments of the same animal hairs that I had noted in the other specimens, only here they were much more numerous. I mentioned my observation to Thorndyke. "They are certainly parts of mammalian hairs," I said, "and they look like the hairs of a cat. Are they from a cat?"

"Rabbit," Thorndyke replied curtly, and even then, I am ashamed to admit, I did not perceive the drift of the investigation.

The room in the Welsbury Town Hall had filled up some minutes before the time fixed for the opening of the inquest, and in the interval, when the jury had retired to view the body in the adjacent mortuary, I looked round the assembly. Mr. Marchmont and Mr. Crowhurst were present, and a youngish, horsey-looking man in cord breeches and leggings, whom I correctly guessed to be Arthur Baxfield. Our friend the Chief Constable of Barwood was also there, and with him Thorndyke exchanged a few words in a retired corner. The rest of the company were strangers.

As soon as the coroner and the jury had taken their places the medical witness was called. The cause of death, he stated, was dislocation of the neck, accompanied by a depressed fracture of the skull. The fracture have been produced by a blow with a heavy weapon, or by the deceased falling on his head. The witness adopted the latter view, as the dislocation showed that deceased had fallen in that manner.

The next witness was Mr. Crowhurst, who repeated to the court what he had told us, and further stated that on leaving deceased's house he went straight home, as he had an appointment with a friend. He was followed by Baxfield, who gave evidence to the same effect, and stated that on leaving the house of the deceased he went to his place of business at Welsbury. He was about to retire when Thorndyke rose to cross-examine.

"At what time did you reach your place of business?" he asked.

The witness hesitated for a few moments and then replied, "Half-past-four."

"And what time did you leave deceased's house?"

"Two o'clock," was the reply.

"What is the distance?"

"In a direct line, about two miles. But I didn't go direct. I took a round in the country by Lenfield."

"That would take you near the race-course on the way back. Did you go to the races?"

"No. The races were just over when I returned."

There was a slight pause and then Thorndyke asked, "Do you smoke much, Mr. Baxfield?"

The witness looked surprised, and so did the jury, but the former replied, "A fair amount. About fifteen cigarettes a day."

"What brand of cigarettes do you smoke, and what kind of tobacco is it?"

"I make my own cigarettes. I make them of shag."

Here protesting murmurs arose from the jury, and the coroner remarked stiffly, "These questions do not appear to have much connection with the subject of this inquiry."

"You may take it, sir," replied Thorndyke, "that they have a very direct bearing on it." Then, turning to the witness he asked, "Do you use a cigarette-tube?"

"Sometimes I do," was the reply.

"Have you lost a cigarette-tube lately?"

The witness directed a startled glance at Thorndyke and replied after some hesitation, "I believe I mislaid one a little time ago."

"When and where did you lose that tube?" Thorndyke asked.

"I – I really couldn't say," replied Baxfield, turning perceptibly pale.

Thorndyke opened his dispatch-box and, taking out the tube that he had saved at so much risk, handed it to the witness. "Is that the tube that you lost?" he asked.

At this question Baxfield turned pale as death, and the hand in which he received the tube shook as if with a palsy. "It may be," he faltered. "I wouldn't swear to it. It is like the one I lost."

Thorndyke took it from him and passed it to the coroner. "I am putting this tube in evidence, sir," said he. Then addressing the witness, he said, "You stated that you did not go to the races. Did you go on the course or inside the grounds at all?"

Baxfield moistened his lips and replied, "I just went in for a minute or two, but I didn't stay. The races were over, and there was a very rough crowd."

"While you were in that crowd, Mr. Baxfield, did you have your pocket picked?"

There was an expectant silence in the court as Baxfield replied in a low voice, "Yes. I lost my watch."

Again Thorndyke opened the dispatch-box and, taking out a watch (it was the one that had been labelled "3"), handed it to the witness. "Is that the watch that you lost?" he asked.

Baxfield held the watch in his trembling hand and replied hesitatingly, "I believe it is, but I won't swear to it.

There was a pause. Then, in grave, impressive tones, Thorndyke said, "Now, Mr. Baxfield, I am going to ask you a question which you need not answer if you consider that by doing so you would prejudice your position in any way. That question is, When your pocket was picked, were any articles besides this watch taken from your person? Don't hurry. Consider your answer carefully."

For some moments Baxfield remained silent, regarding Thorndyke with a wild, affrighted stare. At length he began falteringly, "I don't remember missing any thing – " and then stopped.

"Could the witness be allowed to sit down, sir?" Thorndyke asked. And when the permission had been given and a chair placed, Baxfield sat down heavily and cast a bewildered glance round the court. "I think," he said, addressing Thorndyke, "I had better tell you exactly what happened and take my chance of the consequences. When I left my uncle's house on Monday, I took a circuit through the fields and then entered Gilbert's Copse to wait for my uncle and tell him what I thought of his conduct in leaving the bulk of his property to a stranger. I struck the path that I knew my uncle would take and walked along it slowly to meet him. I did meet him – on the path, just above where he was found – and I began to say what was in my mind. But he wouldn't listen. He flew into a rage, and as I was standing in the middle of the path, he tried to push past me. In doing so he caught his foot in a bramble and staggered back, then he disappeared through the bushes and a few seconds after I heard a thud down below. I pulled the bushes aside and looked down into the chalk-pit, and there I saw him lying with his head all on one side. Now, I happened to know of a short cut down into the pit. It was rather a dangerous climb, but I took it to get down as quickly as possible. It was there that I dropped the cigarette-tube. When I got to my uncle, I could see that he was dead. His skull was battered and his neck was broken. Then the devil put into my head the idea of making away with the will. But I knew that if I took the will only, suspicion would fall on me. So I took most of his valuables – the wallet, his watch and chain, his purse, and his ring. The purse I emptied and threw away, and flung the ring after it. I took the will out of the wallet – it had just been dropped in loose – and put it in an inner pocket. Then I dropped the wallet and the watch and chain into my outside coat pocket.

"I struck across country, intending to make for the race-course and drop the things among the crowd, so that they might be picked up and safely carried away. But when I got there a gang of pickpockets saved me the trouble, they mobbed and hustled me and cleared my pockets of everything but my keys and the will."

"And what has become of the will?" asked Thorndyke.

"I have it here." He dipped into his breast pocket and produced a folded paper, which he handed to Thorndyke, who opened it, and having glanced at it, passed it to the coroner.

That was practically the end of the inquest. The jury decided to accept Baxfield's statement and recorded a verdict of "Death by Misadventure", leaving Baxfield to be dealt with by the proper authorities.

"An interesting and eminently satisfactory case," remarked Thorndyke, as we sat over a rather late dinner. "Essentially simple, too.

122

The elucidation turned, as you probably noticed, on a single illuminating fact."

"I judged that it was so," said I, "though the illumination of that fact has not yet reached me."

"Well," said Thorndyke, "let us first take the general aspect of the case as it was presented by Marchmont. The first thing, of course, that struck one was that the loss of the will might easily have converted Baxfield from a minor beneficiary to the sole heir. But even if the court agreed to recognise the will, it would have to be guided by the statements of the only two men to whom its provisions were even approximately known, and Baxfield could have made any statement he pleased. It was impossible to ignore the fact that the loss of the will was very greatly to Baxfield's advantage.

"When the stolen property was discovered in Fletcher's possession it looked, at the first glance, as if the mystery of the crime were solved. But there were several serious inconsistencies. First, how came Fletcher to be in this solitary wood, remote from any railway or even road? He appeared to be a London pickpocket. When he was killed he was travelling to London by train. It seemed probable that he had come from London by train to ply his trade at the races. Then, as you know, criminological experience shows that the habitual criminal is a rigid specialist. The burglar, the coiner, the pickpocket, each keeps strictly to his own special line. Now, Fletcher was a pickpocket, and had evidently been picking pockets on the race-course. The probabilities were against his being the original robber and in favour of his having picked the pocket of the person who robbed Harewood. But if this were so, who was that person? Once more the probabilities suggested Baxfield. There was the motive, as I have said, and further, the pocket-picking had apparently taken place on the race-course, and Baxfield was known to be a frequenter of race-courses. But again, if Baxfield were the person robbed by Fletcher, then one of the five watches was probably Baxfield's watch. Whether it was so or not might have been very difficult to prove, but here came in the single illuminating fact that I have spoken of."

"You remember that when Marchmont opened the case he mentioned that Baxfield was a manufacturer of felt hats, and Crowhurst told us that he was a sort of foreman or manager of the factory."

"Yes, I remember, now you speak of it. But what is the bearing of the fact?"

"My dear Jervis!" exclaimed Thorndyke. "Don't you see that it gave us a touchstone? Consider, now. What is a felt hat? It is just a mass of agglutinated rabbits' hair. The process of manufacture consists in blowing a jet of the more or less disintegrated hair on to a revolving steel

123

cone which is moistened by a spray of an alcoholic solution of shellac. But, of course, a quantity of the finer and more minute particles of the broken hairs miss the cone and float about in the air. The air of the factory is thus charged with the dust of broken rabbit hairs, and this dust settles on and penetrates the clothing of the workers. But when clothing becomes charged with dust, that dust tends to accumulate in the pockets and find its way into the hollows and interstices of any object carried in those pockets. Thus, if one of the five watches was Baxfield's, it would almost certainly show traces where this characteristic dust had crept under the bezel and settled on the dial. And so it turned out to be. When I inspected those five watches through the Coddington lens, on the dial of No. 3 I saw a quantity of dust of this character. The electrified vulcanite rod picked it all up neatly and transferred it to the slide, and under the microscope its nature was obvious. The owner of this watch was therefore, almost certainly, employed in a felt hat factory. But, of course, it was necessary to show not only the presence of rabbit hair in this watch but its absence in the others and in Fletcher's pockets, which I did.

"Then with regard to Harewood's watch: There was no rabbit hair on the dial, but there was a small quantity on the fluff from the key barrel. Now, if that rabbit hair had come from Harewood's pocket, it would have been uniformly distributed through the fluff. But it was not. It was confined exclusively to the part of the fluff that was exposed. Thus it had come from some pocket other than Harewood's and the owner of that pocket was almost certainly employed in a felt hat factory, and was most probably the owner of watch No. 3. Then there was the cigarette-tube. Its bore was loaded with rabbit hair. But its owner had unquestionably been at the scene of the crime. There was a clear suggestion that his was the pocket in which the stolen watch had been carried and that he was the owner of watch No. 3. The problem was to piece this evidence together and prove definitely who this person was. And that I was able to do by means of a fresh item of evidence, which I acquired when I saw Baxfield at the inquest. I suppose you noticed his boots?"

"I am afraid I didn't," I had to admit.

"Well, I did. I watched his feet constantly, and when he crossed his legs I could see that he had iron toe-tips on his boots. That was what gave me confidence to push the cross-examination."

"It was certainly a rather daring cross-examination – and rather irregular, too," said I.

"It was extremely irregular," Thorndyke agreed. "The coroner ought not to have permitted it. But it was all for the best. If the coroner had disallowed my questions, we should have had to take criminal proceedings against Baxfield, whereas now that we have recovered the will, it is possible that no one will trouble to prosecute him."

Which, I subsequently ascertained, is what actually happened."

A Fisher of Men

"The man," observed Thorndyke, "who would successfully practise the scientific detection of crime must take all knowledge for his province. There is no single fact which may not, in particular circumstances, acquire a high degree of evidential value, and in such circumstances success or failure is determined by the possession or non-possession of the knowledge wherewith to interpret the significance of that fact."

This obiter dictum was thrown off apropos of our investigation of the case rather magniloquently referred to in the press as "The Blue Diamond Mystery", and more particularly of an incident which occurred in the office of our old friend, Superintendent Miller, at Scotland Yard. Thorndyke had called to verify the few facts which had been communicated to him, and having put away his notebook and picked up his green canvas-covered research-case, had risen to take his leave, when his glance fell on a couple of objects on a side-table – a leather handbag and a walking-stick, lashed together with string, to which was attached a descriptive label.

He regarded them for a few moments reflectively and then glanced at the superintendent.

"Derelicts?" he inquired, "or jetsam?"

"Jetsam," the superintendent replied. "Literally jetsam – thrown overboard to lighten the ship."

Here Inspector Badger, who had been a party to the conference, looked up eagerly.

"Yes," he broke in. "Perhaps the doctor wouldn't mind having a look at them. It's quite a nice little problem, Doctor, and entirely in your line."

"What is the problem?" asked Thorndyke.

"It's just this," said Badger. "Here is a bag. Now the question is: Whose bag is it? What sort of person is the owner? Where did he come from and where has he gone to?"

Thorndyke chuckled. "That seems quite simple," said he. "A cursory inspection ought to dispose of trivial details like those. But how did you come by the bag?"

"The history of the derelicts," said Miller, "is this, About four o'clock this morning, a constable on duty in King's Road, Chelsea, saw a man walking on the opposite side of the road, carrying a handbag. There was nothing particularly suspicious in this, but still the constable thought

126

he would cross and have a closer look at him. As he did so, the man quickened his pace and, of course, the constable quickened his. Then the man broke into a run, and so did the constable, and a fine, stern chase started. Suddenly the man shot down a by-street, and as the constable turned the corner he saw his quarry turn into a sort of alley. Following him into this, and gaining on him perceptibly, he saw that the alley ended in a rather high wall. When the fugitive reached the wall, he dropped his bag and stick and went over like a harlequin. The constable went over after him, but not like a harlequin – he wasn't dressed for the part. By the time he got over, into a large garden with a lot of fruit trees in it, my nabs had disappeared. He traced him by his footprints across the garden to another wall, and when he climbed over that he found himself in by-street. But there was no sign of our agile friend. The constable ran up and down the street to the next crossings, blowing his whistle, but of course it was no go. So he went back across the garden and secured the bag and stick, which were at once sent here for examination."

"And no arrest has been made?"

"Well," replied Miller with a faint grin, "a constable in Oakley Street who had heard the whistle arrested a man who was carrying a suspicious-looking object. But he turned out to be a cornet player coming home from the theatre."

"Good," said Thorndyke. "And now let us have a look at the bag, which I take it has already been examined?

"Yes, we've been through it," replied Miller, "but everything has been put back as we found it."

Thorndyke picked up the bag and proceeded to make a systematic inspection of its exterior.

"A good bag," he commented. "Quite an expensive one originally, though it has seen a good deal of service. You noticed the muddy marks on the bottom?"

"Yes," said Miller. "Those were probably made when he dropped the bag to jump over the wall."

"Possibly," said Thorndyke, "though they don't look like street mud. But we shall probably get more information from the contents." He opened the bag, and after a glance at its interior, spread out on the table a couple of sheets of foolscap from the stationery rack, on which he began methodically to deposit the contents of the bag, accompanying the process with a sort of running commentary on their obvious characteristics.

"Item one, a small leather dressing-wallet. Rather shabby, but originally of excellent quality. It contains two Swedish razors, a little Washita hone, a diminutive strop, a folding shaving-brush, which is

127

slightly damp to the fingers and has a scent similar to that of the stick of shaving soap. You notice that the hone is distinctly concave in the middle and that the inscription on the razors, '*Arensburg, Eskilsruna, Sweden*', is partly ground away. Then there is a box containing a very dry cake of soap, a little manicure set, a well-worn toothbrush, a nailbrush, dental-brush, button-hook, corn-razor, a small clothesbrush, and a pair of small hairbrushes. It seems to me, Badger, that this wallet suggests – mind, I only say 'suggests' – a pretty complete answer to one of your questions."

"I don't see how," said the inspector. "Tell me what it suggests to you."

"It suggests to me," replied Thorndyke, laying down the lens through which he had been inspecting the hair-brushes, "a middle-aged or elderly man with a shaven upper lip and a beard; a well-preserved, healthy man, neat, orderly, provident, and careful as to his appearance; a man long habituated to travelling, and – though I don't insist on this, but the appearances suggest that he had been living for some time in a particular households and that at the time when he lost the bag, he was changing his residence."

"He was that," cackled the inspector, "if the constable's account of the way he went over that wall is to be trusted. But still, I don't see how you have arrived at all those facts."

"Not facts, Badger," Thorndyke corrected. "I said suggestions. And those suggestions may be quite misleading. There may be some factor, such as change of ownership of the wallet, which we have not allowed for. But, taking the appearances at their face value, that is what they suggest. There is the wallet itself, for instance – strong, durable, but shabby with years of wear. And observe that it is a travelling-wallet and would be subjected to wear only during travel. Then further, as to the time factor, there are the hone and the razors. It takes a good many years to wear a Washita hone hollow or to wear away the blade of a Swedish razor until the maker's mark is encroached on. The state of health, and to some extent the age, are suggested by the tooth brush and the dental-brush. He has lost some teeth, since he wears a plate, but not many, and he is free from pyorrhoea and alveolar absorption. You don't wear a toothbrush down like this on half-a-dozen rickety survivors. But a man whose teeth will bear hard brushing is probably well-preserved and healthy."

"You say that he shaves his upper lip but wears a beard," said the inspector. "How do you arrive at that?"

"It is fairly obvious," replied Thorndyke. "We see that he has razors and uses them, and we also see that he has a beard."

128

"Do we?" exclaimed Badger. "How do we?"

Thorndyke delicately picked a hair from one of the hairbrushes and held it up. "That is not a scalp hair," said he. "I should say that it came from the side of the chin."

Badger regarded the hair with evident disfavour. "Looks to me," he remarked, "as if a small tooth-comb might have been useful."

"It does," Thorndyke agreed, "but the appearance is deceptive. This is what is called a moniliform hair – like a string of beads. But the bead-like swellings are really parts of the hair. It is a diseased, or perhaps we should say an abnormal, condition." He handed me the hair together with his lens, through which I examined it and easily recognised the characteristic swellings.

"Yes," said I, "it is an early case of *tricliorrexis nodosa.*"

"Good Lord!" murmured the inspector. "Sounds like a Russian nobleman. Is it a common complaint?"

"It is not a rare disease – if you can call it a disease," I replied, "but it is a rare condition, taking the population as a whole."

"It is rather a remarkable coincidence that it should happen to occur in this particular case," the superintendent observed.

"My dear Miller," exclaimed Thorndyke, "surely your experience must have impressed on you the astonishing frequency of the unusual and the utter failure of the mathematical laws of probability in practice. Believe me, Miller, the bread-and-butterfly was right. It is the exceptional that always happens."

Having discharged this paradox, he once more dived into the bag, and this time handed out a singular and rather unsavoury-looking parcel, the outer investment of which was formed by what looked like an excessively dirty towel, but which, as Thorndyke delicately unrolled it, was seen to be only half a towel which was supplemented by a still dirtier and excessively ragged coloured handkerchief. This, too, being opened out, disclosed an extremely soiled and rather frayed collar (which, like the other articles, bore no name or mark), and a mass of grass, evidently used as packing material.

The inspector picked up the collar and quoted reflectively, "He is a man, neat, orderly and careful as to his appearance," after which he dropped the collar and ostentatiously wiped his fingers.

Thorndyke smiled grimly but refrained from repartee as he carefully separated the grass from the contained objects, which turned out to be a small telescopic jemmy, a jointed auger, a screwdriver, and a bunch of skeleton keys.

"One understands his unwillingness to encounter the constable with these rather significant objects in his possession," Thorndyke remarked.

"They would have been difficult to explain away." He took up the heap of grass between his hands and gently compressed it to test its freshness. As he did so a tiny, cigar-shaped object dropped on the paper.

"What is that?" asked the superintendent. "It looks like a chrysalis."

"It isn't," said Thorndyke. "It is a shell, a species of *Clausilia*, I think." He picked up the little shell and closely examined its mouth through his lens. "Yes," he continued, "it is a *Clausilia*. Do you study our British *mollusca*, Badger?"

"No, I don't," the inspector replied with emphasis.

"Pity," murmured Thorndyke. "If you did, you would be interested to learn that the name of this little shell is *Clausilia biplicata*."

"I don't care what its beastly name is," said Badger. "I want to know whose bag this is, what the owner is like, and where he came from, and where he has gone to. Can you tell us that?"

Thorndyke regarded the inspector with wooden gravity. "It is all very obvious," said he, "very obvious. But still, I think I should like to fill in a few details before making a definite statement. Yes, I think I will reserve my judgment until I have considered the matter a little further."

The inspector received this statement with a dubious grin. He was in somewhat of a dilemma. My colleague was addicted to a certain dry facetiousness, and was probably pulling the inspector's leg. But, on the other hand, I knew, and so did both the detectives, that it was perfectly conceivable that he had actually solved Badger's problem, impossible as it seemed, and was holding back his knowledge until he had seen whither it led.

"Shall we take a glance at the stick?" said he, picking it up as he spoke and running his eye over its not very distinctive features. It was a common ash stick, with a crooked handle polished and darkened by prolonged contact with an apparently ungloved hand, and it was smeared for about three inches from the tip with a yellowish mud. The iron shoe of the ferrule was completely worn away and the deficiency had been made good by driving a steel boot-stud into the exposed end.

"A thrifty gentleman, this," Thorndyke remarked, pointing to the stud as he measured the diameter of the ferrule with his pocket calliper-gauge. "Twenty-three-thirty-seconds is the diameter," he added, looking gravely at the inspector. "You had better make a note of that, Badger."

The inspector smiled sourly as Thorndyke laid down the stick, and once more picking up the little green canvas case that contained his research outfit, prepared to depart.

"You will hear from us, Miller," he said, "if we pick up anything that will be useful to you. And now, Jervis, we must really take ourselves off."

130

As the tinkling hansom bore us down Whitehall towards Waterloo, I remarked, "Badger half suspects you of having withheld from him some valuable information in respect of that bag."

"He does," Thorndyke agreed with a mischievous smile, "and he doesn't in the least suspect me of having given him a most illuminating hint."

"But did you?" I asked, rapidly reviewing the conversation and deciding that the facts elicited from the dressing-wallet could hardly be described as hints.

"My learned friend," he replied, "is pleased to counterfeit obtuseness. It won't do, Jervis. I've known you too long."

I grinned with vexation. Evidently I had missed the point of a subtle demonstration, and I knew that it was useless to ask further questions, and for the remainder of our journey in the cab I struggled vainly to recover the "illuminating hint" that the detectives – and I – had failed to note. Indeed, so preoccupied was I with this problem that I rather overlooked the fact that the jettisoned bag was really no concern of ours, and that we were actually engaged in the investigation of a crime of which, at present, I knew practically nothing. It was not until we had secured an empty compartment and the train had begun to move that this suddenly dawned on me, whereupon I dismissed the bag problem and applied to Thorndyke for details of the "The Brentford Train Mystery".

"To call it a mystery," said he, "is a misuse of words. It appears to be a simple train robbery. The identity of the robber is unknown, but there is nothing very mysterious in that, and the crime otherwise is quite commonplace. The circumstances are these:

"Some time ago, Mr. Lionel Montague, of the firm Lyons, Montague, and Salaman, art dealers, bought from a Russian nobleman a very valuable diamond necklace and pendant. The peculiarity of this necklace was that the stones were all of a pale blue colour and pretty accurately matched, so that in addition to the aggregate value of the stones – which were all of large size and some very large – was the value of the piece as a whole due to this uniformity of colour. Mr. Montague gave £70,000 for it, and considered that he had made an excellent bargain. I should mention that Montague was the chief buyer for the firm, and that he spent most of his time travelling about the Continent in search of works of art and other objects suitable for the purposes of his firm, and that, naturally, he was an excellent judge of such things. Now, it seems that he was not satisfied with the settings of this necklace, and as soon as he had purchased it he handed it over to Messrs. Binks, of Old Bond Street, to have the settings replaced by others of better design. Yesterday morning he was notified by Binks that the resetting was

131

completed, and in the afternoon he called to inspect the work and take the necklace away if it was satisfactory. The interview between Binks and Montague took place in a room behind the shop, but it appears that Montague came out into the shop to get a better light for his inspection and Mr. Binks states that as his customer stood facing the door, examining the new settings, he, Binks, noticed a man standing by the doorway furtively watching Mr. Montague."

"There is nothing very remarkable in that," said I. "If a man stands at a shop door with a necklace of blue diamonds in his hand, he is rather likely to attract attention."

"Yes," Thorndyke agreed. "But the significance of an antecedent is apt to be more appreciated after the consequences have developed. Binks is now very emphatic about the furtive watcher. However, to continue, Mr. Montague, being satisfied with the new settings, replaced the necklace in its case, put the latter into his bag – which he had brought with him from the inner room – and a minute or so later left the shop. That was about five p.m., and he seems to have gone direct to the flat of his partner, Mr. Salaman, with whom he had been staying for a fortnight, at Queen's Gate. There he remained until about half-past eight, when he came out accompanied by Mr. Salaman. The latter carried a small suit-case, while Montague carried a handbag in which was the necklace. It is not known whether it contained anything else.

"From Queen's Gate the two men proceeded to Waterloo, walking part of the way and covering the remainder by omnibus."

"By omnibus!" I exclaimed, "with seventy-thousand pounds of diamonds about them!"

"Yes, it sounds odd. But people who habitually handle portable property of great value seem to resemble those who habitually handle explosives. They gradually become unconscious of the risks. At any rate, that is how they went, and they arrived safely at Waterloo in time to catch the 9:15 train for Isleworth. Mr. Salaman saw his partner established in an empty first-class compartment and stayed with him, chatting, until the train started.

"Mr. Montague's destination was Isleworth, in which rather unlikely neighbourhood Mr. Jacob Lowenstein, late of Chicago, and now of Berkeley Square, has a sort of river-side villa with a motorboat house attached. Lowenstein had secured the option of purchasing the blue diamond necklace, and Montague was taking it down to exhibit it and carry out the deal. He was proposing to stay a few days with Lowenstein, and then he was proceeding to Brussels on one of his periodic tours. But he never reached Isleworth. When the train stopped at Brentford, a porter noticed a suit-case on the luggage-rack of an apparently empty first-class

132

compartment. He immediately entered to take possession of it, and was in the act of reaching up to the rack when his foot came in contact with something soft under the seat. Considerably startled, he stooped and peered under, when, to his horror, he perceived the body of a man, quite motionless and apparently dead. Instantly he darted out and rushed up the platform in a state of wild panic until he, fortunately, ran against the station master, with whom and another porter he returned to the compartment. When they drew the body out from under the seat it was found to be still breathing, and they proceeded at once to apply such restoratives as cold water and fresh air, pending the arrival of the police and the doctor, who had been sent for.

"In a few minutes the police arrived accompanied by the police surgeon, and the latter, after a brief examination, decided that the unconscious man was suffering from the effects of a large dose of chloroform, violently and unskilfully administered, and ordered him to be carefully removed to a local nursing home. Meanwhile, the police had been able, by inspecting the contents of his pockets, to identify him as Mr. Lionel Montague."

"The diamonds had vanished, of course?" said I.

"Yes. The handbag was not in the compartment, and later an empty handbag was picked up on the permanent way between Barnes and Chiswick, which seems to indicate the locality where the robbery took place."

"And what is our present objective?"

"We are going, on instructions from Mr. Salaman, to the nursing home to see what information we can pick up. If Montague has recovered sufficiently to give an account of the robbery, the police will have a description of the robber, and there may not be much for us to do. But you will have noticed that they do not seem to have any information at Scotland Yard at present, beyond what I have given you. So there is a chance yet that we may earn our fees."

Thorndyke's narrative of this somewhat commonplace crime, with the discussion which followed it, occupied us until the train stopped at Brentford Station. A few minutes later we halted in one of the quiet by-streets of this old-world town, at a soberly painted door on which was a brass plate inscribed "*St. Agnes Nursing Home*". Our arrival had apparently been observed, for the door was opened by a middle-aged lady in a nurse's uniform.

"Dr. Thorndyke?" she inquired, and as my colleague bowed assent she continued, "Mr. Salaman told me you would probably call. I am afraid I haven't very good news for you. The patient is still quite unconscious."

"That is rather remarkable," said Thorndyke.

"It is. Dr. Kingston, who is in charge of the case, is somewhat puzzled by this prolonged stupor. He is inclined to suspect a narcotic – possibly a large dose of morphine – in addition to the effects of the chloroform and the shock."

"He is probably right," said I, "and the marvel is that the man is alive at all after such outrageous treatment."

"Yes," Thorndyke agreed. "He must be pretty tough. Shall we be able to see him?"

"Oh, yes," the matron replied. "I am instructed to give you every assistance. Dr. Kingston would like to have your opinion on the case."

With this she conducted us to a pleasant room on the first floor, where, in a bed placed opposite a large window – left uncurtained – with the strong light falling full on his face, a man lay with closed eyes, breathing quietly and showing no sign of consciousness when we somewhat noisily entered the room. For some time Thorndyke stood by the bedside, looking down at the unconscious man, listening to the breathing and noting its frequency by his watch. Then he felt the pulse, and raising both eyelids, compared the two pupils.

"His condition doesn't appear alarming," was his conclusion. "The breathing is rather shallow, but it is quite regular, and the pulse is not bad though slow. The contracted pupils strongly suggest opium, or more probably morphine. But that could easily be settled by a chemical test. Do you notice the state of the face, Jervis?"

"You mean the chloroform burns? Yes, the handkerchief or pad must have been saturated. But I was also noticing that he corresponds quite remarkably with the description you were giving Badger of the owner of the dressing-wallet. He is about the age you mentioned – roughly about fifty – and he has the same old-fashioned treatment of the beard, the shaven upper lip, and the monkey-fringe under the chin. It is rather an odd coincidence."

Thorndyke looked at me keenly. "The coincidence is closer than that, Jervis. Look at the beard itself."

He handed me his lens and, stooping down, I brought it to bear on the patient's beard. And then I started back in astonishment, for by the bright light I could see plainly that a considerable proportion of the hairs were distinctly moniliform. This man's beard, too, was affected by an early stage of *trichorrexis nodosa*!

"Well!" I exclaimed, "this is really an amazing coincidence. I wonder if it is anything more."

"I wonder," said Thorndyke. "Are those Mr. Montague's things, Matron?"

134

"Yes," she replied, turning to the side table on which the patient's effects were neatly arranged. "Those are his clothes and the things which were taken from his pockets, and that is his bag. It was found on the line and sent on here a couple of hours ago. There is nothing in it."

Thorndyke looked over the various objects – keys, card-case, pocket-book, *etcetera* – that had been turned out of the patient's pockets, and then picked up the bag, which he turned over curiously and then opened to inspect the interior. There was nothing distinctive about it. It was just a plain, imitation leather bag, fairly new, though rather the worse for its late vicissitudes, lined with coarse linen to which two large, wash-leather pockets had been roughly stitched. As he laid the bag down and picked up his own canvas case, he asked, "What time did Mr. Salaman come to see the patient?"

"He came here about ten o'clock this morning, and he was not able to stay more than half-an-hour as he had an appointment. But he said he would look in again this evening. You can't stay to see him, I suppose?"

"I'm afraid not," Thorndyke replied. "In fact, we must be off now, for both Dr. Jervis and I have some other matters to attend to."

"Are you going straight back to the chambers, Jervis?" Thorndyke asked, as we walked down the main street towards the station.

"Yes," I replied in some surprise. "Aren't you?"

"No. I have a little expedition in view."

"Oh, have you?" I exclaimed, and as I spoke it began to dawn on me that I had overestimated the importance of my other business.

"Yes," said Thorndyke. "The fact is that – Ha! Excuse me one moment, Jervis." He had halted abruptly outside a fishing-tackle shop and now, after a brief glance in through the window, entered with an air of business. I immediately bolted in after him, and was just in time to hear him demand a fishing-rod of a light and inexpensive character. When this had been supplied he asked for a line and one or two hooks, and I was a little surprised – and the vendor was positively scandalised – at his indifference to the quality or character of these appliances. I believe he would have accepted cod-line and a shark-hook if they had been offered.

"And now I want a float," said he.

The shopkeeper produced a tray containing a varied assortment of floats over which Thorndyke ran a critical eye, and finally reduced the shopman to stupefaction by selecting a gigantic, pot-bellied scarlet-and-green atrocity that looked like a juvenile telegraph buoy.

I could not let this outrage pass without comment. "You must excuse me, Thorndyke," I said, "if I venture to point out that the Greenland whale no longer frequents the upper reaches of the Thames."

135

"You mind your own business," he retorted, stolidly pocketing the telegraph buoy when he had paid for his purchases. "I like a float that you can see."

Here the shopman, recovering somewhat from the shock of surprise, remarked deferentially that it was a long time since a really large pike had been caught in the neighbourhood, whereupon Thorndyke finished him off by replying, "Yes, I've no doubt. They don't use the right sort of floats, you know. Now, when the pike see my float, they will just come tumbling over one another to get on the hook." With this he tucked the rod under his arm and strolled out, leaving the shopman breathing hard and staring harder.

"But what on earth," I asked, as we walked down the street (watched by the shopman who had come out on the pavement to see the last of us), "do you want with such an enormous float? Why, it will be visible a quarter-of-a-mile away."

"Exactly," said Thorndyke. "And what more could a fisher of men require?"

This rejoinder gave me pause. Evidently Thorndyke had something in hand of more than common interest, and again it occurred to me that my own business engagements were of no special urgency. I was about to mention this fact when Thorndyke again halted – at an oilshop this time.

"I think I will step in here and get a little burnt umber," said he.

I followed him into the shop, and while the powder-colour was being weighed and made up into a little packet I reflected profoundly. Fishing-tackle and burnt umber had no obvious associations. I began to be mystified and correspondingly inquisitive.

"What do you want the burnt umber for?" I asked as soon as we were outside.

"To mix with plaster," he replied readily.

"But why do you want to colour the plaster? And what are you going to do with it?"

"Now, Jervis," he admonished with mock severity, "you are not doing yourself justice. An investigator of your experience shouldn't ask for explanations of the obvious."

"And why," I continued, "did you want to know if I was going straight back to the chambers?

"Because I may want some assistance later. Probably Polton will be able to do all that I want, but I wished to know that you would both be within reach of a telegram."

"But," I exclaimed, "what nonsense it is to talk of sending a telegram to me when I'm here!"

136

"But I may not want any assistance, after all."

"Well," I said doggedly, "you are going to have it whether you want it or not. You've got something on and I'm going to be in it."

"I like your enthusiasm, Jervis," he chuckled, "but it is quite possible that I shall merely find a mare's nest."

"Very well," said I. "Then I'll help you to find it. I've had plenty of experience in that line, to say nothing of my natural gifts. So lead on."

He led on, with a resigned smile, to the station, where we were fortunate enough to find a train just ready to start. But our journey was not a long one, for at Chiswick Thorndyke got out of the train, and on leaving the station struck out eastward with a very evident air of business. As we entered the outskirts of Hammersmith, he turned into a by-street which presently brought us out into Bridge Road. Here he turned sharply to the right and, at the same brisk pace, crossed Hammersmith Bridge and made his way to the towing path. As he now slowed down perceptibly, I ventured to inquire whether this was the spot on which he proposed to exhibit his super-float.

"This, I think, will be our fishing-ground," he replied, "but we will look over it carefully and select a suitable pitch."

He continued to advance at an easy pace, and I noticed that, according to his constant habit, he was studying the peculiarities of the various feet that had trodden the path within the last day or two — keeping for this purpose on the right-hand side, where the shade of a few pollard willows overhanging an indistinct dry ditch had kept the ground soft. We had walked on for nearly half-a-mile when he halted and looked round.

"I think we had better turn back a little way," said he. "We seem to have overshot our mark."

I made no comment on this rather mysterious observation, and we retraced our steps for a couple-of-hundred yards, Thorndyke still walking on the side farthest from the river and still keeping his eyes fixed on the ground. Presently he again halted, and looking up and down the path, of which we were at the moment the only occupants, placed the canvas case on the ground, and unfastened its clasps.

"This, I think, will be our pitch," said he.

"What are you going to do?" I asked.

"I am going to make one or two casts. And meanwhile you had better get the fishing-rod fixed together so as to divert the attention of any passers-by."

I proceeded to make ready the fishing-tackle, but at the same time kept a close watch on my colleague's proceedings. And very curious proceedings they were. First he dipped up a little water from the river in

137

the rubber mixing bowl with which he mixed a bowlful of plaster, and into this he stirred a few pinches of burnt umber, whereby its dazzling white was changed to a muddy buff. Then, having looked up and down the path, he stooped and carefully poured the plaster into a couple of impressions of a walking-stick that were visible at the edge of the path and finished up by filling a deep impression of the same stick, at the margin of the ditch, where it had apparently been stuck in the soft, clayey ground.

As I watched this operation, a sudden suspicion flashed into my mind. Dropping the fishing-rod, I walked quickly along the path until I was able to pick up another impression of the stick. A very brief examination of it confirmed my suspicion. At the centre of the little shallow pit was a semicircular impression – clearly that of a half-worn boot-stud.

"Why!" I exclaimed, "this is the stick that we saw at Scotland Yard!"

"I should expect it to be and I believe it is," said Thorndyke. "But we shall be better able to judge from the casts. Pick up your rod. There are two men coming down the path."

He closed his "research-case" and drawing the fishing-line from his pocket, began meditatively to unwind it.

"I could wish," said I, "that our appearance was more in character with the part of the rustic angler, and for the Lord's sake keep the float out of sight, or we shall collect a crowd."

Thorndyke laughed softly. "The float," said he, "was intended for Polton. He would have loved it. And the crowd would have been rather an advantage – as you will appreciate when you come to use it."

The two men – builder's labourers, apparently – now passed us with a glance of faint interest at the fishing-tackle, and as they strolled by I appreciated the value of the burnt umber. If the casts bad been made of the snow-white plaster they would have stared conspicuously from the ground and these men would almost certainly have stopped to examine them and see what we were doing. But the tinted plaster was practically invisible.

"You are a wonderful man, Thorndyke," I said, as I announced my discovery. "You foresee everything."

He bowed his acknowledgments, and having tenderly felt one of the casts and ascertained that the plaster had set hard, he lifted it with infinite care, exhibiting a perfect facsimile of the end of the stick, on which the worn boot-stud was plainly visible, even to the remains of the pattern. Any doubt that might have remained as to the identity of the stick was removed when Thorndyke produced his calliper-gauge.

138

"Twenty-three-thirty-seconds was the diameter, I think," said he as he opened the jaws of the gauge and consulted his notes. He placed the cast between the jaws, and as they were gently slid into contact, the index marked twenty-three-thirty-seconds.

"Good," said Thorndyke, picking up the other two casts and establishing their identity with the one which we had examined. "This completes the first act." Dropping one cast into his case and throwing the other two into the river, he continued, "Now we proceed to the next and hope for a like success. You notice that he stuck his stick into the ground. Why do you suppose he did that?"

"Presumably to leave his hands free."

"Yes. And now let us sit down here and consider why he wanted his hands free. Just look around and tell me what you see."

I gazed rather hopelessly at the very indistinctive surroundings and began a bald catalogue. "I see a shabby-looking pollard willow, an assortment of suburban vegetation, an obsolete tin saucepan – unserviceable – and a bald spot where somebody seems to have pulled up a small patch of turf."

"Yes," said Thorndyke. "You will also notice a certain amount of dry, powdered earth distributed rather evenly over the bottom of the ditch. And your patch of turf was cut round with a large knife before it was pulled up. Why do you suppose it was pulled up?"

I shook my head. "It's of no use making mere guesses."

"Perhaps not," said he, "though the suggestion is fairly obvious when considered with the other appearances. Between the roots of the willow you notice a patch of grass that looks denser than one would expect from its position. I wonder – "

As he spoke, he reached forward with his stick and prised vigorously at the edge of the patch, with the result that the clump of grass lifted bodily, and when I picked it up and tried it on the bald spot, the nicety with which it fitted left no doubt as to its origin.

"Ha!" I exclaimed, looking at the obviously disturbed earth between the roots of the willow, which the little patch of turf had covered, "the plot thickens. Something seems to have been either buried or dug up there, more probably buried."

"I hope and believe that my learned friend is correct," said Thorndyke, opening his case to abstract a large, powerful spatula.

"What do you expect to find there?" I asked.

"I have a faint hope of finding something wrapped in the half of a very dirty towel," was the reply.

"Then you had better find it quickly," said I, "for there is a man coming along the path from the Putney direction."

He looked round at the distant figure, and driving the spatula into the loose earth stirred it up vigorously.

"I can feel something," he said, digging away with powerful thrusts and scooping the earth out with his hands. Once more he looked round at the approaching stranger – who seemed now to have quickened his pace but was still four- or five-hundred yards distant. Then, thrusting his hands into the hole, he gave a smart pull. Slowly there came forth a package, about ten-inches-by-six, enveloped in a portion of a peculiarly filthy towel and loosely secured with string. Thorndyke rapidly cast off the string and opened out the towel, disclosing a handsome morocco case with an engraved gold plate.

I pounced on the case and, pressing the catch, raised the lid, and though I had expected no less, it was with something like a shock of surprise that I looked on the glittering row and the dazzling cluster of steely-blue diamonds.

As I closed the casket and deposited it in the green canvas case, Thorndyke, after a single glance at the treasure and another along the path, crammed the towel into the hole and began to sweep the loose earth in on top of it. The approaching stranger was for the moment hidden from us by a bend of the path and a near clump of bushes, and Thorndyke was evidently working to hide all traces before he should appear. Having filled the hole, he carefully replaced the sod of turf and then, moving over to the little bare patch from whence the turf had been removed, he began swiftly to dig it up.

"There," said he, flinging on the path a worm which he had just disinterred, "that will explain our activities. You had better continue the excavation with your pocket knife, and then proceed to the capture of the leviathans. I must run up to the police station and you must keep possession of this pitch. Don't move away from here on any account until I come back or send somebody to relieve you. I will hand you over the float, you'll want that." With a malicious smile he dropped the gaudy monstrosity on the path, and having wiped the spatula and replaced it in the case, picked up the latter and moved away towards Putney.

At this moment the stranger reappeared, walking as if for a wager, and I began to peck up the earth with my pocket-knife.

As the man approached he slowed down by degrees until he came up at something like a saunter. He was followed at a little distance by Thorndyke, who had turned as if he had changed his mind, and now passed me with the remark that, "Perhaps Hammersmith would be better." The stranger cast a suspicious glance at him and then turned his attention to me.

"Lookin' for worms?" he inquired, halting and surveying me inquisitively.

I replied by picking one up (with secret distaste) and holding it aloft, and he continued, looking wistfully at Thorndyke's retreating figure, "Your pal seems to have had enough."

"He hadn't got a rod," said I, "but he'll be back presently."

"Ah!" said he, looking steadily over my shoulder in the direction of the willow. "Well, you won't do any good here. The place where they rises is a quarter-of-a-mile farther down – just round the bend there. That's a prime pitch. You just come along with me and I'll show you."

"I must stay here until my friend comes back," said I. "But I'll tell him what you say."

With this I seated myself stolidly on the bank and, having flung the baited hook into the stream, sat and glared fixedly at the preposterous float. My acquaintance fidgeted about me uneasily, endeavouring from time to time to lure me away to the "prime pitch" round the bend. And so the time dragged on until three-quarters of an hour had passed.

Suddenly I observed two taxicabs crossing the bridge, followed by three cyclists. A minute or two later Thorndyke reappeared, accompanied by two other men, and then the cyclists came into view, approaching at a rapid pace.

"Seems to be a regular procession," my friend remarked, viewing the new arrivals with evident uneasiness. As he spoke, one of the cyclists halted and dismounted to examine his tyre, while the other two approached and shot past us. Then they, too, halted and dismounted, and having deposited their machines in the ditch, they came back towards us. By this time I was able – with a good deal of surprise – to identify Thorndyke's two companions as Inspector Badger and Superintendent Miller. Perhaps my acquaintance also recognised them, or possibly the proceedings of the third cyclist – who had also laid down his machine and was approaching on foot – disturbed him. At any rate he glanced quickly from the one group to the other and, selecting the smaller one, sprang suddenly between the two cyclists and sped away along the path like a hare.

In a moment there was a wild stampede. The three cyclists, remounting their machines, pedalled furiously after the fugitive, followed by Badger and Miller on foot. Then the fugitive, the cyclists, and finally the two officers disappeared round the bend of the path.

"How did you know that he was the man?" I asked, when my colleague and I were left alone.

"I didn't, though I had pretty strong grounds for suspicion. But I merely brought the police to set a watch on the place and arrange an ambush. Their encircling movement was just an experimental bluff, they might have been chary of arresting the fellow if he hadn't taken fright and bolted. We have been fortunate all round, for, by a lucky chance, Badger and Miller were at Chiswick making inquiries and I was able to telephone to them to meet me at the bridge."

At this moment the procession reappeared, advancing briskly, and my late adviser marched at the centre, securely handcuffed. As he was conducted past me, he glared savagely and made some impolite references to a "blooming nark".

"You can take him in one of the taxis," said Miller, "and put your bicycles on top." Then, as the procession moved on towards the bridge he turned to Thorndyke. "I suppose he's the right man, Doctor, but he hasn't got any of the stuff on him."

"Of course he hasn't," said Thorndyke.

"Well, do you know where it is?"

Thorndyke opened his case and taking out the casket, handed it to the superintendent. "I shall want a receipt for it," said he.

Miller opened the casket, and at the sight of the glittering jewels both the detectives uttered an exclamation of amazement, and the superintendent demanded, "Where did you get this, sir?"

"I dug it up at the foot of that willow."

"But how did you know it was there?"

"I didn't," replied Thorndyke, "but I thought I might as well look, you know," and he bestowed a smile of exasperating blandness on the astonished officer.

The two detectives gazed at Thorndyke, then they looked at one another and then they looked at me, and Badger observed, with profound conviction, that it was a "knock-out".

"I believe the doctor keeps a tame clairvoyant," he added.

"And may I take it, sir," said Miller, "that you can establish a *prima facie* case against this man, so that we can get a remand until Mr. Montague is well enough to identify him?"

"You may," Thorndyke replied. "Let me know when and where he is to be charged and I will attend and give evidence."

On this Miller wrote out a receipt for the jewels and the two officers hurried off to their taxicab, leaving us, as Badger put it, "to our fishing."

As soon as they were out of sight, Thorndyke opened his case and mixed another bowlful of plaster. "We want two more casts," said he, "one of the right foot of the man who buried the jewels and one of the right foot of the prisoner. They are obviously identical, as you can see by the arrangement of the nails and the shape of the new patch on the sole. I shall put the casts in evidence and compare them with the prisoner's right boot."

I understood now why Thorndyke had walked away towards Putney and then returned in rear of the stranger. He had suspected the man and had wanted to get a look at his footprints. But there was a good deal in this case that I did not understand at all.

"There," said Thorndyke, as he deposited the casts, each with its pencilled identification, in his canvas case, "that is the end of 'The Blue Diamond Mystery'."

"I beg your pardon," said I, "but it isn't. I want a full explanation. It is evident that from the house at Brentford you made a bee-line to that willow. You knew then pretty exactly where the necklace was hidden. For all I know, you may have had that knowledge when we left Scotland Yard."

"As a matter of fact, I had," he replied. "I went to Brentford principally to verify the ownership of the wallet and the bag."

"But what was it that directed you with such certainty to the Hammersmith towing-path?"

It was then that he made the observation that I have quoted at the beginning of this narrative.

"In this case," he continued, "a curious fact, well known to naturalists, acquired vital evidential importance. It associated a bag, found in one locality, with another apparently unrelated locality. It was the link that joined up the two ends of a broken chain. I offered that fact to Inspector Badger, who, lacking the knowledge wherewith to interpret it, rejected it with scorn."

"I remember that you gave him the name of that little shell that dropped out of the handful of grass."

"Exactly," said Thorndyke. "That was the crucial fact. It told us where the handful of grass had been gathered."

"I can't imagine how," said I. "Surely you find shells all over the country?"

"That is, in general, quite true," he replied, "but *Clausilia biplicata* is one of the rare exceptions. There are four British species of these queer little univalves (which are so named from the little spring door with which the entrance of the shell is furnished), *Clausilia laminata, rolphii, rugose*, and *biplicata*. The first three species have what we may call a normal distribution, whereas the distribution of *biplicata* is abnormal. This seems to be a dying species. It is in process of becoming extinct in this island. But when a species of animal or plant becomes extinct, it does not fade away evenly over the whole of its habitat, but it disappears in patches, which gradually extend, leaving, as it were, islands of survival. This is what has happened to *Clausilia biplicata*. It has disappeared from this country with the exception of two localities. One of these is in Wiltshire, and the other is the right bank of the Thames at Hammersmith. And this latter locality is extraordinarily restricted. Walk down a few hundred yards towards Putney, and you have walked out of its domain. Walk up a few hundred yards towards the bridge, and again you have walked out of its territory. Yet within that little area it is fairly plentiful. If you know where to look – it lives on the bark or at the roots of willow trees – you can usually find one or two specimens. Thus, you see, the presence of that shell associated the handful of grass with a certain willow tree, and that willow was either in Wiltshire or by the Hammersmith towing-path. But there was nothing otherwise to connect it with Wiltshire, whereas there was something to connect it with Hammersmith. Let us for a moment dismiss the shell and consider the other suggestions offered by the bag and stick.

"The bag, as you saw, contained traces of two very different persons. One was a middle-class man, probably middle-aged or elderly, cleanly, careful as to his appearance and of orderly habits, the other, uncleanly, slovenly and apparently a professional criminal. The bag itself seemed to appertain to the former person. It was an expensive bag and showed signs of years of careful use. This, and the circumstances in which it was found, led us to suspect that it was a stolen bag. Now, we knew that the contents of a bag had been stolen. We knew that an empty bag had been picked up on the line between Barnes and Chiswick, and it was probable that the thief had left the train at the latter station. The empty bag had been assumed to be Mr. Montague's, whereas the probabilities – as for instance, the fact of its having been thrown out on the line – suggested that it was the thief's bag, and that Mr. Montague's had been taken away with its contents.

"The point, then, that we had to settle when we left Scotland Yard was whether this apparently stolen bag had any connection with the train robbery. But as soon as we saw Mr. Montague it was evident that he corresponded exactly with the owner of the dressing-wallet, and when we saw the bag that had been found on the line – a shoddy, imitation leather bag – it was practically certain that it was *not* his, while the roughly-stitched leather pockets, exactly suited to the dimensions of house-breaking tools, strongly suggested that it was a burglar's bag. But if this were so, then Mr. Montague's bag had been stolen, and the robber's effects stuffed into it.

"With this working hypothesis, we were now able to take up the case from the other end. The Scotland Yard bag was Montague's bag. It had been taken from Chiswick to the Hammersmith towpath, where –

144

judging from the clay smears on the bottom – it had been laid on the ground, presumably close to a willow tree. The use of the grass as packing suggested that something had been removed from the bag at this place – something that had wedged the tools together and prevented them from rattling, and there appeared to be half a towel missing. Clearly, the towpath was our next field of exploration.

"But, small as this area was geographically, it would have taken a long time to examine in detail. Here, however, the stick gave us invaluable aid. It had a perfectly distinctive tip, and it showed traces of having been stuck about three inches into earth similar to that on the bag. What we had thus to look for was a hole in the ground about three inches deep, and having at the bottom the impression of a half-worn boot-stud. This hole would probably be close to a willow.

"The search turned out even easier than I had hoped. Directly we reached the towpath I picked up the track of the stick, and not one track only, but a double track, showing that our friend had returned to the bridge. All that remained was to follow the track until it came to an end and there we were pretty certain to find the hole in the ground, as, in fact, we did."

"And why," I asked, "do you suppose he buried the stuff?"

"Probably as a precaution, in case he had been seen and described. This morning's papers will have told him that he had not been. Probably, also, he wanted to make arrangements with a fence and didn't want to have the booty about him."

There is little more to tell. When the case was heard on the following morning, Thorndyke's uncannily precise and detailed description of the course of events, coupled with the production of the stolen property, so unnerved the prisoner that he pleaded guilty forthwith.

As to Mr. Montague, he recovered completely in a few days, and a handsome pair of Georgian silver candlesticks may even to this day be seen on our mantelpiece testifying to his gratitude and appreciation of Thorndyke's brilliant conduct of the case.

The Stolen Ingots

"In medico-legal practice," Thorndyke remarked, "one must be constantly on one's guard against the effects of suggestion, whether intentional or unconscious. When the facts of a case are set forth by an informant, they are nearly always presented, consciously or unconsciously, in terms of inference. Certain facts, which appear to the narrator to be the leading facts, are given with emphasis and in detail, while other facts, which appear to be subordinate or trivial, are partially suppressed. But this assessment of evidential value must never be accepted. The whole case must be considered and each fact weighed separately, and then it will commonly happen that the leading fact turns out to be the one that had been passed over as negligible."

The remark was made apropos of a case, the facts of which had just been stated to us by Mr. Halethorpe, of the Sphinx Assurance Company. I did not quite perceive its bearing at the time, but looking back when the case was concluded, I realised that I had fallen into the very error against which Thorndyke's warning should have guarded me.

"I trust," said Mr. Halethorpe, "that I have not come at an inconvenient time. You are so tolerant of unusual hours – "

"My practice," interrupted Thorndyke, "is my recreation, and I welcome you as one who comes to furnish entertainment. Draw your chair up to the fire, light a cigar, and tell us your story."

Mr. Halethorpe laughed, but adopted the procedure suggested, and having settled his toes upon the kerb and selected a cigar from the box, he opened the subject of his call.

"I don't quite know what you can do for us," he began, "as it is hardly your business to trace lost property, but I thought I would come and let you know about our difficulty. The fact is that our company looks like dropping some four-thousand pounds, which the directors won't like. What has happened is this,

"About two months ago, the London House of the Akropong Gold Fields Company applied to us to insure a parcel of gold bars that were to be consigned to Minton and Borwell, the big manufacturing jewellers. The bars were to be shipped at Accra and landed at Bellhaven, which is the nearest port to Minton and Borwell's works. Well, we agreed to underwrite the risk – we have done business with the Akropong people before – and the matter was settled. The bars were put on board the Labadi at Accra, and in due course were landed at Belhaven, where they were delivered to Minton's agents. So far, so good. Then came the catastrophe. The case of bars was put on the train at Belhaven, and consigned to Anchester, where Minton's have their factory. But the line doesn't go to Anchester direct. The junction is at Garbridge, a small country station close to the river Crouch, and here the case was put out and locked up in the station-master's office to wait for the Anchester train. It seems that the station-master was called away and detained longer than he had expected, and when the train was signalled he hurried back in a mighty twitter. However, the case was there all right, and he personally superintended its removal to the guard's van and put it in the guard's charge. All went well for the rest of the journey. A member of the firm was waiting at Anchester Station with a closed van. The case was put into it and taken direct to the factory, where it was opened in the private office – and found to be full of lead pipe."

"I presume," said Thorndyke, "that it was not the original case."

"No," replied Halethorpe, "but it was a very fair imitation. The label and the marks were correct, but the seals were just plain wax. Evidently the exchange had been made in the station office, and it transpires that although the door was securely locked, there was an unfastened window which opened on to the garden, and there were plain marks of feet on the flower-bed outside."

"What time did this happen?" asked Thorndyke.

"The Anchester train came in at a quarter-past-seven, by which time, of course, it was quite dark."

"And when did it happen?"

"The day before yesterday. We heard of it yesterday morning."

"Are you contesting the claim?"

"We don't want to. Of course, we could plead negligence, but in that case I think we should make a claim on the railway company. But, naturally, we should much rather recover the property. After all, it can't be so very far away."

"I wouldn't say that," said Thorndyke. "This was no impromptu theft. The dummy case was prepared in advance, and evidently by somebody who knew what the real case was like, and how and when it was to be despatched from Belhaven. We must assume that the disposal of the stolen case has been provided for with similar completeness. How far is Garbridge from the river?"

"Less than half-a-mile across the marshes. The detective-inspector – Badger, I think you know him – asked the same question."

"Naturally," said Thorndyke. "A heavy object like this case is much more easily and inconspicuously conveyed by water than on land. And then, see what facilities for concealment a navigable river offers. The case could be easily stowed away on a small craft, or even in a boat, or the bars could be taken out and stowed amongst the ballast, or even, at a pinch, dropped over board at a marked spot and left until the hue and cry was over."

"You are not very encouraging," Halethorpe remarked gloomily. "I take it that you don't much expect that we shall recover those bars."

"We needn't despair," was the reply, "but I want you to understand the difficulties. The thieves have got away with the booty, and that booty is an imperishable material which retains its value even if broken up into unrecognisable fragments. Melted down into small ingots, it would be impossible to identify."

"Well," said Halethorpe, "the police have the matter in hand – Inspector Badger, of the C.I.D., is in charge of the case – but our directors would be more satisfied if you would look into it. Of course we would give you any help we could. What do you say?"

"I am willing to look into the case," said Thorndyke, "though I don't hold out much hope. Could you give me a note to the shipping company and another to the consignees, Minton and Borwell?"

"Of course I will. I'll write them now. I have some of our stationery in my attaché case. But, if you will pardon my saying so, you seem to be starting your inquiry just where there is nothing to be learned. The case was stolen after it left the ship and before it reached the consignees – although their agent had received it from the ship."

"The point is," said Thorndyke, "that this was a preconcerted robbery, and that the thieves possessed special information. That information must have come either from the ship or from the factory. So, while we must try to pick up the track of the case itself, we must seek the beginning of the clue at the two ends – the ship and the factory one of which it must have started."

"Yes, that's true," said Halethorpe. "Well, I'll write those two notes and then I must run away, and we'll hope for the best."

He wrote the two letters asking for facilities from the respective parties, and then took his departure in a somewhat chastened frame of mind.

"Quite an interesting little problem," Thorndyke remarked as Halethorpe footsteps died away on the stairs, "but not much in our line. It is really a police case – a case for patient and intelligent inquiry. And that is what we shall have to do – make some careful inquiries on the spot."

"Where do you propose to begin?" I asked.

"At the beginning," he replied. "Belhaven. I propose that we go down there to-morrow morning and pick up the thread at that end."

"What thread?" I demanded. "We know that the package started from there. What else do you expect to learn?"

"There are several curious possibilities in this case, as you must have noticed," he replied "The question is whether any of them are probabilities. That is what I want to settle before we begin a detailed investigation."

"For my part," said I, "I should have supposed that the investigation would start from the scene of the robbery. But I presume that you have seen some possibilities that I have overlooked."

Which eventually turned out to be the case.

"I think," said Thorndyke as we alighted at Belhaven on the following morning, "we had better go first to the Customs and make quite certain, if we can, that the bars were really in the case when it was delivered to the consignees' agents. It won't do to take it for granted that the substitution took place at Garbridge, although that is by far the most probable theory." Accordingly we made our way to the harbour, where an obliging mariner directed us to our destination.

At the Custom House we were received by a genial officer, who, when Thorndyke had explained his connection with the robbery, entered into the matter with complete sympathy and a quick grasp of the situation.

"I see," said he. "You want clear evidence that the bars were in the case when it left here. Well, I think we can satisfy you on that point. Bullion is not a customable commodity, but it has to be examined and reported. If it is consigned to the Bank of England or the Mint, the case is passed through with the seals unbroken, but as this was a private consignment, the seals will have been broken and the contents of the case examined. Jeffson, show these gentlemen the report on the case of gold bars from the Labadi."

"Would it be possible," Thorndyke asked, "for us to have a few words with the officer who opened the case? You know the legal partiality for personal testimony."

"Of course it would. Jeffson, when these gentlemen have seen the report, find the officer who signed it and let them have a talk with him."

We followed Mr. Jeffson into an adjoining office, where he produced the report and handed it to Thorndyke. The particulars that it gave were in effect those that would be furnished by the ship's manifest and the bill of lading. The case was thirteen inches long by twelve wide and nine inches deep, outside measurement, and its gross weight was one-hundred-and-seventeen-pounds-three-ounces, and it contained four

149

bars of the aggregate weight of one hundred-and-thirteen-pounds two-ounces.

"Thank you," said Thorndyke, handing back the report. "And now can we see the officer – Mr. Byrne, I think – just to fill in the details?"

"If you will come with me," replied Mr. Jeffson, "I'll find him for you. I expect he is on the wharf."

We followed our conductor out on to the quay among a litter of cases, crates and barrels, and eventually, amidst a battalion of Madeira wine casks, found the officer deep in problems of "content and ullage", and other customs mysteries. As Jeffson introduced us, and then discreetly retired, Mr. Byrne confronted us, with a mahogany face and truculent blue eye.

"With reference to this bullion," said Thorndyke, "I understand that you weighed the bars separately from the case?"

"Oi did," replied Mr. Byrne.

"Did you weigh each bar separately?"

"Oi did not," was the concise reply.

"What was the appearance of the bars – I mean as to shape and size? Were they of the usual type?

"Oi've not had a great deal to do with bullion," said Mr. Byrne, "but Oi should say that they were just ordinary gold bars, about nine-inches-long-by-four-wide and about two inches deep."

"Was there much packing material in the case?"

"Very little. The bars were wrapped in thick canvas and jammed into the case. There wouldn't be more than about half-an-inch clearance all round to allow for the canvas. The case was inch-and-a-half stuff strengthened with iron bands."

"Did you seal the case after you had closed it up?"

"Oi did. 'Twas all shipshape when it was passed back to the mate. And Oi saw him hand it over to the consignees' agent, so 'twas all in order when it left the wharf."

"That was what I wanted to make sure of," said Thorndyke and, having pocketed his notebook and thanked the officer, he turned away among the wilderness of merchandise.

"So much for the Customs," said he. "I am glad we went there first. As you have no doubt observed, we have picked up some useful information."

"We have ascertained," I replied, "that the case was intact when it was handed over to the consignees' agents, so that our investigations at Garbridge will start from a solid basis. And that, I take it, is all you wanted to know."

"Not quite all," he rejoined. "There are one or two little details that I should like to fill in. I think we will look in on the shipping agents and present Halethorpe's note. We may as well learn all we can before we make our start from the scene of the robbery."

"Well," I said, "I don't see what more there is to learn here. But apparently you do. That seems to be the office, past those sheds."

The manager of the shipping agent's office looked us up and down as he sat at his littered desk with Halethorpe's letter in his hand.

"You've come about that bullion that was stolen," he said brusquely. "Well, it wasn't stolen here. Hadn't you better inquire at Garbridge, where it was?"

"Undoubtedly," replied Thorndyke. "But I am making certain preliminary inquiries. Now, first, as to the bill of lading, who has that – the original, I mean?

"The captain has it at present, but I have a copy."

"Could I see it?" Thorndyke asked.

The manager raised his eyebrows protestingly, but produced the document from a file and handed it to Thorndyke, watching him inquisitively as he copied the particulars of the package into his notebook.

"I suppose," said Thorndyke as he returned the document, "you have a copy of the ship's manifest?"

"Yes," replied the manager, "but the entry in the manifest is merely a copy of the particulars given in the bill of lading."

"I should like to see the manifest, if it is not troubling you too much."

"But," the other protested impatiently, "the manifest contains no information respecting this parcel of bullion excepting the one entry – which, as I have told you, has been copied from the bill of lading."

"I realise that," said Thorndyke, "but I should like to look over it, all the same."

Our friend bounced into an inner office and presently returned with a voluminous document, which he slapped down on a side-table.

"There, sir," he said. "That is the manifest. This is the entry relating to the bullion that you are inquiring about. The rest of the document is concerned with the cargo, in which I presume you are not interested."

In this, however, he was mistaken, for Thorndyke, having verified the bullion entry, turned the leaves over and began systematically, though rapidly, to run his eye over the long list from the beginning, a proceeding that the manager viewed with frenzied impatience.

"If you are going to read it right through, sir," the latter observed, "I shall ask you to excuse me. Art is long but life is short," he added with a sour smile.

Nevertheless he hovered about uneasily, and when Thorndyke proceeded to copy some of the entries into his notebook, he craned over and read them without the least disguise, though not without comment.

"Good God, sir!" he exclaimed. "What possible bearing on this robbery can that parcel of scrivelloes have? And do you realise that they are still in the ship's hold?"

"I inferred that they were, as they are consigned to London," Thorndyke replied, drawing his finger down the "description" column and rapidly scanning the entries in it. The manager watched that finger, and as it stopped successively at a bag of gum copal, a case of quartz specimens, a case of six-inch brass screw-bolts, a bag of beni-seed and a package of kola nuts, he breathed hard and muttered like an angry parrot. But Thorndyke was quite unmoved. With calm deliberation he copied out each entry, conscientiously noting the marks, descriptions of packages and contents, gross and net weights, dimensions, names of consignors and consignees, ports of shipment and discharge and, in fact, the entire particulars. It was certainly an amazing proceeding, and I could make no more of it than could our impatient friend.

At last Thorndyke closed and pocketed his notebook, and the manager heaved a slightly obtrusive sigh. "Is there nothing more, sir?" he asked. "You don't want to examine the ship, for instance?"

The next moment, I think, he regretted his sarcasm, for Thorndyke inquired, with evident interest, "Is the ship still here?

"Yes," was the unwilling admission. "She finishes unloading here at midday to-day and will probably haul into the London Docks to-morrow morning."

"I don't think I need go on board," said Thorndyke, "but you might give me a card in case I find that I want to."

The card was somewhat grudgingly produced, and when Thorndyke had thanked our entertainer for his help, we took our leave and made our way towards the station.

"Well," I said, "you have collected a vast amount of curious information, but I am hanged if I can see that any of it has the slightest bearing on our inquiry."

Thorndyke cast on me a look of deep reproach. "Jervis!" he exclaimed. "You astonish me, you do, indeed. Why, my dear fellow, it stares you in the face!"

"When you say 'it'," I said a little irritably, "you mean – ?"

"I mean the leading fact from which we may deduce the *modus operandi* of this robbery. You shall look over my notes in the train and sort out the data that we have collected. I think you will find them extremely illuminating."

"I doubt it," said I. "But, meanwhile, aren't we wasting a good deal of time? Halethorpe wants to get the gold back, he doesn't want to know how the thieves contrived to steal it."

"That is a very just remark," answered Thorndyke. "My learned friend displays his customary robust common sense. Nevertheless, I think that a clear understanding of the mechanism of this robbery will prove very helpful to us, though I agree with you that we have spent enough time on securing our preliminary data. The important thing now is to pick up a trail from Garbridge. But I see our train is signalled. We had better hurry."

As the train rumbled into station, we looked out for an empty smoking compartment and, having been fortunate enough to secure one, we settled ourselves in opposite corners and lighted our pipes. Then Thorndyke handed me his notebook and as I studied, with wrinkled brows, the apparently disconnected entries, he sat and observed me thoughtfully and with the faintest suspicion of a smile. Again and again I read through those notes with ever-dwindling hopes of extracting the meaning that "stared me in the face". Vainly did I endeavour to connect gum copal, scrivelloes, or beni-seed with the methods of the unknown robbers. The entries in the notebook persisted obstinately in remaining totally disconnected and hopelessly irrelevant. At last I shut the book with a savage snap and handed it back to its owner.

"It's no use, Thorndyke," I said. "I can't see the faintest glimmer of light."

"Well," said he, "it isn't of much consequence. The practical part of our task is before us, and it may turn out a pretty difficult part. But we have got to recover those bars if it is humanly possible. And here we are at our jumping-off place. This is Garbridge Station – and I see an old acquaintance of ours on the platform."

I looked out, as the train slowed down, and there, sure enough, was no less a person than Inspector Badger of the Criminal Investigation Department.

"We could have done very well without Badger," I remarked.

"Yes," Thorndyke agreed, "but we shall have to take him into partnership, I expect. After all, we are on his territory and on the same errand. How do you do, Inspector?" he continued, as the officer, having observed our descent from the carriage, hurried forward with unwonted cordiality.

"I rather expected to see you here, sir," said he. "We heard that Mr. Halethorpe had consulted you. But this isn't the London train."

"No," said Thorndyke. "We've been to Belhaven, just to make sure that the bullion was in the case when it started."

"I could have told you that two days ago," said Badger. "We got on to the Customs people at once. That was all plain sailing, but the rest of it isn't."

"No clue as to how the case was taken away?"

"Oh, yes, that is pretty clear. It was hoisted out, and the dummy hoisted in, through the window of the Station-master's office. And the same night, two men were seen carrying a heavy package, about the size of the bullion-case, towards the marshes. But there the clue ends. The stuff seems to have vanished into thin air. Of course our people are on the look-out for it in various likely directions, but I am staying here with a couple of plain-clothes men. I've a conviction that it is still somewhere in this neighbourhood, and I mean to stick here in the hope that I may spot somebody trying to move it."

As the inspector was speaking we had been walking slowly from the station towards the village, which was on the opposite side of the river. On the bridge Thorndyke halted and looked down the river and over the wide expanse of marshy country.

"This is an ideal place for a bullion robbery," he remarked. "A tidal river near to the sea and a network of creeks, in any one of which one could hide a boat or sink the booty below tide-marks. Have you heard of any strange craft having put in here?"

"Yes. There's a little ramshackle bawley from Leigh – but her crew of two ragamuffins are not Leigh men. And they've made a mess of their visit – got their craft on the mud on the top of the spring tide. There there she'll be till next spring tide. But I've been over her carefully and I'll swear the stuff isn't aboard her. I had all the ballast out and emptied the lazarette and the chain locker."

"And what about the barge?"

"She's a regular trader here. Her crew – the skipper and his son – are quite respectable men and they belong here. There they go in that boat. I expect they are off on this tide. But they seem to be making for the bawley."

As he spoke, the inspector produced a pair of glasses, through which he watched the movement of the barge's jolly, and a couple of elderly fishermen, who were crossing the bridge, halted to look on. The barge's boat ran alongside the stranded bawley, and one of the rowers hailed, whereupon two men tumbled up from the cabin and dropped into the boat, which immediately pushed off and headed for the barge.

154

"Them bawley blokes seems to be taking a passage along of old Bill Somers," one of the fishermen remarked, levelling a small telescope at the barge as the boat drew alongside and the four men climbed on board. "Going to work their passage, too," he added as the two passengers proceeded immediately to man the windlass while the crew let go the brails and hooked the main block to the traveller.

"Rum go," commented Badger, glaring at the barge through his glasses, "but they haven't taken anything aboard with them. I could see that."

"You have overhauled the barge, I suppose?" said Thorndyke.

"Yes. Went right through her. Nothing there. She's light. There was no place aboard her where you could hide a split-pea."

"Did you get her anchor up?"

"No," replied Badger. "I didn't. I suppose I ought to have done so. However, they're getting it up themselves now." As he spoke, the rapid clink of a windlass-pawl was borne across the water, and through my prismatic glasses I could see the two passengers working for all they were worth at the cranks. Presently the clink of the pawl began to slow down somewhat and the two bargemen, having got the sails set, joined the toilers at the windlass, but even then there was no great increase of speed.

"Anchor seems to come up uncommon heavy," one of the fishermen remarked.

"Aye," the other agreed. "Got foul of an old mooring, maybe."

"Look out for the anchor, Badger," Thorndyke said in a low voice, gazing steadily through his binocular. "It is out of the ground. The cable is up and down and the barge is drifting off on the tide."

Even as he spoke, the ring and stock of the anchor rose slowly out of the water, and now I could see that a second chain was shackled loosely to the cable, down which it had slid until it was stopped by the ring of the anchor. Badger had evidently seen it too, for he ejaculated, "Hallo!" and added a few verbal flourishes which I need not repeat. A few more turns of the windlass brought the flukes of the anchor clear of the water, and dangling against them was an undeniable wooden case, securely slung with lashings of stout chain. Badger cursed volubly and, turning to the fishermen, exclaimed in a rather offensively peremptory tone, "I want a boat. Now. This instant."

The elder piscator regarded him doggedly and replied. "All right. I ain't got no objection."

"Where can I get a boat?" the inspector demanded, nearly purple with excitement and anxiety.

155

"Where do you think?" the mariner responded, evidently nettled by the inspector's masterful tone. "Pastrycook's? Or livery stables?"

"Look here," said Badger. "I'm a police officer and I want to board that barge, and I am prepared to pay handsomely. Now where can I get a boat?"

"We'll put you aboard of her," replied the fisherman, " – that is, if we can catch her. But I doubt it. She's off, that's what she is. And there's something queer a-going on aboard of her," he added in a somewhat different tone.

There was. I had been observing it. The case had been, with some difficulty, hoisted on board, and then suddenly there had broken out an altercation between the two bargees and their passengers, and this had now developed into what look like a free fight. It was difficult to see exactly what was happening, for the barge was drifting rapidly down the river, and her sails, blowing out first on one side and then on the other, rather obscured the view. Presently, however, the sails filled and a man appeared at the wheel, then the barge jibed round, and with a strong ebb tide and a fresh breeze, very soon began to grow small in the distance.

Meanwhile the fishermen had bustled off in search of a boat, and the inspector had raced to the bridge-head, where he stood gesticulating frantically and blowing his whistle, while Thorndyke continued placidly to watch the receding barge through his binocular.

"What are we going to do?" I asked, a little surprised at my colleague's inaction.

"What can we do?" he asked in reply. "Badger will follow the barge. He probably won't overtake her, but he will prevent her from making a landing until they get out into the estuary, and then he may possibly get assistance. The chase is in his hands."

"Are we going with him?"

"I am not. This looks like being an all-night expedition, and I must be at our chambers to-morrow morning. Besides, the chase is not our affair. But if you would like to join Badger there is no reason why you shouldn't. I can look after the practice."

"Well," I said, "I think I should rather like to be in at the death, if it won't inconvenience you. But it is possible that they may get away with the booty."

"Quite," he agreed, "and then it would be useful to know exactly how and where it disappears. Yes, go with them, by all means, and keep a sharp look-out."

At this moment Badger returned with the two plain clothes men whom his whistle had called from their posts, and simultaneously a boat was seen approaching the steps by the bridge, rowed by the two

156

fishermen. The inspector looked at us inquiringly. "Are you coming to see the sport?" he asked.

"Doctor Jervis would like to come with you," Thorndyke replied. "I have to get back to London. But you will be a fair boat-load without me."

This appeared to be also the view of the two fishermen, as they brought up at the steps and observed the four passengers, but they made no demur beyond inquiring if there were not any more, and when we had taken our places in the stern sheets, they pushed off and pulled through the bridge and away down stream. Gradually, the village receded and the houses and the bridge grew small and more distant, though they remained visible for a long time over the marshy levels, and still, as I looked back through my glasses, I could see Thorndyke on the bridge, watching the pursuit with his binocular to his eyes.

Meanwhile the fugitive barge, having got some two miles start, seemed to be drawing ahead. But it was only at intervals that we could see her, for the tide was falling fast and we were mostly hemmed in by the high, muddy banks. Only when we entered a straight reach of the river could we see her sails over the land, and every time that she came into view, she appeared perceptibly smaller.

When the river grew wider, the mast was stepped and a good-sized lug-sail hoisted, though one of the fishermen continued to ply his oar on the weather side, while the other took the tiller. This improved our pace appreciably, but still, whenever we caught a glimpse of the barge, it was evident that she was still gaining.

On one of these occasions the man at the tiller, standing up to get a better view, surveyed our quarry intently for nearly a minute and then addressed the inspector.

"She's a-going to give us the go-by, mister," he observed with conviction.

"Still gaining?" asked Badger.

"Aye. She's a-going to slip across the tail of Foulness Sand into the deep channel. And that's the last we shall see of her."

"But can't we get into the channel the same way?" demanded Badger.

"Well, d'ye see," replied the fisherman, "'tis like this. Tide's a-running out, but there'll be enough for her. It'll just carry her out through the Whitaker Channel and across the spit. Then it'll turn, and up she'll go, London way, on the flood. But we shall catch the flood-tide in the Whitaker Channel, and a rare old job we'll have to get out, and when we do get out, that barge'll be miles away."

The inspector swore long and earnestly. He even alluded to himself as a "blithering idiot". But that helped matters not at all. The fisherman's dismal prophecy was fulfilled in every horrid detail. When we were approaching the Whitaker Channel the barge was just crossing the spit, and the last of the ebb-tide was trickling out. By the time we were fairly in the Channel the tide had turned and was already flowing in with a speed that increased every minute, while over the sand we could see the barge, already out in the open estuary, heading to the west on the flood-tide at a good six knots.

Poor Badger was frantic. With yearning eyes fixed on the dwindling barge, he cursed, entreated, encouraged, and made extravagant offers. He even took an oar and pulled with such desperate energy that he caught a crab and it turned a neat back somersault into the fisherman's lap. The two mariners pulled until their oars bent like canes, but still the sandy banks crept by, inch by inch, and ever the turbid water seemed to pour up the channel more and yet more swiftly. It was a fearful struggle and seemed to last for hours, and when, at last, the boat crawled out across the spit and the exhausted rowers rested on their oars, the sun was just setting and the barge had disappeared into the west.

I was really sorry for Badger. His oversight in respect of the anchor was a very natural one for a landsman, and he had evidently taken infinite pains over the case and shown excellent judgment in keeping a close watch on the neighbourhood of Garbridge, and now, after all his care, it looked as if both the robbers and their booty had slipped through his fingers. It was desperately bad luck.

"Well," said the elder fisherman, "they've give us a run for our money, but they've got clear away. What's to be done now, mister?"

Badger had nothing to suggest excepting that we should pull or sail up the river in the hope of getting some assistance on the way. He was in the lowest depths of despair and dejection. But now, when Fortune seemed to have deserted us utterly, and failure appeared to be an accomplished fact, Providence intervened.

A small steam vessel that had been approaching from the direction of the East Swin suddenly altered her course and bore down as if to speak us. The fisherman who had last spoken looked at her attentively for a few moments and then slapped his thigh. "Saved by gum!" he exclaimed. "This'll do your trick, mister. Here comes a Customs cruiser."

Instantly the two fishermen bent to their oars to meet the oncoming craft, and in a few minutes we were alongside, Badger hailing like a bull of Bashan. A brief explanation to the officer in charge secured a highly sympathetic promise of help. We all scrambled up on deck, the boat was dropped astern at the scope of her painter, the engine-room bell jangled merrily, and the smart, yacht-like vessel began to forge ahead.

"Now then," said the officer, as his craft gathered way, "give us a description of this barge. What is she like?

"She's a small stumpy," the senior fisherman explained, "flying light, wants paint badly, steers with a wheel, green transom with *Bluebell Maldon* cut in and gilded. Seemed to be keeping along the north shore."

With these particulars in his mind, the officer explored the western horizon with a pair of night-glasses, although it was still broad daylight. Presently he reported, "There's a stumpy in a line with the Blacktail Spit buoy. Just take a look at her." He handed his glasses to the fisherman, who, after a careful inspection of the stranger, gave it as his opinion that she was our quarry. "Probably makin' for Southend or Leigh," said he, and added, "I'll bet she's bound for Benfleet Creek. Nice quiet place, that, to land the stuff."

Our recent painful experience was now reversed, for as our swift little vessel devoured the miles of water, the barge, which we were all watching eagerly, loomed up larger every minute. By the time we were abreast of the Mouse Lightship, she was but a few hundred yards ahead, and even through my glasses, the name *Bluebell* was clearly legible. Badger nearly wept with delight, the officer in charge smiled an anticipatory smile, the deck-hands girded up their loins for the coming capture, and the plain-clothes men each furtively polished a pair of handcuffs.

At length the little cruiser came fairly abreast of the barge – not unobserved by the two men on her deck. Then she sheered in suddenly and swept alongside. One hand neatly hooked a shroud with a grappling iron and made fast while a couple of preventive officers, the plain men, and the inspector jumped down simultaneously on to the barge's deck. For a moment, the two bawley men were inclined to show fight, but the odds were too great. After a perfunctory scuffle they both submitted to be handcuffed and were at once hauled up on board the cruiser and lodged in the fore-peak under guard. Then the chief officer, the two fishermen, and I jumped on board the barge and followed Badger down the companion hatch to the cabin.

It was a curious scene that was revealed in that little cupboard-like apartment by the light of Badger's electric torch. On each of the two lockers was stretched a man, securely lashed with lead-line and having drawn over his face a knitted stocking cap, while on the little triangular fixed table rested an iron-bound box which I instantly identified by my recollection of the description of the bullion-case in the ship's manifest. It was but the work of a minute to liberate the skipper and his son and send them up, wrathful but substantially uninjured, to refresh on the cruiser, and then the ponderous treasure-chest was borne in triumph by

159

two muscular deck-hands, up the narrow steps, to be hoisted to the Government vessel.

"Well, well," said the inspector, mopping his face with his handkerchief, "all's well that ends well, but I thought I had lost the men and the stuff that time. What are you going to do? I shall stay on board as this boat is going right up to the Custom House in London, but if you want to get home sooner, I dare say the chief officer will put you ashore at Southend."

I decided to adopt this course, and I was accordingly landed at Southend Pier with a telegram from Badger to his head-quarters, and at Southend I was fortunate enough to catch an express train which brought me to Fenchurch Street while the night was still young.

When I reached our chambers, I found Thorndyke seated by the fire, serenely studying a brief. He stood up as I entered and, laying aside the brief, remarked, "You are back sooner than I expected. How sped the chase? Did you catch the barge?"

"Yes. We've got the men and we've got the bullion. But we very nearly lost both," and here I gave him an account of the pursuit and the capture, to which he listened with the liveliest interest. "That Customs cruiser was a piece of sheer luck," said he, when I had concluded. "I am delighted. This capture simplifies the case for us enormously."

"It seems to me to dispose of the case altogether," said I. "The property is recovered and the thieves are in custody. But I think most of the credit belongs to Badger."

Thorndyke smiled enigmatically. "I should let him have it all, Jervis," he said, and then, after a reflective pause, he continued, "We will go round to Scotland Yard in the morning to verify the capture. If the package agrees with the description in the bill of lading, the case, as you say, is disposed of."

"It is hardly necessary," said I. "The marks were all correct and the Customs seals were unbroken – but still, I know you won't be satisfied until you have verified everything for yourself. And I suppose you are right."

It was past eleven in the following forenoon when we invaded Superintendent Miller's office at Scotland Yard. That genial officer looked up from his desk as we entered and laughed joyously. "I told you so, Badger," he chuckled, turning to the inspector, who had also looked up and was regarding us with a foxy smile. "I knew the doctor wouldn't be satisfied until he had seen it with his own eyes. I suppose that is what you have come for, sir?"

"Yes," was the reply. "It is a mere formality, of course, but, if you don't mind – "

"Not in the least," replied Miller. "Come along, Badger, and show the doctor your prize."

The two officers conducted us to a room, which the superintendent unlocked, and which contained a small table, a measuring standard, a weighing machine, a set of Snellen's test-types, and the now historic case of bullion. The latter Thorndyke inspected closely, checking the marks and dimensions by his notes.

"I see you haven't opened it," he remarked.

"No," replied Miller. "Why should we? The Customs seals are intact."

"I thought you might like to know what was inside," Thorndyke explained.

The two officers looked at him quickly and the inspector exclaimed, "But we do know. It was opened and checked at the Customs."

"What do you suppose is inside?" Thorndyke asked.

"I don't suppose," Badger replied testily. "I know. There are four bars of gold inside."

"Well," said Thorndyke, "as the representative of the Insurance Company, I should like to see the contents of that case."

The two officers stared at him in amazement, as also, I must admit, did I. The implied doubt seemed utterly contrary to reason.

"This is scepticism with a vengeance!" said Miller. "How on earth is it possible – but there, I suppose if you are not satisfied, we should be justified – "

He glanced at his subordinate, who snorted impatiently, "Oh, open it and let him see the bars. And then, I suppose, he will want us to make an assay of the metal."

The superintendent retired with wrinkled brows and presently returned with a screwdriver, a hammer, and a case-opener. Very deftly he broke the seals, extracted the screws, and prised up the lid of the case, inside which were one or two folds of thick canvas. Lifting these with something of a flourish, he displayed the upper pair of dull, yellow bars.

"Are you satisfied now, sir?" demanded Badger. "Or do you want to see the other two?"

Thorndyke looked reflectively at the two bars, and the two officers looked inquiringly at him (but one might as profitably have watched the expression on the face of a ship's figure). Then he took from his pocket a folding foot-rule and quickly measured the three dimensions of one of the bars.

"Is that weighing machine reliable?" he asked.

"It is correct to an ounce," the superintendent replied, gazing at my colleague with a slightly uneasy expression. "Why?"

By way of reply Thorndyke lifted out the bar that he had measured and carrying it across to the machine, laid it on the platform, and carefully adjusted the weights.

"Well?" the superintendent queried anxiously, as Thorndyke took the reading from the scale.

"Twenty-nine pounds, three-ounces," replied Thorndyke.

"Well?" repeated the superintendent. "What about it?"

Thorndyke looked at him impassively for a moment, and then, in the same quiet tone, answered, "Lead."

"What!" the two officers shrieked in unison, darting across to the scale and glaring at the bar of metal. Then Badger recovered himself and expostulated, not without temper, "Nonsense, sir. Look at it. Can't you see that it is gold?"

"I can see that it is gilded," replied Thorndyke.

"But," protested Miller, "the thing is impossible! What makes you think it is lead?"

"It is just a question of specific gravity," was the reply. "This bar contains seventy-two cubic inches of metal and it weighs twenty pounds, three ounces. Therefore it is a bar of lead. But if you are still doubtful, it is quite easy to settle the matter. May I cut a small piece off the bar?"

The superintendent gasped and looked at his subordinate. "I suppose," said he, "under the circumstances, eh, Badger? Yes. Very well, doctor."

Thorndyke produced a strong pocket-knife and, having lifted the bar to the table, applied the knife to one corner and tapped it smartly with the hammer. The blade passed easily through the soft metal, and as the detached piece fell to the floor, the two officers and I craned forward eagerly. And then all possible doubts were set at rest. There was no mistaking the white, silvery lustre of the freshly-cut surface.

"Snakes!" exclaimed the superintendent. "This is a fair knock-out! Why, the blighters have got away with the stuff, after all! Unless," he added, with a quizzical look at Thorndyke, "you know where it is, doc

r. I expect you do."

"I believe I do," said Thorndyke, "and if you care to come down with me to the London Docks, I think I can hand it over to you."

The superintendent's face brightened appreciably. Not so Badger's. That afflicted officer flung down the chip of metal that he had been examining, and turning to Thorndyke, demanded sourly, "Why didn't you tell us this before, sir? You let me go off chivvying that damn barge, and you knew all the time that the stuff wasn't on board."

"My dear Badger," Thorndyke expostulated, "don't you see that these lead bars are essential to our case? They prove that the gold bars

162

were never landed and that they are consequently still on the ship. Which empowers us to detain any gold that we may find on her."

"There, now, Badger," said the superintendent, "it's no use for you to argue with the doctor. He's like a giraffe. He can see all round him at once. Let us get on to the Docks."

Having locked the room, we all sallied forth and, taking a train at Charing Cross Station, made our way by Mark Lane and Fenchurch Street to Wapping, where, following Thorndyke, we entered the Docks and proceeded straight to a wharf near the Wapping entrance. Here Thorndyke exchanged a few words with a Customs official, who hurried away and presently returned, accompanied by an officer of higher rank. The latter, having saluted Thorndyke and cast a slightly amused glance at our little party, said, "They've landed that package that you spoke about. I've had it put in my office for the present. Will you come and have a look at it?"

We followed him to his office behind a long row of sheds, where, on a table, was a strong wooden case, somewhat larger than the "bullion"-case, while on the desk a large, many-leaved document lay open.

"This is your case, I think," said the official, "but you had better check it by the manifest. Here is the entry, 'One case containing seventeen-and-three-quarter dozen brass six-inch by three-eighths screw-bolts with nuts. Dimensions, sixteen-inches-by-thirteen-by-nine. Gross weight a hundred-and-nineteen pounds, net weight a hundred-and-thirteen-pounds.' Consigned to '*Jackson and Walker, 593 Great Alie Street, London, E.*' Is that the one?"

"That is the one," Thorndyke replied.

"Then," said our friend, "we'll get it open and have a look at those brass screw-bolts."

With a dexterity surprising in an official of such high degree, he had the screws out in a twinkling, and prising up the lid, displayed a fold of coarse canvas. As he lifted this the two police officers peered eagerly into the case, and suddenly the eager expression on Badger's face changed to one of bitter disappointment.

"You've missed fire this time, sir," he snapped. "This is just a case of brass bolts."

"Gold bolts, inspector," Thorndyke corrected, placidly. He picked out one and handed it to the astonished detective. "Did you ever feel a brass bolt of that weight?" he asked.

"Well, it certainly is devilish heavy," the inspector admitted, weighing it in his hand and passing it on to Miller.

163

"Its weight, as stated on the manifest," said Thorndyke, "works out at well over eight-and-a-half ounces, but we may as well check it," He produced from his pocket a little spring balance, to which he slung the bolt. "You see," he said, "it weighs eight-ounces-and-two-thirds. But a brass bolt of the same size would weigh only three-ounces-and-four-fifths. There is not the least doubt that these bolts are gold, and as you see that their aggregate weight is a hundred-and-thirteen while the weight of the four missing bars is a hundred-and-thirteen-pounds-two-ounces, it is a reasonable inference that these bolts represent those bars, and an uncommonly good job they made of the melting to lose only two ounces. Has the consignee's agent turned up yet?"

"He is waiting outside," replied the officer, with a pleased smile, "hopping about like a pea in a frying-pan. I'll call him in."

He did so, and a small, seedy man approached the door with nervous caution and a rather pale face. But when his beady eye fell on the open case and the portentous assembly in the office, he turned about and fled along the wharf as if the hosts of the Philistines were at his heels.

"Of course it is all perfectly simple, as you say," I replied to Thorndyke as we strolled back up Nightingale Lane, "but I don't see where you got your start. What made you think that the stolen case was a dummy?"

"At first," Thorndyke replied, "it was just a matter of alternative hypotheses. It was purely speculative. The robbery described by Halethorpe was a very crude affair. It was planned in quite the wrong way. Noting this, I naturally asked myself, What is the right way to steal a case of gold ingots? Now, the outstanding difficulty in such a robbery arises from the ponderous nature of the thing stolen, and the way to overcome that difficulty is to get away with the booty at leisure before the robbery is discovered – the longer the better. It is also obvious that if you can delude someone into stealing your dummy you will have covered up your tracks most completely, for if that someone is caught, the issues are extremely confused, and if he is not caught, all the tracks lead away from you. Of course, he will discover the fraud when he tries to dispose of the swag, but his lips are sealed by the fact that he has, himself, committed a felony. So that is the proper strategical plan and, though it was wildly improbable, and there was nothing whatever to suggest it, still, the possibility that this crude robbery might cover a more subtle one had to be borne in mind. It was necessary to make absolutely certain that the gold bars were really in the case when it left Belhaven. I had practically no doubt that they were. Our visit to the Custom House was little more than a formality, just to give us an undeniable datum from

164

which to make our start. We had to find somebody who had actually seen the case open and verified the contents, and when we found that man – Mr. Byrne – it instantly became obvious that the wildly improbable thing had really happened. The gold bars had already disappeared. I had calculated the approximate size of the real bars. They would contain forty-two cubic inches, and would be about seven-inches-by-three-by-two. The dimensions given by Byrne – evidently correct, as shown by those of the case, which the bars fitted pretty closely – were impossible. If those bars had been gold, they would have weighed two-hundred pounds, instead of the hundred-and-thirteen pounds shown on his report. The astonishing thing is that Byrne did not observe the discrepancy. There are not many Customs officers who would have let it pass."

"Isn't it rather odd," I asked, "that the thieves should have gambled on such a remote chance?"

"It is pretty certain," he replied, "that they were unaware of the risk they were taking. Probably they assumed – as most persons would have done – that a case of bullion would be merely inspected and passed. Few persons realise the rigorous methods of the Customs officers. But to resume, It was obvious that the 'gold' bars that Byrne had examined were dummies. The next question was, where were the real bars? Had they been made away with, or were they still on the ship? To settle this question, I decided to go through the manifest and especially through the column of net weights. And there, presently, I came upon a package the net weight of which was within two ounces of the weight of stolen bars. And that package was a parcel of brass screw-bolts – on a homeward-bound ship! But who on earth sends brass bolts from Africa to London? The anomaly was so striking that I examined the entry more closely, and then I found – by dividing the net weight by the number of bolts – that each of these little bolts weighed over half-a-pound. But, if this were so, those bolts could be of no other metal than gold or platinum, and were almost certainly gold. Also, their aggregate weight was exactly that of the stolen bars, less two ounces, which probably represented loss in melting."

"And the scrivelloes," said I, "and the gum copal and the kola nuts – what was their bearing on the inquiry? I can't, even now, trace any connection."

Thorndyke cast an astonished glance at me, and then replied with a quiet chuckle, "There wasn't any. Those notes were for the benefit of the shipping gentleman. As he would look over my shoulder, I had to give him something to read and think about. If I had noted only the brass bolts, I should have virtually informed him of the nature of my suspicions."

"Then, really, you had the case complete when we left Belhaven?"

"Theoretically, yes. But we had to recover the stolen case, for without those lead ingots we could not prove that the gold bolts were stolen property, any more than one could prove a murder without evidence of the death of the victim."

"And how do you suppose the robbery was carried out? How was the gold got out of the ship's strong-room?"

"I should say it was never there. The robbers, I suspect, are the ship's mate, the chief engineer, and possibly the purser. The mate controls the stowage of cargo, and the chief engineer controls the repair shop and has the necessary skill and knowledge to deal with the metal. On receiving the advice of the bullion consignment, I imagine they prepared the dummy case in agreement with the description. When the bullion arrived, the dummy case would be concealed on deck and the exchange made as soon as the bullion was put on board. The dummy would be sent to the strong-room and the real case carried to a prepared hiding place. Then the engineer would cut up the bars, melt them piecemeal, and cast them into bolts in an ordinary casting flask, using an iron bolt as a model, and touching up the screw-threads with a die. The mate could enter the case on the manifest when he pleased, and send the bill of lading by post to the nominal consignee. That is what I imagine to have been the procedure."

Thorndyke's solution turned out to be literally correct. The consignee, pursued by Inspector Badger along the quay, was arrested at the dock gates and immediately volunteered King's evidence. Thereupon the mate, the chief engineer, and the purser of the steamship *Labadi* were arrested and brought to trial, when they severally entered a plea of guilty and described the method of the robbery almost in Thorndyke's words.

The Funeral Pyre

Thorndyke did not often indulge in an evening paper, and was even disposed to view that modern institution with some disfavor. Whence it happened that when I entered our chambers shortly before dinner time with a copy of *The Evening Gazette* in my hand, he fixed upon the folded news-sheet an inquiring and slightly disapproving eye.

"'Orrible discovery near Dartford," I announced, quoting the juvenile vendor.

The disapproval faded from his face, but the inquiring expression remained.

"What is it?" he asked.

"I don't know," I replied, "but it seems t be something in our line."

"My learned friend does us an injustice," he rejoined, with his eye riveted on the paper. "Still, if you are going to make my flesh creep, I will try to endure it."

Thus invited, I opened the paper and read out as follows:

> *A shocking tragedy has come to light in a meadow about a mile from Dartford. About two o'clock this morning, a rural constable observed a rick on fire out on the marshes near the creek. By the time he reached it, the upper half of the rick was burning fiercely in the strong wind, and as he could do nothing alone, he went to the adjacent farm-house and gave the alarm. The farmer and two of his sons accompanied the constable to the scene of the conflagration, but the rick was now a blazing mass, roaring in the wind and giving out an intense heat. As it was obviously impossible to save any part of it, and as there were no other ricks near, the farmer decided to abandon it to its fate and went home.*
>
> *At eight o'clock, he returned to the spot and found the rick still burning, though reduced to a heap of glowing cinders and ashes, and approaching it, he was horrified to perceive a human skull grinning out from the cindery mass. Closer examination showed other bones – all calcined white and chalky – and close to the skull a stumpy clay pipe. The explanation of this dreadful occurrence seems quite simple. The rick was not quite finished, and when the farm hands knocked off work they left the ladder in position. It is assumed that some tramp, in search of a night's lodging,*

167

observed the ladder, and climbing up it, made himself comfortable in the loose hay at the top of the rick, where he fell asleep with his lighted pipe in his mouth. This ignited the hay and the man must have been suffocated by the fumes without awakening from his sleep.

"A reasonable explanation," was Thorndyke's comment, "and quite probable, but of course it is pure hypothesis. As a matter of fact, any one of the three conceivable causes of violent death is possible in this case: Accident, suicide, or homicide."

"I should have supposed," said I, "that we could almost exclude suicide. It is difficult to imagine a man electing to roast himself to death."

"I cannot agree with my learned friend," Thorndyke rejoined. "I can imagine a case – and one of great medico-legal interest – that would exactly fit the present circumstances. Let us suppose a man, hopelessly insolvent, desperate, and disgusted with life, who decides to provide for his family by investing the few pounds that he has left in insuring his life heavily and then making away with himself. How would he proceed? If he should commit suicide by any of the orthodox methods he would simply invalidate his policy. But now, suppose he knows of a likely rick, that he provides himself with some rapidly-acting poison, such as potassium cyanide – he could even use prussic acid if he carried it in a rubber or celluloid bottle, which would be consumed in the fire, that he climbs on to the rick, sets fire to it, and as soon as it is fairly alight, takes his dose of poison and falls back dead among the hay. Who is to contest his family's claim? The fire will have destroyed all traces of the poison, even if they should be sought for. But it is practically certain that the question would never be raised. The claim would be paid without demur."

I could not help smiling at this calm exposition of a practicable crime. "It is a mercy, Thorndyke," I remarked, "that you are an honest man. If you were not – "

"I think," he retorted, "that I should find some better means of livelihood than suicide. But with regard to this case, it will be worth watching. The tramp hypothesis is certainly the most probable, but its very probability makes an alternative hypothesis at least possible. No one is likely to suspect fraudulent suicide, but that immunity from suspicion is a factor that increases the probability of fraudulent suicide. And so, to a less extent, with homicide. We must watch the case and see if there are any further developments."

168

Further developments were not very long in appearing. The report in the morning paper disposed effectually of the tramp theory without offering any other.

> *The tragedy of the burning rick,* [it said] *is taking a somewhat mysterious turn. It is now clear that the unknown man, who was assumed to have been a tramp, must have been a person of some social position, for careful examination of the ashes by the police have brought to light various articles which would have been carried only by a man of fair means. The clay pipe was evidently one of a pair – of which the second one has been recovered – probably silver-mounted and carried in a case, the steel frame of which has been found. Both pipes are of the "Burns Cutty" pattern and have neatly scratched on the bowls the initials "R. R." The following articles have also been found: Remains of a watch, probably gold, and a rather singular watch-chain, having alternate links of platinum and gold. The gold links have partly disappeared, but numerous beads of gold have been found, derived apparently from the watch and chain. The platinum links are intact and are fashioned of twisted square wire. A bunch of keys, partly fused, a rock-crystal seal, apparently from a ring, a little porcelain mascot figure, with a hole for suspension – possibly from the watch-chain – and a number of artificial teeth. In connection with the latter, a puzzling and slightly sinister aspect has been given to the case by the finding of an upper dental plate by a ditch some two-hundred yards from the rick. The plate has two gaps and, on comparison with the skull of the unknown man, these have been found by the police surgeon to correspond with two groups of remaining teeth. Moreover, the artificial teeth found in the ashes all seem to belong to a lower plate. The presence of this plate, so far from the scene of the man's death, is extremely difficult to account for.*

As Thorndyke finished reading the extract he looked at me as if inviting some comment.

"It is a most remarkable and mysterious affair," said I, "and naturally recalls to my mind the hypothetical case that you suggested yesterday. If that case was possible then, it is actually probable now. It fits these new facts perfectly not only in respect of the abundant means of identification but even to this dental plate – if we assume that he took the poison as he was approaching the rick, and that the poison was of an acrid or irritating character which caused him to cough or retch. And I can think of no other plausible explanation."

"There are other possibilities," said Thorndyke, "but fraudulent suicide is certainly the most probable theory on the known facts. But we shall see. As you say, the body can hardly fail to be identified at a pretty early date."

As a matter of fact it, was identified in the course of that same day. Both Thorndyke and I were busily engaged until evening in the courts and elsewhere and had not had time to give this curious case any consideration. But as we walked home together, we encountered Mr. Stalker of the Griffin Life Assurance Company pacing up and down King's Bench Walk near the entry of our chambers.

"Ha!" he exclaimed, striding forward to meet us near the Mitre Court gateway, "you are just the very men I wanted to see. There is a little matter that I want to consult you about. I shan't detain you long."

"It won't matter much if you do," said Thorndyke. "We have finished our routine work for the day and our time is now our own." He led the way up to our chambers, where, having given the fire a stir, he drew up three arm-chairs.

"Now, Stalker," said he. "Warm your toes and tell us your troubles."

Mr. Stalker spread out his hands to the blaze began reflectively,

"It will be enough, I think, if I give you the facts – and most of them you probably know already. You have heard about this man whose remains were found in the ashes of a burnt rick? Well, it turns out that he was a certain Mr. Reginald Reed, an outside broker, as I understand, but what is of more interest to us is that he was a client of ours. We have issued a policy on his life for three-thousand pounds. I thought I remembered the name when I saw it in the paper this afternoon, so I looked up our files and there it was, sure enough."

"When was the policy issued?" Thorndyke asked.

"Ah!" exclaimed Stalker. "That's the exasperating feature of the case. The policy was issued less than a year ago. He has only paid a single premium. So we stand to drop practically the whole three-thousand. Of course, we have to take the fat with the lean, but we don't like to take it in such precious large lumps."

"Of course you don't," agreed Thorndyke. "But now you have come to consult me – about what?"

"Well," replied Stalker, "I put it to you: Isn't there something obviously fishy about the case? Are the circumstances normal? For instance, how the devil came a respectable city gentleman to be smoking his pipe in a haystack out in a lonely meadow at two o'clock in the morning, or thereabouts?"

"I agree," said Thorndyke, "that the circumstances are highly abnormal. But there is no doubt that the man is dead. Extremely dead, if I may use the expression. What is the point that you wish to raise?"

"I am not raising any point," replied Stalker. "We should like you to attend the inquest and watch the case for us. Of course, in our policies, as you know, suicide is expressly ruled out, and if this should turn out to have been a case of suicide – "

"What is there to suggest that it was?" asked Thorndyke.

"What is there to suggest that it wasn't?" retorted Stalker.

"Nothing," rejoined Thorndyke. "But a negative plea is of no use to you. You will have to furnish positive proof of suicide, or else pay the claim."

"Yes, I realise that," said Stalker, "and I am not suggesting – But there, it is of no use discussing the matter while we know so little. I leave the case in your hands. Can you attend the inquest?"

"I shall make it my business to do so," replied Thorndyke.

"Very well," said Stalker, rising and putting on his gloves. "Then we will leave it at that, and we couldn't leave it in better case."

When our visitor had gone I remarked to Thorndyke, "Stalker seems to have conceived the same idea as my learned senior – fraudulent suicide."

"It is not surprising," he replied. "Stalker is a shrewd man and he perceives that when an abnormal thing has happened we may look for an abnormal explanation. Fraudulent suicide was a speculative possibility yesterday, to-day, in the light of these new facts, it is the most probable theory. But mere probabilities won't help Stalker. If there is no direct evidence of suicide – and there is not likely to be any – the verdict will be 'Death by Misadventure', and the Griffin Company will have to pay."

"I suppose you won't do anything until you have heard what transpires at the inquest?"

"Yes," he replied. "I think we should do well to go down and just go over the ground. At present we have the facts at third-hand, and we don't know what may have been overlooked. As to-morrow is fairly free, I propose that we make an early start and see the place ourselves."

"Is there any particular point that you want to clear up?"

"No, I have nothing definite in view. The circumstances are compatible with either accident, suicide, or homicide, with an undoubted leaning towards suicide. But at present, I have a completely open mind. I am, in fact, going down to Dartford in the hope of getting a lead in some definite direction."

171

When we alighted at Dartford Station on the following morning, Thorndyke looked inquiringly up and down the platform until he espied an inspector, when he approached the official and asked for a direction to the site of the burnt rick.

The official glanced at Thorndyke's canvas-covrered research-case and at my binocular and camera as he replied with a smile, "You are not the first, by a long way, that has asked that question. There has been a regular procession of Press gentlemen that way this morning. The place is about a mile from here. You take the foot-path to Joyce Green and turn off towards the creek opposite Temple Farm. This is about where the rick stood," he added, as Thorndyke produced his one-inch Ordnance Map and a pencil, "a few yards from that dyke."

With this direction and the open map we set forth from the station, and taking our way along the unfrequented path soon left the town behind. As we crossed the second stile, where the path rejoined the road, Thorndyke paused to survey the prospect.

"Stalker's question," he remarked, "was not unreasonable. This road leads nowhere but to the river, and one does rather wonder what a city man can have been doing out on these marshes in the small hours of the morning. I think that will be our objective, where you see those men at work by the shepherd's hut, or whatever it is."

We struck off across the level meadows, out of which arose the red sails of a couple of barges, creeping down the invisible creek, and as we approached our objective the shepherd's hut resolved itself into a contractor's office van, and the men were seen to be working with shovels and sieves on the ashes of the rick. A police inspector was superintending the operations, and when we drew near he accosted us with a civil inquiry as to our business.

Thorndyke presented his card and explained that he was watching the case in the interests of the Griffin Insurance Company. "I suppose," he added, "I shall be given the necessary facilities?"

"Certainly," replied the officer, glancing at my colleague with an odd mixture of respect and suspicion, "and if you can spot anything that we've overlooked, you are very welcome. It's all for the public good. Is there anything in particular that you want to see?"

"I should like to see everything that has been recovered so far. The remains of the body have been removed, I suppose?"

"Yes, sir. To the mortuary. But I have got all the effects here."

He led the way to the office – a wooden hut on low wheels – and unlocking the door, invited us to enter. "Here are the things that we have saved," he said, indicating a table covered with white paper on which the

172

various articles were neatly set out, "and I think it's about the lot. We haven't come on anything fresh for the last hour or so."

Thorndyke looked over the collection thoughtfully, picked up and examined successively the two clay pipes – each with the initials "*R. R.*" neatly incised on the bowl – the absurd little mascot figure, so incongruous with its grim surroundings and the tragic circumstances, the distorted keys, the platinum chain-links to several of which shapeless blobs of gold adhered, and the crystal seal, and then, collecting the artificial teeth, arranged them in what appeared to be their correct order and compared them with the dental plate.

"I think," said he, holding the latter in his fingers, "that as the body is not here, I should like to secure the means of comparison of these teeth with the skull. There will be no objection to that, I presume?"

"What did you wish to do?" the inspector asked.

"I should like to take a cast of the plate and a wax impression of the loose teeth. No damage will be done to the originals, of course."

The inspector hesitated, his natural official tendency to refuse permission apparently contending with a desire to see with his own eyes how the famous expert carried out his mysterious methods of research. In the end the latter prevailed and the official sanction was given, subject to a proviso. "You won't mind my looking on while you do it?"

"Of course not," replied Thorndyke. "Why should I?"

"I thought that perhaps your methods were a sort of trade secret."

Thorndyke laughed softly as he opened the research case. "My dear inspector," said he, "the people who have trade secrets are those who make a profound mystery of simple processes that any schoolboy could carry out with one showing. That is the necessity for the secrecy."

As he was speaking, he half-filled a tiny aluminium saucepan with water, and having dropped into it a couple of cakes of dentist's moulding composition, put it to heat over a spirit-lamp. While it was heating, he greased the dental plate and the loose teeth, and prepared the little rubber basin and the other appliances for mixing the plaster.

The inspector was deeply interested. With almost ravenous attention, he followed these proceedings and eagerly watched Thorndyke roll the softened composition into the semblance of a small sausage and press it firmly on the teeth of the plate, peered into the plaster tin, and when the liquid plaster was mixed and applied, first to the top and then to the lower surface of the plate, not only observed the process closely but put a number of very pertinent questions.

While the plaster and composition were setting, Thorndyke renewed his inspection of the salvage from the rick, picking out a number of iron boot protectors which he placed apart in a little heap.

Then he proceeded to roll out two flat strips of softened composition, into one of which he pressed the loose teeth in what appeared to be their proper order, and into the other the boot protectors – eight in number – after first dusting the surface with powdered French chalk. By this time the plaster had set hard enough to allow of the mould being opened and the dental plate taken out. Then Thorndyke, having painted the surfaces of the plaster pieces with knotting, put the mould together again and tied it firmly with string, mixed a fresh bowl of plaster, and poured it into the mould.

While this was setting Thorndyke made a careful inventory, with my assistance, of the articles found in the ashes and put a few discreet questions to the inspector. But the latter knew very little about the case. His duty was merely to examine and report on the rick for the information of the coroner. The investigation of the case was evidently being conducted from headquarters. There being no information to be gleaned from the officer, we went out and inspected the site of the rick. But here, also, there was nothing to be learned, the surface of the ground was now laid bare and the men who were working with the sieves reported no further discoveries. We accordingly returned to the hut and, as the plaster had now set hard, Thorndyke proceeded with infinite care to open the mould. The operation was a complete success, and as my colleague extracted the cast – a perfect replica, in plaster, of the dental plate – the inspector's admiration was unbounded. "Why," he exclaimed, "excepting for the colour, you couldn't tell one from the other. But all the same, I don't quite see what you want it for."

"I want it to compare with the skull," replied Thorndyke, "if I have time to call at the mortuary. As I can't take the original plate with me, I shall need this copy to make the comparison. Obviously, it is important to make sure that this is Reed's plate and not that of some other person. By the way, can you show us the spot where the plate was picked up?"

"Yes," replied the inspector. "You can see the place from here. It was just by that gate at the crossing of the ditch."

"Thank you, inspector," said Thorndyke. "I think we will walk down and have a look at the place." He wrapped the new cast in a soft cloth and, having repacked his research – case, shook hands with the officer and prepared to depart.

"You will notice, Jervis," he remarked as we walked towards the gate, "that this denture was picked up at a spot beyond the rick – farther from the town, I mean. Consequently, if the plate is Reed's, he must have dropped it while he was approaching the rick from the direction of the river. It will be worthwhile to see if we can find out whence he came."

174

"Yes," I agreed. "But the dropping of the plate is a rather mysterious affair. It must have happened when he took the poison – assuming that he really did poison himself, but one would have expected that he would wait until he got to the rick to take his dose."

"We had better not make too many assumptions while we have so few facts," said Thorndyke. He put down his case beside the gate, which guarded a bridge across a broad ditch, or drainage dyke, and opened his map.

"The question is," said he, "did he come through this gate or was he only passing it? This dyke, you see, opens into the creek about three-quarters of a mile farther down. The probability is, therefore, that if he came up from the river across the marshes, he would be on this side of the ditch and would pass the gate. But we had better try both sides. Let us leave our things by the gate and explore the ground for a few hundred yards, one on either side of the ditch. Which side will you take?"

I elected to take the side nearer the creek and, having put my camera down by the research-case, climbed over the padlocked gate and began to walk slowly along by the side of the ditch, scanning the ground for footprints showing the impression of boot-protectors. At first the surface was far from favourable for imprints of any kind, being, like that immediately around the gate, covered with thick turf. About a hundred-and-fifty yards down, however, I came upon a heap of worm-casts on which was plainly visible the print of a heel with a clear impression of a kidney-shaped protector such as I had seen in the hut. Thereupon I hailed Thorndyke and, having stuck my stick in the ground beside the heel-print, went back to meet him at the gate.

"This is rather interesting, Jervis," he remarked, when I had described my find. "The inference seems to be that he came from the creek – unless there is another gate farther down. We had better have our compo impressions handy for comparison." He opened his case and taking from it the strip of composition – now as hard as bone – on which were the impressions of the boot-protectors, slipped it into his outer pocket. We then took up the case and the camera and proceeded to the spot marked by my stick.

"Well," said Thorndyke, "it is not very conclusive, seeing that so many people use boot-protectors, but it is probably Reed's foot-print. Let us hope that we shall find something more distinctive farther on."

We resumed our march, keeping a few yards apart and examining the ground closely as we went. For a full quarter-of-a-mile we went on without detecting any trace of a foot-print on the thick turf. Suddenly we perceived ahead of us a stretch of yellow mud occupying a slight hollow, across which the creek had apparently overflowed at the last spring tide.

175

When we reached it we found that the mud was nearly dry, but still soft enough to take an impression, and the surface was covered with a maze of foot-prints.

We halted at the edge of the patch and surveyed the complicated pattern, and then it became evident that the whole group of prints had been produced by two pairs of feet, with the addition of a row of sheep-tracks.

"This seems to raise an entirely new issue," I remarked.

"It does," Thorndyke agreed. "I think we now begin to see a definite light on the case. But we must go cautiously. Here are two sets of foot-prints of which one is apparently Reed's – to judge by the boot-protectors – while the other prints have been made by a man, whom we will call X, who wore boots or shoes with rubber soles and heels. We had better begin by verifying Reed's." He produced the composition strip from his pocket and, stooping over one pair of footprints, continued, "I think we may assume that these are Reed's feet. We have on the compo strip impressions of eight protectors from the rick, and on each foot-print there are four protectors. Moreover, the individual protectors are the same on the compo and on the foot-prints. Thus the compo shows two pairs of half-protectors, two single edge-pieces, and two kidney-shaped protectors, while each foot-print shows a pair of half-protectors on the outside of the sole, a single one on the inside, and a kidney-shaped piece on the heel. Furthermore, in both cases the protectors are nearly new and show no appreciable signs of wear. The agreement is complete."

"Don't you think," said I, "that we ought to take plaster records of them?"

"I do," he replied, "seeing that a heavy shower or a high tide would obliterate them. If you will make the casts I will, meanwhile, make a careful drawing of the whole group to show the order of imposition."

We fell to work forthwith upon our respective tasks, and by the time I had filled four of the clearest of the foot-prints with plaster, Thorndyke had completed his drawing with the aid of a set of coloured pencils from the research-case. While the plaster was setting, he exhibited and explained the drawing.

"You see, Jervis, that there are four lines of prints and a set of sheep-tracks. The first in order of time are these prints of X, drawn in blue. Then come the sheep, which trod on X's foot-prints. Next comes Reed, alone and after some interval, for he has trodden both on the sheep-tracks and on the tracks of X. Both men were going towards the river. Then we have the tracks of the two men coming back. This time they were together, for their tracks are parallel and neither treads into the prints of the other. Both tracks are rather sinuous, as if the men were

176

walking unsteadily, and both have trodden on the sheep-tracks and on the preceding tracks. Next, we have the tracks of X going alone towards the river and treading on all the others excepting number four, which is the tracks of X coming from the river and turning off towards that gate, which opens on to the road. The sequence of events is therefore pretty clear.

"First, X came along here alone to some destination which we have yet to discover. Later – how much later we cannot judge – came Reed, alone. The two men seem to have met, and later returned together, apparently the worse for drink. That is the last we see of Reed. Next comes X, walking back – quite steadily, you notice – towards the river. Later, he returns, but this time, for some reason – perhaps to avoid the neighbourhood of the rick – he crosses the ditch at that gate, apparently to get on the road, though you see by the map that the road is much the longer route to the town. And now we had better get on and see if we can discover the rendezvous to and from which these two men went and came."

As the plaster had now set quite hard I picked up the casts, and when I had carefully packed them in the case we resumed our progress riverwards. I had already noticed, some distance ahead, the mast of what looked like a small cutter yacht standing up above the marshes, and I now drew Thorndyke's attention to it. But he had already observed it and, like me, had marked it as the probable rendezvous of the two men. In a few minutes the probability became a certainty, for a bend in the creek showed us the little vessel – with the name *Moonbeam* newly painted on the bow – made fast alongside a small wooden staging, and when we reached this the bare earth opposite the gangway was seen to be covered with the foot-prints of both men.

"I wonder," said I, "which of them was the owner of the yacht."

"It is pretty obvious, I think," said Thorndyke, "that X was the owner if either of them was. He came to the yacht alone, and he wore rubber-soled shoes such as yachtsmen favour, whereas Reed came when the other man was there, and he wore iron boot-protectors, which no yacht owner would do if he had any respect for his deck-planks. But they may have had a joint interest – appearances suggest that they were painting the woodwork when they were here together, as some of the paint is fresh and some of it old and shabby." He gazed at the yacht reflectively for some time and then remarked, "It would be interesting – and perhaps instructive – to have a look at the inside."

"It would be a flagrant trespass, to put it mildly," said I.

"It would be more than trespass if that padlock is locked," he replied. "But we need not take a pedantic view of the legal position. My learned friend has a serviceable pair of glasses and commands an unobstructed view of a mile or so, and if he maintains an observant attitude while I make an inspection of the premises, any trifling irregularity will be of no consequence." As he spoke he felt in his pocket and produced the instrument which our laboratory assistant, Polton, had made from a few pieces of stiff steel wire, and which was euphemistically known as a 'smoker's companion'. With this appliance in his hand, he dropped down on to the yacht's deck, and after a quick look round, tried the padlock. Finding it locked, he proceeded to operate on it with the smoker's companion, and in a few moments it fell open, and he pushed back the sliding hatch and stepped down into the little cabin.

His exploration did not take long. In a few minutes he reappeared and climbed the short ladder to the staging. "There isn't much to see," he reported, "but what there is is highly suggestive. If you slip down and have a look round, I think you will have no difficulty in forming a plausible reconstruction of the recent events. You had better take the camera. There is light enough for a time exposure."

I handed him the glasses and, dropping on to the deck, stepped down through the open hatch into the cabin. It was an absurd little cave, barely four feet high from the floor to the coach-roof, open to the fore-peak and lighted by a little skylight and two portholes. Of the two sleeping berths, one had evidently been used as a seat, while the other appeared to have been slept in, to judge by the indented pillow and the tumbled blankets, left just as the occupant had crawled out of them. But the whole interior was in a stale of squalid disorder. Paint-pots and unwashed brushes lay about the floor, in company with a couple of whisky-bottles – one empty and one half-full – two tumblers, a pair of empty siphons, and a litter of playing cards scattered broadcast and evidently derived from two packs. It was, as Thorndyke had said, easy to reconstruct the scene of sordid debauchery that the light of the two candles – each in its congealed pool of grease – must have displayed on that night of horror whose dreadful secret had been disclosed by the ashes of the rick. But I could see nothing that would enable me to give a name to the dead man's mysterious companion.

When I had completed my inspection and taken a photograph of the interior, I rejoined Thorndyke, who then descended and replaced the padlock on the closed hatch, relocking it with the invaluable smoker's companion.

"Well, Jervis," said he, as we turned our faces towards the town, "it seems as if we had accomplished our task, so far as Stalker is concerned. It is still possible that this was a case of suicide, but it is no longer probable. All the appearances point to homicide. I think my learned friend will agree with me in that."

"Undoubtedly," I replied. "And to me there is a strong suggestion of premeditation. I take it that X, the owner of the yacht, enticed Reed out here, possibly to prepare for a cruise, that the two men worked at the repainting while the daylight lasted and then spent the evening drinking and gambling. The fact that they used several packs of cards suggests that they played for pretty heavy stakes. Then, I think, Reed became drunk and X offered to see him safely off the marshes. It is evident that X was not drunk, because, although both tracks appear unsteady when the men were walking together, the tracks of X returning to the yacht are quite steady and straight. I should say that the actual murder took place just after they had got over the gate, that Reed's false teeth fell out while his body was being dragged to the rick, and that this was unnoticed by X owing to the darkness. Then X dragged the body up the ladder and laid it in the middle of the rick at the top, set fire to the rick – probably on the lee side – and at once made off back to the yacht. There he passed the night, and in the morning he returned to the town along the road, giving the neighbourhood of the rick a wide berth. That is my reading of the evidence."

"Yes," said Thorndyke, "that seems to be the interpretation of the facts. And now all that remains is to give a name to the mysterious X, and I should think that will present no difficulties."

"Are you proposing to inspect the remains at the mortuary?" I asked.

"No," he replied. "It would be interesting, but it is not necessary. We have all the available data for identification, and our concern is now not with Reed but with X. We had better get back to London."

On our arrival at the station, we found the bookstall keeper in the act of sticking up a placard of the evening paper on which was the legend, "*Rick Tragedy. Sensational Development*".

We immediately provided ourselves each with a copy of the paper, and sitting down on a seat, proceeded to read the heavily-leaded report.

> *A new and startling aspect has been given to the rick tragedy by some further inquiries that the police have made. It seems that the dead man, Reed, was a member of the firm of Reed and Jarman, outside brokers, and it now transpires that his partner, Walter Jarman, is also missing. There has been no one at the office this week, but the caretaker states that on Monday evening at about eight o'clock, he saw Mr. Jarman*

179

let himself into the office with his key (the rick was first seen to be on fire at two o'clock on Monday morning). It appears that three cheques, payable to the firm and endorsed by Jarman, were paid into the bank – Patmore's – by the first post on Tuesday morning, and that, also on Tuesday morning, Jarman purchased a parcel of diamonds of just over a thousand pounds in value from a diamond merchant in Hatton Garden, who accepted a cheque in payment after telephoning to the bank. It further appears that on the previous Saturday morning, Reed and Jarman visited the bank together and drew out in cash practically their whole balance, leaving only thirty-two pounds. The diamond merchant's cheque was met by the cheques that had just been paid in. It is premature to make any comments, but we may expect some strange disclosures at the inquest, which will be held at Dartford the day after to-morrow.

"I assume," said I, "that the identity of *X* is no longer a mystery. It looks as if these two men had agreed to realise their assets and abscond, and had then spent the night gambling for the swag and, oddly enough, Reed appears to have been the winner, for otherwise there would have been no need to murder him."

"That is so," Thorndyke agreed, "assuming that *X* is Jarman, which is probable, though not certain. But we mustn't go beyond our facts, and we mustn't construct theories from newspaper reports. I think we had better call at Scotland Yard on our way home and verify those particulars."

The report and our own observations occupied us during the journey to London, though our discussion produced no further conclusions. As soon as we arrived at Charing Cross, Thorndyke and I sprang out of the train and, emerging from the station, walked swiftly towards Whitehall.

Our visit was fortunately timed, for as we approached the entrance to the head-quarters, our old friend, Superintendent Miller, came out. He smiled as he saw us and halted to utter the laconic query,

"Rick Case?"

"Yes," replied Thorndyke. "We have come to verify the particulars given in the evening paper. Have you seen the report?"

"Yes, and you may take it as correct. Anything else?"

"I should have liked to look over a series of the cheques drawn by the firm. The last two, I suppose, are inaccessible?"

"Yes. They will be at the bank, and we couldn't inspect them without an order of the court. But, as to the others, if they are at the

180

office, I think you could see them. I'll come along with you now if you like, and have a look round myself. Our people are in possession."

We at once closed with the superintendent's offer and proceeded with him by the Underground Railway to the Mansion House, from whence we made our way to Queen Victoria Street, where Reed and Jarman had their offices. A sergeant was in charge at the moment, and to him the superintendent addressed himself.

"Have you found any returned cheques?"

"Yes, sir," replied the sergeant, "lots of 'em. We've been through them all."

As he spoke he produced several bundles of cheques and laid them on a desk, the drawers of which all stood open.

"Well," said Miller, "there they are, Doctor. I don't know what you want to find out, but I expect you do." He placed a chair by the desk and, as Thorndyke sat down and proceeded to turn the cheques over, he watched him with politely-suppressed curiosity.

"It appears," said Thorndyke, "as if these two men had mixed up their private affairs with the business account. Here, for instance, is a cheque drawn by Reed for the Picardy Wine Company. But that company could hardly have been a client. And this one of Jarman's for the Secretary of the St. John's Nursing Home must be a private cheque, and so I should say are these two for F. Waller, Esq., F.R.C.S., and for Andrew Darton, Esq., L.D.S. They are drawn for professional men and both are – like the Nursing Home cheque – stated in even amounts of guineas, whereas the business cheques are in uneven amounts of pounds, shillings, and pence."

"I think you are right, sir," said Miller. "The business seems to have been conducted in a very casual manner. And just look at those signatures! Never twice alike. The banks hate that sort of thing, naturally. When a customer signs in the signature book he has given a specimen for reference and he ought to keep to it strictly. A man who varies his signature is asking for trouble."

"He is," Thorndyke agreed, as he rapidly entered a few particulars of the cheques in his notebook, "particularly in the case of a firm with a staff of clerks."

He stood up and, having pocketed his notebook, held out his hand.

"I am very much obliged to you, Superintendent," he said.

"Seen all that you wanted to see?" Miller asked.

"Thank you, yes," Thorndyke replied.

"I should very much like to know what you have seen," Miller rejoined, to which my colleague replied by waving his hand towards the cheques, as he turned to go.

181

"I don't quite see the bearing of those cheques on our inquiry," I said, as we took our way homeward along Cheapside.

"It is not very direct," Thorndyke replied, "but the cheques help us to understand the characters of these two men and their relations with one another, which may be very necessary when we come to the inquest."

During the following day I saw very little of Thorndyke, for our excursion to Dartford had put our work somewhat in arrear and we had to secure a free day for the inquest on the morrow. We met at dinner after the day's work, but, beyond settling the programme for the next day, nothing of importance passed with reference to the "Rick Case".

The opening phases of the inquest, though of thrilling interest to the numerous spectators and Press men, did not particularly concern us. The evidence of the rural constable, the farmer, and the police inspector – with whom Thorndyke had a little confidential talk and apparently surprised the officer considerably – merely amplified what we knew already. Of more interest was that of a local dentist who testified to having examined the dental plate and to having compared it with the skull of the dead man. "The plate and the jaw of deceased," he said, "agree completely. The jaw contains five natural teeth in two groups, and the plate has two spaces which exactly correspond to those two groups of teeth. I have tried the plate on the jaw and have no doubt whatever that it belonged to deceased."

"That is a very important fact," Thorndyke remarked to me as the witness retired. "It is the indispensable link in the chain."

"But surely it was obvious?" said I.

"No doubt," he replied. "But now it is proved and in evidence."

I was somewhat puzzled by Thorndyke's remark, but the appearance of a new witness forbade discussion. Mr. Arthur Gerrard was an alert-looking, rather tall man, with bushy, Mephistophelian eyebrows and a small, dark moustache, who wore a pair of large bifocal spectacles, and to whom a small mole at the corner of the mouth imparted the effect of a permanent one-sided smile.

"It was on your information," said the coroner, "that the identity of the deceased was established."

"Yes," replied the witness, who spoke with a slight, but perceptible, Irish accent. "I saw the description in the papers of the things that had been found in the rick and at once recognised them as Reed's. I knew deceased intimately and had often noticed his peculiar watch-chain and the little china mascot and seen him smoking the clay pipe with his initials scratched on it, and I knew that he wore false teeth."

"Did you meet him frequently?"

"Oh, yes. For more than a year he was my partner in business, and we remained friends after I had dissolved the partnership."

"Why did you dissolve the partnership?"

"I had to. Reed was impossible in a business sense. He gambled incessantly in stocks and I had to pay his losses. I lent him, for this purpose, at one time and another, over two-thousand pounds. He gave me bills for the loans, but he was never able to meet them, and in the end, when we dissolved, I got him to insure his life for three-thousand pounds and to draw up a document making his debt to me the first charge on his estate in the event of his death."

"Had you ever any reason to suppose that he contemplated suicide?

"None whatever. After he left me, he entered into partnership with a Mr. Walter Jarman, and whenever I met him, he seemed to be quite happy and contented, though I gathered that he was still gambling a good deal. I saw him a week ago to-day and he then told me that he proposed to take a short yachting holiday with his partner, who owned a small cutter. That was the last time that I saw him alive."

As the witness was about to retire, Thorndyke rose, and having obtained the coroner's permission to cross-examine, asked, "You have spoken of a yacht. Do you know what her name is and where she has been kept lately?"

"Her name is the *Moonbeam*, and I believe Jarman kept her somewhere in the Thames, but I don't know where."

"And as to Jarman himself: What do you know about him, as to his character, for instance?"

"I knew him very slightly. He appeared to be rather a dissipated man. Drank a good deal, I should say, and I think he was a bit of a gambler."

"Do you know if he was a heavy smoker?"

"He didn't smoke at all, but he was an inveterate snuff-taker."

At this point the foreman of the jury interposed with the audible remark that "he didn't see what this had to do with the inquiry," and the coroner looked dubiously at Thorndyke, but as my colleague sat down, the objection was not pursued.

The next witness was the caretaker of the building in which Reed and Jarman's office was situated. His evidence was to the effect that on the previous Monday evening at about eight o'clock, he saw Mr. Jarman let himself into the office with his key. "I don't know how long he stayed there," he continued, in reply to the coroner's question. "I had finished my work and was going up to my rooms at the top of the building. I didn't see him again."

"Did you notice anything unusual in his appearance?" asked Thorndyke, rising to cross-examine. "Was his face at all flushed, for instance?"

"I couldn't say. I was going up the stairs and I just looked back over my shoulder when I heard him. His face was turned away from me."

"But you had no difficult in recognising him?"

"No, I should have known him a mile off. He had his overcoat on, and it is a very peculiar overcoat – light brown with a sort of greenish check. You couldn't possibly mistake it."

"What should you say was Mr. Jarman's height?"

"About five-feet-nine or ten, I should say."

Here the foreman of the jury again interposed. "Aren't we wasting time, sir?" he inquired impatiently. "These details about Jarman may be very important to the police, but they don't concern us. We are inquiring into the death of Mr. Reginald Reed."

The coroner looked deprecatingly at Thorndyke and remarked, "There is some truth in what the foreman says."

"I submit, sir," replied Thorndyke, "that there is no truth in it at all. We are not inquiring into the death of Reginald Reed, but into that of a man whose remains were found in a burned rick."

"But the body has been identified as that of Reginald Reed."

"Then," said Thorndyke, "I submit that it has been wrongly identified. I suggest that the body is that of Walter Jarman and I am prepared to produce witnesses who will prove that it is."

"But," exclaimed the coroner, "we have just heard the evidence of a witness who states that he saw Jarman alive eighteen hours after the rick was fired."

"I beg your pardon, sir," said Thorndyke. "We have heard the witness say that he saw Jarman's overcoat. He expressly stated that he did not see the man's face."

The coroner hastily conferred with the jury – who openly scoffed at Thorndyke's suggestion – and then said, "I find what you say perfectly incredible and so do the jury. It is utterly irreconcilable with the facts. You had better call your witnesses and let us dispose of this extraordinary suggestion."

Thorndyke bowed to the coroner and called Mr. Andrew Darton, whereupon a middle-aged man of markedly professional aspect came forward and, having been sworn, gave evidence as follows, "I am a dental surgeon. A little over two years ago, Mr. Walter Jarman was under my care. I extracted some loose teeth from both jaws and made him two plates – an upper and a lower."

"Could you identify those plates?"

"Yes. I have with me the plaster model on which those plates were made." He opened a bag and produced a plaster cast of a pair of jaws fitted with a brass hinge so that the jaws could be opened and shut. On the upper jaw were two groups of teeth separated by a space of bare gums, while the lower jaw bore a single group of four front teeth.

"This model," the witness explained, "is an exact replica of the patient's jaws, and the two plates were actually moulded on it." He picked up the dental plate from the table and, amidst a hush of breathless expectancy, opened the mouth of the model and applied the plate to the upper jaw. At a glance, it was obvious that it fitted perfectly. The two groups of the plaster teeth slipped exactly into the spaces on the plate, making a complete row of teeth. Then the witness covered the lower gums with strips of plastic wax, and taking the loose teeth from the table, attached them to the wax, and again the correspondence was evident. The teeth thus applied exactly filled the vacant spaces.

"Can you now identify that plate?" Thorndyke asked.

"Yes," was the reply. "I am quite certain that this is the plate I made for Mr. Jarman and that those loose teeth are from his lower plate."

Thorndyke looked at the coroner, who nodded emphatically. "This evidence seems perfectly conclusive," he admitted. "What do you say, gentlemen?" he added, turning to the jury.

There was no doubt as to their sentiments. With one voice they declared their complete conviction. Had they not seen the demonstration with their own eyes?

"And now, sir," said the coroner, "as you appear to know more than anyone else about this case, and as it is perfectly incomprehensible to me, and probably also to the jury, I suggest that you give us an explanation. And you had better make it a sworn statement, so that it can go into the depositions."

"Yes," Thorndyke agreed, "especially as I have some evidence to give." He was accordingly sworn and then proceeded to make the following statement,

"The first thing that struck me on reading the report of this case was the very remarkable character of the objects found in the ashes of the rick. They included objects composed of platinum, of pipe-clay, of iron, and of porcelain – all substances practically indestructible by fire. And these imperishable objects were all highly distinctive and easily identifiable, and two of them actually bore the initials of their owner. There was almost a suggestion of the body having been prepared for identification after burning. This mere suggestion, however, gave place to definite suspicion when I saw the dental plate. That plate presented a most striking discrepancy. Here it is, sir, and you see that it is a clean

185

polished plate of red vulcanite, with not a trace of stain or discoloration. But associated with that plate were two clay pipes.

"Now, the man who smokes a clay pipe is not only – as a rule – a heavy smoker, but he smokes strong and dark-coloured tobacco. And if he wears a dental plate, that plate becomes encrusted with a black deposit which is very difficult to remove. There is, as you see, no trace of any such deposit, or of any tobacco stain in the interstices of the teeth. It appeared to be almost certainly the plate of a non-smoker. But if that were so, it could not be Reed's. But it had been ascertained by the police surgeon that it fitted the jaw of the skull and undoubtedly belonged to the burned body. Consequently if the plate was not Reed's plate, the skull was not Reed's skull, and the body was not Reed's body. But the watch-chain was Reed's, the pipes were his, and the mascot was his. That is to say that the very identifiable and fire-proof property of Reed was associated with the burned body of some other person – that, in other words, the body of some unknown person had been deliberately prepared to counterfeit the body of Reed. This offered a further suggestion and raised a question. The suggestion was that the unknown person had been murdered – presumably somewhere near the spot where the dental plate was found. The question was: What was the object of causing the body to counterfeit that of Reed?

"Now, I knew, from the insurance company, that Reed had insured his life for three-thousand pounds. Therefore, somebody stood to gain three-thousand pounds by his death. The question was – Who was that somebody? I proceeded to make certain investigations on the spot," – and here Thorndyke gave a summary of our discoveries on the marsh and on the yacht. "It thus appeared," he continued, "that there were two men on the marshes that night, going towards the rick. One of them was the person whose body was found in the ashes, the other, who went back alone to the yacht, was presumably the person who stood to gain three-thousand pounds by Reed's death."

"Have you formed any opinion as to who that person was?" the coroner asked.

"Yes," replied Thorndyke. "I have very little doubt that he was Reginald Reed."

"But," exclaimed the coroner, "we have heard in evidence that it was Mr. Arthur Gerrard who stood to gain the three-thousand pounds!"

"Precisely," said Thorndyke, and for a while he and the coroner looked at one another without speaking.

Suddenly the latter cast a searching look around the court. "Where is Mr. Gerrard?" he demanded.

"He left the court about ten minutes ago," said Thorndyke, "and a police inspector left immediately afterwards. I had advised him not to lose sight of Mr. Gerrard."

"Then I take it that you suspect Gerrard of being in collusion with Reed?"

"I suspect that Arthur Gerrard and Reginald Reed are one and the same person."

As Thorndyke made this statement, a murmur of astonishment arose from the jurymen and the spectators. The coroner, after a few moments' puzzled reflection, remarked, "You are not forgetting that Reed's caretaker was present while Gerrard was giving his evidence?" Then, turning to the caretaker, he asked, "What do you say? Was that Mr. Reed who gave evidence under the name of Gerrard?"

The caretaker, who had evidently been thinking furiously, was by no means confident. "I should say not," he replied, "unless he was made up a good deal. He was certainly about the same height and build and colour, but he had a moustache, whereas Mr. Reed was clean-shaved, he had a mole on his face, which Mr. Reed hadn't, he had bushy eyebrows, whereas Mr. Reed had hardly any eyebrows to speak of, and he wore spectacles, which Mr. Reed didn't, and he spoke like an Irishman, whereas Mr. Reed was English. Still it is possible – "

Before he could finish, the door rattled to a heavy concussion. Then it flew open, and Mr. Gerrard staggered into the room, thrust forward by the police inspector. His appearance was marvellously changed, for he had lost his spectacles, and one of his eyebrows had disappeared, as had also the mole and a portion of the built-up moustache. The caretaker started up with an exclamation, but at this moment Gerrard, with a violent effort, wrenched himself free. The inspector sprang forward to recapture him. But he was too late. The prisoner's hand flew upwards, there was a ringing report, and Arthur Gerrard – or Reginald Reed – fell back across a bench with a trickle of blood on his temple and a pistol still clutched in his hand.

"And so," said Stalker, when he called on us the next day for details, "it was a suicide after all. Very lucky, too, seeing that there was no provision in the policy for death by judicial hanging."

188

The Puzzle Lock

R. AUSTIN FREEMAN

Dr. Thorndyke solves more mysteries.

H&S

1925 Hodder & Stoughton, London Cover

190

The Puzzle Lock

I do not remember what was the occasion of my dining with Thorndyke at Giamborini's on the particular evening that is now in my mind. Doubtless, some piece of work completed had seemed to justify the modest festival. At any rate, there we were, seated at a somewhat retired table selected by Thorndyke, with our backs to the large window through which the late June sunlight streamed. We had made our preliminary arrangements, including a bottle of Barsac, and were inspecting dubiously a collection of semi-edible *hors d'oeuvres*, when a man entered and took possession of a table just in front of ours, which had apparently been reserved for him, since he walked directly to it and drew away the single chair that had been set aslant against it.

I watched with amused interest his methodical procedure, for he was clearly a man who took his dinner seriously. A regular customer, too, I judged, by the waiter's manner and the reserved table with its single chair. But the man himself interested me. He was out of the common and there was a suggestion of character, with perhaps a spice of oddity, in his appearance. He appeared to be about sixty years of age, small and spare, with a much-wrinkled, mobile, and rather whimsical face, surmounted by a crop of white, upstanding hair. From his waistcoat pocket protruded the ends of a fountain-pen, a pencil and a miniature electric torch such as surgeons use, a silver-mounted Coddington lens hung from his watch-guard, and the middle finger of his left hand bore the largest seal ring that I have ever seen.

"Well," said Thorndyke, who had been following my glance, "what do you make of him?"

"I don't quite know," I replied. "The Coddington suggests a naturalist or a scientist of some kind, but that blatant ring doesn't. Perhaps he is an antiquary or a numismatist or even a philatelist. He deals with small objects of some kind."

At this moment, a man who had just entered strode up to our friend's table and held out his hand, which the other shook, with no great enthusiasm, as I thought. Then the newcomer fetched a chair and, setting it by the table, seated himself and picked up the menu card, while the other observed him with a shade of disapproval. I judged that he would rather have dined alone, and that the personality of the new arrival – a flashy, bustling, obtrusive type of man – did not commend him.

From this couple my eye was attracted to a tall man who had halted near the door and stood looking about the room as if seeking someone.

191

Suddenly he spied an empty, single table and, bearing down on it, seated himself and began anxiously to study the menu under the supervision of a waiter. I glanced at him with slight distavour. One makes allowances for the exuberance of youth, but when a middle-aged man presents the combination of heavily-greased hair parted in the middle, a waxed moustache of a suspiciously intense black, a pointed imperial, and a single eye-glass, evidently ornamental in function, one views him with less tolerance. However, his get-up was not my concern, whereas my dinner was, and I had given this my undivided attention for some minutes when I heard Thorndyke emit a soft chuckle.

"Not bad," he remarked, setting down his glass.

"Not at all," I agreed, "for a restaurant wine."

"I was not alluding to the wine," said he "but to our friend Badger."

"The inspector!" I exclaimed. "He isn't here, is he? I don't see him."

"I am glad to hear you say that, Jervis," said he. "It is a better effort than I thought. Still, he might manage his properties a little better. That is the second time his eye-glass has been in the soup."

Following, the direction of his glance, I observed the man with the waxed moustache furtively wiping his eye-glass, and the temporary absence of the monocular grimace enabled me to note a resemblance to the familiar features of the detective officer.

"If you say that is Badger, I suppose it is," said I. "He is certainly a little like our friend. But I shouldn't have recognised him."

"I don't know that I should," said Thorndyke, "but for the little unconscious tricks of movement. You know the habit he has of stroking the back of his head, and of opening his mouth and scratching the side of his chin. I saw him do it just now. He had forgotten his imperial until he touched it, and then the sudden arrest of movement was very striking. It doesn't do to forget a false beard."

"I wonder what his game is," said I. "The disguise suggests that he is on the look-out for somebody who might know him, but apparently that somebody has not turned up yet. At any rate, he doesn't seem to be watching anybody in particular."

"No," said Thorndyke. "But there is somebody whom he seems rather to avoid watching. Those two men at the table in front of ours are in his direct line of vision, but he hasn't looked at them once since he sat down, though I noticed that he gave them one quick glance before he selected his table. I wonder if he has observed us. Probably not, as we have the strong light of the window behind us and his attention is otherwise occupied."

192

I looked at the two men and from them to the detective, and I judged that my friend was right. On the inspector's table was a good-sized fern in an ornamental pot, and this he had moved so that it was directly between him and the two strangers, to whom he must have been practically invisible, and now I could see that he did, in fact, steal an occasional glance at them over the edge of the menu card. Moreover, as their meal drew to an end, he hastily finished his own and beckoned to the waiter to bring the bill.

"We may as well wait and see them off," said Thorndyke, who had already settled our account. "Badger always interests me. He is so ingenious and he has such shockingly bad luck."

We had not long to wait. The two men rose from the table and walked slowly to the door, where they paused to light their cigars before going out. Then Badger rose, with his back towards them and his eyes on the mirror opposite, and as they went out, he snatched up his hat and stick and followed. Thorndyke looked at me inquiringly.

"Do we indulge in the pleasures of the chase?" he asked, and as I replied in the affirmative, we, too, made our way out and started in the wake of the inspector.

As we followed Badger at a discreet distance, we caught an occasional glimpse of the quarry ahead, whose proceedings evidently caused the inspector some embarrassment, for they had a way of stopping suddenly to elaborate some point that they were discussing, whereby it became necessary for the detective to drop farther in the rear than was quite safe, in view of the rather crowded state of the pavement. On one of these occasions, when the older man was apparently delivering himself of some excruciating joke, they both turned suddenly and looked back, the joker pointing to some object on the opposite side of the road. Several people turned to see what was being pointed at and, of course, the inspector had to turn, too, to avoid being recognised. At this moment the two men popped into an entry, and when the inspector once more turned they were gone.

As soon as he missed them, Badger started forward almost at a run, and presently halted at the large entry of the Celestial Bank Chambers, into which he peered eagerly. Then, apparently sighting his quarry, he darted in, and we quickened our pace and followed. Halfway down the long hall we saw him standing at the door of a lift, frantically pressing the call-button.

"Poor Badger!" chuckled Thorndyke, as we walked past him unobserved. "His usual luck! He will hardly run them to earth now in this enormous building. We may as well go through to the Blenheim Street entrance."

We pursued our way along the winding corridor and were close to the entrance when I noticed two men coming down the staircase that led to the ball.

"By Jingo! Here they are!" I exclaimed. "Shall we run back and give Badger the tip?"

Thorndyke hesitated. But it was too late. A taxi had just driven up and was discharging its fare. The younger man, catching the driver's eye, ran out and seized the door-handle, and when his companion had entered the cab, he gave an address to the driver and, stepping in quickly, slammed the door. As the cab moved off, Thorndyke pulled out his notebook and pencil and jotted down the number of the vehicle. Then we turned and retraced our steps, but when we reached the lift-door, the inspector had disappeared. Presumably, like the incomparable Tom Bowling, he had gone aloft.

"We must give it up, Jervis," said Thorndyke. "I will send him anonymously the number of the cab, and that is all we can do. But I am sorry for Badger."

With this we dismissed the incident from our minds – at least, I did, assuming that I had seen the last of the two strangers. Little did I suspect how soon and under what strange and tragic circumstances I should meet with them again!

It was about a week later that we received a visit from our old friend, Superintendent Miller of the Criminal Investigation Department. The passing years had put us on a footing of mutual trust and esteem, and the capable, straightforward detective officer was always a welcome visitor.

"I've just dropped in," said Miller, cutting off the end of the inevitable cigar, "to tell you about a rather queer case that we've got in hand. I know you are always interested in queer cases."

Thorndyke smiled blandly. He had heard that kind of preamble before, and he knew, as did I, that when Miller became communicative we could safely infer that the Millerian bark was in shoal water.

"It is a case," the superintendent continued, "of a very special brand of crook. Actually there is a gang, but it is the managing director that we have particularly got our eye on."

"Is he a regular 'habitual', then?" asked Thorndyke.

"Well," replied Miller, "as to that, I can't positively say. The fact is that we haven't actually seen the man to be sure of him."

"I see," said Thorndyke, with a grim smile. "You mean to say that you have got your eye on the place where he isn't."

"At the present moment," Miller admitted, "that is the literal fact. We have lost sight of the man we suspected, but we hope to pick him up again presently. We want him badly, and his pals too. It is probably quite a small gang, but they are mighty fly, a lot too smart to be at large. And they'll take some catching, for there is someone running the concern with a good deal more brains than crooks usually have."

"What is their lay?" I asked.

"Burglary," he replied. "Jewels and plate, but principally jewels, and the special feature of their work is that the swag disappears completely every time. None of the stuff has ever been traced. That is what drew our attention to them. After each robbery we made a round of all the fences, but there was not a sign. The stuff seemed to have vanished into smoke. Now that is very awkward. If you never see the men and you can't trace the stuff, where are you? You've got nothing to go on."

"But you seem to have got a clue of some kind." I said.

"Yes. There isn't a lot in it, but it seemed worth following up. One of our men happened to travel down to Colchester with a certain man, and when he came back two days later, he noticed this same man on the platform at Colchester and saw him get out at Liverpool Street. In the interval there had been a jewel robbery at Colchester. Then there was a robbery at Southampton, and our man went at once to Waterloo and saw all the trains in. On the second day, behold! The Colchester sportsman turns up at the barrier, so our man, who had a special taxi waiting, managed to track him home and afterwards got some particulars about him. He is a chap named Shemmonds, belongs to a firm of outside brokers. But nobody seems to know much about him and he doesn't put in much time at the office.

"Well, then, Badger took him over and shadowed him for a day or two, but just as things were looking interesting, he slipped off the hook. Badger followed him to a restaurant and, through the glass door, saw him go up to an elderly man at a table and shake hands with him. Then he took a chair at the table himself, so Badger popped in and took a seat near them where he could keep them in view. They went out together and Badger followed them, but he lost them in the Celestial Bank Chambers. They went up in the lift just before he could get to the door and that was the last he saw of them. But we have ascertained that they left the building in a taxi and that the taxi set them down at Great Turnstile."

"It was rather smart of you to trace the cab," Thorndyke remarked.

"You've got to keep your eyes skinned in our line of business," said Miller. "But now we come to the real twister. From the time those two men went down Great Turnstile, nobody has set eyes on either of them. They seem to have vanished into thin air."

"You found out who the other man was, then?" said I.

195

"Yes. The restaurant manager knew him, an old chap named Luttrell. And we knew him, too, because he has a thumping burglary insurance, and when he goes out of town he notifies his company, and they make arrangements with us to have the premises watched."

"What is Luttrell?" I asked.

"Well, he is a bit of a mug, I should say – at least that's his character in the trade. Goes in for being a dealer in jewels and antiques, but he'll buy anything – furniture, pictures, plate, any blooming thing. Does it for a hobby, the regular dealers say. Likes the sport of bidding at the sales. But the knock-out men hate him, never know what he's going to do. Must have private means, for though he doesn't often drop money, he can't make much. He's no salesman. It is the buying that he seems to like. But he is a regular character, full of cranks and oddities. His rooms in Thavies Inn look like the British Museum gone mad. He has got electric alarms from all the doors up to his bedroom and the strong-room in his office is fitted with a puzzle lock instead of keys."

"That doesn't seem very safe," I remarked.

"It is," said Miller. "This one has fifteen alphabets. One of our men has calculated that it has about forty billion changes. No one is going to work that out, and there are no keys to get lost. But it is that strong-room that is worrying us, as well as the old joker himself. The Lord knows how much valuable stuff there is in it. What we are afraid of is that Shemmonds may have made away with the old chap and be lying low, waiting to swoop down on that strong-room."

"But you said that Luttrell goes away sometimes," said I.

"Yes, but then he always notifies his insurance company and he seals up his strong-room with a tape round the door-handle and a great seal on the door-post. This time he hasn't notified the company and the door isn't sealed. There's a seal on the door-post – left from last time, I expect – but only the cut ends of tape. I got the caretaker to let me see the place this morning and, by the way, Doctor, I have taken a leaf out of your book. I always carry a bit of squeezing wax in my pocket now and a little box of French chalk. Very handy they are, too. As I had 'em with me this morning, I took a squeeze of the seal. May want it presently for identification."

He brought out of his pocket a small tin box from which he carefully extracted an object wrapped in tissue paper. When the paper had been tenderly removed there was revealed a lump of moulding wax, one side of which was flattened and bore a sunk design.

"It's quite a good squeeze," said Miller, handing it to Thorndyke. "I dusted the seal with French chalk so that the wax shouldn't stick to it."

My colleague examined the "squeeze" through his lens, and passing it and the lens to me, asked, "Has this been photographed, Miller?"

"No," was the reply, "but it ought to be before it gets damaged."

"It ought, certainly," said Thorndyke, "if you value it. Shall I get Polton to do it now?"

The superintendent accepted the offer gratefully and Thorndyke accordingly took the squeeze up to the laboratory, where he left it for our assistant to deal with. When he returned, Miller remarked, "It is a baffling case, this. Now that Shemmonds has dropped out of sight, there is nothing to go on and nothing to do but wait for something else to happen – another burglary or an attempt on the strong-room."

"Is it clear that the strong-room has not been opened?" asked Thorndyke.

"No, it isn't," replied Miller. "That's part of the trouble. Luttrell has disappeared and he may be dead. If he is, Shemmonds will probably have been through his pockets. Of course there is no strong-room key. That is one of the advantages of a puzzle lock. But it is quite possible that Luttrell may have kept a note of the combination and carried it about him. It would have been risky to trust entirely to memory. And he would have had the keys of the office about him. Any one who had those could have slipped in during business hours without much difficulty. Luttrell's premises are empty, but there are people in and out all day going to the other offices. Our man can't follow them all in. I suppose you can't make any suggestion, Doctor?"

"I am afraid I can't," answered Thorndyke. "The case is so very much in the air. There is nothing against Shemmonds but bare suspicion. He has disappeared only in the sense that you have lost sight of him, and the same is true of Luttrell – though there is an abnormal element in his case. Still, you could hardly get a search-warrant on the facts that are known at present."

"No," Miller agreed, "they certainly would not authorise us to break open the strong-room, and nothing short of that would be much use."

Here Polton made his appearance with the wax squeeze in a neat little box such as jewellers use.

"I've got two enlarged negatives," said he, "nice clear ones. How many prints shall I make for Mr. Miller?"

"Oh, one will do, Mr. Polton," said the superintendent. "If I want any more I'll ask you." He took up the little box and, slipping it in his pocket, rose to depart. "I'll let you know, Doctor, how the case goes on, and perhaps you wouldn't mind turning it over a bit in the interval. Something might occur to you."

197

Thorndyke promised to think over the case, and when we had seen the superintendent launched down the stairs, we followed Polton up to the laboratory, where we each picked up one of the negatives and examined it against the light. I had already identified the seal by its shape – a *vesica piscis* or boat-shape – with the one that I had seen on Mr. Luttrell's finger. Now, in the photograph, enlarged three diameters, I could clearly make out the details. The design was distinctive and curious rather than elegant. The two triangular spaces at the ends were occupied respectively by a *memento mori* and a winged hour-glass and the central portion was filled by a long inscription in Roman capitals, of which I could at first make nothing.

"Do you suppose this is some kind of cryptogram?" I asked.

"No," Thorndyke replied. "I imagine the words were run together merely to economise space. This is what I make of it."

He held the negative in his left hand, and with his right wrote down in pencil on a slip of paper the following four lines of doggerel verse,

> *Eheu alas how fast the dam fugaces*
> *Labuntur anni especially in the cases*
> *Of poor old blokes like you and me Posthumus*
> *Who only wait for vermes to consume us.*

"Well," I exclaimed, "it is a choice specimen, one of old Luttrell's merry conceited jests, I take it. But the joke was hardly worth the labour of engraving on a seal."

"It is certainly a rather mild jest," Thorndyke admitted. "But there may be something more in it than meets the eye."

He looked at the inscription reflectively and appeared to read it through once or twice. Then he replaced the negative in the drying rack and, picking up the paper, slipped it into his pocket-book.

"I don't quite see," said I, "why Miller brought this case to us or what he wants you to think over. In fact, I don't see that there is a case at all."

"It is a very shadowy case," Thorndyke admitted. "Miller has done a good deal of guessing, and so has Badger, and it may easily turn out that they have found a mare's nest. Nevertheless there is something to think about."

"As, for instance – ?"

"Well, Jervis, you saw the men, you saw how they behaved, you have heard Miller's story, and you have seen Mr. Luttrell's seal. Put all those data together and you have the material for some very interesting speculation, to say the least. You might even carry it beyond speculation."

I did not pursue the subject, for I knew that when Thorndyke used the word "speculation", nothing would induce him to commit himself to an opinion. But later, bearing in mind the attention that he had seemed to bestow on Mr. Luttrell's schoolboy verses, I got a print from the negative and studied the foolish lines exhaustively. But if it had any hidden meaning – and I could imagine no reason for supposing that it had – that meaning remained hidden, and the only conclusion at which I could arrive was that a man of Luttrell's age might have known better than to write such nonsense.

The superintendent did not leave the matter long in suspense. Three days later he paid us another visit. and half-apologetically reopened the subject.

"I am ashamed to come badgering you like this," he said, "but I can't get this case out of my head. I've a feeling that we ought to get a move of some kind on. And, by the way – though that is nothing to do with it – I've copied out the stuff on that seal and I can't make any sense of it. What the deuce are *fugaces*? I suppose '*vermes*' are worms, though I don't see why he spelt it that way."

"The verses," said Thorndyke, "are apparently a travesty of a Latin poem, one of the Odes of Horace which begins:

Eheu fugaces, Postume, Postume, Labuntur anni

"which means, in effect, '*Alas! Postume, the flying years slip by*'."

"Well," said Miller, "any fool knows that – any middle-aged fool, at any rate. No need to put it into Latin. However, it's of no consequence. To return to this case, I've got an authority to look over Luttrell's premises – not to pull anything about, you know, just to look round. I called in on my way here to let the caretaker know that I should be coming in later. I thought that perhaps you might like to come with me. I wish you would, Doctor. You've got such a knack of spotting things that other people overlook."

He looked wistfully at Thorndyke, and as the latter was considering the proposal, he added, "The caretaker mentioned a rather odd circumstance. It seems that he keeps an eye on the electric meters in the building and that he has noticed a leakage of current in Mr. Luttrell's. It is only a small leak, about thirty watts an hour. But he can't account for it in any way. He has been right through the premises to see if any lamp has been left on in any of the rooms. But all the switches are off everywhere, and it can't be a short circuit. Funny, isn't it?"

It was certainly odd, but there seemed to me nothing in it to account for the expression of suddenly awakened interest that I detected in Thorndyke's face. However, it evidently had some special significance for him, for he asked almost eagerly "When are you making your inspection?"

"I am going there now," replied Miller, and he added coaxingly, "Couldn't you manage to run round with me?"

Thorndyke stood up. "Very well," said he. "Let us go together. You may as well come, too, Jervis, if you can spare an hour."

I agreed readily, for my colleague's hardly disguised interest in the inspection suggested a definite problem in his mind, and we at once issued forth and made our way by Mitre Court and Fetter Lane to the abode of the missing dealer, an old-fashioned house near the end of Thavies Inn.

"I've been over the premises once," said Miller, as the caretaker appeared with the keys, "and I think we had better begin the regular inspection with the offices. We can examine the stores and living-rooms afterwards."

We accordingly entered the outer office, and as this was little more than a waiting-room, we passed through into the private office, which had the appearance of having been used also as a sitting-room or study. It was furnished with an easy-chair, a range of book-shelves, and a handsome bureau book-case, while in the end wall was the massive iron door of the strong-room. On this, as the chief object of interest, we all bore down, and the superintendent expounded its peculiarities.

"It is quite a good idea," said he, "this letter-lock. There's no keyhole – though a safe-lock is pretty hopeless to pick even if there was a keyhole – and no keys to get lost. As to guessing what the 'open sesame' may be – well, just look at it. You could spend a lifetime on it and be no forrader."

The puzzle lock was contained in the solid iron door post, through a slot in which a row of fifteen A's seemed to grin defiance on the would-be safe-robber. I put my finger on the milled edges of one or two of the letters and rotated the discs, noticing how easily and smoothly they turned.

"Well," said Miller, "it's no use fumbling with that. I'm just going to have a look through his ledger and see who his customers were. The book-case is unlocked. I tried it last time. And we'd better leave this as we found it."

He put back the letters that I had moved, and turned away to explore the book-case, and as the letter-lock appeared to present nothing but an insoluble riddle, I followed him, leaving Thorndyke earnestly gazing at the meaningless row of letters.

The superintendent glanced back at him with an indulgent smile.

"The doctor is going to work out the combination," he chuckled. "Well, well. There are only forty billion changes and he's a young man for his age."

With this encouraging comment, he opened the glass door of the book-case, and reaching down the ledger, laid it on the desk-like slope of the bureau.

"It is a poor chance," said he, opening the ledger at the index, "but some of these people may be able to give us a hint where to look for Mr. Luttrell, and it is worth while to know what sort of business he did."

He ran his finger down the list of names and had just turned to the account of one of the customers when we were startled by a loud click from the direction of the strong-room. We both turned sharply and beheld Thorndyke grasping the handle of the strong-room door, and I saw with amazement that the door was now slightly ajar.

"God!" exclaimed Miller, shutting the ledger and starting forward, "he's got it open!" He strode over to the door, and directing an eager look at the indicator of the lock, burst into a laugh. "Well, I'm hanged!" he exclaimed. "Why, it was unlocked all the time! To think that none of us had the sense to tug the handle! But isn't it just like old Luttrell to have a fool's answer like that to the blessed puzzle!"

I looked at the indicator, not a little astonished to observe the row of fifteen A's, which apparently formed the key combination. It may have been a very amusing joke on Mr. Luttrell's part, but it did not look very secure. Thorndyke regarded us with an inscrutable glance and still grasped the handle, holding the door a bare half-inch open.

"There is something pushing against the door," said he. "Shall I open it?

"May as well have a look at the inside," replied Miller. Thereupon Thorndyke released the handle and quickly stepped aside. The door swung slowly open and the dead body of a man fell out into the room and rolled over on to its back.

"Mercy on us!" gasped Miller, springing back hastily and staring with horror and amazement at the grim apparition. "That is not Luttrell." Then, suddenly starting forward and stooping over the dead man, he exclaimed, "Why, it is Shemmonds. So that is where he disappeared to. I wonder what became of Luttrell?"

"There is somebody else in the strong-room," said Thorndyke, and now, peering in through the doorway, I perceived a dim light, which seemed to come from a hidden recess, and by which I could see a pair of feet projecting round the corner. In a moment Miller had sprung in, and I followed. The strong-room was L-shaped in plan, the arm of the L formed by a narrow passage at right angles to the main room. At the end of this a single small electric bulb was burning, the light of which showed the body of an elderly man stretched on the floor of the passage. I recognised him instantly in spite of the dimness of the light and the disfigurement caused by a ragged wound on the forehead.

"We had better get him out of this," said Miller, speaking in a flurried tone, partly due to the shock of the horrible discovery and partly to the accompanying physical unpleasantness, "and then we will have a look round, This wasn't just a mere robbery. We are going to find things out."

With my help he lifted Luttrell's corpse and together we carried it out, laying it on the floor of the room at the farther end, to which we also dragged the body of Shemmonds.

"There is no mystery as to how it happened," I said, after a brief inspection of the two corpses. "Shemmonds evidently shot the old man from behind with the pistol close to the back of the head. The hair is all scorched round the wound of entry and the bullet came out at the forehead."

"Yes," agreed Miller, "that is all clear enough. But the mystery is why on earth Shemmonds didn't let himself out. He must have known that the door was unlocked. Yet instead of turning the handle, he must have stood there like a fool, battering at the door with his fists. Just look at his hands."

"The further mystery," said Thorndyke who, all this time, had been making a minute examination of the lock both front without and within, "is how the door came to be shut. That is quite a curious problem."

"Quite," agreed Miller. "But it will keep. And there is a still more curious problem inside there. There is nearly all the swag from that Colchester robbery. Looks as if Luttrell was in it."

Half reluctantly he re-entered the strong-room and Thorndyke and I followed. Near the angle of the passage he stooped to pick up an automatic pistol and a small, leather book, which he opened and looked into by the light of the lamp. At the first glance he uttered an exclamation and shut the book with a snap.

"Do you know what this is?" he asked, holding it out to us. "It is the nominal roll, address book, and journal of the gang. We've got them in the hollow of our hand, and it is dawning upon me that old Luttrell was the managing director whom I have been looking for so long. Just run your eyes along those shelves. That's loot, every bit of it. I can identify the articles from the lists that I made out."

He stood looking gloatingly along the shelves with their burden of jewellery, plate and other valuables. Then his eye lighted on a drawer in the end wall just under the lamp, an iron drawer with a disproportionately large handle and bearing a very legible label inscribed "*Unmounted Stones*".

"We'll have a look at his stock of unmounted gems," said Miller, and with that he bore down on the drawer, and seizing the handle, gave a vigorous pull. "Funny," said he. "It isn't locked, but something seems to be holding it back."

He planted his foot on the wall and took a fresh purchase on the handle. "Wait a moment, Miller," said Thorndyke, but even as he spoke, the superintendent gave a mighty heave, the drawer came out a full two feet, there was a loud click, and a moment later the strong-room door slammed.

"Good God!" exclaimed Miller, letting go the drawer, which immediately slid in with another click. "What was that?"

"That was the door shutting," replied Thorndyke. "Quite a clever arrangement, like the mechanism of a repeater watch. Pulling out the drawer wound up and released a spring that shut the door. Very ingenious."

"But," gasped Miller, turning an ashen face to my colleague, "we're shut in."

"You are forgetting," said I – a little nervously, I must admit – "that the lock is as we left it."

The superintendent laughed, somewhat hysterically. "What a fool I am!" said he. "As bad as Shemmonds. Still we may as well – " Here he started along the passage and I heard him groping his way to the door, and later heard the handle turn. Suddenly the deep silence of the tomb-like chamber was rent by a yell of terror.

"The door won't move! It's locked fast!"

On this I rushed along the passage with a sickening fear at my heart. And even as I ran, there rose before my eyes the horrible vision of the corpse with the battered hands that had fallen out when we opened the door of this awful trap. He had been caught as we were caught. How soon might it not be that some stranger would be looking in on our corpses.

In the dim twilight by the door I found Miller clutching the handle and shaking it like a madman. His self-possession was completely shattered. Nor was my own condition much better. I flung my whole weight on the door in the faint hope that the lock was not really closed, but the massive iron structure was as immovable as a stone wall. I was nevertheless gathering myself up for a second charge when I heard Thorndyke's voice close behind me.

"That is no use, Jervis. The door is locked. But there is nothing to worry about."

As he spoke, there suddenly appeared a bright circle of light from the little electric lamp that he always carried in his pocket. Within the circle, and now clearly visible, was a second indicator of the puzzle lock on the inside of the door-post. Its appearance was vaguely reassuring, especially in conjunction with Thorndyke's calm voice, and it evidently appeared so to Miller, for he remarked, almost in his natural tones,

"But it seems to be unlocked still. There is the same row of A's it showed when we came in."

It was perfectly true. The slot of the letter-lock still showed the range of fifteen A's, just as it had when the door was open. Could it be that the lock was a dummy and that there was some other means of opening the door? I was about to put this question to Thorndyke when he put the lamp into my hand and, gently pushing me aside, stepped up to the indicator.

"Keep the light steady, Jervis," said he, and forthwith he began to manipulate the milled edges of the letter discs, beginning, as I noticed, at the right or reverse end of the slot and working backwards. I watched him with feverish interest and curiosity, as also did Miller, looking to see some word of fifteen letters develop in the slot. Instead of which, I saw, to my amazement and bewilderment my colleague's finger transforming the row of A's into a succession of M's, which, however, were presently followed by an L and some X's. When the row was completed it looked like some remote, antediluvian date set down in Roman numerals.

"Try the handle now, Miller," said Thorndyke.

The superintendent needed no second bidding. Snatching at the handle, he turned it and bore heavily on the door. Almost instantly a thin line of light appeared at the edge, there was a sharp click, and the door swung right open. We fell out immediately – at least the superintendent and I did – thankful to find ourselves outside and alive. But, as we emerged, we both became aware of a man, white-faced and horror-stricken of aspect, stooping over the two corpses at the other end of the room. Our appearance was so sudden and unexpected – for the massive solidity of the safe-door had rendered our movements inaudible outside – that, for a moment or two, he stood immovable, staring at us, wild-eyed and open-mouthed. Then, suddenly, he sprang up erect and, darting to the door, opened it, and rushed out with Miller close on his heels.

He did not get very far. Following the superintendent, I saw the fugitive wriggling in the embrace of a tall man on the pavement, who, with Miller's assistance, soon had a pair of handcuffs snapped on the man's wrists and then departed with his captive in search of a cab.

"That's one of 'em, I expect," said Miller, as we returned to the office, then, as his glance fell on the open strong-room door, he mopped his face with his handkerchief. "That door gives me the creeps to look at it," said he. "Lord I what a shake-up that was! I've never had such a scare in my life. When I heard that door shut and I remembered how that poor devil, Shemmonds, came tumbling out – phoo!" He wiped his brow again and, walking towards the strong-room door, asked, "By the way, what was the magic word after all?" He stepped up to the indicator and, after a quick glance, looked round at me in surprise. "Why!" he exclaimed, "blow me if it isn't a row of A's still! But the doctor altered it, didn't he?"

At this moment Thorndyke appeared from the strong-room, where he had apparently been conducting some explorations, and to him the superintendent turned for an explanation.

"It is an ingenious device," said he. "In fact, the whole strong-room is a monument of ingenuity, somewhat misapplied, but perfectly effective, as Mr. Shemmonds's corpse testifies. The key-combination is a number expressed in Roman numerals, but the lock has a fly-back mechanism which acts as soon as the door begins to open. That was how Shemmonds was caught. He, no doubt purposely, avoided watching Luttrell set the lock – or else Luttrell didn't let him – but as he went in with his intended victim, he looked at the indicator and saw the row of A's, which he naturally assumed to be the key. Then, when he tried to let himself out, of course, the lock wouldn't open."

"It is rather odd that he didn't try some other combinations," said I.

"He probably did," replied Thorndyke, "but when they failed he would naturally come back to the A's, which he had seen when the door was open. This is how it works."

He shut the door, and then, closely watched by the superintendent and me, turned the milled rims of the letter-discs until the indicator showed a row of numerals thus, *MMMMMMMCCCLXXXV*. Grasping the handle, he turned it and gave a gentle pull, when the door began to open. But the instant it started from its bed, there was a loud click and all the letters of the indicator flew back to A.

"Well, I'm jiggered!" exclaimed Miller. "It must have been an awful suck-in for that poor blighter, Shemmonds. Took me in, too. I saw those A's and the door open, and I thought I knew all about it. But what beats me, Doctor, is how you managed to work it out. I can't see what you had to go on. Would it be allowable to ask how it was done?"

"Certainly," replied Thorndyke "but we had better defer the explanation. You have got those two bodies to dispose of and some other matters, and we must get back to our chambers. I will write down the key-combination, in case you want it, and then you must come and see us and let us know what luck you have had."

He wrote the numerals on a slip of paper, and when he had handed it to the superintendent, we took our leave.

"I find myself," said I, as we walked home, "in much the same position as Miller. I don't see what you had to go on. It is clear to me that you not only worked out the lock-combination – from the seal inscription, as I assume – but that you identified Luttrell as the director of the gang. I don't, in the least, understand how you did it."

"And yet, Jervis," said he, "it was an essentially simple case. If you review it and cast up the items of evidence, you will see that we really had all the facts. The problem was merely to co-ordinate them and extract their significance. Take first the character of Luttrell. We saw the man in company with another, evidently a fairly intimate acquaintance. They were being shadowed by a detective, and it is pretty clear that they detected the sleuth, for they shook him off quite neatly. Later, we learn from Miller that one of these men is suspected to be a member of a firm of swell burglars and that the other is a well-to-do, rather eccentric, and very miscellaneous dealer, who has a strong-room fitted with a puzzle lock. I am astonished that the usually acute Miller did not notice how well Luttrell fitted the part of the managing director whom he was looking for. Here was a dealer who bought and sold all sorts of queer but valuable things, who must have had unlimited facilities for getting rid of stones, bullion and silver, and who used a puzzle lock. Now, who uses a puzzle lock? No one, certainly, who can conveniently use a key. But to the manager of a gang of thieves it would be a valuable safeguard, for he might at any moment be robbed of his keys, and perhaps made away with. But he could not be robbed of the secret passwords and his possession of it would be a security against murder. So you see that the simple probabilities pointed to Luttrell as the head of the gang.

"And now consider the problem of the lock. First, we saw that Luttrell wore on his left hand a huge, cumbrous seal ring, that he carried a Coddington lens on his watch-guard, and a small electric lamp in his pocket. That told us very, little. But when Miller told us about the lock and showed us the squeeze of the seal, and when we saw that the seal bore a long inscription in minute lettering, a connection began to appear. As Miller justly observed, no man – especially no elderly man – could trust the key combination exclusively to his memory. He would carry about him some record to which he could refer in case his memory failed him. But that record would hardly be one that anybody could read, or the secrecy and safety of the lock would be gone. It would probably be some kind of cryptogram, and when we saw this inscription and considered it in conjunction with the lens and the lamp, it seemed highly probable that the key-combination was contained in the inscription, and that probability was further increased when we saw the nonsensical doggerel of which the inscription was made up. The suggestion was that the verses had been made for some purpose independent of their sense. Accordingly I gave the inscription very careful consideration.

"Now we learned from Miller that the puzzle lock had fifteen letters. The key might be one long word, such as 'superlativeness', a number of short words, or some chemical or other formula. Or it was possible that it might be of the nature of a chronogram. I have never heard of chronograms being used for secret records or messages, but it has often occurred to me that they would be extremely suitable. And this was an exceptionally suitable case."

"Chronogram," said I. "Isn't that something connected with medals?"

"They have often been used on medals," he replied. "In effect, a chronogram is an inscription some of the letters of which form a date connected with the subject of the inscription. Usually the date letters are cut larger than the others for convenience in reading, but, of course, this is not essential. The principle of a chronogram is this. The letters of the Roman alphabet are of two kinds, those that are simply letters and nothing else, and those that are numerals as well as letters. The numeral letters are *M* equals a thousand, *D* five-hundred, *C* one-hundred, *L* fifty, *X* ten, *V* five, and *I* equals one. Now, in deciphering a chronogram, you pick out all the numeral letters and add them up without regard to their order. The total gives you the date.

"Well, as I said, it occurred to me that this might be of the nature of a chronogram, but as the lock had letters and not figures, the number, if there was one, would have to be expressed in Roman numerals, and it would have to form a number of fifteen numeral letters. As it was thus quite easy to put my hypothesis to the test, I proceeded to treat the inscription as a chronogram and decipher it, and behold! It yielded a number of fifteen letters, which, of course, was as near certainty as was possible, short of actual experiment."

"Let us see how you did the decipherment," I said, as we entered our chambers and shut the door. I procured a large note-block and pencil and, laying them on the table, drew up two chairs.

"Now," said I, "fire away."

"Very well," he said. "We will begin by writing the inscription in proper chronogram form with the numeral letters double size and treating the *U*'s as *V*'s and the *W*'s as double *V*'s according to the rules."

Here he wrote out the inscription in Roman capitals thus,

eheV aLas hoVV fast the DaM fVgaCes
LabVntVr annI espeCIaLLy In the Cases
of poor oLD bLokes LIke yoV anD Me posthVMVs
VVho onLy VVaIt for VerMes to ConsVMe Vs.

"Now," said he, "let us make a column of each line and add them up, thus,

1. V=5, L=50, VV=10, D=500, M=1000, V=5, C=100 –
Total 1670

2. L=50, V=5, V=5, I=1, C=100, I=1, L=50, L=50, I=1,
C=100 – Total 363

3. L=50, D=500, L=50, L=50, I=1, V=5, D=500, M=1000,
V=5, M=1000, V=5 – Total 3166

4. VV=10, L=50, VV=10, I=1, V=5, M=1000, C=100, V=5,
M=1000, V=5 – Total 2186

"Now," he continued "we take the four totals and add them together, thus:"

1670+363+3166+2186 = 7385

" . . . and we get the grand total of seven-thousand-three-hundred-and-eighty-five and this, expressed in Roman numerals, is *MMMMMMMCCCLXXXV*. Here, then, is a number consisting of fifteen letters, the exact number of spaces in the indicator of the puzzle lock, and I repeat that this striking coincidence, added to, or rather multiplied into, the other probabilities, made it practically certain that this was the key-combination. It remained only to test it by actual experiment."

"By the way," said I, "I noticed that you perked up rather suddenly when Miller mentioned the electric meter."

"Naturally," he replied. "It seemed that there must be a small lamp switched on somewhere in the building, and the only place that had not been examined was the strong-room. But if there was a lamp alight there, someone had been in the strong-room. And, as, the only person who was known to be able to get in was missing, it seemed probable that he was in there still. But if he was, he was pretty certainly dead, and there was quite a considerable probability that someone else was in there with him, since his companion was missing, too, and both had disappeared at the same time. But I must confess that that spring drawer was beyond my expectations, though I suspected it as soon as I saw Miller pulling at it. Luttrell was an ingenious old rascal, he almost deserved a better fate. However, I expect his death will have delivered the gang into the hands of the police."

Events fell out as Thorndyke surmised. Mr. Luttrell's little journal, in conjunction with the confession of the spy who had been captured on the premises, enabled the police to swoop down on the disconcerted gang before any breath of suspicion had reached them, with the result that they are now secured in strong-rooms of another kind whereof the doors are fitted with appliances as effective as, though less ingenious than, Mr. Luttrell's puzzle lock.

The Green Check Jacket

The visits of our old friend, Mr. Brodribb, even when strictly professional, usually took the outward form of a friendly call. On the present occasion there was no such pretence. The old solicitor entered our chambers carrying a small suit-case (the stamped initials on which, "*R.M.*", I noticed, instantly attracted an inquisitive glance from Thorndyke, being obviously not Mr. Brodribb's own) which he placed on the table and then shook hands with an evident air of business.

"I have come, Thorndyke," he said, with unusual directness, "to ask your advice on a matter which is causing me some uneasiness. Do you know Reginald Merrill?"

"Slightly," was the reply. "I meet him occasionally in court and, of course, I know him as the author of that interesting book on prehistoric flint mines."

"Well," said Brodribb, "he has disappeared. He is missing. I don't like to use the expression, but when a responsible man is absent from his usual places of resort, when he apparently had no expectation of being so absent, and when he has made no provision for such absence, I think we may regard him as having disappeared in a legal sense. His absence calls for active inquiry."

"Undoubtedly," agreed Thorndyke, "and I take it that you are the person on whom the duty devolves?"

"I think so. I am his solicitor and the executor of his will – at least I believe so, and the only near relative of his whom I know is his nephew and heir, Ethelbert Crick, his sister's son. But Crick seems to have disappeared, too, and about the same time as Merrill. It is an extraordinary affair."

"You say that you believe you are Merrill's executor. Haven't you seen the will?"

"I have seen a will. I have it in my safe. But Merrill said he was going to draw up another, and he may have done so. But if he has, he will almost certainly have appointed me his executor, and I shall assume that he has and act accordingly."

"Was there any special reason for making a new will?" Thorndyke asked.

"Yes," replied Brodribb. "He has just come into quite a considerable fortune, and he was pretty well off before. Under the old will, practically the whole of his property went to Crick. There was a small bequest to a man named Samuel Horder, his cousin's son, and Horder was the alternative legatee if Crick should die before Merrill. Now, I understood Merrill to say that, in view of this extra fortune, he wished to do rather more for Horder, and I gathered that he proposed to divide the estate more or less equally between the two men. The whole estate was more than he thought necessary for Crick. And now, as we have cleared up the preliminaries, I will give you the circumstances of the disappearance.

"Last Wednesday, the fifth, I had a note from him saying that he would have some reports ready for me on the following day, but that he would be away from his office from 10:30 a.m. to about 6:30, and suggesting that I should send round in the evening if I wanted the papers particularly. Now it happened that my clerk, Page, had to go to a place near London Bridge on Thursday morning and, oddly enough, he saw Mr. Merrill come out of Edginton's, the ship-fitters, with a man who was carrying a largish hand-bag. There was nothing in it, of course, but Page is an observant man and he noticed Merrill's companion so far as to observe that he was wearing a Norfolk jacket of a greenish shepherd's plaid and a grey tweed hat. He also noted the time by the big clock in the street near to Edginton's – 11:46 – and that Merrill looked up at it, and that the two men then walked off rather quickly in the direction of the station. Well, in the evening, I sent Page round to Merrill's chambers in Figtree Court to get the papers. He arrived there just after 6:30, but he found the door shut, and though he rapped at the door on the chance that Merrill might have come in – he lives in the chambers adjoining the office – there was no answer. So he went for a walk round the Temple, deciding to return a little later.

"Well, he had gone as far as the cloisters and was loitering there to look in the window of the wig shop when he saw a man in a greenish shepherd's plaid jacket and a tweed hat coming up Pump Court. As the man approached Page thought he recognised him. In fact, he felt so sure that he stopped him and asked him if he knew what time Mr. Merrill would be home. But the man looked at him in astonishment. 'Merrill?' said he. 'I don't know anyone of that name.' Thereupon Page apologised and explained how he had been misled by the pattern and colour of the jacket.

"After walking about for nearly half-an-hour, Page went back to Merrill's chambers, but the door was shut and he could get no answer by rapping with his stick, so he scribbled a note and dropped it into the letter-box and came away. The next morning I sent him round again, but the chambers were still shut up, and they have been shut up ever since, and nothing whatever has been seen or heard of Merrill.

"On Saturday, thinking it possible that Crick might be able to give me some news of his uncle, I called at his lodgings, and then, to my astonishment, I learned that he also was missing. He had gone away early on Thursday morning, saying that he had to go on business to Rochester, and that he might not be home to dinner. But he never came home at all. I called again on Sunday evening and, as he had still not returned, I decided to take more active measures.

"This afternoon, immediately after lunch, I called at the Porter's Lodge and, having briefly explained the circumstances and who I was, asked the porter to bring the duplicate key – which he had for the laundress – and accompany me to Mr. Merrill's chambers to see if, by chance, the tenant might be lying in them dead or insensible. He assured me that this could not be the case, since he had given the key every morning to the laundress, who had, in fact, returned it to him only a couple of hours previously. Nevertheless, he took the key and looked up the laundress, who had rooms near the lodge, who was fortunately at home and who turned out to be a most respectable and intelligent elderly woman, and we went together to Merrill's chambers. The porter admitted us, and when we had been right through the set and ascertained definitely that Merrill was not there, he handed the key to the laundress, Mrs. Butler, and went away.

"When he was gone, I had a talk with Mrs. Butler, from which some rather startling facts transpired. It seemed that on Thursday, as Merrill was going to be out all day, she took the opportunity to have a grand clean-up of the chambers, to tidy up the lobby, and to look over the chests of drawers and the wardrobe and shake out and brush the clothes and see that no moths had got in. 'When I had finished,' she said, 'the place was like the inside of a band-box, just as he liked to see it.'

"'And, after all, Mrs. Butler,' said I, 'he never did see it.'

"'Oh, yes, he did,' says she. 'I don't know when he came in, but when I let myself in the next morning, I could see that he had been in since I left.'

"'How did you know that?' I asked.

"'Well,' says she, 'I left the carpet-sweeper standing against the wardrobe door. I remembered it after I left and would have gone back and moved it, but I had already handed the key in at the Porter's Lodge. But when I went in next morning it wasn't there. It had been moved into the corner by the fireplace. Then the looking-glass had been moved. I could see that, because, before I went away, I had tidied my hair by it, and being short, I had to tilt it to see my face in it. Now it was tilted to suit a tall person and I could not see myself in it. Then I saw that the shaving soap had been moved, and when I put it back in its place, I found it was damp. It wouldn't have kept damp for twenty-four hours at this time of year.' That was perfectly true, you know, Thorndyke."

"Perfectly," agreed Thorndyke, "that woman is an excellent observer."

"Well," continued Brodribb, "on this she examined the shaving soap and the sponge and found them both perceptibly damp. It appeared practically certain that Merrill had been in on the preceding evening and had shaved, but by way of confirmation, I suggested that she should look over his clothes and see whether he had changed any of his garments. She did so, beginning with those that were hanging in the wardrobe, which she took down one at a time. Suddenly she gave a cry of surprise, and I got a bit of a start myself when she handed out a greenish shepherd's plaid Norfolk jacket.

"'That,' she said, 'was not here when I brushed these clothes,' and it was obvious from its dusty condition that it could not have been, 'and,' she added, 'I have never seen it before to my knowledge, and I think I should have remembered it.' I asked her if there was any coat missing and she answered that she had brushed a grey tweed jacket that seemed to have disappeared.

"Well, it was a queer affair. The first thing to be done was to ascertain, if possible whether that jacket was or was not Merrill's. That, I thought, you would be able to judge better than I, so I borrowed his suit-case and popped the jacket into it, together with another jacket that was undoubtedly his, for comparison. Here is the suit-case and the two jackets are inside."

"It is really a question that could be better decided by a tailor," said Thorndyke. "The differences of measurement can't be great if they could both be worn by the same person. But we shall see." He rose, and having spread some sheets of newspaper over the table, opened the suit-case and took out the two jackets, which he laid out side by side. Then, with his spring-tape, he proceeded systematically to measure the two garments, entering each pair of measurements on a slip of paper divided into two columns. Mr. Brodribb and I watched him expectantly and compared the two sets of figures as they were written down, and very soon it became evident that they were, at least, not identical. At length Thorndyke laid down the tape, and picking up the paper, studied it closely.

"I think," he said, "we may conclude that these two jackets were not made for the same person. The differences are not great, but they are consistent. The elbow creases, for instance, agree with the total length of the sleeves. The owner of the green jacket has longer arms and a bigger span than Merrill, but his chest measurement is nearly two inches greater and he has much more sloping shoulders. He could hardly have buttoned Merrill's jacket."

"Then," said Brodribb, "the next question is, did Merrill come home in some other man's coat or did some other man enter his chambers? From what Page has told us it seems pretty evident that a stranger must have got into those chambers. But if that is so, the questions arise, What the deuce was the fellow's object in changing into Merrill's clothes and shaving? How did he get into Merrill's chambers? What was he doing there? What has become of Merrill? And what is the meaning of the whole affair?"

"To some of those questions," said Thorndyke, "the answers are fairly obvious. If we assume, as I do, that the owner of the green jacket is the man whom Page saw at London Bridge and afterwards in the cloisters, the reason for the change of garments becomes plain enough. Page told the man that he had identified him by this very distinctive jacket as the person with whom Merrill was last seen alive. Evidently that man's safety demanded that he should get rid of the incriminating jacket without delay. Then, as to his having shaved, did Page give you any description of the man?"

"Yes, he was a tallish man, about thirty-five, with a large dark moustache and a torpedo beard."

"Very well," said Thorndyke, "then we may say that the man who went into Merrill's chambers was a moustached bearded man in a green jacket and that the man who came out was a clean-shaved man in a grey jacket, whom Page himself would probably have passed without a second glance. That is clear enough. And as to how he got into the chambers, evidently he let himself in with Merrill's key, and if he did, I am afraid we can make a pretty shrewd guess as to what has become of Merrill, and only hope that we are guessing wrong. As to what this man was doing in those chambers and what is the meaning of the whole affair, that is a more difficult question. If the man had Merrill's latchkey, we may assume that he had the rest of Merrill's keys, that he had, in fact, free access to any locked receptacles in those chambers. The circumstances suggest that he entered the chambers for the purpose of getting possession of some valuable objects contained in them. Do you happen to know whether Merrill had any property of considerable value on the premises?

"I don't," replied Brodribb. "He had a safe, but I don't know what he kept in it. Principally documents, I should think. Certainly not money, in any considerable amounts. The only thing of value that I actually know of is the new will, and that would only be valuable in certain circumstances."

The abrupt and rather ambiguous conclusion of Mr. Brodribb's statement was not lost either on Thorndyke or on me. Apparently the cautious old lawyer had suddenly realised, as I had, that if anything had happened to Merrill, those "certain circumstances" had already come into being. From what he had told us it appeared that, under the new will, Crick stood to inherit a half of Mr. Merrill's fortune, whereas under the old will he stood to inherit nearly the whole. And it was a great fortune. The loss or destruction of the new will would be worth a good many thousand pounds to Mr. Crick.

"Well," said Brodribb, after a pause, "what is to be done? I suppose I ought to communicate with the police."

"You will have to, sooner or later," said Thorndyke, "but meanwhile, leave these two jackets – or, at least, the green one – with me for the present and let me see if I can extract any further information from it."

"You won't find anything in the pockets but dirt. I've tried them."

"I hope you left the dirt," said Thorndyke.

"I did," replied Brodribb, "excepting what came out on my fingers. Very well, I'll leave the coats with you for to-day, and I will see if I can get any further news of Crick from his landlady."

With this the old solicitor shook hands and went off with such an evident air of purpose that I remarked, "Brodribb is off to find out whether Mr. Crick was the proprietor of a green plaid Norfolk jacket."

Thorndyke smiled. "It was rather quaint," said he, "to see the sudden way in which he drew in his horns when the inwardness of the affair dawned on him. But we mustn't start with a preconceived theory. Our business is to get hold of some more facts. There is little enough to go on at present. Let us begin by having a good look at this green jacket."

He picked it up and carried it to the window, where we both looked it over critically.

"It is rather dusty," I remarked, "especially on the front, and there is a white mark on the middle button."

"Yes. Chalk, apparently, and if you look closely, there are white traces on the other buttons and on the front of the coat. The back is much less dusty."

As he spoke, Thorndyke turned the garment round, and then, from the side of the skirt, picked a small, hair-like object which he felt between his finger and thumb, looked at closely and handed to me.

"A bit of barley beard," said I, "and there are two more on the other side. He must have walked along a narrow path through a barley field – the state of the front of his coat almost suggests that he had crawled."

215

"Yes, it is earthy dust, but Polton's extractor will give us more information about that. We had better hand it over to him, but first we will go through the pockets in spite of Brodribb's discouragement."

"By Jove!" I exclaimed, as I thrust my hand into one of the side pockets, "he was right about the dirt. Look at this." I drew out my hand with a quite considerable pinch of dry earth and one or two little fragments of chalk. "It looks as if he had been crawling in loose earth."

"It does," Thorndyke agreed, inspecting his own "catch" – a pinch of reddish earth and a fragment of chalk of the size of a large pea. "The earth is very characteristic, this red-brown loam that you find overlying the chalk. All his outside pockets seem to have caught more or less of it. However, we can leave Polton to collect it and prepare it for examination. I'll take the coat up to him now, and while he is working at it I think I will walk round to Edginton's and see if I can pick up any further particulars."

He went up to the laboratory floor, where our assistant, Polton, carried on his curious and varied activities, and when he returned we sallied forth together. In Fleet Street we picked up a disengaged taxicab, by which we were whisked across Blackfriars Bridge and a few minutes later set down at the corner of Tooley Street. We made our way to the ship-chandler's shop, where Thorndyke proceeded to put a few discreet questions to the manager, who listened politely and with sympathetic interest.

"The difficulty is," said he, "that there were a good many gentlemen in here last Thursday. You say they came about 11:45. If you could tell me what they bought, we could look at the bill-duplicate book and that might help us."

"I don't actually know what they bought," said Thorndyke. "It might have been a length of rope – a rope, perhaps, say twelve or fourteen fathoms or perhaps more. But I may be wrong."

I stared at Thorndyke in amazement. Long as I known him, this extraordinary faculty of instantaneous induction always came on me as a fresh surprise. I had supposed that in this case we had absolutely nothing to go on, and yet here he was with at least a tentative suggestion before the inquiry appeared to have begun. And that suggestion was clear evidence that he had already arrived at a hypothetical solution of the mystery. I was still pondering on this astonishing fact when the manager approached with an open book and accompanied by an assistant.

"I see," said he, "that there is an entry, apparently about mid-day on Thursday, of the sale of a fifteen-fathom length of deep-sea lead-line, and my friend, here, remembers selling it."

216

"Yes," the assistant confirmed, "I remember it because he wanted to get it into his hand-bag, and it took the three of us to stuff it in. Thick lead-line is pretty stiff when it's new."

"Do you remember what these gentlemen were like and how they were dressed?"

"One was a rather elderly gentleman, clean-shaved, I think. The other I remember better because he had rather queer-looking eyes – very pale grey. He had a pointed beard and he wore a greenish check coat and a cloth hat. That's all I remember about him."

"It is more than most people would have remembered," said Thorndyke. "I am very much obliged to you, and I think I will ask you to let me have a fifteen-fathom length of that same lead-line."

By this time my capacity for astonishment was exhausted. What on earth could my colleague want with a deep-sea lead-line? But, after all, why not? If he had then and there purchased a Trotman's anchor, a shark-hook, and a set of International code signals, I should have been prepared to accept the proceeding without comment. Thorndyke was a law unto himself.

Nevertheless, as I walked homeward by his side, carrying the coil of rope, I continued to speculate on this singular case. Thorndyke had arrived at a hypothetical solution of Mr. Brodribb's problem, and it was evidently correct, so far, as the entry in the bill-book proved. But what was the connection between a dusty jacket and a length of thin rope? And why this particular length? I could make nothing of it. But I determined, as soon as we got home, to see what new facts Polton's activities had brought to light.

The results were disappointing. Polton's dust extractor had been busy, and the products in the form of tiny heaps of dust were methodically set out on a sheet of white paper, each little heap covered with a watch-glass and accompanied by its written particulars as to the part of the garment from which it had come. I examined a few samples under the microscope, but though curious and interesting, as all dust is, they showed nothing very distinctive. The dust might have come from anyone's coat. There was, of course, a good deal of yellowish sandy loam, a few particles of chalk, a quantity of fine ash, clinker, and particles of coal – railway dust from a locomotive – ordinary town and house dust, and some oddments such as pollen grains, including those of the sow-thistle, mallow, poppy, and valerian, and in one sample I found two scales from the wing of the common blue butterfly. That was all, and it told me nothing but that the owner of the coat had recently been in a chalk district and that he had taken a railway journey.

While I was working with the microscope, Polton was busy with an occupation that I did not understand. He had cemented the little pieces of chalk that we had found in the pockets to a plate of glass by means of pitch, and he was now brushing them under water with a soft brush and from time to time decanting the milky water into a tall sediment glass. Now, as most people know, chalk is largely composed of microscopic shells – *foraminifera* – which can be detached by gently brushing the chalk under water. But what was the object? There was no doubt that the material was chalk, and we knew that *foraminifera* were there. Why trouble to prove what is common knowledge? I questioned Polton, but he knew nothing of the purpose of the investigation. He merely beamed on me like a crinkly old graven image and went on brushing. I dipped up a sample of the white sediment and examined it under the microscope. Of course there were *foraminifera*, and very beautiful they were. But what about it? The whole proceeding looked purposeless. And yet I knew that it was not. Thorndyke was the last man in the world to expend his energies in flogging a dead horse.

Presently he came up to the laboratory and, when he had looked at the dust specimens and confirmed my opinion of them, he fell to work on the chalk sediment. Having prepared a number of slides, he sat down at the microscope with a sharp pencil and a block of smooth paper with the apparent purpose of cataloguing and making drawings of the *foraminifera*. And at this task I left him while I went forth to collect some books that I had ordered from a bookseller in the Charing Cross Road.

When I returned with my purchases about an hour later, I found him putting back in a press a portfolio of large-scale Ordnance Maps of Kent which he had apparently been consulting, and I noticed on the table his sheet of drawings and a monograph of the fossil *foraminifera*.

"Well, Thorndyke," I said cheerfully, "I suppose this time, you know exactly what has become of Merrill."

"I can guess," he replied, "and so can you. But the actual data are distressingly vague. We have certain indications, as you will have noticed. The trouble will be to bring them to a focus. It is a case for constructive imagination on the one hand and the method of exclusion on the other. I shall make a preliminary circle-round to-morrow."

"Meaning by that?"

"I have a hypothesis. It is probably wrong. If it is, we must try another, and yet another. Every time we fail we shall narrow the field of inquiry until by eliminating one possibility after another, we may hope to arrive at the solution. My first essay will take me down into Kent."

"You are not going into those wild regions alone, Thorndyke," said I. "You will need my protection and support, to say nothing of my invaluable advice. I presume you realise that?"

"Undoubtedly." he replied gravely. "I was reckoning on a two-man expedition. Besides, you are as much interested in the case as I am. And now, let us go forth and dine and fortify ourselves for the perils of to-morrow."

In the course of dinner I led the conversation to the products of Polton's labours and remarked upon their very indefinite significance, but Thorndyke was more indefinite still, as he usually was in cases of a highly speculative character.

"You are expecting too much from Polton," he said with a smile. "This is not a matter of *foraminifera* or pollen or butterfly-scales, they are only items of circumstantial evidence. What we have to do is to consider the whole body of facts in our possession, what Brodribb has told us, what we know for ourselves and what we have ascertained by investigation. The case is still very much in the air, but it is not so vague as you seem to imply."

This was all I could get out of him, and as the "whole body of facts" yielded no suggestion at all to me, I could only possess my soul in patience and hope for some enlightenment on the morrow.

About a quarter-to-eleven on the following morning, while Thorndyke was giving final instructions to Polton and I was speculating on the contents of the suit-case that was going to accompany us, footsteps became audible on our stairs. Their crescendo terminated in a flourish on our little brass knocker which I recognised as Brodribb's knock. I accordingly opened the door, and in walked our old friend. His keen blue eye took in at once our informal raiment and the suit-case and lighted up with something like curiosity.

"Off on an expedition?" he asked.

"Yes," replied Thorndyke. "A little trip down into Kent. Gravesend, in fact."

"Gravesend," repeated Brodribb with further awakened interest. "That was rather a favourite resort of poor Merrill's. By the way, your expedition is not connected with his disappearance, I suppose?"

"As a matter of fact it is," replied Thorndyke. "Just a tentative exploration, you know."

"I know," said Brodribb, all agog now, "and I'm coming with you. I've got a clear day and I'm not going to take a refusal."

"No refusal was contemplated," rejoined Thorndyke. "You'll probably waste a day, but we shall benefit by your society. Polton will let your clerk know that you haven't absconded, or you can look in at the office yourself. We have plenty of time."

Brodribb chose the latter plan, which enabled him to exchange his tall hat and morning coat for a soft hat and jacket, and we accordingly made our way to Charing Cross via Lincoln's Inn, where Brodribb's office was situated. I noticed that Brodribb, with his customary discretion, asked no questions, though he must have observed, as I had, the striking fact that Thorndyke had in some way connected Merrill with Gravesend, and in fact with the exception of Brodribb's account of his failure to get any news of Mr. Crick, no reference was made to the nature of our expedition until we alighted at our destination.

On emerging from the station, Thorndyke turned to the left and led the way out of the approach into a street, on the opposite side of which a rather grimy statue of Queen Victoria greeted us with a supercilious stare. Here we turned to the south along a prosperous thoroughfare, and presently crossing a main road, followed its rather sordid continuation until the urban squalor began to be tempered by traces of rusticity, and the suburb became a village. Passing a pleasant looking inn and a smithy, which seemed to have an out-patient department for invalid carts, we came into a quiet lane offering a leafy vista with glimpses of thatched and tiled cottages whose gardens were gay with summer flowers. Opposite these, some rough stone steps led up to a stile by the side of an open gate which gave access to a wide cart-track. Here Thorndyke halted, and producing his pocket map-case, compared the surroundings with the map. At length he pocketed the case and, turning towards the cart-track, said, "This is our way, for better or worse. In a few minutes we shall probably know whether we have found a clue or a mare's nest."

We followed the track up a rise until, reaching the crest of the hill, we saw stretching away below us a wide, fertile valley with wooded heights beyond, over the brow of which peeped the square tower of some village church.

"Well," said Brodribb, taking off his hat to enjoy the light breeze, "clue or no clue, this is perfectly delightful and well worth the journey. Just look at those charming little blue butterflies fluttering round that mallow. What a magnificent prospect And where, but in Kent, will you see such a barley field as that?"

It was, indeed, a beautiful landscape. But as my eye travelled over the enormous barley field, its tawny surface rippling in golden waves before the summer breeze, it was not the beauty of the scene that occupied my mind. I was thinking of those three ends of barley beard that we had picked from the skirts of the green jacket. The cart-track had now contracted to a foot path, but it was a broader path than I should

220

have looked for, running straight across the great field to a far-away stile, and halfway along it on the left hand side I could see, rising above the barley, the top of a rough fence around a small, square enclosure that looked like a pound – though it was in an unlikely situation.

We pursued the broad path across the field until we were nearly abreast of the pound, and I was about to draw Thorndyke's attention to it, when I perceived a narrow lane through the barley – hardly a path, but rather a track, trodden through the crop by some persons who had gone to the enclosure. Into this track Thorndyke turned as if he had been looking for it, and walked towards the enclosure, closely scrutinising the ground as he went. Brodribb and I, of course, followed in single file, brushing through the barley as we went, and as we drew nearer we could see that there was an opening in the enclosing fence and that inside was a deep hollow the edges of which were fringed with clumps of pink valerian. At the opening of the fence Thorndyke halted and looked back.

"Well," said Brodribb, "is it going to be a mare's nest?"

"No," replied Thorndyke. "It is a clue, and something more!"

As he spoke, he pointed to the foot of one of the principal posts of the fence, to which was secured a short length of rope, the frayed ends of which suggested that it had broken under a heavy strain. And now I could see what the enclosure was. Inside it was a deep pit, and at the bottom of the pit, to one side, was a circular hole, black as night, and apparently leading down into the bowels of the earth.

"That must be a dene hole," said I, looking at the yawning cavity.

"It is," Thorndyke replied.

"Ha," said Brodribb, "so that is a dene hole, is it? Damned unpleasant looking place. Dene holes were one of poor Merrill's hobbies. He used to go down to explore them. I hope you are not suggesting that he went down this one."

"I am afraid that is what has happened, Brodribb," was the reply. "That end of rope looks like his. It is deep-sea lead-line. I have a length of it here, bought at the same place as he bought his, and probably cut from the same sample." He opened the suit-case, and taking out the coil of line that we had bought, flung it down by the foot of the post. Obviously it was identical with the broken end. "However," he added, "we shall see."

"We are going down, are we?" asked Brodribb.

"We?" repeated Thorndyke. "I am going down if it is practicable. Not otherwise. If it is an ordinary seventy-foot shaft with perpendicular sides, we shall have to get proper appliances. But you had better stay above, in any case."

"Nonsense!" exclaimed Brodribb. "I am not such a back number as you think. I have been a mountain-climber in my time and I'm not a bit nervous. I can get down all right if there is any foothold, and I've got a rope to hang on to. And you can see for yourself that somebody has been down with a rope only."

"Yes," replied Thorndyke, "but I don't see that that somebody has come up again."

"No," Brodribb admitted, "that's true. The rope seems to have broken, and you say your rope is the same stuff?"

Thorndyke looked at me inquiringly as I stooped and examined the frayed end of the strange rope.

"What do you say, Jervis?" he asked.

"That rope didn't break," I replied. "It has been chafed or sawn through. It is quite different in appearance from a broken end."

"That was what I decided as soon as I saw it," said Thorndyke. "Besides, a new rope of this size and quality couldn't possibly break under the weight of a man."

Brodribb gazed at the frayed end with an expression of horror.

"What a diabolical thing!" he exclaimed. "You mean that some wretch deliberately cut the rope and let another man drop down the shaft! But it can't be. I really think you must be mistaken. It must have been a defective rope."

"Well, that is what it looks like," replied Thorndyke. He made a 'running bowline' at the end of our rope and slipped the loop over his shoulders, drawing it tight under his arms. Then he turned towards the pit. "You had better take a couple of turns round the foot of the post, Jervis," said he, "and pay out just enough to keep the rope taut."

He took an electric inspection-lamp from the suit case, slipped the battery in his pocket, and hooked the bull's-eye to a button-hole, and when all was ready, he climbed down into the pit, crossed the sloping floor, and crouching down, peered into the forbidding hole, throwing down it a beam of light from his bull's-eye. Then he stood up and grasped the rope.

"It is quite practicable," said he, "only about twenty feet deep, and good foothold all the way." With this he crouched once more, backed into the hole and disappeared from view. He evidently descended pretty quickly, to judge by the rate at which I had to pay out the rope, and in quite a short time I felt the tension slacken and began to haul up the line. As the loop came out of the hole, Mr. Brodribb took possession of it, and regardless of my protests, proceeded to secure it under his arms.

"But how the deuce am I going to get down?" I demanded.

"That's all right, Jervis," he replied persuasively. "I'll just have a look round and then come up and let you down."

It being obviously useless to argue, I adjusted the rope and made ready to pay out. He climbed down into the pit with astonishing agility, backed into the hole and disappeared, and the tension of the rope informed me that he was making quite a rapid descent. He had nearly reached the bottom when there were borne to my ears the hollow reverberations of what sounded like a cry of alarm. But all was apparently well, for the rope continued to draw out steadily, and when at last its tension relaxed, I felt an unmistakable signal shake, and at once drew it up.

As my curiosity made me unwilling to remain passively waiting for Brodribb's return, I secured the end of the rope to the post with a "fisherman's bend" and let myself down into the pit. Advancing to the hole, I lay down and put my head over the edge. A dim light from Thorndyke's lamp came up the shaft and showed me that we were by no means the first explorers, for there were foot-holes cut in the chalk all the way down, apparently of some considerable age. With the aid of these and the rope, it appeared quite easy to descend and I decided to go down forthwith. Accordingly I backed towards the shaft, found the first of the foot-holes, and grasping the rope with one hand and using the other to hang on to the upper cavities, easily let myself down the well-like shaft. As I neared the bottom the light of the lamp was thrown full on the shaft-wall, a pair of hands grasped me and I heard Thorndyke's voice saying, "Look where you are treading, Jervis," on which I looked down and saw immediately below me a man lying on his face by an irregular coil of rope.

I stepped down carefully on to the chalk floor and looked round. We were in a small chamber in one side of which was the black opening of a low tunnel. Thorndyke and Brodribb were standing at the feet of the prostrate figure examining a revolver which the solicitor held.

"It has certainly been fired," said the latter. "One chamber is empty and the barrel is foul."

"That may be," replied Thorndyke, "but there is no bullet wound. This man died from a knife wound in the chest." He threw the light of his lamp on the corpse and as I turned it partly over to verify his statement, he added, "This is poor Mr. Merrill. We found the revolver lying by his side."

"The cause of death is clear enough," said I, "and it certainly wasn't suicide. The question is – " At this moment Thorndyke stooped and threw a beam of light down the tunnel, and Brodribb and I simultaneously uttered an exclamation. At the extreme end, about forty

223

feet away, the body of another man lay. Instantly Brodribb started forward, and stooping to clear the low roof – it was about four-feet-six-inches high – hurried along the tunnel. Thorndyke and I followed close behind. As we reached the body, which was lying supine with a small electric torch by its side, and the light of Thorndyke's lamp fell on the upturned face, Brodribb gasped, "God save us! It's Crick! And here is the knife." He was about to pick up the weapon when Thorndyke put out his hand.

"That knife," said he, "must be touched by no hand but the one that dealt the blow. It may be crucial evidence."

"Evidence of what?" demanded Brodribb. "There is Merrill with a knife wound in his chest and a pistol by his side. Here is Crick with a bullet wound in his breast, a knife by his side and the empty sheath secured round his waist. What more evidence do you want?"

"That depends on what you seek to prove," said Thorndyke. "What is your interpretation of the facts that you have stated?

"Why, it is as plain as daylight," answered Brodribb, "incredible as the affair seems, having regard to the characters of the two men. Crick stabbed Merrill and Merrill shot him dead. Then Merrill tried to escape, but the rope broke, he was trapped and he bled to death at the foot of the shaft."

"And who do you say died first?" Thorndyke asked.

It was a curious question and it caused me to look inquisitively at my colleague. But Brodribb answered promptly, "Why, Crick, of course. Here he lies where he fell. There is a track of blood along the floor of the tunnel, as you can see, and there is Merrill at the entrance, dead in the act of trying to escape."

Thorndyke nodded in a rather mysterious way and there was a brief silence. Then I ventured to remark, "You seem to be losing sight of the man with the green jacket."

Brodribb started and looked at me with a frown of surprise.

"Bless my soul!" he exclaimed. "So I am. I had clean forgotten him in these horrors. But what is your point? Is there any evidence that he has been here?"

"I don't know," said I. "He bought the rope and he was seen with Merrill apparently going towards London Bridge Station. And I gather that it was the green jacket that piloted Thorndyke to this place."

"In a sense," Thorndyke admitted, "that is so. But we will talk about that later. Meanwhile there are one or two facts that I will draw your attention to. First as to the wounds: They are almost identical in position. Each is on the left side, just below the nipple – a vital spot, which would be fully exposed by a man who was climbing down holding on to a rope.

Then, if you look along the floor where I am throwing the light, you can see a distinct trace of something having been dragged along, although there seems to have been an effort to obliterate it, and the blood marks are more in the nature of smears than drops." He gently turned the body over and pointed to the back, which was thickly covered with chalk. "This corpse has obviously been dragged along the floor," he continued. "It wouldn't have been marked in that way by merely falling. Further, the rope, when last seen, was being stuffed into a hand-bag. The rope is here, but where is the hand-bag? Finally, the rope was cut by someone outside, and evidently after the murders had been committed."

As he concluded, he spread his handkerchief over the knife, and wrapping it up carefully without touching it with his fingers, placed it in his outside breast-pocket. Then we went back towards the shaft, where Thorndyke knelt down by the body of Merrill and systematically emptied the pockets.

"What are you searching for?" asked Brodribb.

"Keys," was the reply, "and there aren't any. It is a vital point, seeing that the man with the green jacket evidently let himself into Merrill's chambers that same day."

"Yes," Brodribb agreed with a reflective frown, "it is. But tell us, Thorndyke, how you reconstruct this horrible crime."

"My theory," said Thorndyke, "is that the three men came here together. They made the rope fast to the post. The stranger in the green jacket came down first and waited at the foot of the shaft. Merrill came down next, and the stranger stabbed him just as he reached the bottom, while his arms were still up hanging on to the rope. Crick followed and was shot in the same place and the same manner. Then the stranger dragged Crick's body along the tunnel, swept away the marks as well as he could, put the knife and the lamp by the body, dropped the revolver by Merrill's corpse, took the keys and went up, sawed through the rope – probably with a pocket saw – and threw the end down the shaft. Then he took the next train to London and went straight to Merrill's chambers, where he opened the safe or other receptacles and took possession of what he wanted."

Brodribb nodded. "It was a diabolically clever scheme," said he.

"The scheme was ingenious enough," Thorndyke agreed, "but the execution was contemptible. He has left traces at every turn. Otherwise we shouldn't be here. He has acted on the assumption that the world contains no one but fools. But that is a fool's assumption."

When we had ascended, in the reverse order of our descent, Thorndyke detached our rope and also the frayed end, which we took with us, and we then took our way back towards the town, and I noted that as we stood by the dene hole, there was not a human creature in sight, nor did we meet a single person until we were close to the village. It was an ideal spot for a murder.

"I suppose you will notify the police?" said Brodribb.

"Yes," replied Thorndyke. "I shall call on the Chief Constable and give him the facts and advise him to keep some of them to himself for the present, and also to arrange for an adjournment of the inquest. Our friend with the green jacket must be made to think that he has played a trump card."

Apparently the Chief Constable was a man who knew all the moves of criminal investigation, for at the inquest the discovery was attributed to the local police acting on information received from somebody who had "noticed the broken rope."

None of us was summoned to give evidence, nor were our names mentioned, but the inquest was adjourned for three weeks, for further inquiries.

But in those three weeks there were some singular developments, of which the scene was the clerks' office at Mr. Brodribb's premises in Lincoln's Inn. There, late on a certain forenoon, Thorndyke and I arrived, each provided with a bag and a sheaf of documents, and were duly admitted by Mr. Page.

"Now," said Thorndyke, "are you quite confident, Mr. Page, that you would recognise this man, even if he had shaved off his beard and moustache?"

"Quite confident," replied Page. "I should know him by his eyes. Very queer eyes they were. Light, greenish grey. And I should know his voice, too."

"Good," said Thorndyke, and as Page disappeared into the private office, we sat down and examined our documents, eyed furtively by the junior clerk. Some ten minutes later the door opened and a man entered, and the first glance at him brought my nerves to concert pitch. He was a thick-set, muscular man, clean-shaved and rather dark. But my attention was instantly arrested by his eyes – singularly pale eyes which gave an almost unhuman character to his face. He reminded me of a certain species of lemur that I once saw.

"I have got an appointment with Mr. Brodribb," he said, addressing the clerk. "My name is Horder."

The clerk slipped off his stool and moved towards the door of the private office, but at that moment Page came out. As his eyes met Horder's, he stopped dead, and instantly the two men seemed to stiffen like a couple of dogs that have suddenly met at a street corner. I watched

Horder narrowly. He had been rather pale when he came in. Now he was ghastly, and his whole aspect indicated extreme nervous tension.

"Did you wish to see Mr. Brodribb?" asked Page, still gazing intently at the other.

"Yes," was the irritable reply, "I have given my name once – Horder."

Mr. Page turned and re-entered the private office, leaving the door ajar.

"Mr. Horder to see you, sir," I heard him say. He came out and shut the door. "If you will sit down, Mr. Brodribb will see you in a minute or two," he said, offering a chair, he then took his hat from a peg, glanced at his watch, and went out.

A couple of minutes passed. Once, I thought I heard stealthy footsteps out in the entry, but no one came in or knocked. Presently the door of the private office opened and a tall gentleman came out. And then, once more, my nerves sprang to attention. The tall gentleman was Detective-Superintendent Miller.

The superintendent walked across the office, opened the door, looked out, and then, leaving it ajar, came back to where Horder was sitting.

"You are Mr. Samuel Horder, I think," said he.

"Yes, I am," was the reply. "What about it?"

"I am a police officer, and I arrest you on a charge of having unlawfully entered the premises of the late Reginald Merrill, and it is my duty to caution you – "

Here Horder, who had risen to his feet, and slipped his right hand under the skirt of his coat, made a sudden spring at the officer. But in that instant Thorndyke had gripped his right arm at the elbow and wrist and swung him round, the superintendent seized his left arm while I pounced upon the revolver in his right hand and kept its muzzle pointed to the floor. But it was an uncomfortable affair. Our prisoner was a strong man and he fought like a wild beast, and he had his finger hooked round the trigger of the revolver. The four of us, locked together, gyrated round the office, knocking over chairs and bumping against the walls. The junior clerk skipped round the room with his eyes glued on the pistol and old Brodribb charged out of his sanctum, flourishing a long ruler. However, it did not last long. In the midst of the uproar, two massive constables stole in and joined the fray. There was a yell from the prisoner, the revolver rattled to the floor and then I heard two successive metallic clicks.

"He'll be all right now," murmured the constable who had fixed on the handcuffs, with the manner of one who has administered a soothing remedy.

"I notice," said Thorndyke, when the prisoner had been removed, "that you charged him only with unlawful entry."

"Yes," replied Miller, "until we have taken his finger-prints. Mr. Singleton has developed up three fingers and a thumb, beautifully clear, on that knife that you gave us. If they prove to be Horder's finger-prints, of course, it is a true bill for the murder."

The finger-prints on the knife proved undoubtedly to be Horder's. But the case did not rest on them alone. When his rooms were searched, there were found not only Mr. Merrill's keys but also Mr. Merrill's second will, which had been missed from the safe when it was opened by the maker's locksmith, thus illustrating afresh the perverse stupidity of the criminal mind.

"A satisfactory case," remarked Thorndyke, "in respect of the result, but there was too much luck for us to take much credit from it. On Brodribb's opening statement, it was pretty clear that a crime had been committed. Merrill was missing and someone had possession of his keys and had entered his premises. It also appeared nearly certain that the thing stolen must be the second will, since there was nothing else of value to steal, and the will was of very great value to two persons, Crick and Horder, to each of whom its destruction was worth many thousands of pounds. To both of them its value was conditional on the immediate death of Merrill, before another will could be made, and to Horder it was further conditional on the death of Crick and that he should die before Merrill − for otherwise the estate would go to Crick's heirs or next of kin. The *prima facie* suspicion therefore fell on these two men. But Crick was missing, and the question was, had he absconded or was he dead?

"And now as to the investigation. The green jacket showed earthy dust and chalk on the front and chalk-marks on the buttons. The indication was that the wearer had either crawled on chalky ground or climbed up a chalky face. But the marks on the buttons suggested climbing, for a horizontal surface is usually covered by soil, whereas on a vertical surface the chalk is exposed. But the time factor showed us that this man could not have travelled far from London. He was seen going towards London Bridge Station about the time when a train was due to go down to Kent. That train went to Maidstone and Gillingham, calling at Gravesend, Strood, Snodland, Rochester, Chatham and other places abounding in chalk and connected with the cement industry. In that district there were no true cliffs, but there were numerous chalk-pits, railway embankments, and other excavations. The evidence pointed to one of these excavations. Then Crick was known to have gone to Rochester – earlier in the day – which further suggested the district, though Rochester is the least chalky part of it.

"The question was, what kind of excavation had been climbed into? And for what purpose had the climbing been performed? But here the personality of the missing man gave us a hint. Merrill had written a book to prove that dene holes were simply prehistoric flint-mines. He had explored a number of dene holes and described them in his book. Now the district through which this train had passed was peculiarly rich in dene holes, and then there was the suggestive fact that Merrill had been last seen coming out of a rope-seller's shop. This latter fact was so important that I followed it up at once by calling at Edginton's. There I ascertained that Merrill or his companion had bought a fifteen-fathom length of deep-sea lead-line. Now this was profoundly significant. The maximum depth of a dene hole is about seventy feet. Fifteen fathoms – ninety feet – is therefore the exact length required, allowing for loops and fastenings. This new fact converted the dene-hole hypothesis into what was virtually a certainty, especially when one considered how readily these dangerous pits lent themselves either to fatal accidents or to murder. I accordingly adopted the dene-hole suggestion as a working hypothesis.

"The next question was, 'Where was this dene-hole?' And an uncommonly difficult question it was. I began to fear that the inquiry would fail from the impossibility of solving it. But at this point I got some help from a new quarter. I had given the coat to Polton to extract the dust and I had told him to wash the little lumps of chalk for *foraminifera*."

"What are *foraminifera*?" asked Brodribb.

"They are minute sea shells. Chalk is largely composed of them, and although chalk is in no sense a local rock, there is nevertheless a good deal of variation in the species of *foraminifera* found in different localities. So I had the chalk washed out as a matter of routine. Well, the dust was confirmatory but not illuminating. There was railway dust of the South Eastern type – I expect you know it – chalk, loam dust, pollen-grains of the mallow, and valerian (which grows in chalk-pits and railway cuttings) and some wing scales of the common blue butterfly, which haunts the chalk – I expect he had touched a dead butterfly. But all this would have answered for a good part of Kent. Then I examined the foraminifera and identified the species by the plates in Warnford's *Monograph*. The result was most encouraging. There were nine species in all, and of these five were marked as '*found in the Gravesend chalk*', two more '*from the Kentish chalk*', and the other two '*from the English chalk'*. This was a very striking result. More than half the contained *foraminifera* were from the Gravesend chalk.

"The problem now was to determine the geologic meaning of the term *Gravesend*. I ruled out Rochester, as I had heard of no dene holes in that neighbourhood, and I consulted Merrill's book and the large-scale Ordnance Map. Merrill had worked in the Gravesend district and the adjacent part of Essex, and he gave a list of the dene holes that he had explored, including the Clapper Napper Hole in Swanscombe Wood. But checking his list by the Ordnance Map, I found that there was one dene hole marked on the map which was not in his list. As it was evidently necessary to search all the dene holes in the district, I determined to begin with the one that he seemed to have missed. And there luck favoured us. It turned out to be the right one."

"I don't see that there was much luck in it," said Brodribb. "You calculated the probabilities and adopted the greatest."

"At any rate," said Thorndyke, "there was Merrill and there was Crick, and as soon as I saw them I knew that Horder was the murderer. For the whole tableau had obviously been arranged to demonstrate that Crick died before Merrill and establish Horder as Merrill's heir."

"A diabolical plot," commented Brodribb. "Horribly ingenious, too. By the way – which of them *did* die first in your opinion?"

"Merrill, I should say, undoubtedly," replied Thorndyke.

"That will be good hearing for Crick's next of kin," said Brodribb. "And you haven't done with this case yet, Thorndyke. I shall retain you on the question of survivorship."

The Seal of
Nebuchadnezzar

"I suppose, Thorndyke," said I, "footprints yield quite a lot of information if you think about them enough?"

The question was called forth by the circumstance of my friend halting and stooping to examine the little pit made in the loamy soil of the path by the walking stick of some unknown wayfarer. Ever since we had entered this path – to which we had been directed by the station-master of Pinwell Junction as a short-cut to our destination – I had noticed my friend scanning its surface, marked with numerous footprints, as if he were mentally reconstructing the personalities of the various travellers who had trodden it before us. This I knew to be a habit of his, almost unconsciously pursued, and the present conditions certainly favoured it, for here, as the path traversed a small wood, the slightly moist, plastic surface took impressions with the sharpness of moulding wax.

"Yes," he answered, "but you must do more than think. You need to train your eyes to observe in conspicuous characteristics."

"Such as these, for instance," said. I, with a grin, pointing to a blatant print of a Cox's "*Invicta*" rubber sole with its prancing-horse trade-mark.

Thorndyke smiled. "A man," said he, "who wears a sole like that is a mere advertising agent. He who runs may read those characteristics, but as there are thousands of persons wearing '*Invicta*' soles, the observation merely identifies the wearer as a member of a large genus. It has to be carried a good deal further to identify him as an individual – otherwise, a standardised sole is apt to be rather misleading than helpful. Its gross distinctiveness tends to divert the novice's attention from the more specific characteristics which he would seek in a plain footprint like that of this man's companion."

"Why companion?" I asked. "The two men were walking the same way, but what evidence is there that they were companions?"

"A good deal, if you follow the series of tracks, as I have been doing. In the first place, there is the stride. Both men were rather tall, as shown by the size of their feet, but both have a distinctly short stride. Now the leather-soled man's short stride is accounted for by the way in which he put down his stick. He held it stiffly, leaning upon it to some extent and helping himself with it. There is one impression of the stick to every two paces – every impression of his left foot has a stick impression opposite to it. The suggestion is that he was old, weak, or infirm. But the rubber-soled man walked with his stick in the ordinary way – one stick impression to every four paces. His abnormally short stride is not to be accounted for excepting by the assumption that he stepped short to keep pace with the other man.

"Then the two sets of footprints are usually separate. Neither man has trodden nor set his stick on the other man's tracks, excepting in those places where the path is too narrow for them to walk abreast, and there, in the one case I noticed the rubber soles treading on the prints of the leather soles, whereas at this spot the prints of the leather soles are imposed on those of the rubber soles. That, of course, is conclusive evidence that the two men were here at the same time."

"Yes," I agreed, "that settles the question without troubling about the stride. But after all, Thorndyke, this is a matter of reasoning, as I said – of thinking about the footprints and their meaning. No special acuteness of observation or training of vision comes into it. The mere facts are obvious enough. It is their interpretation that yields the knowledge."

"That is true so far," said he, "but we haven't exhausted our material. Look carefully at the impressions of the two sticks and tell me if you see anything remarkable in either of them?"

I stooped and examined the little pits that the two sticks had made in the path and, to tell the truth, found them extremely unilluminating.

"They seem very much alike," I said. "The rubber-soled man's stick is rather larger than the other and the leather-soled man's stick has made deeper holes – probably because it was smaller and he was leaning on it more heavily."

Thorndyke shook his head. "You've missed the point, Anstey, and you've missed it because you have failed to observe the visible facts. It is quite a neat point, too, and might in certain circumstances be a very important one."

"Indeed," said I. "What is the point?"

"That," said he, "I shall leave you to infer from the visible facts, which are these: First, the impressions of the smaller stick are on the right-hand side of the man who made them, and second, that each impression is shallowest towards the front and the right-hand side."

I examined the impressions carefully and verified Thorndyke's statement.

"Well," I said, "what about it? What does it prove?"

Thorndyke smiled in his exasperating fashion. "The proof," said he, "is arrived at by reasoning from the facts. My learned friend has the facts. If he will consider them, the conclusion will emerge."

"But," said I, "I don't see your drift. The impression is shallower on one side, I suppose, because the ferrule of the stick was worn away on that side. But I repeat, what about it? Do you expect me to infer why the fool that it belonged to wore his stick away all at one side?"

"Now, don't get irritable, Anstey," said he. "Preserve a philosophic calm. I assure you that this is quite an interesting problem."

"So it may be," I replied. "But I'm hanged if I can imagine why he wore his stick down in that way. However, it doesn't really matter. It isn't my stick – and by Jingo, here is old Brodribb. Caught us in the act of wasting our time on academic chin-wags and delaying his business. The debate is adjourned."

Our discussion had brought us to the opening of the wood, which now framed the figure of the solicitor. As he caught sight of us, he hurried forward, holding out his hand.

"Good men and true!" he exclaimed. "I thought you would probably come this way, and it is very good of you to have come at all, especially as it is a mere formality."

"What is?" asked Thorndyke. "Your telegram spoke of an 'alleged suicide'. I take it that there is some ground for inquiry?"

"I don't know that there is," replied Brodribb. "But the deceased was insured for three-thousand pounds, which will be lost to the estate if the suicide is confirmed. So I put it to my fellow that it was worth an expert's fee to make sure whether or not things are what they seem. A verdict of death by misadventure will save us three-thousand pounds. *Verbum sap.*" As he concluded, the old lawyer winked with exaggerated cunning and stuck his elbow into my ribs.

Thorndyke ignored the facetious suggestion of bribery and corruption and inquired dryly, "What are the circumstances of the case?"

"I'd better give you a sketch of them before we get to the house," replied Brodribb. "The dead man is Martin Rowlands, the brother of my neighbour in New Square, Tom Rowlands. Poor old Tom found the telegram waiting when he got to his office this morning and immediately rushed into my office with it and begged me to come down here with him. So I came. Couldn't refuse a brother solicitor. He's waiting at the house now.

"The circumstances are these. Last evening, when he had finished dinner, Rowlands went out for a walk. That is his usual habit in the summer months – it is light until nearly half-past nine nowadays. Well, that is the last time he was seen alive by the servants. No one saw him come in. But there was nothing unusual in that, for he had a private entrance to the annexe in which his library, museum, and workrooms were situated, and when he returned from his walk, he usually entered the house that way and went straight to his study or workroom and spent the evening there. So the servants very seldom saw him after dinner.

"Last night he evidently followed his usual custom. But, this morning, when the housemaid went to his bedroom with his morning tea, she was astonished to find the room empty and the bed undisturbed. She at once reported to the housekeeper, and the pair made their way to the annexe. There they found the study door locked, and as there was no answer after repeated knockings, they went out into the grounds to reconnoitre. The study window was closed and fastened, but the workroom window was unbolted, so that they were able to open it from outside. Then the housemaid climbed in and went to the side door, which she opened and admitted the housekeeper. The two went to the workroom, and as the door which communicated with the study was open, they were able to enter the latter, and there they found Martin Rowlands, sitting in an arm-chair by the table, stone-dead, cold and stiff. On the table were a whisky decanter, a siphon of soda water, a box of cigars, an ash-bowl with the stump of a cigar in it, and a bottle of photographic tabloids of cyanide of potassium.

"The housekeeper immediately sent off for a doctor and dispatched a telegram to Tom Rowlands at his office. The doctor arrived about nine and decided that the deceased had been dead about twelve hours. The cause of death was apparently cyanide poisoning, but, of course, that will be ascertained or disproved by the *post mortem*. Those are all the known facts at present. The doctor helped the servants to place the body on a sofa, but as it is as stiff as a frozen sheep, they might as well have left it where it was."

"Have the police been communicated with?" I asked.

"No," replied Brodribb. "There were no suspicious circumstances, so far as any of us could see, and I don't know that I should have felt justified in sending for you – though I always like to have Thorndyke's opinion in a case of sudden death – if it had not been for the insurance."

Thorndyke nodded. "It looks like a straightforward case of suicide," said he. "As to the state of deceased's affairs, his brother will be able to give us any necessary information, I suppose?

"Yes," replied Brodribb. "As a matter of fact, I think Martin has been a bit worried just lately, but Tom will tell you about that. This is the place."

We turned in at a gateway that opened into the grounds of a substantial though unpretentious house, and as we approached the front

234

door, it was opened by a fresh-coloured, white-haired man whom we both knew pretty well in our professional capacities. He greeted us cordially, and though he was evidently deeply shocked by the tragedy, struggled to maintain a calm, business-like manner.

"It is good of you to come down," said he, "but I am afraid we have troubled you rather unnecessarily. Still, Brodribb thought it best – *ex abundanti cautela*, you know – to have the circumstances reviewed by a competent authority. There is nothing abnormal in the affair excepting its having happened. My poor brother was the sanest of men, I should say, and we are not a suicidal family. I suppose you had better see the body first?"

As Thorndyke assented, he conducted us to the end of the hall and into the annexe, where we entered the study, the door of which was now open, though the key was still in the lock. The table still bore the things that Brodribb had described, but the chair was empty, and its late occupant lay on a sofa, covered with a large table-cloth. Thorndyke advanced to the sofa and gently drew away the cloth, revealing the body of a man, fully dressed, lying stiffly and awkwardly on its back with the feet raised and the stiffened limbs extended. There was something strangely and horribly artificial in the aspect of the corpse, for, though it was lying down, it had the posture of a seated figure, and thus bore the semblance of a hideously realistic effigy which had been picked up from a chair and laid down. I stood looking at it from a little distance with a layman's distaste for the presence of a dead body, but still regarding it with attention and some curiosity. Presently my glance fell on the soles of the shoes – which were, indeed, exhibited plainly enough – and I noted, as an odd coincidence that they were "*Invicta*" rubber soles, like those which we had just been discussing in the wood, that it was even possible that those very footprints had been made by the feet of this grisly figure.

"I expect, Thorndyke," Brodribb said tactfully, "you would rather make your inspection alone. If you should want us, you will find us in the dining room," and with this he retired, taking Mr. Rowlands with him.

As soon as they were gone I drew Thorndyke's attention to the rubber soles.

"It is a queer thing," said I, "but we may have actually been discussing this poor fellow's own prints."

"As a matter of fact, we were," he replied, pointing to a drawing-pin that had been trodden on and had stuck into one of the rubber heels. "I noticed this at the time, and apparently you did not, which illustrates what I was saying about the tendency of these very distinctive types of sole to distract attention from those individual peculiarities which are the ones that really matter."

"Then," said I, "if they were his footprints, the man with the remarkable stick was with him. I wonder who he was. Some neighbour who was walking home from the station with him, I expect."

"Probably," said Thorndyke, "and as the prints were quite recent – they might even have been made last night – that person may be wanted as a witness at the inquest as the last person who saw deceased alive. That depends on the time the prints were made."

He walked back to the sofa and inspected the corpse very methodically, giving close attention to the mouth and hands. Then he made a general inspection of the room, examined the objects on the table and the floor under it, strayed into the adjoining workshop, where he peered into the deep laboratory sink, took an empty tumbler from a shelf, held it up to the light and inspected the shelf – where a damp ring showed that the tumbler had been put there to drain – and from the workshop wandered into a little lobby and from thence out at the side door, down the flagged path to the side gate and back again.

"It is all very negative," he remarked discontentedly as we returned to the study, "except that bottle of tabloids, which is pretty positive evidence of premeditation. That looks like a fresh box of cigars. Two missing. One stump in the ash-tray and more ash than one cigar would account for. However, let us go into the dining and hear what Rowlands has to tell us." And with this he walked out and crossed the hall and I followed him.

As we entered the dining the two men looked at us and Brodribb asked, "Well, what is the verdict?"

"At present," Thorndyke replied, "it is an open verdict. Nothing has come to light that disagrees with the obvious appearances. But I should like to hear more of the antecedents of the tragedy. You were saying that deceased had been somewhat worried lately. What does that amount to?"

"It amounts to nothing," said Rowlands. "At least, I should have thought so, in the case of a level-headed man like my brother. Still, as it is all there is, so far as I know, to account for what has happened, I had better give you the story. It seems trivial enough.

"Some short time ago, a Major Cohen, who had just come home from Mesopotamia, sold to a dealer named Lyon a small gold cylinder seal that he had picked up in the neighbourhood of Baghdad. The Lord knows how he came by it, but he had it and he showed it to Lyon, who bought it off him for a matter of twenty pounds. Cohen, of course, knew nothing about the thing, and Lyon didn't know much more, for although he is a dealer, he is no expert. But he is a very clever faker – or rather, I

236

should say, restorer, for he does quite a legitimate trade. He was a jeweller and watch-jobber originally, a most ingenious workman, and his line is to buy up damaged antiques and restore them. Then he sells them to minor collectors, though quite honestly as restorations, so I oughtn't to call him a faker. But, as I said, he has no real knowledge of antiques, and all he saw in Cohen's seal was a gold cylinder seal, apparently ancient and genuine, and on that he bought it for about twice the value of the gold and thought no more about it.

"About a fortnight later, my brother Martin went to his shop in Petty France, Westminster, to get some repairs done, and Lyon, knowing that my brother was a collector of Babylonian antiquities, showed him the seal, and Martin, seeing at once that it was genuine and a thing of some interest and value, bought it straight-way for forty pounds without examining it at all minutely, as it was obviously worth that much in any case. But when he got home and took a rolled impression of it on moulding wax, he made a most astonishing discovery. The impression showed a mass of minute cuneiformic characters, and on deciphering these he learned with amazement and delight that this was none other than the seal of Nebuchadnezzar.

"Hardly able to believe in his good fortune, he hurried off to the British Museum and showed his treasure to the Keeper of the Babylonian Antiquities, who fully confirmed the identity of the seal and was naturally eager to acquire it for the Museum. Of course, Martin wouldn't sell it, but he allowed the keeper to take a record of its weight and measurements and to make an impression on clay to exhibit in the case of seal-rollings.

"Meanwhile, it seems that Cohen, before disposing of the seal, had amused himself by making a number of rolled impressions on clay. Some of these he took to Lyon, who bought them for a few shillings and put one of them in his shop window as a curio. There it was seen and recognised by an American Assyriologist, who went in and bought it and then began to question Lyon closely as to whence he had obtained it. The dealer made no secret of the matter, but gave Cohen's name and address – saying nothing, however, about the seal. In fact, he was unaware of the connection between the seal and the rollings as Cohen had sold him the latter as genuine clay tablets which he said he had found in Mesopotamia. But, of course, the expert saw that it was a recent rolling and that someone must have the seal.

"Accordingly, off he went to Cohen and questioned him closely, whereupon Cohen began to smell a rat. He admitted that he had had the seal, but refused to say what had become of it until the expert told him what it was and how much it was worth. This the expert did, very reluctantly and in strict confidence, and when Cohen learned that it was the seal of Nebuchadnezzar and that it was worth anything up to ten-thousand pounds, he nearly fainted, and then he and the expert together bustled off to Lyon's shop.

"But now Lyon smelt a rat, too. He refused absolutely to disclose the whereabouts of the seal, and having, by now, guessed that the seal-rollings were those of the seal, he took one of them to the British Museum, and then, of course, the murder was out. And further to complicate the matter, the Assyriologist, Professor Bateman, seems to have talked freely to his American friends at his hotel, with the result that Lyon's shop was besieged by wealthy American collectors, all roaring for the seal and all perfectly regardless of cost. Finally, as they could get no change out of Lyon, they went to the British Museum, where they learned that my brother had the seal and got his address – or rather mine, for he had, fortunately for himself, given my office as his address. Then they proceeded to bombard him with letters, as also did Cohen and Lyon.

"It was an uncomfortable situation. Cohen was like a madman. He swore that Lyon had swindled him and he demanded to have the seal returned or the proper price paid. Lyon, for his part, went about like a roaring lion of Judah, making a similar demand, and the millionaire collectors offered wild sums for the seal. Poor Martin was very much worried about it. He was particularly unhappy about Cohen, who had actually found the seal and who was a disabled soldier – he had been wounded in both legs and was permanently lame. As to Lyon, he had no grievance, for he was a dealer and it was his business to know the value of his own stock, but still it was hard luck even on him. And then there were the collectors, pestering him daily with entreaties and extravagant offers. It was very worrying for him. They would probably have come down here to see him, but he kept his private address a close secret.

"I don't know what he meant to do about it. What he did was to arrange with me for the loan of my private office and have a field day, interviewing the whole lot of them – Lyon, the Professor, and the assorted millionaires. That was three days ago, and the whole boiling of them turned up, and by the same token one of them was the kind of pestilent fool that walks off with the wrong hat or umbrella."

"Did he walk off with your hat?" asked Brodribb.

"No, but he took my stick, a nice old stick that belonged to my father."

"What sort of stick did he leave in its place?" Thorndyke asked.

"Well," replied Rowlands, "I must admit that there was some excuse, for the stick that he left was almost a facsimile of my own. I don't think I should have noticed it but for the feel. When I began to walk with it, I was aware of something unusual in the feel of it."

"Perhaps it was not quite the same length as yours," Thorndyke suggested.

"No, it wasn't that," said Rowlands. "The length was all right, but there was some more subtle difference. Possibly, as I am left-handed and carry my stick on the left side, it may in the course of years have acquired a left-handed bias, if such a thing is possible. I'll go and get the stick for you to see."

He went out of the room and returned in a few moments with an old-fashioned Malacca cane, the ivory handle of which was secured by a broad silver band. Thorndyke took it from him and looked it over with a degree of interest and attention that rather surprised me, for the loss of Rowlands' stick was a trivial incident and no concern of ours. Nevertheless, my colleague inspected it most methodically – handle, silver band, and ferrule, especially the ferrule, which he examined as if it were quite a rare and curious object.

"You needn't worry about your stick, Tom," said Brodribb with a mischievous smile. "Thorndyke will get it back if you ask him nicely."

"It oughtn't to be very difficult," said Thorndyke, handing back the stick, "if you have a list of the visitors who called that day."

"Their names will be in the appointments book," said Rowlands. "I must look them up. Some of them I remember – Cohen, Lyon, Bateman, and two or three of the collectors. But to return to our history. I don't know what passed at the interviews or what Martin intended to do, but I have no doubt he made some notes on the subject. I must search for them, for, of course, we shall have to dispose of the seal."

"By the way," said Thorndyke, "where is the seal?"

"Why, it is here in the safe," replied Rowlands, "and it oughtn't to be. It should have been taken to the bank."

"I suppose there is no doubt that it is in the safe?" said Thorndyke.

"No," replied Rowlands, "at least – " He stood up suddenly. "I haven't seen it," he said. "Perhaps we had better make sure."

He led the way quickly to the study, where he halted and stood looking at the shrouded corpse. "The key will be in his pocket," he said, almost in a whisper. Then, slowly and reluctantly, he approached the sofa, and gently drawing away the cover from the body, began to search the dead man's pockets.

"Here it is," he said at length, producing a bunch of keys and separating one, which he apparently knew. He crossed to the safe, and inserting the key, threw open the door.

"Ha!" he exclaimed with evident relief, "it is all right.. Your question gave me quite a start. Is it necessary to open the packet?"

He held out a little sealed parcel on which was written "*The Seal of Nebuchadnezzar*", and looked inquiringly at Thorndyke.

"You spoke of making sure," the latter replied with a faint smile.

"Yes, I suppose it would be best," said Rowlands, and with that, he cut the thread with which it was fastened, broke the seal, and opened the package, disclosing a small cardboard box in which lay a cylindrical object rolled up in a slip of paper.

Rowlands picked it out and, removing the paper, displayed a little cylinder of gold pitted all over with minute cuneiform characters. It was about an inch-and-a-quarter long by half-an-inch thick and had a hole bored through its axis from end to end.

"This paper, I see," said Rowlands, "contains a copy of the keeper's description of the seal – its weight, dimensions, and so on. We may as well take care of that."

He handed the little cylinder to Thorndyke, who held it delicately in his fingers and looked at it with a gravely reflective air. Indeed, small as it was, there was something very impressive in its appearance and in the thought that it had been handled by and probably worn on the person of the great king in those remote, almost mythical times, so familiar and yet so immeasurably far away. So I reflected as I watched Thorndyke inspecting the venerable little object in his queer, exact, scientific way, examining the minute characters through his lens, scrutinising the ends, and even peering through the central hole.

"I notice," he said, glancing at the paper which Rowlands held, "that the keeper has given only one transverse diameter, apparently assuming that it is a true cylinder. But it isn't. The diameter varies. It is not quite circular in section and the sides are not perfectly parallel."

He produced his pocket calliper-gauge and, closing the jaws on the cylinder, took the reading of the vernier. Then he turned the cylinder, on which the gauge became visibly out of contact.

"There is a difference of nearly two millimetres," he said when he had again closed the gauge and taken the reading.

"Ah, Thorndyke," said Brodribb, "that keeper hadn't got your mathematically exact eye and, in fact, the precise measurements don't seem to matter much."

"On the other hand," retorted Thorndyke, "inexact measurements are of no use at all."

When we had all handled and inspected the seal, Rowlands repacked it and returned it to the safe, and we went back to the dining-room.

"Well, Thorndyke," said Brodribb, "how does the insurance question stand? What is our position?"

"I think," Thorndyke replied, "that we will leave the question open until the inquest has been held. You must insist on an expert analysis, and perhaps that may throw fresh light on the matter. And now we must be off to the station. I expect you have plenty to do."

"We have," said Brodribb, "so I won't offer to walk with you. You know the way."

Politely but firmly declining Rowlands' offer of material hospitality, Thorndyke took up his research-case and, having shaken hands with our hosts, we followed them to the door and took our departure.

"Not a very satisfactory case," I remarked as we set forth along the road, "but you can't make a bull's-eye every time."

"No," he agreed, "you can only observe and note the facts. Which reminds me that we have some data to collect in the wood. I shall take casts of those footprints in case they should turn out to be of importance. It is always a useful precaution, seeing that footprints are fugitive."

It seemed to me an excessive precaution, but I made no comment, and when we arrived at the footpath through the wood and he had selected the sharpest footprints, I watched him take out from his case the plaster-tin, water-bottle, spoon, and little rubber bowl, and wondered what was in his mind. The "*Invicta*" footprints were obviously those of the dead man. But what if they were? And of what use were the casts of the other man's feet? The man was unknown, and as far as I could see, there was nothing suspicious in his presence here. But when Thorndyke had poured the liquid plaster into the two pairs of footprints, he went on to a still more incomprehensible proceeding. Mixing some fresh plaster, he filled up with it two adjoining impressions of the strange man's stick. Then, taking a reel of thread from the case, he cut off about two yards, and stretching it taut, held it exactly across the middle of the two holes, until the plaster set and fixed it in position. After waiting for the plaster to set hard, and having, meanwhile, taken up and packed the casts of the footprints, he gently raised, first the one and then the other cast, each of which was a snowy-white facsimile of the tip of the stick which had made the impression the two casts, being joined by a length of thread which gave the exact distance apart of the two impressions.

"I suppose," said I, as he made a pencil mark on one of the casts, "the thread is to show the length of the stride?"

"No," he answered. "It is to show the exact direction in which the man was walking and to mark the front and back of the stick."

I could make nothing of this. It was highly ingenious, but what on earth was the use of it? What could it possibly prove?

I put a few tentative questions, but could get no explanation beyond the obvious truth that it was of no use to postpone the collection of evidence until after the event. What event he was referring to, I did not gather, nor was I any further enlightened when, on arriving at Victoria, he hailed a taxicab and directed the driver to set him down at Scotland Yard.

"You had better not wait," he said, as he got out. "I have some business to talk over with Miller or the Assistant Commissioner and may be detained some time. But I shall be at home all the evening."

Taking this as an invitation to drop in at his chambers, I did so after dinner and made another ineffectual attempt to pump him.

"I am sorry to be so evasive," said he, "but this case is so extremely speculative that I cannot come to any definite conclusion until I have more data. I may have been theorising in the air, but I am going forth to-morrow morning at half-past eight in the hope of putting some of my inferences to the test. If my learned friend would care to lend his distinguished support to the expedition, his society would be appreciated. But it will be a case of passive observation and quite possibly nothing will happen."

"Well, I will come and look on," said I. "Passive observation is my speciality." And with this I took my departure, rather more mystified than ever.

Punctually, next morning at half-past eight, I arrived at the entry of Thorndyke's chambers. A taxicab was already waiting at the kerb and, as I stepped on the threshold, my colleague appeared on the stairs. Together we entered the cab which at once moved off, and proceeding down Middle Temple Lane to the Embankment, headed westward. Our first stopping-place was New Scotland Yard, but there Thorndyke remained only a minute or two. Our further progress was in the direction of Westminster, and in a few minutes we drew up at the corner of Petty France, where we alighted and paid off the taxi. Sauntering slowly westward and passing a large, covered car that was drawn up by the pavement, we presently encountered no less a person than Mr. Superintendent Miller, dressed in the height of fashion and smoking a cigar. The meeting was not, apparently, unexpected, for Miller began, without preamble, "It's all right, so far, Doctor, unless we are too late. It will be an awful suck-in if we are. Two plain-clothes men have been here ever since you called yesterday evening, and nothing has happened yet."

"You mustn't treat it as a certainty, Miller," said Thorndyke. "We are only acting on reasonable probabilities. But it may be a false shot, after all."

242

Miller smiled indulgently. "I know, sir. I've heard you say that sort of thing before. At any rate, he's there at present, I saw him just now through the shop window – and, by gum! Here he is!"

I followed the superintendent's glance and saw a tallish, elderly man advancing on the opposite side of the street. He walked stiffly with the aid of a stick and with a pronounced stoop as if suffering from some weakness of the back, and he carried in his free hand a small wooden case suspended by a rug-strap. But what instantly attracted my attention was his walking-stick, which appeared, so far as I could remember, to be an exact replica of the one that Tom Rowlands had shown us.

We continued to walk westward, allowing Mr. Lyon – as I assumed him to be – to pass us. Then we turned back and followed at a little distance, and I noticed that two tall, military-looking men whom we had met kept close behind us. At the corner of Petty France Mr. Lyon hailed a taxicab, and Miller quickened his pace and bore down on the big covered car.

"Jump in," he said, opening the door as Lyon entered the cab. "We mustn't lose sight of him." And with this he fairly shoved Thorndyke and me into the car and, having spoken a word to the driver, stepped in himself and was followed by the two plain-clothes men. The car started forward, and having made a spurt which brought it within a few yards of the taxi, slowed down to the pace of the latter and followed it through the increasing traffic until we turned into Whitehall, where our driver allowed the taxi to draw ahead somewhat. At Charing Cross, however, we closed up and kept immediately behind our quarry in the dense traffic of the Strand, and when it turned to cross opposite the Acropolis Hotel, we still followed and swept past it in the hotel courtyard so that we reached the main entrance first. By the time that Mr. Lyon had paid his fare we had already entered and were waiting in the hall of the hotel.

As he followed us in, he paused and looked about him until his glance fell on a stoutish, clean-shaved man who was sitting in a wicker chair, who, on catching his eye, rose and advanced towards him. At this moment Superintendent Miller touched him on the shoulder, causing him to spin round with an expression of very distinct alarm.

"Mr. Maurice Lyon, I think," said Miller. "I am a detective officer." He paused and looked hard at the dealer, who had turned deathly pale. Then he continued, "You are carrying a walking-stick which I believe is not your property."

Lyon gave a gasp of relief. "You are quite right," said he. "But I don't know whose property it is. If you do, I shall be pleased to return it in exchange for my own, which I left by mistake."

He held it out in an irresolute fashion, and Miller took it from him and handed it to Thorndyke.

"Is that the stick?" he asked.

Thorndyke looked the stick over quickly, and then, inverting it, made a minute examination of the ferrule, finishing up by taking its dimensions in two diameters and comparing the results with some written notes.

Mr. Lyon fidgeted impatiently. "There's no need for all this fuss," said he. "I have told you that the stick is not mine."

"Quite so," said Miller, "but we must have a few words privately about that stick."

Here he turned to an hotel official, who had just arrived under the guidance of one of the plain-clothes men, and who suggested rather anxiously that our business would be better transacted in a private room at the back of the building than in the public hall. He was just moving off to show us the way when the clean-shaved stranger edged up to Lyon and extended his hand towards the wooden case.

"Shall I take this?" he asked suavely.

"Not just now, sir," said Miller, firmly fending him off. "Mr. Lyon will talk to you presently."

"But that case is my property," the other objected truculently, "and who are you, anyway?"

"I am a police officer," replied Miller. "But if that is your property, you had better come with us and keep an eye on it."

I have never seen a man look more uncomfortable than did the owner of that case – with the exception of Mr. Lyon, whose complexion had once more taken on a tallowy whiteness. But as the manager led the way to the back of the hall the two men followed silently, shepherded by the superintendent and the rest of our party, until we reached a small, marble-floored lobby or ante-room, when our conductor shut us in and retired.

"Now," said Miller, "I want to know what is in that case."

"I can tell you," said the stranger. "It is a piece of sculpture, and it belongs to me."

Miller nodded. "Let us have a look at it," said he.

There being no table, Lyon sat down on a chair, and resting the case on his knees, unfastened the straps with trembling fingers on which a drop of sweat fell now and again from his forehead. When the case was free, he opened the lid and displayed the head of a small plaster bust, a miniature copy of Donatello's "St. Cecilia", the shoulders of which were wedged in with balls of paper. These Lyon picked out clumsily, and when he had removed the last of them, he lifted out the bust with infinite care and held it out for Miller's inspection. The officer took it from him tenderly – after an eager glance into the empty case – and holding it with both hands, looked at it rather blankly.

"Feels rather damp," he remarked with a some what nonplussed air, and then he cast an obviously inquiring glance at Thorndyke, who took the bust from him, and holding it poised in the palm of his hand, appeared to be estimating its weight. Glancing past him at Lyon, I noticed with astonishment that the dealer was watching him with a ghastly stare of manifest terror, while the stranger was hardly less disturbed.

"For God's sake, man, be careful!" the latter exclaimed, starting forward. "You'll drop it!"

The prediction was hardly uttered before it was verified. Drop it he did, and in a perfectly deliberate, purposeful manner, so that the bust fell on its back on the marble floor and was instantly shattered into a hundred fragments. It was an amazing affair. But what followed was still more amazing. For, as the snowy fragments scattered to right and left, from one of them a little yellow metal cylinder detached itself and rolled slowly along the floor. The stranger darted forward and stooped to seize it, but Miller stooped, too, and I judged that the superintendent's cranium was the harder, for he rose, rubbing his head with one hand and with the other holding out the cylinder to Thorndyke.

"Can you tell us what this is, Doctor?" he asked.

"Yes," was the reply. "It is the Seal of Nebuchadnezzar, and it is the property of the executors of the late Martin Rowlands, who was murdered the night before last."

As he finished speaking, Lyon slithered from his chair and lay upon the floor insensible, while the stranger made a sudden burst for the door, where he was instantly folded in the embrace of a massive plain-clothes man, who held him immovable while his colleague clicked on the handcuffs.

"So," I remarked, as we walked home, "your casts of the stick and the footprints were not wanted after all."

"On the contrary," he replied, "they are wanted very much. If the seal should fail to hang Mr. Lyon, the casts will assuredly fit the rope round his neck." (This, by the way, actually happened. The defence that Lyon received the seal from some unknown person was countered by the unexpected production in court of the casts of Lyon's feet and the stick, which proved that the prisoner had been at Pinwell, and in the company of the deceased at or about the date of the murder, and secured his conviction.)

"By the way," said I, "how did you fix this crime on Lyon? It began, I think, with those stick impressions in the wood. What was there peculiar about those impressions?"

"Their peculiarity was that they were the impressions of a stick which apparently did not belong to the person who was carrying it."

"Good Lord, Thorndyke!" I exclaimed, "is that possible? How could an impression on the ground suggest ownership?

"It is a curious point," he replied, "though essentially simple, which turns on the way in which the ferrule of a stick becomes worn. In a plain, symmetrical stick without a handle, the ferrule wears evenly all round, but in a stick with a crook or other definite handle, which is grasped in a particular way and always put down in the same position, the ferrule becomes worn on one side – the side opposite the handle, or the front of the stick. But the important point is that the bevel of wear is not exactly opposite the handle. It is slightly to one side, for this reason. A man puts his stick down with the handle fore and aft, but as he steps forward, his hand swings away from his body, rotating the stick slightly outward. Consequently, the wear on the ferrule is slightly inward. That is to say, that in a right-handed man's stick the wear is slightly to the left and in a left-handed man's stick the wear is slightly to the right. But if a right-handed man walks with a left-handed stick, the impression on the ground will show the bevel of wear on the right side – which is the wrong side, and the right-handed rotation will throw it still farther to the right. Now in this case, the impressions showed a shallow part, corresponding to the bevel of wear, on the right side. Therefore it was a left-handed stick. But it was being carried in the right hand. Therefore it – apparently – did not belong to the person who was carrying it.

"Of course, as the person was unknown, the point was merely curious and did not concern us. But see how quickly circumstantial evidence mounts up. When we saw the feet of deceased, we knew that the footprints in the wood were his. Consequently the man with the stick was in his company, and that man at once came into the picture. Then Tom Rowlands told us that he had lost his stick and that he was left-handed, and he showed us the stick that he had got in exchange, and behold! That is a right-handed stick, as I ascertained by examining the ferrule. Here, then, is a left-handed man who has lost a stick and got a right-handed one in exchange, and there, in the wood, was a right-handed man who was carrying a left-handed stick and who was in company with the deceased. It was a striking coincidence. But further, the suggestion was that this unknown man was one of those who had called at Tom's office, and therefore one who wanted to get possession of the seal. This

246

instantly suggested the question, Did he succeed in getting possession of the seal? We went to the safe and at once it became obvious that he did."

"The seal in the safe was a forgery, of course?"

"Yes, and a bad forgery, though skilfully done. It was an electrotype, it was unsymmetrical, it did not agree with the keeper's measurements, and the perforation, though soiled at the ends, was bright in the middle from the boring tool."

"But how did you know that Lyon had made it?"

"I didn't. But he was by far the most probable person. He had a seal-rolling, from which an electro could be made, and he had the great skill that was necessary to turn a flat electro into a cylinder. He was an experienced faker of antiques, and he was a dealer who would have facilities for getting rid of the stolen seal. But it was only a probability, though, as time pressed, we had to act on it. Of course, when we saw him with the stick in his hand, it became virtually a certainty."

"And how did you guess that the seal was in the bust?"

"I had expected to find it enclosed in some plaster object, that being the safest way to hide it and smuggle it out of this country and into the United States. When I saw the bust, it was obvious. It was a hastily-made copy of one of Brucciani's busts. The plaster was damp – Brucciani's bake theirs dry – and had evidently been made only a few hours. So I broke it. If I had been mistaken I could have replaced it for five shillings, but the whole circumstances made it practically a certainty."

"Have you any idea as to how Lyon administered the poison?"

"We can only surmise," he replied. "Probably he took with him some solution of cyanide – if that was what was used – and poured it into Rowlands' whisky when his attention was otherwise occupied. It would be quite easy, and a single gulp of a quick-acting poison like that would finish the business in a minute or two. But we are not likely ever to know the details."

The evidence at the inquest showed that Thorndyke was probably right, and his evidence at the trial clinched the case against Lyon. As to the other man – who proved to be an American dealer well known to the New York Customs officials – the case against him broke down from lack of evidence that he was privy either to the murder or the theft. And so ended the case of Nebuchadnezzar's Seal, a case that left Mr. Brodribb more than ever convinced that Thorndyke was either gifted with a sixth sense which enabled him to smell out evidence or was in league with some familiar demon who did it for him.

Phyllis Annesley's Peril

"One is sometimes disposed to regret," said Thorndyke, as we sat waiting for the arrival of Mr. Mayfield, the solicitor, "that our practice is so largely concerned with the sordid and the unpleasant."

"Yes," I agreed. "Medical Jurisprudence is not always a particularly delicate subject. But it is our line of practice and we have got to take it as we find it."

"A philosophic conclusion, Jervis," he rejoined, "and worthy of my learned friend. It happens that the most intimate contact of Law and Medicine is in crimes against the person and consequently the proper study of the Medical Jurist is crime of that type. It is a regrettable fact, but we must accept it."

"At the same time," said I, "there don't seem to be any Medico-legal issues in this Bland case. The woman was obviously murdered. The only question is, who murdered her? And the answer to that question seems pretty obvious."

"It does," said Thorndyke. "But we shall be better able to judge when we have heard what Mayfield has to tell us. And I think I hear him coming up the stairs now."

I rose to open the door for our visitor and, as he entered, I looked at him curiously. Mr. Mayfield was quite a young man, and the mixture of deference and nervousness in his manner as he entered the room suggested no great professional experience.

"I am afraid, sir," said he, taking the easy-chair that Thorndyke offered him, "that I ought to have come to you sooner, for the inquest, or, at least, the police court proceedings."

"You reserved your defence, I think?" said Thorndyke.

"Yes," replied the solicitor, with a wry smile. "I had to. There seemed to be nothing to say. So I put in a plea of 'Not Guilty' and reserved the defence in the hope that something might turn up. But I am gravelled completely. It looks a perfectly hopeless case. I don't know how it strikes you, sir."

"I have seen only the newspaper reports," said Thorndyke. "They are certainly not encouraging. But let us disregard them. I suggest that you recite the facts of the case and I can ask any questions that are necessary to elucidate it further."

"Very well, sir," said Mayfield. "Then I will begin with the disappearance of Mrs. Lucy Bland. That occurred about the eighteenth of last May. At that time she was living, apart from her husband, at

248

Wimbledon, in furnished lodgings. After lunch on the eighteenth she went out, saying that she should not be home until night. She was seen by someone who knew her at Wimbledon Station on the down side about three o'clock. At shortly after six, probably on the same day, she went to the Post Office at Lower Ditton to buy some stamps. The postmistress, who knew her by sight, is certain that she called there, but cannot swear to the exact date. At any rate, she did not go home that night and was never seen alive again. Her landlady communicated with her husband and he at once applied to the police. But all the inquiries that were made led to nothing. She had disappeared without leaving a trace.

"The discovery was made four months later, on the sixteenth of September. On that day some workmen went to 'The Larches', a smallish, old-fashioned, riverside house just outside Lower Ditton, to examine the electric wiring. The house was let to a new tenant, and as the meter had shown an unaccountable leakage of current during the previous quarter, they went to see what was wrong.

"To get at the main, they had to take up part of the floor of the dining-room, and when they got the boards up, they were horrified to discover a pair of feet – evidently a woman's feet – projecting from under the next board. They immediately went to the police station and reported what they had seen, whereupon the inspector and a sergeant accompanied them back to the house and directed them to take up several more boards – which they did – and there, jammed in between the joists, was the body of a woman who was subsequently identified as Mrs. Lucy Bland. The corpse appeared to be perfectly fresh and only quite recently dead, but at the *post mortem* it was discovered that it had been embalmed or preserved by injecting a solution of formaldehyde and might have been dead three or four months. The cause of death was given at the inquest as suffocation, probably preceded by the forcible administration of chloroform."

"The house, I understand," said Thorndyke, "belongs to one of the accused?"

"Yes. Miss Phyllis Annesley. It is her freehold, and she lived in it until recently. Last autumn, however, she took to travelling about and then partly dismantled the house and stored most of the furniture, but she kept two bedrooms furnished and the kitchen and dining room in just usable condition, and she used to put up there for a day or two in the intervals of her journeys, either alone or with her maid."

"And as to Miss Annesley's relations with the Blands?"

"She had known them both for some years. With Leonard Bland she was admittedly on affectionate terms, though there is no suggestion of improper relations between them. But Bland used to visit her when she lived there and they used to go for picnics on the river in the boat belonging to the house. Mrs. Bland also occasionally visited Miss Annesley, and they seem to have been on quite civil terms. Of course, she knew about her husband's affection for the lady, but she doesn't seem to have had any strong feeling about it."

"And what were the relations of the husband and wife?" asked Thorndyke.

"Rather queer. They didn't suit one another, so they simply agreed to go their own ways. But they don't seem to have been unfriendly, and Mr. Bland was most scrupulous in regard to his financial obligations to his wife. He not only allowed her liberal maintenance, but went out of his way to make provision for her. I will give you an instance, which impressed me very much.

"An old acquaintance of his, a Mr. Julius Wicks, who had been working for some years in the film studio at Los Angeles, came to England about a year ago and proposed to Bland that they should start one or two picture theatres in the provinces, Bland to find the money – which he was able to do – and Wicks to provide the technical knowledge and do the actual management. Bland agreed, and a partnership was arranged on the basis of two-thirds of the profits to Bland and one-third to Wicks, with the proviso that if Bland should die, all his rights as partner should be vested in his wife."

"And supposing Wicks should die?"

"Well, Wicks was not married, though he was engaged to a film actress. On his death, his share would go to Bland, and similarly, on Bland's death, if he should die after his wife, his share would go to his partner."

"Bland seems to have been a fairly good business man," said I.

"Yes," Mayfield agreed. "The arrangement was all in his favour. But he was the capitalist, you see. However, the point is that Bland was quite mindful of his wife's interests. There was nothing like enmity."

"Then," said Thorndyke, "one motive is excluded. Was the question of divorce ever raised?"

"It couldn't be," said Mayfield. "There were no grounds on either side. But it seems to have been recognised and admitted that if Bland had been free he would have married Miss Annesley. They were greatly attached to one another."

"That seems a fairly solid motive," said I.

"It appears to be," Mayfield admitted. "But to me, who have known these people for years and have always had the highest opinion of them, it seems – Well, I can't associate this atrocious crime with them at all. However, that is not to the point. I must get on with the facts.

"Very soon after the discovery at 'The Larches', the police learned that there had been rumours in Lower Ditton for some time past of strange happenings at the house and that two labourers named Brodie and Stanton knew something definite. They accordingly looked up these two men and examined them separately, when both men made substantially identical statements, which were to this effect:

"About the middle of May – neither of them was able to give an exact date – between nine and ten in the evening, they were walking together along the lane in which 'The Larches' is situated when they saw a man lurking in the front garden of the house. As they were passing, he came to the gate and beckoned to them, and when they approached he whispered, 'I say, mates, there's something rummy going on in this house.'

"'How do you know?' asked Brodie.

"'I've been looking in through a hole in the shutter,' the man replied. 'They seem to be hiding something under the floor. Come and have a look.'

"The two men followed him up the garden to the back of the house, where he took them to one of the windows of a ground-floor room and pointed to two holes in the outside shutters.

"'Just take a peep in through them,' said he.

"Each of the men put an eye to one of the holes and looked in, and this is what they both saw: There were two rooms, communicating, with a wide arch between them. Through the arch and at the far end of the second room were two persons, a man and a woman. They were on their hands and knees, apparently doing something to the floor. Presently the man, who had on a painter's white blouse, rose and picked up a board which he stood on end against the wall. Then he stooped again and seemed to lay hold of something that lay on the floor – something that looked like a large bundle or a roll of carpet. At this moment something passed across in front of the holes and shut out the view – so that there must have been a third person in the room. When the obstructing body moved away again, the man was kneeling on the floor looking down at the bundle and the woman had come forward and was standing just in the arch with a pair of pincers in her hand. She was dressed in a spotted pinafore with a white sailor collar, and both the men recognised her at once as Miss Annesley."

"They knew her by sight, then?" said Thorndyke.

"Yes. They were Ditton men. It is a small place and everybody in it must have known Miss Annesley – and Bland, too, for that matter. Well, they saw her standing in the archway quite distinctly. Neither of the men has the least doubt as to her identity. They watched her for perhaps half-a-minute. Then the invisible person inside moved in front of the peepholes and shut out the scene.

"When the obstruction moved away, the woman was back in the farther room, kneeling on the floor. The bundle had disappeared and the man was in the act of taking the board, which he had rested against the wall, and laying it in its place in the floor. After this, the obstruction kept coming and going, so that the watchers only got occasional glimpses of what was going on. They saw the man apparently hammering nails into the floor and they heard faint sounds of knocking. On one occasion, towards the end of the proceedings, they saw the man standing in the archway with his face towards them, apparently looking at something in his hand. They couldn't see what the thing was, but they clearly recognised the man as Mr. Bland, whom they both knew well by sight. Then the view was shut out again, and when they next saw Mr. Bland, he was standing by Miss Annesley in the farther room, looking down at the floor and taking off his blouse. As it seemed that the business was over and that Bland and Miss Annesley would probably be coming out, the men thought it best to clear off, lest they should be seen.

"As they walked up the lane, they discussed the mysterious proceedings that they had witnessed, but could make nothing of them. The stranger suggested that perhaps Miss Annesley was hiding her plate or valuables to keep them safe while she was travelling, and hinted that it might be worth someone's while to take the floor up later on and see what was there. But this suggestion Brodie and Stanton, who are most respectable men, condemned strongly, and they agreed that, as the affair was no concern of theirs, they had better say nothing about it. But they evidently must have talked to some extent, for the affair got to be spoken about in the village and, of course, when the body was discovered under the floor, the gossip soon reached the ears of the police."

"Has the third man come forward to give evidence?" Thorndyke asked.

"No, he has not been found yet. He was a stranger to both the men, apparently a labourer or farm-hand or tramp. But nothing is known about him. So that is the case, and it is about as hopeless as it is possible to be. Of course, there is the known character of the accused, but against that is a perfectly intelligible motive and the evidence of two eye-witnesses. Do you think you would be disposed to undertake the defence, sir? I realise that it is asking a great deal of you."

"I should like to think the matter over," said Thorndyke, "and make a few preliminary inquiries. And I should want to read over the depositions in full detail. Can you let me have them?"

"I have a verbatim report of the police court proceedings and of the inquest. I will leave them with you now. And when may I hope to have your decision?"

"By the day after to-morrow at the latest," was the reply, on which the young solicitor produced a bundle of papers from his bag and, having laid them on the table, thanked us both and took his leave.

"Well, Thorndyke," I said when Mayfield had gone, "I am fairly mystified. I know you would not undertake a merely formal defence, but what else you could do is, I must confess, beyond my imagination. It seems to me that the prosecution have only to call the witnesses and the verdict of 'Guilty' follows automatically."

"That is how it appears to me," said Thorndyke. "And if it still appears so when I have read the reports and made my preliminary investigations, I shall decline the brief. But appearances are sometimes misleading."

With this, he took the reports and the notebook, in which he had made a few brief memoranda of Mayfield's summary of the case, and drawing a chair to the table, proceeded, with quiet concentration, to read through and make notes on the evidence. When he had finished, he passed the reports to me and rose, pocketing his notebook and glancing at his watch.

"Read the evidence through carefully, Jervis," said he, "and tell me if you see any possible way out. I have one or two calls to make, but I shall not be more than an hour. When I come back, I should like to hear your views on the case."

During his absence, I read the reports through with the closest attention. Something in Thorndyke's tone had seemed to hint at a possible flaw in the case for the prosecution. But I could find no escape from the conviction that these two persons were guilty. The reports merely amplified what Mayfield had told us, and the added detail, especially in the case of the eye witnesses, only made the evidence more conclusive. I could not see the material for even a formal defence.

In less than an hour, my colleague re-entered the room, and I was about to give him my impressions of the evidence when he said, "It is rather early, Jervis, but I think we had better go and get some lunch. I have arranged to go down to Ditton this afternoon and have a look at the house. Mayfield has given me a note to the police sergeant, who has the key and is virtually in possession."

"I don't see what you will gain by looking at the house," said I.

"Neither do I," he replied. "But it is a good rule always to inspect the scene of a crime and all the evidence as far as possible."

"Well," I said, "it is a forlorn hope. I have read through the evidence and it seems to me that the accused are as good as convicted. I can see no line of defence at all. Can you?"

"At present I cannot," he replied. "But there are one or two points that I should like to clear up before I decide whether or not to undertake the defence. And I have a great belief in first-hand observation."

We consumed a simplified lunch at one of our regular haunts in Fleet Street and from thence were conveyed by a taxi to Waterloo, where we caught the selected train to Lower Ditton. I had put the reports in my pocket, and during our journey I read them over again, to see if I could discover any point that would be cleared up by an inspection of the premises.

For, in spite of the rather vague purpose implied by Thorndyke's explanation, something in my colleague's manner, coupled with long experience of his method, made me suspect that he had some definite object in view. But nothing was said by either of us during the journey, nor did we discuss the case, indeed, so far as I could see, there was nothing to discuss.

Our reception at the Lower Ditton Police Station was something more than cordial. The sergeant recognised Thorndyke instantly – it appeared that he was an enthusiastic admirer of my colleague – and after a brief glance at Mayfield's note, took a key from his desk and put on his helmet.

"Lord bless you, sir," said he, "I don't need to be told who you are. I've seen you in court, and heard you. I'll come along with you to the house myself."

I suspected that Thorndyke would have gladly dispensed with this attention, but he accepted it with genial courtesy, and we went forth through the village and along the quiet lane in which the ill-omened house was situated. And as we went, the sergeant commented on the case with curiously unofficial freedom.

"You've got your work cut out, sir, if you are going to conduct the defence. But I wish you luck. I've known Miss Annesley for some years – she was well known in the village here – and a nicer, gentler, more pleasant lady you wouldn't wish to meet. To think of her in connection with a murder – and such a murder, too – such a brutal, callous affair! Well, it's beyond me. And yet there it is, unless those two men are lying."

"Is there any reason to suppose that they are?" I asked.

"Well, no, there isn't. They are good, sober, decent men. And it would be such an atrociously wicked lie. And they both knew the prisoners, and liked them. Everybody liked Mr. Bland and Miss

254

Annesley, though their friendship for one another may not have been quite in order. But I can tell you, sir, these two men are frightfully cut up at having to give evidence. This is the house!"

He opened a gate and we entered the garden, beyond which was a smallish, old-fashioned house, of which the ground-floor windows were protected by outside shutters. We walked round to the back of the house, where was another garden with a lawn and a path leading down to the river.

"Is that a boat-house?" Thorndyke asked, pointing to a small gable that appeared above a clump of lilac bushes.

"Yes," replied the sergeant. "And there is a boat in it, a good, beamy, comfortable tub that Miss Annesley and her friend used to go out picnicking in. This is the window that the men peeped in at, but you can't see much now because the room is all dark."

I looked at the two French windows, which opened on to the lawn, and reflected on this new instance of the folly of wrong-doers. Each window was fitted with a pair of strong shutters, which bolted on the inside, and each shutter was pierced, about five feet from the sill, by a circular hole a little over an inch in diameter. It seemed incredible that two sane persons, engaged in the concealment of a murdered body, should have left those four holes uncovered for any chance eavesdropper to spy on their doings.

But my astonishment at this lack of precaution was still greater when the sergeant admitted us and we stood inside the room, for both the windows, as well as the pair in the farther room, were furnished with heavy curtains.

"Yes," said the sergeant, in answer to my comment, "it's a queer thing how people overlook matters of vital importance. You see, they drew the drawing-room curtains all right, but they forgot these. Is there anything in particular that you want to see, sir?"

"I should like to see where the body was hidden," said Thorndyke, "but I will just look round the rooms first."

He walked slowly to-and-fro, looking about him and evidently fixing the appearance of the rooms on his memory. Not that there was much to see or remember. The two nearly square rooms communicated through a wide arch, once closed by curtains, as shown by the brass curtain-rod. The back room had been completely dismantled with the exception of the window curtains, but the front room, although the floor and the walls, were bare, was not entirely unfurnished. The sideboard was still in position and bore at each end a tall electric light standard, as did also the mantelpiece. There were three dining chairs and a good-sized gate-leg table stood closed against the wall.

"I see you have not had the floor-boards nailed down," said Thorndyke.

"No, sir, not yet. So we can see where the body was hidden and where the electric main is. The electricians took up the wrong board at first – that is how they came to discover the body. And one of them said that the boards over the main had been raised recently, and he thought that the – er – the accused had meant to hide the body there, but when they got the floor up they struck the main and had to choose a fresh place."

He stooped, and lifting the loose boards, which he stood on end against the mantelpiece, exposed the joists and the earth floor about a foot below them. In one of the spaces the electric main ran and in the adjoining one the apparently disused gas main.

"This is where we found poor Mrs. Bland," said the sergeant, pointing to an empty space. "It was an awful sight. Gave me quite a turn. The poor lady was lying on her side jammed down between the joists and her nose flattened up against one of the timbers. They must have been brutes that did it, and I can't – I really can't believe that Miss Annesley was one of them."

"It looks a narrow place for a body to lie in," said I.

"The joists are sixteen inches apart," said Thorndyke, laying his pocket rule across the space, "and two and a half inches thick. Heavy timber and wide spaces."

He stood up, and turning round, looked towards the windows of the back room. I followed his glance and noted, almost with a start, the two holes in the shutter of the left-hand window (the right-hand window, of course, from outside) glaring into the darkened room like a pair of inquisitive, accusing eyes. The holes in the other window were hardly visible, and the reason for the difference was obvious. The one window had small panes and thick muntins, or sash-bars, whereas the other was glazed, with large sheets of plate glass and had no muntins.

"Of course it would be dark at the time," I said in response to his unspoken comment, "and this room would be lighted up, more or less."

"Not so very dark in May," he replied. "There is a furnished bedroom, isn't there, sergeant?"

"Two, sir," was the reply, and the sergeant forthwith opened the door and led the way across the hall and up the stairs.

"This is Miss Annesley's room," he said, opening a door gingerly and peering in.

We entered the room and looked about us with vague curiosity. It was a simply-furnished room, but dainty and tasteful, with its small four-post bedstead, light easy chair, and little, ladylike writing-table.

"That's Mr. Bland," said the sergeant, pointing to a double photograph-frame on the table, "and the lady is Miss Annesley herself."

I took up the frame and looked curiosity at the two portraits. For a pair of murderers, they were certainly uncommonly prepossessing. The man, who looked about thirty-five, was a typical good-looking, middle-class Englishman, while the woman was distinctly handsome, with a thoughtful, refined and gentle cast of face.

"She has something of a Japanese air," said I, "with that coil on the top of the head and the big ivory hairpin stuck through it."

I passed the frame to Thorndyke, who regarded each portrait attentively, and then, taking both photographs out of the frame, closely examined each in turn, back and front, before replacing them.

"The other bedroom," said the sergeant as Thorndyke laid down the frame, "is the spare room. There's nothing to see in it."

Nevertheless he conducted us into it, and when we had verified his statement we returned downstairs.

"Before we go," said Thorndyke, "I will just see what is opposite those holes."

He walked to the window and was just looking out through one of the holes when the sergeant, who had followed him closely, suddenly slid along the floor and nearly fell.

"Well, I never!" he exclaimed, recovering himself and stooping to pick up some small object. "There's a dangerous thing to leave lying about the floor. Bit of slate pencil – at least, that is what it looks like."

He handed it to Thorndyke, who glanced at it and remarked, "Yes, things that roll under the foot are apt to produce broken bones, but I think you had better take care of it. I may have to ask you something about it at the trial."

We bade the sergeant farewell at the bottom of the lane, and as we turned into the footpath to the station I said, "We don't seem to have picked up very much more than Mayfield told us – excepting that bit of slate pencil. By the way, why did you tell the sergeant to keep it?"

"On the broad principle of keeping everything, relevant or irrelevant. But it wasn't slate pencil, it was a fragment of a small carbon rod."

"Presumably dropped by the electricians who had been working in the room," said I, and then asked, "Have you come to any decision about this case?"

"Yes, I shall undertake the defence."

"Well," I said, "I can't imagine what line you will take. Strong suspicion would have fallen on these two persons even if there had been no witnesses, but the evidence of those two eye-witnesses seems to clench the matter."

"Precisely," said Thorndyke. "That is my position. I rest my case on the evidence of those two men – as I hope it will appear under cross-examination."

This statement of Thorndyke's gave me much food for reflection during the days that followed. But it was not very nourishing food, for the case still remained perfectly incomprehensible. To be sure, if the evidence of the two eye-witnesses could be shown to be false, the ease against the prisoners would break down, since it would bring another suspected person into view. But their evidence was clearly not false. They were men of known respectability and no one doubted the truth of their statements.

Nor was the obscurity of the case lightened in any way by Thorndyke's proceedings. We called together on the two prisoners, but from neither did we elicit any fresh facts. Neither could establish a clear alibi or suggest any explanation of the eye-witnesses' statements. They gave a simple denial of having been in the house at that time or of having ever taken up the floor.

Both prisoners, however, impressed me favourably. Bland, whom we interviewed at Brixton, seemed a pleasant, manly fellow, frank and straightforward, though quite shrewd and business-like, while Miss Annesley, whom we saw at Holloway, was a really charming young lady – sweet-faced, dignified, and very gracious and gentle in manner. In one respect, indeed, I found her disappointing. The picturesque coil had disappeared from the top of her head and her hair had been shortened ("bobbed" is, I believe, the correct term) into a mere fringe. Thorndyke also noticed the change, and in fact commented on it.

"Yes," she admitted, "it is a disimprovement in my case. It doesn't suit me. But I really had no choice. When I was in Paris in the spring I had an accident. I was having my hair cleaned with petrol when it caught fire. It was most alarming. The hairdresser had the presence of mind to throw a damp towel over my head, and that saved my life. But my hair was nearly all burnt. There was nothing for it but to have it trimmed as evenly as possible. But it looked horrid at first. I had my photograph taken by Barton soon after I came home, just as a record, you know, and it looks awfully odd. I look like a Bluecoat boy."

"By the way," said Thorndyke, "when did you return?"

"I landed in England about the middle of April and went straight to my little flat at Paddington, where I have been living ever since."

"You don't remember where you were on the eighteenth of May?

"I was living at my flat, but I can't remember what I did on that day. You don't, as a rule, unless you keep a diary, which I do not."

This was not very promising. As we came away from the prison, I felt, on the one hand, a conviction that this sweet, gracious lady could have had no hand in this horrible crime, and on the other an utter despair of extricating her from the web of circumstances in which she had become enmeshed.

From Thorndyke I could gather nothing, except that he was going on with his investigations – a significant fact, in his case. To my artfully disguised questions he had one invariable reply, "My dear Jervis, you have read the evidence, you have seen the house, you have all the facts. Think the case over and consider the possibilities of cross-examination." And that was all I could get out of him.

He was certainly very busy, but his activities only increased my bewilderment. He sent a well-known architect down to make a scale-plan of the house and grounds, and he dispatched Polton to take photographs of the place from every possible point of view. The latter, indeed, was up to his eyes in work, and enjoying himself amazingly, but as secret as an oyster. As he went about, beaming with happiness and crinkling with self-complacency, he exasperated me to that extent that I could have banged his little head against the wall. In short, though I had watched the development of the case from the beginning, I was still without a glimmer of understanding of it even when I took my seat in court on the morning of the trial.

It was a memorable occasion, and every incident in it is still vivid in my memory. Particularly do I remember looking with a sort of horrified fascination at the female prisoner, standing by her friend in the dock, pale but composed and looking the very type and picture of womanly beauty and dignity, and reflecting with a shudder that the graceful neck – looking longer and more slender from the shortness of the hair – might very probably be, within a matter of days, encircled by the hangman's rope. These lugubrious reflections were interrupted by the entrance of two persons, a man and a woman, who were apparently connected with the case, since as they took their seats they both looked towards the dock and exchanged silent greetings with the prisoners.

"Do you know who those people are, Mayfield?" I asked.

"That is Mr. Julius Wicks, Mr. Bland's partner, and his fiancée, Miss Eugenia Kropp, the film actress," he replied.

I was about to ask him if they were here to give evidence when, the preliminaries having come to an end, the counsel for the Crown, Sir John Turville, rose and began his opening speech.

259

It was a good speech and eminently correct, but its very moderation made it the more damaging. It began with an outline of the facts, almost identical with Mayfield's summary, and a statement of the evidence which would presently be given by the principal witnesses.

"And now," said Sir John, when he had finished his recital, "let us bring these facts to a focus. Considered as a related group, this is what they show us. On the sixteenth of September there is found, concealed under the floor of a certain room in a certain house, the body of a woman who has evidently been murdered. That woman is the separated wife of a man who is on affectionate terms with another woman whom he would admittedly wish to marry and who would be willing to marry him. This murdered woman is, in short, the obstacle to the marriage desired by these two persons. Now the house in which the corpse is concealed is the property of one of those two persons, and both of them have access to it, and no other person has access to it. Here, then, to begin with, is a set of profoundly suspicious circumstances.

"But there are others far more significant. That unfortunate lady, the unwanted wife of the prisoner, Bland, disappeared mysteriously on the eighteenth of last May, and witnesses will prove that the body was deposited under the floor on or about that date. Now, on or about that same date, in that same house, in that same room, in the same part of that room, those two persons, the prisoners at the bar, were seen by two eminently respectable witnesses in the act of concealing some large object under the floor. What could that object have been? The floor of the room has been taken up and nothing whatever but the corpse of this poor murdered lady has been found under it. The irresistible conclusion is that those two persons were then and there engaged in concealing that corpse.

"To sum up, then, the reasons or believing that the prisoners are guilty of the crime with which they are charged are threefold. They had an intelligible and strong motive to commit that crime, they had the opportunity to commit it, and we have evidence from two eye-witnesses which makes it practically an observed fact that the prisoners did actually commit that crime."

As the Crown counsel sat down, pending the swearing of the first witness, I turned to Thorndyke and said anxiously, "I can't imagine what you are going to reply to that."

"My reply," he answered quietly, "will be largely governed by what I am able to elicit in cross-examination." Here the first witness was called – the electrician who discovered the body – and gave his evidence, but Thorndyke made no cross-examination. He was followed by the sergeant, who described the discovery in more detail. As the Crown counsel sat down, Thorndyke rose, and I pricked up my ears.

"Have you mentioned everything that you saw or found in this room?" he asked.

"Yes, at that time. Later – on the second of October – I found a small piece of a carbon pencil on the floor of the front room near the window."

He produced from his pocket an envelope from which he extracted the fragment of the alleged "slate pencil" and passed it to Thorndyke, who, having passed to the judge with the intimation that he wished it to be put in evidence, sat down. The judge inspected the fragment curiously and then cast an inquisitive glance at Thorndyke – as he had done once or twice before – for my colleague's appearance in the role of counsel was a rare event, and one usually productive of surprises.

To the long succession of witnesses who followed, Thorndyke listened attentively but did not cross-examine, I saw the judge look at him curiously from time to time, and my own curiosity grew more and more intense. Evidently he was saving himself up for the crucial witnesses. At length the name of James Brodie was called, and a serious-looking elderly workman entered the box. He gave his evidence clearly and confidently, though with manifest reluctance, and I could see that his vivid description of that sinister scene made a great impression on the jury. When the examination in chief was finished, Thorndyke rose, and the judge settled himself to listen with an air of close attention.

"Have you ever been inside 'The Larches'?" Thorndyke asked.

"No, sir. I've passed the house twice every day for years, but I've never been inside it."

"When you looked in through the shutter, was the room well lighted?"

"No, 'twas very dim. I could only just see what the people were doing."

"Yet you recognised Miss Annesley quite clearly?"

"Not at first, I didn't. Not until she came and stood in the archway. The light seemed quite good there."

"Did you see her come out of the front room and walk to the arch?"

"No. I saw her in the front room and then something must have stopped up the hole, for 'twas all dark. Then the hole got clear again and I saw her standing in the arch. But I only saw her for a moment or two. Then the hole got stopped again and when it opened she was back in the front room."

"How did you know that the woman in the front room was Miss Annesley? Could you see her face in that dim light?"

261

"No, but I could tell her by her dress. She wore a striped pinafore with a big, white sailor-collar. Besides, there wasn't nobody else there."

"And with regard to Mr. Bland: Did you see him walk out of the front room and up to the arch?"

"No. 'Twas the same as with Miss Annesley. Something kept passing across the hole. I see him in the front room, then I see him in the arch and then I see him in the front room again."

"When they were in the archway, were they moving or standing still?"

"They both seemed to be standing quite still."

"Was Miss Annesley looking straight towards you?"

"No. Her face was turned away a little."

"I want you to look at these photographs and tell us if any of them shows the head in the position in which you saw it."

He handed a bundle of photographs to the witness, who looked at them, one after another, and at length picked out one.

"That is exactly how she looked," said he. "She might have been standing for this very picture."

He passed the photograph to Thorndyke, who noted the number written on it and passed it to the judge, who also noted the number and laid it on his desk. Thorndyke then resumed, "You say the light was very dim in the front room. Were the electric lamps alight?"

"None that I could see were alight."

"How many electric lamps could you see?"

"Well, there was three hanging from the ceiling and there was two standards on the mantelpiece and one on the sideboard. None of them was alight."

"Was there only one standard on the sideboard?"

"There may have been more, but I couldn't see 'em because I could only see just one corner of the sideboard."

"Could you see the whole of the mantelpiece?"

"Yes. There was a standard lamp at each end."

"Could you see anything on the near side of the mantelpiece?"

"There was a table there, a folding table with twisted legs. But I could only see part of that. The side of the arch cut it off."

"You have said that you could see Miss Annesley quite clearly and could see how she was dressed. Could you see how her hair was arranged?"

"Yes. 'Twas done up on the top of her head in what they calls a bun and there was a sort of a skewer stuck through it."

As the witness gave this answer, a light broke on me. Not a very clear light, for the mystery was still unsolved. But I could see that

262

Thorndyke had a very definite strategic plan. And, glancing at the dock, I was immediately aware that the prisoners had seen the light, too.

"You have described what looked like a hole in the floor," Thorndyke resumed, "where some boards had been raised, near the middle of the room. Was that hole nearer the sideboard or nearer the mantelpiece?"

"It was nearer the mantelpiece," the witness replied, on which Thorndyke sat down, the witness left the box, and both the judge and the counsel for the prosecution rapidly turned over their notes with evident surprise.

The next witness was Albert Stanton and his evidence was virtually a repetition of Brodie's, and when, in cross Thorndyke put over again the same series of questions, he elicited precisely the same answers even to the recognition of the same photograph. And again I began to see a glimmer of light. But only a glimmer.

Stanton being the last of the witnesses for the Crown, his brief re-examination by Sir John Turville completed the case for the prosecution. Thereupon Thorndyke rose and announced that he called witnesses, and forthwith the first of them appeared in the box. This was Frederick Stokes, A.R.I.B.A., architect, and he deposed that he had made a careful survey of the house called "The Larches" at Lower Ditton and prepared a plan on the scale of half-an-inch-to-a-foot. He swore that the plan – of which he produced the original and a number of lithographed duplicates – was true and exact in every respect. Thorndyke took the plans from him and passing them to the judge asked that the original should be put in evidence and the duplicates handed to the jury.

The next witness was Joseph Barton of Kensington, photographer. He deposed to having taken photographs of Miss Annesley on various occasions, the last being on the twenty-third of last April. He produced copies of them all with the date written on each. He swore that the dates written were the correct dates. The photographs were handed up to the judge, who looked them over, one by one. Suddenly he seemed, as it were, to stiffen and turned quickly from the photographs to his notes, and I knew that he had struck the last portrait – the one with the short hair.

As the photographer left the box, his place was taken by no less a person than our ingenious laboratory assistant, who, having taken his place, beamed on the judge, the jury, and the court in general, with a face wreathed in crinkly smiles. Nathaniel Polton, being sworn, deposed that, on the fifteenth of October, he proceeded to "The Larches" at Lower Ditton and took three photographs of the ground-floor rooms. The first was taken through the right-hand hole of the shutter marked "A"in the plan, the second through the left-hand hole, and the third from a point inside the back room between the windows and nearer to the window marked "*B*". He produced those photographs with the particulars written on each. He had also made some composite photographs showing the two prisoners dressed as the witnesses, Brodie and Stanton, had described them. The bodies in those photographs were the bodies of Miss Winifred Blake and Mr. Robert Anstey, K.C., respectively. On these bodies the heads of the prisoners had been printed, and here Polton described the method of substitution in detail. The purpose of the photographs was to show that a photograph could be produced with the head of one person and the body of another. He also deposed to having seen and taken possession of two photographs, one of each of the two prisoners, which he found in the bedroom and which he now produced and passed to the judge. And this completed his evidence.

Thorndyke now called the prisoner, Bland, and having elicited from him a sworn denial of the charge, proceeded to examine him respecting the profits from his three picture theatres, which, it appeared, amount to over six-thousand pounds-per-annum.

"In the event of your death, what becomes of this valuable property?"

"If my wife had been alive it would have gone to her, but as she is dead, it goes to my partner and manager, Mr. Julius Wicks."

"In whose custody was the house at Ditton while Miss Annesley was in France?"

"In mine. The keys were in my possession."

"Were the keys ever out of your possession?"

"Only for one day. My partner, Mr. Wicks, asked to be allowed to use the boat for a trip on the river and to take a meal in the house. So I lent him the keys, which he returned the next day."

After a short cross-examination, Bland returned to the dock and was succeeded by Miss Annesley, who, having given a sworn denial of the charge, described her movements in France and in London about the period of the crime. She also described, in answer to a question, the circumstances under which she had lost her hair.

"Can you remember the date on which this accident happened?" Thorndyke asked.

"Yes. It was on the thirtieth of March. I made a note of the date, so that I could see how long my hair took to grow."

As Thorndyke sat down, the counsel for the prosecution rose and made a somewhat searching cross-examination, but without in any way shaking the prisoner's evidence. When this was concluded and Miss Annesley had returned to the dock, Thorndyke rose to address the court for the defence.

"I shall not occupy your time, gentlemen," he began, "by examining the whole mass of evidence nor by arguing the question of motive. The guilt or innocence of the prisoners turns on the accuracy or inaccuracy of the evidence of the two witnesses, Brodie and Stanton, and to the examination of that evidence I shall confine myself.

"Now that evidence, as you may have noticed, presents some remarkable discrepancies. In the first place, both witnesses describe what they saw in identical terms. They saw exactly the same things in exactly the same relative positions. But this is a physical impossibility, if they were really looking into a room, for they were looking in from different points of view, through different holes, which were two feet six inches apart. But there is another much more striking discrepancy.

"Both these men have described, most intelligently, fully and clearly, a number of objects in that room which were totally invisible to both of them, and they have described as only partly visible other objects which were in full view. Both witnesses, for instance, have described the mantelpiece with its two standard lamps and a table with twisted legs on the near side of it, and both saw one corner only of the sideboard. But if you look at the architect's plan and test it with a straight-edge, you will see that neither the mantelpiece nor the table could possibly be seen by either. The whole of that side of the room was hidden from them by the jamb of the arch. While as to the sideboard, the whole of it, with its two standards, was visible to Brodie, and to Stanton the whole of it, excepting a small portion of the near side. But further, if you lay the straight-edge on the point marked "C" and test it against the sides of the arch, you will see that a person standing at that spot would get the exact view described by both the witnesses.

"I pass round duplicate plans with pencil lines ruled on them, but in case you find any difficulty in following the plans, I have put in the photographs of the room taken by Polton. The first photograph was taken through the hole used by Brodie, and shows exactly what he would have seen on looking through that hole, and you see that it agrees completely with the plan but disagrees totally with his description. The second photograph shows what was visible to Stanton, and the third photograph, taken from the point marked "C", shows exactly the view described by both the witnesses, but which neither of them could possibly have seen under the circumstances stated.

"Now what is the explanation of these extraordinary discrepancies? No one, I suppose, doubts the honesty of these witnesses. I certainly do not. I have no doubt whatever that they were telling the truth to the best of their belief. Yet they have stated that they saw things which it is physically impossible that they could have seen. How can these amazing contradictions be reconciled?"

He paused, and in the breathless silence, I noticed that the judge was gazing at him with an expression of intense expectancy, an expression that was reflected on the jury and indeed on every person present.

"Well, gentlemen," he resumed, "there is one explanation which completely reconciles these contradictions, and that explanation also reconciles all the other strange contradictions and discrepancies which you may have noticed. If we assume that these two men, instead of looking through an arch into a room, as they believed, were really looking at a moving picture thrown on a screen stretched across the arch, all the contradictions vanish. Everything becomes perfectly plain, consistent and understandable."

"Thus both men, from two different points of view, saw exactly the same scene, naturally, if they were both looking at the same picture, but otherwise quite impossible. Again, both men, from the point "*A*", saw a view which was visible only from the point "*C*. Perfectly natural if they were both looking at a picture taken from the point "*C*, for a picture is the same picture from whatever point of view it is seen. But otherwise a physical impossibility.

"You may object that these men would have seen the difference between a picture and a real room. Perhaps they would, even in that dim light – if they had looked at the scene with both eyes. But each man was looking with only one eye – through a small hole. Now it requires the use of both eyes to distinguish between a solid object and a flat picture. To a one-eyed man there is no difference – which is probably the reason that one-eyed artists are such accurate draughtsmen – they see the world around them as a flat picture, just as they draw it, whereas a two-eyed artist has to turn the solid into the flat. For the same reason, if you look at a picture with one eye shut it tends to look solid, really because the frame and the solid objects around it have gone flat. So that, if this picture was coloured, as it must have been, it would have been indistinguishable, to these one-eyed observers, from the solid reality.

"Then, let us see how the other contradictions disappear. There is the appearance of the prisoner Annesley. She was seen – on or after the eighteenth of May – with her long hair coiled on the top of her head. But at that date her hair was quite short. You have heard the evidence and you have the photograph taken on the twenty-third of April showing her with short hair, like a man's. Here is a contradiction which vanishes at once if you realise that these men were not looking at Miss Annesley at all, but at a photograph of her taken more than a year previously.

266

"And everything agrees with this assumption. The appearance of Miss Annesley has been declared by the witnesses to be identical with that photograph – a copy of which was in the house and could have been copied by anyone who had access to the house. Her figure was perfectly stationary. She appeared suddenly in the arch and then disappeared, she was not seen to come or to go. And the light kept coming and going, with intervals of darkness which are inexplicable, but that exactly fitted these appearances and disappearances. Then the figure was well lighted, though the room was nearly dark. Of course it was well lighted. It had to be recognised. And of course the rest of the room was dimly lighted, because the film-actors in the background had to be unrecognised.

"Then there is the extraordinary dress, the striped pinafore with the great white collar and the painter's blouse worn by Bland. Why this ridiculous masquerade? Its purpose is obvious. It was to make these observers believe that the portraits in the arch – which they mistook for real people – were the same persons as the film-actors in the background, whose features they could not distinguish. And Mr. Polton has shown us how the clothing of the portraits was managed.

"Then there is the lighting of the room. How was it lighted? None of the electric lamps was alight. But – a piece of a carbon pencil from an arc lamp, such as kinematographers use, has been found near the point "C", from which spot the picture would have been taken and exhibited, and the electric light meter showed, about this date, an unaccountable leakage of current such as would be explained by the use of an arc lamp.

"Then the evidence of the witnesses shows the hole in the floor in the wrong place. Of course it could not have been a real hole, for the gas and electric mains were just underneath. It was probably an oblong of black paper. But why was it in the wrong place? The explanation, I suggest, is that the picture was taken before the murder (and probably shown before the murder, too), that the spot shown was the one in which it was intended to bury the body, but that when the floor was taken up after the murder, the mains were found underneath and a new spot had to be chosen.

"Finally – as to the discrepancies – what has become of the third spectator? The mysterious man who came to the gate and called in these two men from the lane – along which they were known to pass every day at about the same time? Who is this mysterious individual? And where is he? Can we give him a name? Can we say that he is at this moment in this court, sitting amongst the spectators, listening to the pleadings in defence of his innocent victims, the prisoners who stand at the bar on their deliverance? I affirm, gentlemen, that we can. And more than that it is not permitted to me to say."

He paused, and a strange, impressive hush fell on the court. Men and women furtively looked about them, the jury stared openly into the body of the court, and the judge, looking up from his notes, cast a searching glance among the spectators. Suddenly my eye lighted on Mr. Wicks and his fiancée. The man was wiping away the sweat that streamed down his ashen, ghastly face, the woman had rested her head in her hands, and was trembling as if in an ague-fit.

I was not the only observer. One after another – spectators, ushers, jurymen, counsel, judge – noticed the terror-stricken pair, until every eye in the court was turned on them. And the silence that fell on the place was like the silence of the grave.

It was a dramatic moment. The air was electric, the crowded court tense with emotion. And Thorndyke, looking, with his commanding figure and severe impassive face, like a personification of Fate and Justice, stood awhile motionless and silent, letting emotion set the coping-stone on reason.

At length he resumed his address. "Before concluding," he began, "I have to say a few words on another aspect of the case. The learned counsel for the prosecution, referring to the motive for this crime, has suggested a desire on the part of the prisoners to remove the obstacle to their marriage. But it has been given in evidence that there are other persons who had a yet stronger and more definite motive for getting rid of the deceased Lucy Bland. You have heard that in the event of Bland's death, his partner, Julius Wicks, stood to inherit property of the value of six-thousand-pounds-per-annum, provided that Bland's wife was already dead. Now, the murder of Lucy Bland has fulfilled one of the conditions for the devolution of this property, and if you should convict and his Lordship should sentence the prisoner, Bland, then his death on the gallows would fulfil the other condition and this great property would pass to his partner, Julius Wicks. This is a material point, as is also the fact that Wicks is, as you have heard, an expert film-producer and kinema operator, that he has been proved to have had access to the house at Ditton, and that he is engaged to a film-actress.

"In conclusion, I submit that the evidence of Brodie and Stanton makes it certain that they were looking at a moving picture, and that all the other evidence confirms that certainty. But the evidence of this moving picture is the evidence of a conspiracy to throw suspicion on the prisoners. But a conspiracy implies conspirators. And there can be no doubt that those conspirators were the actual murderers of Lucy Bland. But if this be so, and I affirm that there can be no possible doubt that it is so, then it follows that the prisoners are innocent of the crime with which

268

they are charged, and I accordingly ask you for a verdict of 'Not Guilty'."

As Thorndyke sat down a faint hum arose in the court, but still all eyes were turned towards Wicks and Eugenia Kropp. A moment later the pair rose and walked unsteadily towards the door. But here, I noticed, Superintendent Miller had suddenly appeared and stood at the portal with a uniformed constable. As Wicks and Miss Kropp reached the door, I saw the constable shake his head. With, or without authority, he was refusing to let them leave the court. There was a brief pause. Suddenly there broke out a confused uproar, a scuffle, a loud shriek, the report of a pistol and the shattering of glass, and then I saw Miller grasping the man's wrists and pinning him to the wall, while the shrieking woman struggled with the constable to get to the door.

After the removal of the disturbers – in custody – events moved swiftly. The Crown counsel's reply was brief and colourless, practically abandoning the charge, while the judge's summing-up was a mere *précis* of Thorndyke's argument with a plain direction for an acquittal. But nothing more was needed, for the jury had so clearly made up their minds that the clerk had hardly uttered his challenge when the foreman replied with the verdict of "Not Guilty". A minute later, when the applause had subsided and after brief congratulations by the judge, the prisoners came down from the dock, into the court, moist-eyed but smiling, to wring Thorndyke's hands and thank him for this wonderful deliverance.

"Yes," agreed Mayfield – himself disposed furtively to wipe his eyes – "that is the word. It was wonderful. And yet it was all so obvious – when you knew."

A Sower of Pestilence

The affectionate relations that existed between Thorndyke and his devoted follower, Polton, were probably due, at least in part, to certain similarities in their characters. Polton was an accomplished and versatile craftsman, a man who could do anything, and do it well, and Thorndyke has often said that if he had not been a man of science, he would, by choice, have been a skilled craftsman. Even as things were, he was a masterly manipulator of all instruments of research, and a good enough workman to devise new appliances and processes and to collaborate with his assistant in carrying them out.

Such a collaboration was taking place when the present case opened. It had occurred to Thorndyke that lithography might be usefully applied to medico-legal research, and on this particular morning he and Polton were experimenting in the art of printing from the stone. In the midst of their labours, the bell from our chambers below was heard to ring, and Polton, reluctantly laying down the inking roller and wiping his hands on the southern aspect of his trousers, departed to open the door.

"It's a Mr. Rabbage," he reported on his return. "Says he has an appointment with you, sir."

"So he has," said Thorndyke. "And, as I understand that he is going to offer us a profound mystery for solution, you had better come down with me, Jervis, and hear what he has to say."

Mr. Rabbage turned out to be a elderly gentleman who, as we entered, peered at us through a pair of deep, concave spectacles and greeted us "with a smile that was childlike and bland." Thorndyke looked him over and adroitly brought him to the point.

"Yes," said Mr. Rabbage, "it is really a most mysterious affair that has brought me here. I have already laid it before a very talented detective officer whom I know slightly – a Mr. Badger – but he frankly admitted that it was beyond him and strongly advised me to consult you."

"Inspector Badger was kind enough to pay me a very handsome compliment," said Thorndyke.

"Yes. He said that you would certainly be able to solve this mystery without any difficulty. So here I am. And perhaps I had better explain who I am, in case you don't happen to know my name. I am the director of the St. Francis Home of Rest for aged, invalid, and destitute cats, an institution where these deserving animals are enabled to convert the autumn of their troubled lives into a sort of Indian Summer of comfort

270

and repose. The home is, I may say, my own venture. I support it out of my own means. But I am open to receive contributions, and to that end there is secured to the garden railings a large box with a wide slit and an inscription inviting donations of money, of articles of value, or of food or delicacies for the inmates."

"And do you get much?" I asked.

"Of money," he replied, "very little. Of articles of value, none at all. As to gifts of food, they are numerous, but they often display a strange ignorance of the habits of the domestic cat. Such things, for instance, as pickles and banana-skins, though doubtless kindly meant, are quite unsuitable as diet. But the most singular donation that I have ever received was that which I found in the box the day before yesterday. There were a number of articles, but all apparently from the same donor, and their character was so mysterious that I showed them to Mr. Badger, as I have told you, who was as puzzled as I was and referred me to you. The collection comprised three ladies' purses, a morocco-leather wallet, and a small aluminium case. I have brought them with me to show you."

"What did the purses contain?" Thorndyke asked.

"Nothing," replied Mr. Rabbage, gazing at us with wide-open eyes. "They were perfectly empty. That is the astonishing circumstance."

"And the leather wallet?"

"Empty, too, excepting for a few odd papers."

"And the aluminium case?"

"Ah!" exclaimed Mr. Rabbage, "that was the most amazing of all. It contained a number of glass tubes! And those tubes contained – now, what do you suppose?" He paused impressively, and then, as neither of us offered a suggestion, be answered his own question. "Fleas and lice! Yes, actually! Fleas and lice! Isn't that an extraordinary donation?"

"It is certainly," Thorndyke agreed. "Anyone might have known that, with a houseful of cats, you could produce your own fleas."

"Exactly," said Mr. Rabbage. "That is what instantly occurred to me, and also, I may say, to Mr. Badger. But let me show you the things."

He produced from a hand-bag and spread out on the table a collection of articles which were, evidently, the "husks" of the gleanings of some facetious pickpocket, to whom Mr. Rabbage's donation-box must have appeared as a perfect God-send. Thorndyke picked up the purses, one after the other, and having glanced at their empty interiors, put them aside. The letter-wallet he looked through more attentively, but without disturbing its contents, and then he took up and opened the aluminium case. This certainly was a rather mysterious affair. It opened like a cigarette case. One side was fitted with six glass specimen-tubes, each provided with a well-fitting parchment cap, perforated with a

271

number of needle-holes, and of the six tubes, four contained fleas – about a dozen in each tube – some of which were dead, but others still alive, and the remaining two lice, all of which were dead. In the opposite side of the case, secured with a catch, was a thin celluloid note-tablet on which some numbers had been written in pencil.

"Well," said Mr. Rabbage, when the examination was finished, "can you offer any solution of the mystery?"

Thorndyke shook his head gravely. "Not offhand," he replied. "This is a matter which will require careful consideration. Leave these things with me for further examination and I will let you know, in the course of a few days, what conclusion we arrive at."

"Thank you," said Mr. Rabbage, rising and holding out his hand. "You have my address, I think."

He glanced at his watch, snatched up his hand-bag, and darted to the door, and a moment later we heard him bustling down the stairs in the hurried, strenuous manner that is characteristic of persons who spend most of their lives doing nothing.

"I'm surprised at you, Thorndyke," I said when he had gone, "encouraging that ass, Badger, in his silly practical jokes. Why didn't you tell this old nincompoop that he had just got a pick-pocket's leavings and have done with it?"

"For the reason, my learned brother, that I haven't done with it. I am a little curious as to whose pocket has been picked, and what that person was doing with a collection of fleas and lice."

"I don't see that it is any business of yours," said I. "And as to the vermin, I should suggest that the owner of the case is an entomologist who specialises in epizoa. Probably he is collecting varieties and races."

"And how," asked Thorndyke, opening the case and handing it to me, "does my learned friend account for the faint scent of aniseed that exhales from this collection?"

"I don't account for it at all," said I. "It is a nasty smell. I noticed it when you first opened the case. I can only suppose that the flea-merchant likes it, or thinks that the fleas do."

"The latter seems the more probable," said Thorndyke, "for you notice that the odour seems to principally from the parchment caps of the four tubes that contain fleas. The caps of the louse tubes don't seem to be scented. And now let us have a little closer look at the letter-wallet."

He opened the wallet and took out its contents, which were unilluminating enough. Apparently it had been gutted by the pickpocket and only the manifestly valueless articles left. One or two bills, recording purchases at shops, a time-table, a brief letter in French, without its envelope and bearing neither address, date, nor signature, and a set of small maps mounted on thin card, this was the whole collection, and not one of the articles appeared to furnish the slightest clue to the identity of the owner.

Thorndyke looked at the letter curiously and read it aloud.

"It is just a little singular," he remarked, "that this note should be addressed to nobody by name, should bear neither address, date, nor signature, and should have had its envelope removed. There is almost an appearance of avoiding the means of identification. Yet the matter is simple and innocent enough, just an appointment to meet at the Mile End Picture Palace. But these maps are more interesting – in fact, they are quite curious."

He took them out of the wallet – lifting them carefully by the edges, I noticed – and laid them out on the table. There were seven cards, and each had a map, or rather a section, pasted on both sides. The sections had been cut out of a street map of London, and as each card was three-inches-by-four-and-a-half, each section represented an area of one-mile-by-a-mile-and-a-half. They had been very carefully prepared, neatly stuck on the cards, and varnished, and every section bore a distinguishing letter. But the most curious feature was a number of small circles drawn in pencil on various parts of the maps, each circle enclosing a number.

"What do you make of those circles, Thorndyke?" I asked.

"One can only make a speculative hypothesis," he replied. "I am disposed to associate them with the fleas and lice. You notice that the maps all represent the most squalid parts of East London – Spitalfields, Bethnal Green, Whitechapel, and so forth, where the material would be plentiful, and you also notice that the celluloid tablet in the insect case bears a number of pencilled jottings that might refer to these maps. Here, for instance, is a note, '$B\ 21\ a + b -$ ', and you observe that each entry has an "a" and a "b" with either a *plus* or a *minus* sign. Now, if we assume that "a" means fleas and "b" lice, or vice versa, the maps and the notes together might form a record of collections or experiments with a geographical basis."

"They might," I agreed, "but there isn't a particle of evidence that they do. It is a most fantastic hypothesis. We don't know, and we have no reason to suppose, that the insect-case and the wallet were the property of the same person. And we have no means of finding out whether they were or were not."

"There I think you do us an injustice, Jervis," said he. "Are we not lithographers?"

"I don't see where the lithography comes in," said I.

"Then you ought to. This is a test case. These maps are varnished, and are thus virtually lithographic transfer paper, and the celluloid tablet also has a non-absorbent surface. Now, if you handle transfer paper carelessly when drawing on it, you are apt to find, when you have transferred to the stone, that your finger-prints ink up, as well as the drawing. So it is possible that if we put these maps and the note-tablet on the stone, we may be able to ink up the prints of the fingers that have handled them and so prove whether they were or were not the same fingers."

"That would be interesting as an experiment," said I, "though I don't see that it matters two straws whether they were the same or not."

"Probably it doesn't," he replied, "though it may. But we have a new method and we may as well try it."

We took the things up to the laboratory and explained the problem to Polton, who entered into the inquiry with enthusiasm. Producing from a cupboard a fresh stone, he picked the maps out of the wallet one by one (with a pair of watchmaker's tweezers) and fell to work forthwith on the task of transferring the invisible – and possibly non-existent – fingerprints from the maps and the note-tablet to the stone. I watched him go through the various processes in his neat, careful, dexterous fashion and hoped that all his trouble would not be in vain. Nor was it, for when he began cautiously ink up the stone, it was evident that something was there, though it was not so evident what that something was. Presently, however, the vague markings took more definite shape, and now could be recognised eight rather confused masses of finger-prints, badly smeared, some incomplete, and all mixed up and superimposed so as to make the identification of any one print almost an impossibility.

Thorndyke looked them over dubiously. "It is a dreadful muddle," said he, "but I think we can pick out the prints well enough for identification if that should be necessary. Which of these is the notes tablet, Polton?"

"The one in the right-hand top corner, sir," was the reply.

"Ah!" said Thorndyke, "then that answers our question. Confused as the impressions are, you can see quite plainly that the left thumb is the same thumb as that on the maps."

"Yes," I agreed after making the comparison, "there is not much doubt that they are the same. And now the question is, what about it?"

"Yes," said Thorndyke, "that is the question." And with this we retired from the laboratory, leaving Polton joyfully pulling off proofs.

During the next few days I had a vague impression that my colleague was working at this case, though with what object I could not imagine. Mr. Rabbage's problem was too absurd to take seriously, and Thorndyke was beyond working out cases, as he used to at one time, for the sake of mere experience. However, a day or two later, a genuine case turned up and occupied our attention to some purpose.

It was about six in the evening when Mr. Nicholas Balcombe called on us by appointment, and proceeded, in a business-like fashion, to state his case.

"I was advised by my friend Stalker, of the Griffin Life Assurance Office, to consult you," said he. "Stalker tells me that you have got him out of endless difficulties, and I am hoping that you will be able to help me out of mine, though they are not so clearly within your province as Stalker's. But you will know about that better than I do.

"I am the manager of Rutherford's Bank – the Cornhill Branch – and I have just had a very alarming experience. The day before yesterday, about three in the afternoon, a deed-box was handed in with a note from one of our customers – Mr. Pilcher, the solicitor, of Pilcher, Markham, and Sudburys – asking us to deposit it in our strong-room and give the bearer a receipt for it. Of course this was done, in the ordinary way of business, but there was one exceptional circumstance that turns out to have been, as it would appear, providential. Owing to the increase of business our strong-room had become insufficient for our needs, and we have lately had a second one built on the most modern lines and perfectly fire-proof. This had not been taken into use when Pilcher's deed-box arrived, but as the old room was very full, I opened the new room and saw the deed-box deposited in it.

"Well, nothing happened up to the time that I left the bank, but about two o'clock in the morning the night watchman noticed a smell of burning, and on investigating, located the smell as apparently proceeding from the door of the new strong-room. He at once reported to the senior clerk, whose turn it was to sleep on the premises, and the latter at once telephoned to the police station. In a few minutes a police officer arrived with a couple of firemen and a hand-extinguisher. The clerk took them down to the strong-room and unlocked the door. As soon as it was opened, a volume of smoke and fumes burst out, and then they saw the deed-box – or rather the distorted remains of it – lying on the floor. The police took possession of what was left, but a very cursory examination on the spot showed that the box was, in effect, an incendiary bomb, with a slow time fuse or some similar arrangement."

"Was any damage done?" Thorndyke asked.

"Mercifully, no," replied Mr. Balcombe. "But just think of what might have happened! If I had put the box in the old strong-room it is certain that thousands of pounds' worth of valuable property would have been destroyed. Or again, if instead of an incendiary bomb the box had contained a high explosive, the whole building would probably have been blown to pieces."

"What explanation does Pilcher give?"

"A very simple one. He knows nothing about it. The note was a forgery, and on the firm's headed paper, or a perfect imitation of it. And mind you," Mr. Balcombe continued, "my experience is not a solitary one. I have made private inquiries of other bank managers, and I find that several of them have been subjected to similar outrages, some with serious results. And probably there are more. They don't talk about these things, you know. Then there are those fires, the great timber fire at Stepney, and those big warehouse fires near the London Docks, there is something queer about them. It looks as if some gang was at work for purposes of pure mischief and destruction."

"You have consulted the police, of course?"

"Yes. And they know something, I feel sure. But they are extremely reticent, so I suppose they don't know enough. At any rate, I should like you to investigate the case independently and so would my directors. The position is most alarming."

"Could you let me see Pilcher's letter?" Thorndyke asked.

"I have brought it with me," said Balcombe. "Thought you would probably want to examine it. I will leave it with you, and if we can give you any other information or assistance, we shall be only too glad."

"Was the box brought by hand?" inquired Thorndyke.

"Yes," replied Balcombe, "but I didn't see the bearer. I can get you a description from the man who received the package, if that would be any use."

"We may as well have it," said Thorndyke, "and the name and address of the person giving it, in case he is wanted as a witness."

"You shall have it," said Balcombe, rising and picking up his hat. "I will see to it myself. And you will let me know, in due course, if any information comes to hand?"

Thorndyke gave the required promise and our client took his leave.

"Well," I said with a laugh, as the brisk footsteps died away on the stairs, "you have had a very handsome compliment paid you. Our friend seems to think that you are one of those master craftsmen who can make bricks, not only without straw, but without clay. There's absolutely nothing to go on."

"It is certainly rather in the air," Thorndyke agreed. "There is this letter and the description of the man who left the packet, when we get it, and neither of them is likely to help us much."

He looked over the letter and its envelope, held the former up to the light and then handed them to me.

276

"We ought to find out whether this is Pilcher's own paper or an imitation," said I, when I had examined the letter and envelope without finding anything in the least degree distinctive or characteristic, "because, if it is their paper, the unknown man must have had some sort of connection with their establishment or staff."

"There must have been some sort of connection in any case," said Thorndyke. "Even an imitation implies possession of an original. But you are quite right. It is a line of inquiry, and practically the only one that offers."

The inquiry was made on the following day, and the fact clearly established that the paper was Pitcher's paper, but the ink was not their ink. The handwriting appeared to be disguised, and no one connected with the firm was able to recognise it. The staff, even to the caretaker, were all eminently respectable and beyond suspicion of being implicated in an affair of the kind.

"But after all," said Mr. Pitcher, "there are a hundred ways in which a sheet of paper may go astray if anyone wants it – at the printer's, the stationer's, or even in this office – for the paper is always in the letter-rack on the table."

Thus our only clue – if so it could be called – came to an end, and I waited with some curiosity to see what Thorndyke would do next. But so far as I could see, he did nothing, nor did he make any reference to this obscure case during the next few days. We had a good deal of other work on hand, and I assumed that this fully occupied his attention.

One evening, about a week later, he made the first reference to the case and a very mysterious communication it seemed to me.

"I have projected a little expedition for to-morrow," said he. "I am proposing to spend the day, or part of it, in the pastoral region of Bethnal Green."

"In connection with any of our cases?" I asked.

"Yes," he replied. "Balcombe's. I have been making some cautious inquiries with Polton's assistance, principally among hawkers and coffee-shop keepers, and I think I have struck a promising track."

"What kind of inquiries have you been making?" said I.

"I have been looking for a man, or men, engaged in giving street entertainments. That is what our data seemed to suggest, among other possibilities."

"Our data!" I exclaimed. "I didn't know we had any."

"We had Balcombe's account of the attempt to burn the bank. That gave us some hint as to the kind of man to look for. And there were certain other data, which my learned friend may recall."

"I don't recall anything suggesting a street entertainer," said I.

277

"Not directly," he replied. "It was one of several hypotheses, but it is probably the correct one, as I have heard of such a person as I had assumed, and have ascertained where he is likely to be found on certain days. To-morrow I propose to go over his beat in the hope of getting a glimpse of him. If you think of coming with me, I may remind you that it is not a dressy neighbourhood."

On the following morning we set forth about ten o'clock, and as raiment which is inconspicuous at Bethnal Green may be rather noticeable in the Temple, we slipped out by the Tudor Street gate and made our way to Blackfriars Station. In place of the usual "research-case," I noticed that Thorndyke was carrying a somewhat shabby wood-fibre attaché case, and that he had no walking-stick. We got out at Aldgate and presently struck up Vallance Street in the direction of Bethnal Green, and by the brisk pace and the direct route adopted, I judged that Thorndyke had a definite objective. However, when we entered the maze of small streets adjoining the Bethnal Green Road, our pace was reduced to a saunter, and at corners and crossroads Thorndyke halted from time to time to look along the streets, and occasionally he referred to a card which he produced from his pocket, on which were written the names of streets and days of the week.

A couple of hours passed in this apparently aimless perambulation of the back streets.

"It doesn't look as if you were going to have much luck," I remarked, suppressing a yawn. "And I am not sure that we are not, in our turn, being 'spotted'. I have noted a man – a small, shabby-looking fellow, apparently keeping us in view from a distance, though I don't see him at the moment."

"It is quite likely," said Thorndyke. "This is a shady neighbourhood, and any native could see that we don't belong to it. Good morning! Taking a little fresh air?"

The latter question was addressed to a man who was standing at the door of a small coffee-shop, having apparently come to the surface for a "breather".

"Dunno about fresh," was the reply, "but it's the best there is. By-the-by, I saw one of them blokes what I was a-tellin' you about go by just now. Foreigner with the rats. If you want to see him give a show, I expect you'll find him in that bit of waste ground off Bolter's Rents."

"Bolter's Rents?" Thorndyke repeated. "Is that a turning out of Salcombe Street?"

"Quite right," was the reply. "Half-way up on the right-hand side."

Thanking our informant, Thorndyke strode off up the street, and as we turned the next corner I glanced back. At the moment, the small man whom I had noticed before stepped out of a doorway and came after us at a pace suggesting anxiety not to lose sight of us.

Bolter's Rents turned out to be a wide paved alley, one side of which opened into a patch of waste ground where a number of old houses had been demolished. This space had an unspeakably squalid appearance, for not only had the debris of the demolished houses been left in unsavoury heaps, but the place had evidently been adopted by the neighbourhood as a general dumping-ground for household refuse. The earth was strewn with vegetable, and even animal, leavings, flies and bluebottles hummed around and settled in hundreds on the garbage, and the air was pervaded by an odour like that of an old-fashioned brick dust-bin.

But in spite of these trifling disadvantages, a considerable crowd had collected, mainly composed of women and children, and at the centre of the crowd a man was giving an entertainment with a troupe of performing rats. We had sauntered slowly up the Rents and now halted to look on. At the moment, a white rat was climbing a pole at the top of which a little flag was stuck in a socket. We watched him rapidly climb the pole, seize the flagstaff in his teeth, lift it out of the socket, climb down the pole and deliver the flag to his master. Then a little carriage was produced and the rat harnessed into it, another white rat being dressed in a cloak and placed in the seat, and the latter – introduced to the audience as Lady Murphy – was taken for a drive round the stage.

While the entertainment was proceeding, I inspected the establishment and its owner. The stage was composed of light hinged boards opened out on a small four-wheeled hand-cart, apparently home-made. At one end was a largish cage, divided by a wire partition into two parts, one of which contained a number of white and piebald rats, while the inmates of the other compartment were all wild rats – but not, I noted, the common brown or Norway rat, but the old-fashioned British black rat. I remarked upon the circumstance to Thorndyke.

"Yes," he said, "they were probably caught locally. The sewers here will be inhabited by brown rats, but the houses, in an old neighbourhood like this, will be infested principally by the black rat. What do you make of the exhibitor?"

I had already noticed him, and now unobtrusively examined him again. He was a medium-sized man with a sallow complexion, dark, restless eyes – which frequently wandered in our direction – a crop of stiff, bushy, upstanding hair – he wore no hat – and a ragged beard.

"A Slav of some kind, I should think," was my reply. "A Russian, or perhaps a Lett. But that beard is not perfectly convincing."

279

"No," Thorndyke agreed, "but it is a good make up. Perhaps we had better move on now. We have a deputy, you observe."

As he spoke, the small man whom I had observed following us strolled up the Rents, and as he drew nearer, revealed to my astonished gaze no less a person than our ingenious laboratory assistant, Polton. Strangely altered, indeed, was our usually neat and spruce artificer with his seedy clothing and grubby hands, but as he sauntered up, profoundly unaware of our existence, a faint reminiscence of the familiar crinkly smile stole across his face.

We were just moving off when a chorus of shrieks mingled with laughter arose from the spectators, who hastily scattered right and left, and I had a momentary glimpse of a big black rat bounding across the space, to disappear into one of the many heaps of debris. It seemed that the exhibitor had just opened the cage to take out a black rat when one of the waiting performers – presumably a new recruit – had seized the opportunity to spring out and escape.

"Well," a grinning woman remarked to me, genially, "there's plenty more where that one came from. You should see this place on a moonlight night! Fair alive with 'em, it is."

We sauntered up the Rents and along the cross street at the top, and as we went, I reflected on the very singular inquiry in which Thorndyke seemed to be engaged. The rat-tamer's appearance was suspicious. He didn't quite look the part, and his beard was almost certainly a make-up – and a skilful one, too, for it was no mere "property" beard, and the restless, furtive eyes, and a certain suppressed excitement in his bearing, hinted at something more than met the eye. But if this was Mr. Balcombe's incendiary, how had Thorndyke arrived at his identity and, above all, by what process of reasoning had he contrived to associate the bank outrage with performing rats? That he had done so, his systematic procedure made quite clear. But how? It had seemed to me that we had not a single fact on which to start an investigation.

We had walked the length of the cross street, and had halted before turning, when a troop of children emerged from the Rents. Then came the exhibitor, towing his cart, with the cage shrouded in a cloth, then more children, and finally, at a little distance, Polton, slouching along idly but keeping the cart in view.

"I think," said Thorndyke, "it would be instructive, as a study in urban sanitation, to have a look round the scene of the late exhibition."

We retraced our steps down Bolter's Rents, now practically deserted, and wandered around the patch of waste land and in among the piles of bricks and rotting timber where the houses had been pulled down.

"Your lady friend was right," said Thorndyke. "This is a perfect Paradise for rats. Convenient residences among the ruins and unlimited provisions to be had for the mere picking up."

"Apparently you were right, too," said I, "as to the species inhabiting these eligible premises. That seems to be a black rat," and I pointed to a deceased specimen that lay near the entrance to a burrow.

Thorndyke stooped over the little corpse, and after a brief inspection, drew a glove on his right hand.

"Yes," he said, "this is a typical specimen of *Mus rattus*, though it is unusually light in colour. I think it will be worth taking away to examine at our leisure."

Glancing round to see that we were unobserved, he opened his attaché case and took from it a largish tin canister and removed the lid – which, I noted, was anointed at the joint with vaseline. Stooping, he picked up the dead rat by the tail with his gloved fingers dropped it into the canister, clapped on the lid, and replaced it in the attaché case. Then he pulled off the glove and threw it on a rubbish heap.

"You are mighty particular," said I.

"A dead rat is a dirty thing," said he, "and it was only an old glove."

On our way home, I made various cautious attempt to extract from Thorndyke some hint as to the purpose of his investigation and his mode of procedure. But I could extract nothing from him beyond certain generalities.

"When a man," said he, "introduces an incendiary bomb into the strong-room of a bank, we may reasonably inquire as to his motives. And when we have reached the fairly obvious conclusion as to what those motives must be, we may ask ourselves what kind of conduct such motives will probably generate – that is, what sort of activities will be likely to be associated with such motives and with the appropriate state of mind. And when we have decided on that, too, we may look for a person engaged in those activities, and if we find such a person we may consider that we have a *prima facie* case. The rest is a matter of verification."

"That is all very well, Thorndyke," I objected, "but if I find a man trying to set fire to a bank, I don't immediately infer that his customary occupation is exhibiting performing rats in a back street of Bethnal Green."

Thorndyke laughed quietly. "My learned friend's observation is perfectly just. It is not a universal rule. But we are dealing with a specific case in which certain other facts are known to us. Still, the connection, if there is one, has yet to be established. This exhibitor may turn out not to be Balcombe's man after all."

"And if he is not?"

"I think we shall want him all the same, but I shall know better in a couple of hours' time."

What transpired during those two hours I did not discover at the time, for I had an engagement to dine with some legal friends and must needs hurry away as soon as I had purified myself from the effects of our travel in the unclean East. When I returned to our chambers, about half-past ten, I found Thorndyke seated in his easy chair immersed in a treatise on old musical instruments. Apparently he had finished with the case.

"How did Polton get on?" I asked.

"Admirably," replied Thorndyke. "He shadowed our entertaining friend from Bethnal Green to a by-street in Ratcliff, where he apparently resides. But he did more than that. We had made up a little book of a dozen leaves of transfer paper in which I wrote in French some infallible rules for taming rats. Just as the man was going into his house, Polton accosted him and asked him for an expert opinion on these directions. The foreign gentleman was at first impatient and huffy, but when he had glanced at the book, he became interested, and a good deal amused, and finally read the whole set of rules through attentively. Then he handed the book back to Polton and recommended him to follow the rules carefully, offering to supply him with a few rats to experiment on, an offer which Polton asked him to hold over for a day or two.

"As soon as he got home, Polton dismembered the book and put the leaves down on the stone, with this result."

He took from his pocket-book a number of small pieces of paper, each of which was marked more or less distinctly with lithographed reproductions of finger-prints, and laid them on the table. I looked through them attentively, and with a faint sense of familiarity.

"Isn't that left thumb," said I, "rather similar to the print on the maps from Mr. Rabbage's letter wallet?"

"It is identical," he replied. "Here are the proofs of the map-prints and the note-tablet. If you compare them, you can see that not only the left thumb, but the other prints are the same in all."

Careful comparison showed that this was so.

"But," I exclaimed, "I don't understand this at all. These are the finger-prints of Mr. Rabbage's mysterious entomologist. I thought you were looking for Balcombe's man."

"My impression," he replied "is that they are the same person, though the evidence is far from conclusive. But we shall soon know. I have sworn an information against the foreign gent, and Miller has arranged to raid the house at Ratcliff early to-morrow and as it promises to be a highly interesting event, I propose to be present. Shall I have the pleasure of my learned friend's company?"

"Most undoubtedly," I replied, "though I am absolutely in the dark as to the meaning of the whole affair."

"Then," said Thorndyke, "I recommend you to go over the history of both cases systematically in the interval."

Six o'clock on the following morning found us in an empty house in Old Gravel Lane, Ratcliff, in company with Superintendent Miller and three stalwart plain clothes men, awaiting the report of a patrol. We were all dressed in engineers' overalls, reeking with naphthalin. Our trousers were tucked into our socks, and socks and boots were thickly smeared with vaseline, as were our wrists, around which our sleeves were bound closely with tape. These preparations, together with an automatic pistol served out to each of us, gave me some faint inkling of the nature of the case, though it was still very confused in my mind.

About a quarter-past-six, a messenger arrived and reported that the house which was to be raided was open. Thereupon Miller and one of his men set forth, and the rest of us followed at short intervals. On arriving at the house, which was but a short distance from our rendezvous, we found a stolid plain-clothes man guarding the open door and a frowsy-looking woman who carried a jug of milk, angrily demanding in very imperfect English to be allowed to pass into her house. Pushing past the protesting housekeeper, we entered the grimy passage, where Miller was just emerging from a ground-floor room.

"That is the woman's quarters," said he, "and the kitchen seems to be a sort of rat-menagerie. We'd better try the first-floor."

He led the way up the stairs, and when he reached the landing he tried the handle of the front room. Finding the door locked or bolted, he passed on to the back room and tried the door of that, with the same result. Then, holding up a warning finger, he proceeded to whistle a popular air in a fine, penetrating tone, and to perform a double shuffle on the bare floor. Almost immediately an angry voice was heard in the front room, and slippered feet padded quickly across the floor. Then a bolt was drawn noisily, the door flew open, and for an instant I had a view of the rat-show man, clothed in a suit of very soiled pyjamas. But it was only for an instant. Even as our eyes met, he tried to slam the door to, and failing – in consequence of an intruding constabulary foot – he sprang back, leaped over a bed. and darted through a communicating doorway into the back room and shut and bolted the door.

"That's unfortunate," said Miller. "Now we're going to have trouble."

The superintendent was right. On the first attempt to force the door, a pistol-shot from within blew a hole in the top panel and made a notch in the ear of the would-be invader. The latter replied through the hole, and there followed a sort of snarl and the sound of a shattered bottle. Then, as the constable stood aside and shot after shot came from within, the door became studded with ragged holes. Meanwhile Miller, Thorndyke, and I tiptoed out on the landing, and taking as long a run as was possible, flung ourselves, simultaneously on the back-room door. The weight of three large men was too much for the crazy woodwork. As we fell on it together, there was a bursting crash, the hinges tore away, the door flew inwards, and we staggered into the room.

It was a narrow shave for some of us. Before we could recover our footing, the showman had turned with his pistol pointing straight at Miller's head. A bare instant before it exploded, Thorndyke, whose momentum had carried him half-way across the room, caught it with an upward snatch, and its report was followed by a harmless shower of plaster from the ceiling. Immediately our quarry changed his tactics. Leaving the pistol in Thorndyke's grasp, he darted across the room towards a work-bench on which stood a row of upright, cylindrical tins. He was in the act of reaching out for one of these when Thorndyke grasped his pyjamas between the shoulders and dragged him back, while Miller rushed forward and seized him. For a few moments there was a frantic and furious struggle, for the fellow fought with hands and feet and teeth with the ferocity of a wild cat and, overpowered as he was, still strove to drag his captors towards the bench. Suddenly, once more, a pistol-shot rang out, and then all was still. By accident or design the struggling man had got hold of the pistol that Thorndyke still grasped and pressed the trigger, and the bullet had entered his own head just above the ear.

"Pooh!" exclaimed Miller, rising and wiping his forehead, "that was a near one. If you hadn't stopped him, Doctor, we'd all have gone up like rockets."

"You think those things are bombs, then?" said I.

"Think!" he repeated. "I removed two exactly like them from the General Post Office, and they turned out to be charged with T.N.T. And those square ones on the shelf are twin brothers of the one that went off in Rutherford's Bank."

As we were speaking, I happened to glance round at the doorway, and there, to my surprise, was the woman whom we had seen below, still holding the jug of milk and staring in with an expression of horror at the dead revolutionary. Thorndyke also observed her, and stepping across to where she stood, asked, "Can you tell me if there has been, or is now, anyone sick in this house?

"Yes," the woman replied, without removing her eyes from the dead man. "Dere is a chentleman sick upstairs. I haf not seen him. He used to look after him," and she nodded to the dead body of the showman.

"I think we will go up and have a look at this sick gentleman," said Thorndyke. "You had better not come, Miller."

We started together up the stairs, and as we went I asked, "Do you suppose this is a case of plague?"

"No," he replied. "I fancy the plague department is in the kitchen, but we shall see."

He looked round the landing which we had now reached and then opened the door of the front room, Immediately I was aware of a strange, intensely fetid odour, and glancing into the room, I perceived a man lying, apparently in a state of stupor, in a bed covered with indescribably filthy bed-clothes. Thorndyke entered and approached the bed, and I followed. The light was rather dim, and it was not until we were quite close that I suddenly recognised the disease.

"Good God!" I exclaimed, "it is typhus!"

"Yes," said Thorndyke, "and look at the bed clothes, and look at the poor devil's neck. We can see now how that villain collected his specimens."

I stooped over the poor, muttering, unconscious wretch and was filled with horror. Bed-clothes, pillow, and patient were all alike crawling with vermin.

"Of course," I said as we walked homewards, "I see the general drift of this case, but what I can't under stand is how you connected up the facts."

"Well," replied Thorndyke, "let us set out the argument and trace the connections. The starting-point was the aluminium case that Mr. Rabbage brought us. Those tubes of fleas and lice were clearly an abnormal phenomenon. They might, as you suggested, have belonged to a scientific collector, but that was not probable. The fleas were alive, and were meant to remain alive, as the perforated caps of the tubes proved, And the lice had merely died, as lice quickly do if they are not fed. They did not appear to have been killed. But against your view there were two very striking facts, one of which I fancy you did not observe. The fleas were not the common human flea. They were Asiatic rat-fleas."

"You are quite right," I admitted. "I did not notice that."

"Then," he continued, "there was the aniseed with which the parchment caps of the tubes were scented. Now aniseed is irresistible to rats. It is an infallible bait. But it is not specially attractive to fleas. What then was the purpose of the scent? The answer, fantastic as it was, had to be provisionally accepted because it was the only one that suggested Itself. If one of these tubes had been exposed to rats – dropped down a rat-hole, for instance – it is certain that the rats would have gnawed off the parchment cap. Then the fleas would have been liberated, and as they were rat-fleas, they would have immediately fastened upon the rats. The tubes, therefore, appeared to be an apparatus for disseminating rat-fleas.

"But why should anyone want to disseminate rat-fleas? That question at once brought into view another striking fact, Here, in these tubes, were rat-fleas and body-lice, both carriers of deadly disease. The rat-flea is a carrier of plague, the body-louse is a carrier of typhus. It was an impressive coincidence. It suggested that the dissemination of rat-fleas might be really the dissemination of plague, and if the lice were distributed, too, that might mean the distribution of typhus.

"And now consider the maps. The circles on them all marked old slum-areas tenanted by low-class aliens. But old slums abound in rats, and low-class aliens abound in body-lice. Here was another coincidence. Then there was the note-tablet bearing numbers associated with the letters 'a' and 'b' and plus and minus signs. The letters 'a' and 'b' might mean rat and louse or plague and typhus, and the plus and minus might mean a success or a failure to produce an outbreak of disease. That was merely speculative, but it was quite consistent.

"So far we were dealing with a hypothesis based on simple observation. But that hypothesis could be proved or disproved. The question was, Were these insects infected insects, or were they not? To settle this I took one flea from each of the four tubes and 'sowed' it on agar, with the result that from each flea I got a typical culture of plague bacillus, which I verified with Haffkine's 'Stalactite Test.' I also examined one louse from each of the two tubes, and in each case got a definite typhus reaction. So the insects were infected and the hypothesis was confirmed.

"The next thing was to find the owner of the tubes. Now the circles on the maps indicated some sort of activity, presumably connected with rats and carried on in these areas.

"I visited those areas and got into conversation with the inhabitants on the subject of rats, rat-catchers, rat pits, sewermen, and everything bearing on rats, and at length I heard of an exhibitor of performing rats. You know the rest. We found the man, we observe that all his rats, excepting the tame white ones, were black rats – the special plague-carrying species – and we found on this spot a dead rat, which I ascertained on examining the body, had died of plague. Finally there was Polton's little book giving us the finger-prints of the owner of the

286

aluminium case. That completed the identification, and inquiries at the Local Government Board showed that cases of plague and typhus had occurred in the marked areas."

"Had not the authorities taken any steps in the matter?" I asked.

"Oh, yes," he replied. "They had carried out an energetic rat campaign in the London Docks, the likeliest source of infection. Naturally, they would not think of a criminal lunatic industriously sowing plague broadcast."

"Then how did you connect this man with the bank outrage?"

"I never did, very conclusively," he replied. "It was mostly a matter of inference. You see, the two crimes were essentially similar. They were varieties of the same type. Both were cases of idiotic destructiveness, and the agent in each was evidently a moral imbecile who was a professed enemy of society. Such persons are rare in this country, and when they occur are usually foreigners, most commonly Russians, or East Europeans of some kind. The only actual clue was the date on Pilcher's letter, the rather peculiar figures of which were extraordinarily like those on the maps and the note-tablet. Still, it was little more than a guess, though it happens to have turned out correct."

"And how do you suppose this fellow avoided getting plague and typhus himself?"

"It was quite likely that he had had both. But he could easily avoid the typhus by keeping himself clean and his clothing disinfected, and as to the plague, he could have used Haffkine's plague-prophylactic and given it to the woman. Clearly it would not have suited him to have a case of plague in the house and have the health officer inspecting the premises."

That was the end of the case, unless I should include in the history a very handsome fee sent to my colleague by the President of the Local Government Board.

"I think we have earned it," said Thorndyke, "and yet I am not sure that Mr. Rabbage is not entitled to a share."

And in fact, when that benevolent person called a few days later to receive a slightly ambiguous report and tender his fee, he departed beaming, bearing a donation wherewith to endow an additional bed, cot, or basket, in the St. Francis Home of Rest.

Rex v. Burnaby

It is a normal incident in general medical practice that the family doctor soon drifts into the position of a family friend. The Burnabys had been among my earliest patients, and mutual sympathies had quickly brought about the more intimate relationship. It was a pleasant household, pervaded by a quiet geniality and a particularly attractive, homely, unaffected culture. It was an interesting household, too, for the disparity in age between the husband and wife made the domestic conditions a little unusual and invited speculative observation. And there were other matters, to be referred to presently.

Frank Burnaby was a somewhat delicate man of about fifty, quiet, rather shy, gentle, kindly, and singularly innocent and trustful. He held a post at the Records Office, and was full of quaint and curious lore derived from the ancient documents on which he worked, selections from which he would retail in the family circle with a picturesque imagination and a fund of quiet, dry humour that made them delightful to listen to. I have never met a more attractive man, or one whom I liked better or respected more.

Equally attractive, in an entirely different way, was his wife, an extremely charming and really beautiful woman of under thirty – little more than a girl, in fact – amiable, high-spirited, and full of fun and frolic, but nevertheless an accomplished, cultivated woman with a strong interest in her husband's pursuits. They appeared to me an exceedingly happy and united couple, deeply attached to one another and in perfect sympathy. There were four children – three boys and a girl – of Burnaby's by his first wife, and their devotion to their young stepmother spoke volumes for her care of them.

But there was a fly in the domestic ointment – at least, that was what I felt. There was another family friend, a youngish man named Cyril Parker. Not that I had anything against him, personally, but I was not quite happy about the relationship. He was a markedly good-looking man, pleasant, witty, and extremely well-informed, for he was a partner in a publishing house and acted as reader for the firm, whence it happened that he, like Mr. Burnaby, gathered stores of interesting matter from his professional reading. But I could not disguise from myself that his admiration and affection for Mrs. Burnaby were definitely inside the danger zone, and that the intimacy – on his side, at any rate – was growing rather ominously. On her side there seemed nothing more than frank, though very pronounced, friendship. But I looked at the relationship askance. She was a woman whom any man might have fallen in love with, and I did not like the expression that I sometimes detected in Parker's eyes when he was looking at her. Still, there was nothing in the conduct of either to which the slightest exception could have been taken or which in any way foreshadowed the terrible disaster which was so shortly to befall.

The starting-point of the tragedy was a comparatively trivial event. By much poring over crabbed manuscripts, Mr. Burnaby developed symptoms of eye-strain, which caused me to send him to an oculist for an opinion and a prescription for suitable spectacles. On the evening of the day on which he had consulted the oculist, I received an urgent summons from Mrs. Burnaby and, on arriving at the house, found her husband somewhat seriously ill. His symptoms were rather puzzling, for they corresponded to no known disease. His face was flushed, his temperature slightly raised, his pulse rapid, though the breathing was slow, his throat was excessively dry, and his pupils widely dilated. It was an extraordinary condition, resembling nothing within my knowledge excepting atropine poisoning.

"Has he been taking medicine of any kind?" I asked.

Mrs. Burnaby shook her head. "He never takes any drugs or medicine but what you prescribe, and it couldn't be anything that he has taken, because the attack came on quite soon after he came home, before he had either food or drink."

It was very mysterious and the patient himself could throw no light on the origin of the attack. While I was reflecting on the matter, I happened to glance at the mantelpiece, on which I noticed a drop labelled *"The Eye Drops"* and a prescription envelope. Opening the latter, I found the oculist's prescription for the drops – a very weak solution of atropine sulphate.

"Has he had any of these drops?" I asked.

"Yes," replied Mrs. Burnaby. "I dropped some into his eyes as soon as he came in, two drops in each eye, according to the directions."

It was very odd. The amount of atropine in those four drops was less than a hundredth-of-a-grain, an impossibly small dose to produce the symptoms. Yet he had all the appearance of having taken a poisonous dose, which he obviously had not, since the drop-bottle was nearly full. I could make nothing of it. However, I treated it as a case of atropine poisoning, and as the treatment produced marked improvement, I went home, more mystified than ever.

When I called on the following morning, I learned that he was practically well, and had gone to his office. But that evening I had another urgent message, and on hurrying round to Burnaby's house, found him suffering from an attack similar to, but even more severe than, the one on the previous day. I immediately administered an injection of pilocarpine and other appropriate remedies, and had the satisfaction of seeing a rapid improvement in his condition. But whereas the efficacy of the treatment proved that the symptoms were really due to atropine, no atropine appeared to have been taken excepting the minute quantity contained in the eye-drops.

It was very mysterious. The most exhaustive inquiries failed to suggest any possible source of the poison excepting the drops, and as each attack had occurred a short time after the use of them, it was impossible to ignore the apparent connection, in spite of the absurdly minute dose.

"I can only suppose," said I, addressing Mrs. Burnaby and Mr. Parker, who had called to make inquiries, "that Burnaby is the subject of an idiosyncrasy – that he is abnormally sensitive to this drug."

"Is that a known condition?" asked Parker.

"Oh, yes," I replied. "People vary enormously in the way in which they react to drugs. Some are so intolerant of particular drugs – iodine, for instance – that ordinary medicinal doses produce poisonous effects, while others have the most extraordinary tolerance. Christisori, in his *Treatise on Poisons*, gives a case of a man, unaccustomed to opium, who took nearly an ounce of laudanum without any effect – a dose that would have killed an ordinary man. These drugs are terrible pitfalls for the doctor who doesn't know his patient. Just think what might have happened to Burnaby if someone had given him a full medicinal dose of belladonna."

"Does belladonna have the same effect as atropine?" asked Mrs. Burnaby.

"It is the same," I replied. "Atropine is the active principle of belladonna."

"What a mercy," she exclaimed, "that we discovered this idiosyncrasy in time. I suppose he had better discontinue the drops?"

"Yes," I answered, "most emphatically, and I will write to Mr. Haines and let him know that the atropine is impracticable."

I accordingly wrote to the oculist, who was politely sceptical as to the connection between the drops and the attacks. However, Burnaby settled the matter by refusing point-blank to have any further dealings with atropine, and his decision was so far justified that, for the time being, the attacks did not recur.

A couple of months passed. The incident had, to a great extent, faded from my mind. But then it was revived in a way that not only filled me with astonishment but caused me very grave anxiety. I was just about to set out on my morning round when Burnaby's housemaid met me at my door, breathing quickly and carrying a note. It was from Mrs. Burnaby, begging me to call at once and telling me that her husband had been seized by an attack similar to the previous ones. I ran back for my emergency bag and then hurried round to the house, where I found Burnaby lying on a sofa, very flushed, rather alarmed, and exhibiting well-marked symptoms of atropine poisoning. The attack, however, was not a very severe one, and the application of the appropriate remedies soon produced a change for the better.

"Now, Burnaby," I said, as he sat up with a sigh of relief, "what have you been up to? Haven't been tinkering with those drops again?"

"No," he replied. "Why should I? Haines has finished with my eyes."

"Well, you've been taking something with atropine in it."

"I suppose I have, but I can't imagine what. I have had no medicine of any kind."

"No pills, lozenges, liniment, plaster, or ointment?"

"Nothing medicinal of any sort," he replied. "In fact, I have swallowed nothing to-day but my breakfast, and the attack came on directly after, though it was a simple enough meal, goodness knows – just a couple of pigeon's eggs and some toast and tea."

"Pigeon's eggs," said I, with a grin. "Why not sparrow's?"

"Cyril sent them – as a joke, I think," Mrs. Burnaby explained (Cyril, of course, was Mr. Parker), "but I must say Frank enjoyed them. You see, Cyril has taken lately to keeping pigeons and rabbits and other edible beasts, and I think he has done it principally for Frank's sake, as you have ordered him a special diet. We are constantly getting things from Cyril now – pigeons and rabbits especially, and much younger than we can buy them at the shops."

"Yes," said Burnaby, "he is most generous. I should think he supplies more than half my diet. I hardly like to accept so much from him."

"It gives him pleasure to send these gifts," said Mrs. Burnaby, "but I wish it gave him pleasure to slaughter the creatures first. He always brings or sends them alive, and the cook hates killing them. As to me, I couldn't do it, though I deal with the corpses afterwards. I prepare nearly all Frank's food myself."

"Yes," said Burnaby, with a glance of deep affection at his wife, "Margaret is an artist in kickshaws and I consume the works of art. I can tell you, doctor, I live like a fighting cock."

This was all very well, but it was beside the question, which was, where did the atropine come from? If Burnaby had swallowed nothing

291

but his breakfast, it would seem that the atropine must have been in that. I pointed this out.

"But you know, doctor," said Burnaby, "that isn't possible. We can write the eggs off. You can't get poison into an egg without making a hole in the shell, and these eggs were intact. And as to the bread and butter, and the tea – we all had the same, and none of the others seem any the worse."

"That isn't very conclusive," said I. "A dose of atropine that would be poisonous to you would probably have no appreciable effect on the others. But, of course, the real mystery is how on earth atropine could have got into any of the food."

"It couldn't," said Burnaby, and that really was my own conviction. But it was an unsatisfactory conclusion, for it left the mystery unexplained, and when a length I took my leave to continue my rounds of visits, it was with the uncomfortable feeling that I had failed to trace the origin of the danger or to secure my patient against its recurrence.

Nor was my uneasiness unjustified. Little more than a week had passed when a fresh summons brought me to Burnaby's house, full of bewilderment and apprehension. And indeed there was good cause for apprehension, for when I arrived, to find Burnaby lying speechless and sightless, his blue eyes turned to blank discs of black, glittering with the unnatural "belladonna sparkle" – when I felt his racing pulse and watched his vain efforts to swallow a sip of water – I began to ask myself whether he was not beyond recall. The same question was asked mutely by the terrified eyes of his wife, who rose like a ghost from his bedside as I entered the room. But once more he responded to the remedies, though more slowly this time, and at the end of an hour I was relieved to see that the urgent danger was past, although he still remained very ill.

Meanwhile, inquiries failed utterly to elicit any explanation of the attack. The symptoms had set in shortly after dinner, a simple meal consisting of a pigeon cooked *en casserole* by Mrs. Burnaby herself, vegetables, and a light pudding which had been shared by the rest of the family, and a little Chablis from a bottle that had been unsealed and opened in the dining-room. Nothing else had been taken and no medicaments of any kind used. On the other hand, any doubts as to the nature of the attack were set at rest by a chemical test made by me and confirmed by the Clinical Research Association, Atropine was demonstrably present, though the amount was comparatively small. But its source remained an impenetrable mystery.

It was a profoundly disturbing state of affairs. The last attack had narrowly missed a fatal termination and the poison was still untraced. From the same unknown source a fresh charge might be delivered at any moment, and who could say what the result would be? Poor Burnaby was in a state of chronic terror and his wife began to look haggard and worn with constant anxiety and apprehension. Nor was I in much better case myself, for, whatever should befall, the responsibility was mine. I racked my brains for some possible explanation, but could think of none, though there were times when a horrible thought would creep into my mind, only to be indignantly cast out.

One evening a few days after the last attack, I received a visit from Burnaby's brother, a pathologist attached to one of the London hospitals, but not in practice. Very different was Dr. Burnaby from his gentle, amiable brother – a strong, resolute, energetic man and none too suave in manner. We were already acquainted, so no introductions were necessary, and he came to the point with characteristic directness.

"You can guess what I have come about, Jardine – this atropine business. What is being done in the matter?"

"I don't know that anything is being done," I answered lamely. "I can make nothing of it."

"Waiting for the next attack and the inquest, hmm? Well, that won't do, you know. This affair has got to be stopped before it is too late. If you don't know where the poison comes from, somebody does. Hmm! And it is time to find out who that somebody is. There aren't many to choose from. I am going there now to have a look round and make a few inquiries. You'd better come with me."

"Are they expecting you?" I asked.

"No," he answered gruffly, "but I'm not a stranger and neither are you."

I decided to go round with him, though I didn't much like his manner. This was evidently meant to be a surprise visit, and I had no great difficulty in guessing at what was in his mind. On the other hand, I was not sorry to share the responsibility with a man of his position and a relative of the patient. Accordingly, I set forth with him willingly enough, and it is significant of my state of mind at this time, that I took my emergency bag with me.

When we arrived Burnaby and his wife were just sitting down to dinner – the children took their evening meal by themselves – and they welcomed us with the ready hospitality that made this such a pleasant household. Dr. Burnaby's place was laid opposite mine, and I was faintly amused to note his eye furtively travelling over the table, evidently assessing each article of food as a possible vehicle of atropine. "If you had only let us know you were coming, Jim," said Mrs. Burnaby when the joint made its appearance, "we would have had something better than saddle of mutton. As it is, you must take pot-luck."

"Saddle of mutton is good enough for me," replied Dr. Burnaby. "But what on earth is that stuff that Frank has got?" he added, as Burnaby lifted the lid from a little casserole.

"That," she answered, "is a fricassee of rabbit. Such a tiny creature it was, a mere infant. Cook nearly wept at having to kill it."

"Kill it!" exclaimed the doctor. "Do you buy your rabbits alive?"

"We didn't buy this one," she replied. "It was brought by Cyril – Mr. Parker, you know," she added hastily and with a slight flush, as she caught a grim glance of interrogation. "He sends quite a lot of poultry and rabbits and things for Frank from his little farm."

"Ha!" said the doctor with a reflective eye on the casserole. "Hmm! Breeds them himself, hey? Whereabouts is his farm?"

"At Eltham. But it isn't really a farm. He just keeps rabbits and fowls and pigeons in a place at the back of his garden."

"Is your cook English?" Dr. Burnaby asked, glancing again at the casserole. "That affair of Frank's has rather a French look."

"Bless you, Jim," said Burnaby, "I am not dependent on mere cooks. I am a pampered gourmet. Margaret prepares most of my food with her own sacred hands. Cooks can't do this sort of thing." And he helped himself afresh from the casserole.

Dr. Burnaby seemed to reflect profoundly upon this explanation. Then he abruptly changed the subject from cookery to the Lindisfarne Gospels and thereby set his brother's chin wagging to a new tune. For Burnaby's affections as a scholar were set on seventh- and eighth-century manuscripts, and his knowledge of them was as great as his enthusiasm.

"Oh, get on with your dinner, Frank, you old windbag," exclaimed Mrs. Burnaby. "You are letting everything get cold."

"So I am, dear," he admitted, "but – I won't be a minute. I just want Jim to see those collotypes of the Durham Book. Excuse me."

He sprang up from the table and darted into the adjoining library, whence he returned almost immediately carrying a small portfolio.

"These are the plates," he said, handing the portfolio to his brother. "Have a look at them while I dispose of the arrears."

He took up his knife and fork and made as if to resume his meal. Then he laid them down and leaned back in his chair. "I don't think I want any more, after all," he said.

The tone in which he spoke caused me to look at him critically, for my talk with his brother had made me a little nervous and apprehensive of further trouble. What I now saw was by no means reassuring. A slight flush and a trace of anxiety in his expression made me ask, with outward composure but inward alarm, "You are feeling quite fit, I hope, Burnaby?"

"Well, not so very," he replied. "My eyes are going a bit misty and my throat – " Here he worked his lips and swallowed as if with some effort.

I rose hastily and, catching a terrified glance from his wife, went to him and looked into his eyes. And thereupon my heart sank. For already his pupils were twice their natural size and the darkened eyes exhibited the too-familiar sparkle. I was sensible of a thrill of terror and, as I looked into Burnaby's now distinctly alarmed face, his brother's ominous words echoed in my ears. Had I waited "for the next attack and the inquest"?

The symptoms, once started, developed apace. From moment to moment he grew worse, and the rapid enlargement of the pupils gave an alarming hint as to the intensity of the poisoning. I darted out into the hall for my bag, and as I re-entered, I saw him rise, groping blindly with his hands, until his wife, ashen-faced and trembling, took his arm and led him to the door.

"I had better give him a dose of pilocarpine at once," I said, getting out my hypodermic syringe and glancing at Dr. Burnaby, who watched me with stony composure.

"Yes," he agreed, "and a little morphine, too! And he will probably need some stimulant. I won't come up, only be in the way."

I followed the patient up to the bedroom and administered the antidotes forthwith. Then, while he was getting partially undressed with his wife's help, I went downstairs in search of brandy and hot water, I was about to enter the dining-room when, through the partly-open door, I saw Dr. Burnaby standing by the fireplace with his open hand-bag – which he had fetched in from the hall – on the table before him, and in his hand a little Bohemian glass jar from the mantelpiece. Involuntarily, I halted for a moment, and as I did so, he carefully deposited the little ornament in the bag and closed the latter, locking it with a small key which he then put in his pocket.

It was an excessively odd proceeding, but, of course, it was no concern of mine. Nevertheless, instead of entering the dining-room, I stole softly towards the kitchen and fetched the hot water myself. When I returned, the bag was back on the hall table and I found Dr. Burnaby grimly pacing up and down the dining room. He asked me a few questions while I was looking for the brandy, and then, somewhat to my surprise, proposed to come up and lend a hand with the patient.

On entering the bedroom, we found poor Burnaby lying half-undressed on the bed and in a very pitiable state, terrified, physically

295

distressed, and inclined to ramble mentally. His wife knelt by the bed, white-faced, red-eyed and evidently panic-stricken, though she was quite quiet and self-restrained. As we entered, she rose to make way for us, and while we were examining the patient's pulse and listening to his racing heart, she silently busied herself with the preparations for administering the stimulants.

"You don't think he is going to die, do you?" she whispered, as Dr. Burnaby handed me back my stethoscope.

"It is no use thinking," he replied dryly – and I thought rather callously. "We shall see." And with this he turned his back to her and looked at his brother with a gloomy frown.

For more than an hour that question was an open one. From moment to moment I expected to feel the wildly-racing pulse flicker out, to hear the troubled breathing die away in an expiring rattle. From time to time we cautiously increased the antidotes and administered restoratives, but I must confess that I had little hope. Dr. Burnaby was undisguisedly pessimistic. And as the weary minutes dragged on, and I looked momentarily for the arrival of the dread messenger, there would keep stealing into my mind a question that I hardly dared to entertain. What was the meaning of it all? Whence had the poison come? And why, in this household, had it found its way to Burnaby alone – the one inmate to whom it was specially deadly?

At last – at long last – there came a change, hardly perceptible at first, and viewed with little confidence. But after a time it became more pronounced, and then, quite rapidly, the symptoms began to clear up. The patient swallowed with ease, and great relish, a cup of coffee, the heart slowed down, the breathing became natural, and presently, as the morphine began to take effect, he sank into a doze which passed by degrees into a quiet sleep.

"I think he will do now," said Dr. Burnaby, "so I won't stay any longer. But it was a near thing, Jardine, most uncomfortably near."

He walked to the door, where, as he went out, he turned and bowed stiffly to his sister-in-law. I followed him down the stairs, rather expecting him to revert to the subject of his visit to me. But he made no reference to it, nor, indeed, did he say anything until he stood on the doorstep with his bag in his hand. Then he made a somewhat cryptic remark, "Well, Jardine," he said, "the Durham Book saved him. But for those collotypes, he would be a dead man." And with that he walked away, leaving me to interpret as best I could this decidedly obscure remark.

A quarter-of-an-hour later, as Burnaby was peacefully asleep and apparently out of all danger, I took my own departure, and as soon as I was outside the house, I proceeded to put into execution a plan that had been forming in my mind during the last hour. There was some mystery in this case that was evidently beyond my powers to solve. But solved it had to be, if Burnaby's life was to be saved, to say nothing of my own reputation, so I had decided to put the facts before my friend and former teacher, Dr. Thorndyke, and seek his advice, and if necessary, his assistance.

It was now past ten o'clock, but I determined to take my chance of finding him at his chambers, and accordingly, having found a taxi, I directed the driver to set me down at the gate of Inner Temple Lane. My former experience of Thorndyke's habits led me to be hopeful, and my hopes were not unjustified on this occasion, for when I had mounted to the first pair landing of No. 5A King's Bench Walk, and assaulted the knocker of the inner door, I was relieved to find him not only at home, but alone and disengaged. "It's a deuce of a time to come knocking you up," I said, as he shook my hand, "but I am in rather a hole, and the matter is urgent, so – "

"So you paid me the compliment of treating me as a friend," said he. "Very proper of you. What is the nature of your difficulty?"

"Why, I've got a case of recurrent atropine poisoning and I can make absolutely nothing of it."

Here I began to give a brief outline sketch of the facts, but after a minute or two he stopped me.

"It is of no use being sketchy, Jardine," said he. "The night is young. Let us have a complete history of the case, with particulars of all the persons concerned and their mutual relations. And don't spare detail."

He seated himself with a notebook on his knee, and when he had lighted his pipe, I plunged into the narrative of the case, beginning with the eye-drop incident and finishing with the alarming events of the present evening.

He listened with close attention, refraining from interrupting me excepting occasionally to ask for a date, which he jotted down with a few other notes. When I had finished, he laid aside his notebook and, as he knocked out his pipe, observed, "A very remarkable case, Jardine, and interesting by reason of the unusual nature of the poison."

"Oh, hang the interest!" I exclaimed. "I am not a toxicologist. I am a general practitioner, and I want to know what the deuce I ought to do."

"I think," said he, "that your duty is perfectly obvious. You ought to communicate with the police, either alone or in conjunction with some member of the family."

I looked at him in dismay. "But," I faltered, "what have I got to tell the police?"

"What you have told me," he replied, "which, put in a nutshell, amounts to this: Frank Burnaby has had three attacks of atropine poisoning, disregarding the eye-drops. Each attack has appeared to be associated with some article of food prepared by Mrs. Burnaby and supplied by Mr. Cyril Parker."

"But, good God!" I exclaimed. "You don't suspect Mrs. Burnaby?"

"I suspect nobody," he replied. "It may not be criminal poisoning at all. But Mr. Burnaby has to be protected, and the case certainly needs investigation."

"You don't think I could make a few inquiries myself first?" I suggested.

He shook his head. "The risk is too great," he replied. "The man might die before you reached a conclusion, whereas a few inquiries made by the police would probably put a stop to the affair, unless the poisoning is in some inconceivable way inadvertent."

That was what his advice amounted to, and I felt that he was right. But it put on me a horribly unpleasant duty, and as I wended homewards I tried to devise some means of mitigating its unpleasantness. Finally I decided to try to persuade Mrs. Burnaby to make a joint communication with me.

But the necessity never arose. When I made my morning visit, I found a taxicab drawn up opposite the door and the housemaid who admitted me looked as if she had seen a ghost.

"Why, what is the matter, Mabel?" I asked, as she ushered me funereally into the drawing-room.

She shook her head. "I don't know, sir. Something awful, I'm afraid. I'll tell them you are here." With this she shut the door and departed.

The housemaid's manner and the unusually formal reception filled me with vague forebodings. But even as I was wondering what could have happened, the question was answered by the entry of a tall man who looked like a guardsman in mufti.

"Dr. Jardine?" he asked, and as I nodded, he explained, presenting his card, "I am Detective Lane. I have been instructed to make some inquiries in respect of certain information which we have received. It is stated that Mr. Frank Burnaby is suffering from the effects of poison. So far as you know, is that true?"

"I hope he is recovered now," I replied, "but he was suffering last night from what appeared to be atropine poisoning."

"Have there been any previous attacks of the same kind?" the sergeant asked.

"Yes," I answered. "This was the fifth attack, but the first two were evidently due to some eye-drops that he had used."

"And in the case of the other three, have you any idea as to how the poison came to be taken? Whether it was in the food, for instance?"

"I have no idea, Sergeant. I know nothing more than what I have told you and, of course, I am not going to make any guesses. Is it admissible to ask who gave the information?"

"I am afraid not, sir," he replied. "But you will soon know. There is a definite charge against Mrs. Burnaby – I have just made the arrest – and we shall want your evidence for the prosecution."

I stared at him in utter consternation. "Do you mean," I gasped, "that you have arrested Mrs. Burnaby?"

"Yes," he replied, "on a charge of having administered poison to her husband."

I was absolutely thunderstruck. And yet, when I remembered Thorndyke's words and recalled my own dim and hastily-dismissed surmises, there was nothing so very surprising in this shocking turn of events.

"Could I have a few words with Mrs. Burnaby?" I asked.

"Not alone," he replied, "and better not at all. Still, if you have any business – "

"I have," said I, whereupon he led the way to the dining-room, where I found Mrs. Burnaby seated rigidly in a chair, pale as death, but quite calm though rather dazed. Opposite her a military-looking man sat stiffly by the table with an air of being unconscious of her presence, and he took no notice as I walked over to his prisoner and silently pressed her hand.

"I've come, Mrs. Burnaby," said I, "to ask if there is anything that you want me to do. Does Burnaby know about this horrible affair?"

"No," she answered. "You will have to tell him if he is fit to hear it, and if not, I want you to let my father know as soon as you can. That is all, and you had better go now, as we mustn't detain these gentlemen. Good-bye."

She shook my hand unemotionally, and when I had faltered a few words of vague encouragement and sympathy, I went out of the room, but waited in the hall to see the last of her.

The police officers were most polite and considerate. When she came out, they attended her in quite a deferential manner. As the sergeant was in the act of opening the street door, the bell rang, and when the door opened, it disclosed Mr. Parker standing on threshold. He was about to address Mrs. Burnaby but she passed him with a slight bow, and descended the steps, preceded by the sergeant and followed by the detective. The former held the door of the cab open while she entered, when he entered also and shut the door. The detective took his seat beside the driver and the cab moved off.

"What is in the wind, Jardine?" Parker asked looking at me with a distinctly alarmed expression. "Those fellows look like plain-clothes policemen."

"They are," said I. "They have just arrest Mrs. Burnaby on a charge of having attempted to poison her husband."

I thought Parker would have fallen. As it was, he staggered to a hall chair and dropped on it in a state of collapse. "Good God!" he gasped. "What a frightful thing! But there can't possibly be any evidence – any real grounds for suspecting her. It must be just a wild guess. I wonder who started it."

On this subject I had pretty strong suspicions, but I did not mention them, and when I had seen Parker into the dining-room and explained matters a little further I went upstairs, bracing myself for my very disagreeable task.

Burnaby was quite recovered, though rather torpid from the effects of the morphine. But my news roused him most effectually. In a moment he was out of bed, hurriedly preparing to dress, and though his pale, set face told how deeply the catastrophe had shocked him, he was quite collected and had all his wits about him.

"It's of no use letting our emotions loose, Doctor," said he, in reply to my expressions of sympathy. "Margaret is in a very dangerous position. You have only to consider what she is – a young, beautiful woman – and what I am, to realise that. We must act promptly. I shall go and see her father – he is a very capable lawyer – and we must get a first-class counsel."

This seemed to be an opportunity for mentioning Thorndyke's peculiar qualifications in a case of this kind, and I did so. Burnaby listened attentively, apparently not unimpressed, but he replied cautiously, "We shall have to leave the choice of the counsel to Harratt, but if you care, meanwhile, to consult with Dr. Thorndyke, you have my authority. I will tell Harratt."

On this I took my departure, not a little relieved at the way he had taken the evil tidings, and as soon as I had disposed of the more urgent part of my work, I betook myself to Thorndyke's chambers, just in time to catch him on his return from the Courts.

"Well, Jardine," he said, when I had brought the history up to date, "what is it that you want me to do?"

300

"I want you to do what you can to establish Mrs. Burnaby's innocence," I replied.

He looked at me reflectively for a few moments. Then he said, quietly but rather significantly, "It is not my practice to give *ex parte* evidence. An expert witness cannot act as an advocate. If I investigate the evidence in this case, it will have to be at your risk, as representing the accused, since any fact, no matter how damaging, which is in the possession of the witness must be disclosed in accordance with the terms of the oath, to say nothing of the obvious duty of every person to further the ends of justice. Speaking as a lawyer, and taking the known facts at their face value, I do not advise you to employ me to investigate the case at large. You might find that you had merely strengthened the hand of the prosecution.

"But I will make a suggestion. There seems to me to be in this case a very curious and interesting possibility. Let me investigate that independently. If my inquiries yield a positive result, I will let you know and you can call me as a witness. If they yield a negative result, you had better leave me out of the case."

To this suggestion I necessarily agreed, but when I took my leave of Thorndyke I went away with a sense of discouragement and failure. His reference to "the face value of the known facts" clearly implied that those facts were adverse to the accused, while the "curious possibility" suggested nothing but a forlorn hope from which he had no great expectations.

I need not follow the weary business in detail. At the first hearing before the magistrate the police merely stated the charge and gave evidence of arrest, both they and the defence asking for a remand and neither apparently desiring to show their hand. Accordingly the case was adjourned for seven days, and as bail was refused, the prisoner was detained in custody.

During those seven dreary days, I spent as much time as I could with Burnaby, and though I was filled with admiration of his fortitude and self, his drawn and pallid face wrung my heart. In those few days, he seemed to have changed into an old man. At his house, I also met Mr. Harratt, Mrs. Burnaby's father, a fine, dignified man and a typical old lawyer, and it was unspeakably pathetic to see the father and the husband of the accused woman each trying to support the courage of the other while both were torn with anxiety and apprehension. On one occasion, Mr. Parker was present and looked more haggard and depressed than either. But Mr. Harratt's manner towards him was so frigid and forbidding that he did not repeat his visit. At these meetings we discussed the case freely, which was a further affliction to me. For even I

301

could not fail to see that any evidence that I could give directly supported the case for the prosecution.

So six of the seven days ran out, and all the time there was no word from Thorndyke. But on the evening of the sixth day I received a letter from him, curt and dry, but still giving out a ray of hope. This was the brief message:

> *I have gone into the question of which I spoke to you and consider that the point is worth raising. I have accordingly written to Mr. Harratt advising him to that effect.*

It was a somewhat colourless communication, but I knew Thorndyke well enough to realise that his promises usually understated his intentions. And when, on the following morning, I met Mr. Harratt and Burnaby at the court, something in their manner – a new vivacity and expectancy – suggested that Thorndyke had been more explicit in his communication to the lawyer. But, all the same, their anxiety, for all their outward courage, was enough to have touched a heart of stone.

The spectacle that that court presented when the case was called forms a *tableau* that is painted on my memory in indelible colours. The mingling of squalor and tragedy, of frivolity and dread solemnity – the grave magistrate on the bench, the stolid policemen, the busy, preoccupied lawyers, and the gibbering crowd of spectators, greedy for sensation, with eager eyes riveted on the figure in the dock – offered such a medley of contrasts as I hope never to look upon again.

As to the prisoner herself, her appearance brought my heart into my mouth. Rigid as a marble statue and nearly as void of colour, she stood in the dock, guarded by two constables, looking with stony bewilderment on the motley scene, outwardly calm, but with the calm of one who looks death in the face, and when the prosecuting counsel rose to open the case for the police, she looked at him as a victim on the scaffold might look upon the executioner.

As I listened to the brief opening address, my heart sank, though the counsel, Sir Harold Layton, K.C., presented his case with that scrupulous fairness to the accused that makes an English court of justice a thing without parallel in the world. But the mere facts, baldly stated without comment, were appalling. No persuasive rhetoric was needed to show that they led direct to the damning conclusion.

Frank Burnaby, an elderly man, married to a young and beautiful woman, had on three separate occasions had administered to him a certain deadly poison – to wit, atropine. It would be proved that he had suffered from the effects of that poison, that the symptoms followed the taking of certain articles of food of which he alone had partaken, that the said food did actually contain the said poison, and that the food which contained the poison was specially prepared for his sole consumption by his wife, the accused, with her own hands. No evidence was at present available as to how the accused obtained the poison or that she had any such poison in her possession, nor would any suggestion be offered as to the motive of the crime. But, on the evidence of the actual administration of the poison, he would ask that the prisoner be committed for trial. He then proceeded to call the witnesses, of whom I was naturally the first. When I had been sworn and given my description, the counsel asked a few questions which elicited the history of the case and which I need not repeat. He then continued:

"Have you any doubt as to the cause of Mr. Burnaby's symptoms?"

"No. They were certainly due to atropine poisoning."

"Has Mr. Burnaby any constitutional peculiarity in respect of atropine?"

"Yes. He is abnormally susceptible to the effects of atropine."

"Was this peculiar susceptibility known to the accused?"

"Yes. It was communicated to her by me."

"Was it known, so far as you are aware, to any other persons?"

"Mr. Parker was present when I told her, and Mr. Burnaby and his brother, Dr. Burnaby, were also informed."

"Is there any way, so far as you know, in which the accused could have obtained possession of atropine?"

"Only by having the oculist's prescription for the eye-drops made up."

"Do you know of any medium, other than the food, by which atropine might have been taken by Mr. Burnaby?"

"I do not," I replied, and this concluded my evidence. But as I stepped out of the witness-box, I reflected gloomily that every word that I had spoken was a rivet in the fetters of the silent figure in the dock.

The next witness was the cook. She testified that she had killed and skinned the rabbit and had then handed it to the accused, who made it into a fricassee and prepared it for the table. Witness took no part in the preparation and she was absent from the kitchen on one occasion for several minutes, leaving the accused there alone.

When the cook had concluded her evidence, the name of James Burnaby was called, and the doctor entered the witness-box, looking distinctly uncomfortable, but grim and resolute. The first few questions elicited the circumstances of his visit to his brother's house and of the sudden attack of illness. That illness he had at once recognised as acute atropine poisoning, and had assumed that the poison was in the specially prepared food.

"Did you take any measures to verify this opinion?" counsel asked.

"Yes. As soon as I was alone, I took part of the remainder of the rabbit and put it in a glass jar which I found on the mantelpiece and which I first rinsed out with water. Later, I carried the sample of food to Professor Berry, who analysed it in my presence and found it to contain atropine. He obtained from it a thirtieth of a grain of atropine sulphate."

"Is that a poisonous dose?"

"Not to an ordinary person, though it is considerably beyond the medicinal dose. But it would have been a poisonous dose to Frank Burnaby. If he had swallowed this, in addition to what he had already taken, I feel no doubt that it would have killed him."

This concluded the case for the prosecution, and a black case it undoubtedly looked. There was no cross-examination, and as Thorndyke had arrived some time previously and conferred with Mr. Harratt and his counsel, I concluded that the defence would take the form of a counter-attack by the raising of a fresh issue. And so it turned out. When Thorndyke entered the witness-box and had disposed of the preliminaries, the counsel for the defence "gave him his head".

"You have made certain investigations in regard to this case, I believe?" Thorndyke assented, and the counsel continued, "I will not ask you specific questions, but will request you to describe your investigations and their result, and tell us what caused you to make them."

"This case," Thorndyke began, "was brought to my notice by Dr. Jardine, who gave me all the facts known to him. These facts were very remarkable and, taken together, they suggested a possible explanation of the poisoning. There were four striking points in the case. First, there was the very unusual nature of the poison. Second, the abnormal susceptibility of Mr. Burnaby to this particular poison. Third, the fact that all the food in which the poison appeared to have been conveyed came from the same source: It was sent by Mr. Cyril Parker. Fourth, that food consisted of pigeon's eggs, pigeon's flesh, and rabbit's flesh."

"What is there remarkable about that?" the counsel asked.

"The remarkable point is that the pigeon and the rabbit have an extraordinary immunity to atropine. Most vegetable-feeding birds and animals are more or less immune to vegetable poisons. Many birds and animals are largely immune to atropine, but among birds the pigeon is exceptionally immune, while the rabbit is the most extreme instance among animals. A single rabbit can take without the slightest harm more than a hundred times the quantity of atropine that would kill a man, and

304

rabbits habitually feed freely on the leaves and berries of the belladonna or deadly nightshade."

"Does the deadly nightshade contain atropine?" the counsel asked.

"Yes. Atropine is the active principle of the belladonna plant and gives to it its poisonous properties."

"And if an animal, such as a rabbit, were to feed on the nightshade plant, would its flesh be poisonous?"

"Yes. Cases of belladonna poisoning from eating rabbit have been recorded – by Firth and Bentley, for instance."

"And you suspected that the poison in this case had been contained in the pigeon and the rabbit themselves?"

"Yes. It was a striking coincidence that the poisoning should follow the consumption of these two specially immune animals. But there was a further reason for connecting them. The symptoms were strictly proportionate to the probable amount of poison in each case. Thus the symptoms were only slight after eating the pigeon's eggs. But the eggs of a poisoned pigeon could contain only a minute quantity of the poison. After eating the pigeon the symptoms were much more severe, and the body of a pigeon which had fed on belladonna would contain much more atropine than could be contained in an egg. Finally, after eating the rabbit, the symptoms were extremely violent, but a rabbit has the greatest immunity and is the most likely to have eaten large quantities of belladonna leaves."

"Did you take any measures to put your theory to the test?"

"Yes. Last Monday I went to Eltham, where I had ascertained that Mr. Cyril Parker lives, and inspected his premises from the outside. At the end of his garden is a small paddock enclosed by a wall. Approaching this across a meadow and looking over the wall, I saw that the enclosure was provided with small fowl-houses, pigeon-cotes, and rabbit hutches. All these were open and their inmates were roaming about the paddock. On one side of the enclosure, by the wall was a dense mass of deadly nightshade plants, extending the whole length of the wall and about a couple of yards in width. At one part of this was a ring fence of wire netting, and inside it were five half-grown rabbits. There was a basket containing a small quantity of cabbage leaves and other green stuff, but as I watched, I saw the young rabbits browsing freely on the nightshade plants in preference to the food provided for them.

"On the following day I went to Eltham again taking with me an assistant who carried a young rabbit in a small hamper. We watched the paddock until the coast was clear. Then my assistant got over the wall and abstracted a young rabbit from inside the ring fence and handed it to me. He then took the rabbit from the hamper and dropped it inside the fence. As soon as we were clear of the meadow, we killed the captured rabbit – to prevent any possible elimination of any poison that it might have swallowed. On arriving in London, I at once took the dead rabbit to St. Margaret's Hospital, where, in the chemical laboratory, and in the presence of Dr. Woodford, the Professor of Chemistry, I skinned it and prepared it as if for cooking by removing the viscera. I then separated the flesh from the bones and handed the former to Dr. Woodford, who, in my presence, carried out an exhaustive chemical test for atropine. The result was that atropine was found to be present in all the muscles and, on making a quantitative test, the muscles alone yielded no less than .93 grain."

"Is that a poisonous dose?" the counsel asked.

"Yes, it is a poisonous dose for a normal man. In the case of an abnormally susceptible person like Mr. Burnaby it would certainly be a fatal dose."

This completed Thorndyke's evidence. There was no cross and the magistrate put no questions. When Dr. Woodford had been called and had given confirmatory evidence, Mrs. Burnaby's counsel proceeded to address the bench. But the magistrate cut him short.

"There is really no case to argue," said he. "The evidence of the expert witnesses makes it perfectly clear that the poison was already in the food when it came into the hands of the accused. Consequently the charge against her of introducing the poison falls to the ground and the case must be dismissed. I am sure everyone will sympathise with the unfortunate lady who has been the victim of these extraordinary circumstances, and will rejoice, as I do, at the clearing up of the mystery. The prisoner is discharged."

It was a dramatic moment when, amidst the applause of the spectators, Mrs. Burnaby stepped down from the dock and clasped her husband's outstretched hand But, overwhelmed as they both were by the sudden relief, I thought it best not to linger, but, after congratulations, to take myself off with Thorndyke. But one pleasant incident I witnessed before I went: Dr. Burnaby had been standing apart, evidently some what embarrassed, when suddenly Mrs. Burnaby ran to him and held out her hand.

"I suppose, Margaret," he said gruffly, "you think I'm an old beast?"

"Indeed I don't," she replied. "You acted quite properly, and I respect you for having the moral courage to do it. And don't forget, Jim, that you action has saved Frank's life. But for you, there would have been no Dr. Thorndyke, and but for Dr. Thorndyke, there would have been another poisoned rabbit."

306

"What do you make of this case?" I asked, as Thorndyke and I walked away from the court. "Do you suppose the poisoning was accidental?"

He shook his head. "No, Jardine," he replied. "There are too many coincidences. You notice that the poisoned animals did not appear until after Mr. Parker had learned from you that Burnaby was abnormally sensitive to atropine and could consequently be poisoned by an ordinary medicinal dose. Then the sending of the animals alive looks like a precaution divert suspicion from himself and confuse the issue. Again, that ring fence among the belladonna plans has a fishy look, and the plants themselves were not only abnormally numerous but many of them very young and looked as if they had been planted. Further, I happen to know that Parker's firm published, only last year, a book on toxicology in which the immunity of pigeons and rabbits was mentioned and which Parker probably read."

"Then do you believe that he intended to let Mrs. Burnaby – the woman with whom he was in love – bear the brunt of his crime? It seems incredibly villainous and cowardly."

"I do not," he replied. "I imagine that the rabbit that I captured, or one of the others, would have been sent to Burnaby in a few days' time. The cook would probably have prepared it for him and it would almost certainly have killed him, and his death would have been proof of Mrs. Burnaby's innocence. Suspicion would have been transferred to the cook. But I don't suppose any action will be taken against him, for it is practically certain that no jury would convict him on my evidence."

Thorndyke was right in his opinion. No proceedings were taken against Parker. But the house of the Burnabys knew him no more.

A Mystery of the Sand-Hills

I have occasionally wondered how often Mystery and Romance present themselves to us ordinary men of affairs, only to be passed by without recognition. More often, I suspect, than most of us imagine. The uncanny tendency of my talented friend John Thorndyke to become involved in strange, mysterious, and abnormal circumstances has almost become a joke against him. But yet, on reflection, I am disposed to think that his experiences have not differed essentially from those of other men, but that his extraordinary powers of observation and rapid inference have enabled him to detect abnormal elements in what, to ordinary men, appeared to be quite commonplace occurrences. Certainly this was so in the singular Roscoff case, in which, if I had been alone, I should assuredly have seen nothing to merit more than a passing attention.

It happened that on a certain summer morning – it was the fourteenth of August, to be exact – we were discussing this very subject as we walked across the golf-links from Sandwich towards the sea. I was spending a holiday in the old town with my wife, in order that she might paint the ancient streets, and we had induced Thorndyke to come down and stay with us for a few days. This was his last morning, and we had come forth betimes to stroll across the sand-hills to Shellness.

It was a solitary place in those days. When we came off the sand-hills on to the smooth, sandy beach, there was not a soul in sight, and our own footprints were the first to mark the firm strip of sand between high-water mark and the edge of the quiet surf.

We had walked a hundred yards or so when Thorndyke stopped and looked down at the dry sand above tide-marks and then along the wet beach.

"Would that be a shrimper?" he cogitated, referring to some impressions of bare feet in the sand. "If so, he couldn't have come from Pegwell, for the River Stour bars the way. But he came out of the sea and seems to have made straight for the sand-hills."

"Then he probably was a shrimper," said I, not deeply interested.

"Yet," said Thorndyke, "it was an odd time for a shrimper to be at work."

"What was an odd time?" I demanded. "When was he at work?"

"He came out of the sea at this place," Thorndyke replied, glancing at his watch, "at about half-past eleven last night, or from that to twelve."

"Good Lord, Thorndyke!" I exclaimed, "how on earth do you know that?"

"But it is obvious, Anstey," he replied. "It is now half-past-nine, and it will be high-water at eleven, as we ascertained before we came out. Now, if you look at those footprints on the sand, you see that they stop short – or rather begin – about two-thirds of the distance from high-water mark to the edge of the surf. Since they are visible and distinct, they must have been made after last high-water. But since they do not extend to the water's edge, they must have been made when the tide was going out, and the place where they begin is the place where the edge of the surf was when the footprints were made. But the place is, as we see, about an hour below the high-water mark, Therefore, when the man came out of the sea, the tide had been going down for an hour, roughly. As it is high-water at eleven this morning, it was high-water at about ten-forty last night, and as the man came out of the sea about an hour after high-water, he must have come out at, or about, eleven-forty. Isn't that obvious?"

"Perfectly," I replied, laughing. "It is as simple as sucking eggs when you think it out. But how the deuce do you manage always to spot these obvious things at a glance? Most men would have just glanced at those footprints and passed them without a second thought."

"That", he replied, "is a mere matter of habit, the habit of trying to extract the significance of simple appearances. It has become almost automatic with me."

During our discussion we had been walking forward slowly, straying on to the edge of the sand-hills. Suddenly, in a hollow between the hills, my eye lighted upon a heap of clothes, apparently, to judge by their orderly disposal, those of a bather. Thorndyke also had observed them and we approached together and looked down on them curiously.

"Here is another problem for you," said I. "Find the bather. I don't see him anywhere."

"You won't find him here," said Thorndyke. "These clothes have been out all night. Do you see the little spider's web on the boots with a few dewdrops still clinging to it? There has been no dew forming for a good many hours. Let us have a look at the beach."

We strode out through the loose sand and stiff, reedy grass to the smooth beach, and here we could plainly see a line of prints of naked feet leading straight down to the sea, but ending abruptly about two-thirds of the way to the water's edge.

"This looks like our nocturnal shrimper," said I. "He seems to have gone into the sea here and come out at the other place. But if they are the same footprints, he must have forgotten to dress before he went home. It is a quaint affair."

"It is a most remarkable affair," Thorndyke agreed, "and if the footprints are not the same it will be still more inexplicable."

He produced from his pocket a small spring tape-measure with which he carefully took the lengths of two of the most distinct footprints and the length of the stride. Then we walked back along the beach to the other set of tracks, two of which he measured in the same manner.

"Apparently they are the same," he said, putting away his tape. "Indeed, they could hardly be otherwise. But the mystery is, what has become of the man? He couldn't have gone away without his clothes, unless he is a lunatic, which his proceedings rather suggest. There is just the possibility that he went into the sea again and was drowned. Shall we walk along towards Shellness and see if we can find any further traces?"

We walked nearly half-a-mile along the beach, but the smooth surface of the sand was everywhere unbroken. At length we turned to retrace our steps, and at this moment I observed two men advancing across the sand-hills. By the time we had reached the mysterious heap of garments they were quite near and, attracted no doubt by the intentness with which we were regarding the clothes, they altered their course to see what we were looking at. As they approached, I recognized one of them as a barrister named Hallet, a neighbour of mine in the Temple, whom I had already met in the town, and we exchanged greetings.

"What is the excitement?" he asked, looking at the heap of clothes and then glancing along the deserted beach, "and where is the owner of the togs? I don't see him anywhere."

"That is the problem," said I. "He seems to have disappeared."

"Gad!" exclaimed Hallett, "if he has gone home without his clothes, he'll create a sensation in the town! What?"

Here the other man, who carried a set of golf clubs, stooped over the clothes with a look of keen interest.

"I believe I recognize these things, Hallett. In fact, I am sure I do. That waistcoat, for instance. You must have noticed that waistcoat. I saw you playing with the chap a couple of days ago. Tall, clean-shaven, dark fellow. Temporary member, you know. What was his name? Popoff, or something like that?"

"Roscoff," said Hallett. "Yes, by Jove, I believe you are right. And now I come to think of it, he mentioned to me that he sometimes came up here for a swim. He said he particularly liked a paddle by moonlight, and I told him he was a fool to run the risk of bathing in a lonely place like this, especially at night."

"Well, that is what he seems to have done," said Thorndyke, "for these clothes have certainly been here all night, as you can see by that spider's web."

"Then he has come to grief, poor beggar!" said Hallett. "Probably got carried away by the current. There is a devil of a tide here on the flood."

He started to walk towards the beach, and the other man, dropping his clubs, followed.

"Yes," said Hallett, "that is what has happened. You can see his footprints plainly enough going down to the sea, but there are no tracks coming back."

"There are some tracks of bare feet coming out of the sea farther up the beach," said I, "which seem to be his."

Hallett shook his head. "They can't be his," he said, "for it is obvious that he never did come back. Probably they are the tracks of some shrimper. The question is, what are we to do! Better take his things to the dormy-house and then let the police know what has happened."

We went back and began to gather up the clothes, each of us taking one or two articles.

"You were right, Morris," said Hallett, as he picked up the shirt. "Here's his name, 'P. Roscoff', and I see it is on the vest and the shorts, too. And I recognize the stick now – not that that matters, as the clothes are marked."

On our way across the links to the dormy-house, mutual introductions took place. Morris was a London solicitor, and both he and Hallett knew Thorndyke by name.

"The coroner will have an expert witness," Hallett remarked as we entered the house. "Rather a waste in a simple case like this. We had better put the things in here."

He opened the door of a small room furnished with a good-sized table and a set of lockers, into one of which he inserted a key.

"Before we lock them up," said Thorndyke, "I suggest that we make and sign a list of them and of the contents of the pockets to put with them."

"Very well," agreed Hallett. "You know the ropes in these cases. I'll write down the descriptions, if you will call them out."

Thorndyke looked over the collection and first enumerated the articles, a tweed jacket and trousers, light, knitted wool waistcoat, black-and-yellow stripes, blue cotton shirt, net vest and shorts, marked in ink "P. Roscoff", brown merino socks, brown shoes, tweed cap, and a walking-stick – a mottled Malacca cane with a horn crooked handle. When Hallett had written down this list, Thorndyke laid the clothes on the table and began to empty the pockets, one at a time, dictating the descriptions of the articles to Hallett while Morris took them from him and laid them on a sheet of newspaper. In the jacket pockets were a handkerchief, marked "*P.R.*", a letter-case containing a few stamps, one or two hotel bills and local tradesmen's receipts, and some visiting cards inscribed "*Mr. Peter Roscoff, Bell Hotel, Sandwich*", a leather cigarette-case, a 3B pencil fitted with a point-protector, and a fragment of what Thorndyke decided to be vine charcoal.

"That lot is not very illuminating," remarked Morris, peering into the pockets of the letter-case. "No letter or anything indicating his permanent address. However, that isn't our concern." He laid aside the letter-case and, picking up a pocket-knife that Thorndyke had just taken from the trousers pocket, examined it curiously. "Queer knife, that," he remarked, "Steel blade – mighty sharp, too – Nail file, and an ivory blade. Silly arrangement, it seems. A paperknife is more convenient carried loose, and you don't want a handle to it."

"Perhaps it was meant for a fruit-knife," suggested Hallett, adding it to the list and glancing at a little heap of silver coins that Thorndyke had just laid down. "I wonder," he added, "what has made that money turn so black. Looks! As if he had been taking some medicine containing sulphur. What do you think, Doctor?"

"It is quite a probable explanation," replied Thorndyke, "though we haven't the means of testing it. But you notice that this vesta-box from the other pocket is quite bright, which is rather against your theory."

He held out a little silver box bearing the engraved monogram "*P.R.*", the burnished surface of which contrasted strongly with the dull brownish-black of the coins. Hallett looked at it with an affirmative grunt and, having entered it in his list and added a bunch of keys and a watch from the waistcoat pocket, laid down his pen.

"That's the lot, is it?" said he, rising and beginning to gather up the clothes. "My word! Look at the sand on the table! Isn't it astonishing how saturated with sand one's clothes become after a day on the links here? When I undress at night, the bathroom floor is like the bottom of a bird-cage. Shall I put the things in the locker now?"

"I think", said Thorndyke, "that, as I may have to give evidence, I should like to look them over before you put them away."

Hallett grinned. "There's going to be some expert evidence after all," he said. "Well, fire away, and let me know when you have finished. I am going to smoke a cigarette outside."

With this, he and Morris sauntered out, and I thought it best to go with them, though I was a little curious as to my colleague's object in examining these derelicts. However, my curiosity was not entirely baulked, for my friends went no farther than the little garden that surrounded the house, and from the place where we stood I was able to look in through the window and observe Thorndyke's proceedings.

Very methodical they were. First he laid on the table a sheet of newspaper and on this deposited the jacket, which he examined carefully all over, picking some small object off the inside near the front, and giving special attention to a thick smear of paint which I had noticed on the left cuff. Then, with his spring tape, he measured the sleeves and other principal dimensions. Finally, holding the jacket upside down, he beat it gently with his stick, causing a shower of sand to fall on the paper. He then laid the jacket aside and, taking from his pocket one or two seed envelopes (which I believe he always carried), very carefully shot the sand from the paper into one of them and wrote a few words on it – presumably the source of the sand – and similarly disposing of the small object that he had picked off the surface.

This rather odd procedure was repeated with the other garments – a fresh sheet of newspaper being used for each and with the socks, shoes, and cap. The latter he examined minutely, especially as to the inside, from which he picked out two or three small objects which I could not see, but assumed to be hairs. Even the walking-stick was inspected and measured, and the articles from the pockets scrutinized afresh, particularly the curious pocket-knife, the ivory blade of which he examined on both sides through his lens.

Hallett and Morris glanced in at him from time to time with indulgent smiles, and the former remarked, "I like the hopeful enthusiasm of the real *pukka* expert, and the way he refuses to admit the existence of the ordinary and commonplace. I wonder what he has found out from those things. But here he is. Well, Doctor, what's the verdict? Was it temporary insanity or misadventure?"

Thorndyke shook his head. "The inquiry is adjourned pending the production of fresh evidence," he replied, adding, "I have folded the clothes up and put all the effects together in a paper parcel, excepting the stick."

When Hallett had deposited the derelicts in the locker, he came out and looked across the links with an air of indecision.

"I suppose," said he, "we ought to notify the police. I'll do that. When do you think the body is likely to wash up, and where?"

"It is impossible to say," replied Thorndyke. "The set of the current is towards the Thames, but the body might wash up anywhere along the coast. A case is recorded of a bather drowned off Brighton whose body came up six weeks later at Walton-on-the-Naze. But that was quite exceptional. I shall send the coroner and the Chief Constable a note with my address, and I should think you had better do the same. And that is all that we can do, until we get the summons for the inquest, if there ever is one."

313

To this we all agreed, and as the morning was now spent, we walked back together across the links to the town, where we encountered my wife returning homeward with her sketching kit. This Thorndyke and I took possession of and, having parted from Hallett and Morris opposite the Barbican, we made our way to our lodgings in quest of lunch. Naturally, the events of the morning were related to my wife and discussed by us all, but I noted that Thorndyke made no reference to his inspection of the clothes, and accordingly I said nothing about the matter before my wife, and no opportunity of opening the subject occurred until the evening, when I accompanied him to the station. Then, as we paced the platform while waiting for his train, I put my question,

"By the way, did you extract any information from those garments? I saw you going through them very thoroughly."

"I got a suggestion from them," he replied, "but it is such an odd one that I hardly like to mention it. Taking the appearances at their face value, the suggestion was that the clothes were not all those of the same man. There seemed to be traces of two men, one of whom appeared to belong to this district, while the other would seem to have been associated with the eastern coast of Thanet between Ramsgate and Margate, and by preference, on the scale of probabilities, to Dumpton or Broadstairs."

"How on earth did you arrive at the localities?" I asked.

"Principally," he replied, "by the peculiarities of the sand which fell from the garments and which was not the same in all of them. You see, Anstey," he continued, "sand is analogous to dust. Both consist of minute fragments detached from larger masses, and just as, by examining microscopically the dust of a room, you can ascertain the colour and material of the carpets, curtains, furniture coverings, and other textiles, detached particles of which form the dust of that room, so, by examining sand, you can judge of the character of the cliffs, rocks, and other large masses that occur in the locality, fragments of which become ground off by the surf and incorporated in the sand of the beach. Some of the sand from these clothes is very characteristic and will probably be still more so when I examine it under the microscope."

"But," I objected, "isn't there a fallacy in that line of reasoning? Might not one man have worn the different garments at different times and in different places?"

"That is certainly a possibility that has to be borne in mind," he replied. "But here comes my train. We shall have to adjourn this discussion until you come back to the mill."

As a matter of fact, the discussion was never resumed, for, by the time that I came back to "the mill", the affair had faded from my mind, and the accumulations of grist monopolized my attention, and it is probable that it would have passed into complete oblivion but for the circumstance of its being revived in a very singular manner, which was as follows.

One afternoon about the middle of October my old friend, Mr. Brodribb, a well-known solicitor, called to give me some verbal instructions. When he had finished our business, he said, "I've got a client waiting outside, whom I am taking up to introduce to Thorndyke. You'd better come along with us."

"What is the nature of your client's case?" I asked.

"Hanged if I know," chuckled Brodribb. "He won't say. That's why I am taking him to our friend. I've never seen Thorndyke stumped yet, but I think this case will put the lid on him. Are you coming?"

"I am, most emphatically," said I, "if your client doesn't object."

"He's not going to be asked," said Brodribb. "He'll think you are part of the show. Here he is."

In my outer office we found a gentlemanly, middle-aged man to whom Brodribb introduced me, and whom he hustled down the stairs and up King's Bench Walk to Thorndyke's chambers. There we found my colleague earnestly studying a will with the aid of a watchmaker's eye-glass, and Brodribb opened the proceedings without ceremony.

"I've brought a client of mine, Mr. Capes, to see you, Thorndyke. He has a little problem that he wants you to solve."

Thorndyke bowed to the client and then asked, "What is the nature of the problem?"

"Ah!" said Brodribb, with a mischievous twinkle, "that's what you've got to find out. Mr. Capes is a somewhat reticent gentleman."

Thorndyke cast a quick look at the client and from him to the solicitor. It was not the first time that old Brodribb's high spirits had overflowed in the form of a "leg-pull", though Thorndyke had no more whole-hearted admirer than the shrewd, facetious old lawyer.

Mr. Capes smiled a deprecating smile. "It isn't quite so bad as that," he said. "But I really can't give you much information. It isn't mine to give. I am afraid of telling someone else's secrets, if I say very much."

"Of course you mustn't do that," said Thorndyke. "But, I suppose you can indicate in general terms the nature of your difficulty and the kind of help you want from us."

"I think I can," Mr. Capes replied. "At any rate, I will try. My difficulty is that a certain person with whom I wish to communicate has disappeared in what appears to me to be a rather remarkable manner. When I last heard from him, he was staying at a certain seaside resort and he stated in his letter that he was returning on the following day to his rooms in London. A few days later, I called at his rooms and found that he had not yet returned. But his luggage, which he had sent on independently, had arrived on the day which he had mentioned. So it is evident that he must have left his seaside lodgings. But from that day to this I have had no communication from him, and he has never returned to his rooms nor written to his landlady."

"About how long ago was this?" Thorndyke asked.

"It is just about two months since I heard from him."

"You don't wish to give the name of the seaside resort where he was staying."

"I think I had better not," answered Mr. Capes. "There are circumstances – they don't concern me, but they do concern him very much – which seem to make it necessary for me to say as little as possible."

"And there is nothing further that you can tell us?"

"I am afraid not, excepting that, if I could get into communication with him, I could tell him of something very much to his advantage and which might prevent him from doing something which it would be much better that he should not do."

Thorndyke cogitated profoundly while Brodribb watched him with undisguised enjoyment. Presently my colleague looked up and addressed our secretive client.

"Did you ever play the game of "Clump", Mr. Capes? It is a somewhat legal form of game in which one player asks questions of the others, who are required to answer 'yes' or 'no' in the proper witness-box style."

"I know the game," said Capes, looking a little puzzled, "but – "

"Shall we try a round or two?" asked Thorndyke, with an unmoved countenance. "You don't wish to make any statements, but if I ask you certain specific questions, will you answer 'yes' or 'no'?"

Mr. Capes reflected awhile. At length he said, "I am afraid I can't commit myself to a promise. Still, if you like to ask a question or two, I will answer them if I can."

"Very well," said Thorndyke. "Then, as a start, supposing I suggest that the date of the letter that you received was the thirteenth of August? What do you say? Yes or no?"

Mr. Capes sat bolt upright and stared at Thorndyke open-mouthed.

"How on earth did you guess that?" he exclaimed in an astonished tone. "It's most extraordinary! But you are right. It was dated the thirteenth."

316

"Then," said Thorndyke, "as we have fixed the time we will have a try at the place. What do you say if I suggest that the seaside resort was in the neighbourhood of Broadstairs?"

Mr. Capes was positively thunderstruck. As he sat gazing at Thorndyke, he looked like amazement personified.

"But," he exclaimed, "you can't be guessing! You *know*! You *know* that he was at Broadstairs. And yet, how could you? I haven't even hinted at who he is."

"I have a certain man in my mind," said Thorndyke, "who may have disappeared from Broadstairs. Shall I suggest a few personal characteristics?"

Mr. Capes nodded eagerly and Thorndyke continued,

"If I suggest, for instance, that he was an artist – a painter in oil – " Capes nodded again " – that he was somewhat fastidious as to his pigments?"

"Yes," said Capes. "Unnecessarily so in my opinion, and I am an artist myself. What else?"

"That he worked with his palette in his right hand and held his brush with his left?"

"Yes, yes," exclaimed Capes, half-rising from his chair. "And what was he like?"

"By gum," murmured Brodribb, "we haven't stumped him after all."

Evidently we had not, for he proceeded,

"As to his physical characteristics, I suggest that he was a shortish man – about five-feet-seven – rather stout, fair hair, slightly bald and wearing a rather large and ragged moustache."

Mr. Capes was astounded – and so was I, for that matter – and for some moments there was a silence, broken only by old Brodribb, who sat chuckling softly and rubbing his hands. At length Mr. Capes said, "You have described him exactly, but I needn't tell you that. What I do not understand at all is how you knew that I was referring to this particular man, seeing that I mentioned no name. By the way, sir, may I ask when you saw him last?"

"I have no reason to suppose," replied Thorndyke, "that I have ever seen him at all," an answer that reduced Mr. Capes to a state of stupefaction and brought our old friend Brodribb to the verge of apoplexy. "This man," Thorndyke continued, "is a purely hypothetical individual whom I have described from certain traces left by him. I have reason to believe that he left Broadstairs on the fourteenth of August, and I have certain opinions as to what became of him thereafter. But a few more details would be useful, and I shall continue my interrogation. Now

317

this man sent his luggage on separately. That suggests a possible intention of breaking his journey to London. What do you say?"

"I don't know," replied Capes, "but I think it probable."

"I suggest that he broke his journey for the purpose of holding an interview with some other person."

"I cannot say," answered Capes, "but if he did break his journey it would probably be for that purpose."

"And supposing that interview to have taken place, would it be likely to be an amicable interview?"

"I am afraid not. I suspect that my – er – acquaintance might have made certain proposals which would have been unacceptable, but which he might have been able to enforce. However, that is only surmise," Capes added hastily. "I really know nothing more than I have told you, except the missing man's name, and that I would rather not mention."

"It is not material," said Thorndyke, "at least, not at present. If it should become essential, I will let you know."

"Mmm – yes," said Mr. Capes. "But you were saying that you had certain opinions as to what has become of this person."

"Yes," Thorndyke replied, "speculative opinions. But they will have to be verified. If they turn out to be correct – or incorrect either – I will let you know in the course of a few days. Has Mr. Brodribb your address?"

"He has, but you had better have it, too."

He produced his card and, after an ineffectual effort to extract a statement from Thorndyke, took his departure.

The third act of this singular drama opened in the same setting as the first, for the following Sunday morning found my colleague and me following the path from Sandwich to the sea. But we were not alone this time. At our side marched Major Robertson, the eminent dog trainer, and behind him trotted one of his superlatively educated fox-hounds.

We came out on the shore at the same point as on the former occasion, and turning towards Shellness, walked along the smooth sand with a careful eye on the not very distinctive landmarks. At length Thorndyke halted.

"This is the place," said he. "I fixed it in my mind by that distant tree, which coincides with the chimney of that cottage on the marshes. The clothes lay in that hollow between the two big sand-hills."

We advanced to the spot, but, as a hollow is useless as a landmark, Thorndyke ascended the nearest sand-hill and stuck his stick in the summit and tied his handkerchief to the handle.

"That," he said, "will serve as a centre which we can keep in sight, and if we describe a series of gradually widening concentric circles round it, we shall cover the whole ground completely."

"How far do you propose to go?" asked the major.

"We must be guided by the appearance of the ground," replied Thorndyke. "But the circumstances suggest that if there is anything buried, it can't be very far from where the clothes were laid. And it is pretty certain to be in a hollow."

The major nodded, and when he had attached a long leash to the dog's collar, we started, at first skirting the base of the sand-hill, and then, guided by our own footmarks in the loose sand, gradually increasing the distance from the high mound, above which Thorndyke's handkerchief fluttered in the light breeze. Thus we continued, walking slowly, keeping close to the previously made circle of footprints and watching the dog, who certainly did a vast amount of sniffing, but appeared to let his mind run unduly on the subject of rabbits.

In this way half-an-hour was consumed, and I was beginning to wonder whether we were going after all to draw a blank, when the dog's demeanour underwent a sudden change. At the moment we were crossing a range of high sand-hills, covered with stiff, reedy grass and stunted gorse, and before us lay a deep hollow, naked of vegetation and presenting a bare, smooth surface of the characteristic greyish-yellow sand. On the side of the hill the dog checked and, with upraised muzzle, began to sniff the air with a curiously suspicious expression, clearly unconnected with the rabbit question. On this, the major unfastened the leash, and the dog, left to his own devices, put his nose to the ground and began rapidly to cast to and fro, zig-zagging down the side of the hill and growing every moment more excited. In the same sinuous manner he proceeded across the hollow until he reached a spot near the middle, and here he came to a sudden stop and began to scratch up the sand with furious eagerness.

"It's a find, sure enough!" exclaimed the major, nearly as excited as his pupil and, as he spoke, he ran down the hillside, followed by me and Thorndyke, who, as he reached the bottom, drew from his "poacher's pocket" a large fern-trowel in a leather sheath. It was not a very efficient digging implement, but it threw up the loose sand faster than the scratchings of the dog.

It was easy ground to excavate. Working at the spot that the dog had located, Thorndyke had soon hollowed out a small cavity some eighteen inches deep. Into the bottom of this he thrust the pointed blade of the big trowel. Then he paused and looked round at the major and me, who were craning eagerly over the little pit.

"There is something there," said he. "Feel the handle of the trowel."

I grasped the wooden handle and, working it gently up and down, was aware of a definite but somewhat soft resistance. The major verified my observation, and then Thorndyke resumed his digging, widening the pit and working with increased caution. Ten minutes more careful excavation brought into view a recognizable shape – a shoulder and upper arm, and following the lines of this, further diggings disclosed the form of a head and shoulders plainly discernable though still shrouded in sand. Finally, with the point of the trowel and a borrowed handkerchief – mine – the adhering sand was cleared away, and then, from the bottom of the deep, funnel-shaped hole, there looked up at us, with a most weird and horrible effect, the discoloured face of a man.

In that face, the passing weeks had wrought inevitable changes, on which I need not dwell. But the features were easily recognizable, and I could see at once that the man corresponded completely with Thorndyke's description. The cheeks were full, the hair on the temples was of a pale, yellowish brown, a straggling, fair moustache covered the mouth and, when the sand had been sufficiently cleared away, I could see a small, tonsure-like bald patch near the back of the crown. But I could see something more than this. On the left temple, just behind the eyebrow, was a ragged, shapeless wound such as might have been made by a hammer.

"That turns into certainty what we have already surmised," said Thorndyke, gently pressing the scalp around the wound. "It must have killed him instantly. The skull is smashed in like an egg-shell. And this is undoubtedly the weapon," he added, drawing out of the sand beside the body a big, hexagon-headed screw-bolt, "very prudently buried with the body. And that is all that really concerns us. We can leave the police to finish the disinterment, but you notice, Anstey, that the corpse is nude with the exception of the vest and probably the pants. The shirt has disappeared. Which is exactly what we should have expected."

Slowly, but with the feeling of something accomplished, we took our way back to the town, having collected Thorndyke's stick on the way. Presently, the major left us, to look up a friend at the clubhouse on the links. As soon as we were alone, I put in a demand for an elucidation.

"I see the general trend of your investigations," said I "but I can't imagine how they yielded so much detail, as to the personal appearance of this man, for instance."

"The evidence in this case," he replied, "was analogous to circumstantial evidence. It depended on the cumulative effect of a number of facts, each separately inconclusive, but all pointing to the same conclusion. Shall I run over the data in their order and in accordance with their connections?"

I gave an emphatic affirmative, and he continued,

"We begin, naturally, with the first fact – which is, of course, the most interesting and important, the fact which arrests attention, which shows that something has to be explained and possibly suggests a line of inquiry. You remember that I measured the footprints in the sand for comparison with the other footprints. Then I had the dimensions of the feet of the presumed bather. But as soon as I looked at the shoes which purported to be those of that bather, I felt a conviction that his feet would never go into them.

"Now, that was a very striking fact – if it really was a fact – and it came on top of another fact hardly less striking, The bather had gone into the sea, and at a considerable distance he had unquestionably come out again. There could be no possible doubt. In foot-measurement and length of stride the two sets of tracks were identical, and there were no other tracks. That man had come ashore and he had remained ashore. But yet he had not put on his clothes. He couldn't have gone away naked, but obviously he was not there. As a criminal lawyer, you must admit that there was *prima facie* evidence of something very abnormal and probably criminal.

"On our way to the dormy-house, I carried the stick in the same hand as my own and noted that it was very little shorter. Therefore it was a tall man's stick. Apparently, then, the stick did not belong to the shoes, but to the man who had made the footprints. Then, when we came to the dormy-house, another striking fact presented itself. You remember that Hallett commented on the quantity of sand that fell from the clothes on to the table. I am astonished that he did not notice the very peculiar character of that sand. It was perfectly unlike the sand which would fall from his own clothes. The sand on the sand-hills is dune sand – wind-borne sand, or, as the legal term has it, æolian sand, and it is perfectly characteristic. As it has been carried by the wind, it is necessarily fine. The grains are small, and as the action of the wind sorts them out, they are extremely uniform in size. Moreover, by being continually blown about and rubbed together, they become rounded by mutual attrition. And then dune sand is nearly pure sand, composed of grains of silica unmixed with other substances.

"Beach sand is quite different. Much of it is half-formed, freshly broken down silica and is often very coarse and, as I pointed out at the time, it is mixed with all sorts of foreign substances derived from masses in the neighbourhood. This particular sand was loaded with black and white particles, of which the white were mostly chalk, and the black particles of coal. Now there is very little chalk in the Shellness sand, as there are no cliffs quite near, and chalk rapidly disappears from sand by reason of its softness, and there is no coal."

"Where does the coal come from?" I asked.

"Principally from the Goodwins," he replied. "It is derived from the cargoes of colliers whose wrecks are embedded in those sands, and from the bunkers of wrecked steamers. This coal sinks down through the seventy odd feet of sand and at last works out at the bottom, where it drifts slowly across the floor of the sea in a north-westerly direction until some easterly gale throws it up on the Thanet shore between Ramsgate and Foreness Point. Most of it comes up at Dumpton and Broadstairs, there you may see the poor people, in the winter, gathering coal pebbles to feed their fires.

"This sand, then, almost certainly came from the Thanet coast, but the missing man, Roscoff, had been staying in Sandwich, playing golf on the sand-hills. This was another striking discrepancy, and it made me decide to examine the clothes exhaustively, garment by garment. I did so, and this is what I found.

"The jacket, trousers, socks, and shoes were those of a shortish, rather stout man, as shown by measurements, and the cap was his, since it was made of the same cloth as the jacket and trousers.

"The waistcoat, shirt, underclothes, and stick were those of a tall man.

"The garments, socks and shoes of the short man were charged with Thanet beach sand, and contained no dune sand, excepting the cap, which might have fallen off on the sand-hills.

"The waistcoat was saturated with dune sand and contained no beach sand, and a little dune sand was obtained from the shirt and under-garments. That is to say, that the short man's clothes contained beach sand only, while the tall man's clothes contained only dune sand.

"The short man's clothes were all unmarked, the tall man's clothes were either marked or conspicuously recognizable, as the waistcoat and also the stick.

"The garments of the short man which had been left were those that could not have been worn by a tall man without attracting instant attention and the shoes could not have been put on at all, whereas the garments of the short man which had disappeared – the waistcoat, shirt, and underclothes – were those that could have been worn by a tall man without attracting attention. The obvious suggestion was that the tall man had gone off in the short man's shirt and waistcoat but otherwise in his own clothes.

322

"And now as to the personal characteristics of the short man. From the cap I obtained five hairs. They were all blond, and two of them were of the peculiar, atrophic, "point of exclamation" type that grow at the margin of a bald area. Therefore he was a fair man and partially bald. On the inside of the jacket, clinging to the rough tweed, I found a single long, thin, fair moustache hair, which suggested a long, soft moustache. The edge of the left cuff was thickly marked with oil-paint – not a single smear, but an accumulation such as a painter picks up when he reaches with his brush hand across a loaded palette. The suggestion – not very conclusive – was that he was an oil-painter and left-handed. But there was strong confirmation. There was an artist's pencil – *3B* – and a stump of vine charcoal such as an oil-painter might carry. The silver coins in his pocket were blackened with sulphide as they would be if a piece of artist's soft, vulcanized rubber has been in the pocket with them. And there was the pocket-knife. It contained a sharp steel pencil-blade, a charcoal file, and an ivory palette-blade, and that palette-blade had been used by a left-handed man."

"How did you arrive at that?" I asked.

"By the bevels worn at the edges," he replied. "An old palette-knife used by a right-handed man shows a bevel of wear on the under side of the left-hand edge and the upper side of the right-hand edge, in the case of a left-handed man the wear shows on the under side of the right-hand edge and the upper side of the left-hand edge. This being an ivory blade, showed the wear very distinctly and proved conclusively that the user was left-handed, and as an ivory palette-knife is used only by fastidiously careful painters for such pigments as the cadmiums, which might be discoloured by a steel blade, one was justified in assuing that he was somewhat fastidious as to his pigments."

As I listened to Thorndyke's exposition I was profoundly impressed. His conclusions, which had sounded like mere speculative guesses, were, I now realized, based upon an analysis of the evidence as careful and as impartial as the summing up of a judge. And these conclusions he had drawn instantaneously from the appearances of things that had been before my eyes all the time and from which I had learned nothing.

"What do you suppose is the meaning of the affair?" I asked presently. "What was the motive of the murder?"

"We can only guess," he replied. "But, interpreting Capes' hints, I should suspect that our artist friend was a blackmailer, that he had come over here to squeeze Roscoff – perhaps not for the first time – and that his victim lured him out on the sand-hills for a private talk and then took the only effective means of ridding himself of his persecutor. That is my view of the case, but, of course, it is only surmise."

Surmise as it was, however, it turned out to be literally correct. At the inquest, Capes had to tell all that he knew, which was uncommonly little, though no one was able to add to it. The murdered man, Joseph Bertrand, had fastened on Roscoff and made a regular income by blackmailing him. That much Capes knew, and he knew that the victim had been in prison and that that was the secret. But who Roscoff was and what was his real name – for Roscoff was apparently a *nom de guerre* – he had no idea. So he could not help the police. The murderer had got clear away and there was no hint as to where to look for him, and so far as I know, nothing has ever been heard of him since.

The Apparition of
Burling Court

Thorndyke seldom took a formal holiday. He did not seem to need one. As he himself put it, "A holiday implies the exchange of a less pleasurable occupation for one more pleasurable. But there is no occupation more pleasurable than the practice of Medical Jurisprudence." Moreover, his work was less affected by terms and vacations than that of an ordinary barrister, and the Long Vacation often found him with his hands full. Even when he did appear to take a holiday the appearance tended to be misleading, and it was apt to turn out that his disappearance from his usual haunts was associated with a case of unusual interest at a distance.

Thus it was on the occasion when our old friend, Mr. Brodribb, of Lincoln's Inn, beguiled him into a fortnight's change at St. David's-at-Cliffe, a seaside hamlet on the Kentish coast. There was a case in the background, and a very curious case it turned out to be, though at first it appeared to me quite a commonplace affair, and the manner of its introduction was as follows.

One hot afternoon in the early part of the Long Vacation, the old solicitor dropped in for a cup of tea and a chat. That, at least, was how he explained his visit, but my experience of Mr. Brodribb led me to suspect some ulterior purpose in the call, and as he sat by the open window, teacup in hand, looking, with his fine pink complexion, his silky white hair, and his faultless "turn out" the very type of the courtly, old-fashioned lawyer, I waited expectantly for the matter of his visit to transpire. And, presently, out it came.

"I am going to take a little holiday down at St. David's," said he. "Just a quiet spell by the sea, you know. Delightful place. So quiet and restful and so breezy and fresh. Ever been there?"

"No," replied Thorndyke. "I only just know the name."

"Well, why shouldn't you come down for a week or so? Both of you. I shall stay at Burling Court, the Lumleys' place. I can't invite you there as I'm only a guest, but I know of some comfortable rooms in the village that I could get for you. I wish you would come down, Thorndyke," he added after a pause. "I'm rather unhappy about young Lumley – I'm the family lawyer, you know, and so was my father and my grandfather, so I feel almost as if the Lumleys were my own kin – and I should like to have your advice and help."

"Why not have it now?" suggested Thorndyke.

"I will," he replied, "but I should like your help on the spot too. I'd like you to see Lumley have a talk with him and tell me what you think of him."

"What is amiss with him?" Thorndyke asked.

"Well," answered Brodribb, "it looks uncomfortably like insanity. He has delusions – sees apparitions and that sort of thing. And there is some insanity in the family. But I had better give you the facts in their natural order.

"About four months ago Giles Lumley of Burling Court died, and as he was a widower without issue, the estate passed to his nearest male relative, my present client, Frank Lumley, who was also the principal beneficiary under the will. At the time of Giles' death Frank was abroad, but a cousin of his, Lewis Price, was staying at the house with his wife as a more or less permanent guest, and as Price's circumstances were not very flourishing, and as he is the next heir to the estate, Frank – who is a bachelor – wrote to him at once telling him to look upon Burling Court as his home for as long as he pleased."

"That was extremely generous of him," I remarked

"Yes," Brodribb agreed, "Frank is a good fellow, a very high-minded gentleman and a very sweet man but a little queer – very queer just now. Well, Frank came back from abroad and took up his abode at the house, and for a time all went well. Then, one day, Price called on me and gave me some very unpleasant news. It seemed that Frank, who had always been rather neurotic and imaginative, had been interesting himself a good deal in psychical research and – and balderdash of that kind, you know. Well, there was no great harm in that, perhaps. But just lately he had taken to seeing visions and – what was worse – talking about them, so much so that Price got uneasy and privately invited a mental specialist down to lunch, and the specialist, having had a longish talk with Frank Price confidentially stated that he (Frank) was obviously suffering from insane delusions. Thereupon Price called me and begged me to see Frank myself and what ought to be done, so I made an occasion for him to come and see me at the office."

"And what did you think of him?" asked Thorndyke.

"I was horrified – horrified," said Mr. Brodribb. "I assure you, Thorndyke, that that poor young man sat in my office and talked like a stark lunatic. Quite quietly, you know. No excitement, though he was evidently anxious and unhappy. But there he sat gravely talking the damnedest nonsense you ever heard."

"As, for instance – ?"

"Well, his infernal visions. Luminous birds flying about in the dark, and a human head suspended in mid air – upside down, too. But I had better give you his story as he told it. I made full shorthand notes as he was talking, and I've brought them with me, though I hardly need them.

"His trouble seems to have begun soon after he took up his quarters at Burling Court. Being a bookish sort of fellow, he started to go through his library systematically, and presently he came across a small manuscript book, which turned out to be a sort of family history, or rather a collection of episodes. It was rather a lurid little book, for it apparently dwelt chiefly on the family crime, the family spectre, and the family madness."

"Did you know about these heirlooms?" Thorndyke asked.

"No, it was the first I'd heard of 'em. Price knew there was some soft of family superstition, but he didn't know what it was, and Giles knew about it – so Price tells me – but didn't care to talk about it. He never mentioned it to me."

"What is the nature of the tradition?" inquired Thorndyke.

"I'll tell you," said Brodribb, taking out his notes. "I've got it all down, and poor Frank reeled the stuff off as if he had learned it by heart. The book, which is dated 1819, was apparently written by a Walter Lumley and the story of the crime and the spook runs thus:

"About 1720 the property passed to a Gilbert Lumley, a naval officer, who then gave up the sea, married, and settled down at Burling Court. A year or two later some trouble arose about his wife and a man named Glynn, a neighbouring squire. With or without cause, Lumley became violently jealous, and the end of it was that he lured Glynn to a large cavern in the cliffs and there murdered him. It was a most ferocious and vindictive crime. The cavern, which was then used by smugglers, had a beam across the roof bearing a tackle for hoisting out boat cargoes, and this tackle Lumley fastened to Glynn's ankles – having first pinioned him – and hoisted him up so that he hung head downwards a foot or so clear of the floor of the cave. And there he left him hanging until the rising tide flowed into the cave and drowned him.

"The very next day the murder was discovered, and as Lumley was the nearest justice of the peace, the discoverers reported to him and took him to the cave to the body. When he entered the cave the corpse was stilt hanging as he had left the living man, and a bat was flittering round and round the dead man's head. He had the body taken down and carried to Glynn's house and took the necessary measures for the inquest. Of course, everyone suspected him of the murder, but there was no evidence against him. The verdict was murder by some person unknown, and as

Gilbert Lumley was not sensitive, everything seemed to have gone quite satisfactorily.

"But it hadn't. One night, exactly a month after murder, Gilbert retired to his bedroom in the dark. He was in the act of feeling along the mantelpiece for the tinder-box, when he became aware of a dim light moving about the room. He turned round quickly and then saw that it was a bat – a most uncanny and abnormal bat that seemed to give out a greenish ghostly light – flitting round and round his bed. On this, remembering the bat in the cavern, he rushed out of the room in the very devil of a fright. Presently he returned with one of the servants and a couple of candles, but the bat had disappeared.

"From that time onward, the luminous bat haunted Gilbert, appearing in dark rooms, on staircases and passages and corridors, until his nerves were all on end and he did not dare to move about the house at night without a candle or a lantern. But that was not the worst. Exactly two months after the murder the next stage of the haunting began. He had retired to his bedroom and was just about to get into bed when he remembered that he had left his watch in the little dressing-room that adjoined his chamber. With a candle in his hand he went to the dressing-room and flung open the door. And then he stopped dead and stood as if turned into stone, for, within a couple of yards of him, suspended in mid-air, was a man's head hanging upside down.

"For some seconds he stood rooted to the spot, unable to move. Then he uttered a cry of horror and rushed back to his room and down to the hall. There was no doubt whose head it was, strange and horrible as it looked in that unnatural, inverted position, for he had seen it twice before in that very position hanging in the cavern. Evidently he had not got rid of Glynn.

"That night, and every night henceforward, he slept in his wife's room. And all through the night he was conscious of a strange and dreadful impulse to rise and go down to the shore, to steal into the cavern and wait for the flowing tide. He lay awake, fighting against the invisible power that seemed to be drawing him to destruction, and by the morning the horrid impulse began to weaken. But he went about in terror, not daring to go near the shore and afraid to trust himself alone.

"A month passed. The effect of the apparition grew daily weaker and an abundance of lights in the house protected him from the visitation of the bat. Then, exactly three months after the murder, he saw the head again. This time it was in the library, where he had gone to fetch a book. He was standing by the book shelves and had just taken out a volume, when, as he turned away, there the hideous thing was hanging in that awful, grotesque posture, chin upwards and the scanty hair dropping down like wet fringe. Gilbert dropped the book that he was holding and fled from the room with a shriek, and all that night invisible hands seemed to be plucking at him to draw him away to where the voices of the waves were reverberating in the cavern.

"This second visitation affected him profoundly. He could not shake off that sinister impulse to steal away to the shore. He was a broken man, the victim of an abiding terror, clinging for protection to the very servants, creeping abroad with shaking limbs and an apprehensive eye towards the sea. And ever in his ears was the murmur of the surf and the hollow echoes of the cavern.

"Already he had sought forgetfulness in drink, and sought it in vain. Now he took refuge in opiates. Every night, before retiring to the dreaded bed, he mingled laudanum with the brandy that brought him stupor if not repose. And brandy and opium began to leave their traces in the tremulous hand, the sallow cheek, and the bloodshot eye. And so another month passed.

"As the day approached that would mark the fourth month, his terror of the visitation that he now anticipated reduced him to a state of utter prostration. Sleep – even drugged sleep – appeared that night to be out of the question, and he decided to sit up with his family, hoping by that means to escape the dreaded visitor. But it was a vain hope. Hour after hour he sat in his elbow chair by the fire, while his wife dozed in her chair opposite, until the clock in the hall struck twelve. He listened and counted the strokes of the bell, leaning back with his eyes closed. Half the weary night was gone. As the last stroke sounded and a deep silence fell on the house, he opened his eyes – and looked into the face of Glynn within a few inches of his own.

"For some moments he sat with dropped jaw and dilated eyes staring in silent horror at this awful thing, then with an agonised screech he slid from his chair into a heap on the floor.

"At noon on the following day he was missed from the house. A search was made in the grounds and in the neighbourhood, but he was nowhere to be found. At last someone thought of the cavern, of which he had spoken in his wild mutterings and a party of searchers made their way thither. And there they found him when the tide went out, lying on the wet sand with the brown sea-tangle wreathed about his limbs and the laudanum bottle – now full of sea water – by his side.

"With the death of Gilbert Lumley it seemed that the murdered man's spirit was appeased. During the lifetime of Gilbert's son, Thomas, the departed Glynn made no sign. But on his death and the succession of his son Arthur – then a middle-aged man – the visitations began again, and in the same order. At the end of the first month the luminous bat appeared, at the end of the second, the inverted head made its entry, and again at the third and the fourth months, and within twenty-four hours of the last visitation, the body of Arthur Lumley was found in the cavern. And so it has been from that time onward. One generation escapes untouched by the curse, but in the next, Glynn and the sea claim their own."

"Is that true, so far as you know?" asked Thorndyke.

"I can't say," answered Brodribb. "I am now only quoting Walter Lumley's infernal little book. But I remember that, in fact, Giles' father was drowned. I understood that his boat capsized, but that may have been only a story to cover the suicide.

"Well now, I have given you the gruesome history from this book that poor Frank had the misfortune to find. You see that he had it all off by heart and had evidently read it again and again. Now I come to his own story, which he told me very quietly but with intense conviction and very evident forebodings.

"He found this damned book a few days after his arrival at Burling Court, and it was clear to him that, if the story was true, he was the next victim, since his predecessor, Giles, had been left in peace. And so it turned out. Exactly a month after his arrival, going up to his bedroom in the dark – no doubt expecting this apparition – as soon as he opened the door he saw a thing like a big glow-worm or firefly flitting round the room. It is evident that he was a good deal upset, for he rushed downstairs in a state of great agitation and fetched Price up to see it. But the strange thing was – though perhaps not so very strange, after all – that, although the thing was still there, flitting about the room, Price could see nothing. However, he pulled up the blind – the window was wide open – and the bat flopped out and disappeared.

"During the next month the bat reappeared several times, in the bedroom, in corridors, and once in a garret, when it flew out as Frank opened the door."

"What was he doing in the garret?" asked Thorndyke.

"He went up to fetch an ancient coffin-stool that Mrs. Price had seen there and was telling him about. Well, this went on until the end of the second month. And then came the second act. It seems that by some infernal stupidity, he was occupying the bedroom that had been used by Gilbert. Now on this night, as soon as he had gone up, he must needs pay a visit to the little dressing-room, which is now known as 'Gilbert's Cabin' – so he tells me, for I was not aware of it – and where Gilbert's cutlass, telescope, quadrant and the old navigator's watch are kept."

"Did he take a light with him?" inquired Thorndyke.

"I think not. There is a gas jet in the corridor and presumably he lit that. Then he opened the door of the cabin, and immediately he saw, a few feet in front of him, a man's head, upside down, apparently hanging in mid-air. It gave him a fearful shock – the more so, perhaps, because he half expected it – and, as before, he ran downstairs, all of a tremble. Price had gone to bed but Mrs. Price came up with him, and he showed her the horrible thing which was still hanging in the middle of the dark room.

"But Mrs. Price could see nothing. She assured him that it was all his imagination, and in proof of it, she walked into the room, right through the head, as it seemed, and when she had found the matches, she lit the gas. Of course, there was nothing whatever in the room.

"Another month passed. The bat appeared at intervals and kept poor Frank's nerves in a state of constant tension. On the night of the appointed day, as you will anticipate, Frank went again to Gilbert's cabin, drawn there by an attraction that one can quite understand. And there, of course, was the confounded head as before. That was a fortnight ago. So, you see, the affair is getting urgent. Either there is some truth in this weird story – which I don't believe for a moment – or poor old Frank is ripe for the asylum. But in any case something will have to be done."

"You spoke just now," said Thorndyke, "of some insanity in the family. What does it amount to, leaving these apparitions out of the question?"

"Well, a cousin of Frank's committed suicide in an asylum."

"And Frank's parents?"

"They were quite sane. The cousin was the son of Frank's mother's sister, and she was all right, too. But the boy's father had to be put away."

"Then," said Thorndyke, "the insanity doesn't seem to be in Frank's family at all, in a medical sense. Legal inheritance and physiological inheritance do not follow the same lines. If his mother's sister married a lunatic, he might inherit that lunatic's property, but he could not inherit his insanity. There was no blood relationship."

"No, that's true," Brodribb admitted, "though Frank certainly seems as mad as a hatter. But now, to come back to the holiday question: What do you say to a week or so at St. David's?"

Thorndyke looked at me interrogatively. "What says my learned friend?" he asked.

"I say, Let us put up the shutters and leave Polton in charge," I replied, and Thorndyke assented without a murmur.

Less than a week later, we were installed in the very comfortable rooms that Mr. Brodribb had found for us in the hamlet of St. David's, within five minutes' walk of the steep gap-way that led down to the beach. Thorndyke entered into the holiday with an enthusiasm that would have astonished the denizens of King Bench Walk. He explored the village, he examined the church, inside and out, he sampled all the footpaths with the aid of the Ordnance Map, he foregathered with the fishermen on the beach and renewed his acquaintance with boat-craft, and he made a pilgrimage to the historic cavern – it was less than a mile along the shore – and inspected its dark and chilly interior with the most lively curiosity.

We had not been at St. David's twenty-four hours before we made the acquaintance of Frank Lumley. Mr. Brodribb saw to that, for the old solicitor was profoundly anxious about his client – he took his responsibilities very seriously, did Mr. Brodribb. His "family" clients were to him as his own kin, and their interests his own interests – and his confidence in Thorndyke's wisdom was unbounded. We were very favourably impressed by the quiet, gentle, rather frail young man, and for my part, I found him, for a certifiable lunatic, a singularly reasonable and intelligent person. Indeed, apart from his delusions – or rather hallucinations – he seemed perfectly sane, for a somewhat eager interest in psychical and supernormal phenomena (of which he made no secret) is hardly enough to create a suspicion of a man's sanity.

But he was clearly uneasy about his own mental condition. He realised that the apparitions might be the products of a disordered brain, though that was not his own view of them, and he discussed them with us in the most open and ingenuous manner.

"You don't think," Thorndyke suggested, "that these apparitions may possibly be natural appearances which you have misinterpreted or exaggerated in consequence of having read that very circumstantial story?"

Lumley shook his head emphatically. "It is impossible," said he. "How could I? Take the case of the bat. I have seen it on several occasions quite distinctly. It was obviously a bat, but yet it seemed full of a ghostly, greenish light like that of a glow-worm. If it was not what it appeared, what was it? And then the head. There it was, perfectly clear and solid and real, hanging in mid-air within three or four feet of me. I could have touched it if I had dared."

"What size did it appear?" asked Thorndyke.

Lumley reflected. "It was not quite life-size. I should say about two-thirds the size of an ordinary head."

"Should you recognise the face if you saw it again?

"I can't say," replied Lumley. "You see, it was upside down. I haven't a very clear picture of it – I mean as to what the face would have been like the right way up."

332

"Was the room quite dark on both occasions?" Thorndyke asked.

"Yes, quite. The gas jet in the corridor is just above the door and does not let any light into the room."

"And what is there opposite the door?"

"There is a small window, but that is usually kept shuttered nowadays. Under the window is a small folding dressing-table that belonged to Gilbert Lumley. He had it made when he came home from the sea."

Thus Lumley was quite lucid and coherent in his answers. His manner was perfectly sane, it was only the matter that was abnormal. Of the reality of the apparitions he had not the slightest doubt, and he never varied in the smallest degree in his description of their appearance. The fact that they had been invisible both to Mr. Price and his wife he explained by pointing out that the curse applied only to the direct descendants of Gilbert Lumley, and to those only in alternate generations.

After one of our conversations, Thorndyke expressed a wish to see the little manuscript book that had been the cause of all the trouble – or at least had been the forerunner – and Lumley promised to bring it to our rooms on the following afternoon. But then came an interruption to our holiday, not entirely unexpected, an urgent telegram from one of our solicitor friends asking consultation on an important and intricate case that had just been put into his hands, and making it necessary for us to go up to town by an early train on the following morning.

We sent a note to Brodribb, telling him that we should be away from St. David's for perhaps a day or two, and on our way to the station he overtook us.

"I am sorry you have had to break your holiday," he said, "but I hope you will be back before Thursday."

"Why Thursday, in particular?" inquired Thorndyke.

"Because Thursday is the day on which that damned head is due to make its third appearance. It will be an anxious time. Frank hasn't said anything, but I know his nerves are strung up to concert pitch."

"You must watch him," said Thorndyke. "Don't let him out of your sight if you can help it."

"That's all very well," said Brodribb, "but he isn't a child, and I am not his keeper. He is the master of the house and I am just his guest. I can't follow him about if he wants to be alone."

"You mustn't stand on politeness, Brodribb," rejoined Thorndyke. "It will be a critical time and you must keep him in sight."

"I shall do my best," Brodribb said anxiously, "but I do hope you will be back by then."

He accompanied us dejectedly to the platform and stayed with us until our train came in. Suddenly, just as we were entering our carriage, he thrust his hand into his pocket.

"God bless me!" he exclaimed, "I had nearly forgotten this book. Frank asked me to give it to you." As he spoke, he drew out a little rusty calf-bound volume and handed it to Thorndyke. "You can look through it at your leisure," said he, "and if you think it best to chuck the infernal thing out of the window, do so. I suspect poor Frank is none the better for conning it over perpetually as he does."

I thought there was a good deal of reason in Brodribb's opinion. If Lumley's illusions were, as I suspected, the result of suggestion produced by reading the narrative, that suggestion would certainly tend to be reinforced by conning it over and over again. But the old lawyer's proposal was hardly practicable.

As soon as the train had fairly started, Thorndyke proceeded to inspect the little volume, and his manner of doing so was highly characteristic. An ordinary person would have opened the book and looked through the contents, probably seeking out at once the sinister history of Gilbert Lumley.

Not so Thorndyke. His inspection began at the very beginning and proceeded systematically to deal with every fact that the book had to disclose. First he made an exhaustive examination of the cover, scrutinised the corners, inspected the bottom edges and compared them with the top edges, and compared the top and bottom head-caps. Then he brought out his lens and examined the tooling, which was simple in character and worked in "blind" – *i.e.* not gilt. He also inspected the head-bands through the glass, and then he turned his attention to the interior. He looked carefully at both end-papers, he opened the sections and examined the sewing-thread, he held the leaves up to the light and tested the paper by eye and by touch and he viewed the writing in several places through his lens. Finally he handed the book and the lens to me without remark.

It was a quaint little volume with a curiously antique air, though it was but a century old. The cover was of rusty calf, a good deal rubbed, but not in bad condition, for the joints were perfectly sound, but then it had probably had comparatively little use. The paper – a laid paper with very distinct wire-lines but no watermark – had turned with age to a pale, creamy buff, the writing had faded to a warm brown, but was easily legible and very clearly and carefully written. Having noted these points, I turned over the leaves until I came to the story of Gilbert Lumley and the ill-fated Glynn, which I read through attentively, observing that Mr.

Brodribb's notes had given the whole substance of the narrative with singular completeness.

"This story," I said, as I handed the book back to Thorndyke, "strikes me as rather unreal and unconvincing. One doesn't see how Walter Lumley got his information."

"No," agreed Thorndyke. "It is on the plane of fiction. The narrator speaks in the manner of a novelist with complete knowledge of events and actions which were apparently known only to the actors."

"Do you think it possible that Walter Lumley was simply romancing?"

"I think it quite possible, and in fact very probable that the whole narrative is fictitious," he replied. "We shall have to go into that question later on. For the present, I suppose, we had better give our attention to the case that we have in hand at the moment."

The little volume was accordingly put away, and for the rest of the journey our conversation was occupied with the matter of the consultation that formed our immediate business. As this, however, had no connection with the present history, I need make no further reference to it beyond stating that it kept us both busy for three days and that we finished with it on the evening of the third.

"Do you propose to go down to St. David's to-night or to-morrow?" I asked, as we let ourselves into our chambers.

"To-night," replied Thorndyke. "This is Thursday, you know, and Brodribb was anxious that we should be back some time to-day. I have sent him a telegram saying that we shall go down by the train that arrives about ten o'clock. So if he wants us, he can meet us it the station or send a message."

"I wonder," said I, "if the apparition of Glynn's head will make its expected visitation to-night."

"It probably will if there is an opportunity," Thorndyke replied. "But I hope that Brodribb will manage to prevent the opportunity from occurring. And, talking of Lumley, as we have an hour to spare, we may as well finish our inspection of his book. I snipped off a corner of one of the leaves and gave it to Polton to boil up in weak caustic soda. It will be ready for examination by now."

"You don't suspect that the book has been faked, do you?" said I.

"I view that book with the deepest suspicion," he replied, opening a drawer and producing the little volume. "Just look at it, Jervis. Look at the cover, for instance."

"Well," I said, turning the book over in my hand, "the cover looks ancient enough to me, typical old, rusty calf with a century's wear on it."

335

"Oh, there's no doubt that it is old calf," said he, "just the sort of leather that you could skin off the cover of an old quarto or folio. But don't you see that the signs of wear are all in the wrong places? How does a book wear in use? Well, first there are the bottom edges, which rub on the shelf. Then the corners, which are the thinnest leather and the most exposed. Then the top head-cap, which the finger hooks into in pulling the book from the shelf. Then the joint or hinge, which wears through from frequent opening and shutting. The sides get the least wear of all. But in this book, the bottom edges, the corners, the top head-cap and the joints are perfectly sound. They are not more worn than the sides, and the tooling is modern in character. It looks quite fresh and the tool-marks are impressed on the marks of wear instead of being themselves worn. The appearances suggest to me a new binding with old leather.

"Then look at the paper. It professes to be discoloured by age. But the discoloration of the leaves of an old book occurs principally at the edges, where the paper has become oxidised by exposure to the air. The leaves of this book are equally discoloured all over. To me they suggest a bath of weak tea rather than old age.

"Again, there is the writing. Its appearance is that of faded writing done with the old-fashioned writing ink – made with iron sulphate and oak-galls. But it doesn't look quite the right colour. However, we can easily test that. If it is old iron-gall ink, a drop of ammonium sulphide will turn it black. Let us take the book up to the laboratory and try it – and we had better have a 'control' to compare it with."

He ran his eye along the book-shelves and took down a rusty-looking volume of Humphry Clinker, the end-paper of which bore several brown and faded signatures.

"Here is a signature dated 1803," said he. "That will be near enough," and with the two books in his hand he led the way upstairs to the laboratory. Here he took down the ammonium sulphide bottle, and dipping up a little of the liquid in a fine glass tube, opened the cover of Humphry Clinker and carefully deposited a tiny drop on the figure '3' in the date. Almost immediately the ghostly brown began to darken until it at length became jet black. Then, in the same way, he opened Walter Lumley's manuscript book and on the 9th of the date, 1819, he deposited a drop of the solution. But this time there was no darkening of the pale brown writing – on the contrary, it faded rapidly to a faint and muddy violet.

"It is not an iron ink," said Thorndyke, "and it looks suspiciously like an aniline brown. But let us see what the paper is made of. Have you boiled up that fragment, Polton?"

"Yes, sir," answered our laboratory assistant, "and I've washed the soda out of it, so it's all ready."

He produced a labelled test-tube containing a tiny corner of paper floating in water, which he carefully emptied into a large watch-glass. From this Thorndyke transferred the little pulpy fragment to a microscope slide and, with a pair of mounted needles, broke it up into its constituent fibres. Then he dropped on it a drop of aniline stain, removed the surplus with blotting-paper, added a drop of glycerine and put on it a large cover-slip.

"There, Jervis," said he, handing me the slide, "let us have your opinion on Walter Lumley's paper."

I placed the slide on the stage of the microscope and proceeded to inspect the specimen. But no exhaustive examination was necessary. The first glance settled the matter.

"It is nearly all wood," I said. "Mechanical wood fibre, with some esparto, a little cotton and a few linen fibres."

"Then," said Thorndyke, "it is a modern paper. Mechanical wood-pulp – prepared by Keller's process – was first used in paper-making in 1840. 'Chemical wood-pulp' came in later, and esparto was not used until 1860. So we can say with confidence that this paper was not made until more than twenty years after the date that is written on it. Probably it is of quite recent manufacture."

"In that case," said I, "this book is a counterfeit – presumably fraudulent."

"Yes. In effect it is a forgery."

"But that seems to suggest a conspiracy."

"It does," Thorndyke agreed, "especially if it is considered in conjunction with the apparitions. The suggestion is that this book was prepared for the purpose of inducing a state of mind favourable to the acceptance of supernatural appearances. The obvious inference is that the apparitions themselves were an imposture produced for fraudulent purposes. But it is time for us to go."

We shook hands with Polton and, having collected our suit-cases from the sitting-room, set forth for the station.

During the journey down I reflected on the new turn that Frank Lumley's affairs had taken. Apparently, Brodribb had done his client an injustice. Lumley was not so mad as the old lawyer had supposed. He was merely credulous and highly suggestible. The "hallucinations" were real phenomena which he had simply misinterpreted. But who was behind these sham illusions? And what was it all about? I tried to open the question with Thorndyke, but though he was willing to discuss the sham manuscript book and the technique of its production, he would commit himself to nothing further.

On our arrival at St. David's, Thorndyke looked up and down the platform and again up the station approach. "No sign of Brodribb or any messenger," he remarked, "so we may assume that all is well at Burling Court up to the present. Let us hope that Brodribb's presence has had an inhibitory effect on the apparitions."

Nevertheless, it was evident that he was not quite easy in his mind. During supper he appeared watchful and preoccupied, and when, after the meal, he proposed a stroll down to the beach, he left word with our landlady as to where he was to be found if he should be wanted.

It was about a quarter-to-eleven when we arrived at the shore, and the tide was beginning to run out. The beach was deserted with the exception of a couple of fishermen who had apparently come in with the tide and who were making their boat secure for the night before going home. Thorndyke approached them and, addressing the older fisherman, remarked, "That is a big, powerful boat. Pretty fast, too, isn't she?"

"Aye, sir," was the reply, "fast and weatherly, she is. What we calls a 'galley-punt'. Built at Deal for the hovelling trade – salvage, you know, sir – but there ain't no hovelling nowadays, not to speak of."

"Are you going out to-morrow?" asked Thorndyke.

"Not as I knows of, sir. Was you thinking of a bit of fishing?"

"If you are free," said Thorndyke, "I should like to charter the boat for to-morrow. I don't know what time I shall be able to start, but if you will stand by ready to put off at once when I come down we can count the waiting as sailing."

"Very well, sir," said the fisherman, "the boat's yours for the day to-morrow. Any time after six, or earlier, if you like, if you come down here you'll find me and my mate standing by with a stock of bait and the boat ready to push off."

"That will do admirably," said Thorndyke, and the morrow's programme being thus settled, we wished the fishermen good-night and walked slowly back to our lodgings, where, after a final pipe, we turned in.

On the following morning, just as we were finishing a rather leisurely breakfast, we saw from our window our friend Mr. Brodribb hurrying down the street towards our house. I ran out and opened the door, and as he entered I conducted him into our sitting-room. From his anxious and flustered manner it was obvious that something had gone wrong, and his first words confirmed the sinister impression.

"I'm afraid we're in for trouble, Thorndyke," said he. "Frank is missing."

338

"Since when?" asked Thorndyke.

"Since about eight o'clock this morning. He is nowhere about the house and he hasn't had any breakfast."

"When was he last seen?" Thorndyke asked. "And where?"

"About eight o'clock, in the breakfast-room. Apparently he went in there to say 'Good-bye' to the Prices – they have gone on a visit for the day to Folkestone and were having an early breakfast so as to catch the eight-thirty train. But he didn't have breakfast with them. He just went in and wished them a pleasant journey and then it appears that he went out for a stroll in the grounds. When I came down to breakfast at half-past-eight, the Prices had gone and Frank hadn't come in. The maid sounded the gong, and as Frank still did not appear, she went out into the grounds to look for him, and presently I went out myself. But he wasn't there and he wasn't anywhere in the house. I don't like the look of it at all. He is usually very regular and punctual at meals. What do you think we had better do, Thorndyke?"

My colleague looked at his watch and rang the bell.

"I think, Brodribb," said he, "that we must act on the obvious probabilities and provide against the one great danger that is known to us. Mrs. Robinson," he added, addressing the landlady, who, had answered the bell in person, "can you let us have a jug of strong coffee at once?"

Mrs. Robinson could, and bustled away to prepare it, while Thorndyke produced from a cupboard a large vacuum flask.

"I don't quite follow you, Thorndyke," said Mr. Brodribb. "What probabilities and what danger do you mean?"

"I mean that, up to the present, Frank Lumley has exactly reproduced in his experiences and his actions the experiences and actions of Gilbert Lumley as set forth in Walter Lumley's narrative. The overwhelming probability is that he will continue to reproduce the story of Gilbert to the end. He probably saw the apparition for the third time last night, and is even now preparing for the final act."

"Good God!" gasped Brodribb. "What a fool I am! You mean the cave? But we can never get there now. It will be high water in an hour and the beach at St. David's Head will be covered already. Unless we can get a boat," he added despairingly.

"We have got a boat," said Thorndyke. "I chartered one last night."

"Thank the Lord!" exclaimed Brodribb. "But you always think of everything – though I don't know what you want that coffee for."

"We may not want it at all," said Thorndyke, as he poured the coffee, which the landlady had just brought, into the vacuum flask, "but on the other hand we may."

He deposited the flask in a hand-bag, in which I observed a small emergency-case, and then turned to Brodribb.

"We had better get down to the beach now," said he.

As we emerged from the bottom of the gap-way we saw our friends of the previous night laying a double line of planks across the beach from the boat to the margin of the surf, for the long galley-punt, with her load of ballast, was too heavy over the shingle. They had just got the last plank laid as we reached the boat, and as they observed us they came running back with half-a-dozen of their mates.

"Jump aboard, gentlemen," said our skipper, with a slightly dubious eye on Mr. Brodribb – for the boat's gunwale was a good four feet above the beach. "We'll have her afloat in a jiffy."

We climbed in and hauled Mr. Brodribb in after us. The tall mast was already stepped – against the middle thwart in the odd fashion of galley-punts – and the great sail was hooked to the traveller and the tack-hook ready for hoisting. The party of boatmen gathered round and each took a tenacious hold of gunwale or thole. The skipper gave time with a jovial "Yo-ho!" His mates joined in with a responsive howl and heaved as one man. The great boat moved forward, and gathering way, slid swiftly along the greased planks towards the edge of the surf. Then her nose splashed into the sea, the skipper and his mate sprang in over the transom, the tall lug-sail soared up the mast and filled, and the skipper let the rudder slide down its pintles and grasped the tiller.

"Did you want to go anywheres in particklar?" he inquired.

"We want to make for the big cave round St. David's Head," said Thorndyke, " and we want to get there well before high water."

"We'll do that easy enough, sir," said the skipper "with this breeze. 'Tis but about a mile and we've got three-quarters-of-an-hour to do it in."

He took a pull at the main sheet and, putting the helm down, brought the boat on a course parallel to the coast. Quietly but swiftly the water slipped past, one after another fresh headlands opened out till, in about a quarter-of-an-hour, we were abreast of St. David's Head with the sinister black shape of the cavern in full view over the port bow. Shortly afterwards the sail was lowered and our crew, reinforced by Thorndyke and me, took to the oars, pulling straight towards the shore with the cavern directly ahead.

As the boat grounded on the beach Thorndyke, Brodribb and I sprang out and hurried across the sand and shingle to the gloomy and forbidding hole in white cliff. At first, coming out of the bright sunlight we seemed to be plunged in absolute darkness, and groped our way insecurely over the heaps of slippery sea-tangle that littered the floor.

340

Presently our eyes grew accustomed to the dim light, and we could trace faintly the narrow, tunnel-like passage with its slimy green and the jagged roof nearly black with age. At the farther end it grew higher, and here I could see the small, dark bodies of bats hanging from the roof and clinging to the walls, and one or two fluttering blindly and noiselessly like large moths in the hollows of the vault above. But it was not the bats that engrossed my attention. Far away, at the extreme end, I could dimly discern the prostrate figure of a man lying motionless on a patch of smooth sand, a dreadful shape that seemed to sound the final note of tragedy to which the darkness, the clammy chill of the cavern and the ghostly forms of he bats had been a fitting prelude.

"My God!" gasped Brodribb, "we're too late!" He broke into a shambling run and Thorndyke and I darted on ahead. The man was Frank Lumley, of course, and a glance at him gave us at least a ray of hope. He was lying in an easy posture with closed eyes and was still breathing, though his respiration was shallow and slow. Beside him on the sand lay a little bottle and near it a cork. I picked up the former and read on the label "*Laudanum, Poison*" and a local druggist's name and address. But it was empty save for a few drops, the appearance and smell of which confirmed the label.

Thorndyke, who had been examining the unconscious man's eyes with a little electric lamp, glanced at the bottle.

"Well," said he, "we know the worst. That is a two-drachm phial, so if he took the lot his condition is not hopeless."

As he spoke he opened the hand-bag and, taking out the emergency-case, produced from it a hypodermic syringe and a tiny bottle of atropine solution. I drew up Lumley's sleeve while the syringe was filled and Thorndyke then administered the injection.

"It is opium poisoning, I suppose?" said I.

"Yes," was the answer. "His pupils are like pin points, but his pulse is not so bad. I think we can safely move him down to the boat."

Thereupon we lifted him, and with Brodribb supporting his feet, we moved in melancholy procession down the cave. Already the waves were lapping the beach at the entrance and even trickling in amongst the seaweed, and the boat, following the rising tide, had her bows within the cavern. The two fishermen, who were steadying the boat with their oars, greeted our appearance, carrying the body, with exclamations of astonishment. But they asked no questions, simply taking the unconscious man from us and laying him gently on the grating in the stern-sheets.

"Why, 'tis Mr. Lumley!" exclaimed the skipper.

"Yes," said Thorndyke, and having given them a few words of explanation, he added, "I look to you to keep this affair to yourselves."

To this the two men agreed heartily, and the boat having been pushed off and the sail hoisted, the skipper asked, "Do we sail straight back, sir?"

"Yes," replied Thorndyke, "but we won't land yet. Stand on and off opposite the gap-way."

Already, as a result of the movement, the patient's stupor appeared less profound. And now Thorndyke took definite measures to rouse him, shaking him gently and constantly changing his position. Presently Lumley drew a deep sighing breath, and opened his eyes for a moment. Then Thorndyke sat him up, and producing the vacuum-flask, made him swallow a few teaspoonful of coffee. This procedure was continued for over an hour while the boat cruised up and down opposite the landing-place half-a-mile or so from the shore. Constantly our patient relapsed into stuporous sleep, only to be roused again and given a sip of coffee.

At length he recovered so far as to be able to sit up – lurching from side to side as the boat rolled – and drowsily answer questions spoken loudly in his ears. A quarter-of-an-hour later, as he still continued to improve, Thorndyke ordered the skipper to bring the boat to the landing-place.

"I think he could walk now," said he, "and the exercise will rouse him more completely."

The boat was accordingly beached and Lumley assisted to climb out, and though at first he staggered as if he would fall, after a few paces he was able to walk fairly steadily, supported on either side by me and Thorndyke. The effort of ascending the steep gap-way revived him further, and by the time we reached the gate of Burling Court – half-a-mile across the fields – he was almost able to stand alone.

But even when he had arrived home he was not allowed to rest, earnestly as he begged to be left in peace. First Thorndyke insisted on his taking a light meal, and then proceeded to question him as to the events of the previous night.

"I presume, Lumley," said he, "that you saw the apparition of Glynn's head?"

"Yes. After Mr. Brodribb had seen me to bed, I got up and went to Gilbert's cabin. Something seemed to draw me to it. And as soon as I opened the door, there was the head hanging in the air within three feet of me. Then I knew that Glynn was calling me, and – well, you know the rest."

"I understand," said Thorndyke. "But now I want you to come to Gilbert's cabin with me and show me exactly where you were and where the head was."

Lumley was profoundly reluctant and tried to postpone the demonstration. But Thorndyke would listen to no refusal, and at last Lumley rose wearily and conducted his tormentor up the stairs, followed by Brodribb and me.

We went first to Lumley's bedroom and from that into a corridor, into which some other bedrooms opened. The corridor was dimly lighted by a single window, and when Thorndyke had drawn the thick curtain over this, the place was almost completely dark. At one end of the corridor was the small, narrow door of the "cabin", over which was a gas bracket. Thorndyke lighted the gas and opened the door and we then saw that the room was in total darkness, its only window being closely shuttered and the curtains drawn. Thorndyke struck a match and lit the gas and we then looked curiously about the little room.

It was a quaint little apartment, to which its antique furniture and contents gave an old-world air. An ancient hanger, quadrant, and spy-glass hung on the wall, a large, dropsical-looking watch, inscribed "*Thomas Tompion, Londini fecit*," reposed on a little velvet cushion in the middle of a small, black mahogany table by the window, and a couple of Cromwellian chairs stood against the wall. Thorndyke looked curiously at the table, which was raised on wooden blocks, and Lumley explained, "That was Gilbert's dressing-table. He had it made for his cabin on board ship."

"Indeed," said Thorndyke. "Then Gilbert was a rather up-to-date gentleman. There wasn't much mahogany furniture before 1720. Let us have a look at the interior arrangements."

He lifted the watch and, having placed it on a chair, raised the lid of the table, disclosing a small wash basin, a little squat ewer, and other toilet appliances. The table lid, which was held upright by a brass strut, held a rather large dressing-mirror enclosed in a projecting case.

"I wonder," said I, "why the table was stood on those blocks."

"Apparently," said Thorndyke, "for the purpose of bringing the mirror to the eye-level of a person standing up."

The answer gave Brodribb an idea. "I suppose, Frank," said he, "it was not your own reflection in the mirror that you saw?"

"How could it be?" demanded Lumley. "The head was upside down, and besides, it was quite near to me."

"No, that's true," said Brodribb, and turning away from the table he picked up the old navigator's watch. "A queer old timepiece, this," he remarked.

"Yes," said Lumley, "but it's beautifully made. Let me show you the inside."

He took off the outer case and opened the inner one, exhibiting the delicate workmanship of the interior to Brodribb and me, while Thorndyke continued to pore over the inner fittings of the table. Suddenly my colleague said, "Just go outside, you three, and shut the door. I want to try an experiment."

Obediently we all filed out and closed the door, waiting expectantly in the corridor. In a couple of minutes Thorndyke came out and before he shut the door I noticed that the little room was now in darkness. He walked us a short distance down the corridor and then, halting, said, "Now, Lumley, I want you to go into the cabin and tell us what you see."

Lumley appeared a little reluctant to go in alone, but eventually he walked towards the cabin and opened the door. Instantly he uttered a cry of horror, and closing the door, ran back to us, trembling, agitated, wild-eyed.

"It is there now!" he exclaimed. "I saw it distinctly."

"Very well," said Thorndyke. "Now you go and look, Brodribb."

Mr. Brodribb showed no eagerness. With very obvious trepidation he advanced to the door and threw it open with a jerk. Then, with a sharp exclamation, he slammed it to, and came hurrying back, his usually pink complexion paled down to a delicate mauve.

"Horrible! Horrible!" he exclaimed. "What the devil is it, Thorndyke?"

A sudden suspicion flashed into my mind. I strode forward, and turning the handle of the door, pulled it open. And then I was not surprised that Brodribb had been startled. Within a yard of my face, clear, distinct and solid, was an inverted head, floating in mid-air in the pitch-dark room. Of course, being prepared for it, I saw at a glance what it was, recognised my own features, strangely and horribly altered as they were by their inverted position. But even now that I knew what it was, the thing had a most appalling, uncanny aspect.

"Now," said Thorndyke, "let us go in and explode the mystery. Just stand outside the door, Jervis, while I demonstrate."

He produced a sheet of white paper from his pocket, and smoothing it out, let our two friends into the room.

"First," said he, holding the paper out flat at the eye-level, "you see on this paper a picture of Dr. Jervis's head upside down."

"So there is," said Brodribb, "like a magic-lantern picture."

"Exactly like," agreed Thorndyke, "and of exactly the same nature. Now let us see how it is produced."

He struck a match and lit the gas, and instantly all our eyes turned towards the open dressing-table.

"But that is not the same mirror that we saw just now," said Brodribb.

"No," replied Thorndyke. "The frame is reversible on a sliding hinge and I have turned it round. On one side is the ordinary flat looking-glass which you saw before, on the other is this concave shaving-mirror. You observe that, if you stand close to it, you see your face the right way up and magnified, if you go back to the door, you see your head upside down and smaller."

"But," objected Lumley, "the head looked quite solid and seemed to be right out in the room."

"So it was, and is still. But the effect of reality is destroyed by the fact that you can now see the frame of the mirror enclosing the image, so that the head appears to be in the mirror. But in the dark, you could only see the image. The mirror was invisible."

Brodribb reflected on this explanation. Presently he said, "I don't think I quite understand it now."

Thorndyke took a pencil from his pocket and began to draw a diagram on the sheet of paper that he still held:

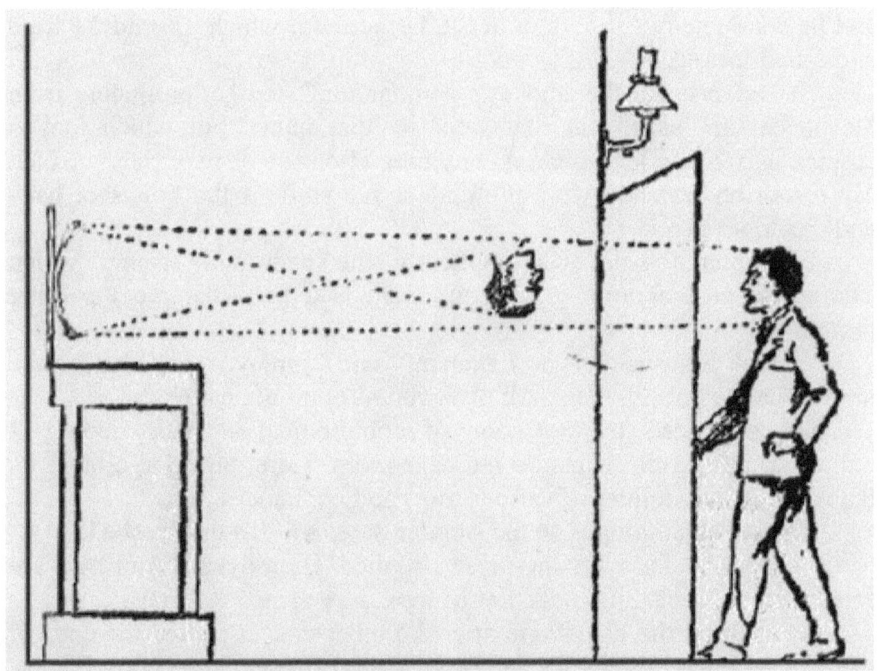

The Apparition of Burling Court

345

"The figure that you see in an ordinary flat looking glass," he explained, "is what is called a 'virtual image'. It appears to be behind the mirror, but of course it is not there. It is an optical illusion. But the image from a concave mirror is in front of the mirror and is a real image like that of a magic-lantern or a camera and, like them, inverted. This diagram will explain matters. Here is Lumley standing at the open door of the room. His figure is well lighted by the gas over the door (which, however, throws no light into the room) and is clearly reflected by the mirror, which throws forward a bright inverted image. But, as the room is dark and the mirror invisible, he sees only the image, which looks like – and in fact is – a real object standing in mid-air."

"But why did I see only the head?" asked Lumley.

"Because the head occupied the whole of the mirror. If the mirror had been large enough you would have seen the full-length figure."

Lumley reflected for a moment. "It almost looks if this had been arranged," he said at length.

"Of course it has been arranged," said Thorndyke, "and very cleverly arranged, too. And now let us go and see if anything else has been arranged. Which is Mr. Price's room?"

"He has three rooms, which open out of this corridor," said Lumley, and he conducted us to a door at the farther end, which Thorndyke tried and found locked.

"It is a case for the smoker's companion," said he, producing from his pocket an instrument that went by that name, but which looked suspiciously like a lock-pick. At any rate, after one or two trials – which Mr. Brodribb watched with an appreciative smile – the bolt shot back and the door opened.

We entered what was evidently the bedroom, around which Thorndyke cast a rapid glance and then asked, "What are the other rooms?"

"I think he uses them to tinker in," said Lumley, "but I don't quite know what he does in them. All three rooms communicate."

We advanced to the door of communication and, finding it unlocked, passed through into the next room. Here, on a large table by the window, was a litter of various tools and appliances.

"What is that thing with the wooden screws?" Brodribb asked.

"A bookbinder's sewing-press," replied Thorndyke. "And here are some boxes of finishing tools. Let us look over them."

He took up the boxes one after the other and inspected the ends of the tools – brass stamps for impressing the ornaments on book covers. Presently he lifted out two, a leaf and a flower. Then he produced from

346

his coat pocket the little manuscript book, and laying it on the table, picked up from the floor a little fragment of leather. Placing this also on the table, he pressed two of the tools on it, leaving a clear impression of a leaf and a flower. Finally he laid the scrap of leather on the book, when it was obvious that the leaf and flower were identical replicas of the leaves and flowers which formed the decoration of the book cover.

"This is very curious," said Lumley. "They seem to be exactly alike."

"They are exactly alike," said Thorndyke. "I affirm that the tooling on that book was done with these tools, and the leaves sewn on that press."

"But the book is a hundred years old," objected Lumley.

Thorndyke shook his head. "The leather is old," said he, "but the book is new. We have tested the paper and found it to be of recent manufacture. But now let us see what is in that little cupboard. There seem to be some bottles there."

He ran his eye along the shelves, crowded with bottles and jars of varnish, glair, oil, cement, and other material.

"Here," he said, taking down a small bottle of dark-coloured powder, "is some aniline brown. That probably produced the ancient and faded writing. But this is more illuminating – in more senses than one." He picked out a little, wide-mouthed bottle labelled *Radium Paint for the Hands and Figures of Luminous Watches.*"

"Ha!" exclaimed Brodribb. "A very illuminating discovery, as you say."

"And that," said Thorndyke, looking keenly round the room, "seems to be all there is here. Shall we take a glance at the third room?"

We passed through the communicating doorway and found ourselves in a small apartment practically unfurnished and littered with trunks, bags, and various lumber. As we stood looking about us, Thorndyke sniffed suspiciously.

"I seem to detect a sort of mousy odour," said he, glancing round inquisitively. "Do you notice it, Jervis?"

I did, and with the obvious idea in my mind began I to prowl round the room in search of the source, Suddenly my eye lighted on a smallish box, in the top of which a number of gimlet-holes had been bored. I raised the lid and peered in. The interior was covered with filth and on the bottom lay a dead bat.

We all stood for a few seconds looking in silence at the little corpse. Then Thorndyke closed the box and tucked it under his arm.

"This completes the case, I think," said he. "What time does Price return?"

347

"He is expected home about seven o'clock," said Lumley. Then he added with a troubled expression, "I don't understand all this. What does it mean?"

"It is very simple," replied Thorndyke. "You have a sham ancient book containing an evidently fabulous story of supernatural events, and you have a series of appliances and arrangements for producing illusions which seem to repeat those events. The book was planted where it was certain to be found and read, and the illusions began after it was known that it actually had been read. It is a conspiracy."

"But why?" demanded Lumley. "What was the object?"

"My dear Frank," said Brodribb, "you seem forget that Price is the next of kin and the heir to your estate on your death."

Lumley's eyes filled. He seemed overcome with grief and disgust. "It is incredible," he murmured huskily. "The baseness of it is beyond belief."

Price and his wife arrived home at about seven o'clock, A meal had been prepared for them, and when they had finished, a servant was sent in to ask Mr. Price to speak with Mr. Brodribb in the study. There we all awaited him, Lumley being present by his own wish, and on the table were deposited the little book, the scrap of leather, the two finishing tools, the pot of radium paint and the box containing the dead bat. Presently Price entered, accompanied by his wife, and at the sight of the objects on the table they both turned deathly pale. Mr. Brodribb placed chairs for them, and when they were seated he began in a dry, stern voice,

"I have sent for you, Mr. Price, to give you certain information. These two gentlemen, Dr. Thorndyke and Dr. Jervis, are eminent criminal lawyers whom I have commissioned to make investigations and to advise me in this matter. Their investigations have disclosed the existence of a forged manuscript, a dead bat, a pot of luminous paint and a concave mirror. I need not enlarge on those discoveries. My intention is to prosecute you and your wife for conspiracy to procure the suicide of Mr. Frank Lumley. But, at Mr. Lumley's request, I have consented to delay the proceedings for forty-eight hours. During that period you will be at liberty to act as you think best."

For some seconds there was a tense silence. The two crestfallen conspirators sat with their eyes fixed on the floor, and Mrs. Price choked down a half-hysterical sob. Then they rose, and Price, without looking at any of us, said in a low voice, "Very well. Then I suppose we had better clear out."

"And the best thing, too," remarked Brodribb, when they had gone, "for I doubt if we could have carried our bluff into court."

348

On the wall of our sitting-room in the Temple there hang, to this day, two keys. One is that of the postern gate of Burling Court, and the other belongs to the suite of rooms that were once occupied by Mr. Lewis Price, and they hang there, by Frank Lumley's wish, as a token that Burling Court is a country home to which we have access at all hours and seasons as tenants in virtue of an inalienable right.

The Mysterious Visitor

"**S**o," said Thorndyke, looking at me reflectively, "you are a full-blown medical practitioner with a practice of your own. How the years slip by! It seems but the other day that you were a student, gaping at me from the front bench of the lecture theatre."

"Did I gape?" I asked incredulously.

"I use the word metaphorically," said he, "to denote ostentatious attention. You always took my lecture very seriously. May I ask if you have ever found them of use in your practice?"

"I can't say that I have ever had any very thrilling medico-legal experiences since that extraordinary cremation case that you investigated – the case of Septimus Maddock, you know. But that reminds me that there is a little matter that I meant to speak to you about. It is of no interest, but I just wanted your advice, though it isn't even my business, strictly speaking. It concerns a patient of mine, a man named Crofton, who has disappeared rather unaccountably."

"And do you call that a case of no medico-legal interest?" demanded Thorndyke.

"Oh, there's nothing in it. He just went away for a holiday and he hasn't communicated with his friends very recently. That is all. What makes me a little uneasy is that there is a departure from his usual habits – he is generally a fairly regular correspondent – that seems a little significant in view of his personality. He is markedly neurotic and his family history is by no means what one would wish."

"That is an admirable thumb-nail sketch, Jardine," said Thorndyke, "but it lacks detail. Let us have a full-size picture."

"Very well," said I, "but you mustn't let me bore you. To begin with Crofton: He is a nervous, anxious, worrying sort of fellow, everlastingly fussing about money affairs, and latterly this tendency has been getting worse. He fairly got the jumps about his financial position, felt that he was steadily drifting into bankruptcy, and couldn't get that out of his mind. It was all bunkum. I am more or less a friend of the family, and I know that there was nothing to worry about. Mrs. Crofton assured me that, although they were a trifle hard up, they could rub along quite safely.

"As he seemed to be getting the hump worse and worse, I advised him to go away for a change and stay in a boarding house where he would see some fresh faces. Instead of that, he elected to go down to a bungalow that he has at Seasalter, near Whitstable, and lets out in the

350

season. He proposed to stay by himself and spend his time in sea-bathing and country walks. I wasn't very keen on this, for solitude was the last thing that he wanted. There was a strong family history of melancholia and some unpleasant rumours of suicide. I didn't like his being alone at all. However, another friend of the family, Mrs. Crofton's brother in fact, a chap named Ambrose, offered to go down and spend a week-end with him to give him a start, and afterwards to run down for an afternoon whenever he was able. So off he went with Ambrose on Friday, the sixteenth of June, and for a time all went well. He seemed to be improving in health and spirits and wrote to his wife regularly two or three times a week. Ambrose went down as often as he could to cheer him up, and the last time brought back the news that Crofton thought of moving on to Margate for a further change. So, of course, he didn't go down to the bungalow again.

"Well, in due course, a letter came from Margate, it had been written at the bungalow, but the postmark was Margate and bore the same date – the sixteenth of July – as the letter itself. I have it with me. Mrs. Crofton sent it for me to see and I haven't returned it yet. But there is nothing of interest in it beyond the statement that he was going on to Margate by the next train and would write again when he had found rooms there. That was the last that was heard of him. He never wrote and nothing is known of his movements excepting that he left Seasalter and arrived at Margate. This is the letter."

I handed it to Thorndyke, who glanced at the mark and then laid it on the table for examination later. "Have any inquiries been made?" he asked.

"Yes. His photograph has been sent to the Margate police, but, of course – well, you know what Margate like in July. Thousands of strangers coming and going every day. It is hopeless to look for him in that crowd and it is quite possible that he isn't there now. But his disappearance is most inopportune, for a big legacy that's just fallen in and, naturally, Mrs. Crofton is frantically anxious to let him know. It is a matter of about thirty-thousand pounds."

"Was this legacy expected?" asked Thorndyke.

"No. The Croftons knew nothing about it. They didn't know that the old lady – Miss Shuler – had made a will or that she had very much to leave, and they didn't know that she was likely to die, or even that she was ill. Which is rather odd, for she was ill for a month or two and, as she suffered from a malignant abdominal tumour, it was known that she couldn't recover."

"When did she die?"

"On the thirteenth of July."

Thorndyke raised his eyebrows. "Just three days before the date of this letter," he remarked, "so that if he should never reappear, this letter will be the sole evidence that he survived her. It is an important document. It may come to represent a value of thirty-thousand pounds."

"It isn't so important as it looks," said I. "Miss Shuler's will provides that if Crofton should die before the *estatrix*, the legacy should go to his wife. So whether he is alive or not, the legacy is quite safe. But we must hope that he is alive, though I must confess to some little anxiety on his account."

Thorndyke reflected a while on this statement. Presently he asked, "Do you know if Crofton has made a will?"

"Yes, he has," I replied, "quite recently. I was one of the witnesses and I read it through at Crofton's request. It was full of the usual legal verbiage, but it might have been stated in a dozen words. He leaves practically everything to his wife, but instead of saying so it enumerates the property item by item."

"It was drafted, I suppose, by the solicitor?"

"Yes, another friend of the family named Jobson, and he is the executor and residuary legatee."

Thorndyke nodded and again became deeply reflective. Still meditating, he took up the letter, and as he inspected it, I watched him curiously and not without a certain secret amusement. First he looked over the envelope, back and front. Then he took from his pocket a powerful Coddington lens and with this examined the flap and the postmark. Next, he drew out the letter, held it up to the light, then read it through and finally examined various parts of the writing through his lens. "Well," I asked, with an irreverent grin, "I should think you have extracted the last grain of meaning from it."

He smiled as he put away his lens and handed the letter back to me.

"As this may have to be produced in proof of survival," said he, "it had better be put in a place of safety. I notice that he speaks of returning later to the bungalow. I take it that it has been ascertained that he did not return there?"

"I don't think so. You see, they have been waiting for him to write. You think that someone ought – "

I paused, for it began to be borne in on me that Thorndyke was taking a somewhat gloomy view of the case.

"My dear Jardine," said he, "I am merely following your own suggestion. Here is a man with an inherited tendency to melancholia and suicide who has suddenly disappeared. He went away from an empty house and announced his intention of returning to it later. As that house is the only known locality in which he could be sought, it is obvious that

352

it ought to have been examined. And even if he never came back there, the house might contain some clues to his present whereabouts."

This last sentence put an idea into my mind which I was a little shy of broaching. What was a clue to Thorndyke might be perfectly meaningless to an ordinary person. I recalled his amazing interpretations of most commonplace facts in the mysterious Maddock case and the idea took fuller possession. At length I said tentatively, "I would go down myself if I felt competent. To-morrow is Saturday, and I could get a colleague to look after my practice, there isn't much doing just now. But when you speak of clues, and when I remember what duffer I was last time – I wish it were possible for you to have a look at the place."

To my surprise, he assented almost with enthusiasm.

"Why not?" said he. "It is a week-end. We can put up at the bungalow, I suppose, and have a little gipsy holiday. And there are undoubtedly points of interest in the case. Let us go down to-morrow. We can lunch in the train and have the afternoon before us. You had better get a key from Mrs. Crofton, or, if she hasn't got one, an authority to visit the house. We may want that if we have to enter without a key. And we go alone, of course."

I assented joyfully. Not that I had any expectations as to what we might learn from our inspection. But something in Thorndyke's manner gave me the impression that he had extracted from my account of the case some significance that was not apparent to me.

The bungalow stood on a space of rough ground a little way behind the sea-wall, along which we walked towards it from Whitstable, passing on our way a ship-builder's yard and a slipway, on which a collier brigantine was hauled up for repairs. There were one or two other bungalows adjacent, but a considerable distance apart, and we looked at them as we approached to make out the names painted on the gates.

"That will probably be the one," said Thorndyke, indicating a small building enclosed within a wooden fence and provided, like the others, with a bathing hut just above high-water mark. Its solitary, deserted aspect and lowered blinds supported his opinion, and when we reached the gate, the name "*Middlewick*" painted on it settled the matter.

"The next question is," said I, "how the deuce we are going to get in? The gate is locked, and there is no bell. Is it worthwhile to hammer at the fence?"

"I wouldn't do that," replied Thorndyke. "The place is pretty certainly empty or the gate wouldn't be locked. We shall have to climb over unless there is a back gate unlocked, so the less noise we make the better."

We walked round the enclosure, but there was no other gate, nor was there any tree or other cover to disguise our rather suspicious proceedings.

"There's no help for it, Jardine," said Thorndyke, "so here goes."

He put his green canvas suit-case on the ground, grasped the top of the fence with both hands and went over like a harlequin. I picked up the case and handed it over to him and, having taken a quick glance round, followed my leader.

"Well," I said, "here we are. And now, how are we to get into the house?"

"We shall have to pick a lock if there is no door open, or else go in by a window. Let us take a look round." We walked round the house to the back door, but found it not only locked, but bolted top and bottom, as Thorndyke ascertained with his knifeblade. The windows were all casements and all fastened with their catches.

"The front door will be the best," said Thorndyke. "It can't be bolted unless he got out by the chimney and I think my 'smoker's companion' will be able to cope with an ordinary door-lock. It looked like a common builder's fitting."

As he spoke, we returned to the front of the house and he produced the 'smoker's companion' from his pocket. (I don't know what kind of smoker it was designed to accompany.) The lock was apparently a simple affair, for the second trial with the 'companion' shot back the bolt, and when I turned the handle, the door opened. As a precaution, I called out to inquire if there was anybody within, and then, as there was no answer, we entered, walking straight into the living-room, as there was no hall or lobby.

A couple of paces from the threshold we halted to look round the room, and on me the aspect of the place produced a vague sense of discomfort. Though it was early in a bright afternoon, the room was almost completely dark, for not only were the blinds lowered, but the curtains were drawn as well.

"It looks," said I, peering about the dim and gloomy apartment with sun-dazzled eyes, "as if he had gone away at night. He wouldn't have drawn the curtains in the daytime."

"One would think not," Thorndyke agreed, "but it doesn't follow."

He stepped to the front window and, drawing back the curtains, pulled up the blind, revealing a half-curtain of green serge over the lower part of the window. As the bright daylight flooded the room, he stood with his back to the window looking about with deep attention, letting his eyes travel slowly over the walls, the furniture, and especially the floor. Presently he stooped to pick up a short match-end which lay just under the table opposite the door, and as he looked at it thoughtfully, he pointed to a couple of spots of candle grease on the linoleum near the table. Then he glanced at the mantelpiece and from that to an ash-bowl on the table.

"These are only trifling discrepancies," said he, "but they are worth noting. You see," he continued in response to my look of inquiry, "that this room is severely trim and orderly. Everything seems to be in place. The match-box, for instance, has its fixed receptacle above the mantelpiece, and there is a bowl for the burnt matches, regularly used, as its contents show. Yet there is a burnt match thrown on the floor, although the bowl is on the table quite handy. And the match, you notice, is not of the same kind as those in the box over the mantelpiece, which is a large Bryant and May, or as the burnt matches in the bowl which have evidently come from it. But if you look in the bowl," he continued, picking it up, "you will see two burnt matches of this same kind – apparently the small size Bryant and May – one burnt quite short and one only half burnt. The suggestion is fairly obvious, but, as I say, there is a slight discrepancy."

"I don't know," said I, "that either the suggestion or the discrepancy is very obvious to me."

He walked over to the mantelpiece and took the match box from its case.

"You see," said he, opening it, "that this box is nearly full. It has an appointed place and it was in that place. We find a small match, burnt right out, under the table opposite the door, and two more in the bowl under the hanging lamp. A reasonable inference is that someone came in in the dark and struck a match as he entered. That match must have come from a box that he brought with him in his pocket. It burned out and he struck another, which also burned out while he was raising the chimney of the lamp, and he struck a third to light the lamp. But if that person was Crofton, why did he need to strike a match to light the room when the match-box was in its usual place, and why did he throw the match-end on the floor?"

"You mean that the suggestion is that the person was not Crofton, and I think you are right. Crofton doesn't carry matches in his pocket. He uses wax vestas and carries them in a silver case."

"It might possibly have been Ambrose," Thorndyke suggested.

"I don't think so," said I. "Ambrose uses a petrol lighter."

Thorndyke nodded. "There may be nothing in it," said he, "but it offers a suggestion. Shall we look over the rest of the premises?"

He paused for a moment to glance at a small key board on the wall on which one or two keys were hanging, each distinguished by a little ivory label and by the name written underneath the peg, then he opened a door in the corner of the room. As this led into the kitchen, I closed it and opened an adjoining one which gave access to a bedroom.

"This is probably the extra bedroom," he remarked as we entered. "The blinds have not been drawn down, and there is a general air of trimness that suggests the tidy up of an unoccupied room. And the bed looks if it had been out of use."

After an attentive look round, he returned to the living room and crossed to the remaining door. As he opened it, we looked into a nearly dark room, both the windows being covered by thick serge curtains.

"Well," he observed, when he had drawn back the curtains and raised the blinds, "there is nothing painfully tidy here. That is a very roughly-made bed, and the blanket is outside the counterpane."

He looked critically about the room and especially the bedside table.

"Here are some more discrepancies," said he. "There are two candlesticks, in one of which the candle has burned itself right out, leaving a fragment of wick. There are five burnt matches in it, two large ones from the box by its side and three small ones, of which two are mere stumps. The second candle is very much guttered, and I think – " He lifted it out of the socket. "Yes, it has been used out of the candlestick. You see that the grease has run down right to the bottom and there is a distinct impression of a thumb – apparently a left thumb – made while the grease was warm. Then you notice the mark on the table of a tumbler which had contained some liquid that was not water, but there is no tumbler. However, it may be an old mark, though it looks fresh."

"It is hardly like Crofton to leave an old mark on the table," said I. "He is a regular old maid. We had better see if the tumbler is in the kitchen."

"Yes," agreed Thorndyke. "But I wonder what he was doing with that candle. Apparently he took it out-of-doors, as there is a spot on the floor of the living-room, and you see that there are one or two spots on the floor here." He walked over to a chest of drawers near the door and was looking into a drawer which he had pulled out, and which I could see was full of clothes, when I observed a faint smile spreading over his face. "Come round here, Jardine," he said in a low voice, "and take a peep through the crack of the door."

I walked round and, applying my eye to the crack, looked across the living-room at the end window. Above the half-curtain I could distinguish the unmistakable top of a constabulary helmet.

"Listen," said Thorndyke. "They are in force."

As he spoke, there came from the neighbourhood of the kitchen a furtive scraping sound, suggestive of a pocket knife persuading a window-catch. It was followed by the sound of an opening window and then of a stealthy entry. Finally, the kitchen door opened softly, someone tip-toed across the living-room and a burly police-sergeant appeared, framed in the bedroom doorway.

"Good afternoon, Sergeant," said Thorndyke, with a genial smile.

"Yes, that's all very well," was the response, "but the question is, who might you be, and what might you be doing in this house?"

Thorndyke briefly explained our business and, when, we had presented our cards and Mrs. Crofton's written authority, the sergeant's professional stiffness vanished like magic.

"It's all right, Tomkins," he sang out to an invisible myrmidon. "You had better shut the window and go out by the front door. You must excuse me, gentlemen," he added, "but the tenant of the next bungalow cycled down and gave us the tip. He watched you through his glasses and saw you pick the front-door lock. It did look a bit queer, you must admit."

Thorndyke admitted it freely with a faint chuckle, and we walked across the living-room to the kitchen. Here, the sergeant's presence seemed to inhibit comments, but I noticed that my colleague cast a significant glance at a frying-pan that rested on a Primus stove. The congealed fat in it presented another "discrepancy", for I could hardly imagine the fastidious Crofton going away and leaving it in that condition.

Noting that there was no unwashed tumbler in evidence, I followed my friend back to the living-room, where he paused with his eye on the key-board.

"Well," remarked the sergeant, "if he ever did come back here, it's pretty clear that he isn't here now. You've been all over the premises, I think?"

"All excepting the bathing-hut," replied Thorndyke and, as he spoke, he lifted the key so labelled from its hook.

The sergeant laughed softly. "He's not very likely to have taken up quarters there," said he. "Still, there nothing like being thorough. But you notice that the key of the front door and that of the gate have both been taken away, so we can assume that he has taken himself away too."

"That is a reasonable inference," Thorndyke admitted, "but we may as well make our survey complete."

With this he led the way out into the garden and to the gate, where he unblushingly produced the 'smoker's companion' and insinuated its prongs into the keyhole.

"Well, I'm sure!" exclaimed the sergeant as the lock clicked and the gate opened. "That's a funny sort of tool, and you seem quite handy with it, too. Might I have a look at it?"

He looked at it so very long and attentively, when Thorndyke handed it to him, that I suspected him of an intention to infringe the patent. By the time he had finished his inspection we were at the bottom of the bank below the sea-wall and Thorndyke had inserted the key into the lock of the bathing-hut. As the sergeant returned the 'companion', Thorndyke took it and pocketed it, and then he turned the key and pushed the door open, and the officer started back with a shout of amazement.

It was certainly a grim spectacle that we looked in on. The hut was a small building about six feet square, devoid of any furniture or fittings, excepting one or two pegs high up the wall. The single, unglazed window was closely shuttered, and on the bare floor in the farther corner a man was sitting, leaning back into the corner, with his head dropped forward on his breast. The man was undoubtedly Arthur Crofton. That much I could say with certainty, notwithstanding the horrible changes wrought by death and the lapse of time. "But," I added when I had identified the body, "I should have said that he had been dead more than a fortnight. He must have come straight back from Margate and done this. And that will probably be the missing tumbler," I concluded, pointing to one that stood on the floor close to the right hand of the corpse.

"No doubt," replied Thorndyke, somewhat abstractedly. He had been looking critically about the interior of the hut, and now remarked, "I wonder why he did not shoot the bolt instead of locking himself in, and what has become of the key? He must have taken it out of the lock and put it in his pocket."

He looked interrogatively at the sergeant who, having no option but to take the hint, advanced with an expression of horrified disgust and proceeded very gingerly to explore the dead man's clothing.

"Ah!" he exclaimed at length, "here we are." He drew from the waistcoat pocket a key with a small ivory label attached to it. "Yes, this is the one. You see, it is marked '*Bathing-hut*'."

He handed it to Thorndyke, who looked at it attentively, and even with an appearance of surprise, and then, producing an indelible pencil from his pocket, wrote on the label, "*Found on body*".

"The first thing," said he, "is to ascertain it fits the lock."

"Why, it must," said the sergeant, "if he locked himself in with it."

"Undoubtedly," Thorndyke agreed, "but that is the point. It doesn't look quite similar to the other one."

He drew out the key which we had brought from the house and gave it to me to hold. Then he tried the key from the dead man's pocket, but it not only did not fit, it would not even enter the keyhole.

The sceptical indifference faded suddenly from the sergeant's face. He took the key from Thorndyke, having tried it with the same result, stood up and stared, round-eyed, at my colleague.

"Well!" he exclaimed. "This is a facer! It's the wrong key!"

"There may be another key on the body," said Thorndyke. "It isn't likely, but you had better make sure."

The sergeant showed no reluctance this time. He searched the dead man's pockets thoroughly and produced a bunch of keys. But they were all quite small keys, none of them in the least resembling that of the hut door. Nor, I noticed, did they include those of the bungalow door or the garden gate. Once more the officer drew himself up and stared at Thorndyke.

"There's something rather fishy about this affair," said he.

"There is," Thorndyke agreed. "The door was certainly locked, and as it was not locked from within, it must have been locked from without. Then that key – the *wrong* key – was presumably placed in the dead man's pocket by some other person. And there are some other suspicious facts. A tumbler has disappeared from the bedside table, and there is a tumbler here. You notice one or two spots of candle-grease on the floor here, and it looks as if a candle had been stood in that corner near the door. There is no candle here now, but in the bedroom there is a candle which has been carried without a candle stick and which, by the way, bears an excellent impression of a thumb. The first thing to do will be to take the deceased's finger-prints. Would you mind fetching my case from the bedroom, Jardine?"

I ran back to the house (not unobserved by the gentleman in the next bungalow) and, catching up the case, carried it down to the hut. When I arrived there I found Thorndyke holding the tumbler delicately in his gloved left hand while he examined it against the light with the aid of his lens. He handed the latter to me and observed.

"If you look at this carefully, Jardine, you will see a very interesting thing. There are the prints of two different thumbs – both left hands, and therefore of different persons. You will remember that the tumbler stood by the right hand of the body and that the table, which bore the mark of a tumbler, was at the left-hand side of the bed."

When I had examined the thumb-prints he placed the tumbler carefully on the floor and opened his "research-case", which was fitted as a sort of portable laboratory. From this he took a little brass box containing an ink-tube, a tiny roller, and some small cards and, using the box-lid as an inking plate, he proceeded methodically to take the dead man's finger-prints, writing the particulars on each card.

"I don't quite see what you want with Crofton's finger-prints," said I. "The other man's would be more to the point."

"Undoubtedly," Thorndyke replied. "But we have to prove that they are another man's – that they are not Crofton's. And there is that print on the candle. That is a very important point to settle, and as we have finished here, we had better go and settle it at once."

He closed his case and, taking up the tumbler with his gloved hand, led the way back to the house, the sergeant following when he had locked the door. We proceeded directly to the bedroom, where Thorndyke took the candle from its socket and, with the aid of his lens, compared it carefully with the two thumb-prints on the card, and then with the tumbler.

"It is perfectly clear," said he. "This is a mark of a left thumb. It is totally unlike Crofton's and it appears to be identical with the strange thumb-print on the tumbler – from which it seems to follow that the stranger took the candle from this room to the hut and brought it back. But he probably blew it out before leaving the house and lit it again in the hut."

The sergeant and I examined the cards, the candle, and the tumbler, and then the former asked, "I suppose you have no idea whose thumb-print that might be? You don't know, for instance, of anyone who might have had any motive for making away with Mr. Crofton?"

"That," replied Thorndyke, "is rather a question for the coroner's jury."

"So it is," the sergeant agreed. "But there won't be much question about their verdict. It is a pretty clear case of wilful murder."

To this Thorndyke made no reply, excepting to give some directions as to the safe-keeping of the candle and tumbler, and our proposed "gipsy holiday" being now evidently impossible, we took our leave of the sergeant – who already had our cards – and wended back to the station.

"I suppose," said I, "we shall have to break the news to Mrs. Crofton."

"That is hardly our business," he replied. "We can leave that to the solicitor or to Ambrose. If you know the lawyer's address, you might send him a telegram, arranging a meeting at eight o'clock to-night. Give no particulars. Just say 'Crofton found', but mark the telegram 'Urgent' so that he will keep the appointment."

On reaching the station, I sent off the telegram, and very soon afterwards the London train was signalled. It turned out to be a slow train, which gave us ample time to discuss the case and me ample time for reflection. And in fact, I reflected a good deal, for there was a rather uncomfortable question in my mind – the very question that the sergeant had raised and that Thorndyke had obviously evaded. Was there anyone who might have had a motive for making away with Crofton? It was an awkward question when one remembered the great legacy that had just fallen in and the terms of Miss Shuler's will, which expressly provided that, if Crofton died before his wife, the legacy should go to her. Now, Ambrose was the wife's brother, and Ambrose had been in the bungalow alone with Crofton, and nobody else was known to have been there at all. I meditated on these facts uncomfortably and would have liked to put the case to Thorndyke, but his reticence, his evasion of the sergeant's question, and his decision to communicate with the solicitor rather than with the family showed pretty clearly what was in his mind and that he did not wish to discuss the matter.

Promptly at eight o'clock, having dined at a restaurant, we presented ourselves at the solicitor's house and were shown into the study, where we found Mr. Jobson seated at a writing-table. He looked at Thorndyke with some surprise, and when the introductions had been made, said somewhat dryly, "We may take it that Dr. Thorndyke is in some way connected with our rather confidential business?"

"Certainly," I replied. "That is why he is here."

Jobson nodded. "And how is Crofton?" he asked, "and where did you dig him up?"

"I am sorry to say," I replied, "that he is dead. It is a dreadful affair. We found his body locked in the bathing-hut. He was sitting in a corner with a tumbler on the floor by his side."

"Horrible! Horrible!" exclaimed the solicitor. "He ought never to have gone there alone. I said so at the time. And it is most unfortunate on account of the insurance, though that is not a large amount. Still the suicide clause, you know – "

"I doubt whether the insurance will be affected," said Thorndyke. "The coroner's finding will almost certainly be wilful murder."

Jobson was thunderstruck. In a moment his face grew livid and he gazed at Thorndyke with an expression of horrified amazement.

"Murder!" he repeated incredulously. "But you said he was locked in the hut. Surely that is clear proof of suicide."

"He hadn't locked himself in, you know. There was no key inside."

"Ah!" The solicitor spoke almost in a tone relief. "But, perhaps – did you examine his pockets?"

361

"Yes, and we found a key labelled '*Bathing hut*'. But it was the wrong key. It wouldn't go into the lock. There is no doubt whatever that the door was locked from the outside."

"Good God!" exclaimed Jobson, in a faint voice. "It does look suspicious. But still, I can't believe – It seems quite incredible."

"That may be," said Thorndyke, "but it is all perfectly clear. There is evidence that a stranger entered the bungalow at night and that the affair took place in the bedroom. From thence the stranger carried the body down to the hut and he also took a tumbler and a candle from the bedside table. By the light of the candle – which was stood on the floor of the hut in a corner – he arranged the body, having put into its pocket a key from the board in the living-room. Then he locked the hut, went back to the house, put the key on its peg and the candle in its candlestick. Then he locked up the house and the garden gate and took the keys away with him."

The solicitor listened to this recital in speechless amazement. At length he asked, "How long ago do you suppose this happened?"

"Apparently on the night of the fifteenth of this month," was the reply.

"But," objected Jobson, "he wrote home on the sixteenth."

"He wrote," said Thorndyke, "on the sixth. Somebody put a one in front of the six and posted the letter at Margate on the sixteenth. I shall give evidence to that effect at the inquest."

I was becoming somewhat mystified. Thorndyke's dry, stern manner – so different from his usual suavity – and the solicitor's uncalled-for agitation, seemed to hint at something more than met the eye. I watched Jobson as he lit a cigarette – with a small Bryant and May match, which he threw on the floor – and listened expectantly for his next question. At length he asked, "Was there any sort of – er – clue as to who this stranger might be?"

"The man who will be charged with the murder? Oh, yes. The police have the means of identifying him with absolute certainty."

"That is, if they can find him," said Jobson.

"Naturally. But when all the very remarkable facts have transpired at the inquest, that individual will probably come pretty clearly into view."

Jobson continued to smoke furiously with his eyes fixed on the floor, as if he were thinking hard. Presently he asked, without looking up, "Supposing they do find this man. What then? What evidence is there that he murdered Crofton?"

"You mean direct evidence?" said Thorndyke. "I can't say, as I did not examine the body, but the circumstantial evidence that I have given you would be enough to convict unless there were some convincing explanation other than murder. And I may say," he added, "that if the suspected person has a plausible explanation to offer, he would be well advised to produce it before he is charged. A voluntary statement has a good deal more weight than the same statement made by a prisoner in answer to a charge."

There was an interval of silence, in which I looked bewilderment from Thorndyke's stern visage to the pale face of the solicitor. At length the latter rose abruptly and, after one or two quick strides up and down the room, halted by the fireplace and, still avoiding Thorndyke's eye, said, somewhat brusquely, though in a low, husky voice, "I will tell you how it happened. I went down to Seasalter, as you said, on the night of the fifteenth, on the chance of finding Crofton at the bungalow. I wanted to tell him of Miss Shuler's death and of the provisions her will."

"You had some private information on that subject, I presume?" said Thorndyke.

"Yes. My cousin was her solicitor and he kept me informed about the will."

"And about the state of her health?"

"Yes. Well, when I arrived at the bungalow, it was in darkness. The gate and the front door were unlocked, so I entered, calling out Crofton's name. As no one answered, I struck a match and lit the lamp. Then I went into the bedroom and struck a match there, and by its light I could see Crofton lying on the bed, quite still. I spoke to him, but he did not answer or move. Then I lighted a candle on his table, and now I could see what I had already guessed, that he was dead, and that he had been dead some time – probably more than a week.

"It was an awful shock to find a dead man in this solitary house, and my first impulse was to rush out and give the alarm. But when I went into the living-room, I happened to see a letter lying on writing-table and noticed that it was in his own hand and addressed to his wife. Unfortunately, I had the curiosity to take it out of the unsealed envelope and read it. It was dated the sixth and stated his intention of going to Margate for a time and then coming back to the bungalow.

"Now, the reading of that letter exposed me to an enormous temptation. By simply putting a one in front of the six and thus altering the date from the sixth to the sixteenth and posting the letter at Margate, I stood to gain thirty-thousand pounds. I saw that at a glance. But I did not decide immediately to do it. I pulled down the blinds, drew the curtains, and locked up the house while I thought it over. There seemed to be practically no risk, unless someone should come to the bungalow and notice that the state of the body did not agree with the altered date on the letter. I went back and looked at the dead man. There was a burnt-out candle by his side and a tumbler containing the dried-up remains of some brown liquid. He had evidently poisoned himself. Then it occurred to me that, if I put the body and the tumbler in some place where they were not likely to be found for some time, the discrepancy between the condition of the body and the date of the letter would not be noticed.

"For some time I could think of no suitable place, but at last I remembered the bathing-hut. No one would look there for him. If they came to the bungalow and didn't find him there, they would merely conclude that he had not come back from Margate. I took the candle and the key from the key-board and went down to the hut, but there was a key in the door already, so I brought the other key back and put it in Crofton's pocket, never dreaming that it might not be the duplicate. Of course, I ought to have tried it in the door.

"Well, you know the rest. I took the body down about two in the morning, locked up the hut, brought away the key and hung it on the board, took the counterpane off the bed, as it had some marks on it, and re-made the bed with the blanket outside. In the morning I took the train to Margate, posted the letter after altering the date, and threw the gate-key and that of the front door into the sea.

"That is what really happened. You may not believe me, but I think you will as you have seen the body and will realise that I had no motive for killing Crofton before the fifteenth, whereas Crofton evidently died before that date."

"I would not say 'evidently'," said Thorndyke, "but, as the date of his death is the vital point in your defence, you would be wise to notify the coroner of the importance of the issue."

"I don't understand this case," I said, as we walked homewards. (I was spending the evening with Thorndyke.) "You seemed to smell a rat from the very first. And I don't see how you spotted Jobson. It is a mystery to me."

"It wouldn't be if you were a lawyer," he replied. "The case against Jobson was contained in what you told me at our first interview. You yourself commented on the peculiarity of the will that he drafted for Crofton. The intention of the latter was to leave all his property to his wife. But instead of saying so, the will specified each item of property, and appointed a residuary legatee, which was Jobson himself. This might have appeared like mere legal verbiage, but when Miss Shuler's legacy was announced, the transaction took on a rather different aspect. For this legacy was not among the items specified in the will. Therefore it did not go to Mrs. Crofton. It would be included in the residue of the estate and would go to the residuary legatee."

"The deuce it would!" I exclaimed.

"Certainly, until Crofton revoked his will or made a fresh one. This was rather suspicious. It suggested that Jobson had private information as to Miss Shuler's will and had drafted Crofton's will in accordance with it, and as she died of malignant disease, her doctor must have known for some time that she was dying and it looked as if Jobson had information on that point, too. Now the position of affairs that you described to me was this:

"Crofton, a possible suicide, had disappeared, and had made no fresh will.

"Miss Shuler died on the thirteenth, leaving thirty-thousand pounds to Crofton, if he survived her, or if he did not, then to Mrs. Crofton. The important question then was whether Crofton was alive or dead, and if he was dead, whether he had died before or after the thirteenth. For if he died before the thirteenth the legacy went to Mrs. Crofton, but if he died after that date the legacy went to Jobson.

"Then you showed me that extraordinarily opportune letter dated the sixteenth. Now, seeing that that date was worth thirty-thousand pounds to Jobson, I naturally scrutinised it narrowly. The letter was written with ordinary blue-black ink. But this ink, even in the open, takes about a fortnight to blacken completely. In a closed envelope it takes considerably longer. On examining this date through a lens, the one was very perceptibly bluer than the six. It had therefore been added later. But for what reason? And by whom?

"The only possible reason was that Crofton was dead and had died before the thirteenth. The only person who had any motive for making the alteration was Jobson. Therefore, when we started for Seasalter, I already felt sure that Crofton was dead and that the letter had been posted at Margate by Jobson. I had further no doubt that Crofton's body was concealed somewhere on the premises of the bungalow. All that I had to do was to verify those conclusions."

"Then you believe that Jobson has told us the truth?"

"Yes. But I suspect that he went down there with the deliberate intention of making away with Crofton before he could make a fresh will. The finding of Crofton's body must have been a fearful disappointment, but I must admit that he showed considerable resource in dealing with the situation, and he failed only by the merest chance. I think his defence against the murder charge will be admitted, but, of course, it will involve plea of guilty to the charge of fraud in connection with the legacy."

365

Thorndyke's forecast turned out to be correct. Jobson was acquitted of the murder of Arthur Crofton, but is at present "doing time" in respect of the forged letter and the rest of his too-ingenious scheme.

1927 Hodder & Stoughton, London Cover

The Magic Casket

It was in the near neighbourhood of King's Road, Chelsea, that chance, aided by Thorndyke's sharp and observant eyes, introduced us to the dramatic story of the Magic Casket. Not that there was anything strikingly dramatic in the opening phase of the affair, nor even in the story of the casket itself. It was Thorndyke who added the dramatic touch, and most of the magic, too, and I record the affair principally as an illustration of his extraordinary capacity for producing odd items of out-of-the-way knowledge and instantly applying them in the most unexpected manner.

Eight o'clock had struck on a misty November night when we turned out of the main road and, leaving behind the glare of the shop windows, plunged into the maze of dark and narrow streets to the north. The abrupt change impressed us both, and Thorndyke proceeded to moralise on it in his pleasant, reflective fashion.

"London is an inexhaustible place," he mused. "Its variety is infinite. A minute ago we walked in a glare of light, jostled by a multitude. And now look at this little street. It is as dim as a tunnel, and we have got it absolutely to ourselves. Anything might happen in a place like this."

Suddenly he stopped. We were, at the moment, passing a small church or chapel, the west door of which was enclosed in an open porch, and as my observant friend stepped into the latter and stooped, I perceived in the deep shadow against the wall, the object which had evidently caught his eye.

"What is it?" I asked, following him in.

"It is a handbag," he replied, "and the question is, what is it doing here?"

He tried the church door, which was obviously locked, and coming out, looked at the windows.

"There are no lights in the church." said he. "The place is locked up, and there is nobody in sight. Apparently the bag is derelict. Shall we have a look at it?"

Without waiting for an answer, he picked it up and brought it out into the mitigated darkness of the street, where we proceeded to inspect it. But at the first glance it told its own tale, for it had evidently been locked, and it bore unmistakable traces of having been forced open.

"It isn't empty," said Thorndyke. "I think we had better see what is in it. Just catch hold while I get a light."

He handed me the bag while he felt in his pocket for the tiny electric lamp which he made a habit of carrying, and an excellent habit it is. I held the mouth of the bag open while he illuminated the interior, which we then saw to be occupied by several objects neatly wrapped in brown paper. One of these Thorndyke lifted out, and untying the string and removing the paper, displayed a Chinese stoneware jar. Attached to it was a label, bearing the stamp of the Victoria and Albert Museum, on which was written:

Miss Mabel Bonnet
168 Willow Walk
Fulham Road, W.

"That tells us all that we want to know," said Thorndyke, re-wrapping the jar and tenderly replacing it in the bag. "We can't do wrong in delivering the things to their owner, especially as the bag itself is evidently her property, too." And he pointed to the gilt initials, "*M. B.*," stamped on the morocco.

It took us but a few minutes to reach the Fulham Road, but we then had to walk nearly a mile along that thoroughfare before we arrived at Willow Walk – to which an obliging shopkeeper had directed us – and, naturally, No. 168 was at the farther end.

As we turned into the quiet street we almost collided with two men, who were walking at a rapid pace, but both looking back over their shoulders. I noticed that they were both Japanese – well-dressed, gentlemanly-looking men – but I gave them little attention, being interested, rather, in what they were looking at. This was a taxicab which was dimly visible by the light of a street lamp at the farther end of the walk, and from which four persons had just alighted. Two of these had hurried ahead to knock at a door, while the other two walked very slowly across the pavement and up the steps to the threshold. Almost immediately the door was opened, two of the shadowy figures entered, and the other two returned slowly to the cab and as we came nearer, I could see that these latter were policemen in uniform. I had just time to note this fact when they both got into the cab and were forthwith spirited away.

"Looks like a street accident of some kind," I remarked, and then, as I glanced at the number of the house we were passing, I added, "Now, I wonder if that house happens to be – yes, by Jove! It is. It is *168*! Things have been happening, and this bag of ours is one of the *dramatis personae*."

The response to our knock was by no means prompt. I was, in fact, in the act of raising my hand to the knocker to repeat the summons when the door opened and revealed an elderly servant-maid who regarded us inquiringly and, as I thought, with something approaching alarm.

"Does Miss Mabel Bonney live here?" Thorndyke asked.

"Yes, sir," was the reply, "but I am afraid you can't see her just now, unless it is something urgent. She is rather upset, and particularly engaged at present."

"There is no occasion whatever to disturb her," said Thorndyke. "We have merely called to restore this bag, which seemed to have been lost." And with this he held it out towards her. She grasped it eagerly with a cry of surprise and, as the mouth fell open, she peered into it.

"Why," she exclaimed, "they don't seem to have taken anything, after all. Where did you find it, sir?"

"In the porch of a church in Spelton Street," Thorndyke replied, and was turning away when the servant said earnestly, "Would you kindly give me your name and address, sir? Miss Bonney will wish to write and thank you."

"There is really no need," said he, but she interrupted anxiously. "If you would be so kind, sir. Miss Bonney will be so vexed if she is unable to thank you, and besides, she may want to ask you some questions about it."

"That is true," said Thorndyke (who was restrained only by good manners from asking one or two questions himself). He produced his card-case and, having handed one of his cards to the maid, wished her "Good-evening" and retired.

"That bag had evidently been pinched," I remarked, as we walked back towards the Fulham Road.

"Evidently," he agreed, and was about to enlarge on the matter when our attention was attracted to a taxi, which was approaching from the direction of the main road. A man's head was thrust out of the window, and as the vehicle passed a street lamp, I observed that the head appertained to an elderly gentleman with very white hair and a very fresh face.

"Did you see who that was?" Thorndyke asked.

"It looked like old Brodribb," I replied.

"It did, very much. I wonder where he is off to."

He turned and followed, with a speculative eye, the receding taxi, which presently swept alongside the kerb and stopped, apparently opposite the house from where we had just come. As the vehicle came to rest, the door flew open and the passenger shot out like an elderly, but agile, Jack-in-the-box, and bounced up the steps.

"That is Brodribb's knock, sure enough," said I, as the old-fashioned flourish reverberated up the quiet street. "I have heard it too often on our own knocker to mistake it. But we had better not let him see us watching him."

As we went once more on our way, I took a sly glance, now and again, at my friend, noting with a certain malicious enjoyment his profoundly cogitative air. I knew quite well what was happening in his mind, for his mind reacted to observed facts in an invariable manner. And here was a group of related facts: The bag, stolen, but deposited intact; the museum label; the injured or sick person – probably Miss Bonney, herself – brought home under police escort; and the arrival, post-haste, of the old lawyer – a significant group of facts. And there was Thorndyke, under my amused and attentive observation, fitting them together in various combinations to see what general conclusion emerged. Apparently my own mental state was equally clear to him, for he remarked, presently, as if response to an unspoken comment, "Well, I expect we shall know all about it before many days have passed if Brodribb sees my card, as he most probably will. Here comes an omnibus that will suit us. Shall we hop on?"

He stood at the kerb and raised his stick, and as the accommodation on the omnibus was such that our seats were separated, there was no opportunity to pursue the subject further, even if there had been anything to discuss.

But Thorndyke's prediction was justified sooner than I had expected. For we had not long finished our supper, and had not yet closed the "oak", when there was heard a mighty flourish on the knocker of our inner door.

"Brodribb, by Jingo!" I exclaimed, and hurried across the room to let him in.

"No, Jervis," he said as I invited him to enter, "I am not coming in. Don't want to disturb you at this time of night. I've just called to make an appointment for to-morrow with a client."

"Is the client's name Bonney?" I asked.

He started and gazed at me in astonishment. "Gad, Jervis!" he exclaimed, "you are getting as bad as Thorndyke. How the deuce did you know that she was my client?"

"Never mind how I know. It is our business to know everything in these chambers. But if your appointment concerns Miss Mabel Bonney, for the Lord's sake come in and give Thorndyke a chance of a night's rest. At present, he is on broken bottles, as Mr. Bumble would express it."

On this persuasion, Mr. Brodribb entered, nothing loath – very much the reverse, in fact – and having bestowed a jovial greeting on Thorndyke, glanced approvingly round the room.

"Ha!" said he, "you look very cosy. If you are really sure I am not –"

I cut him short by propelling him gently towards the fire, beside which I deposited him in an easy chair, while Thorndyke pressed the electric bell which rang up in the laboratory.

"Well," said Brodribb, spreading himself out comfortably before the fire like a handsome old tom-cat, "if you are going to let me give you a few particulars – but perhaps you would rather that I should not talk shop?"

"Now you know perfectly well, Brodribb," said Thorndyke, "that 'shop' is the breath of life to us all. Let us have those particulars."

Brodribb sighed contentedly and placed his toes on the fender (and at this moment the door opened softly and Polton looked into the room. He took a single, understanding glance at our visitor, and withdrew, shutting the door without a sound).

"I am glad," pursued Brodribb, "to have this opportunity of a preliminary chat, because there are certain things that one can say better when the client is not present, and I am deeply interested in Bonney's affairs. The crisis in those affairs which has brought me here is of quite recent date – in fact, it dates from this evening. But I know your partiality for having events related in their proper sequence, so I will leave today's happenings for the moment and tell you the story – the whole of which is material to the case – from the beginning."

Here there was a slight interruption, due to Polton's noiseless entry with a tray on which was a decanter, a biscuit box, and three port glasses. This he deposited on a small table which he placed within convenient reach of our guest. Then, with a glance of altruistic satisfaction at our old friend, he stole out like a benevolent ghost.

"Dear, dear!" exclaimed Brodribb, beaming on the decanter, "this is really too bad. You ought not to indulge me in this way."

"My dear Brodribb," replied Thorndyke, "you are a benefactor to us. You give us a pretext for taking a glass of port. We can't drink alone, you know."

"I should, if I had a cellar like yours," chuckled Brodribb, sniffing ecstatically at his glass. He took a sip, with his eyes closed, savoured it solemnly, shook his head, and set the glass down on the table.

"To return to our case," he resumed, "Miss Bonney is the daughter of a solicitor, Harold Bonney – you may remember him. He had offices in Bedford Row, and there, one morning, a client came to him and asked him to take care of some property while he, the said client, ran over to Paris, where he had some urgent business. The property in question was a collection of pearls of most unusual size and value, forming a great necklace, which had been unstrung for the sake of portability. It is not clear where they came from, but as the transaction occurred soon after the Russian Revolution, we may make a guess. At any rate, there they were, packed loosely in a leather bag, the string of which was sealed with the owner's seal.

"Bonney seems to have been rather casual about the affair. He gave the client a receipt for the bag, stating the nature of the contents, which he had not seen, and deposited it, in the client's presence, in the safe in his private office. Perhaps he intended to take it to the bank or transfer it to his strong-room, but it is evident that he did neither, for his managing clerk, who kept the second key of the strong-room – without which the room could not be opened – knew nothing of the transaction. When he went home at about seven o'clock, he left Bonney hard at work in his office, and there is no doubt that the pearls were still in the safe.

"That night, at about a quarter-to-nine, it happened that a couple of C.I.D. officers were walking up Bedford Row when they saw three men come out of one of the houses. Two of them turned up towards Theobald's Road, but the third came south, towards them. As he passed them, they both recognised him as a Japanese named Uyenishi, who was believed to be a member of a cosmopolitan gang and whom the police were keeping under observation. Naturally, their suspicions were aroused. The first two men had hurried round the corner and were out of sight, and when they turned to look after Uyenishi, he had mended his pace considerably and was looking back at them. Thereupon one of the officers named Barker decided to follow the man, while the other, Holt, reconnoitred the premises.

"Now, as soon as Barker turned, the Japanese broke into a run. It was just such a night as this – dark and slightly foggy. In order to keep his man in sight, he had to run, too, and he found that he had a sprinter to deal with. From the bottom of Bedford Row, Uyenishi darted across and shot down Hand Court like a lamp-lighter. Barker followed, but at the Holborn end his man was nowhere to be seen. However, he presently learned from a man at a shop door that the fugitive had run past and turned up Brownlow Street, so off he went again in pursuit. But when he got to the top of the street, back in Bedford Row, he was done. There was no sign of the man, and no one about from whom he could make inquiries. All he could do was to cross the road and walk up Bedford Row to see if Holt had made any discoveries.

"As he was trying to identify the house, his colleague came out on to the doorstep and beckoned him in and this was the story that he told. He had recognised the house by the big lamp-standard, and as the place was all dark, he had gone into the entry and tried the office door. Finding it unlocked, he had entered the clerks' office, lit the gas, and tried the door of the private office, but found it locked. He knocked at it, but getting no answer, had a good look round the clerk's office, and there, presently, on the floor in a dark corner, he found a key. This he tried in the door of the private office, and finding that it fitted, turned it and opened the door. As he did so, the light from the outer office fell on the body of a man lying on the floor just inside.

"A moment's inspection showed that the man had been murdered – first knocked on the head and then finished with a knife. Examination of the pockets showed that the dead man was Harold Bonney, and also that no robbery from the person seemed to have been committed. Nor was there any sign of any other kind of robbery. Nothing seemed to have been disturbed, and the safe had not been broken into, though that was not very conclusive, as the safe key was in the dead man's pocket. However, a murder had been committed, and obviously Uyenishi was either the murderer or an accessory, so Holt had, at once, rung up Scotland Yard on the office telephone, giving all the particulars.

"I may say at once that Uyenishi disappeared completely and at once. He never went to his lodgings at Limehouse, for the police were there before he could have arrived. A lively hue and cry was kept up. Photographs of the wanted man were posted outside every police station, and a watch was set at all the ports. But he was never found. He must have got away at once on some outward-bound tramp from the Thames. And there we will leave him for the moment.

"At first it was thought that nothing had been stolen, since the managing clerk could not discover that anything was missing. But a few days later the client returned from Paris, and presenting his receipt, asked for his pearls. But the pearls had vanished. Clearly they had been the object of the crime. The robbers must have known about them and traced them to the office. Of course the safe had been opened with its own key, which was then replaced in the dead man's pocket.

"Now, I was poor Bonney's executor, and in that capacity I denied his liability in respect of the pearls on the ground that he was a gratuitous bailee – there being no evidence that any consideration had been demanded – and that being murdered cannot be construed as negligence. But Miss Mabel, who was practically the sole legatee, insisted on accepting liability. She said that the pearls could have been secured in the bank or the strong-room, and that she was morally, if not legally, liable for their loss, and she insisted on handing to the owner the full amount at which he valued them. It was a wildly foolish proceeding, for he would certainly have accepted half the sum. But still I take my hat off to a person – man or woman – who can accept poverty in preference to a broken covenant." And here Brodribb, being in fact that sort of person himself, had to be consoled with a replenished glass.

"And mind you," he resumed, "when I speak of poverty, I wish to be taken literally. The estimated value of those pearls was fifty-thousand pounds – if you can imagine anyone out of Bedlam giving such a sum for a parcel of trash like that – and when poor Mabel Bonney had paid it, she was left with the prospect of having to spread her butter mighty thin for the rest of her life. As a matter of fact, she has had to sell one after another of her little treasures to pay just her current expenses, and I'm hanged if I can see how she is going to carry on when she has sold the last of them. But there, I mustn't take up your time with her private troubles. Let us return to our muttons.

"First, as to the pearls They were never traced, and it seems probable that they were never disposed of. For, you see, pearls are different from any other kind of gems. You can cut up a big diamond, but you can't cut up a big pearl. And the great value of this necklace was due not only to the size, the perfect shape and 'orient' of the separate pearls, but to the fact that the whole set was perfectly matched. To break up the necklace was to destroy a good part of its value.

"And now as to our friend Uyenishi. He disappeared, as I have said, but he reappeared at Los Angeles, in custody of the police, charged with robbery and murder. He was taken red-handed and was duly convicted and sentenced to death, but for some reason – or more probably, for no reason, as we should think – the sentence was commuted to imprisonment for life. Under these circumstances, the English police naturally took no action, especially as they really had no evidence against him.

"Now Uyenishi was, by trade, a metal-worker, a maker of those pretty trifles that are so dear to the artistic Japanese, and when he was in prison he was allowed to set up a little workshop and practise his trade on a small scale. Among other things that he made was a little casket in the form of a seated figure, which he said he wanted to give to his brother as a keepsake. I don't know whether any permission was granted for him to make this gift, but that is of no consequence, for Uyenishi got influenza and was carried off in a few days by pneumonia, and the prison authorities learned that his brother had been killed, a week or two previously, in a shooting affair at San Francisco. So the casket remained on their hands.

376

"About this time, Miss Bonney was invited to accompany an American lady on a visit to California, and accepted gratefully. While she was there she paid a visit to the prison to inquire whether Uyenishi had ever made any kind of statement concerning the missing pearls. Here she heard of Uyenishi's recent death, and the governor of the prison, as he could not give her any information, handed over to her the casket as a sort of memento. This transaction came to the knowledge of the press, and – well, you know what the Californian press is like. There were 'some comments,' as they would say, and quite an assortment of Japanese, of shady antecedents, applied to the prison to have the casket 'restored' to them as Uyenishi's heirs. Then Miss Bonney's rooms at the hotel were raided by burglars – but the casket was in the hotel strong-room – and Miss Bonney and her hostess were shadowed by various undesirables in such a disturbing fashion that the two ladies became alarmed and secretly made their way to New York. But there another burglary occurred, with the same unsuccessful result, and the shadowing began again. Finally, Miss Bonney, feeling that her presence was a danger to her friend, decided to return to England, and managed to get on board the ship without letting her departure be known in advance.

"But even in England she has not been left in peace. She has had an uncomfortable feeling of being watched and attended, and has seemed to be constantly meeting Japanese men in the streets, especially in the vicinity of her house. Of course, all the fuss is about this infernal casket, and when she told me what was happening, I promptly popped the thing in my pocket and took it, to my office, where I stowed it in the strong-room. And there, of course, it ought to have remained. but it didn't. One day Miss Bonney told me that she was sending some small things to a loan exhibition of oriental works of art at the South Kensington Museum, and she wished to include the casket. I urged her strongly to do nothing of the kind, but she persisted, and the end of it was that we went to the museum together, with her pottery and stuff in a handbag and the casket in my pocket.

"It was a most imprudent thing to do, for there the beastly casket was, for several months, exposed in a glass case for anyone to see, with her name on the label, and what was worse, full particulars of the origin of the thing. However, nothing happened while it was there – the museum is not an easy place to steal from – and all went well until it was time to remove the things after the close of the exhibition. Now, to-day was the appointed day and, as on the previous occasion, she and I went to the museum together. But the unfortunate thing is that we didn't come away together. Her other exhibits were all pottery, and these were dealt with first, so that she had her handbag packed and was ready to go before

377

they had begun on the metal work cases. As we were not going the same way, it didn't seem necessary for her to wait, so she went off with her bag and I stayed behind until the casket was released, when I put it in my pocket and went home, where I locked the thing up again in the strong-room.

"It was about seven when I got home. A little after eight I heard the telephone ring down in the office, and down I went, cursing the untimely ringer, who turned out to be a policeman at St. George's Hospital. He said he had found Miss Bonney lying unconscious in the street and had taken her to the hospital, where she had been detained for a while, but she was now recovered and he was taking her home. She would like me, if possible, to go and see her at once. Well, of course, I set off forthwith and got to her house a few minutes after her arrival, and just after you had left.

"She was a good deal upset, so I didn't worry her with many questions, but she gave me a short account of her misadventure, which amounted to this: She had started to walk home from the museum along the Brompton Road, and she was passing down a quiet street between that and Fulham Road when she heard soft footsteps behind her. The next moment, a scarf or shawl was thrown over her head and drawn tightly round her neck. At the same moment, the bag was snatched from her hand. That is all that she remembers, for she was so terrified that she fainted, and knew no more until she found herself in a cab with two policemen who were taking her to the hospital.

"Now it is obvious that her assailants were in search of that damned casket, for the bag had been broken open and searched, but nothing taken or damaged, which suggests the Japanese again, for a British thief would have smashed the crockery. I found your card there, and I put it to Miss Bonney that we had better ask you to help us – I told her all about you – and she agreed emphatically. So that is why I am here, drinking your port and robbing you of your night's rest."

"And what do you want me to do?" Thorndyke asked.

"Whatever you think best," was the cheerful reply. "In the first place, this nuisance must be put a stop to – this shadowing and hanging about. But apart from that, you must see that there is something queer about this accursed casket. The beastly thing is of no intrinsic value. The museum man turned up his nose at it. But it evidently has some extrinsic value, and no small value either. If it is good enough for these devils to follow it all the way from the States, as they seem to have done, it is good enough for us to try to find out what its value is. That is where you come in. I propose to bring Miss Bonney to see you to-morrow, and I will bring the infernal casket, too. Then you will ask her a few questions,

378

take a look at the casket – through the microscope, if necessary – and tell us all about it in your usual necromantic way."

Thorndyke laughed as he refilled our friend's glass. "If faith will move mountains, Brodribb," said he, "you ought to have been a civil engineer. But it is certainly a rather intriguing problem."

"Ha!" exclaimed the old solicitor, "then it's all right. I've known you a good many years, but I've never known you to be stumped, and you are not going to be stumped now. What time shall I bring her? Afternoon or evening would suit her best."

"Very well," replied Thorndyke, "bring her to tea – say, five o'clock. How will that do?"

"Excellently, and here's good luck to the adventure." He drained his glass and, the decanter being now empty, he rose, shook our hands warmly, and took his departure in high spirits.

It was with a very lively interest that I looked forward to the prospective visit. Like Thorndyke, I found the case rather intriguing. For it was quite clear, as our shrewd old friend had said, that there was something more than met the eye in the matter of this casket.

Hence, on the following afternoon, when, on the stroke of five, footsteps became audible on our stairs, I awaited the arrival of our new client with keen curiosity, both as to herself and her mysterious property.

To tell the truth, the lady was better worth looking at than the casket. At the first glance, I was strongly prepossessed in her favour, and so, I think, was Thorndyke. Not that she was a beauty, though comely enough. But she was an example of a type that seems to be growing rarer – quiet, gentle, soft-spoken, and a lady to her finger-tips, a little sad-faced and care worn, with a streak or two of white in her prettily-disposed black hair, though she could not have been much over thirty-five. Altogether a very gracious and winning personality.

When we had been presented to her by Brodribb – who treated her as if she had been a royal personage – and had enthroned her in the most comfortable easy-chair, we inquired as to her health, and were duly thanked for the salvage of the bag. Then Polton brought in the tray, with an air that seemed to demand an escort of choristers, the tea was poured out, and the informal proceedings began.

She had not, however, much to tell, for she had not seen her assailants, and the essential facts of the case had been fully presented in Brodribb's excellent summary. After a very few questions, therefore, we came to the next stage, which was introduced by Brodribb's taking from his pocket a small parcel which he proceeded to open.

"There," said he, "that is the *fons et origo mali*. Not much to look at, I think you will agree." He set the object down on the table and glared at it malevolently, while Thorndyke and I regarded it with a more impersonal interest. It was not much to look at. Just an ordinary Japanese casket in the form of a squat, shapeless figure with a silly little grinning face, of which the head and shoulders opened on a hinge – a pleasant enough object, with its quiet, warm colouring, but certainly not a masterpiece of art.

Thorndyke picked it up and turned it over slowly for preliminary inspection, then he went on to examine it detail by detail, watched closely, in his turn, by Brodribb and me. Slowly and methodically, his eye – fortified by a watchmaker's eyeglass – travelled over every part of the exterior. Then he opened it, and I having examined the inside of the lid, scrutinised the bottom from within, long and attentively. Finally, he turned the casket upside down and examined the bottom from without, giving to it the longest and most rigorous inspection of all – which puzzled me somewhat, for the bottom was absolutely plain. At length, he passed the casket and the eyeglass to me without comment.

"Well," said Brodribb, "what is the verdict?"

"It is of no value as a work of art," replied Thorndyke. "The body and lid are just castings of common white metal – an antimony alloy, I should say. The bronze colour is lacquer."

"So the museum man remarked," said Brodribb.

"But," continued Thorndyke, "there is one very odd thing about it. The only piece of fine metal in it is in the part which matters least. The bottom is a separate plate of the alloy known to the Japanese as *Shakudo* – an alloy of copper and gold."

"Yes," said Brodribb, "the museum man noted that, too, and couldn't make out why it had been put there."

"Then," Thorndyke continued, "there is another anomalous feature. The inside of the bottom is covered with elaborate decoration – just the place where decoration is most inappropriate, since it would be covered up by the contents of the casket. And, again, this decoration is etched, not engraved or chased. But etching is a very unusual process for this purpose, if it is ever used at all by Japanese metal-workers. My impression is that it is not, for it is most unsuitable for decorative purposes. That is all that I observe, so far."

"And what do you infer from your observations?" Brodribb asked.

"I should like to think the matter over," was the reply. "There is an obvious anomaly, which must have some significance. But I won't embark on speculative opinions at this stage. I should like, however, to take one or two photographs of the casket, for reference, but that will occupy some time. You will hardly want to wait so long."

380

"No," said Brodribb. "But Miss Bonney is coming with me to my office to go over some documents and discuss a little business. When we have finished, I will come back and fetch the confounded thing."

"There is no need for that," replied Thorndyke. "As soon as I have done what is necessary, I will bring it up to your place."

To this arrangement Brodribb agreed readily, and he and his client prepared to depart. I rose, too, and as I happened to have a call to make in Old Square, Lincoln's Inn, I asked permission to walk with them.

As we came out into King's Bench Walk, I noticed a smallish, gentlemanly-looking man who had just passed our entry and now turned in at the one next door, and by the light of the lamp in the entry he looked to me like a Japanese. I thought Miss Bonney had observed him, too, but she made no remark, and neither did I. But, passing up Inner Temple Lane, we nearly overtook two other men, who – though I got but a back view of them and the light was feeble enough – aroused my suspicions by their neat, small figures. As we approached, they quickened their pace, and one of them looked back over his shoulder, and then my suspicions were confirmed, for it was an unmistakable Japanese face that looked round at us. Miss Bonney saw that I had observed the men, for she remarked, as they turned sharply at the Cloisters and entered Pump Court, "You see, I am still haunted by Japanese."

"I noticed them," said Brodribb. "They are probably law students. But we may as well be cornpanionable." And with this, he, too, headed for Pump Court.

We followed our Oriental friends across the Lane into Fountain Court, and through that and Devereux Court out to Temple Bar, where we parted from them, they turning westward and we crossing to Bell Yard, up which we walked, entering New Square by the Carey Street gate. At Brodribb's doorway we halted and looked back, but no one was in sight. I accordingly went my way, promising to return anon to hear Thorndyke's report, and the lawyer and his client disappeared through the portal.

My business occupied me longer than I had expected, but nevertheless, when I arrived at Brodribb's premises – where he lived in chambers over his office – Thorndyke had not yet made his appearance. A quarter-of-an-hour later, however, we heard his brisk step on the stairs, and as Brodribb threw the door open, he entered and produced the casket from his pocket.

"Well," said Brodribb, taking it from him and locking it, for the time being, in a drawer, "has the oracle spoken, and if so, what did he say?"

"Oracles," replied Thorndyke, "have a way of being more concise than explicit. Before I attempt to interpret the message, I should like to view the scene of the escape, to see if there was any intelligible reason why this man Uyenishi should have returned up Brownlow Street into what must have been the danger zone. I think that is a material question."

"Then," said Brodribb, with evident eagerness, "let us all walk up and have a look at the confounded place. It is quite close by."

We all agreed instantly, two of us, at least, being on the tip-toe of expectation. For Thorndyke, who habitually understated his results, had virtually admitted that the casket had told him something, and as we walked up the Square to the gate in Lincoln's Inn Fields, I watched him furtively, trying to gather from his impassive face a hint as to what the something amounted to, and wondering how the movements of the fugitive bore on the solution of the mystery. Brodribb was similarly occupied, and as we crossed from Great Turnstile and took our way up Brownlow Street, I could see that his excitement was approaching bursting-point.

At the top of the street, Thorndyke paused and looked up and down the rather dismal thoroughfare which forms a continuation of Bedford Row and bears its name. Then he crossed to the paved island surrounding the pump which stands in the middle of the road, and from thence surveyed the entrances to Brownlow Street and Hand Court, and then he turned and looked thoughtfully at the pump.

"A quaint old survivor, this," he remarked, tapping the iron shell with his knuckles. "There is a similar one, you may remember, in Queen Square, and another at Aldgate. But that is still in use."

"Yes," Brodribb assented, almost dancing with impatience and inwardly damning the pump, as I could see. "I've noticed it."

"I suppose," Thorndyke proceeded, in a reflective tone, "they had to remove the handle. But it was rather a pity."

"Perhaps it was," growled Brodribb, whose complexion was rapidly developing affinities to that of a pickled cabbage. "But what the d – "

Here he broke off short and glared silently at Thorndyke, who had raised his arm and squeezed his hand into the opening once occupied by the handle. He groped in the interior with an expression of placid interest, and presently reported, "The barrel is still there, and so, apparently, is the plunger – " (Here I heard Brodribb mutter huskily, "Damn the barrel and the plunger too!") " – but my hand is rather large for the exploration. Would you, Miss Bonney, mind slipping your hand in and telling me if I am right?"

We all gazed at Thorndyke in dismay, but in a moment Miss Bonney recovered from her astonishment, and with a deprecating smile,

382

half shy, half amused, she slipped off her glove, and reaching up – it was rather high for her – inserted her hand into the narrow slit. Brodribb glared at her and gobbled like a turkey-cock, and I watched her with a sudden suspicion that something was going to happen. Nor was I mistaken. For, as I looked, the shy, puzzled smile faded from her face and was succeeded by an expression of incredulous astonishment. Slowly she withdrew her hand, and as it came out of the slit it dragged something after it. I started forward, and by the light of the lamp above the pump I could see that the object was a leather bag secured by a string from which hung a broken seal.

"It can't be!" she gasped as, with trembling fingers, she untied the string. Then, as she peered into the open mouth, she uttered a little cry. "It is! It is! It is the necklace!"

Brodribb was speechless with amazement. So was I, and I was still gazing open-mouthed at the bag in Miss Bonney's hands when I felt Thorndyke touch my arm. I turned quickly and found him offering me an automatic pistol. "Stand by, Jervis," he said quietly, looking towards Gray's Inn.

I looked in the same direction, and then perceived three men stealing round the corner from Jockey's Fields. Brodribb saw them, too, and snatching the bag of pearls from his client's hands, buttoned it into his breast pocket and placed himself before its owner, grasping his stick with a war-like air. The three men filed along the pavement until they were opposite us, when they turned simultaneously and bore down on the pump – each man, as I noticed, holding his right hand behind him. In a moment, Thorndyke's hand, grasping a pistol, flew up – as did mine, also – and he called out sharply, "Stop! If any man moves a hand, I fire."

The challenge brought them up short, evidently unprepared for this kind of reception. What would have happened next it is impossible to guess. But at this moment a police whistle sounded and two constables ran out from Hand Court. The whistle was instantly echoed from the direction of Warwick Court, whence two more constabulary figures appeared through the postern gate of Gray's Inn. Our three attendants hesitated but for an instant. Then, with one accord, they turned tail and flew like the wind round into Jockey's Fields, with the whole posse of constables close on their heels.

"Remarkable coincidence," said Brodribb, "that those policemen should happen to be on the look-out. Or isn't it a coincidence?"

"I telephoned to the station superintendent before I started," replied Thorndyke, "warning him of a possible breach of the peace at this spot."

Brodribb chuckled. "You're a wonderful man, Thorndyke. You think of everything. I wonder if the police will catch those fellows."

"It is no concern of ours," replied Thorndyke. "We've got the pearls, and that finishes the business. There will be no more shadowing, in any case."

Miss Bonney heaved a comfortable little sigh and glanced gratefully at Thorndyke. "You can have no idea what a relief that is!" she exclaimed, "to say nothing of the treasure-trove."

We waited some time, but as neither the fugitives nor the constables reappeared, we presently made our way back down Brownlow Street. And there it was that Brodribb had an inspiration.

"I'll tell you what," said be. "I will just pop these things in my strong-room – they will be perfectly safe there until the bank opens to-morrow – and then we'll go and have a nice little dinner. I'll pay the piper."

"Indeed you won't!" exclaimed Miss Bonney. "This is my thanksgiving festival, and the benevolent wizard shall be the guest of the evening."

"Very well, my dear," agreed Brodribb. "I will pay and charge it to the estate. But I stipulate that the benevolent wizard shall tell us exactly what the oracle said. That is essential to the preservation of my sanity."

"You shall have his *ipsissima verba*," Thorndyke promised, and the resolution was carried, *nem. con.*

An hour-and-a-half later we were seated around a table in a private room of a café to which Mr. Brodribb had conducted us. I may not divulge its whereabouts, though I may, perhaps, hint that we approached it by way of Wardour Street. At any rate, we had dined, even to the fulfilment of Brodribb's ideal, and coffee and liqueurs furnished a sort of gastronomic doxology. Brodribb had lighted a cigar and Thorndyke had produced a vicious-looking little black cheroot, which he regarded fondly and then returned to its abiding-place as unsuited to the present company.

"Now," said Brodribb, watching Thorndyke fill his pipe (as understudy of the cheroot aforesaid), "we are waiting to hear the words of the oracle."

"You shall hear them," Thorndyke replied. "There were only five of them. But first, there are certain introductory matters to be disposed of. The solution of this problem is based on two well-known physical facts – one metallurgical and the other optical."

"Ha!" said Brodribb. "But you must temper the wind to the shorn lamb, you know, Thorndyke. Miss Bonney and I are not scientists."

"I will put the matter quite simply, but you must have the facts. The first relates to the properties of malleable metals – excepting iron and steel – and especially of copper and its alloys. If a plate of such metal or alloy – say, bronze, for instance – is made red-hot and quenched in water, it becomes quite soft and flexible – the reverse of what happens in the case of iron. Now, if such a plate of softened metal be placed on a steel anvil and hammered, it becomes extremely hard and brittle."

"I follow that," said Brodribb.

"Then see what follows. If, instead of hammering the soft plate, you put on it the edge of a blunt chisel and strike on that chisel a sharp blow, you produce an indented line. Now the plate remains soft, but the metal forming the indented line has been hammered and has become hard. There is now a line of hard metal on the soft plate. Is that clear?"

"Perfectly," replied Brodribb, and Thorndyke accordingly continued, "The second fact is this: If a beam of light falls on a polished surface which reflects it, and if that surface is turned through a given angle, the beam of light is deflected through double that angle."

"Hmm!" grunted Brodribb. "Yes. No doubt. I hope we are not going to get into any deeper waters, Thorndyke."

"We are not," replied the latter, smiling urbanely. "We are now going to consider the application of these facts. Have you ever seen a Japanese magic mirror?

"Never, nor even heard of such a thing."

"They are bronze mirrors, just like the ancient Greek or Etruscan mirrors – which were probably 'magic' mirrors, too. A typical specimen consists of a circular or oval plate of bronze, highly polished on the face and decorated on the back with chased ornament – commonly a dragon or some such device – and furnished with a handle. The ornament is, as I have said – chased, that is to say – it is executed in indented lines made with chasing tools, which are, in effect, small chisels, more or less blunt, which are struck with a chasing-hammer.

"Now these mirrors have a very singular property. Although the face is perfectly plain, as a mirror should be, yet, if a beam of sunlight is caught on it and reflected, say, on to a white wall, the round or oval patch of light on the wall is not a plain light patch. It shows quite clearly the ornament on the back of the mirror."

"But how extraordinary!" exclaimed Miss Bonney.

"It sounds quite incredible." I said.

"It does," Thorndyke agreed. "And yet the explanation is quite simple. Professor Sylvanus Thompson pointed it out years ago. It is based on the facts which I have just stated to you. The artist who makes one of these mirrors begins, naturally, by annealing the metal until it is quite soft. Then he chases the design on the back, and this design then shows slightly on the face. But he now grinds the face perfectly flat with fine emery and water so that the traces of the design are complete obliterated. Finally, he polishes the face with rouge on a soft buff.

"But now observe that wherever the chasing-tool has made a line, the metal is hardened right through, so that the design is in hard metal on a soft matrix. But the hardened metal resists the wear of the polishing buffer more than the soft metal does. The result is that the act of polishing causes the design to appear in faint relief on the face. Its projection is infinitesimal – less than the hundred-thousandth of an inch – and totally invisible to the eye. But, minute as it is, owing to the optical law which I mentioned – which, in effect, doubles the projection – it is enough to influence the reflection of light. As a consequence, every chased line appears on the patch of light as a dark line with a bright border, and so the whole design is visible. I think that is quite clear."

"Perfectly clear," Miss Bonney and Brodribb agreed.

"But now," pursued Thorndyke, "before we come to the casket, there is a very curious corollary which I must mention. Supposing our artist, having finished the mirror, should proceed with a scraper to erase the design from the back, and on the blank, scraped surface to etch a new design. The process of etching does not harden the metal, so the new design does not appear on the reflection. But the old design would. For although it was invisible on the face and had been erased from the back, it would still exist in the substance of the metal and continue to influence the reflection. The odd result would be that the design which would be visible in the patch of light on the wall would be a different one from that on the back of the mirror.

"No doubt, you see what I am leading up to. But I will take the investigation of the casket as it actually occurred. It was obvious, at once, that the value of the thing was extrinsic. It had no intrinsic value, either in material or workmanship. What could that value be? The clear suggestion was that the casket was the vehicle of some secret message or information. It had been made by Uyenishi, who had almost certainly had possession of the missing pearls, and who had been so closely pursued that be never had an opportunity to communicate with his confederates. It was to be given to a man who was almost certainly one of those confederates and, since the pearls had never been traced, there was a distinct probability that the (presumed) message referred to some hiding-place in which Uyenishi had concealed them during his flight, and where they were probably still hidden.

"With these considerations in my mind, I examined the casket, and this was what I found. The thing, itself, was a common white-metal casting, made presentable by means of lacquer. But the white metal bottom had been cut out and replaced by a plate of fine bronze – *Shakudo*. The inside of this was covered with an etched design, which immediately aroused my suspicions. Turning it over, I saw that the

386

outside of the bottom was not only smooth and polished, it was a true mirror. It gave a perfectly undistorted reflection of my face. At once, I suspected that the mirror held the secret – that the message, whatever it was, had been chased on the back, had then been scraped away and an etched design worked on it to hide the traces of the scraper.

"As soon as you were gone, I took the casket up to the laboratory and threw a strong beam of parallel light from a condenser on the bottom, catching the reflection on a sheet of white paper. The result was just what I had expected. On the bright oval patch on the paper could be seen the shadowy, but quite distinct, forms of five words in the Japanese character.

"I was in somewhat of a dilemma, for I have no knowledge of Japanese, whereas the circumstances were such as to make it rather unsafe to employ a translator. However, as I do just know the Japanese characters and possess a Japanese dictionary, I determined to make an attempt to fudge out the words myself. If I failed, I could then look for a discreet translator.

"However, it proved to be easier than I had expected, for the words were detached, they did not form a sentence, and so involved no questions of grammar. I spelt out the first word and then looked it up in the dictionary. The translation was 'pearls.' This looked hopeful, and I went on to the next, of which the translation was 'pump.' The third word floored me. It seemed to be '*jokkis*', or '*jokkish*', but there was no such word in the dictionary, so I turned to the next word, hoping that it would explain its predecessor. And it did. The fourth word was 'fields,' and the last word was evidently 'London.' So the entire group read 'Pearls, Pump, *Jokkis*, Fields, London.'

"Now, there is no pump, so far as I know, in Jockey Fields, but there is one in Bedford Row close to the corner of the Fields, and exactly opposite the end of Brownlow Street And by Mr. Brodribb's account, Uyenishi, in his flight, ran down Hand Court and returned up Brownlow Street, as if he were making for the pump. As the latter is disused and the handle-hole is high up, well out of the way of children, it offers quite a good temporary hiding-place, and I had no doubt that the bag of pearls had been poked into it and was probably there still. I was tempted to go at once and explore, but I was anxious that the discovery should be made by Miss Bonney, herself, and I did not dare to make a preliminary exploration for fear of being shadowed. If I had found the treasure I should have had to take it and give it to her, which would have been a flat ending to the adventure. So I had to dissemble and be the occasion of much smothered objurgation on the part of my friend Brodribb. And that is the whole story of my interview with the oracle."

Our mantelpiece is becoming a veritable museum of trophies of victory, the gifts of grateful clients. Among them is a squat, shapeless figure of a Japanese gentleman of the old school, with a silly grinning little face – *The Magic Casket*. But its possession is no longer a menace. Its sting has been drawn, its magic is exploded, its secret is exposed, and its glory departed.

The Contents of a
Mare's Nest

"It is very unsatisfactory," said Mr. Stalker, of the Griffin Life Assurance Company at the close of a consultation on a doubtful claim. "I suppose we shall have to pay up.

"I am sure you will," said Thorndyke. "The death was properly certified, the deceased is buried, and you have not a single fact with which to support an application for further inquiry.

"No," Stalker agreed. "But I am not satisfied. I don't believe that doctor really knew what she died from. I wish cremation were more usual.

"So, I have no doubt, has many a poisoner," Thorndyke remarked dryly

Stalker laughed, but stuck to his point. "I know you don't agree," said he, "but from our point of view it is much more satisfactory to know that the extra precautions have been taken. In a cremation case, you have not to depend on the mere death certificate – you have the cause of death verified by an independent authority, and it is difficult to see how any miscarriage can occur.

Thorndyke shook his head. "It is a delusion, Stalker. You can't provide in advance for unknown contingencies. In practice, your special precautions degenerate into mere formalities. If the circumstances of a death appear normal, the independent authority will certify. If they appear abnormal, you won't get a certificate at all. And if suspicion arises only after the cremation has taken place, it can neither be confirmed nor rebutted.

"My point is," said Stalker, "that the searching examination would lead to discovery of a crime before cremation."

"That is the intention," Thorndyke admitted. "But no examination, short of an exhaustive *post mortem*, would make it safe to destroy a body so that no reconsideration of the cause of death would be possible."

Stalker smiled as he picked up his hat. "Well," he said, "to a cobbler there is nothing like leather, and I suppose that to a toxicologist there is nothing like an exhumation." And with this parting shot he took his leave.

We had not seen the last of him, however. In the course of the same week he looked in to consult us on a fresh matter.

"A rather queer case has turned up," said he. "I don't know that we are deeply concerned in it, but we should like to have your opinion as to how we stand. The position is this: Eighteen months ago, a man named Ingle insured with us for fifteen-hundred pounds, and he was then accepted as a first-class life. He has recently died – apparently from heart failure, the heart being described as fatty and dilated – and his wife, Sibyl, who is the sole legatee and executrix, has claimed payment.

"But just as we were making arrangements to pay, a *caveat* has been entered by a certain Margaret Ingle, who declares that *she* is the wife of the deceased and claims the estate as next-of-kin. She states that the alleged wife, Sibyl, is a widow named Huggard who contracted a bigamous marriage with the deceased, knowing that he had a wife living."

"An interesting situation," commented Thorndyke, "but, as you say, it doesn't particularly concern you. It is a matter for the Probate Court."

"Yes," agreed Stalker. "But that is not all. Margaret Ingle not only charges the other woman with bigamy – she accuses her of having made away with the deceased."

"On what grounds?"

"Well, the reasons she gives are rather shadowy. She states that Sibyl's husband, James Huggard, also died under suspicious circumstances – there seems to have been some suspicion that he had been poisoned – and she asserts that Ingle was a healthy, sound man and could not have died from the causes alleged."

"There is some reason in that," said Thorndyke, "if he was really a first-class life only eighteen months ago. As to the first husband, Huggard, we should want some particulars as to whether there was an inquest, what was the alleged cause of death, and what grounds there were for suspecting that he had been poisoned. If there really were any suspicious circumstances, it would be advisable to apply to the Home Office for an order to exhume the body of Ingle and verify the cause of death."

Stalker smiled somewhat sheepishly. "Unfortunately," said he, "that is not possible. Ingle was cremated."

"Ah!" said Thorndyke, "that is, as you say, unfortunate. It clearly increases the suspicion of poisoning, but destroys the means of verifying that suspicion."

"I should tell you," said Stalker, "that the cremation was in accordance with the provisions of the will."

"That is not very material," replied Thorndyke. "In fact, it rather accentuates the suspicious aspect of the case, for the knowledge that the death of the deceased would be followed by cremation might act as a

390

further inducement to get rid of him by poison. There were two death certificates, of course?"

"Yes. The confirmatory certificate was given by Dr. Halbury, of Wimpole Street. The medical attendant was a Dr. Barber, of Howland Street. The deceased lived in Stock-Orchard Crescent, Holloway."

"A good distance from Howland Street," Thorndyke remarked. "Do you know if Halbury made a *post mortem*? I don't suppose he did."

"No, he didn't," replied Stalker.

"Then," said Thorndyke, "his certificate is worthless. You can't tell whether a man has died from heart failure by looking at his dead body. He must have just accepted the opinion of the medical attendant. Do I understand that you want me to look into this case?"

"If you will. It is not really our concern whether or not the man was poisoned, though I suppose we should have a claim on the estate of the murderer. But we should like you to investigate the case, though how the deuce you are going to do it I don't quite see."

"Neither do I," said Thorndyke. "However, we must get into touch with the doctors who signed the certificates, and possibly they may be able to clear the whole matter up."

"Of course," said I, "there is the other body – that of Huggard – which might be exhumed – unless he was cremated, too."

"Yes," agreed Thorndyke, "and for the purposes of the criminal law, evidence of poisoning in that case would be sufficient. But it would hardly help the Griffin Company, which is concerned exclusively with Ingle deceased. Can you let us have a *précis* of the facts relating to this case, Stalker?"

"I have brought one with me," was the reply, "a short statement, giving names, addresses, dates, and other particulars. Here it is." And he handed Thorndyke a sheet of paper bearing a tabulated statement.

When Stalker had gone, Thorndyke glanced rapidly through the *précis* and then looked at his watch. "If we make our way to Wimpole Street at once," said he, "we ought to catch Halbury. That is obviously the first thing to do. He signed the 'C' certificate, and we shall be able to judge from what he tells us whether there is any possibility of foul play. Shall we start now?"

As I assented, he slipped the *précis* in his pocket and we set forth. At the top of Middle Temple Lane we chartered a taxi by which we were shortly deposited at Dr. Halbury's door, and a few minutes later were ushered into his consulting room and found him shovelling a pile of letters into the waste-paper basket.

"How d'ye do?" he said briskly, holding out his hand. "I'm up to my eyes in arrears, you see. Just back from my holiday. What can I do for you?"

"We have called," said Thorndyke, "about a man named Ingle."

"Ingle – Ingle," repeated Halbury. "Now, let me see – "

"Stock-Orchard Crescent, Holloway," Thorndyke explained.

"Oh, yes. I remember him. Well, how is he?"

"He's dead," replied Thorndyke.

"Is he really?" exclaimed Halbury. "Now that shows how careful one should be in one's judgments. I half suspected that fellow of malingering. He was supposed to have a dilated heart, but I couldn't make out any appreciable dilatation. There was excited, irregular action. That was all. I had a suspicion that he had been dosing himself with trinitrine. Reminded me of the cases of cordite chewing that I used to meet with in South Africa. So he's dead, after all. Well, it's queer. Do you know what the exact cause of death was?"

"Failure of a dilated heart is the cause stated on the certificates – the body was cremated, and the 'C' Certificate was signed by you."

"By me!" exclaimed the physician. "Nonsense! It's a mistake. I signed a certificate for a Friendly Society. Ingle brought it here for me to sign – but I didn't even know he was dead. Besides, I went away for my holiday a few days after I saw the man and only came back yesterday. What makes you think I signed the death certificate?"

Thorndyke produced Stalker's *précis* and handed it to Halbury, who read out his own name and address with a puzzled frown. "This is an extraordinary affair," said he. "It will have to be looked into."

"It will, indeed," assented Thorndyke, "especially as a suspicion of poisoning has been raised."

"Ha!" exclaimed Halbury. "Then it *was* trinitrine, you may depend. But I suspected him unjustly. It was somebody else who was dosing him, perhaps that sly-looking baggage of a wife of his. Is anyone in particular suspected?

"Yes. The accusation, such as it is, is against the wife."

"Hmm. Probably a true bill. But she's done us. Artful devil. You can't get much evidence out of an urnful of ashes. Still, somebody has forged my signature. I suppose that is what the hussy wanted that certificate for – to get a specimen of my handwriting. I see the 'B' certificate was signed by a man named Meeking. Who's he? It was Barber who called me in for an opinion."

"I must find out who he is," replied Thorndyke. "Possibly Dr. Barber will know. I shall go and call on him now."

"Yes," said Dr. Halbury, shaking hands as we rose to depart, "you ought to see Barber. He knows the history of the case, at any rate."

From Wimpole Street we steered a course for Howland Street, and here we had the good fortune to arrive just as Dr. Barber's car drew up at the door. Thorndyke introduced himself and me, and then introduced the subject of his visit, but said nothing, at first, about our call on Dr. Halbury.

"Ingle," repeated Dr. Barber. "Oh, yes, I remember him. And you say he is dead. Well, I'm rather surprised. I didn't regard his condition as serious."

"Was his heart dilated?" Thorndyke asked.

"Not appreciably. I found nothing organic, no valvular disease. It was more like a tobacco heart. But it's odd that Meeking didn't mention the matter to me – he was my *locum*, you know. I handed the case over to him when I went on my holiday. And you say he signed the death certificate?"

"Yes, and the '*B*' certificate for cremation, too."

"Very odd," said Dr. Barber. "Just come in and let us have a look at the day book."

We followed him into the consulting room, and there, while he was turning over the leaves of the day book, I ran my eye along the shelf over the writing-table from which he had taken it, on which I observed the usual collection of case books and books of certificates and notification forms, including the book of death certificates.

"Yes," said Dr. Barber, "here we are. '*Ingle, Mr., Stock-Orchard Crescent.*' The last visit was on the 4th of September, and Meeking seems to have given some sort of certificate. Wonder if he used a printed form." He took down two of the books and turned over the counterfoils.

"Here we are," he said presently. "'*Ingle, Jonathan, 4 September. Now recovered and able to resume duties.*' That doesn't look like dying, does it? Still, we may as well make sure."

He reached down the book of death certificates and began to glance through the most recent entries.

"No," he said, turning over the leaves, "there doesn't seem to be – Hullo! What's this? Two blank counterfoils, and about the date, too, between the 2nd and 13th of September. Extraordinary! Meeking is such a careful, reliable man."

He turned back to the day book and read through the fortnight's entries. Then he looked up with an anxious frown.

"I can't make this out," he said. "There is no record of any patient having died in that period."

"Where is Dr. Meeking at present?" I asked.

"Somewhere in the South Atlantic," replied Barber. "He left here three weeks ago to take up a post on a Royal Mail Boat. So he couldn't have signed the certificate in any case."

That was all that Dr. Barber had to tell us, and a few minutes later we took our departure.

"This case looks pretty fishy," I remarked, as we turned down Tottenham Court Road.

"Yes," Thorndyke agreed. "There is evidently something radically wrong. And what strikes me especially is the cleverness of the fraud, the knowledge and judgment and foresight that are displayed."

"She took pretty considerable risks," I observed.

"Yes, but only the risks that were unavoidable. Everything that could be foreseen has been provided for. All the formalities have been complied with – in appearance. And you must notice, Jervis, that the scheme did actually succeed. The cremation has taken place. Nothing but the incalculable accident of the appearance of the real Mrs. Ingle, and her vague and apparently groundless suspicions, prevented the success from being final. If she had not come on the scene, no questions would ever have been asked."

"No," I agreed. "The discovery of the plot is a matter of sheer bad luck. But what do you suppose has really happened?"

Thorndyke shook his head.

"It is very difficult to say. The mechanism of the affair is obvious enough, but the motives and purpose are rather incomprehensible. The illness was apparently a sham, the symptoms being produced by nitro-glycerine or some similar heart poison. The doctors were called in, partly for the sake of appearances and partly to get specimens of their handwriting. The fact that both the doctors happened to be away from home and one of them at sea at the time when verbal questions might have been asked – by the undertaker, for instance – suggests that this had been ascertained in advance. The death certificate forms were pretty certainly stolen by the woman when she was left alone in Barber's consulting-room and, of course, the cremation certificates could be obtained on application to the crematorium authorities. That is all plain sailing. The mystery is, what is it all about? Barber or Meeking would almost certainly have given a death certificate, although the death was unexpected, and I don't suppose Halbury would have refused to confirm it. They would have assumed that their diagnosis had been at fault."

"Do you think it could have been suicide, or an inadvertent overdose of trinitrine?"

"Hardly. If it was suicide, it was deliberate, for the purpose of getting the insurance money for the woman, unless there was some

394

further motive behind. And the cremation, with all its fuss and formalities, is against suicide, while the careful preparation seems to exclude inadvertent poisoning. Then, what was the motive for the sham illness except as a preparation for an abnormal death?"

"That is true," said I. "But if you reject suicide, isn't it rather remarkable that the victim should have provided for his own cremation?"

"We don't know that he did," replied Thorndyke. "There is a suggestion of a capable forger in this business. It is quite possible that the will itself is a forgery."

"So it is!" I exclaimed. "I hadn't thought of that."

"You see," continued Thorndyke, "the appearances suggest that cremation was a necessary part of the programme – otherwise these extraordinary risks would not have been taken. The woman was sole executrix and could have ignored the cremation clause. But if the cremation was necessary, *why* was it necessary? The suggestion is that there was something suspicious in the appearance of the body, something that the doctors would certainly have observed or that would have been discovered if an exhumation had taken place."

"You mean some injury or visible signs of poisoning?"

"I mean something discoverable by examination, even after burial."

"But what about the undertaker? Wouldn't he have noticed anything palpably abnormal?"

"An excellent suggestion, Jervis. We must see the undertaker. We have his address, Kentish Town Road – a long way from deceased's house, by the way. We had better get on a bus and go there now."

A yellow omnibus was approaching as he spoke. We hailed it and sprang on, continuing our discussion as we were borne northward.

Mr. Burrell, the undertaker, was a pensive-looking, profoundly civil man who was evidently in a small way, for he combined with his funeral functions general carpentry and cabinet making. He was perfectly willing to give any required information, but he seemed to have very little to give.

"I never really saw the deceased gentleman," he said in reply to Thorndyke's cautious inquiries. "When I took the measurements, the corpse was covered with a sheet, and as Mrs. Ingle was in the room, I made the business as short as possible."

"You didn't put the body in the coffin, then?"

"No. I left the coffin at the house, but Mrs. Ingle said that she and the deceased gentleman's brother would lay the body in it."

"But didn't you see the corpse when you screwed the coffin-lid down?"

"I didn't screw it down. When I got there it was screwed down already. Mrs. Ingle said they had to close up the coffin, and I dare say it was necessary. The weather was rather warm, and I noticed a strong smell of formalin."

"Well," I said, as we walked back down the Kentish Town Road, "we haven't got much more forward."

"I wouldn't say that," replied Thorndyke. "We have a further instance of the extraordinary adroitness with which this scheme was carried out, and we have confirmation of our suspicion that there was something unusual in the appearance of the body. It is evident that this woman did not dare to let even the undertaker see it. But one can hardly help admiring the combination of daring and caution, the boldness with which these risks were taken, and the care and judgment with which they were provided against. And again I point out that the risks were justified by the result. The secret of that man's death appears to have been made secure for all time."

It certainly looked as if the mystery with which we were concerned was beyond the reach of investigation. Of course, the woman could be prosecuted for having forged the death certificates, to say nothing of the charge of bigamy. But that was no concern of ours or Stalker's. Jonathan Ingle was dead, and no one could say how he died.

On our arrival at our chambers we found a telegram that had just arrived, announcing that Stalker would call on us in the evening, and as this seemed to suggest that he had some fresh information we looked forward to his visit with considerable interest. Punctually at six o'clock, he made his appearance and at once opened the subject.

"There are some new developments in this Ingle case," said he. "In the first place, the woman, Huggard, has bolted. I went to the house to make a few inquiries and found the police in possession. They had come to arrest her on the bigamy charge, but she had got wind of their intentions and cleared out. They made a search of the premises, but I don't think they found anything of interest except a number of rifle cartridges, and I don't know that they are of much interest either, for she could hardly have shot him with a rifle."

"What kind of cartridges were they?" Thorndyke asked.

Stalker put his hand in his pocket.

"The inspector let me have one to show you," said he, and he laid on the table a military cartridge of the pattern of some twenty years ago. Thorndyke picked it up and, taking from a drawer a pair of pliers, drew the bullet out of the case and inserted into the latter a pair of dissecting forceps. When he withdrew the forceps, their points grasped one or two short strings of what looked like cat-gut.

396

"Cordite!" said I. "So Halbury was probably right, and this is how she got her supply." Then, as Stalker looked at me inquiringly, I gave him a short account of the results of our investigations.

"Ha!" he exclaimed, "the plot thickens. This juggling with the death certificates seems to connect itself with another kind of juggling that I came to tell you about. You know that Ingle was Secretary and Treasurer to a company that bought and sold land for building estates. Well, I called at their office after I left you and had a little talk with the chairman. From him, I learned that Ingle had practically complete control of the financial affairs of the company, that he received and paid all moneys and kept the books. Of late, however, some of the directors have had a suspicion that all was not well with the finances, and at last it was decided to have the affairs of the company thoroughly overhauled by a firm of chartered accountants. This decision was communicated to Ingle, and a couple of days later a letter arrived from his wife saying that he had had a severe heart attack and asking that the audit of the books might be postponed until he recovered and was able to attend at the office."

"And was it postponed?" I asked.

"No," replied Stalker. "The accountants were asked to get to work at once, which they did, with the result that they discovered a number of discrepancies in the books and a sum of about three-thousand pounds unaccounted for. It isn't quite obvious how the frauds were carried out, but it is suspected that some of the returned cheques are fakes with forged endorsements."

"Did the company communicate with Ingle on the subject?" asked Thorndyke.

"No. They had a further letter from Mrs. Ingle – that is, Huggard – saying that Ingle's condition was very serious, so they decided to wait until he had recovered. Then, of course, came the announcement of his death, on which the matter was postponed pending the probate of the will. I suppose a claim will be made on the estate, but as the executrix has absconded, the affair has become rather complicated."

"You were saying," said Thorndyke, "that the fraudulent death certificates seem to be connected with these frauds on the company. What kind of connection do you assume?"

"I assume – or at least, suggest," replied Stalker, "that this was a case of suicide. The man, Ingle, saw that his frauds were discovered, or were going to be, and that he was in for a long term of penal servitude, so he just made away with himself. And I think that if the murder charge could be dropped, Mrs. Huggard might be induced to come forward and give evidence as to the suicide."

Thorndyke shook his head.

397

"The murder charge couldn't be dropped," said he. "If it was suicide, Huggard was certainly an accessory, and in law, an accessory to suicide is an accessory to murder. But, in fact, no official charge of murder has been made, and at present there are no means of sustaining such a charge. The identity of the ashes might be assumed to be that stated in the cremation order, but the difficulty is the cause of death. Ingle was admittedly ill. He was attended for heart disease by three doctors. There is no evidence that he did not die from that illness."

"But the illness was due to cordite poisoning," said I, "That is what we believe. But no one could swear to it. And we certainly could not swear that he died from cordite poisoning."

"Then," said Stalker, "apparently there is no means of finding out whether his death was due to natural causes, suicide, or murder?"

"There is only one chance," replied Thorndyke. "It is just barely possible that the cause of death might be ascertainable by an examination of the ashes."

"That doesn't seem very hopeful," said I. "Cordite poisoning would certainly leave no trace."

"We mustn't assume that he died from cordite poisoning," said Thorndyke. "Probably he did not. That may have masked the action of a less obvious poison, or death might have been produced by some new agent."

"But," I objected, "how many poisons are there that could be detected in the ashes? No organic poison would leave any traces, nor would metallic poisons such as mercury, antimony, or arsenic."

"No," Thorndyke agreed. "But there are other metallic poisons which could be easily recovered from the ashes – lead, tin, gold, and silver, for instance. But it is useless to discuss speculative probabilities. The only chance that we have of obtaining any new facts is by an examination of the ashes. It seems infinitely improbable that we shall learn anything from it, but there is the bare possibility and we ought not to leave it untried."

Neither Stalker nor I made any further remark, but I could see that the same thought was in both our minds. It was not often that Thorndyke was "gravelled", but apparently the resourceful Mrs. Huggard had set him a problem that was beyond even his powers. When an investigator of crime is reduced to the necessity of examining a potful of ashes in the wild hope of ascertaining from them how the deceased met his death, one may assume that he is at the very end of his tether. It is a forlorn hope indeed.

Nevertheless, Thorndyke seemed to view the matter quite cheerfully, his only anxiety being lest the Home Secretary should refuse to make the order authorising the examination. And this anxiety was dispelled a day or two later by the arrival of a letter giving the necessary authority, and informing him that a Dr. Hemming – known to us both as an expert pathologist – had been deputed to be present at the examination and to confer with him as to the necessity for a chemical analysis.

On the appointed day Dr. Hemming called at our chambers and we set forth together for Liverpool Street, and as we drove thither it became evident to me that his view of our mission was very similar to my own. For, though he talked freely enough, and on professional topics, he maintained a most discreet silence on the subject of the forthcoming inspection – indeed, the first reference to the subject was made by Thorndyke himself just as the train was approaching Corfield, where the crematorium was situated.

"I presume," said he, "you have made all necessary arrangements, Hemming?"

"Yes," was the reply. "The superintendent will meet us and will conduct us to the catacombs, and there, in our presence, will take the casket from its niche in the columbarium and have it conveyed to the office, where the examination will be made. I thought it best to use these formalities, though, as the casket is sealed and bears the name of the deceased, there is not much point in them."

"No," said Thorndyke, "but I think you were right. It would be easy to challenge the identity of a mass of ashes if all precautions were not taken, seeing that the ashes themselves are unidentifiable."

"That was what I felt," said Hemming, and then, as the train slowed down, he added, "This is our station, and that gentleman on the platform, I suspect, is the superintendent."

The surmise turned out to be correct, but the cemetery official was not the only one present bearing that title, for as we were mutually introducing ourselves, a familiar tall figure approached up the platform from the rear of the train – our old friend Superintendent Miller of the Criminal Investigation Department.

"I don't wish to intrude," said he, as he joined the group and was presented by Thorndyke to the strangers, "but we were notified by the Home Office that an investigation was to be made, so I thought I would be on the spot to pick up any crumbs of information that you may drop. Of course, I am not asking to be present at the examination."

"You may as well be present as an additional witness to the removal of the urn," said Thorndyke, and Miller accordingly joined the party, which now made its way from the station to the cemetery.

The catacombs were in a long, low arcaded building at the end of the pleasantly-wooded grounds, and on our way thither we passed the crematorium, a smallish, church-like edifice with a perforated chimney-shaft partly concealed by the low spire. Entering the catacombs, we were conducted to the "columbarium", the walls of which were occupied by a multitude of niches or pigeon-holes, each niche accommodating a terra-cotta urn or casket. The superintendent proceeded to near the end of the gallery, where he halted and, opening the register, which he had brought with him, read out a number and the name *Jonathan Ingle*, and then led us to a niche bearing that number and name, in which reposed a square casket, on which was inscribed the name and date of death. When we had verified these particulars, the casket was tenderly lifted from its place by two attendants, who carried it to a well-lighted room at the end of the building, where a large table by a window had been covered with white paper. Having placed the casket on the table, the attendants retired, and the superintendent then broke the seals and removed the cover.

For a while we all stood looking in at the contents of the casket without speaking, and I found myself contrasting them with what would have been revealed by the lifting of a coffin-lid. Truly corruption had put on incorruption. The mass of snow-white, coral-like fragments, delicate, fragile, and lace-like in texture, so far from being repulsive in aspect, were almost attractive. I ran my eye, with an anatomist's curiosity, over these dazzling remnants of what had lately been a man, half-unconsciously seeking to identify and give a name to particular fragments, and a little surprised at the difficulty of determining that this or that irregularly-shaped white object was a part of any one of the bones with which I had thought myself so familiar.

Presently Hemming looked up at Thorndyke and asked, "Do you observe anything abnormal in the appearance of these ashes? I don't."

"Perhaps," replied Thorndyke, "we had better turn them out on to the table, so that we can see the whole of them."

This was done very gently, and then Thorndyke proceeded to spread out the heap, touching the fragments with the utmost delicacy – for they were extremely fragile and brittle – until the whole collection was visible.

"Well," said Hemming, when we had once more looked them over critically, "what do you say? I can see no trace of any foreign substance. Can you?"

"No," replied Thorndyke. "And there are some other things that I can't see. For instance, the medical referee reported that the proposer had a good set of sound teeth. Where are they? I have not seen a single

400

fragment of a tooth. Yet teeth are far more resistant to fire than bones, especially the enamel caps."

Hemming ran a searching glance over the mass of fragments and looked up with a perplexed frown.

"I certainly can't see any sign of teeth," he admitted, "and it is rather curious, as you say. Does the fact suggest any particular significance to you?"

By way of reply, Thorndyke delicately picked up a flat fragment and silently held it out towards us. I looked at it and said nothing, for a very strange suspicion was beginning to creep into my mind.

"A piece of a rib," said Hemming. "Very odd that it should have broken across so cleanly. It might have been cut with a saw."

Thorndyke laid it down and picked up another, larger fragment, which I had already noticed.

"Here is another example," said he, handing it to our colleague.

"Yes," agreed Hemming. "It is really rather extraordinary. It looks exactly as if it had been sawn across."

"It does," agreed Thorndyke. "What bone should you say it is?"

"That is what I was just asking myself," replied Hemming, looking at the fragment with a sort of half-vexed smile. "It seems ridiculous that a competent anatomist should be in any doubt with as large a portion as this, but really I can't confidently give it a name. The shape seems to me to suggest a tibia, but of course it is much too small. Is it the upper end of the ulna?"

"I should say no," answered Thorndyke. Then he picked out another of the larger fragments, and handing it to Hemming, asked him to name it.

Our friend began to look somewhat worried.

"It is an extraordinary thing, you know," said he, "but I can't tell you what bone it is part of. It is clearly the shaft of a long bone, but I'm hanged if I can say which. It is too big for a metatarsal and too small for any of the main limb bones. It reminds one of a diminutive thigh bone."

"It does," agreed Thorndyke, "very strongly." While Hemming had been speaking he had picked out four more large fragments, and these he now laid in a row with the one that had seemed to resemble a tibia in shape. Placed thus together, the five fragments bore an obvious resemblance.

"Now," said he, "look at these. There are five of them. They are parts of limb bones, and the bones of which they are parts were evidently exactly alike, excepting that three were apparently from the left side and two from the right. Now, you know, Hemming, a man has only four limbs and of those only two contain similar bones. Then two of them show distinct traces of what looks like a saw-cut."

Hemming gazed at the row of fragments with a frown of deep cogitation.

"It is very mysterious," he said. "And looking at them in a row they strike me as curiously like tibia in shape, not in size."

"The size," said Thorndyke is about that of a sheep's tibia."

"A sheep's?" exclaimed Hemming, staring in amazement, first at the calcined bones and then at my colleague.

"Yes, the upper half, sawn across in the middle of the shank."

Hemming was thunderstruck. "It is an astounding affair!" he exclaimed. "You mean to suggest – "

"I suggest," said Thorndyke, "that there is not a sign of a human bone in the whole collection. But there are very evident traces of at least five legs of mutton."

For a few moments there was a profound silence, broken only by a murmur of astonishment from the cemetery official and a low chuckle from Superintendent Miller, who had been listening with absorbed interest. At length Hemming spoke.

"Then, apparently, there was no corpse in the coffin at all?"

"No," answered Thorndyke. "The weight was made up, and the ashes furnished, by joints of butcher's meat. I dare say, if we go over the ashes carefully, we shall be able to judge what they were. But it is hardly necessary. The presence of five legs of mutton and the absence of a single recognisable fragment of a human skeleton, together with the forged certificates, gives us a pretty I conclusive case. The rest, I think we can leave to Superintendent Miller."

"I take it, Thorndyke," said I, as the train moved out of the station, "that you came here expecting to find what you did find?"

"Yes," he replied. "It seemed to me the only possibility, having regard to all the known facts."

"When did it first occur to you?"

"It occurred to me as a possibility as soon as we discovered that the cremation certificates had been forged, but it was the undertaker's statement that seemed to clench the matter."

"But he distinctly stated that he measured the body."

"True. But there was nothing to show that it was a dead body. What was perfectly clear was that there was something that must on no account be seen, and when Stalker told us of the embezzlement we had a body of evidence that could point to only one conclusion. Just consider that evidence.

"Here we had a death, preceded by an obviously sham illness and followed by cremation with forged certificates. Now, what was it that had happened? There were four possible hypotheses. Normal death, suicide, murder, and fictitious death. Which of these hypotheses fitted the facts?

"Normal death was apparently excluded by the forged certificates.

"The theory of suicide did not account for the facts. It did not agree with the careful, elaborate preparation. And why the forged certificates? If Ingle had really died, Meeking would have certified the death. And why the cremation? There was no purpose in taking those enormous risks.

"The theory of murder was unthinkable. These certificates were almost certainly forged by Ingle himself, who we know was a practised forger. But the idea of the victim arranging for his own cremation is an absurdity.

"There remained only the theory of fictitious death, and that theory fitted all the facts perfectly. First, as to the motive. Ingle had committed a felony. He had to disappear. But what kind of disappearance could be so effectual as death and cremation? Both the prosecutors and the police would forthwith write him off and forget him. Then there was the bigamy – a criminal offence in itself. But death would not only wipe that off, after 'death' he could marry Huggard regularly under another name, and he would have shaken off his deserted wife for ever. And he stood to gain fifteen-hundred pounds from the Insurance Company. Then see how this theory explained the other facts. A fictitious death made necessary a fictitious illness. It necessitated the forged certificates, since there was no corpse. It made cremation highly desirable, for suspicion might easily have arisen, and then the exhumation of a coffin containing a dummy would have exploded the fraud. But successful cremation would cover up the fraud for ever. It explained the concealment of the corpse from the undertaker, and it even explained the smell of formalin which he noticed."

"How did it?" I asked.

"Consider, Jervis," he replied. "The dummy in this coffin had to be a dummy of flesh and bone which would yield the correct kind of ash. Joints of butcher's meat would fulfil the conditions. But the quantity required would be from a hundred-and-fifty to two-hundred pounds. Now Ingle could not go to the butcher and order a whole sheep to be sent the day before the funeral. The joints would have to be bought gradually and stored. But the storage of meat in warm weather calls for some kind of preservative, and formalin is highly effective, as it leaves no trace after burning.

"So you see that the theory of fictitious death agreed with all the known circumstances, whereas the alternative theories presented inexplicable discrepancies and contradictions. Logically, it was the only possible theory and, as you have seen, experiment proved it to be the true one."

As he concluded, Dr. Hemming took his pipe from his mouth and laughed softly.

"When I came down to-day," said he, "I had all the facts which you had communicated to the Home Office, and I was absolutely convinced that we were coming to examine a mare's nest. And yet, now I have heard your exposition, the whole thing looks perfectly obvious."

"That is usually the case with Thorndyke's conclusions," said I. "They are perfectly obvious – when you have heard the explanation."

Within a week of our expedition, Ingle was in the hands of the police. The apparent success of the cremation adventure had misled him to a sense of such complete security that he had neglected to cover his tracks, and he had accordingly fallen an easy prey to our friend Superintendent Miller. The police were highly gratified, and so were the directors of the Griffin Life Assurance Company.

The Stalking Horse

As Thorndyke and I descended the stairs of the foot bridge at Densford Junction, we became aware that something unusual had happened. The platform was nearly deserted save at one point, where a small but dense crowd had collected around the open door of a first-class compartment of the down train, heads were thrust out of the windows of the other coaches, and at intervals doors opened and inquisitive passengers ran along to join the crowd, from which an excited porter detached himself just as we reached the platform.

"You'd better go for Dr. Pooke first," the station-master called after him.

On this, Thorndyke stepped forward.

"My friend and I," said he, "are medical men. Can we be of any service until the local doctor arrives?"

"I'm very much afraid not, sir," was the reply, "but you'll see." He cleared a way for us and we approached the open door.

At the first glance there appeared to be nothing to account for the awe-stricken expression with which the bystanders peered into the carriage and gazed at its solitary occupant. For the motionless figure that sat huddled in the corner seat, chin on breast, might have been a sleeping man. But it was not. The waxen pallor of the face and the strange, image-like immobility forbade the hope of any awakening.

"It looks almost as if he had passed away in his sleep," said the stationmaster when we had concluded our brief examination and ascertained certainly that the man was dead. "Do you think it was a heart attack, sir?"

Thorndyke shook his head and touched with his finger a depressed spot on the dead man's waistcoat. When he withdrew his finger it was smeared with blood.

"Good God!" the official gasped, in a horrified whisper. "The man has been murdered!" He stared incredulously at the corpse for a few moments and then turned and sprang out of the compartment, shutting the door behind him, and we heard him giving orders for the coach to be separated and shunted into the siding.

"This is a gruesome affair, Jervis," my colleague said as he sat down on the seat opposite the dead man and cast a searching glance round the compartment. "I wonder who this poor fellow was and what was the object of the murder? It looks almost too determined for a common robbery and, in fact, the body does not appear to have been robbed." Here he stooped suddenly to pick up one or two minute fragments of glass which seemed to have been trodden into the carpet, and which he examined closely in the palm of his hand. I leaned over and looked at the fragments, and we agreed that they were portions of the bulb of an electric torch or flash-lamp.

"The significance of these – if they have any," said Thorndyke, "we can consider later. But if they are recent, it would appear that the metal part of the bulb has been picked up and taken away. That might be an important fact. But on the other hand, the fragments may have been here some time and have no connection with the tragedy, though you notice that they were lying opposite the body and opposite the seat which the murderer must have occupied when the crime was committed."

As he was speaking, the uncoupled coach began slowly to move towards the siding, and we both stooped to make a further search for the remainder of the lamp-bulb, And then, almost at the same moment, we perceived two objects lying under the opposite seat – the seat occupied by the dead man. One was a small pocket-handkerchief, the other a sheet of notepaper.

"This," said I, as I picked up the former, "accounts for the strong smell of scent in the compartment."

"Possibly," Thorndyke agreed, "though you will notice that the odour does not come principally from the handkerchief, but from the back cushion of the corner seat. But here is something more distinctive – a most incriminating piece of evidence, unless it can be answered by an undeniable alibi." He held out to me a sheet of letter paper, both pages of which were covered with writing in bright blue ink, done with a Hectograph or some similar duplicator. It was evidently a circular letter, for it bore the printed heading, *"Women's Emancipation League, 16 Barnabas Square, S.W."*, and the contents appeared to refer to a *"militant demonstration"* planned for the near future.

"It is dated the day before yesterday," commented Thorndyke, "so that it might have been lying here for twenty-four hours, though that is obviously improbable, and as this is neither the first sheet nor the last, there are – or have been – at least two more sheets. The police will have something to start on, at any rate."

He laid the letter on the seat and explored both of the hat-racks, taking down the dead man's hat, gloves, and umbrella, and noting in the hat the initials *"F. B."* He had just replaced them when voices became audible outside, and the station-master climbed up on the foot-board and opened the door to admit two men, one of whom I assumed to be a doctor, the other being a police inspector.

"The station-master tells me that this is a case of homicide," said the former, addressing us jointly.

"That is what the appearances suggest," replied Thorndyke. "There is a bullet wound, inflicted apparently at quite short range – the waistcoat is perceptibly singed – and we have found no weapon in the compartment."

The doctor stepped past us and proceeded to make a rapid examination of the body.

"Yes," he said, "I agree with you. The position of the wound and the posture of the body both suggest that death was practically instantaneous. If it had been suicide, the pistol would have been in the hand or on the floor. There is no clue to the identity of the murderer, I suppose?"

"We found these on the floor under the dead man's seat," replied Thorndyke, indicating the letter and the handkerchief, "and there is some glass trodden into the carpet – apparently the remains of an electric flash-lamp."

The inspector pounced on the handkerchief and the letter, and having scrutinised the former vainly in search of name or initials, turned to the letter.

"Why, this is a suffragist's letter!" he exclaimed. "But it can't have anything to do with this affair. They are mischievous beggars, but they don't do this sort of thing." Nevertheless, he carefully bestowed both articles in a massive wallet, and approaching the corpse, remarked, "We may as well see who he is while we are waiting for the stretcher."

With a matter-of-fact air, which seemed somewhat to shock the station-master, he unbuttoned the coat of the passive figure in the corner and thrust his hand into the breast pocket, drawing out a letter-case which he opened, and from which he extracted a visiting card. As he glanced at it, his face suddenly took on an expression of amazement.

"God!" he exclaimed in a startled tone. "Who do you think he is, Doctor? He is Mr. Francis Burnham!"

The doctor looked at him with an interrogative frown. "Burnham – Burnham," he repeated. "Let me see, now – "

"Don't you know? The anti-suffrage man. Surely – "

"Yes, yes," interrupted the doctor. "Of course I remember him. The arch-enemy of the suffrage movement and – yes, of course." The doctor's brisk speech changed abruptly into a hesitating mumble. Like the inspector, he had suddenly "seen a great light", and again, like the officer, his perception had begotten a sudden reticence.

Thorndyke glanced at his watch. "Our train is a minute overdue," said he. "We ought to get back to the platform." Taking a card from his case, he handed it to the inspector, who looked at it and slightly raised his eyebrows.

"I don't think my evidence will be of much value," said he, "but, of course, I am at your service if you want it." With this and a bow to the doctor and the station-master, he climbed down to the ground, and when I had given the inspector my card, I followed, and we made our way to the platform.

The case was not long in developing. That very evening, as Thorndyke and I were smoking our after-dinner pipes by the fire, a hurried step was heard on the stair and was followed by a peremptory knock on our door. The visitor was a man of about thirty, with a clean-shaved face, an intense and rather neurotic expression, and a restless, excited manner. He introduced himself by the name of Cadmus Bawley, and thereby, in effect, indicated the purpose of his visit.

"You know me by name, I expect," he said, speaking rapidly and with a sharp, emphatic manner, "and probably you can guess what I have come about. You have seen the evening paper, of course?"

"I have not," replied Thorndyke.

"Well," said Mr. Bawley, "you know about the murder of the man Burnham, because I see that you were present at the discovery, and you know that part of a circular letter from our League was found in the compartment. Perhaps you will not be surprised to learn that Miss Isabel Dalby has been arrested and charged with the murder."

"Indeed!" said Thorndyke.

"Yes. It's an infamous affair! A national disgrace!" exclaimed Bawley, banging the table with his fist. "A manifest plot of the enemies of social reform to get rid of a high-minded, noble-hearted lady whose championship of this great Cause they are unable to combat by fair means in the open. And it is a wild absurdity, too. As to the fellow, Burnham, I can't pretend to feel any regret – "

"May I suggest – " Thorndyke interrupted somewhat stiffly " – that the expression of personal sentiments is neither helpful nor discreet? My methods of defence – if that is what you have come about – are based on demonstration rather than rhetoric. Could you give us the plain facts?"

Mr. Cadmus Bawley looked unmistakably sulky, but after a short pause, he began his recital in a somewhat lower key.

"The bald facts," he said, "are these, This afternoon, at half-past two, Miss Dalby took the train from King's Cross to Holmwood. This is the train that stops at Densford Junction and is the one in which Burnham travelled. She took a first-class ticket and occupied a compartment for ladies only, of which she was the only occupant. She got out at Holmwood and went straight to the house of our Vice-President, Miss

Carleigh – who has been confined to her room for some days – and stayed there about an hour. She came back by the four-fifteen train, and I met her at the station – King's Cross – at a quarter to five. We had tea at a restaurant opposite the station, and over our tea we discussed the plans for the next demonstration, and arranged the rendezvous and the most convenient routes for retreat and dispersal when the police should arrive. This involved the making of sketch plans, and these Miss Dalby drew on a sheet of paper that she took from her pocket, and which happened to be part of the circular letter referring to the raid.

After tea, we walked together down Gray's Inn Road and parted at Theobald's Road, I going on to the head-quarters and she to her rooms in Queen Square. On her arrival home, she found two detectives waiting outside her house, and then – and then, in short, she was arrested, like a common criminal, and taken to the police station, where she was searched and the remainder of the circular letter found in her pocket. Then she was formally charged with the murder of the man Burnham, and she was graciously permitted to send a telegram to head-quarters. It arrived just after I got there and, of course, I at once went to the police station. The police refused to accept bail, but they allowed me to see her to make arrangements for the defence."

"Does Miss Dalby offer any suggestion," asked Thorndyke, "as to how a sheet of her letter came to be in the compartment with the murdered man?"

"Oh, yes!" replied Mr. Bawley. "I had forgotten that. It wasn't her letter at all. She destroyed her copy of the letter as soon as she had read it."

"Then," inquired Thorndyke, "how came the letter to be in her pocket?"

"Ah," replied Bawley, "that is the mystery. She thinks someone must have slipped it into her pocket to throw suspicion on her."

"Did she seem surprised to find it in her pocket when you were having tea together?"

"No. She had forgotten having destroyed her copy. She only remembered it when I told her that the sheet had been found in Burnham's carriage."

"Can she produce the fragments of the destroyed letter?"

"No, she can't. Unfortunately she burned it."

"Do these circular letters bear any distinguishing mark? Are they addressed to members by name?"

"Only on the envelopes. The letters are all alike. They are run off a duplicator. Of course, if you don't believe the story – "

"I am not judging the case," interrupted Thorndyke, "I am simply collecting the facts. What do you want me to do?"

"If you feel that you could undertake the defence, I should like you to do so. We shall employ the solicitors to the League, Bird and Marshall, but I know they will be willing and glad to act with you."

"Very well," said Thorndyke. "I will investigate the case and consult with your solicitors. By the way, do the police know about the sheet of the letter on which the plans were drawn?"

"No. I thought it best to say nothing about that, and I have told Miss Dalby not to mention it."

"That is just as well," said Thorndyke. "Have you the sheet with the plan on it?"

"I haven't it about me," was the reply. "It is in my desk at my chambers."

"You had better let me have it to look at," said Thorndyke.

"You can have it if you want it, of course," said Bawley, "but it won't help you. The letters are all alike, as I have told you."

"I should like to see it, nevertheless," said Thorndyke, "and perhaps you could give me some account of Mr. Burnham. What do you know about him?"

Mr. Bawley shut his lips tightly, and his face took on an expression of vindictiveness verging on malignity.

"All I know about Burnham," he said, "is that he was a fool and a ruffian. He was not only an enemy of the great reform that our League stands for, he was a treacherous enemy – violent, crafty, and indefatigably active. I can only regard his death as a blessing to mankind."

"May I ask," said Thorndyke, "if any members of your League have ever publicly threatened to take personal measures against him?

"Yes," snapped Bawley. "Several of us – including myself – have threatened to give him the hiding that he deserved. But a hiding is a different thing from murder, you know."

"Yes," Thorndyke agreed somewhat dryly. Then he asked, "Do you know anything about Mr. Burnham's occupation and habits?"

"He was a sort of manager of the London and Suburban Bank. His job was to supervise the suburban branches, and his habit was to visit them in rotation. He was probably going to the branch at Holmwood when he was killed. That is all I can tell you about him."

"Thank you," said Thorndyke, and as our visitor rose to depart he continued, "Then I will look into the case and arrange with your solicitors to have Miss Dalby properly represented at the inquest, and I

410

shall be glad to have that sheet of the letter as soon as you can send or leave it."

"Very well," said Bawley, "though, as I have told you, it won't be of any use to you. It is only a duplicated circular."

"Possibly," Thorndyke assented. "But the other sheets will be produced in Court, so I may as well have an opportunity of examining it beforehand."

For some minutes after our client had gone, Thorndyke remained silent and reflective, copying his rough notes into his pocket-book and apparently amplifying and arranging them. Presently he looked up at me with an unspoken question in his eyes.

"It is a queer case," said I. "The circumstantial evidence seems to be strongly against Miss Dalby, but it is manifestly improbable that she murdered the man."

"It seems so," he agreed. "But the case will be decided on the evidence, and the evidence will be considered by a judge, not by a Home Secretary. You notice the importance of Burnham's destination?"

"Yes. He was evidently dead when the train arrived at Holmwood. But it isn't clear how long he had been dead."

"The evidence," said Thorndyke, "points strongly to the tunnel between Cawden and Holmwood as the place where the murder was committed. You will remember that the up-express passed our train in the tunnel. If the adjoining compartments were empty, the sound of a pistol shot would be completely drowned by the noise of the express thundering past. Then you will remember the fragments of the electric bulb that we picked up, and that there was no light on in the carriage. That is rather significant. It not only suggests that the crime was committed in the dark, but there is a distinct suggestion of preparation – arrangement and premeditation. It suggests that the murderer knew what the circumstances would be and provided for them."

"Yes, and that is rather a point against our client. But I don't quite see what you expect to get out of that sheet of the letter. It is the presence of the letter, rather than its matter, that constitutes the evidence against Miss Dalby."

"I don't expect to learn anything from it," replied Thorndyke, "but the letter will be the prosecution's trump card, and it is always well to know in advance exactly what cards your opponent holds. It is a mere matter of routine to examine everything, relevant or irrelevant."

The inquest was to be held at Densford on the third day after the discovery of the body. But in the interval certain new facts had come to light. One was that the deceased was conveying to the Holmwood branch of the bank a sum of three-thousand pounds, of which one-thousand was in gold and the remainder in Bank of England notes, the whole being contained in a leather handbag. This bag had been found, empty, in a ditch by the side of the road which led from the station to the house of Miss Carleigh, the Vice-President of the Women's Emancipation League. It was further stated that the ticket-collector at Holmwood had noticed that Miss Dalby – whom he knew by sight – was carrying a bag of the kind described when she passed the barrier, and that when she returned, about an hour later, she had no bag with her. On the other hand, Miss Carleigh had stated that the bag which Miss Dalby brought to her house was her (Miss Carleigh's) property, and she had produced it for the inspection of the police. So that already there was some conflict of evidence, with a balance distinctly against Miss Dalby.

"There is no denying," said Thorndyke, as we discussed the case at the breakfast table on the morning of the inquest, "that the circumstantial evidence is formidably complete and consistent, while the rebutting evidence is of the feeblest. Miss Dalby's statement that the letter had been put into her pocket by some unknown person will hardly be taken seriously, and even Miss Carleigh's statement with reference to the bag will not carry much weight unless she can furnish corroboration."

"Nevertheless," said I, "the general probabilities are entirely in favour of the accused. It is grossly improbable that a lady like Miss Dalby would commit a robbery with murder of this cold-blooded, deliberate type."

"That may be," Thorndyke retorted, "but a jury has to find in accordance with the evidence."

"By the way," said I, "did Bawley ever send you that sheet of the letter that you asked for?"

"No, confound him! But I have sent Polton round to get it from him, so that I can look it over carefully in the train – which reminds me that I can't get down in time for the opening of the inquest. You had better travel with the solicitors and see the shorthand writers started. I shall have to come down by a later train."

Half-an-hour later, just as I was about to start, a familiar step was heard on the stair, and then our laboratory assistant, Polton, let himself in with his key.

"Just caught him, sir, as he was starting for the station," he said, with a satisfied, crinkly smile, laying an envelope on the table, and added, "Lord! How he did swear!"

Thorndyke chuckled and, having thanked his assistant, opened the envelope, and handed it to me. It contained a single sheet of letter-paper, exactly similar to the one that we had found in the railway carriage, excepting that the writing filled one-side-and-a-quarter only and, since it concluded with the signature *"Letitia Humboe, President"*, it was evidently the last sheet. There was no water-mark nor anything, so far as I could see, to distinguish it from the dozens of other impressions that had been run off on the duplicator with it, excepting the roughly-pencilled plan on the blank side of the sheet.

"Well," I said as I put on my hat and walked towards the door, "I suspect that Bawley was right. You won't get much help from this to support Miss Dalby's rather improbable statement." And Thorndyke agreed that appearances were not very promising.

The scene in the coffee-room of The Plough Inn at Densford was one with which I was familiar enough. The quiet, business-like coroner, the half-embarrassed jurors, the local police and witnesses and the spectators, penned up at one end of the room, were all well-known characters. The unusual feature was the handsome, distinguished-looking young lady who sat on a plain Windsor chair between two inscrutable policemen, watched intently by Mr. Cadmus Bawley. Miss Dalby was pale and obviously agitated, but quiet, resolute, and somewhat defiant in manner. She greeted me with a pleasant smile when I introduced myself, and hoped that I and my colleague would have no difficulty in disposing of "this grotesque and horrible accusation".

I need not describe the proceedings in detail. Evidence of the identity of the deceased having been taken, Dr. Pooke deposed that death was due to a wound of the heart produced by a spherical bullet, apparently fired from a small, smooth-bore pistol at very short range. The wound was in his opinion not self-inflicted. The coroner then produced the sheet of the circular letter found in the carriage, and I was called to testify to the finding of it. The next witness was Superintendent Miller of the Criminal Investigation Department, who produced the two sheets of the letter which were taken from Miss Dalby's pocket when she was arrested. These he handed to the coroner for comparison with the one found in the carriage with the body of deceased.

"There appear," said the coroner, after placing the three sheets together, "to be one or more sheets missing. The two you have handed me are sheets one and three, and the one found in the railway carriage is sheet two."

"Yes," the witness agreed, "sheet four is missing, but I have a photograph of it. Here is a set of the complete letter," and he laid four unmounted prints on the table.

The coroner examined them with a puzzled frown. "May I ask," he said, "how you obtained these photographs?"

"They are not photographs of the copy that you have," the witness explained, "but of another copy of the same letter which we intercepted in the post. That letter was addressed to a stationer's shop to be called for. We have considered it necessary to keep ourselves informed of the contents of these circulars, so that we can take the necessary precautions, and as the envelopes are marked with the badge and are invariably addressed in blue ink, it is not difficult to identify them."

"I see," said the coroner, glaring stonily at Mr. Bawley, who had accompanied the superintendent's statement with audible and unfavourable comments. "Is that the whole of your evidence? Thank you. Then, if there is no cross-examination, I will call the next witness. Mr. Bernard Parsons."

Mr. Parsons was the general manager of the London and Suburban Bank, and he deposed that deceased was, on the day when be met his death, travelling to Holmwood to visit and inspect the new local branch of the bank, and that he was taking thither the sum of three-thousand pounds, of which one-thousand was in gold and the remainder in Bank of England notes – mostly five-pound notes. He carried the notes and specie in a strong leather handbag.

"Can you say if either of these is the bag that he carried?" the coroner asked, indicating two largish, black leather bags that his officer had placed on the table.

Mr. Parsons promptly pointed to the larger of the two, which was smeared externally with mud. The coroner noted the answer and then asked, "Did anyone besides yourself know that deceased was making this visit?"

"Many persons must have known," was the reply. "Deceased visited the various branches in a fixed order. He came to Holmwood on the second Tuesday in the month."

"And would it be known that he had this great sum of money with him?"

"The actual amount would not be generally known, but he usually took with him supplies of specie and notes – sometimes very large sums – and this would be known to many of the bank staff, and probably to a good many persons outside. The Holmwood Branch consumes a good deal of specie, as most of the customers pay in cheques and draw out cash for local use."

This was the substance of Mr. Parsons' evidence, and when he sat down the ticket-collector was called. That official identified Miss Dalby as one of the passengers by the train in which the body of deceased was found. She was carrying a bag when she passed the barrier. He could not identify either of the bags, but both were similar to the one that she was carrying. She returned about an hour later and caught an up-train, and he noticed that she was then not carrying a bag. He could not say whether any of the other passengers was carrying a bag. There were very few first-class passengers by that train, but a large number of third-class – mostly fruit-pickers – and they made a dense crowd at the barrier so that he did not notice individual passengers particularly. He noticed Miss Dalby because he knew her by sight, as she often came to Holmwood with other suffragist ladies. He did not see which carriage Miss Dalby came from, and he did not see any first-class compartment with an open door.

The coroner noted down this evidence with thoughtful deliberation, and I was considering whether there were any questions that it would be advisable to ask the witness when I felt a light touch on my shoulder, and looking up perceived a constable holding out a telegram. Observing that it was addressed to *"Dr. Jervis, Plough Inn, Densford"*, I nodded to the constable, and taking the envelope from him, opened it and unfolded the paper. The telegram was from Thorndyke, in the simple code that he had devised for our private use. I was able to decode it without referring to the key – which each of us always carried in his pocket – and it then read:

> *I am starting for Folkestone* in re *Burnham deceased. Follow immediately and bring Miller if you can for possible arrest. Meet me on pier near Ostend boat.*
>
> *Thorndyke*

Accustomed as I was to my colleague's inveterate habit of acting in the least expected manner, I must confess that I gazed at the decoded message in absolute stupefaction. I had been totally unaware of the faintest clue beyond the obvious evidence to which I had been listening, and behold! Here was Thorndyke with an entirely fresh case, apparently cut-and-dried, and the unsuspected criminal in the hollow of his hand. It was astounding.

Unconsciously I raised my eyes – and met those of Superintendent Miller, fixed on me with devouring curiosity. I held up the telegram and beckoned, and immediately he tip-toed across and took a seat by my side. I laid the decoded telegram before him, and when he had glanced through it, I asked in a whisper, "Well, what do you say?"

By way of reply, he whisked out a time-table, conned it eagerly for a few minutes, and then held it towards me with his thumb-nail on the words, *"Densford Junction"*.

"There's a fast train up in seven minutes," he whispered hoarsely. "Get the coroner to excuse us and let your solicitors carry on for you."

A brief, and rather vague, explanation secured the assent of the coroner – since we had both given our evidence – and the less willing agreement of my clients. In another minute the superintendent and I were heading for the station, which we reached just as the train swept up alongside the platform.

"This is a queer start," said Miller, as the train moved out of the station, "but, Lord! There is never any calculating Dr. Thorndyke's moves. Did you know that he had anything up his sleeve?"

"No, but then one never does know. He is as close as an oyster. He never shows his hand until he can play a trump card. But it is possible that he has struck a fresh clue since I left."

"Well," rejoined Miller, "we shall know when we get to the other end And I don't mind telling you that it will be a great relief to me if we can drop this charge against Miss Dalby."

From time to time during the journey to London, and from thence to Folkestone, the superintendent reverted to Thorndyke's mysterious proceedings. But it was useless to speculate. We had not a single fact to guide us, and when, at last, the train ran into Folkestone Central Station, we were as much in the dark as when we started.

Assuming that Thorndyke would have made any necessary arrangements for assistance from the local police, we chartered a cab and proceeded direct to the end of Rendezvous Street – a curiously appropriate destination, by the way. Here we alighted in order that we might make our appearance at the meeting-place as inconspicuously as possible and, walking towards the harbour, perceived Thorndyke waiting on the quay, ostensibly watching the loading of a barge, and putting in their case a pair of prismatic binoculars with which he had apparently observed our arrival.

"I am glad you have come, Miller," he said, shaking the superintendent's hand. "I can't make any promises, but I have no doubt that it is a case for you even if it doesn't turn out all that I hope and expect. *The Cornflower* is our ship, and we had better go on board separately in case our friends are keeping a look-out. I have arranged matters with the captain, and the local superintendent has got some plain-clothes men on the pier."

With this we separated. Thorndyke went on in advance, and Miller and I followed at a discreet interval.

As I descended the gangway a minute or so after Miller, a steward approached me, and having asked my name requested me to follow him, when he conducted me to the purser's office, in which I found Thorndyke and Miller in conversation with the purser.

"The gentlemen you are inquiring for," said the latter, "are in the smoking-room playing cards with another passenger. I have put a tarpaulin over one of the ports, in case you want to have a look at them without being seen."

"Perhaps you had better make a preliminary inspection, Miller," said Thorndyke. "You may know some of them."

To this suggestion the superintendent agreed, and forthwith went off with the purser, leaving me and Thorndyke alone. I at once took the opportunity to demand an explanation. "I take it that you struck some new evidence after I left you?"

"Yes," Thorndyke replied. "And none too soon, as you see. I don't quite know what it will amount to, but I think we have secured the defence, at any rate and that is really all that we are concerned with. The positive aspects of the case are the business of the police. But here comes Miller, looking very pleased with himself, and with the purser."

The superintendent, however, was not only pleased, he was also not a little puzzled.

"Well!" he exclaimed, "this is a quaint affair. We have got two of the leading lights of the suffrage movement in there. One is Jameson, the secretary of the Women's Emancipation League, the other is Pinder, their chief bobbery-monger. Then there are two men named Dorman and Spiller, both of them swell crooks, I am certain, though we have never been able to fix anything on them. The fifth man I don't know."

"Neither do I," said Thorndyke. "My repertoire includes only four. And now we will proceed to sort them out. Could we have a few words with Mr. Thorpe – in here, if you don't mind."

"Certainly," replied the purser. "I'll go and fetch him." He bustled away in the direction of the smoking-room, whence he presently reappeared, accompanied by a tall, lean man who wore large bi-focal spectacles of the old-fashioned, split-lens type, and was smoking a cigar. As the newcomer approached down the alley-way, it was evident that he was nervous and uneasy, though he maintained a certain jaunty swagger that accorded ill with a pronounced, habitual stoop. As he entered the cabin, however, and became aware of the portentous group of strangers, the swagger broke down completely, suddenly his face became ashen and haggard, and he peered through his great spectacles from one to the others, with an expression of undisguisable terror.

"Mr. Thorpe?" queried Thorndyke, and the superintendent murmured, "Alias Pinder."

"Yes," was the reply, in a husky undertone. "What can I do for you?"

Thorndyke turned to the superintendent. "I charge this man," said he, "with having murdered Francis Burnham in the train between London and Holmwood."

The superintendent was visibly astonished, but not more so than the accused, on whom Thorndyke's statement produced the most singular effect. In a moment, his terror seemed to drop from him, the colour returned to his face, the haggard expression of which gave place to one of obvious relief.

Miller stood up, and addressing the accused, began, "It is my duty to caution you – " but the other interrupted, "Caution your grandmother! You are talking a parcel of dam' nonsense. I was in Birmingham when the murder was committed. I can prove it, easily."

The superintendent was somewhat taken aback, for the accused spoke with a confidence that carried conviction.

"In that case," said Thorndyke, "you can probably explain how a letter belonging to you came to be found in the carriage with the murdered man."

"Belonging to me!" exclaimed Thorpe. "What the deuce do you mean? That letter belonged to Miss Dalby. The rest of it was found in her pocket."

"Precisely," said Thorndyke. "One sheet had been placed in the railway carriage and the remainder in Miss Dalby's pocket to fix suspicion on her. But it was *your* letter, and the inference is that you disposed of it in that manner for the purpose that I have stated."

"But," persisted Thorpe, with visibly-growing uneasiness, "this was a duplicated circular. You couldn't tell one copy from another."

"Mr. Pinder," said Thorndyke, in an impressively quiet tone, "if I tell you that I ascertained from that letter that you had taken a passage on this ship in the name of Thorpe, you will probably understand what I mean."

Apparently he did understand, for, once more, the colour faded from his face and he sat down heavily on a locker, fixing on Thorndyke a look of undisguised dismay. Thus he sat for some moments, motionless and silent, apparently thinking hard.

Suddenly he started up. "My God!" he exclaimed, "I see now what has happened. The infernal scoundrel! First he put it on to Miss Dalby, and now he has put it on to me. Now I understand why he looked so startled when I ran against him."

"What do you mean?" asked Thorndyke.

"I'll tell you," replied Pinder. "As I move about a good deal – and for other reasons – I used to have my suffrage letters sent to a stationer's shop in Barlow Street – "

"I know," interrupted the superintendent, "Bedall's. I used to look them over and take photographs of them." He grinned craftily as he made this statement and, rather to my surprise, the accused grinned too. A little later I understood that grin.

"Well," continued Pinder, "I used to collect these letters pretty regularly. But this last letter was delivered while I was away at Birmingham. Before I came back I met a man who gave me certain – er – *instructions* – you know what they were," he added, addressing Thorndyke, "so I did not need the letter. But, of course, I couldn't leave it there uncollected, so when I got back to London, I called for it. That was two days ago. To my astonishment Miss Bedall declared that I had collected it three days previously. I assured her that I was not in London on that day, but she was positive that I had called. 'I remember clearly,' she said, 'giving you the letter myself.' Well, there was no arguing. Evidently she had given the letter to the wrong person – she is very near-sighted, I should say, judging by the way she holds things against her nose – but how it happened I couldn't understand.

"But I think I understand now. There is one person only in the world who knew that I had my letters addressed there, a sort of pal of mine named Payne. He happened to be with me one evening when I called to collect my letters. Now, Payne chanced to be a good deal like me – at least he is tall and thin and stoops a bit, but he does not wear spectacles. He tried on my spectacles once for a joke, and then he really looked extremely like me. He looked in a mirror and remarked on the resemblance himself. Now, Payne did not belong to the Women's League, and I suggest that he took advantage of this resemblance to get possession of this letter. He got a pair of spectacles like mine and personated me at the shop."

"Why should he want to get possession of that letter?" Miller demanded.

"To plant it as he has planted it," replied Pinder, "and set the police on a false trail."

"This sounds pretty thin," said Miller. "You are accusing this man of having murdered Mr. Burnham. What grounds have you for this accusation?"

"My grounds," replied Pinder, "are, first, that he stole this letter which has been found, obviously planted and, second, that he had a grudge against Burnham and knew all about his movements."

"Indeed!" said Miller, with suddenly increased interest. "Then who and what is this man Payne?"

"Why," replied Pinder, "until a month ago, he was assistant cashier at the Streatham branch of the bank. Then Burnham came down and

419

hoofed him out without an hour's notice. I don't know what for, but I can guess."

"Do you happen to know where Payne is at this moment?"

"Yes, I do. He is on this ship, in the smoking-room – only he is Mr. Shenstone now. And mighty sick he was when he found me on board."

The superintendent looked at Thorndyke. "What do you think about it, Doctor?" he asked.

"I think," said Thorndyke, "that we had better have Mr. Shenstone in here and ask him a few questions. Would you see if you can get him to come here?" he added, addressing the purser, who had been listening with ecstatic enjoyment.

"I'll get him to come along all right," replied the purser, evidently scenting a new act in this enthralling drama, and away he bustled, all agog. In less than a minute we saw him returning down the alley-way with a tall, thin man who, at a distance, was certainly a good deal like Pinder, though the resemblance diminished as he approached. He, too, was obviously agitated, and seemed to be plying the purser with questions. But when he came opposite the door of the cabin he stopped dead and seemed disposed to shrink back.

"Is that the man?" Thorndyke demanded sharply and rather loudly, springing to his feet as he spoke.

The effect of the question was electrical. As Thorndyke rose, the new-comer turned and, violently thrusting the purser aside, raced madly down the alley-way and out on to the deck.

"Stop that man!" roared Miller, darting out in pursuit, and at the shout a couple of loitering deck-hands headed the fugitive off from the gangway. Following, I saw the terrified man swerving this way and that across the littered deck to avoid the seamen, who joined in the pursuit, I saw him make a sudden frantic burst for a baggage-slide springing from a bollard up to the bulwark-rail. Then his foot must have tripped on a lashing, for he staggered for a moment, flung out his arms with a wild shriek, and plunged headlong into the space between the ship's side and the quay wall.

In an instant the whole ship was in an uproar. An officer and two hands sprang to the rail with ropes and a boathook, while others manned the cargo derrick and lowered a rope with a running bowline between the ship and the quay.

"He's gone under," a hoarse voice proclaimed from below, "but I can see him jammed against the side."

There were a couple of minutes of sickening suspense. Then the voice from below was heard again. "Heave up!"

420

The derrick-engine rattled, the taut rope came up slowly, and at length out of that horrid gulf arose a limp and dripping shape that, as it cleared the bulwark, was swung inboard and let down gently on the deck. Thorndyke and I stooped over him. But it was a dead man's face that we looked into, and a tinge of blood on the lips told the rest of the tale.

"Cover him up," said the superintendent. "He's out of our jurisdiction now. But what's going on there?"

Following his look, I perceived a small scattered crowd of men all running furiously along the quay towards the town. Some of them I judged to be the late inmates of the smoking-room and some plain-clothes men. The only figure that I recognised was that of Mr. Pinder, and he was already growing small in the distance.

"The local police will have to deal with them," said Miller. Then turning to the purser, he asked, "What baggage had this man?"

"Only two cabin trunks," was the reply. "They are both in his state-room."

To the state-room we followed the purser, when Miller had possessed himself of the dead man's keys, and the two trunks were hoisted on to the bunk and opened. Each trunk contained a large cash-box, and each cash-box contained five hundred pounds in gold and a big bundle of notes. The latter Miller examined closely, checking their numbers by a column of entries in his pocket-book.

"Yes," he reported at length, "it's a true bill. These are the notes that were stolen from Mr. Burnham. And now I will have a look at the baggage of those other four sportsmen."

This being no affair of ours, Thorndyke and I went ashore and slowly made our way towards the town. But presently the superintendent overtook us in high glee, with the news that he had discovered what appeared to be the accumulated "swag" of a gang of swell burglars for whom he had been for some months vainly on the look-out.

"How was it done?" repeated Thorndyke in reply to Miller's question, as we sat at a retired table in the "Lord Warden" Hotel. "Well, it was really very simple. I am afraid I shall disappoint you if you expect anything ingenious and recondite. Of course, it was obvious that Miss Dalby had not committed this atrocious murder and robbery, and it was profoundly improbable that this extremely incriminating letter had been dropped accidentally. That being so, it was almost certain that the letter had been 'planted,' as Pinder expressed it. But that was a mere opinion that helped us not at all. The actual solution turned upon a simple chemical fact with which I happened to be acquainted, which is this: That all the basic coal-tar dyes, and especially methylene blue, dye oxycellulose without requiring a mordant, but do not react in this way on cellulose. Now, good paper is practically pure cellulose, and if you dip a sheet of such paper into certain oxidising liquids, such as a solution of potassium chlorate with a slight excess of hydrochloric acid, the paper is converted into oxycellulose. But if instead of immersing the paper, you write on it with a quill or glass pen dipped in the solution, only the part which has been touched by the pen is changed into oxycellulose. No change is visible to the eye, but if a sheet of paper written on with this colourless fluid is dipped in a solution of, say, methylene blue, the invisible writing immediately becomes visible. The oxycellulose takes up the blue dye.

"Now, when I picked up that sheet of the letter in the railway carriage and noted that the ink used appeared to be methylene blue, this fact was recalled to my mind. Then, on looking at it closely, I seemed to detect a certain slight spottiness in the writing. There were points on some of the letters that were a little deeper in colour than the rest, and it occurred to me that it was possible that these circulars might be used to transmit secret messages of a less innocent kind than those that met the unaided eye, just as these political societies might form an excellent cover for the operations of criminal associations. But if the circulars had been so used, it is evident that the secret writing would not be on all the circulars. The prepared sheets would be used only for the circulars that were to be sent to particular persons, and in those cases the secret writing would probably be in the nature of a personal communication, either to a particular individual or to a small group. The possible presence of a secret message thus became of vital evidential importance, for if it could be shown that this letter was addressed to some person other than Miss Dalby, that would dispose of the only evidence connecting her with the crime.

"It happened, most fortunately, that I was able to get possession of the final sheet of this letter – "

"Of course it did," growled Miller, with a sour smile.

"It reached me," continued Thorndyke, "only after Dr. Jervis had started for Densford. The greater part of one side was blank, excepting for a rough plan drawn in pencil, and this blank side I laid down on a sheet of glass and wetted the written side with a small wad of cotton-wool dipped in distilled water. Of course, the blue writing began to run and dissolve out, and then, very faintly, some other writing began to show through in reverse. I turned the paper over, and now the new writing, though faint, was quite legible, and became more so when I wiped the blue-stained cotton-wool over it a few times. A solution of methylene blue would have made it still plainer, but I used water only, as

422

I judged that the blue writing was intended to furnish the dye for development. Here is the final result."

He drew from his pocket a letter-case, from which he extracted a folded paper which he opened and laid on the table. It was stained a faint blue, through which the original writing could be seen, dim and blurred, while the secret message, though very pale, was quite sharp and clear. And this was the message:

> *. . . so although we are not actually blown on, the position is getting risky and it's time for us to hop. I have booked passages for the four of us to Ostend by* The Cornflower, *which sails on Friday evening next (20th). The names of the four illustrious passengers are, Walsh (that's me), Grubb (Dorman), Jenkins (Spiller) and Thorpe (that's you). Get those names well into your canister – better make a note of them – and turn up in good time on Friday.*

"Well," said Miller, as he handed back the letter, "we can't know everything – unless we are Dr. Thorndyke. But there's one thing I do know."

"What is that?" I asked.

"I know why that fellow Pinder grinned when I told him that I had photographed his confounded letters."

The Naturalist at Law

A hush had fallen on the court as the coroner concluded his brief introductory statement and the first witness took up his position by the long table. The usual preliminary questions elicited that Simon Moffet, the witness aforesaid, was fifty-eight years of age, that he followed the calling of a shepherd, and that he was engaged in supervising the flocks that fed upon the low-lying meadows adjoining the little town of Bantree in Buckinghamshire.

"Tell us how you came to discover the body," said the coroner.

"'Twas on Wednesday morning, about half-past five," Moffet began. "I was getting the sheep through the gate into the big meadow by Reed's Farm when I happened to look down the dyke, and then I noticed a boot sticking up out of the water. Seemed to me as if there was a foot in it by the way it stuck up, so as soon as all the sheep was in, I shut the gate and walked down the dyke to have a look at un. When I got close, I see the toe of another boot just alongside. Looks a bit queer, I thinks, but I couldn't see anything more, 'cause the duck-weed is that thick as it looks as if you could walk on it. Howsever, I clears away the weed with my stick, and then I see 'twas a dead man. Give me a rare turn, it did. He was a-layin' at the bottom of the ditch with his head near the middle and his feet up close to the bank. Just then young Harry Walker comes along the cart-track on his way to work, so I shows him the body and sends him back to the town for to give notice at the police station."

"And is that all you know about the affair?"

"Ay. Later on I see the sergeant come along with a man wheelin' the stretcher, and I showed him where the body was and helped to pull it out and load it on the stretcher. And that's all I know about it."

On this the witness was dismissed and his place taken by a shrewd-looking, business-like police sergeant, who deposed as follows,

"Last Wednesday, the 8th of May, at 6:15 a.m., I received information from Henry Walker that a dead body was lying in the ditch by the cart-track leading from Ponder's Road to Reed's Farm. I proceeded there forthwith, accompanied by Police-Constable Ketchum, and taking with us a wheeled stretcher. On the track I was met by the last witness, who conducted me to the place where the body was lying and where I found it in the position that he has described, but we had to clear away the duck-weed before we could see it distinctly. I examined the bank carefully, but could see no trace of footprints, as the grass grows thickly right down to the water's edge. There were no signs of a struggle or any disturbance on the bank. With the aid of Moffet and Ketchum, I drew the body out and placed it on the stretcher. I could not see any injuries or marks of violence on the body or anything unusual about it. I conveyed it to the mortuary, and with Constable Ketchum's assistance removed the clothing and emptied the pockets, putting the contents of each pocket in a separate envelope and writing the description on each. In a letter-case from the coat pocket were some visiting cards bearing the name and address of Mr. Cyrus Pedley, of 21 Hawtrey Mansions, Kensington, and a letter signed Wilfred Pedley, apparently from deceased's brother. Acting on instructions, I communicated with him and served a summons to attend this inquest."

"With regard to the ditch in which you found the body," said the coroner, "can you tell us how deep it is?"

"Yes, I measured it with Moffet's crook and a tape measure. In the deepest part, where the body was lying, it is four-feet-two-inches deep. From there it slopes up pretty sharply to the bank."

"So far as you can judge, if a grown man fell into the ditch by accident, would he have any difficulty in getting out?"

"None at all, I should say, if he were sober and in ordinary health. A man of medium height, standing in the middle at the deepest part, would have his head and shoulders out of water, and the sides are not too steep to climb up easily, especially with the grass and rushes on the bank to lay hold of."

"You say there were no signs of disturbance on the bank. Were there any in the ditch itself?

"None that I could see. But, of course, signs of disturbance soon disappear in water. The duck-weed drifts about as the wind drives it, and there are creatures moving about on the bottom. I noticed that deceased had some weed grasped in one hand."

This concluded the sergeant's evidence, and as he retired, the name of Dr. Albert Parton was called. The new witness was a young man of grave and professional aspect, who gave his evidence with an extreme regard for clearness and accuracy.

"I have made an examination of the body of the deceased," he began, after the usual preliminaries. "It is that of a healthy man of about forty-five. I first saw it about two hours after it was found. It had then been dead from twelve to fifteen hours. Later I made a complete examination. I found no injuries, marks of violence or any definite bruises, and no signs of disease."

"Did you ascertain the cause of death?" the coroner asked.

"Yes. The cause of death was drowning."

"You are quite sure of that?"

425

"Quite sure. The lungs contained a quantity of water and duck-weed, and there was more than a quart of water mixed with duck-weed and water-weed in the stomach. That is a clear proof of death by drowning. The water in the lungs was the immediate cause of death, by making breathing impossible, and as the water and weed in the stomach must have been swallowed, they furnish conclusive evidence that deceased was alive when he fell into the water."

"The water and weed could not have got into the stomach after death?

"No, that is quite impossible. They must have been swallowed when the head of the deceased was just below the surface, and the water must have been drawn into the lungs by spasmodic efforts to breathe when the mouth was under water."

"Did you find any signs indicating that deceased might have been intoxicated?"

"No. I examined the water from the stomach very carefully with that question in view, but there was no trace of alcohol – or, indeed, of anything else. It was simple ditch-water. As the point is important I have preserved it, and – " here the witness produced a paper parcel which he unfastened, revealing a large glass jar containing about a quart of water plentifully sprinkled with duck-weed. This he presented to the coroner, who waved it away hastily and indicated the jury, to whom it was then offered and summarily rejected with emphatic head-shakes. Finally it came to rest on the table by the place where I was sitting with my colleague, Dr. Thorndyke, and our client, Mr. Wilfred Pedley. I glanced at it with faint interest, noting how the duck-weed plants had risen to the surface and floated, each with its tassel of roots hanging down into the water, and how a couple of tiny, flat shells, like miniature ammonites, had sunk and lay on the bottom of the jar. Thorndyke also glanced at it – indeed, he did more than glance, for he drew the jar towards him and examined its contents in the systematic way in which it was his habit to examine everything. Meanwhile the coroner asked, "Did you find anything abnormal or unusual, or anything that could throw light on how deceased came to be in the water?"

"Nothing whatever," was the reply. "I found simply that the deceased met his death by drowning."

Here, as the witness seemed to have finished his evidence, Thorndyke interposed.

"The witness states, sir, there were no definite bruises. Does he mean that there were any marks that *might* have been bruises?"

The coroner glanced at Dr. Parton, who replied, "There was a faint mark on the outside of the right arm, just above the elbow, which had

426

somewhat the appearance of a bruise, as if the deceased had been struck with a stick. But it was very indistinct. I shouldn't like to swear that it was a bruise at all."

This concluded the doctor's evidence, and when he had retired, the name of our client, Wilfred Pedley, was called. He rose and, having taken the oath and given his name and address, deposed, "I have viewed the body of deceased. It is that of my brother, Cyrus Pedley, who is forty-three years of age. The last time I saw the deceased alive was on Tuesday morning, the day before the body was found."

"Did you notice anything unusual in his manner or state of mind?"

The witness hesitated but at length replied, "Yes. He seemed anxious and depressed. He had been in low spirits for some time past, but on this occasion he seemed more so than usual."

"Had you any reason to suspect that he might contemplate taking his life?"

"No," the witness replied, emphatically, "and I do not believe that he would, under any circumstances, have contemplated suicide."

"Have you any special reason for that belief?"

"Yes. He was a highly conscientious man and he was in my debt. He had occasion to borrow two-thousand pounds from me, and the debt was secured by an insurance on his life. If he had committed suicide, that insurance would be invalidated and the debt would remain unpaid. From my knowledge of him, I feel certain that he would not have done such a thing."

The coroner nodded gravely and then asked, "What was deceased's occupation?"

"He was employed in some way by the Foreign Office, I don't know in what capacity. I know very little about his affairs."

"Do you know if he had any money worries or any troubles or embarrassments of any kind?"

"I have never heard of any, but he was a very reticent man. He lived alone in his flat, taking his meals at his club, and no one knew – at least, I did not – how he spent his time or what was the state of his finances. He was not married, and I am his only near relative."

"And as to deceased's habits. Was he ever addicted to taking more stimulants than was good for him?"

"Never," the witness replied emphatically. "He was a most temperate and abstemious man."

"Was he subject to fits of any kind, or fainting attacks?"

"I have never heard that he was."

"Can you account for his being in this solitary place at this time – apparently about eight o'clock at night?"

"I cannot. It is a complete mystery to me. I know of no one with whom either of us was acquainted in this district. I had never heard of the place until I got the summons to the inquest."

This was the sum of our client's evidence and so far, things did not look very favourable from our point of view – we were retained on the insurance question – to rebut, if possible, the suggestion of suicide. However, the coroner was a discreet man, and having regard to the obscurity of the case – and perhaps to the interests involved – summed up in favour of an open verdict, and the jury, taking a similar view, found that deceased met his death by drowning, but under what circumstances there was no evidence to show.

"Well," I said, as the court rose, "that leaves it to the insurance people to make out a case of suicide if they can. I think you are fairly safe, Mr. Pedley. There is no positive evidence."

"No," our client replied. "But it isn't only the money I am thinking of. It would be some consolation to me for the loss of my poor brother if I had some idea how he met with his death, and could feel sure that it was an unavoidable misadventure. And for my own satisfaction – leaving the insurance out of the question – I should like to have definite proof that it was not suicide."

He looked half-questioningly at Thorndyke, who nodded gravely. "Yes," the latter agreed, "the suggestion of suicide ought to be disposed of if possible, both for legal and sentimental reasons. How far away is the mortuary?"

"A couple of minutes' walk," replied Mr. Pedley. "Did you wish to inspect the body?"

"If it is permissible," replied Thorndyke, "and then I propose to have a look at the place where the body was found."

"In that case," our client said, "I will go down to the Station Hotel and wait for you. We may as well travel up to town together, and you can then tell me if you have seen any further light on the mystery."

As soon as he was gone, Dr. Parton advanced, tying the string of the parcel which once more enclosed the jar of ditch-water.

"I heard you say, sir, that you would like to inspect the body," said he. "If you like, I will show you the way to the mortuary. The sergeant will let us in. Won't you, Sergeant? This gentleman is a doctor as well as a lawyer."

"Bless you, sir," said the sergeant, "I know who Dr. Thorndyke is, and I shall feel it an honour to show him anything he wishes to see."

Accordingly we set forth together, Dr. Parton and Thorndyke leading the way.

"The coroner and the jury didn't seem to appreciate my exhibit," the former remarked with a faint grin, tapping the parcel as he spoke.

"No," Thorndyke agreed, "and it is hardly reasonable to expect a layman to share our own matter-of-fact outlook. But you were quite right to produce the specimen. That ditch-water furnishes conclusive evidence on a vitally material question. Further, I would advise you to preserve that jar for the present, well-covered and under lock-and-key."

Parton looked surprised. "Why?" he asked. "The inquest is over and the verdict pronounced."

"Yes, but it was an open verdict, and an open verdict leaves the case in the air. The inquest has thrown no light on the question as to how Cyrus Pedley came by his death."

"There doesn't seem to me much mystery about it," said the doctor. "Here is a man found drowned in a shallow ditch which he could easily have got out of if he had fallen in by accident. He was not drunk. Apparently he was not in a fit of any kind. There are no marks of violence and no signs of a struggle, and the man is known to have been in an extremely depressed state of mind. It looks like a clear case of suicide, though I admit that the jury were quite right, in the absence of direct evidence."

"Well," said Thorndyke, "it will be my duty to contest that view if the insurance company dispute the claim on those grounds."

"I can't think what you will have to offer in answer to the suggestion of suicide," said Parton.

"Neither can I, at present," replied Thorndyke. "But the case doesn't look to me quite so simple as it does to you."

"You think it possible that an analysis of the contents of this jar may be called for?"

"That is a possibility," replied Thorndyke. "But I mean that the case is obscure, and that some further inquiry into the circumstances of this man's death is by no means unlikely."

"Then," said Parton, "I will certainly follow your advice and lock up this precious jar. But here we are at the mortuary. Is there anything in particular that you want to see?"

"I want to see all that there is to see," Thorndyke replied. "The evidence has been vague enough so far. Shall we begin with that bruise or mark that you mentioned?"

Dr. Parton advanced to the grim, shrouded figure that lay on the slate-topped table, like some solemn effigy on an altar tomb, and drew back the sheet that covered it. We all approached, stepping softly, and stood beside the table, looking down with a certain awesome curiosity at the still, waxen figure that, but a few hours since, had been a living man

429

like ourselves. The body was that of a good-looking, middle-aged man with a refined, intelligent face – slightly disfigured by a scar on the cheek – now set in the calm, reposeful expression that one so usually finds on the faces of the drowned, with drowsy, half-closed eyes and slightly parted lips that revealed a considerable gap in the upper front teeth.

Thorndyke stood awhile looking down on the dead man with a curious questioning expression. Then his eye travelled over the body, from the placid face to the marble-like torso and the hand which, though now relaxed, still lightly grasped a tuft of water-weed. The latter Thorndyke gently disengaged from the limp hand, and after a glance at the dark green, feathery fronds, laid it down and stooped to examine the right arm at the spot above the elbow that Parton had spoken of.

"Yes," he said, "I think I should call it a bruise, though it is very faint. As you say, it might have been produced by a blow with a stick or rod. I notice that there are some teeth missing. Presumably he wore a plate?"

"Yes," replied Parton, "a smallish gold plate with four teeth on it – at least, so his brother told me. Of course, it fell out when he was in the water, but it hasn't been found – in fact, it hasn't been looked for."

Thorndyke nodded and then turned to the sergeant. "Could I see what you found in the pockets?" he asked.

The sergeant complied readily, and my colleague watched his orderly procedure with evident approval. The collection of envelopes was produced from an attaché case and conveyed to a side table, where the sergeant emptied out the contents of each into a little heap, opposite which he placed the appropriate envelope with its written description. Thorndyke ran his eye over the collection – which was commonplace enough – until he came to the tobacco pouch, from which protruded the corner of a scrap of crumpled paper. This he drew forth and smoothed out the creases, when it was seen to be a railway receipt for an excess fare.

"Seems to have lost his ticket or travelled without one," the sergeant remarked. "But not on this line."

"No," agreed Thorndyke. "It is the Tilbury and Southend line. But you notice the date. It is the 18th, and the body was found on the morning of Wednesday, the 19th. So it would appear that he must have come into this neighbourhood in the evening, and that he must have come either by way of London or by a very complicated cross-country route. I wonder what brought him here."

He produced his notebook and was beginning to copy the receipt when the sergeant said, "You had better take the paper, sir. It is of no use to us now, and it isn't very easy to make out."

430

Thorndyke thanked the officer and, handing me the paper, asked, "What do you make of it, Jervis?"

I scrutinised the little crumpled scrap and deciphered with difficulty the hurried scrawl, scribbled with a hard, ill-sharpened pencil.

"It seems to read '*Ldn to C.B*'. or '*S.B*', '*Hlt*' – that is some '*Halt*,' I presume. But the amount, *4/9*, is clear enough, and that will give us a clue if we want one." I returned the paper to Thorndyke, who bestowed it in his pocket-book and then remarked, "I don't see any keys."

"No, sir," replied the sergeant, "there aren't any. Rather queer, that, for he must have had at least a latch key. They must have fallen out into the water."

"That is possible," said Thorndyke, "but it would be worth while to make sure. Is there anyone who could show us the place where the body was found?"

"I will walk up there with you myself, sir, with pleasure," said the sergeant, hastily repacking the envelopes. "It is only a quarter-of-an-hour's walk from here."

"That is very good of you, Sergeant," my colleague responded, "and as we seem to have seen everything here, I propose that we start at once. You are not coming with us, Parton?"

"No," the doctor replied. "I have finished with the case and I have got my work to do." He shook hands with us heartily and watched us – with some curiosity, I think – as we set forth in company with the sergeant.

His curiosity did not seem to me to be unjustified. In fact, I shared it. The presence of the police officer precluded discussion, but as we took our way out of the town I found myself speculating curiously on my colleague's proceedings. To me, suicide was written plainly on every detail of the case. Of course, we did not wish to take that view, but what other was possible? Had Thorndyke some alternative theory? Or was he merely, according to his invariable custom, making an impartial survey of everything, no matter how apparently trivial, in the hope of lighting on some new and informative fact?

The temporary absence of the sergeant, who had stopped to speak to a constable on duty, enabled me to put the question, "Is this expedition intended to clear up anything in particular?"

"No," he replied, "excepting the keys, which ought to be found. But you must see for yourself that this is not a straightforward case. That man did not come all this way merely to drown himself in a ditch. I am quite in the dark at present, so there is nothing for it but to examine everything with our own eyes and see if there is anything that has been overlooked

431

that may throw some light on either the motive or the circumstances. It is always desirable to examine the scene of a crime or a tragedy."

Here the return of the sergeant put a stop to the discussion and we proceeded on our way in silence. Already we had passed out of the town, and we now turned out of the main road into a lane or by-road, bordered by meadows and orchards and enclosed by rather high hedgerows.

"This is Ponder's Road," said the sergeant. "It leads to Renham, a couple of miles farther on, where it joins the Aylesbury Road. The cart track is on the left a little way along."

A few minutes later we came to our turning, a narrow and rather muddy lane, the entrance to which was shaded by a grove of tall elms. Passing through this shady avenue, we came out on a grass-covered track, broken by deep wagon-ruts and bordered on each side by a ditch, beyond which was a wide expanse of marshy meadows.

"This is the place," said the sergeant, halting by the side of the right-hand ditch and indicating a spot where the rushes had been flattened down. "It was just as you see it now – only the feet were just visible sticking out of the duck-weed, which had drifted back after Moffet had disturbed it."

We stood awhile looking at the ditch, with its thick mantle of bright green, spotted with innumerable small dark objects and showing here and there a faint track where a water-vole had swum across.

"Those little dark objects are water-snails, I suppose," said I, by way of making some kind of remark.

"Yes," replied Thorndyke, "the common Amber shell, I think – *Succinea putris*." He reached out his stick and fished up a sample of the duck-weed, on which one or two of the snails were crawling. "Yes," he repeated. "*Succinea putris* it is, a queer little left-handed shell, with the spire, as you see, all lop-sided. They have a habit of swarming in this extraordinary way. You notice that the ditch is covered with them."

I had already observed this, but it hardly seemed to be worth commenting on under the present circumstances – which was apparently the sergeant's view also, for he looked at Thorndyke with some surprise, which developed into impatience when my colleague proceeded further to expand on the subject of natural history.

"These water-weeds," he observed, "are very remarkable plants in their various ways. Look at this duck-weed, for instance. Just a little green oval disc with a single root hanging down into the water, like a tiny umbrella with a long handle, and yet it is a complete plant, and a flowering plant, too." He picked a specimen off the end of his stick and held it up by its root to exhibit its umbrella-like form and, as he did so, he looked in my face with an expression that I felt to be somehow

432

significant, but of which I could not extract the meaning. But there was no difficulty in interpreting the expression on the sergeant's face. He had come here on business and he wanted to "cut the cackle and get to the hosses".

"Well, Sergeant," said Thorndyke, "there isn't much to see, but I think we ought to have a look for those keys. He must have had keys of some kind, if only a latchkey, and they must be in this ditch."

The sergeant was not enthusiastic. "I've no doubt you are right, sir," said he, "but I don't see that we should be much forrader if we found them. However, we may as well have a look, only I can't stay more than a few minutes. I've got my work to do at the station."

"Then," said Thorndyke, "let us get to work at once. We had better hook out the weed and look it over, and if the keys are not in that, we must try to expose the bottom where the body was lying. You must tell us if we are working in the right place."

With this he began, with the crooked handle of his stick, to rake up the tangle of weed that covered the bottom of the ditch and drag the detached masses ashore, piling them on the bank and carefully looking them through to see if the keys should chance to be entangled in their meshes. In this work I took my part under the sergeant's direction, raking in load after load of the delicate, stringy weed, on the pale green ribbon-like leaves of which multitudes of the water-snails were creeping, and sorting over each batch in hopeless and fruitless search for the missing keys. In about ten minutes we had removed the entire weedy covering from the bottom of the ditch over an area of from eight to nine feet – the place which, according to the sergeant, the body had occupied, and as the duck-weed had been caught by the tangled masses of water-weed that we had dragged ashore, we now had an uninterrupted view of the cleared space, save for the clouds of mud that we had stirred up.

"We must give the mud a few minutes to settle," said Thorndyke.

"Yes," the sergeant agreed, "it will take some time, and as it doesn't really concern me now that the inquest is over, I think I will get back to the station, if you will excuse me."

Thorndyke excused him very willingly, I think, though politely and with many thanks for his help. When he had gone I remarked, "I am inclined to agree with the sergeant. If we find the keys, we shan't be much forrader."

"We shall know that he had them with him," he replied. "Though, of course, if we don't find them, that will not prove that they are not here. Still, I think we should try to settle the question."

His answer left me quite unconvinced, but the care with which he searched the ditch and sorted out the weed left me in no doubt that, to

433

him, the matter seemed to be of some importance. However, nothing came of the search. If the keys were there, they were buried in the mud, and eventually we had to give up the search and make our way back towards the station.

As we passed out of the lane into Ponder's Road, Thorndyke stopped at the entrance, under the trees, by a little triangle of turf which marked the beginning of the lane, and looked down at the muddy ground.

"Here is quite an interesting thing, Jervis," he remarked, "which shows us how standardised objects tend to develop an individual character. These are the tracks of a car, or more probably a tradesman's van, which was fitted with Barlow tyres. Now there must be thousands of vans fitted with these tyres, they are the favourite type for light covered vans, and when new they are all alike and indistinguishable. Yet this tyre – of the off-hind wheel – has acquired a character which would enable one to pick it out with certainty from ten-thousand others. First, you see, there is a deep cut in the tyre at an angle of forty-five, then a kidney-shaped 'Blakey' has stuck in the outer tyre without puncturing the inner, and finally some adhesive object – perhaps a lump of pitch from a newly-mended road – has become fixed on just behind the 'Blakey'. Now, if we make a rough sketch of those three marks and indicate their distance apart, thus – " here he made a rapid sketch in his notebook, and wrote in the intervals in inches " – we have the means of swearing to the identity of a vehicle which we have never seen."

"And which," I added, "had for some reason swerved over to the wrong side of the road. Yes, I should say that tyre is certainly unique. But surely most tyres are identifiable when they have been in use for some time."

"Exactly," he replied. "That was my point. The standardised thing is devoid of character only when it is new."

It was not a very subtle point, and as it was fairly obvious I made no comment, but presently reverted to the case of Pedley, deceased.

"I don't quite see why you are taking all this trouble. The insurance claim is not likely to be contested. No one can prove that it was a case of suicide, though I should think no one will feel any doubt that it was – at least that is my own feeling."

Thorndyke looked at me with an expression of reproach.

"I am afraid that my learned friend has not been making very good use of his eyes," said he. "He has allowed his attention to be distracted by superficial appearances."

"You don't think that it was suicide, then?" I asked, considerably taken aback.

"It isn't a question of thinking," he replied. "It was certainly not suicide. There are the plainest indications of homicide and, of course, in the particular circumstances, homicide means murder."

I was thunderstruck. In my own mind I had dismissed the case somewhat contemptuously as a mere commonplace suicide. As my friend had truly said, I had accepted the obvious appearances and let them mislead me, whereas Thorndyke had followed his golden rule of accepting nothing and observing everything. But what was it that he had observed? I knew that it was useless to ask, but still I ventured on a tentative question.

"When did you come to the conclusion that it was a case of homicide?"

"As soon as I had had a good look at the place where the body was found," he replied promptly.

This did not help me much, for I had given very little attention to anything but the search for the keys. The absence of those keys was, of course, a suspicious fact – if it was a fact. But we had not proved their absence, we had only failed to find them.

"What do you propose to do next?" I asked.

"Evidently," he answered, "there are two things to be done. One is to test the murder theory – to look for more evidence for or against it. The other is to identify the murderer, if possible. But really the two problems are one, since they involve the questions: 'Who had a motive for killing Cyrus Pedley?' and 'Who had the opportunity and the means?'"

Our discussion brought us to the station where, outside the hotel, we found Mr. Pedley waiting for us.

"I am glad you have come," said he. "I was beginning to fear that we should lose this train. I suppose there is no new light on this mysterious affair?"

"No," Thorndyke replied. "Rather there is a new problem. No keys were found in your brother's pockets, and we have failed to find them in the ditch – though, of course, they may be there."

"They must be," said Pedley. "They must have fallen out of his pocket and got buried in the mud, unless he lost them previously, which is most unlikely. It is a pity, though. We shall have to break open his cabinets and drawers, which he would have hated. He was very fastidious about his furniture."

"You will have to break into his flat, too," said I.

"No," he replied, "I shan't have to do that. I have a duplicate of his latchkey. He had a spare bedroom which he let me use if I wanted to stay in town." As he spoke, he produced his key-bunch and exhibited a small Chubb latchkey. "I wish we had the others, though," he added.

Here the up-train was heard approaching and we hurried onto the platform, selecting an empty first-class compartment as it drew up. As soon as the train had started, Thorndyke began his inquiries, to which I listened attentively.

"You said that your brother had been anxious and depressed lately. Was there anything more than this? Any nervousness or foreboding?"

"Well, yes," replied Pedley. "Looking back, I seem to see that the possibility of death was in his mind. A week or two ago, he brought his will to me to see if it was quite satisfactory to me as the principal beneficiary and he handed to me his last receipt for the insurance premium. That looks a little suggestive."

"It does," Thorndyke agreed. "And as to his occupation and his associates: What do you know about them?"

"His private friends are mostly my own, but of his official associates I know nothing. He was connected with the Foreign Office, but in what capacity I don't know at all. He was extremely reticent on the subject. I only know that he travelled about a good deal, presumably on official business."

This was not very illuminating, but it was all our client had to tell, and the conversation languished somewhat until the train drew up at Marylebone, when Thorndyke said, as if by an after-thought, "You have your brother's latchkey. How would it be if we just took a glance at the flat? Have you time now?"

"I will make time," was the reply, "if you want to see the flat. I don't see what you could learn from inspecting it, but that is your affair. I am in your hands."

"I should like to look round the rooms," Thorndyke answered, and as our client assented, we approached a taxi-cab and entered while Pedley gave the driver the necessary directions. A quarter-of-an-hour later we drew up opposite a tall block of buildings, and Mr. Pedley, having paid off the cab, led the way to the lift.

The dead man's flat was on the third floor and, like the others, was distinguished only by the number on the door. Mr. Pedley inserted the key into the latch and, having opened the door, preceded us across the small lobby into the sitting-room.

"Ha!" he exclaimed, as he entered. "This solves your problem." As he spoke, he pointed to the table, on which lay a small bunch of keys, including a latch key similar to the one that he had shown us. "But," he continued, "it is rather extraordinary. It just shows what a very disturbed state his mind must have been in."

"Yes," Thorndyke agreed, looking critically about the room, "and as the latchkey is there, it raises the question whether the keys may have been out of his possession. Do you know what the various locked receptacles contain?"

"I know pretty well what is in the bureau, but as to the cupboard above it, I have never seen it open and don't know what he kept in it. I always assumed that he reserved it for his official papers. I will just see if anything seems to have been disturbed."

He unlocked and opened the flap of the old-fashioned bureau and pulled out the small drawers one after the other, examining the contents of each. Then he opened each of the larger drawers and turned over the various articles in them. As he closed the last one, he reported, "Everything seems to be in order – cheque-book, insurance policy, a few share certificates, and so on. Nothing seems to have been touched. Now we will try the cupboard, though I don't suppose its contents would be of much interest to anyone but himself. I wonder which is the key."

He looked at the keyhole and made a selection from the bunch, but it was evidently the wrong key. He tried another and yet another with a like result, until he had exhausted the resources of the bunch.

"It is very remarkable," he said. "None of these keys seems to fit. I wonder if he kept this particular key locked up or hidden. It wasn't in the bureau. Will you try what you can do?"

He handed the bunch to Thorndyke, who tried all the keys in succession with the same result. None of them was the key belonging to the lock. At length, having tried them all, he inserted one and turned it as far as it would go. Then he gave a sharp pull, and immediately the door came open.

"Why, it was unlocked after all!" exclaimed Mr. Pedley. "And there is nothing in it. That is why there was no key on the bunch. Apparently he didn't use the cupboard."

Thorndyke looked critically at the single vacant shelf, drawing his finger along it in two places and inspecting his finger-tips. Then he turned his attention to the lock, which was of the kind that is screwed on the inside of the door, leaving the bolt partly exposed. He took the bolt in his fingers and pushed it out and then in again, and by the way it moved I could see that the spring was broken. On this he made no comment, but remarked, "The cupboard has been in use pretty lately. You can see the trace of a largish volume – possibly a box-file – on the shelf. There is hardly any dust there, whereas the rest of the shelf is fairly thickly coated. However, that does not carry us very far, and the appearance of the rooms is otherwise quite normal."

"Quite," agreed Pedley. "But why shouldn't it be? You didn't suspect – "

"I was merely testing the suggestion offered by the absence of the keys," said Thorndyke. "By the way, have you communicated with the Foreign Office?"

"No," was the reply, "but I suppose I ought to. What had I better say to them?"

"I should merely state the facts in the first instance. But you can, if you like, say that I definitely reject the idea of suicide."

"I am glad to hear you say that," said Pedley. "Can I give any reasons for your opinion?"

"Not in the first place," replied Thorndyke. "I will consider the case and let you have a reasoned report in a day or two, which you can show to the Foreign Office and also to the insurance company."

Mr. Pedley looked as if he would have liked to ask some further questions, but as Thorndyke now made his way to the door, he followed in silence, pocketing the keys as we went out. He accompanied us down to the entry and there we left him, setting forth in the direction of South Kensington Station.

"It looked to me," said I, as soon as we were out of ear-shot, "as if that lock had been forced. What do you think?"

"Well," he answered, "locks get broken in ordinary use, but taking all the facts together, I think you are right. There are too many coincidences for reasonable probability. First, this man leaves his keys, including his latchkey, on the table, which is an extraordinary thing to do. On that very occasion, he is found dead under inexplicable circumstances. Then, of all the locks in his rooms, the one which happens to be broken is the one of which the key is not on the bunch. That is a very suspicious group of facts."

"It is," I agreed. "And if there is, as you say – though I can't imagine on what grounds – evidence of foul play, that makes it still more suspicious. But what is the next move? Have you anything in view?"

"The next move," he replied, "is to clear up the mystery of the dead man's movements on the day of his death. The railway receipt shows that on that day be travelled down somewhere into Essex. From that place, he took a long, cross-country journey of which the destination was a ditch by a lonely meadow in Buckinghamshire. The questions that we have to answer are: What was he doing in Essex? Why did he make that strange journey? Did he make it alone? And, if not, who accompanied him?

"Now, obviously, the first thing to do is to locate that place in Essex, and when we have done that, to go down there and see if we can pick up any traces of the dead man."

"That sounds like a pretty vague quest," said I, "but if we fail, the police may be able to find out something. By the way, we want a new *Bradshaw*."

"An excellent suggestion, Jervis," said he. "I will get one as we go into the station."

A few minutes later, as we sat on a bench waiting for our train, he passed to me the open copy of *Bradshaw*, with the crumpled railway receipt.

"You see," said he, "it was apparently '*G.B.Hlt.*,' and the fare from London was four-and-ninepence. Here is Great Buntingfield Halt, the fare to which is four-and-ninepence. That must be the place. At any rate, we will give it a trial. May I take it that you are coming to lend a hand? I shall start in good time to-morrow morning."

I assented emphatically. Never had I been more completely in the dark than I was in this case, and seldom had I known Thorndyke to be more positive and confident. Obviously, he had something up his sleeve, and I was racked with curiosity as to what that something was.

On the following morning we made a fairly early start, and half-past-ten found us seated in the train, looking out across a dreary waste of marshes, with the estuary of the Thames a mile or so distant. For the first time in my recollection Thorndyke had come unprovided with his inevitable "research case", but I noted that he had furnished himself with a botanist's vasculum – or tin collecting-case – and that his pocket bulged as if he had some other appliances concealed about his person. Also that he carried a walking-stick that was strange to me.

"This will be our destination, I think," he said, as the train slowed down, and sure enough it presently came to rest beside a little makeshift platform on which was displayed the name "*Great Buntingfield Halt*". We were the only passengers to alight, and the guard, having noted the fact, blew his whistle and dismissed the little station with a contemptuous wave of his flag.

Thorndyke lingered on the platform after the train had gone, taking a general survey of the country. Half-a-mile away to the north a small village was visible, while to the south the marshes stretched away to the river, their bare expanse unbroken save by a solitary building whose unredeemed hideousness proclaimed it a factory of some kind. Presently the station-master approached deferentially, and as we proffered our tickets, Thorndyke remarked, "You don't seem overburdened with traffic here."

"No, sir. You're right," was the emphatic reply. "'Tis a dead-alive place. Excepting the people at the Golomite Works and one now and then from the village, no one uses the halt. You're the first strangers I've seen for more than a month."

"Indeed," said Thorndyke. "But I think you are forgetting one. An acquaintance of mine came here last Tuesday – and by the same token, he hadn't got a ticket and had to pay his fare."

"Oh, I remember," the station-master replied. "You mean a gentleman with a scar on his cheek. But I don't count him as a stranger. He has been here before. I think he is connected with the works, as he always goes up their road."

"Do you happen to remember what time he came back?" Thorndyke asked.

"He didn't come back at all," was the reply. "I am sure of that, because I work the halt-and-level crossing by myself. I remember thinking it queer that he didn't come back, because the ticket that he had lost was a return. He must have gone back in the van belonging to the works – that one that you see coming towards the crossing."

As he spoke, he pointed to a van that was approaching down the factory road – a small covered van with the name *"Golomite Works"* painted, not on the cover, but on a board that was attached to it. The station-master walked towards the crossing to open the gates, and we followed, and when the van had passed, Thorndyke wished our friend "Good morning," and led the way along the road, looking about him with lively interest and rather with the air of one looking for something in particular.

We had covered about two-thirds of the distance to the factory when the road approached a wide ditch, and from the attention with which my friend regarded it, I suspected that this was the something for which he had been looking. It was, however, quite unapproachable, for it was bordered by a wide expanse of soft mud thickly covered with rushes and trodden deeply by cattle. Nevertheless, Thorndyke followed its margin, still looking about him keenly, until, about a couple of hundred yards from the factory, I observed a small decayed wooden staging or quay, apparently the remains of a vanished footbridge. Here Thorndyke halted and unbuttoning his coat, began to empty out his pockets, producing first the vasculum, then a small case containing three wide-mouthed bottles – both of which he deposited on the ground – and finally a sort of miniature landing-net, which he proceeded to screw on to the ferrule of his stick.

"I take it," said I, "that these proceedings are a blind to cover some sort of observations."

"Not at all," he replied. "We are engaged in the study of pond and ditch natural history, and a most fascinating and instructive study it is.

440

The variety of forms is endless. This ditch, you observe, like the one at Bantree, is covered with a dense growth of duck-weed, but whereas that ditch was swarming with *succinea*, here there is not a single *succinea* to be seen."

I grunted a sulky assent, and watched suspiciously as he filled the bottles with water from the ditch and then made a preliminary sweep with his net.

"Here is a trial sample," said he, holding the loaded net towards me. "Duck-weed, horn-weed, *Planorbis nautileus*, but no *succinea*. What do you think of it, Jervis?"

I looked distastefully at the repulsive mess, but yet with attention, for I realised that there was a meaning in his question. And then, suddenly, my attention sharpened. I picked out of the net a strand of dark green, plumy weed and examined it. "So this is horn-weed," I said. "Then it was a piece of horn-weed that Cyrus Pedley held grasped in his hand, and now I come to think of it, I don't remember seeing any horn-weed in the ditch at Bantree."

He nodded approvingly. "There wasn't any," said he.

"And these little ammonite-like shells are just like those that I noticed at the bottom of Dr. Parton's jar. But I don't remember seeing any in the Bantree ditch."

"There were none there," said he. "And the duck-weed?"

"Oh, well," I replied, "duck-weed is duck-weed, and there's an end of it."

He chuckled aloud at my answer, and quoting, "'*A primrose by the river's brim, A yellow primrose was to him*'," bestowed a part of the catch in the vasculum, then turned once more to the ditch and began to ply his net vigorously, emptying out each netful on the grass, looking it over quickly and then making a fresh sweep, dragging the net each time through the mud at the bottom. I watched him now with a new and very lively interest, for enlightenment was dawning, mingled with some self-contempt and much speculation as to how Thorndyke had got his start in this case.

But I was not the only interested watcher. At one of the windows of the factory I presently observed a man who seemed to be looking our way. After a few seconds' inspection he disappeared, to reappear almost immediately with a pair of field-glasses, through which he took a long look at us. Then he disappeared again, but in less than a minute I saw him emerge from a side door and advance hurriedly towards us.

"We are going to have a notice of ejectment served on us, I fancy," said I.

Thorndyke glanced quickly at the approaching stranger but continued to ply his net, working, as I noticed, methodically from left to right. When the man came within fifty yards he hailed us with a brusque inquiry as to what our business was. I went forward to meet him and, if possible, to detain him in conversation, but this plan failed, for he ignored me and bore straight down on Thorndyke.

"Now, then," said he, "what's the game? What are you doing here?"

Thorndyke was in the act of raising his net from the water, but he now suddenly let it fall to the bottom of the ditch while he turned to confront the stranger.

"I take it that you have some reason for asking," said he.

"Yes, I have," the other replied angrily and with a slight foreign accent that agreed with his appearance – he looked like a Slav of some sort. "This is private land. It belongs to the factory. I am the manager."

"The land is not enclosed," Thorndyke remarked.

"I tell you the land is private land," the fellow retorted excitedly. "You have no business here. I want to know what you are doing."

"My good sir," said Thorndyke, "there is no need to excite yourself. My friend and I are just collecting botanical and other specimens."

"How do I know that?" the manager demanded. He looked round suspiciously and his eye lighted on the vasculum. "What have you got in that thing?" he asked.

"Let him see what is in it," said Thorndyke, with a significant look at me.

Interpreting this as an instruction to occupy the man's attention for a few moments, I picked up the vasculum and placed myself so that he must turn his back to Thorndyke to look into it. I fumbled awhile with the catch, but at length opened the case and began to pick out the weed strand by strand. As soon as the stranger's back was turned Thorndyke raised his net and quickly picked out of it something which he slipped into his pocket. Then he advanced towards us, sorting out the contents of his net as he came.

"Well," he said, "you see we are just harmless naturalists. By the way, what did you think we were looking for?"

"Never mind what I thought!" the other replied fiercely. "This is private land. You have no business here, and you have got to clear out."

"Very well," said Thorndyke. "As you please. There are plenty of other ditches." He took the vasculum and the case of bottles and, having put them in his pocket, unscrewed his net, wished the stranger, "Good-morning," and turned back towards the station. The man stood watching us until we were near the level crossing, when he, too, turned back and retired to the factory.

442

"I saw you take something out of the net," said I. "What was it?"

He glanced back to make sure that the manager was out of sight. Then he put his hand in his pocket, drew it out closed, and suddenly opened it. In his palm lay a small gold dental plate with four teeth on it.

"My word!" I exclaimed, "this clenches the matter with a vengeance. That is certainly Cyrus Pedley's plate. It corresponds exactly to the description."

"Yes," he replied, "it is practically a certainty. Of course, it will have to be identified by the dentist who made it. But it is a foregone conclusion."

I reflected as we walked towards the station on the singular sureness with which Thorndyke had followed what was to me an invisible trail. Presently I said, "What is puzzling me is how you got your start in this case. What gave you the first hint that it was homicide and not suicide or misadventure?"

"It was the old story, Jervis," he replied. "Just a matter of observing and remembering apparently trivial details. Here, by the way, is a case in point."

He stopped and looked down at a set of tracks in the soft, earth road – apparently those of the van which we had seen cross the line. I followed the direction of his glance and saw the clear impression of a Blakey's protector, preceded by that of a gash in the tyre and followed by that of a projecting lump.

"But this is astounding!" I exclaimed. "It is almost certainly the same track that we saw in Ponder's Road."

"Yes," he agreed. "I noticed it as we came along." He brought out his spring-tape and notebook, and handing the latter to me, stooped and measured the distances between the three impressions. I wrote them down as he called them out, and then we compared them with the note made in Ponder's Road. The measurements were identical, as were the relative positions of the impressions.

"This is an important piece of evidence," said he. "I wish we were able to take casts, but the notes will be pretty conclusive. And now," he continued as we resumed our progress towards the station, "to return to your question. Parton's evidence at the inquest proved that Cyrus Pedley was drowned in water which contained duck-weed. He produced a specimen and we both saw it. We saw the duck-weed in it and also two *Planorbis* shells. The presence of those two shells proved that the water in which he was drowned must have swarmed with them. We saw the body, and observed that one hand grasped a wisp of horn-weed. Then we went to view the ditch and we examined it. That was when I got, not a mere hint, but a crucial and conclusive fact. The ditch was covered with duck-weed, as we expected. But it was the wrong duck-weed."

"The wrong duck-weed!" I exclaimed. "Why, how many kinds of duck-weed are there?"

"There are four British species," he replied. "The Greater Duck-weed, the Lesser Duck-weed, the Thick Duck-weed, and the Ivy-leaved Duck-weed. Now the specimens in Parton's jar I noticed were the Greater Duck-weed, which is easily distinguished by its roots, which are multiple and form a sort of tassel. But the duck-weed on the Bantree ditch was the Lesser Duck weed, which is smaller than the other, but is especially distinguished by having only a single root. It is impossible to mistake one for the other.

"Here, then, was practically conclusive evidence of murder. Cyrus Pedley had been drowned in a pond or ditch. But *not* in the ditch in which his body was found. Therefore his dead body had been conveyed from some other place and put into this ditch. Such a proceeding furnishes *prima facie* evidence of murder. But as soon as the question was raised, there was an abundance of confirmatory evidence. There was no horn-weed or *Planorbis* shells in the ditch, but there were swarms of *succinea*, some of which would inevitably have been swallowed with the water. There was an obscure linear pressure mark on the arm of the dead man, just above the elbow, such a mark as might be made by a cord if a man were pinioned to render him helpless. Then the body would have had to be conveyed to this place in some kind of vehicle, and we found the traces of what appeared to be a motor-van, which had approached the cart-track on the wrong side of the road, as if to pull up there. It was a very conclusive mass of evidence, but it would have been useless but for the extraordinarily lucky chance that poor Pedley had lost his railway ticket and preserved the receipt, by which we were able to ascertain where he was on the day of his death and in what locality the murder was probably committed. But that is not the only way in which Fortune has favoured us. The station-master's information was, and will be, invaluable. Then it was most fortunate for us that there was only one ditch on the factory land, and that that ditch was accessible at only one point, which must have been the place where Pedley was drowned."

"The duck-weed in this ditch is, of course, the Greater Duck-weed?"

"Yes. I have taken some specimens as well as the horn-weed and shells."

He opened the vasculum and picked out one of the tiny plants, exhibiting the characteristic tassel of roots.

"I shall write to Parton and tell him to preserve the jar and the horn-weed if it has not been thrown away. But the duck-weed alone, produced in evidence, would be proof enough that Pedley was not drowned in the Bantree ditch, and the dental plate will show where he was drowned."

"Are you going to pursue the case any farther?" I asked.

"No," he replied. "I shall call at Scotland Yard on my way home and report what I have learned and what I can prove in court. Then I shall have finished with the case. The rest is for the police, and I imagine they won't have much difficulty. The circumstances seem to tell their own story. Pedley was employed by the Foreign Office, probably on some kind of secret service. I imagine that he discovered the existence of a gang of evil-doers – probably foreign revolutionaries, of whom we may assume that our friend the manager of the factory is one, that he contrived to associate himself with them and to visit the factory occasionally to ascertain what was made there besides Golomite – if Golomite is not itself an illicit product. Then I assume that he was discovered to be a spy, that he was lured down here, that he was pinioned and drowned some time on Tuesday night, and his body put into the van and conveyed to a place miles away from the scene of his death, where it was deposited in a ditch apparently identical in character with that in which he was drowned. It was an extremely ingenious and well-thought-out plan. It seemed to have provided for every kind of inquiry, and it very narrowly missed being successful."

"Yes," I agreed. "But it didn't provide for Dr. John Thorndyke."

"It didn't provide for a searching examination of all the details," he replied, "and no criminal plan that I have ever met has done so. The completeness of the scheme is limited by the knowledge of the schemers and, in practice, there is always something overlooked. In this case, the criminals were unlearned in the natural history of ditches."

Thorndyke's theory of the crime turned out to be substantially correct. The Golomite Works proved to be a factory where high explosives were made by a gang of cosmopolitan revolutionaries who were all known to the police. But the work of the latter was simplified by a detailed report which the dead man had deposited at his bank and which was discovered in time to enable the police to raid the factory and secure the whole gang. When once they were under lock-and-key, further information was forthcoming, for a charge of murder against them jointly soon produced King's Evidence sufficient to procure a conviction of the three actual perpetrators of the murder.

Mr. Ponting's Alibi

Thorndyke looked doubtfully at the pleasant-faced athletic-looking clergyman who had just come in, bearing Mr. Brodribb's card as an explanatory credential.

"I don't quite see," said he, "why Mr. Brodribb sent you to me. It seems to be a purely legal matter which he could have dealt with himself, at least as well as I can."

"He appeared to think otherwise," said the clergyman. ("*The Revd. Charles Meade*" was written on the card.)

"At any rate," he added with a persuasive smile, "here I am, and I hope you are not going to send me away."

"I shouldn't offer that affront to my old friend Brodribb," replied Thorndyke, smiling in return, "so we may as well get to business, which, in the first place, involves the setting out of all the particulars. Let us begin with the lady who is the subject of the threats of which you spoke."

"Her name," said Mr. Meade, "is Miss Millicent Fawcett. She is a person of independent means, which she employs in works of charity. She was formerly a hospital sister, and she does a certain amount of voluntary work in the parish as a sort of district nurse. She has been a very valuable help to me and we have been close friends for several years, and I may add, as a very material fact, that she has consented to marry me in about two months' time. So that, you see, I am properly entitled to act on her behalf."

"Yes," agreed Thorndyke. "You are an interested party. And now, as to the threats. What do they amount to?"

"That," replied Meade, "I can't tell you. I gathered quite by chance, from some words that she dropped, that she had been threatened. But she was unwilling to say more on the subject, as she did not take the matter seriously. She is not at all nervous. However, I told her I was taking advice, and I hope you will be able to extract more details from her. For my own part, I am decidedly uneasy."

"And as to the person or persons who have uttered the threats. Who are they? And out of what circumstances have the threats arisen?"

"The person is a certain William Ponting, who is Miss Fawcett's step-brother – if that is the right term. Her father married, as his second wife, a Mrs. Ponting, a widow with one son. This is the son. His mother died before Mr. Fawcett, and the latter, when he died, left his daughter, Millicent, sole heir to his property. That has always been a grievance to Ponting. But now he has another. Miss Fawcett made a will some years ago by which the bulk of her rather considerable property is left to two cousins, Frederick and James Barnett, the sons of her father's sister. A comparatively small amount goes to Ponting. When he heard this he was furious. He demanded a portion at least equal to the others, and has continued to make this demand from time to time. In fact, he has been extremely troublesome, and appears to be getting still more so. I gathered that the threats were due to her refusal to alter the will."

"But," said I, "doesn't he realise that her marriage will render that will null and void?"

"Apparently not," replied Meade, "nor, to tell the truth, did I realise it myself. Will she have to make a new will?"

"Certainly," I replied. "And as that new will may be expected to be still less favourable to him, that will presumably be a further grievance."

"One doesn't understand," said Thorndyke, "why he should excite himself so much about her will. What are their respective ages?"

"Miss Fawcett is thirty-six and Ponting is about forty."

"And what kind of man is he?" Thorndyke asked.

"A very unpleasant kind of man, I am sorry to say. Morose, rude, and violent-tempered. A spendthrift and a cadger. He has had quite a lot of money from Miss Fawcett – loans, which, of course, are never repaid. And he is none too industrious, though he has a regular job on the staff of a weekly paper. But he seems to be always in debt."

"We may as well note his address," said Thorndyke.

"He lives in a small flat in Bloomsbury – alone now, since he quarrelled with the man who used to share it with him. The address is 12 Borneo House, Devonshire Street."

"What sort of terms is he on with the cousins, his rivals?"

"No sort of terms now," replied Meade. "They used to be great friends. So much so that he took his present flat to be near them – they live in the adjoining flat, Number 12 Sumatra House. But since the trouble about the wills, he is hardly on speaking terms with them."

"They live together, then?"

"Yes, Frederick and his wife and James, who is unmarried. They are rather a queer lot, too. Frederick is a singer on the variety stage, and James accompanies him on various instruments. But they are both sporting characters of a kind, especially James, who does a bit on the turf and engages in other odd activities. Of course, their musical habits are a grievance to Ponting. He is constantly making complaints of their disturbing him at his work."

Mr. Meade paused and looked wistfully at Thorndyke, who was making full notes of the conversation.

"Well," said the latter, "we seem to have got all the facts excepting the most important – the nature of the threats. What do you want us to do?"

"I want you to see Miss Fawcett – with me, if possible – and induce her to give you such details as would enable you to put a stop to the nuisance. You couldn't come to-night, I suppose? It is a beast of a night, but I would take you there in a taxi – it is only to Tooting Bec. What do you say?" he added eagerly, as Thorndyke made no objection. "We are sure to find her in, because her maid is away on a visit to her home and she is alone in the house."

Thorndyke looked reflectively at his watch.

"Half-past eight," he remarked, "and half-an-hour to get there. These threats are probably nothing but ill-temper. But we don't know. There may be something more serious behind them and, in law as in medicine, prevention is better than a *post mortem*. What do you say, Jervis?"

What could I say? I would much sooner have sat by the fire with a book than turn out into the murk of a November night. But I felt it necessary, especially as Thorndyke had evidently made up his mind. Accordingly I made a virtue of necessity, and a couple of minutes later we had exchanged the cosy room for the chilly darkness of Inner Temple Lane, up which the gratified parson was speeding ahead to capture a taxi. At the top of the Lane, we perceived him giving elaborate instructions to a taxi-driver as he held the door of the cab open, and Thorndyke, having carefully disposed of his research-case – which, to my secret amusement, he had caught up, from mere force of habit, as we started – took his seat, and Meade and I followed.

As the taxi trundled smoothly along the dark streets, Mr. Meade filled in the details of his previous sketch and, in a simple, manly, unaffected way dilated upon his good fortune and the pleasant future that lay before him. It was not, perhaps, a romantic marriage, he admitted, but Miss Fawcett and he had been faithful friends for years, and faithful friends they would remain till death did them part. So he ran on, now gleefully, now with a note of anxiety, and we listened by no means unsympathetically, until at last the cab drew up at a small, unpretentious house, standing in its own little grounds in a quiet suburban road.

"She is at home, you see," observed Meade, pointing to a lighted ground-floor window. He directed the taxi-driver to wait for the return journey, and striding up the path, delivered a characteristic knock at the door. As this brought no response, he knocked again and rang the bell. But still there was no answer, though twice I thought I heard the sound of a bolt being either drawn or shot softly. Again Mr. Meade plied the knocker more vigorously, and pressed the push of the bell, which we could hear ringing loudly within.

"This is very strange," said Meade, in an anxious tone, keeping his thumb pressed on the bell-push. "She can't have gone out and left the electric light on. What had we better do?"

"We had better enter without more delay," Thorndyke replied. "There were certainly sounds from within. Is there a side gate?"

Meade ran off towards the side of the house, and Thorndyke and I glanced at the lighted window, which was slightly open at the top.

"Looks a bit queer," I remarked, listening at the letter-box.

Thorndyke assented gravely, and at this moment Meade returned, breathing hard.

"The side gate is bolted inside," said he, and at this I recalled the stealthy sound of the bolt that I had heard. "What is to be done?"

Without replying, Thorndyke handed me his research-case, stepped across to the window, sprang up on the sill, drew down the upper sash, and disappeared between the curtains into the room. A moment later the street door opened and Meade and I entered the hall. We glanced through the open doorway into the lighted room, and I noticed a heap of needlework thrown hastily on the dining- table. Then Meade switched on the hall light, and Thorndyke walked quickly past him to the half-open door of the next room. Before entering, he reached in and switched on the light, and as he stepped into the room he partly closed the door behind him.

"Don't come in here, Meade!" he called out. But the parson's eye, like my own, had seen something before the door closed, a great, dark stain on the carpet just within the threshold. Regardless of the admonition, he pushed the door open and darted into the room. Following him, I saw him rush forward, fling his arms up wildly, and with a dreadful, strangled cry, sink upon his knees beside a low couch on which a woman was lying.

"Merciful God!" he gasped. "She is dead! Is she dead, doctor? Can nothing be done?"

Thorndyke shook his head. "Nothing," he said in a low voice. "She is dead."

Poor Meade knelt by the couch, his hands clutching at his hair and his eyes riveted on the dead face, the very embodiment of horror and despair.

"God Almighty!" he exclaimed in the same strangled undertone. "How frightful! Poor, poor Millie! Dear, sweet friend!" Then suddenly – almost savagely – he turned to Thorndyke. "But it can't be, Doctor! It is

449

impossible – Unbelievable. That, I mean!" and he pointed to the dead woman's right hand, which held an open razor.

Our poor friend had spoken my own thought. It was incredible that this refined, pious lady should have inflicted those savage wounds, that gaped scarlet beneath the waxen face. There, indeed, was the razor lying in her hand. But what was its testimony worth? My heart rejected it, but yet, unwillingly, I noted that the wounds seemed to support it, for they had been made from left to right, as they would have been if self-inflicted.

"It is hard to believe," said Thorndyke, "but there is only one alternative. Someone should acquaint the police at once."

"I will go," exclaimed Meade, starting up. "I know the way and the cab is there." He looked once more with infinite pity and affection at the dead woman. "Poor, sweet girl!" he murmured. "If we can do no more for you, we can defend your memory from calumny and call upon the God of Justice to right the innocent and punish the guilty."

With these words and a mute farewell to his dead friend, he hurried from the room, and immediately afterwards we heard the street door close.

As he went out, Thorndyke's manner changed abruptly. He had been deeply moved – as who would not have been – by this awful tragedy that had in a moment shattered the happiness of the genial, kindly parson. Now he turned to me with a face set and stern. "This is an abominable affair, Jervis," he said in an ominously quiet voice.

"You reject the suggestion of suicide, then?" said I, with a feeling of relief that surprised me.

"Absolutely," he replied. "Murder shouts at us from everything that meets our eye. Look at this poor woman, in her trim nurse's dress, with her unfinished needlework lying on the table in the next room, and that preposterous razor loose in her limp hand. Look at the savage wounds. Four of them, and the first one mortal. The great bloodstain by the door, the great bloodstain on her dress from the neck to the feet. The gashed collar, the cap-string cut right through. Note that the bleeding had practically ceased when she lay down. That is a group of visible facts that is utterly inconsistent with the idea of suicide. But we are wasting time. Let us search the premises thoroughly. The murderer has pretty certainly got away, but as he was in the house when we arrived, any traces will be quite fresh."

As he spoke, he took his electric lamp from the research-case and walked to the door.

"We can examine this room later," he said, "but we had better look over the house. If you will stay by the stairs and watch the front and back doors, I will look through the upper rooms."

He ran lightly up the stairs while I kept watch below, but he was absent less than a couple of minutes.

"There is no one there," he reported, "and as there is no basement, we will just look at this floor and then examine the grounds."

After a rapid inspection of the ground-floor rooms, including the kitchen, we went out by the back door, which was unbolted, and inspected the grounds. These consisted of a largish garden with a small orchard at the side. In the former we could discover no traces of any kind, but at the end of the path that crossed the orchard we came an a possible clue. The orchard was enclosed by a five-foot fence, the top of which bristled with hooked nails, and at the point opposite to the path, Thorndyke's lantern brought into view one or two wisps of cloth caught on the hooks.

"Someone has been over here," said Thorndyke, "but as this is an orchard – there is nothing remarkable in the fact. However, there is no fruit on the trees now, and the cloth looks fairly fresh. There are two kinds, you notice, a dark blue and a black-and-white mixture of some kind."

"Corresponding, probably, to the coat and trousers," I suggested.

"Possibly," he agreed, taking from his pocket a couple of the little seed-envelopes of which he always carried a supply. Very delicately, he picked the tiny wisps of cloth from the hooks and bestowed each kind in a separate envelope. Having pocketed these, he leaned over the fence and threw the light of his lamp along the narrow lane or alley that divided the orchard from the adjoining premises. It was ungravelled and covered with a growth of rank grass, which suggested that it was little frequented. But immediately below was a small patch of bare earth, and on this was a very distinct impression of a foot, covering several less distinct prints.

"Several people have been over here at different times," I remarked.

"Yes," Thorndyke agreed. "But that sharp footprint belongs to the last one over, and he is our concern. We had better not confuse the issues by getting over ourselves. We will mark the spot and explore from the other end." He laid his handkerchief over the top of the fence and we then went back to the house.

"You are going to take a plaster cast, I suppose?" said I, and as he assented, I fetched the research-case from the drawing-room. Then we fixed the catch of the front-door latch and went out, drawing the door to after us.

451

We found the entrance to the alley about sixty yards from the gate, and entering it, walked slowly forwards, scanning the ground as we went. But the bright lamplight showed nothing more than the vague marks of trampling feet on the grass until we came to the spot marked by the handkerchief on the fence.

"It is a pity," I remarked, "that this footprint has obliterated the others."

"On the other hand," he replied, "this one, which is the one that interests us, is remarkably clear and characteristic, a circular heel and a rubber sole of a recognisable pattern mended with a patch of cement paste. It is a footprint that could be identified beyond a doubt."

As he was speaking, he took from the research-case the water-bottle, plaster-tin, rubber mixing-bowl and spoon, and a piece of canvas with which to "reinforce" the cast. Rapidly, he mixed a bowlful – extra thick, so that it should set quickly and hard – dipped the canvas into it, poured the remainder into the footprint, and laid the canvas on it.

"I will get you to stay here, Jervis," said he, "until the plaster has set. I want to examine the body rather more thoroughly before the police arrive, particularly the back."

"Why the back?" I asked.

"Did not the appearance of the body suggest to you the advisability of examining the back?" he asked, and then, without waiting for a reply, he went off, leaving the inspection-lamp with me.

His words gave me matter for profound thought during my short vigil. I recalled the appearance of the dead woman very vividly – indeed, I am not likely ever to forget it – and I strove to connect that appearance with his desire to examine the back of the corpse. But there seemed to be no connection at all. The visible injuries were in front, and I had seen nothing to suggest the existence of any others. From time to time I tested the condition of the plaster, impatient to rejoin my colleague but fearful of cracking the thin cast by raising it prematurely. At length the plaster seemed to be hard enough, and trusting to the strength of the canvas, I prised cautiously at the edge, when, to my relief, the brittle plate came up safely and I lifted it clear. Wrapping it carefully in some spare rag, I packed it in the research-case, and then, taking this and the lantern, made my way back to the house.

When I had let down the catch and closed the front door, I went to the drawing-room, where I found Thorndyke stooping over the dark stain at the threshold and scanning the floor as if in search of something. I reported the completion of the cast and then asked him what he was looking for.

452

"I am looking for a button," he replied. "There is one missing from the back, the one to which the collar was fastened."

"Is it of any importance?" I asked.

"It is important to ascertain when and where it became detached," he replied. "Let us have the inspection-lamp."

I gave him the lamp, which he placed on the floor, turning it so that its beam of light travelled along the surface. Stooping to follow the light, I scrutinised the floor minutely but in vain.

"It may not be here at all," said I, but at that moment the bright gleam, penetrating the darkness under a cabinet, struck a small object close to the wall. In a moment I had thrown myself prone on the carpet and, reaching under the cabinet, brought forth a largish mother-of-pearl button.

"You notice," said Thorndyke, as he examined it, "that the cabinet is near the window, at the opposite end of the room to the couch. But we had better see that it is the right button."

He walked slowly towards the couch, still stooping and searching the floor with the light. The corpse, I noticed, had been turned on its side, exposing the back and the displaced collar. Through the strained button-hole of the latter Thorndyke passed the button without difficulty.

"Yes," he said, "that is where it came from. You will notice that there is a similar one in front. By the way," he continued, bringing the lamp close to the surface of the grey serge dress, "I picked off one or two hairs – animal hairs. Cat and dog they looked like. Here are one or two more. Will you hold the lamp while I take them off?"

"They are probably from some pets of hers," I remarked, as he picked them off with his forceps and deposited them in one of the invaluable seed-envelopes. "Spinsters are a good deal addicted to pets, especially cats and dogs."

"Possibly," he replied. "But I could see none in front, where you would expect to find them, and there seem to be none on the carpet. Now let us replace the body as we found it and just have a look at our material before the police arrive. I expected them here before this."

We turned the body back into its original position and, taking the research-case and the lamp, went into the dining-room. Here Thorndyke rapidly set up the little travelling microscope and, bringing forth the seed- envelopes, began to prepare slides from the contents of some while I prepared the others. There was time only for a very hasty examination, which Thorndyke made as soon as the specimens were mounted.

"The clothing," he reported, with his eye at the microscope, "is woollen in both cases. Fairly good quality. The one a blue serge, apparently indigo dyed, the other a mixture of black-and-white, no other colour. Probably a fine tabby or a small shepherd's plaid."

"Serge coat and shepherd's plaid trousers," I suggested. "Now see what the hairs are." I handed him the slide, on which I had roughly mounted the collection in oil of lavender, and he placed it on the stage.

"There are three different kinds of hairs here," he reported, after a rapid inspection. "Some are obviously from a cat – a smoky Persian. Others are long, rather fine tawny hairs from a dog. Probably a Pekinese. But there are two that I can't quite place. They look like monkey's hairs, but they are a very unusual colour. There is a perceptible greenish tint, which is extremely uncommon in mammalian hairs. But I hear the taxi approaching. We need not be expansive to the local police as to what we have observed. This will probably be a case for the C.I.D."

I went out into the hall and opened the door as Meade came up the path, followed by two men, and as the latter came into the light, I was astonished to recognise in one of them our old friend, Detective-Superintendent Miller, the other being, apparently, the station superintendent.

"We have kept Mr. Meade a long time," said Miller, "but we knew you were here, so the time wouldn't be wasted. Thought it best to get a full statement before we inspected the premises. How do, Doctor?" he added, shaking hands with Thorndyke. "Glad to see you here. I suppose you have got all the facts. I understood so from Mr. Meade."

"Yes," replied Thorndyke, "we have all the antecedents of the case, and we arrived within a few minutes of the death of the deceased."

"Ha!" exclaimed Miller. "Did you? And I expect you have formed an opinion on the question as to whether the injuries were self-inflicted?"

"I think," said Thorndyke, "that it would be best to act on the assumption that they were not – and to act promptly."

"Precisely," Miller agreed emphatically. "You mean that we had better find out at once where a certain person was at – What time did you arrive here?"

"It was two-minutes-to nine-when the taxi stopped," replied Thorndyke, "and, as it is now only twenty-five-minutes-to-ten, we have good time if Mr. Meade can spare us the taxi. I have the address."

"The taxi is waiting for you," said Mr. Meade, "and the man has been paid for both journeys. I shall stay here in case the superintendent wants anything." He shook our hands warmly, and as we bade him farewell and noted the dazed, despairing expression and lines of grief that had already eaten into the face that had been so blithe and hopeful, we both thought bitterly of the few fatal minutes that had made us too late to save the wreckage of his life.

We were just turning away when Thorndyke paused and again faced the clergyman. "Can you tell me," he asked, "whether Miss Fawcett had any pets? Cats, dogs, or other animals?"

Meade looked at him in surprise, and Superintendent Miller seemed to prick up his ears. But the former answered simply, "No. She was not very fond of animals. She reserved her affections for men and women."

Thorndyke nodded gravely and, picking up the research-case, walked slowly out of the room, Miller and I following.

As soon as the address had been given to the driver and we had taken our seats in the taxi, the superintendent opened the examination-in-chief.

"I see you have got your box of magic with you, Doctor," he said, cocking his eye at the research-case. "Any luck?"

"We have secured a very distinctive footprint," replied Thorndyke, "but it may have no connection with the case."

"I hope it has," said Miller. "A good cast of a footprint which you can let the jury compare with the boot is first-class evidence." He took the cast, which I had produced from the research-case, and turning it over tenderly and gloatingly, exclaimed, "Beautiful! beautiful! Absolutely distinctive! There can't be another exactly like it in the world. It is as good as a fingerprint. For the Lord's sake take care of it. It means a conviction if we can find the boot."

The superintendent's efforts to engage Thorndyke in discussion were not very successful, and the conversational brunt was borne by me, for we both knew my colleague too well to interrupt him if he was disposed to be meditative. And such was now his disposition. Looking at him as he sat in his corner, silent but obviously wrapped in thought, I knew that he was mentally sorting out the data and testing the hypotheses that they yielded.

"Here we are," said Miller, opening the door as the taxi stopped. "Now what are we going to say? Shall I tell him who I am?"

"I expect you will have to," replied Thorndyke, "if you want him to let us in."

"Very well," said Miller. "But I shall let you do the talking, because I don't know what you have got up your sleeve."

Thorndyke's prediction was verified literally. In response to the third knock, with an obligato accompaniment on the bell, wrathful footsteps – I had no idea footsteps could be so expressive – advanced rapidly along the lobby, the door was wrenched open – but only for a few inches – and an angry, hairy face appeared in the opening.

"Now then," the hairy person demanded, "what the deuce do you want?"

455

"Are you Mr. William Ponting?" the superintendent inquired.

"What the devil is that to do with you?" was the genial answer – in the Scottish mode.

"We have business," Miller began persuasively.

"So have I," the presumable Ponting replied, "and mine won't wait."

"But our business is very important," Miller urged.

"So is mine," snapped Ponting, and would have shut the door but for Miller's obstructing foot, at which he kicked viciously, but with unsatisfactory results, as he was shod in light slippers, whereas the superintendent's boots were of constabulary solidity.

"Now, look here," said Miller, dropping his conciliatory manner very completely, "you'd better stop this nonsense. I am a police officer, and I am going to come in." And with this he inserted a massive shoulder and pushed the door open.

"Police officer, are you?" said Ponting. "And what might your business be with me?"

"That is what I have been waiting to tell you," said Miller. "But we don't want to do our talking here."

"Very well," growled Ponting. "Come in. But understand that I am busy. I've been interrupted enough this evening."

He led the way into a rather barely furnished room with a wide bay-window in which was a table fitted with a writing-slope and lighted by an electric standard lamp. A litter of manuscript explained the nature of his business and his unwillingness to receive casual visitors. He sulkily placed three chairs, and then, seating himself, glowered at Thorndyke and me.

"Are they police officers, too?" he demanded.

"No," replied Miller, "they are medical gentlemen. Perhaps you had better explain the matter, Doctor," he added, addressing Thorndyke, who thereupon opened the proceedings.

"We have called," said he, "to inform you that Miss Millicent Fawcett died suddenly this evening."

"The devil!" exclaimed Ponting. "That's sudden with a vengeance. What time did this happen?"

"About a quarter-to-nine."

"Extraordinary!" muttered Ponting. "I saw her only the day before yesterday, and she seemed quite well then. What did she die of?"

"The appearances," replied Thorndyke, "suggest suicide."

"Suicide!" gasped Ponting. "Impossible! I can't believe it. Do you mean to tell me she poisoned herself?"

456

"No," said Thorndyke, "it was not poison. Death was caused by injuries to the throat inflicted with a razor."

"Good God!" exclaimed Ponting. "What a horrible thing! But," he added, after a pause, "I can't believe she did it herself, and I don't. Why should she commit suicide? She was quite happy, and she was just going to be married to that mealy-faced parson. And a razor, too! How do you suppose she came by a razor? Women don't shave. They smoke and drink and swear, but they haven't taken to shaving yet. I don't believe it. Do you?"

He glared ferociously at the superintendent who replied, "I am not sure that I do. There's a good deal in what you've just said, and the same objections had occurred to us. But you see, if she didn't do it herself, someone else must have done it, and we should like to find out who that someone is. So we begin by ascertaining where any possible persons may have been at a quarter-to-nine this evening."

Ponting smiled like an infuriated cat. "So you think me a possible person, do you?" said he.

"Everyone is a possible person," Miller replied blandly, "especially when he is known to have uttered threats."

The reply sobered Ponting considerably. For a few moments he sat, looking reflectively at the superintendent, then, in comparatively quiet tones, he said, "I have been working here since six o'clock. You can see the stuff for yourself, and I can prove that it has been written since six."

The superintendent nodded, but made no comment, and Ponting gazed at him fixedly, evidently thinking hard. Suddenly he broke into a harsh laugh.

"What is the joke?" Miller inquired stolidly.

"The joke is that I have got another alibi – a very complete one. There are compensations in every evil. I told you I had been interrupted in my work already this evening. It was those fools next door, the Barnetts – cousins of mine. They are musicians, save the mark! Variety stage, you know. Funny songs and jokes for mental defectives. Well, they practise their infernal ditties in their rooms, and the row comes into mine, and an accursed nuisance it is. However, they have agreed not to practise on Thursdays and Fridays – my busy nights – and usually they don't. But to-night, just as I was in the thick of my writing, I suddenly heard the most unholy din, that idiot, Fred Barnett, bawling one of his imbecile songs – '*When the pigs their wings have folded*', and balderdash of that sort – and the other donkey accompanying him on the clarinet, if you please! I stuck it for a minute or two. Then I rushed round to their flat and raised Cain with the bell and knocker. Mrs. Fred opened the door, and I told her what I thought of it. Of course she was very apologetic, said they had forgotten that it was Thursday and promised that she would make her husband stop. And I suppose she did, for by the time I got back to my rooms the row had ceased. I could have punched the whole lot of them into a jelly, but it was all for the best as it turns out."

"What time was it when you went round there?" asked Miller.

"About five-minutes-past-nine," replied Ponting. "The church bell had struck nine when the row began."

"Hmm!" grunted Miller, glancing at Thorndyke. "Well, that is all we wanted to know, so we need not keep you from your work any longer."

He rose, and being let out with great alacrity, stumped down the stairs, followed by Thorndyke and me. As we came out into the street, he turned to us with a deeply disappointed expression.

"Well," he exclaimed, "this is a suck-in. I was in hopes that we had pounced on our quarry before he had got time to clear away the traces. And now we've got it all to do. You can't get round an alibi of that sort."

I glanced at Thorndyke to see how he was taking this unexpected check. He was evidently puzzled, and I could see by the expression of concentration in his face that he was trying over the facts and inferences in new combinations to meet this new position. Probably he had noticed, as I had, that Ponting was wearing a tweed suit, and that therefore the shreds of clothing from the fence could not be his unless he had changed. But the alibi put him definitely out of the picture and, as Miller had said, we now had nothing to give us a lead.

Suddenly Thorndyke came out of his reverie and addressed the superintendent.

"We had better put this alibi on the basis of ascertained fact. It ought to be verified at once. At present we have only Ponting's unsupported statement."

"It isn't likely that he would risk telling a lie," Miller replied gloomily.

"A man who is under suspicion of murder will risk a good deal," Thorndyke retorted, "especially if he is guilty. I think we ought to see Mrs. Barnett before there is any opportunity of collusion."

"There has been time for collusion already," said Miller. "Still, you are quite right, and I see there is a light in their sitting-room, if that is it, next to Ponting's. Let us go up and settle the matter now. I shall leave you to examine the witness and say what you think it best to say."

We entered the building and ascended the stairs to the Barnetts' flat, where Miller rang the bell and executed a double knock. After a short interval the door was opened and a woman looked out at us inquisitively.

"Are you Mrs. Frederick Barnett?" Thorndyke inquired. The woman admitted her identity in a tone of some surprise, and Thorndyke explained, "We have called to make a few inquiries concerning your neighbour, Mr. Ponting, and also about certain matters relating to your family. I am afraid it is a rather unseasonable hour for a visit, but as the affair is of some importance and time is an object, I hope you will overlook that."

Mrs. Barnett listened to this explanation with a puzzled and rather suspicious air. After a few moments' hesitation, she said, "I think you had better see my husband, if you will wait here a moment I will go and tell him." With this, she pushed the door to, without actually closing it, and we heard her retire along the lobby, presumably to the sitting-room, for, during the short colloquy, I had observed a door at the end of the lobby, partly open, through which I could see the end of a table covered with a red cloth.

The "moment" extended to a full minute, and the superintendent began to show signs of impatience.

"I don't see why you didn't ask her the simple question straight out," he said, and the same question had occurred to me. But at this point footsteps were heard approaching, the door opened, and a man confronted us, holding the door open with his left hand, his right being wrapped in a handkerchief. He looked suspiciously from one to the other of us, and asked stiffly, "What is it that you want to know? And would you mind telling me who you are?"

"My name is Thorndyke," was the reply. "I am the legal adviser of the Reverend Charles Meade, and these two gentlemen are interested parties. I want to know what you can tell me of Mr. Ponting's recent movements – to-day, for instance. When did you last see him?"

The man appeared to be about to refuse any conversation, but suddenly altered his mind, reflected for a few moments, and then replied, "I saw him from my window at his – they are bay-windows – about half-past eight. But my wife saw him later than that. If you will come in she can tell you the time exactly." He led the way along the lobby with an obviously puzzled air. But he was not more puzzled than I, or than Miller, to judge by the bewildered glance that the superintendent cast at me, as he followed our host along the lobby. I was still meditating on Thorndyke's curiously indirect methods when the sitting-room door was opened, and then I got a minor surprise of another kind. When I had last looked into the room, the table had been covered by a red cloth. It was now bare, and when we entered the room I saw that the red cover had been thrown over a side table, on which was some bulky and angular object. Apparently it had been thought desirable to conceal that object,

459

whatever it was, and as we took our seats beside the bare table, my mind was busy with conjectures as to what that object could be.

Mr. Barnett repeated Thorndyke's question to his wife, adding, "I think it must have been a little after nine when Ponting came round. What do you say?"

"Yes," she replied, "it would be, for I heard it strike nine just before you began your practice, and he came a few minutes after."

"You see," Barnett explained, "I am a singer, and my brother, here, accompanies me on various instruments, and of course we have to practise. But we don't practise on the nights when Ponting is busy – Thursdays and Fridays – as he said that the music disturbed him. To-night, however, we made a little mistake. I happen to have got a new song that I am anxious to get ready – it has an illustrative accompaniment on the clarinet, which my brother will play. We were so much taken up with the new song that we all forgot what day of the week it was, and started to have a good practice. But before we had got through the first verse, Ponting came round, battering at the door like a madman. My wife went out and pacified him, and of course we shut down for the evening."

While Mr. Barnett was giving his explanation, I looked about the room with vague curiosity. Somehow – I cannot tell exactly how – I was sensible of something queer in the atmosphere of this place, of a certain indefinite sense of tension. Mrs. Barnett looked pale and flurried. Her husband, in spite of his volubility, seemed ill at ease, and the brother, who sat huddled in an easy-chair, nursing a dark-coloured Persian cat, stared into the fire, and neither moved nor spoke. And again I looked at the red table-cloth and wondered what it covered.

"By the way," said Barnett, after a brief pause, "what is the point of these inquiries of yours? About Ponting, I mean. What does it matter to you where he was this evening?"

As he spoke, he produced a pipe and tobacco-pouch, and proceeded to fill the former, holding it in his bandaged right hand and filling it with his left. The facility with which he did this suggested that he was left-handed, an inference that was confirmed by the ease with which he struck the match with his left hand, and by the fact that he wore a wrist-watch on his right wrist.

"Your question is a perfectly natural one," said Thorndyke. "The answer to it is that a very terrible thing has happened. Miss Millicent Fawcett, who is, I think, a connection of yours, met her death this evening under circumstances of grave suspicion. She died, either by her own hand or by the hand of a murderer, a few minutes before nine o'clock. Hence it has become I necessary to ascertain the whereabouts at that time of any persons on whom suspicion might reasonably fall."

"Good God!" exclaimed Barnett. "What a shocking thing!"

The exclamation was followed by a deep silence, amidst which I could hear the barking of a dog in an adjacent room, the unmistakable sharp, treble yelp of a Pekinese. And again I seemed to be aware of a strange sense of tension in the occupants of this room. On hearing Thorndyke's answer, Mrs. Barnett had turned deadly pale and let her head fall forward on her hand. Her husband had sunk on to a chair, and he, too, looked pale and deeply shocked, while the brother continued to stare silently into the fire.

At this moment Thorndyke astonished me by an exhibition of what seemed – under the tragic circumstances – the most outrageous bad manners and bad taste. Rising from his chair with his eyes fixed on a print which hung on the wall above the red-covered table, he said, "That looks like one of Cameron's etchings," and forthwith stepped across the room to examine it, resting his hand, as he leaned forward, on the object covered by the cloth.

"Mind where you are putting your hand, sir!" Fred Barnett called out, springing to his feet.

Thorndyke looked down at his hand, and deliberately raising a corner of the cloth, looked under. "There is no harm done," he remarked quietly, letting the cloth drop, and with another glance at the print, he went back to his chair.

Once more a deep silence fell upon the room, and I had a vague feeling that the tension had increased. Mrs. Barnett was as white as a ghost and seemed to catch at her breath. Her, husband watched her with a wild, angry expression and smoked furiously, while the superintendent – also conscious of something abnormal in the atmosphere of the room – looked furtively from the woman to the man and from him to Thorndyke.

Yet again in the silence the shrill barking of the Pekinese dog broke out, and somehow that sound connected itself in my mind with the Persian cat that dozed on the knees of the immovable man by the fire. I looked at the cat and at the man, and even as I looked, I was startled by a most extraordinary apparition. Above the man's shoulder, slowly rose a little round head like the head of a diminutive, greenish-brown man. Higher and higher the tiny monkey raised itself, resting on its little hands to peer at the strangers. Then, with sudden coyness, like a shy baby, it popped down out of sight.

I was thunderstruck. The cat and the dog I had noted merely as a curious coincidence. But the monkey – and such an unusual monkey, too – put coincidences out of the question. I stared at the man in positive stupefaction. Somehow that man was connected with that unforgettable figure lying upon the couch miles away. But how? When that deed of horror was doing, he had been here in this very room. Yet, in some way, he had been concerned in it. And suddenly a suspicion dawned upon me that Thorndyke was waiting for the actual perpetrator to arrive.

"It is a most ghastly affair," Barnett repeated presently in a husky voice. Then, after a pause, he asked, "Is there any sort of evidence as to whether she killed herself or was killed by somebody else?"

"I think that my friend, here, Detective-Superintendent Miller, has decided that she was murdered." He looked at the bewildered superintendent, who replied with an inarticulate grunt.

"And is there any clue as to who the – the murderer may be? You spoke of suspected persons just now."

"Yes," replied Thorndyke, "there is an excellent clue, if it can only be followed up. We found a most unmistakable footprint, and what is more, we took a plaster cast of it. Would you like to see the cast?"

Without waiting for a reply, he opened the research-case and took out the cast, which he placed in my hands.

"Just take it round and show it to them," he said.

The superintendent had witnessed Thorndyke's amazing proceedings with an astonishment that left him speechless. But now he sprang to his feet and, as I walked round the table, he pressed beside me to guard the precious cast from possible injury. I laid it carefully down on the table, and as the light fell on it obliquely, it presented a most striking appearance – that of a snow-white boot-sole on which the unshapely patch, the circular heel, and the marks of wear were clearly visible.

The three spectators gathered round, as near as the superintendent would let them approach, and I observed them closely, assuming that this incomprehensible move of Thorndyke's was a device to catch one or more of them off their guard. Fred Barnett looked at the cast stolidly enough, though his face had gone several shades paler, but Mrs. Barnett stared at it with starting eyeballs and dropped jaw – the very picture of horror and dismay. As to James Barnett, whom I now saw clearly for the first time, he stood behind the woman with a singularly scared and haggard face, and his eyes riveted on the white boot-sole. And now I could see that he wore a suit of blue serge and that the front both of his coat and waistcoat were thickly covered with the shed hairs of his pets.

There was something very uncanny about this group of persons gathered around that accusing footprint, all as still and rigid as statues and none uttering a sound. But something still more uncanny followed.

462

Suddenly the deep silence of the room was shattered by the shrill notes of a clarinet, and a brassy voice burst forth:

"When the pigs their wings have folded
And the cows are in their nest – "

We all spun round in amazement, and at the first glance the mystery of the crime was solved. There stood Thorndyke with the red table-cover at his feet, and at his side, on the small table, a massively-constructed phonograph of the kind used in offices for dictating letters, but fitted with a convoluted metal horn in place of the rubber ear-tubes.

A moment of astonished silence was succeeded by a wild confusion. Mrs. Barnett uttered a piercing shriek and fell back on to a chair, her husband broke away and rushed at Thorndyke, who instantly gripped his wrist and pinioned him, while the superintendent, taking in the situation at a glance, fastened on the unresisting James and forced him down into a chair. I ran round and, having stopped the machine – for the preposterous song was hideously incongruous with the tragedy that was enacting – went to Thorndyke's assistance and helped him to remove his prisoner from the neighbourhood of the instrument.

"Superintendent Miller," said Thorndyke, still maintaining a hold on his squirming captive, "I believe you are a justice of the peace?"

"Yes," was the reply, *"ex officio."*

"Then," said Thorndyke, "I accuse these three persons of being concerned in the murder of Miss Millicent Fawcett, Frederick Barnett as the principal who actually committed the murder, James Barnett as having aided him by holding the arms of the deceased, and Mrs. Barnett as an accessory before the fact in that she worked this phonograph for the purpose of establishing a false alibi."

"I knew nothing about it!" Mrs. Barnett shrieked hysterically. "They never told me why they wanted me to work the thing."

"We can't go into that now," said Miller. "You will be able to make your defence at the proper time and place. Can one of you go for assistance, or must I blow my whistle?"

"You had better go, Jervis," said Thorndyke. "I can hold this man until reinforcements arrive. Send a constable up and then go on to the station. And leave the outer door ajar."

I followed these directions and, having found the police station, presently returned to the flat with four constables and a sergeant in two taxis.

When the prisoners had been removed, together with the three animals – the latter in charge of a zoophilist constable – we searched the

463

bedrooms. Frederick Barnett had changed his clothing completely, but in a locked drawer – the lock of which Thorndyke picked neatly, to the superintendent's undisguised admiration – we found the discarded garments, including a pair of torn shepherd's plaid trousers, covered with blood stains, and a new, empty razor-case. These things, together with the wax cylinder of the phonograph, Miller made up into a neat parcel and took away with him.

"Of course," said I, as we walked homewards, "the general drift of this case is quite obvious. But it seemed to me that you went to the Barnetts' flat with a definite purpose already formed, and with a definite suspicion in your mind. Now, I don't see how you came to suspect the Barnetts."

"I think you will," he replied, "if you will recall the incidents in their order from the beginning, including poor Meade's preliminary statement. To begin with the appearances of the body, the suggestion of suicide was transparently false. To say nothing of its incongruity with the character and circumstances of the deceased and the very unlikely weapon used, there were the gashed collar and the cut cap-string. As you know, it is a well-established rule that suicides do not damage their clothing. A man who cuts his own throat doesn't cut his collar. He takes it off. He removes all obstructions. Naturally, for he wishes to complete the act as easily and quickly as possible, and he has time for preparation. But the murderer must take things as he finds them and execute his purpose as best he can.

"But further, the wounds were inflicted near the door, but the body was on the couch at the other end of the room. We saw, from the absence of bleeding, that she was dying – in fact, apparently dead – when she lay down. She must therefore have been carried to the couch *after* the wounds were inflicted.

"Then there were the blood-stains. They were all in front, and the blood had run down vertically. Then she must have been standing upright while the blood was flowing. Now there were four wounds, and the first one was mortal – it divided the common carotid artery and the great veins. On receiving that wound, she would ordinarily have fallen down. But she did not fall, or there would have been a blood-stain across the neck. Why did she not fall? The obvious suggestion was that someone was holding her up. This suggestion was confirmed by the absence of cuts on her hands – which would certainly have been cut if someone bad not been holding them. It was further confirmed by the rough crumpling of the collar at the back, so rough that the button was torn off. And we found that button near the door.

"Further, there were the animal hairs. They were on the back only. There were none on the front – where they would have been if derived from the animals – or anywhere else. And we learned that she kept no animals. All these appearances pointed to the presence of two persons, one of whom stood behind her and held her arms while the other stood in front and committed the murder. The cloth on the fence supported this view, being probably derived from two different pairs of trousers. The character of the wounds made it nearly certain that the murderer was left-handed.

"While we were returning in the cab, I reflected on these facts and considered the case generally. First, what was the motive? There was nothing to suggest robbery, nor was it in the least like a robber's crime. What other motive could there be? Well, here was a comparatively rich woman who had made a will in favour of certain persons, and she was going to be married. On her marriage the will would automatically become void, and she was not likely to make another will so favourable to those persons. Here, then, was a possible motive, and that motive applied to Ponting, who had actually uttered threats and was obviously suspect.

"But, apart from those threats, Ponting was not the principal suspect, for he benefited only slightly under the will. The chief beneficiaries were the Barnetts, and Miss Fawcett's death would benefit them, not only by securing the validity of the will, but by setting the will into immediate operation. And there were two of them. They therefore fitted the circumstances better than Ponting did. And when we came to interview Ponting, he went straight out of the picture. His manuscript would probably have cleared him – with his editor's confirmation. But the other alibi was conclusive.

"What instantly struck me, however, was that Ponting's alibi was also an alibi for the Barnetts. But there was this difference: Ponting had been *seen*, the Barnetts had only been *heard*. Now, it has often occurred to me that a very effective false alibi could be worked with a gramophone or a phonograph – especially with one on which one can make one's own records. This idea now recurred to me, and at once it was supported by the appearance of an arranged effect. Ponting was known to be at work. It was practically certain that a blast of 'music' would bring him out. Then he would be available, if necessary, as a witness to prove an alibi. It seemed to be worth while to investigate.

"When we came to the flat we encountered a man with an injured hand – the right. It would have been more striking if it had been his left. But it presently turns out that he is left-handed, which is still more striking as a coincidence. This man is extraordinarily ready to answer

465

questions which most persons would have refused to answer at all. Those answers contain the alibi.

"Then there was the incident of the table – I think you noticed it. That cover was on the large table when we arrived, but it was taken off and thrown over something, evidently to conceal it. But I need not pursue the details. When I had seen the cat, heard the dog, and then seen the monkey, I determined to see what was under the table-cover, and finding that it was a phonograph with the cylinder record still on the drum, I decided to 'go Nap' and chance making a mistake. For until we had tried the record, the alibi remained. If it had failed, I should have advised Miller to hold a boot parade. Fortunately we struck the right record and completed the case."

Mrs. Barnett's defence was accepted by the magistrate and the charge against her was dismissed. The other two were committed for trial, and in due course paid the extreme penalty. "Yet another illustration," was Thorndyke's comment, "of the folly of that kind of criminal who won't let well alone, and who will create false clues. If the Barnetts had not laid down those false tracks, they would probably never have been suspected. It was their clever alibi that led us straight to their door."

Pandora's Box

"**I** see our friend, S. Chapman, is still a defaulter," said I, as I ran my eye over the "Personal" column of *The Times*.

Thorndyke looked up interrogatively.

"Chapman?" he repeated, "let me see – who is he?"

"The man with the box. I read you the advertisement the other day. Here it is again: '*If the box left in the luggage-room by S. Chapman is not claimed within a week from this date, it will be sold to defray expenses. – Alexander Butt, Red Lion Hotel, Stoke Varley, Kent.*' That sounds like an ultimatum, but it has been appearing at intervals for the last month. As the first notice expired about three weeks ago, the question is, why doesn't Mr. Butt sell the box and have done with it?"

"He may have some qualms as to the legality of the proceeding," said Thorndyke. "It would be interesting to know what expenses he refers to and what is the value of the box."

The latter question was resolved a day or two later by the appearance in our chambers of an agitated gentleman, who gave his name as George Chapman. After apologising for his unannounced visit he explained, "I have come to you on the advice of my solicitor and on behalf of my brother, Samuel, who has become involved in a most extraordinary and horrible set of complications. At present he is in custody of the police charged with an atrocious murder."

"That is certainly a rather serious complication," Thorndyke observed dryly. "Perhaps you had better give us an account of the circumstances – the whole set of circumstances, from the beginning."

"I will," said Mr. Chapman, "without any reservations. The only question is, which is the beginning? There are the business and the domestic affairs. Perhaps I had better begin with the business concerns. My brother was a sort of travelling agent for a firm of manufacturing jewellers. He held a stock of the goods, which he used as samples for large orders, but in the case of small retailers he actually supplied the goods himself. When travelling, he usually carried his stock in a small Gladstone bag, but he kept the bulk of it in a safe in his house, and he used to go home at week-ends, or oftener, to replenish his travelling stock. Now, about two months ago he left home on a trip, but instead of taking a selection of his goods, he took the entire stock in a largish wooden box, leaving the safe empty. What he meant to do I don't know, and that's the fact. I offer no opinion. The circumstances were peculiar, as you will hear presently, and his proceedings were peculiar, for he went down to Stoke Varley – a village not far from Folkestone – put up at The Red Lion, and deposited his box in the luggage-room that is kept for the use of commercial travellers, and then, after staying there for a few days, came up to London to make some arrangements for selling or letting his house – which, it seems, he had decided to leave. He came up in the evening, and the very next morning the first of his adventures befell, and a very alarming one it was.

"It appears that, as he was walking down a quiet street, he saw a lady's purse lying on the pavement. Naturally he picked it up, and as it contained nothing to show the name or address of the owner, he put it in his pocket, intending to hand it in at a police station. Shortly after this, he got into an omnibus, and a well-dressed woman entered at the same time and sat down next to him. Just as the conductor was coming in to collect the fares, the woman began to search her pocket excitedly, and then, turning to my brother, called on him loudly to return her purse. Of course, he said that he knew nothing about her purse, whereupon she roundly accused him of having picked her pocket, declaring to the conductor that she had felt him take out her purse, and demanding that the omnibus should be stopped and a policeman fetched. At this moment a policeman was seen on the pavement. The conductor stopped the omnibus and hailed the constable, who came and, having examined the floor of the vehicle without finding the missing purse, and taken the conductor's name and number, took my brother into custody and conducted him and the woman to the police station. Here the inspector took down from the woman a description of the stolen purse and its contents, which my brother, to his utter dismay, recognised as that of the purse which he had picked up and which was still in his pocket. Immediately, he gave the inspector an account of the incident and produced the purse, but it is hardly necessary to say that the inspector refused to take his explanation seriously.

"Then my brother did a thing which was natural enough, but which did not help him. Seeing that he was practically certain to be convicted – for there was really no answer to the charge – he gave a false name and refused his address. He was then locked up in a cell for the night, and the next morning was brought before the magistrate, who, having heard the evidence of the woman and the inspector and having listened without comment to my brother's story, committed him for trial at the Central Criminal Court, and refused bail. He was then removed to Brixton, where he was detained for nearly a month, pending the opening of the sessions.

"At length the day of his trial drew near. But it was then found that the woman who had accused him had left her lodgings and could not be traced. As there was no one to prosecute, and as the disappearance of the woman put a rather new light upon my brother's story, the case against him was allowed to drop, and he was released.

"He went home by train, and at the station he bought a copy of *The Times* to read on the way. Before opening it he chanced to run his eye over the 'Personal' column, and there his attention was arrested by his own name in an advertisement – "

"Relating to a box?" said I.

"Precisely. Then you have seen it. Well, considering the value of the contents of that box, he was naturally rather anxious. At once he sent off a telegram saying that he would call on the following day before noon to claim the box and pay what was owing. And he did so. Yesterday morning, he took an early train down to Stoke Varley and went straight to The Red Lion. On his arrival, he was asked to step into the coffee-room, which he did, and there he found three police officers, who forthwith arrested him on a charge of murder. But before going into the particular of that charge, I had better give you an account of his domestic affairs on which this incredible and horrible accusation turns.

"My brother, I am sorry to say, was living with a woman who was not his wife. He had originally intended to marry her, but his association with her – which lasted over several years – did not encourage that intention. She was a terrible woman, and she led him a terrible life. Her temper was ungovernable, and when she had taken too much to drink – which was a pretty frequent occurrence – she was not only noisy and quarrelsome, but physically violent as well. Her antecedents were disreputable. She had been connected with the seamy side of the music-hall stage, her associations were disreputable, she brought questionable women to my brother's house, she consorted with men of doubtful character, and her relations with them were equally doubtful. Indeed, with one of them, a man named Gamble, I should say that her relations were not doubtful at all, though I understand he was a married man.

"Well, my brother put up with her for years, living a life that cut him off from all decent society. But at last his patience gave way (and I may add that he made the acquaintance of a very desirable lady, who was willing to condone his past and marry him if he could secure a possible future). After a particularly outrageous scene, he ordered the woman – Rebecca Mings was her name – out of the house and declared their relationship at an end.

"But she refused to be shaken off. She kept possession of the street-door key, and she returned again and again, and made a public scandal. The last time she created such an uproar when the door was bolted against her that a crowd collected in the street and my brother was forced to let her in. She stayed with him some hours, alone in the house – for the only servant he had was a daily girl who left at three o'clock – and went away quite quietly about ten at night. But, although a good many people saw her go into the house, no one but my brother seems to have seen her leave it, a most disastrous circumstance, for, from the moment when she left the house, no one ever saw her again. She did not go to her lodgings that night. She disappeared utterly – until – but I must go back now to The Red Lion at Stoke Varley.

"When my brother was arrested on the charge of having murdered Rebecca Mings, certain particulars were given to him, and when I went down there in response to a telegram, I gathered some more. The circumstances are these, About a fortnight after my brother had left to come to London, some of the 'commercials' who used the luggage-room complained of an unpleasant odour in it, which was presently traced to my brother's box. As that box appeared to have been abandoned, the landlord became suspicious and communicated with the police. They telephoned to the London police, who found my brother's house shut up and his whereabouts unknown. Thereupon the local police broke open the box and found in it a woman's left arm and a quantity of blood-stained clothing. On which they caused the advertisement to be put in *The Times*, and meanwhile they made certain inquiries. It appeared that my brother had spent part of his time at Stoke Varley fishing in the little river. On learning this, the police proceeded to dredge the river, and presently they brought up a right arm – apparently the fellow of the one found in the box – and a leg divided into three parts, evidently a woman's. Now, as to the arm found in the box, there could be no question about its identity, for it bore a very distinct tattooed inscription consisting of the initials 'R. M.' above a heart transfixed by an arrow, with the initials 'J. B.' underneath. A few inquiries elicited the fact that the woman, Rebecca Mings, who had disappeared, bore such a tattooed mark on her left arm, and certain persons who had known her, having been sworn to secrecy, were shown the arm, and recognised the mark without hesitation. Further inquiries showed that Rebecca Mings was last seen alive entering my brother's house, as I have described, and on this information the police broke into the house and searched it."

"Do you know if they found anything?" Thorndyke asked.

"I don't," replied Chapman, "but I infer that they did. The police at Stoke Varley were very courteous and kind, but they declined to give any particulars about the visit to the house. However, we shall hear at the inquest if they made any discoveries."

"And is that all that you have to tell us?" asked Thorndyke.

"Yes," was the reply, "and enough, too. I make no comment on my brother's story, and I won't ask whether you believe it. I don't expect you to. The question is whether you would undertake the defence. I suppose it isn't necessary for a lawyer to be convinced of his client's innocence in order to convince the jury."

"You are thinking of an advocate," said Thorndyke. "I am not an advocate, and I should not defend a man whom I believed to be guilty. The most that I can do is to investigate the case. If the result of the investigation is to confirm the suspicions against your brother, I shall go no farther in the case. You will have to get an ordinary criminal barrister to defend your brother. If, on the other hand, I find reasonable grounds for believing him innocent, I will undertake the defence. What do you say to that?"

"I've no choice," replied Chapman, "and I suppose if you find all the evidence against him, the defence won't matter much."

"I am afraid that is so," said Thorndyke. "And, now there are one or two questions to be cleared up. First: Does your brother offer any explanation of the presence of these remains in his box?"

"He supposes that somebody at The Red Lion must have taken the jewellery out and put the remains in. Anyone could get access to the luggage-room by asking for the key at the office."

"Well," said Thorndyke, "that is conceivable. Then, as to the person who might have made this exchange. Is there anyone who had any reason for wishing to make away with deceased?"

"No," replied Chapman. "Plenty of people disliked her, but no one but my brother had any motive for getting rid of her."

"You spoke of a man with whom she was on somewhat intimate terms. There had been no quarrel or breach there, I suppose?"

"The man Gamble, you mean. No, I should say they were the best of friends. Besides, Gamble had no responsibilities in regard to her. He could have dropped her whenever he was tired of her."

"Do you know anything about him?" Thorndyke asked.

"Very little. He has been a rolling stone, and has been in all sorts of jobs, I believe. He was in the New Zealand trade for some time, and dealt in all sorts of things – among others, in smoked human heads. Sold them to collectors and museums, I understand. So he would have had some previous experience," Chapman added with a faint grin.

"Not in dismemberment," said Thorndyke. "Those will have been ancient Maori heads – relics of the old head hunters. There are some in the Hunterian Museum. But, as you say, there seems to be no motive in Gamble's case, even if there had been the opportunity, whereas, in your brother's case, there seem to have been both the motive *and* the opportunity. I suppose your brother never threatened the deceased?"

"I am sorry to say he did," replied Chapman. "On several occasions, and before witnesses, too, he threatened to put her out of the way. Of course he never meant it – he was really the mildest of men. But it was a foolish thing to do and most unfortunate, as things have turned out."

"Well." said Thorndyke, "I will look into the matter and let you know what I think of it. It is unnecessary to remark that appearances are not very encouraging."

"No, I can see that," said Chapman, rising and producing his card-case. "But we must hope for the best." He laid his card on the table and, having shaken hands with us gloomily, took his departure.

"It doesn't do to take things at their face value," I remarked, when he had gone, "but I don't think we have ever had a more hopeless-looking case. All it wants to complete it is the discovery of remains in Chapman's house."

"In that respect," said Thorndyke, "it may already be complete. But it hardly wants that finishing touch. On the evidence that we have, any jury would find a verdict of 'guilty' without leaving the box. The only question for us is whether the face value of the evidence is its real value. If it is, the defence will be a mere formality."

"I suppose," said I, "you will begin the investigation at Stoke Varley?"

"Yes," he replied. "We begin by checking the alleged facts. If they are really as stated, we shall probably need to go no farther. And we had better lose no time, as the remains may be moved into the jurisdiction of a London coroner, and we ought to see everything *in situ* as far as possible. I suggest that we postpone the rest of to-day's business and start at once, taking Scotland Yard on the way to get authority to inspect the remains and the premises."

In a few minutes we were ready for the expedition. While Thorndyke packed the "research-case" with the necessary instruments, I gave instructions to our laboratory assistant, Polton, as to what was to be done in our absence, and then, when we had consulted the time-table, we set forth by way of the Embankment.

At Scotland Yard, on inquiring for our friend, Superintendent Miller, we received the slightly unwelcome news that he was at Stoke Varley, inquiring into the case. However, the authorisation was given readily enough and, armed with this, we made our way to Charing Cross Station, arriving there in good time to catch our train.

We had just given up our tickets and turned out into the pleasant station approach of Stoke Varley when Thorndyke gave a soft chuckle. I looked at him inquiringly, and he explained. "Miller has had a telegram, and we are going to have facilities, with a little supervision." Following the direction of his glance, I now observed the superintendent strolling towards us, trying to look surprised, but achieving only a somewhat sheepish grin.

"Well, I'm sure, gentlemen!" he exclaimed. "This is an unexpected pleasure. You don't mean to say you are engaged in this treasure-trove case?"

"Why not?" asked Thorndyke.

"Well, I'll tell you why not," replied Miller. "Because it's no go. You'll only waste your time and injure your reputation. I may as well let you know, in confidence, that we've been through Chapman's house in London. It wasn't very necessary, but still, if there was a vacancy in his coffin for one or two more nails, we've knocked them in."

"What did you find in his house?" Thorndyke asked.

"We found," replied Miller, "in a cupboard in his bedroom, a good-sized bottle of hyoscine tablets, about two-thirds full – one-third missing. No great harm in that – he might have taken 'em himself. But when we went down into the cellar, we noticed that the place smelt – well, a bit graveyardy, so to speak. So we had a look round. It was a stone-floored cellar, not very even, but so far as we could see, none of the flagstones seemed to have been disturbed. We didn't want the job of digging the whole of them up, so I just filled a bucket with water and poured it over the floor. Then I watched.

"In less than a minute one big flagstone near the middle went nearly dry, while the water still stood on all the others. 'What O!' says I. 'Loose earth underneath here.' So we got a crow-bar and prised up that big flag, and sure enough, underneath it we found a good-sized bundle done up in a sheet. I won't go into unpleasant particulars – not that it would upset you, I suppose – but that bundle contained human remains."

"Any bones?" inquired Thorndyke.

"No. Mostly in'ards and some skin from the front of the body. We handed them over to the Home Office experts, and they examined them and made an analysis. Their report states that the remains are those of a woman of about thirty-five – that was about Mings' age – and that the various organs contained a large quantity of hyoscine – more than enough to have caused death. So there you are. If you are going to conduct the defence, you won't get much glory from it."

"It is very good of you, Miller," said Thorndyke, "to have given us this private information. It is very helpful, though I have not undertaken the defence. I have merely come down to check the facts and see if there is any material for a defence. And I shall go through the routine, as I am here. Where are the remains?"

473

"In the mortuary. I'll show you the way, and as I happen to have the key in my pocket, I can let you in."

We passed through the outskirts of the village, gathering a small train of stealthy followers who dogged us to the door of the mortuary and hungrily watched us as the superintendent let us in and locked the door after us.

"There you are," said Miller, indicating the slate table on which the remains lay, covered by a sheet soaked in an antiseptic. "I've seen all I want to see." And he retired into a corner and lit his pipe.

The remnants of mortality, disclosed by the removal of the sheet, were dreadfully suggestive of crime in its most brutal and horrible form, but they offered little information. The dismemberment had been manifestly rude and unskilful, and the remains were clearly those of a woman of medium size and apparently in the prime of life. The principal interest centred in the left arm, the waxen skin of which bore a very distinct tattoo-mark, consisting of the initials "R. M." over a very symmetrical heart, transfixed by an arrow, beneath which were the initials "J. B." The letters were Roman capitals about half-an-inch high, well-formed and finished with serifs, and the heart and arrow quite well drawn. I looked reflectively at the device, standing out in dull blue from its ivory-like background, and speculated vaguely as to who "J. B." might have been and how many predecessors and successors he had had. And then my interest waned, and I joined the superintendent in the corner. It was a sordid case, and a conviction being a foregone conclusion, it did not seem to call for further attention.

Thorndyke, however, seemed to think otherwise. But that was his way. When he was engaged in an investigation, he put out of his mind everything that he had been told and began from the very beginning. That was what he was doing now. He was inspecting these remains as if they had been the remains of some unidentified person. He made, and noted down, minute measurements of the limbs. He closely examined every square inch of surface. He scrutinised each finger separately, and then with the aid of his portable inking-plate and roller, took a complete set of finger-prints. He measured all the dimensions of the tattoo-marks with a delicate calliper-gauge, and then examined the marks themselves, first with a common lens and then with the high-power Coddington. The principles that he laid down in his lectures at the hospital were, "Accept no statement without verification, observe every fact independently for yourselves, and keep an open mind." And, certainly, no one ever carried out more conscientiously his own precepts.

"Do you know, Dr. Jervis," the superintendent whispered to me as Thorndyke brought his Coddington to bear on the tattoo-marks, "I

474

believe this lens business is becoming a habit with the doctor. It's my firm conviction that if somebody were to blow up the Houses of Parliament, he'd go and examine the ruins through a magnifying glass. Just look at him poring over those tattooed letters that you could read plainly twenty feet away!"

Meanwhile, Thorndyke, unconscious of these criticisms, placidly continued his inspection. From the table, with its gruesome burden, he transferred his attention to the box, which had been placed on a bench by the window, examining it minutely inside and out, feeling with his fingers the dark grey paint with which it was coated and the white-painted initials, "*S. C.*" on the lid, which he also measured carefully. He even copied into his note book the maker's name, which was stamped on a small brass label affixed to the inside of the lid, and the name of the lock-maker, and inspected the screws which had drawn from the wood when it was forced open. At length he put away his notebook, closed the research-case and announced that he had finished, adding the inquiry, "How do you get to The Red Lion from here?"

"It's only a few minutes' walk," said Miller. "I'll show you the way. But you're wasting your time, Doctor, you are indeed. You see," he continued, when he had locked up the mortuary and pocketed the key, "that suggestion of Chapman's is ridiculous on the face of it. Just imagine a man bringing a portmanteau full of human remains into the luggage-room of a commercial hotel, opening it and opening another's man's box, and swapping the contents of the one for the other with the chance of one of the commercials coming in at any moment. Supposing one of 'em had, what would he have had to say? 'Hallo!' says the baggy, 'you seem to have got somebody's arm in your box.' 'So I have,' says Chapman. 'I expect it's my wife's. Careless woman! Must have dropped it in when she was packing the box.' Bah! It's a fool's explanation. Besides, how could he have got Chapman's box open? We couldn't. It was a first-class lock. We had to break it open, but it hadn't been broken open before. No, sir, that cat won't jump. Still, you needn't take my word for it. Here is the place, and here is Mr. Butt, himself, standing at his own front door looking as pleasant as the flowers in May. Like the lump of sugar that you put in a fly-trap to induce 'em to walk in."

The landlord, who had overheard – without difficulty – the concluding passage of Miller's peroration, smiled genially, and when the purpose of the visit had been explained, suggested a "modest quencher" in the private parlour as an aid to conversation.

"I wanted," said Thorndyke, waiving the suggestion of the "quencher", "to ascertain whether Chapman's theory of an exchange of contents could be seriously entertained."

Well, sir," said the landlord, "the fact is that it couldn't. That room is a public room, and people may be popping in there at any time all day. We don't usually keep it locked. It isn't necessary. We know most of our customers, and the contents of the packages that are stowed in the room are principally travellers' samples of no considerable value. The thing would have been impossible in the daytime, and we lock the room up at night."

"Have you had any strangers staying with you in the interval between Chapman's going away and the discovery of the remains?"

"Yes. There was a Mr. Doler. He had two cabin trunks, and a uniform case which went to the luggage-room. And then there was a lady, Mrs. Murchison. She had a lot of stuff in there: A small, flat trunk, a hat-box, and a big dress-basket – one of these great basket pantechnicons that ladies take about with them. And there was another gentleman – I forget his name, but you will see it in the visitors' book – he had a couple of largish portmanteaux in there. Perhaps you would like to see the book?"

"I should," said Thorndyke, and when the book was produced and the names of the guests pointed out, he copied the entries into his notebook, adding the particulars of their luggage.

"And now, sir," said Miller, "I suppose you won't be happy until you've seen the room itself?"

"Your insight is really remarkable, Superintendent," my colleague replied. "Yes, I should like to see the room."

There was little enough to see, however, when we arrived there. The key was in the door, and the latter was not only unlocked but stood ajar, and when we pushed it open and entered we saw a small room, empty save for a collection of portmanteaux, trunks, and Gladstone bags. The only noteworthy fact was that it was at the end of a corridor, covered with linoleum, so that anyone inside would have a few seconds' notice of another person's approach. But evidently that would have been of little use in the alleged circumstances. For the hypothetical criminal must have emptied Chapman's box of the jewellery before he could put the incriminating objects into it, so that, apart from the latter, the arrival of an inopportune visitor would have found him apparently in the act of committing a robbery. The suggestion was obviously absurd.

"By the way," said Thorndyke, as we descended the stairs, "where is the central character of this drama – Chapman? He is not here, I suppose?"

"Yes, he is," replied Miller. "He is committed for trial, but we are keeping him here until we know where the inquest is to be held. You would probably like to have a few words with him? Well, I'll take you along to the police station and tell them who you are, and then perhaps you would like to come back here and have some lunch or dinner before you return to town."

I warmly seconded the latter proposal, and the arrangement having been made, we set forth for the police station, which we gathered from Miller was incorporated with a small local prison. Here we were shown into what appeared to be a private office, and presently a sergeant entered, ushering in a man whom we at once recognised from his resemblance to our client, Mr. George Chapman, disguised though it was by his pallor, his unshaven face, and his air of abject misery. The sergeant, having announced him by name, withdrew with the superintendent and locked the door on the outside. As soon as we were alone, Thorndyke rapidly acquainted the prisoner with the circumstances of his brother's visit and then continued, "Now, Mr. Chapman, you want me to undertake your defence. If I do so, I must have all the facts. If there is anything known to you that your brother has not told me, I ask you to tell it to me without reservation."

Chapman shook his head wearily.

"I know nothing more than you know," said he. "The whole affair is a mystery that I can make nothing of. I don't expect you to believe me. Who would, with all this evidence against me? But I swear to God that I know nothing of this abominable crime. When I brought that box down here, it contained my stock of jewellery and nothing else, and after I put it in the luggage-room, I never opened it."

"Do you know of anybody who might have had a motive for getting rid of Rebecca Mings?"

"Not a soul," replied Chapman. "She led me the devil's own life, but she was popular enough with her own friends. And she was an attractive woman in her way, a fine, well-built woman, rather big – she stood five-feet-seven – with a good complexion and very handsome golden hair. Such as her friends were – they were a shady lot. I think they were fond of her, and I don't believe she had any enemies."

"Some hyoscine was found in your house," said Thorndyke. "Do you know anything about it?"

"Yes. I got it when I suffered from neuralgia. But I never took any. My doctor heard about it and sent me to the dentist. The bottle was never opened. It contained a hundred tablets."

"And with regard to the box," said Thorndyke. "Had you had it long?"

"Not very long. I bought it at Fletchers, in Holborn, about six months ago."

"And you have nothing more to tell us?"

"No," he replied. "I wish I had," and then, after a pause, he asked with a wistful look at Thorndyke, "Are you going to undertake my defence, sir? I can see that there is very little hope, but I should like to be given just a chance."

I glanced at Thorndyke, expecting at the most a cautious and conditional reply. To my astonishment he answered, "There is no need to take such a gloomy view of the case, Mr. Chapman. I shall undertake the defence, and I think you have quite a fair chance of an acquittal."

On this amazing reply I reflected, not without some self-condemnation, during our walk to the hotel and the meal that preceded our departure. For it was evident that I had missed something vital. Thorndyke was a cautious man and little given to making promises or forecasts of results. He must have picked up some evidence of a very conclusive kind, but what that evidence could be, I found it impossible to imagine. The superintendent, too, was puzzled, I could see, for Thorndyke made no secret of his intention to go on with the case. But Miller's delicate attempts to pump him came to nothing, and when he had escorted us to the station and our train moved off, I could see him standing on the platform, gently scratching the back of his head and gazing speculatively at our retreating carriage.

As soon as we were clear of the station, I opened my attack.

"What on earth," I demanded, "did you mean by giving that poor devil, Chapman, hopes of acquittal? I can't see that he has a dog's chance."

Thorndyke looked at me gravely.

"My impression is, Jervis." he said, "that you have not kept an open mind in this case. You have allowed yourself to fall under the suggestive influence of the obvious, whereas the function of the investigator is to consider the possible alternatives of the obvious inference. And you have not brought your usual keen attention to bear on the facts. If you had considered George Chapman's statement attentively, you would have noticed that it contained some very curious and significant suggestions, and if you had examined those dismembered remains critically, you would have seen that they confirmed those suggestions in a very remarkable manner."

"As to George Chapman's statement," said I, "the only suggestive point that I recall is the reference to those Maori heads. But, as you, yourself, pointed out, the dealers in those heads don't do the dismemberment."

Thorndyke shook his head a little impatiently.

"Tut, tut, Jervis," said he, "that isn't the point at all. Any fool can cut up a dead body as this one has been cut up. The point is that that statement, carefully considered, yields a definite and consistent alternative to the theory that Samuel Chapman killed this woman and dismembered her body, and that alternative theory is supported by the appearance of these remains. I think you will see the point if you recall Chapman's statement, and reflect on the possible bearing of the various incidents that he described."

In this, however, Thorndyke was unduly optimistic. I recalled the statement completely enough, and reflected on it frequently and profoundly during the next few days, but the more I thought of it the more conclusive did the case against the accused appear.

Meanwhile, my colleague appeared to be taking no steps in the matter, and I assumed that he was waiting for the inquest. It is true that, when, on one occasion, he had accompanied me towards the City, and leaving me in Queen Victoria Street disappeared into the premises of Messrs. Burden Brothers, lock manufacturers, I was inclined to associate his proceedings with his minute examination of the lock at Stoke Varley. And, again, when our laboratory assistant, Polton, was seen to issue forth, top-hatted and armed with an umbrella and an attaché case, I suspected some sort of "private inquiries", possibly connected with the case. But from Thorndyke I could get no information at all. My tentative "pumpings" elicited one unvarying reply. "You have the facts, Jervis. You heard George Chapman's statement, and you have seen the remains. Give me a reasonable theory and I will discuss it with pleasure." And that was how the matter remained. I had no reasonable theory – other than that of the police – and there was accordingly no discussion.

On a certain evening, a couple of days before the inquest – which had been postponed in the hope that some further remains might be discovered – I observed signs of an expected visitor: A small table placed by the supernumerary arm-chair and furnished with a tray bearing a siphon, a whisky-decanter, and a box of cigars. Thorndyke caught my inquiring glance at these luxuries, for which neither of us had any use, and proceeded to explain.

"I have asked Miller to look in this evening – he is due now. I have been working at this Chapman case and, as it is now complete, I propose to lay my cards on the table."

"Is that safe?" said I. "Supposing the police still go for a conviction and try to forestall your evidence?"

"They won't," he replied. "They couldn't. And it would be most improper to let the case go for trial on a false theory. But here is Miller, and a mighty twitter he is in, I have no doubt."

He was. Without even waiting for the customary cigar, he plumped down into the chair, and dragging a letter from his pocket, fixed a glare of astonishment on my placid colleague.

"This letter of yours, sir," said he, "is perfectly incomprehensible to me. You say that you are prepared to put us in possession of the facts of this Chapman case. But we are in possession of the facts already. We are absolutely certain of a conviction. Let me remind you, sir, of what those facts are. We have got a dead body which has been identified beyond all doubt. Part of that body was found in a box which is the property of Samuel Chapman, which was brought by him and deposited by him at The Red Lion Hotel. Another part of that body was found in his dwelling-house. A supply of poison – an uncommon poison, too – similar to that which killed the dead person, has also been found in his house, and the dead body is that of a woman with whom Chapman was known to be on terms of enmity and whom he has threatened, in the presence of witnesses, to kill. Now, sir, what have you got to say to those facts?"

Thorndyke regarded the agitated detective with a quiet smile. "My comments, Miller," said he, "can be put in a nut-shell. You have got the wrong man, you have got the wrong box, and you have got the wrong body."

The superintendent was thunderstruck, and no wonder. So was I. As to Miller, he drew himself forward until he was sitting on the extreme edge of the chair, and for some moments stared at my impassive colleague in speechless amazement. At length he burst out, "But, my dear sir! This is sheer nonsense – at least, that's what it sounds like, though I know it can't be. Let's begin with the body. You say it's the wrong one."

"Yes. Rebecca Mings was a biggish woman. Her height was five-feet-seven. This woman was not more than five-feet-four."

"Bah!" exclaimed Miller. "You can't judge to an inch or two from parts of a dismembered body. You are forgetting the tattoo-mark. That clenches the identity beyond any possible doubt."

"It does, indeed," said Thorndyke. "That is the crucial evidence. Rebecca Mings had a certain tattoo mark on her left forearm. This woman had not."

"Had not!" shrieked Miller, coming yet farther forward on his chair. (I expected, every moment, to see him sitting on the floor.) "Why, I saw it, and so did you."

"I am speaking of the woman, not of the body," said Thorndyke. "The mark that you saw was a post-mortem tattoo-mark. It was made *after* death. But the fact that it was made after death is good evidence that it was not there during life."

"Moses!" exclaimed the superintendent. "This is a facer. Are you perfectly sure it was done after death?"

"Quite sure. The appearance, through a powerful lens, is unmistakable. Tattoo-marks are made, as you know, of course, by painting Indian ink on the skin and pricking it in with fine needles. In the living skin the needle-wounds heal up at once and disappear, but in the dead skin the needle-holes remain unclosed and can be easily seen with a lens. In this case the skin had been well washed and the surface pressed with some smooth object, but the holes were plainly visible and the ink was still in them."

"Well, I'm sure!" said Miller. "I never heard of tattooing a dead body before."

"Very few people have, I expect," said Thorndyke. "But there is one class of persons who know all about it: The persons who deal in Maori heads."

"Indeed?" queried Miller. "How does it concern them?"

"Those heads are usually elaborately tattooed, and the value of a head depends on the quality of the tattooing. Now, when those heads became objects of trade, the dealers conceived the idea of touching up defective specimens by additional tattooing on the dead head, and from this they proceeded to obtain heads which had no tattoo-marks, and turn them into tattooed heads."

"Well, to be sure," said the superintendent, with a grin, "what wicked men there are in the world, aren't there, Dr. Jervis?"

I murmured a vague assent, but I was principally conscious of a desire to kick myself for having failed to pick this invaluable clue out of George Chapman's statement.

"And now," said Miller, "we come to the box. How do you know it is the wrong one?"

"That," replied Thorndyke, "is proved even more conclusively. The original box was made by Fletchers, in Holborn. It was sold to Chapman, and his initials painted on it, on the 9th of last April. I have seen the entry in the day-book. The locks of these boxes are made by Burden Brothers of Queen Victoria Street, and as they are quite high-class locks each is given a registered number, which is stamped on the lock. The number on the box that you have is *5007*, and Burden's books show that it was made and sold to Fletchers about the middle of July – the sale was dated the 13th. Therefore this can not be Chapman's box."

"Apparently not," Miller agreed. "But whose box is it? And what has become of Chapman's box?"

"That," replied Thorndyke, "was presumably taken away in Mrs. Murchison's dress-basket."

"Then who the deuce is Mrs. Murchison?" demanded the superintendent.

"I should say," replied Thorndyke, "that she was formerly known as Rebecca Mings."

"The deceased!" exclaimed Miller, falling back in his chair with a guffaw. "My eye! What a lark it is! But she must have some sauce, to walk off with the jewellery *and* leave her own dismembered remains in exchange! By the way, whose remains are they?"

"We shall come to that presently," Thorndyke answered. "Now we have to consider the man you have in custody."

"Yes," agreed Miller, "we must settle about him. Of course if it isn't his box, and the body isn't Mings' body, that puts him out of it so far. But there are those remains that we dug up in his cellar. What about them?"

"That question," replied Thorndyke, "will, I think, be answered by a general review of the case. But I must, remind you that if the box is not Chapman's, it is some other person's – that is to say, that if Chapman goes out of the case as to the Stoke Varley incidents, someone else comes in. So, if the body is not Mings' body, it is some other woman's, and that other woman must have disappeared. And now let us review the case as a whole.

"You know about the pocket-picking charge. It was obviously a false charge, deliberately prepared by 'planting' the purse – that is, it was a conspiracy. Now what was the object of this conspiracy? Clearly it was to get Chapman out of the way while the boxes were exchanged at Stoke Varley, and the remains deposited in the river and elsewhere. Then who were the conspirators – other than the agent who planted the purse?

"They – if there were more than one – must have had access to Mings, dead or alive, in order to make the exact copy, or tracing, of her tattoo-mark. They must have had some knowledge of the process of *post mortem* tattooing. They must have had access to Chapman's house. And, since they had in their possession the dead body of a woman, they must have been associated with some woman who has disappeared.

"Who is there who answers this description? Well, of course, Mings had access to herself, though she could hardly have taken a tracing from her own arm, and she had access to Chapman's house, since she had possession of the latchkey. Then there is a man named Gamble, with whom Mings was on terms of great intimacy. Now Gamble was formerly a dealer in tattooed Maori heads, so he may be assumed to know something about *post mortem* tattooing. And I have ascertained that

482

Gamble's wife has disappeared from her usual places of resort. So here are two persons who, together, agree with the description of the conspirators. And now let us consider the train of events in connection with the dates.

"On July the 29th, Chapman came to town from Stoke Varley. On the 30th he was arrested as a pick-pocket. On the 31st he was committed for trial. On the 2nd of August Mrs. Gamble went away to the country. No one seems to have seen her go, but that is the date on which she is reported to have gone. On August the 5th, Mrs. Murchison deposited at Stoke Varley a box which must have been purchased between the 13th of July and the 4th of August, and which contained a woman's arm. On the 14th of August, that box was opened by the police. On the 18th, human remains were discovered in Chapman's house. On the 27th, Chapman was released from Brixton. On the 28th, he was arrested for murder at Stoke Varley. I think, Miller, you will agree that that is a very striking succession of dates."

"Yes," Miller agreed. "It looks like a true bill. If you will give me Mr. Gamble's address, I'll call on him."

"I'm afraid you won't find him at home," said Thorndyke. "He has gone into the country, too, and I gather from his landlord, who holds a returned cheque, that Mr. Gamble's banking account has gone into the country with him."

"Then," said the superintendent "I suppose I must take a trip into the country, too."

"Well, Thorndyke," I said, as I laid down the paper containing the report of the trial of Gamble and Mings for the murder of Theresa Gamble, one morning about four months later, "you ought to be very highly gratified. After sentencing Gamble to death and Mings to fifteen years' penal servitude, the judge took the opportunity to compliment the police on their ingenuity in unravelling this crime, and the Home Office experts on their skill in detecting the counterfeit tattoo-marks. What do you think of that?"

"I think," replied Thorndyke, "that his Lordship showed a very proper and appreciative spirit."

The Trail of Behemoth

Of all the minor dissipations in which temperate men indulge there is none, I think, more alluring than the after-breakfast pipe. I had just lit mine and was standing before the fire with the unopened paper in my hand when my ear caught the sound of hurried footsteps ascending the stair. Now experience has made me somewhat of a connoisseur in footsteps. A good many are heard on our stair, heralding the advent of a great variety of clients, and I have learned to distinguish those which are premonitory of urgent cases. Such I judged the present ones to be, and my judgment was confirmed by a hasty, importunate tattoo on our small brass knocker, Regretfully taking the much-appreciated pipe from my mouth, I crossed the room and threw the door open.

"Good morning, Dr. Jervis," said our visitor, a barrister whom I knew slightly. "Is your colleague at home?"

"No, Mr. Bidwell," I replied. "I am sorry to say he is out of town. He won't be back until the day-after-to-morrow."

Mr. Bidwell was visibly disappointed.

"Ha! Pity!" he exclaimed, and then with quick tact he added. "But still, you are here. It comes to the same thing."

"I don't know about that," said I. "But, at any rate, I am at your service."

"Thank you," said he. "And in that case, I will ask you to come round with me at once to Tanfield Court. A most shocking thing has happened. My old friend and neighbour, Giles Herrington, has been – well, he is dead – died suddenly, and I think there can be no doubt that he was killed. Can you come now? I will give you the particulars as we go."

I scribbled a hasty note to say where I had gone and, having laid it on the table, got my hat and set forth with Mr. Bidwell.

"It has only just been discovered," said he, as we crossed King's Bench Walk. "The laundress who does his chambers and mine was battering at my door when I arrived – I don't live in the Temple, you know. She was as pale as a ghost and in an awful state of alarm and agitation. It seems that she had gone up to Herrington's chambers to get his breakfast ready as usual, but when she went into the sitting-room she found him lying dead on the floor. Thereupon she rushed down to my chambers – I am usually an early bird – and there I found her, as I said, battering at my door, although she has a key.

"Well, I went up with her to my friend's chambers – they are on the first floor, just over mine – and there, sure enough, was poor old Giles lying on the floor, cold and stiff. Evidently he had been lying there all night."

"Were there any marks of violence on the body?" I asked.

"I didn't notice any," he replied, "but I didn't look very closely. What I did notice was that the place was all in disorder – a chair overturned and things knocked off the table. It was pretty evident that there had been a struggle and that he had not met his death by fair means."

"And what do you want us to do?" I asked.

"Well," he replied, "I was Herrington's friend, about the only friend he had, for he was not an amiable or a sociable man, and I am the executor of his will.

"Appearances suggest very strongly that he has been murdered, and I take it upon myself to see that his murderer is brought to account. Our friendship seems to demand that. Of course, the police will go into the affair, and if it turns out to be all plain sailing, there will be nothing for you to do. But the murderer, if there is one, has got to be secured and convicted, and if the police can't manage it, I want you and Thorndyke to see the case through. This is the place."

He hurried in through the entry and up the stairs to the first-floor landing, where he rapped loudly at the closed "oak" of a set of chambers, above which was painted the name of "*Mr. Giles Herrington*".

After an interval, during which Mr. Bidwell repeated the summons, the massive door opened and a familiar face looked out, the face of Inspector Badger of the Criminal Investigation Department. The expression that it bore was not one of welcome, and my experience of the inspector caused me to brace myself up for the inevitable contest.

"What is your business?" he inquired forbiddingly.

Mr. Bidwell took the question to himself and replied, "I am Mr. Herrington's executor, and in that capacity I have instructed Dr. Jervis and his colleague, Dr. Thorndyke, to watch the case on my behalf. I take it that you are a police officer?"

"I am," replied Badger, "and I can't admit any unauthorised persons to these chambers."

"We are not unauthorised persons," said Mr. Bidwell. "We are here on legitimate business. Do I understand that you refuse admission to the legal representatives of the deceased man?"

In the face of Mr. Bidwell's firm and masterful attitude, Badger began, as usual, to weaken. Eventually, having warned us to convey no information to anybody, he grudgingly opened the door and admitted us.

"I have only just arrived, myself," he said. "I happened to be in the porter's lodge on other business when the laundress came and gave the alarm."

As I stepped into the room and looked round, I saw at a glance the clear indications of a crime. The place was in the utmost disorder. The cloth had been dragged from the table, littering the floor with broken glass, books, a tobacco jar, and various other objects. A chair sprawled on its back, the fender was dislodged from its position, the hearth-rug was all awry, and in the midst of the wreckage, on the space of floor between the table and the fireplace, the body of a man was stretched in a not-uneasy posture.

I stooped over him and looked him over searchingly, an elderly man, clean-shaved and slightly bald, with a grim, rather forbidding countenance, which was not, however, distorted or apparently unusual in expression. There were no obvious injuries, but the crumpled state of the collar caused me to look more closely at the throat and neck, and I then saw pretty plainly a number of slightly discoloured marks, such as would be made by fingers tightly grasping the throat. Evidently Badger had already observed them, for he remarked, "There's no need to ask you what he died of, Doctor. I can see that for myself."

"The actual cause of death," said I, "is not quite evident. He doesn't appear to have died from suffocation, but those are very unmistakable marks on the throat."

"Uncommonly," agreed Badger, "and they are enough for my purpose without any medical hair-splittings. How long do you think he has been dead?"

"From nine to twelve hours," I replied, "but nearer nine, I should think."

The inspector looked at his watch.

"That makes it between nine o'clock and midnight, but nearer midnight," said he. "Well, we shall hear if the night porter has anything to tell us. I've sent word for him to come over, and the laundress, too. And here is one of 'em."

It was, in fact, both of them, for when the inspector opened the door, they were discovered conversing eagerly in whispers. "One at a time," said Badger. "I'll have the porter in first," and, having admitted the man, he unceremoniously shut the door on the woman. The night porter saluted me as he came in – we were old acquaintances – and then halted near the door, where he stood stiffly, with his eyes riveted on the corpse.

"Now," said Badger, "I want you to try to remember if you let in any strangers last night, and if so, what their business was."

"I remember quite well," the porter replied. "I let in three strangers while I was on duty. One was going to Mr. Bolter in Fig Tree Court, one was going to Sir Alfred Blain's chambers, and the third said he had an appointment with Mr. Herrington."

"Ha!" exclaimed Badger, rubbing his hands. "Now, what time did you let him in?"

"It was just after ten-fifteen."

"Can you tell us what he was like and how he was dressed?"

"Yes," was the reply. "He didn't know where Tanfield Court was, and I had to walk down and show him, so I was able to have a good look at him. He was a middle-sized man, rather thin, dark hair, small moustache, no beard, and he had a long, sharp nose with a bump on the bridge. He wore a soft felt hat, a loose light overcoat, and he carried a thickish rough stick."

"What class of man was he? Seem to be a gentleman?"

"He was quite a gentlemanly kind of man, so far as I could judge, but he looked a bit shabby as to his clothes."

"Did you let him out?"

"Yes. He came to the gate a few minutes before eleven."

"And did you notice anything unusual about him then?"

"I did," the porter replied impressively. "I noticed that his collar was all crumpled and his hat was dusty and dented. His face was a bit red, and he looked rather upset, as if he had been having a tussle with somebody. I looked at him particularly and wondered what had been happening, seeing that Mr. Herrington was a quiet, elderly gentleman, though he was certainly a bit peppery at times."

The inspector took down these particulars gleefully in a large notebook and asked, "Is that all you know of the affair?" And when the porter replied that it was, he said, "Then I will ask you to read this statement and sign your name below it."

The porter read through his statement and carefully signed his name at the foot. He was about to depart when Badger said, "Before you go, perhaps you had better help us to move the body into the bedroom. It isn't decent to leave it lying there."

Accordingly the four of us lifted the dead man and carried him into the bedroom, where we laid him on the undisturbed bed and covered him with a rug. Then the porter was dismissed, with instructions to send in Mrs. Runt.

The laundress's statement was substantially a repetition of what Mr. Bidwell had told me. She had let herself into the chambers in the usual way, had come suddenly on the dead body of the tenant, and had forthwith rushed downstairs to give the alarm. When she had concluded, the inspector stood for a few moments looking thoughtfully at his notes.

"I suppose," he said presently, "you haven't looked round these chambers this morning? Can't say if there is anything unusual about them, or anything missing?"

The laundress shook her head.

"I was too upset," she said, with another furtive glance at the place where the corpse had lain, "but," she added, letting her eyes roam vaguely round the room, "there doesn't seem to be anything missing, so far as I can see – wait! Yes, there is. There's something gone from that nail on the wall, and it was there yesterday morning, because I remember dusting it."

"Ha!" exclaimed Badger. "Now what was it that was hanging on that nail?"

"Well," Mrs. Runt replied hesitatingly, "I really don't know what it was. Seemed like a sort of sword or dagger, but I never looked at it particularly, and I never took it off its nail. I used to dust it as it hung."

"Still," said Badger, "you can give us some sort of description of it, I suppose?"

"I don't know that I can," she replied. "It had a leather case, and the handle was covered with leather, I think, and it had a sort of loop, and it used to hang on that nail."

"Yes, you said that before," Badger commented sourly. "When you say it had a case, do you mean a sheath?"

"You can call it a sheath if you like," she retorted, evidently ruffled by the inspector's manner. "I call it a case."

"And how big was it? How long, for instance?"

Mrs. Runt held out her hands about a yard apart, looked at them critically, shortened the interval to a foot, extended it to two, and still varying the distance, looked vaguely at the inspector.

"I should say it was about that," she said.

"About what?" snorted Badger. "Do you mean a foot or two feet or a yard? Can't you give us some idea?"

"I can't say no clearer than what I have," she snapped. "I don't go round gentlemen's chambers measuring the things."

It seemed to me that Badger's questions were rather unnecessary, for the wall-paper below the nail gave the required information. A coloured patch on the faded ground furnished a pretty clear silhouette of a broad bladed sword or large dagger, about two-feet-six-inches long, which had apparently hung from the nail by a loop or ring at the end of the handle. But it was not my business to point this out. I turned to Bidwell and asked,

"Can you tell us what the thing was?"

"I am afraid I can't," he replied. "I have very seldom been in these chambers. Herrington and I usually met in mine and went to the club. I have a dim recollection of something hanging on that nail, but I have not the least idea what it was or what it was like. But do you think it really matters? The thing was almost certainly a curio of some kind. It couldn't have been of any appreciable value. It is absurd, on the face of it, to suppose that this man came to Herrington's chambers, apparently by appointment, and murdered him for the sake of getting possession of an antique sword or dagger. Don't you think so?"

I did, and so, apparently, did the inspector, with the qualification that the thing seemed to have disappeared, and its disappearance ought to be accounted for, which was perfectly true, though I did not quite see how the "accounting for" was to be effected. However, as the laundress had told all that she knew, Badger gave her her dismissal and she retired to the landing, where I noticed that the night porter was still lurking. Mr. Bidwell also took his departure, and happening, a few moments later, to glance out of the window, I saw him walking slowly across the court, apparently conferring with the laundress and the porter.

As soon as we were alone, Badger assumed a friendly and confidential manner and proceeded to give advice.

"I gather that Mr. Bidwell wants you to investigate this case, but I don't fancy it is in your line at all. It is just a matter of tracing that stranger and getting hold of him. Then we shall have to find out what property there was on these premises. The laundress says that there is nothing missing, but of course no one supposes that the man came here to take the furniture. It is most probable that the motive was robbery of some kind. There's no sign of anything broken open, but then, there wouldn't be, as the keys were available."

Nevertheless he prowled round the room, examining every receptacle that had a lock and trying the drawers of the writing-table and of what looked like a file cabinet.

"You will have your work cut out," I remarked, "to trace that man. The porter's description was pretty vague."

"Yes," he replied, "there isn't much to go on. That's where you come in," he added with a grin, "with your microscopes and air-pumps and things. Now if Dr. Thorndyke was here he would just sweep a bit of dust from the floor and collect any stray oddments and have a good look at them through his magnifier, and then we should know all about it. Can't you do a bit in that line? There's plenty of dust on the floor. And here's a pin. Wonderful significant thing is a pin. And here's a wax vesta – now, that ought to tell you quite a lot. And here is the end of a leather boot-lace – at least, that is what it looks like. That must have come out of somebody's boot. Have a look at it, Doctor, and see if you can tell me what kind of boot it came out of and whose boot it was."

He laid the fragment, and the match, and the pin on the table and grinned at me somewhat offensively. Inwardly I resented his impertinence – perhaps the more so since I realised that Thorndyke would probably not have been so completely gravelled as I undoubtedly was. But I considered it politic to take his clumsy irony in good part, and even to carry on his elephantine joke. Accordingly, I picked up the three "clues", one after the other, and examined them gravely, noting that the supposed boot-lace appeared to be composed of whalebone or vulcanite.

"Well, Inspector," I said. "I can't give you the answer off-hand. There's no microscope here. But I will examine these objects at my leisure and let you have the information in due course."

With that I wrapped them with ostentatious care in a piece of note and bestowed them in my pocket, a proceeding which the inspector watched with a sour smile.

"I'm afraid you'll be too late," said he. "Our men will probably pick up the tracks while you are doing the microscope stunt. However, I mustn't stay here any longer. We can't do anything until we know what valuables there were on the premises, and I must have the body removed and examined by the police surgeon."

He moved towards the door, and as I had no further business in the rooms, I followed, and leaving him to lock up, I took my way back to our chambers.

When Thorndyke returned to town a couple of days later, I mentioned the case to him. But what Badger had said appeared to be true. It was a case of ascertaining the identity of the stranger who had visited the dead man on that fatal night, and this seemed to be a matter for the police rather than for us. So the case remained in abeyance until the evening following the inquest, when Mr. Bidwell called on us, accompanied by a Mr. Carston, whom he introduced as an old friend of his and of Herrington's family.

"I have called," he said, "to bring you a full report of the evidence at the inquest. I had a shorthand writer there, and this is a typed transcript of his notes. Nothing fresh transpired beyond what Dr. Jervis knows and has probably told you, but I thought you had better have all the information in writing."

"There is no clue as to who the suspicious visitor was, I suppose?" said Thorndyke.

"Not the slightest," replied Bidwell. "The porter's description is all they have to go on, and of course it would apply to hundreds of persons. But, in connection with that, there is a question on which I should like to take your opinion. Poor Herrington once mentioned to me that he was subjected to a good deal of annoyance by a certain person who from time to time applied to him for financial help. I gathered that some sort of claim was advanced, and that the demands for money were more or less of the nature of blackmail. Giles didn't say who the person was, but I got the impression that he was a relative. Now, my friend Carston, who attended the inquest with me, noticed that the porter's description of the stranger would apply fairly well to a nephew of Giles's, whom he knows slightly and who is a somewhat shady character, and the question that Carston and I have been debating is whether these facts ought to be communicated to the police. It is a serious matter to put a man under suspicion on such very slender data, and yet – "

"And yet," said Carston, "the facts certainly fit the circumstances. This fellow – his name is Godfrey Herrington – is a typical ne'er-do-weel. Nobody knows how he lives. He doesn't appear to do any work. And then there is the personality of the deceased. I didn't know Giles Herrington very well, but I knew his brother, Sir Gilbert, pretty intimately, and if Giles was at all like him, a catastrophe might easily have occurred."

"What was Sir Gilbert's special characteristic?" Thorndyke asked.

"Unamiability," was the reply. "He was a most cantankerous, overbearing man, and violent at times. I knew him when I was at the Colonial Office with him, and one of his official acts will show the sort of man he was. You may remember it, Bidwell – the Bekwè affair. There was some trouble in Bekwè, which is one of the minor kingdoms bordering on Ashanti, and Sir Gilbert was sent out as a special commissioner to settle it. And settle it he did – with a vengeance. He took up an armed force, deposed the king of Bekwè, seized the royal stool, message stick, state sword, drums, and the other insignia of royalty, and brought them away with him. And what made it worse was that he treated these important things as mere loot kept some of them himself and gave away others as presents to his friends.

"It was an intolerably high-handed proceeding, and it caused a rare outcry. Even the Colonial Governor protested, and in the end the Secretary of State directed the Governor to reinstate the king and restore the stolen insignia, as these things went with the royal title and were necessary for the ceremonies of reinstatement or the accession of a new king."

"And were they restored?" asked Bidwell.

"Most of them were. But just about this time Gilbert died, and as the whereabouts of one or two of them were unknown, it was impossible to collect them then. I don't know if they have been found since."

Here Thorndyke led Mr. Carston back to the point from which he had digressed.

"You are suggesting that certain peculiarities of temper and temperament on the part of the deceased might have some bearing on the circumstances of his death."

"Yes," said Carston. "If Giles Herrington was at all like his brother – I don't know whether he was – " here he looked inquiringly at Bidwell, who nodded emphatically.

"I should say he was, undoubtedly," said he. "He was my friend, and I was greatly attached to him, but to others, I must admit, he must have appeared a decidedly morose, cantankerous, and irascible man."

"Very well," resumed Carston. "If you imagine this cadging, blackmailing wastrel calling on him and trying to squeeze him, and then you imagine Herrington refusing to be squeezed and becoming abusive and even violent, you have a fair set of antecedents for – for what, in fact, did happen."

"By the way," said Thorndyke, "what exactly did happen, according to the evidence?"

"The medical evidence," replied Bidwell, "showed that the immediate cause of death was heart failure. There were marks of fingers on the throat, as you know, and various other bruises. It was evident that deceased had been violently assaulted, but death was not directly due to the injuries."

"And the finding of the jury?" asked Thorndyke.

"Wilful murder, committed by some person unknown."

"It doesn't appear to me," said I, "that Mr. Carston's suggestion has much present bearing on the case. It is really a point for the defence. But we are concerned with the identity of the unknown man."

"I am inclined to agree with Dr. Jervis," said Bidwell. "We have got to catch the hare before we go into culinary details."

"My point is," said Carston, "that Herrington's peculiar temper suggests a set of circumstances that would render it probable that his visitor was his nephew Godfrey."

"There is some truth in that," Thorndyke agreed. "It is highly speculative, but a reasonable speculation cannot be disregarded when the known facts are so few. My feeling is that the police ought to be informed of the existence of this man and his possible relations with the deceased. As to whether he is or is not the suspected stranger, that could be settled at once if he were confronted with the night porter."

"Yes, that is true," said Bidwell "I think Carston and I had better call at Scotland Yard and give the Assistant Commissioner a hint on the subject. It will have to be a very guarded hint, of course."

"Was the question of motive raised?" Thorndyke asked. "As to robbery, for instance."

"There is no evidence of robbery," replied Bidwell. "I have been through all the receptacles in the chambers, and everything seems intact. The keys were in poor Giles's pocket and nothing seems to have been disturbed – indeed, it doesn't appear that there was any portable property of value on the premises."

"Well," said Thorndyke, "the first thing that has to be done is to establish the identity of the nocturnal visitor. That is the business of the police. And if you call and tell them what you have told us, they will, at least, have something to investigate. They should have no difficulty in proving either that he is or is not the man whom the porter let in at the gate, and until they have settled that question, there is no need for us to take any action."

"Exactly," said Bidwell, rising and taking up his hat. "If the police can complete the case, there is nothing for us to do. However, I will leave you the report of the inquest to look over at your leisure, and will keep you informed as to how the case progresses."

When our two friends had gone, Thorndyke sat for some time turning over the sheets of the report and glancing through the depositions of the witnesses. Presently he remarked, "If it turns out that this man, Godfrey Herrington, is not the man whom the porter let in, the police will be left in the air. Apart from Bidwell's purely speculative suggestion, there seems to be no clue whatever to the visitor's identity."

"Badger would like to hear you say that," said I. "He was very sarcastic respecting our methods of research." And here I gave him an account of my interview with the inspector, including the "clues" with which he had presented me.

"It was like his impudence," Thorndyke commented smilingly, "to pull the leg of my learned junior. Still, there was a germ of sense in what he said. A collection of dust from the floor of that room, in which two men had engaged in a violent struggle, would certainly yield traces of both of them."

"Mixed up with the traces of a good many others," I remarked.

"True," he admitted. "But that would not affect the value of a positive trace of a particular individual. Supposing, for instance, that Godfrey Herrington were known to have dyed hair, and suppose that one or more dyed male hairs were found in the dust from the floor of the room. That would establish a probability that he had been in that room, and also that he was the person who had struggled with the deceased."

"Yes, I see that," said I. "Perhaps I ought to have collected some of the dust. But it isn't too late now, as Bidwell has locked up the chambers, Meanwhile, let me present you with Badger's clues. They came off the floor."

I searched in my pocket and produced the paper packet, the existence of which I had forgotten, and having opened it, offered it to him with an ironical bow. He looked gravely at the little collection and, disregarding the pin and the match, picked out the third object and examined it curiously.

"That is the alleged boot-lace end," he remarked. "It doesn't do much credit to Badger's powers of observation. It is as unlike leather as it could well be."

"Yes," I agreed, "it is obviously whalebone or vulcanite."

"It isn't vulcanite," said he, looking closely at the broken end and getting out his pocket lens for a more minute inspection.

"What do you suppose it is?" I asked, my curiosity stimulated by the evident interest with which he was examining the object.

"We needn't suppose," he replied. "I fancy that if we get Polton to make a cross section of it, the microscope will tell us what it is. I will take it up to him." As he went out and I heard him ascending to the laboratory where our assistant, Polton, was at work, I was conscious of a feeling of vexation and a sense of failure. It was always thus. I had treated this fragment with the same levity as had the inspector, just dropping it into my pocket and forgetting it. Probably the thing was of no interest or importance, but whether it was or not, Thorndyke would not be satisfied until he knew for certain what it was. And that habit of examining everything, of letting nothing pass without the closest scrutiny, was one of the great secrets of his success as an investigator.

When he came down again I reopened the subject.

"It has occurred to me," I said, "that it might be as well for us to have a look at that room. My inspection was rather perfunctory, as Badger was there."

"I have just been thinking the same," he replied. "If Godfrey is not the man, and the police are left stranded, Bidwell will look to us to take up the inquiry, and by that time the room may have been disturbed. I think we will get the key from Bidwell to-morrow morning and make a thorough examination. And we may as well adopt Badger's excellent suggestion respecting the dust. I will instruct Polton to come over with us and bring a full-sized vacuum-cleaner, and we can go over what he collects at our leisure."

Agreeably to this arrangement, we presented ourselves on the following morning at Mr. Bidwell's chambers, accompanied by Polton, who, however, being acutely conscious of the vacuum-cleaner, which was thinly disguised in brown paper, sneaked up the stairs and got out of sight. Bidwell opened the door himself, and Thorndyke explained our intentions to him.

"Of course you can have the key," he said, "but I don't know that it is worth your while to go into the matter. There have been developments since I saw you last night. When Carston and I called at Scotland Yard, we found that we were too late. Godfrey Herrington had come forward and made a voluntary statement."

"That was wise of him," said Thorndyke, "but he would have been wiser still to have notified the porter of what had happened and sent for a doctor. He claims that the death was a misadventure, of course?"

"Not at all," replied Bidwell. "He states that when be left, Giles was perfectly well, so well that he was able to kick him – Godfrey – down the stairs and pitch him out on to the pavement. It seems, according to his account, that he called to try to get some financial help from his uncle. He admits that he was rather importunate and persisted after Giles had definitely refused. Then Giles got suddenly into a rage, thrust him out of the chambers, ran him down the stairs, and threw him out into Tanfield Court. It is a perfectly coherent story, and quite probable up to a certain point, but it doesn't account for the bruises on Giles's body or the finger-marks on his throat."

"No," agreed Thorndyke. "Either he is lying, or he is the victim of some very inexplicable circumstances. But I gather that you have no further interest in the case?"

Bidwell reflected.

"Well," he said, "I don't know about that. Of course I don't believe him, but it is just possible that he is telling the truth. My feeling is that, if he is guilty, I want him convicted, but if by any chance he is innocent – well, he is Giles's nephew, and I suppose it is my duty to see that he has a fair chance. Yes, I think I would like you to watch the case independently – with a perfectly open mind, neither for nor against. But I don't see that there is much that you can do."

"Neither do I," said Thorndyke. "But one can observe and note the visible facts, if there are any. Has anything been done to the rooms?"

"Nothing whatever," was the reply. "They are just as Dr. Jervis and I found them the morning after the catastrophe."

With this, he handed Thorndyke the key and we ascended to the landing, where we found Polton on guard with the vacuum-cleaner, like a sentry armed with some new and unorthodox weapon.

The appearance of the room was unchanged. The half-dislodged table-cloth, the litter of broken glass on the floor, even the displaced fender and hearth-rug, were just as I had last seen them. Thorndyke looked about him critically and remarked "The appearances hardly support Godfrey's statement. There was clearly a prolonged and violent struggle, not a mere ejectment. And look at the table cloth. The uncovered part of the table is that nearest the door, and most of the things have fallen off at the end nearest the fireplace. Obviously, the body that dislodged the cloth was moving away from the door, not towards it, which again suggests something more than an unresisted ejectment."

He again looked round, and his glance fell on the nail and the coloured silhouette on the wall-paper.

"That, I presume," said he, "is where the mysterious sword or dagger hung. It is rather large for a dagger and somewhat wide for a sword, though barbaric swords are of all shapes and sizes."

He produced his spring tape and carefully measured the phantom shape on the wall. "Thirty-one inches long," he reported, "including the loop at the end of the handle, by which it hung, seven-and-a-half inches at the top of the scabbard, tapering rather irregularly to three inches at the tip. A curious shape. I don't remember ever having seen a sword quite like it."

Meanwhile Polton, having picked up the broken glass and other objects, had uncovered the vacuum-cleaner and now started the motor – which was driven by an attached dry battery – and proceeded very systematically to trundle the machine along the floor. At every two or three sweeps he paused to empty the receiver, placing the grey, felt-like mass on a sheet of paper, with a pencilled note of the part of the room from whence it came. The size of these masses of felted dust, and the astonishing change in the colour of the carpet that marked the trail of the cleaner, suggested that Mrs. Runt's activities had been of a somewhat perfunctory character. Polton's dredgings apparently represented the accumulations of years.

"Wonderful lot of hairs in this old dust," Polton remarked as he deposited a fresh consignment on the paper, "especially in this lot. It came from under that looking-glass on the wall. Perhaps that clothes brush that hangs under the glass accounts for it."

"Yes," I agreed, "they will be hairs brushed off Mr. Herrington's collar and shoulders. But," I added, taking the brush from its nail and examining it, "Mrs. Runt seems to have used the glass, too. There are three long hairs still sticking to the brush."

As Thorndyke was still occupied in browsing inquisitively round the room, I proceeded to make a preliminary inspection of the heaps of dust, picking out the hairs and other recognisable objects with my pocket forceps, and putting them on a separate sheet of paper. Of the former, the bulk were pretty obviously those of the late tenant – white or dull black male hairs – but Mrs. Runt had contributed quite liberally, for I picked out of the various heaps over a dozen long hairs, the mousy brown colour of which seemed to identify them as hers. The remainder were mostly ordinary male hairs of various colours, eyebrow hairs and eyelashes, of no special interest, with one exception. This was a black hair which lay flat on the paper in a Close coil, like a tiny watch-spring.

"I wonder who this black man was," said I, inspecting it through my lens.

"Probably some African or West Indian Law student," Thorndyke suggested. "There are always a good many about the Inns of Court."

He came round to examine my collection, and while he was viewing the black man's hair with the aid of my lens, I renewed my investigation of the little dust-heaps. Presently I made a new discovery.

"Why," I exclaimed, "here is another of Badger's boot-laces – another piece of the same one, I think. By the way, did you ascertain what that boot-lace really was?"

"Yes," he replied. "Polton made a section of it and mounted it, and furthermore, he made a magnified photograph of it. I have the photograph in my pocket, so you can answer your own question."

He produced from his letter-case a half-plate print which he handed to me and which I examined curiously.

"It is a singular object," said I, "but I don't quite make it out. It looks rather like a bundle of hairs embedded in some transparent substance."

"That, in effect," he replied, "is what it is. It is an elephant's hair, probably from the tail. But, as you see, it is a compound hair, virtually a group of hairs agglutinated into a single stem. Most very large hairs are compound. A tiger's whiskers, for instance, are large, stiff hairs which, if cut across, are seen to be formed of several largish hairs fused together, and the colossal hair which grows on the nose of the rhinoceros – the so-called nasal horn – is made up of thousands of subordinate hairs."

"It is a remarkable-looking thing," I said, handing back the photograph, "very distinctive – if you happen to know what it is. But the mystery is how on earth it came here. There are no elephants in the Temple."

"I certainly haven't noticed any," he replied, "and, as you say, the presence of an elephant's hair in a room in the middle of London is a rather remarkable circumstance. And yet, perhaps, if we consider all the other circumstances, it may not be impossible to form a conjecture as to how it came here. I recommend the problem to my learned friend for consideration at his leisure. And now, as we have seen all that there is to see – which is mighty little – we may as well leave Polton to finish the collection of data from the floor. We can take your little selection with us."

He folded the paper containing the hairs that I had picked out into a neat packet, which he slipped into his pocket. Then, having handed the key of the outer door to Polton for return to Mr. Bidwell, he went out and I followed. We descended the stairs slowly, both of us deeply reflective. As to the subject of his meditations I could form no opinion, but my own were occupied by the problem which he had suggested, and the more I reflected on it, the less capable of solution did it appear.

We had nearly reached the ground floor when I became aware of quick footsteps descending the stairs behind us. Near the entry our follower overtook us, and as we stood aside to let him pass, I had a brief vision of a shortish, dapper, smartly-dressed black man – apparently an African or West Indian – who carried a small suit-case and a set of golf-clubs.

"Now," said I, in a low tone, "I wonder if that gentleman is the late owner of that hair that I picked up. It seems intrinsically probable as he appears to live in this building, and would be a near neighbour of Herrington's." I halted at the entry and read out the only name painted on the door-post as appertaining to the second floor – Mr. Kwaku Essien.

But Thorndyke was not listening. His long legs were already carrying him, with a deceptively leisurely air, across Tanfield Court in the wake of Mr. Essien, and at about the same pace. I put on a spurt and over took him, a little mystified by his sudden air of purpose and by the fact that he was not walking in the direction of our chambers. Still more mystified was I when it became clear that Thorndyke was following the African and keeping at a constant distance in rear of him, but I made no comment until, having pursued our quarry to the top of Middle Temple Lane, we saw him hail a taxi and drive off. Then I demanded an explanation.

"I wanted to see him fairly out of the precincts," was the reply, "because I have a particular desire to see what his chambers are like. I only hope his door has a practicable latch."

I stared at him in dismay.

"You surely don't contemplate breaking into his chambers!" I exclaimed.

"Certainly not," he replied. "If the latch won't yield to gentle persuasion I shall give it up. But don't let me involve you, Jervis. I admit that it is a slightly irregular proceeding."

498

"Irregular!" I repeated. "It is house-breaking, pure and simple. I can only hope that you won't be able to get in."

The hope turned out to be a vain one, as I had secretly feared. When we had reconnoitred the stairs and established the encouraging fact that the third floor was untenanted, we inspected the door above which our victim's name was painted, and a glance at the yawning key of an old-fashioned draw-latch told me that the deed was as good as done.

"Now, Jervis," said Thorndyke, producing from his pocket the curious instrument that he described as a "smoker's companion – " It was an undeniable pick-lock, made by Polton under his direction. " – you had better clear out and wait for me at our chambers."

"I shall do nothing of the kind," I replied. "I am an accessory before the fact already, so I may as well stay and see the crime committed."

"Then in that case," said he, "you had better keep a look-out from the landing window and call me if any one comes to the house. That will make us perfectly safe."

I accordingly took my station at the window, and Thorndyke, having knocked several times at the "oak" without eliciting any response, set to work with the smoker's companion. In less than a minute the latch clicked, the outer door opened, and Thorndyke, pushing the inner door open, entered, leaving both doors ajar. I was devoured by curiosity as to what his purpose was. Obviously it must be a very definite one to justify this most extraordinary proceeding. But I dared not leave my post for a moment, seeing that we were really engaged in a very serious breach of the law and it was of vital importance that we should not be surprised in the act. I was therefore unable to observe my colleague's proceedings, and I waited impatiently to see if anything came of this unlawful entry.

I had waited thus some ten minutes, keeping a close watch on the pavement below, when I heard Thorndyke quickly cross the room and approach the door. A moment later he came out on the landing, bearing in his hand an object which, while it enlightened me as to the purpose of the raid, added to my mystification.

"That looks like the missing sword from Herrington's room!" I exclaimed, gazing at it in amazement.

"Yes," he replied. "I found it in a drawer in the bedroom. Only it isn't a sword."

"Then what the deuce is it?" I demanded, for the thing looked like a broad-bladed sword in a soft leather scabbard of somewhat rude native workman ship.

By way of reply he slowly drew the object from its sheath, and as it came into sight, I uttered an exclamation of astonishment. To the inexpert eye it appeared an elongated body about nine inches in length covered with coarse, black leather, from either side of which sprang a multitude of what looked like thick, black wires. Above, it was furnished with a leather handle which was surmounted by a suspension loop of plaited leather.

"I take it," said I, "that this is an elephant's tail."

"Yes," he replied, "and a rather remarkable specimen. The hairs are of unusual length. Some of them, you see, are nearly eighteen inches long."

"And what are you going to do now?" I asked.

"I am going to put it back where I found it. Then I shall run down to Scotland Yard and advise Miller to get a search warrant. He is too discreet to ask inconvenient questions."

I must admit that it was a great relief to me when, a minute later, Thorndyke came out and shut the door, but I could not deny that the raid had been justified by the results. What had, presumably, been a mere surmise had been converted into a definite fact on which action could confidently be taken.

"I suppose," said I, as we walked down towards the Embankment en route for Scotland Yard, "I ought to have spotted this case."

"You had the means," Thorndyke replied. "At your first visit, you learned that an object of some kind had disappeared from the wall. It seemed to be a trivial object of no value, and not likely to be connected with the crime. So you disregarded it. But it *had* disappeared. Its disappearance was not accounted for, and that disappearance seemed to coincide in time with the death of Herrington. It undoubtedly called for investigation. Then you found on the floor an object the nature of which was unknown to you. Obviously, you ought to have ascertained what it was."

"Yes, I ought," I admitted, "though I am not sure that I should have been much forrader even then. In fact, I am not so very much forrader even now. I don't see how you spotted this man Essien, and I don't understand why he took all this trouble and risk and even committed a murder to get possession of this trumpery curio. Of course I can make a vague guess. But I should like to hear how you ran the man and the thing to earth."

"Very well," said Thorndyke. "Let me retrace the train of discoveries and inferences in their order. First I learned that an object, supposed to be a barbaric sword of some kind, had disappeared about the time of the murder – if it was a murder. Then we heard from Carston that Sir Gilbert Herrington had appropriated the insignia and ceremonial objects belonging to the King of Bekwè, that some had subsequently been restored, but others had been given to friends as curios. As I

500

listened to that story, the possibility occurred to me that this curio which had disappeared might be one of the missing ceremonial objects. It was not only possible, it was quite probable. For Giles Herrington was a very likely person to have received one of these gifts, and his morose temper made it unlikely that he would restore it. And then, since such an object would be of great value to somebody, and since it was actually stolen property, there would be good reasons why some interested person should take forcible possession of it. This, of course, was mere hypothesis of a rather shadowy kind. But when you produced an object which I at once suspected, and then proved, to be an elephant's hair, the hypothesis became a reasonable working theory. For, among the ceremonial objects which form what we may call the regalia of a West African king is the elephant's tail which is carried before him by a special officer as a symbol of his power and strength. An elephant's tail had pretty certainly been stolen from the king, and Carston said nothing about its having been restored.

"Well, when we went to Herrington's chambers just now, it was clear to me that the thing which had disappeared was certainly not a sword. The phantom shape on the wall did not show much, but it did show plainly that the object had hung from the nail by a large loop at the end of the handle. But the suspension loop of a sword or dagger is always on the scabbard, never on the hilt. But if the thing was not a sword, what was it? The elephant's hair that you found on the floor seemed to answer the question.

"Now, as we came in, I had noticed on the doorpost the West African name, Kwaku Essien. But if this was an elephant's tail, its lawful owner was a black man, and that owner wanted to recover it and was morally entitled to take possession of it. Here was another striking agreement. The chambers over Herrington's were occupied by a black man. Finally, you found among the floor dust a black man's hair. Then a black man had actually been in this room. But from what we know of Herrington, that black man was not there as an invited visitor. All the probabilities pointed to Mr. Essien. But the probabilities were not enough to act on. Then we had a stroke of sheer luck. We got the chance to explore Essien's chambers and seek the crucial fact. But here we are at Scotland Yard."

That night, at about eight o'clock, a familiar tattoo on our knocker announced the arrival of Mr. Superintendent Miller, not entirely unexpected as I guessed.

"Well," he said, as I let him in, "the fellow has come home. I've just had a message from the man who was detailed to watch the premises."

"Are you going to make the arrest now?" asked Thorndyke.

501

"Yes, and I should be glad if you could come across with me. You know more about the case than I do."

Thorndyke assented at once, and we set forth together. As we entered Tanfield Court we passed a man who was lurking in the shadow of an entry, and who silently indicated the lighted windows of the chambers for which we were bound. Ascending the stairs up which I had lately climbed with unlawful intent, we halted at Mr. Essien's door, on which the superintendent executed an elaborate flourish with his stick, there being no knocker. After a short interval we heard a bolt with drawn, the door opened a short distance, and in the interval a man's face appeared looking out at us suspiciously.

"Who are you, and what do you want?" the owner of the face demanded gruffly.

"You are Mr. Kwaku Essien, I think?" said Miller, unostentatiously insinuating his foot into the door opening.

"Yes," was the reply. "But I don't know you. What is your business?"

"I am a police officer," Miller replied, edging his foot in a little farther, "and I hold a warrant to arrest you on the charge of having murdered Mr. Giles Herrington."

Before the superintendent had fairly finished his sentence, the man vanished and the door slammed violently – onto the superintendent's massive foot. That foot was instantly reinforced by a shoulder and for a few moments there was a contest of forces, opposite but not equal. Suddenly the door flew open and the superintendent charged into the room. I had a momentary vision of a flying figure, closely pursued, darting through into an inner room, of the slamming of a second door – once more on an intercepting foot. And then – it all seemed to have happened in a few seconds – a dejected figure, sitting on the edge of a bed, clasping a pair of manacled hands and watching Miller as he drew the elephant's tail out of a drawer in the dressing-chest.

"This – er – article," said Miller, "belonged to Mr. Herrington, and was stolen from his premises on the night of the murder."

Essien shook his head emphatically.

"No," he replied. "You are wrong. I stole nothing, and I did not murder Mr. Herrington. Listen to me and I will tell you all about it."

Miller administered the usual caution and the prisoner continued, "This elephant-brush is one of many things stolen, years ago, from the King of Bekwè. Some of those things – most of them – have been restored, but this could not be traced for a long time. At last it became known to me that Mr. Herrington had it, and I wrote to him asking him to give it up and telling him who I was – I am the eldest living son of the

502

king's sister, and therefore, according to our law, the heir to the kingdom. But he would not give it up or even sell it. Then, as I am a student of the Inn, I took these chambers above his, intending, when I had an opportunity, to go in and take possession of my uncle's property.

The opportunity came that night that you have spoken of. I was coming up the stairs to my chambers when, as I passed his door, I heard loud voices inside as of people quarrelling. I had just reached my own door and opened it when I heard his door open, and then a great uproar and the sound of a struggle. I ran down a little way and looked over the banisters, and then I saw him thrusting a man across the landing and down the lower stairs. As they disappeared, I ran down, and finding his door ajar, I went in to recover my property. It took me a little time to find it, and I had just taken it from the nail and was going out with it when, at the door, I met Mr. Herrington coming in. He was very excited already, and when he saw me he seemed to go mad. I tried to get past him, but he seized me and dragged me back into the room, wrenching the thing out of my hand.

He was very violent. I thought he wanted to kill me, and I had to struggle for my life. Suddenly he let go his hold of me, staggered back a few paces, and then fell on the floor. I stooped over him, thinking that he was taken ill, and wondering what I had better do. But soon I saw that he was not ill, he was dead. Then I was very frightened. I picked up the elephant brush and put it back into its case, and I went out very quietly, shut the door, and ran up to my rooms. That is what happened. There was no robbery and murder."

"Well," said Miller, as the prisoner and his escort disappeared towards the gate, "I suppose, in a technical sense, it is murder, but they are hardly likely to press the charge."

"I don't think it is even technically," said Thorndyke. "My feeling is that he will be acquitted if he is sent for trial. Meanwhile, I take it that my client, Godfrey Herrington, will be released from custody at once."

"Yes, Doctor," replied Miller, "I will see to that now. He has had better luck than he deserved, I suspect, in having his case looked after by you. I don't fancy he would have got an acquittal if he had gone for trial."

Thorndyke's forecast was nearly correct, but there was no acquittal, since there was no trial. The case against Kwaku Essien never got farther than the Grand Jury.

The Pathologist to the Rescue

"**I** hope," said I, as I looked anxiously out of our window up King's Bench Walk, "that our friend, Foxley, will turn up to time, or I shall lose the chance of hearing his story. I must be in court by half-past-eleven. The telegram said that he was a parson, didn't it?"

"Yes," replied Thorndyke. "The Reverend Arthur Foxley."

"Then perhaps this may be he. There is a parson crossing from the Row in this direction, only he has a girl with him. He didn't say anything about a girl, did he?"

"No. He merely asked for the appointment. However," he added, as he joined me at the window and watched the couple approaching with their eyes apparently fixed on the number above our portico, "this is evidently our client, and punctual to the minute."

In response to the old-fashioned flourish on our little knocker, he opened the inner door and invited the clergyman and his companion to enter, and while the mutual introductions were in progress, I looked critically at our new clients. Mr. Foxley was a typical and favourable specimen of his class, a handsome, refined, elderly gentleman, prim as to his speech, suave and courteous in bearing, with a certain engaging simplicity of manner which impressed me very favourably. His companion I judged to be a parishioner, for she was what ladies are apt to describe as "not quite" – that is to say, her social level appeared to appertain to the lower strata of the middle-class. But she was a fine, strapping girl, very sweet-faced and winsome, quiet and gentle in manner and obviously in deep trouble, for her clear grey eyes – fixed earnestly, almost devouringly, on Thorndyke – were reddened and swimming with unshed tears.

"We have sought your aid, Dr. Thorndyke," the clergyman began, "on the advice of my friend, Mr. Brodribb, who happened to call on me on some business. He assured me that you would be able to solve our difficulties if it were humanly possible, so I have come to lay those difficulties before you. I pray to God that you may be able to help us, for my poor young friend here, Miss Markham, is in a most terrible position, as you will understand when I tell you that her future husband, a most admirable young man named Robert Fletcher, is in the custody of the police, charged with robbery and murder."

Thorndyke nodded gravely, and the clergyman continued. "I had better tell you exactly what has happened. The dead man is one Joseph Riggs, a maternal uncle of Fletcher's, a strange, eccentric man, solitary, miserly, and of a violent, implacable temper. He was quite well-to-do, though penurious and haunted constantly by an absurd fear of poverty. His nephew, Robert, was apparently his only known relative and, under his will, was his sole heir. Recently, however, Robert has become engaged to my friend, Miss Lilian, and this engagement was violently opposed by his uncle, who had repeatedly urged him to make what he called a 'profitable' marriage. For Miss Lilian is a dowerless maiden – dowerless save for those endowments with which God has been pleased to enrich her, and which her future husband has properly prized above mere material wealth. However, Riggs declared, in his brutal way, that he was not going to leave his property to the husband of a shop-woman, and that Robert might look out for a wife with money or be struck out of his will.

"The climax was reached yesterday when Robert, in response to a peremptory summons, went to see his uncle. Mr. Riggs was in a very intractable mood. He demanded that Robert should break off his engagement unconditionally and at once, and when Robert bluntly insisted on his right to choose his own wife the old man worked himself up into a furious rage, shouting, cursing, using the most offensive language and even uttering threats of personal violence. Finally, he drew his gold watch from his pocket and laid it with its chain on the table then, opening a drawer, he took out a bundle of bearer bonds and threw them down by the watch.

"'There, my friend,' said he, 'that is your inheritance. That is all you will get from me, living or dead. Take it and go, and don't let me ever set eyes on you again.'

"At first Robert refused to accept the gift, but his uncle became so violent that eventually, for peace's sake, he took the watch and the bonds, intending to return them later, and went away. He left at half-past-five, leaving his uncle alone in the house."

"How was that?" Thorndyke asked. "Was there no servant?"

"Mr. Riggs kept no resident servant. The young woman who did his housework came at half-past eight in the morning and left at half-past-four. Yesterday she waited until five to get tea ready, but then, as the uproar in the sitting-room was still unabated, she thought it best to go. She was afraid to go in to lay the tea-things.

"This morning, when she arrived at the house, she found the front door unlocked, as it always was during the day. On entering, her attention was at once attracted by two or three little pools of blood on the floor of the hall, or passage. Somewhat alarmed by this, she looked into the sitting-room, and finding no one there, and being impressed by the silence in the house, she went along the passage to a back room – a sort

505

of study or office, which was usually kept locked when Mr. Riggs was not in. Now, however, it was unlocked and the door was ajar, so having first knocked and receiving no answer, she pushed open the door and looked in, and there, to her horror, she saw her employer lying on the floor, apparently dead, with a wound on the side of his head and a pistol on the floor by his side.

"Instantly she turned and rushed out of the house, and she was running up the street in search of a policeman when she encountered me at a corner and burst out with her dreadful tidings. I walked with her to the police station, and as we went she told me what had happened on the previous afternoon. Naturally, I was profoundly shocked and also alarmed, for I saw that − rightly or wrongly − suspicion must immediately fall on Robert Fletcher. The servant, Rose Turnmill, took it for granted that he had murdered her master, and when we found the station inspector, and Rose had repeated her statement to him, it was evident that he took the same view.

"With him and a sergeant, we went back to the house, but on the way we met Mr. Brodribb, who was staying at The White Lion and had just come out for a walk. I told him, rapidly, what had occurred and begged him to come with us, which, with the inspector's consent, he did, and as we walked I explained to him the awful position that Robert Fletcher might be placed in, and asked him to advise me what to do. But, of course, there was nothing to be said or done until we had seen the body and knew whether any suspicion rested on Robert.

"We found the man Riggs lying as Rose had said. He was quite dead, cold and stiff. There was a pistol wound on the right temple, and a pistol lay on the floor at his right side. A little blood − but not much − had trickled from the wound and lay in a small pool on the oilcloth. The door of an iron safe was open and a bunch of keys hung from the lock, and on a desk one or two share certificates were spread out. On searching the dead man's pockets, it was found that the gold watch which the servant told us he usually carried was missing, and when Rose went to the bedroom to see if it was there, it was nowhere to be found.

"Apart from the watch, however, the appearances suggested that the man had taken his own life. But against this view was the blood on the hall floor. The dead man appeared to have fallen at once from the effects of the shot, and there had been very little bleeding. Then how came the blood in the hall? The inspector decided that it could not have been the blood of the deceased, and when we examined it and saw that there were several little pools and that they seemed to form a track towards the street door, he was convinced that the blood had fallen from some person who had been wounded and was escaping from the house. And, under the circumstances, he was bound to assume that that person was Robert Fletcher, and on that assumption, he dispatched the sergeant forthwith to arrest Robert.

"On this I held a consultation with Mr. Brodribb, who pointed out that the case turned principally on the blood in the hall. If it was the blood of deceased, and the absence of the watch could be explained, a verdict of suicide could be accepted. But if it was the blood of some other person, that fact would point to murder. The question, he said, would have to be settled, if possible, and his advice to me, if I believed Robert to be innocent – which, from my knowledge of him, I certainly did – was this: Get a couple of small, clean, labelled bottles from a chemist and – with the inspector's consent – put in one a little of the blood from the hall and in the other some of the blood of the deceased. Seal them both in the inspector's presence and mine and take them up to Dr. Thorndyke. If it is possible to answer the question, Are they or are they not from the same person? He will answer it.

"Well, the inspector made no objection, so I did what he advised. And here are the specimens. I trust they may tell us what we want to know."

Here Mr. Foxley took from his attaché case a small cardboard box and, opening it, displayed two little wide-mouthed bottles carefully packed in cotton wool. Lifting them out tenderly, he placed them on the table before Thorndyke. They were both neatly corked, sealed – with Brodribb's seal, as I noticed – and labelled, the one inscribed "*Blood of Joseph Riggs*", and the other "*Blood of Unknown Origin*", and both signed "*Arthur Foxley*" and dated. At the bottom of each was a small mass of gelatinous blood-clot.

Thorndyke looked a little dubiously at the two bottles, and addressing the clergyman, said, "I am afraid Mr. Brodribb has rather over-estimated our resources. There is no known method by which the blood of one person can be distinguished with certainty from that of another."

"Dear, dear!" exclaimed Mr. Foxley. "How disappointing! Then these specimens are useless, after all?"

"I won't say that, but it is in the highest degree improbable that they will yield any information. You must build no expectations on them."

"But you will examine them and see if anything is to be gleaned," the parson urged, persuasively.

"Yes, I will examine them. But you realise that if they should yield any evidence, that evidence might be unfavourable?"

"Yes, Mr. Brodribb pointed that out, but we are willing to take the risk – and so, I may say, is Robert Fletcher, to whom I put the question."

"Then you have seen Mr. Fletcher since the discovery?"

"Yes, I saw him at the police station after his arrest. It was then that he gave me – and also the police – the particulars that I have repeated to you. He had to make a statement, as the dead man's watch and the bonds were found in his possession."

"With regard to the pistol. Has it been identified?"

"No. It is an old-fashioned derringer which no one has ever seen before, so there is no evidence as to whose property it was."

"And as to those share certificates which you spoke of as lying on the desk. Do you happen to remember what they were?"

"Yes, they were West African mining shares – Abusum Pa-pa was the name, I think."

"Then," said Thorndyke, "Mr. Riggs had been losing money. The Abusum Pa-pa Company has just gone into liquidation. Do you know if anything had been taken from the safe?"

"It is impossible to say, but apparently not, as there was a good deal of money in the cash-box, which we unlocked and inspected. But we shall hear more to-morrow at the inquest, and I trust we shall hear something there from you. But in any case, I hope you will attend to watch the proceedings on behalf of poor Fletcher. And if possible, to be present at the autopsy at eleven o'clock. Can you manage that?"

"Yes. And I shall come down early enough to make an inspection of the premises, if the police will give the necessary facilities."

Mr. Foxley thanked him effusively, and when the details as to the trains had been arranged, our clients rose to depart. Thorndyke shook their hands cordially, and as he bade farewell to Miss Markham he murmured a few words of encouragement. She looked up at him gratefully and appealingly as she naïvely held his hand.

"You will try to help us, Dr. Thorndyke, won't you?" she urged. "And you will examine that blood very, very carefully. Promise that you will. Remember that poor Robert's life may hang upon what you can tell about it."

"I realise that, Miss Markham," he replied gently, "and I promise you that the specimens shall be most thoroughly examined, and further, that no stone shall be left unturned in my endeavours to bring the truth to light."

At his answer, spoken with infinite kindliness and sympathy, her eyes filled and she turned away with a few broken words of thanks, and the good clergyman – himself not unmoved by the little episode – took her arm and led her to the door.

"Well," I remarked as their retreating footsteps died away, "old Brodribb's enthusiasm seems to have let you in for a queer sort of task, and I notice that you appear to have accepted Fletcher's statement."

"Without prejudice," he replied. "I don't know Fletcher, but the balance of probabilities is in his favour. Still, that blood-track in the hall is a curious feature. It certainly requires explanation."

"It does, indeed!" I exclaimed, "and you have got to find the explanation! Well, I wish you joy of the job. I suppose you will carry out the farce to the bitter end as you have promised?"

"Certainly," he replied. "But it is hardly a farce. I should have looked the specimens over in any case. One never knows what illuminating fact a chance observation may bring into view."

I smiled sceptically.

"The fact that you are asked to ascertain is that these two samples of blood came from the same person. If there are any means of proving that, they are unknown to me. I should have said it was an impossibility."

"Of course," he rejoined, "you are quite right, speaking academically and in general terms. No method of identifying the blood of individual persons has hitherto been discovered. But yet I can imagine the possibility, in particular and exceptional cases, of an actual, personal identification by means of blood. What does my learned friend think?"

"He thinks that his imagination is not equal to the required effort," I answered, and with that I picked up my brief-bag and went forth to my duties at the courts.

That Thorndyke would keep his promise to poor Lilian Markham was a foregone conclusion, preposterous as the examination seemed. But even my long experience of my colleague's scrupulous conscientiousness had not prepared me for the spectacle which met my eyes when I returned to our chambers. On the table stood the microscope, flanked by three slide-boxes. Each box held six trays, and each tray held six slides – a hundred-and-eight slides in all!

But why three boxes? I opened one. The slides – carefully mounted blood-films – were labelled "*Joseph Riggs*". Those in the second box were labelled, "*Blood from Hall Floor*". But when I opened the third box, I beheld a collection of empty slides labelled "*Robert Fletcher*"!

I chuckled aloud. Prodigious! Thorndyke was going even one better than his promise. He was not only going to examine – probably had examined – the two samples produced, he was actually going to collect a third sample for himself!

I picked out one of Mr. Riggs's slides and laid it on the stage of the microscope. Thorndyke seemed to have been using a low-power objective – the inch-and-a-half. After a glance through this, I swung round the nose-piece to the high power. And then I got a further surprise. The brightly-coloured "white" corpuscles showed that Thorndyke had actually been to the trouble of staining the films with eosin! Again I murmured, "Prodigious!" and put the slide back in its box. For, of course, it showed just what one expected, blood – or rather, broken-up blood-clot. From its appearance I could not even have sworn that it was human blood.

I had just closed the box when Thorndyke entered the room. His quick eye at once noted the changed objective and he remarked, "I see you have been having a look at the specimens."

"A specimen." I corrected. "Enough is as good as a feast."

"Blessed are they who are easily satisfied," he retorted, and then he added, "I have altered my arrangements, though I needn't interfere with yours. I shall go down to Southaven to-night. In fact, I am starting in a few minutes."

"Why?" I asked.

"For several reasons. I want to make sure of the *post mortem* to-morrow morning, I want to pick up any further facts that are available, and finally, I want to prepare a set of blood-films from Robert Fletcher. We may as well make the series complete," he added with a smile, to which I replied by a broad grin.

"Really, Thorndyke," I protested. "I'm surprised at you, at your age, too. She is a nice girl, but she isn't so beautiful as to justify a hundred-and-eight blood-films."

I accompanied him to the taxi, followed by Polton, who carried his modest luggage, and then returned to speculate on his probable plan of campaign. For, of course, he had one. His purposive, resolute manner told me that he had seen farther into this case than I had. I accepted that as natural and inevitable. Indeed, I may admit that my disrespectful badinage covered a belief in his powers hardly second even to old Brodribb's. I was, in fact, almost prepared to discover that those preposterous blood-films had, after all, yielded some "illuminating fact" which had sent him hurrying down to Southaven in search of corroboration.

When I alighted from the train on the following day at a little past noon, I found him waiting on the platform, ready to conduct me to his hotel for an early lunch.

"All goes well, so far," he reported. "I attended the *post mortem*, and examined the wound thoroughly. The pistol was held in the right hand not more than two inches from the head, probably quite close, for the skin is scorched and heavily tattooed with black powder grains. I find that Riggs was right-handed. So the *prima facie* probabilities are in favour of suicide, and the recent loss of money suggests a reasonable motive."

"But what about that blood in the hall?"

"Oh, we have disposed of that. I completed the blood-film series last night."

I looked at him quickly to see if he was serious or only playing a facetious return-shot. But his face was as a face of wood.

"You are an exasperating old devil, Thorndyke!" I exclaimed with conviction. Then, knowing that cross-examination would be futile, I asked, "What are we going to do after lunch?"

"The inspector is going to show us over 'the scene of the tragedy', as the newspapers would express it."

I noted gratefully that he had reserved this item for me, and dismissed professional topics for the time being, concentrating my attention on the old-world, amphibious streets through which we were walking. There is always something interesting in the aspect of a sea-port town, even if it is only a small one like Southaven.

The inspector arrived with such punctuality that he found us still at the table and was easily induced to join us with a cup of coffee and to accept a cigar – administered by Thorndyke, as I suspected, with the object of hindering conversation. I could see that his interest in my colleague was intense and not unmingled with awe – a fact which, in conjunction with the cigar, restrained him from any undue manifestations of curiosity, but not from continuous, though furtive, observation of my friend. Indeed, when we arrived at the late Mr. Riggs's house, I was secretly amused by the close watch that he kept on Thorndyke's movements, unsensational as the inspection turned out to be.

The house, itself, presented very little of interest excepting its picturesque old-world exterior, which fronted on a quiet by-street and was furnished with a deep bay which, as Thorndyke ascertained, commanded a clear view of the street from end to end. It was a rather shabby, neglected little house, as might have been expected, and our examination of it yielded, so far as I could see, only a single fact of any significance, which was that there appeared to be no connection whatever between the blood-stain on the study floor and the train of large spots from the middle of the hall to the street door. And on this piece of evidence – definitely unfavourable from our point of view – Thorndyke concentrated his attention when he had made a preliminary survey.

Closely followed by the watchful inspector, he browsed round the little room, studying every inch of the floor between the blood-stain and the door. The latter he examined minutely from top to bottom, especially as to the handle, the jambs, and the lintel. Then he went out into the hall, scrutinising the floor inch by inch, poring over the walls, and even looking behind the framed prints that hung on them. A reflector lamp suspended by a nail on the wall received minute and prolonged attention, as did also a massive lamp-hook screwed into one of the beams of the low ceiling, of which Thorndyke remarked as he stooped to pass under it, that it must have been fixed there by a dwarf.

"Yes," the inspector agreed, "and a fool. A swinging lamp hung on that hook would have blocked the whole fairway. There isn't too much room as it is. What a pity we weren't a bit more careful about footprints in this place. There are plenty of tracks of wet feet here on this oil-cloth, faint, but you could have made them out all right if they hadn't been all on top of one another. There's Mr. Foxley's, the girl's, mine, and the men who carried out the body, but I'm hanged if I can tell which is which. It's a regular mix up."

"Yes," I agreed, "it is all very confused. But I notice one rather odd thing. There are several faint traces of a large right foot, but I can't see any sign of the corresponding left foot. Can you?"

"Perhaps this is it," said Thorndyke, pointing to a large, vague oval mark. "I have noticed that it seems to occur in some sort of connection with the big right foot, but I must admit that it is not a very obvious foot-print."

"I shouldn't have taken it for a foot-print at all, or at any rate, not a human foot-print. It is more like the spoor of some big animal."

"It is," Thorndyke agreed, "but whatever it is, it seems to have been here before any of the others arrived. You notice that wherever it occurs, it seems to have been trodden on by some of the others."

"Yes, I had noticed that, and the same is true of the big right foot, so it seems probable that they are connected, as you say. But I am hanged if I can make anything of it. Can you, Inspector?"

The inspector shook his head. He could not recognise the mark as a foot-print, but he could see very plainly that he had been a fool not to have taken more care to protect the floor.

When the examination of the hall was finished, Thorndyke opened the door and looked at the big, flat doorstep. "What was the weather like here on Wednesday evening?" he asked.

"Showery," the inspector replied, "and there were one or two heavy showers during the night. You were noticing that there are no blood-tracks on the doorstep. But there wouldn't be in any case, for if a man had come out of this door dropping blood, the blood would have dropped on wet stone and got washed away at once."

Thorndyke admitted the truth of this, and so another item of favourable evidence was extinguished. The probability that the blood in the hall was that of some person other than the deceased remained undisturbed, and I could not see that a single fact had been elicited by our inspection of the house that was in any way helpful to our client. Indeed, it appeared to me that there was absolutely no case for the defence, and I even asked myself whether we were not, in fact, merely trying to fudge up a defence for an obviously guilty man. It was not like Thorndyke to do that. But how did the case stand? There was a suggestion of suicide, but a clear possibility of homicide. There was strong evidence that a second person had been in the house, and that person appeared to have received a wound. But a wound suggested a struggle, and the servant's evidence was to the effect that when she left the house a violent altercation was in progress. The deceased was never again seen alive, and the other party to the quarrel bad been found with property of the dead man in his possession. Moreover, there was a clear motive for the crime, stupid as that crime was. For the dead man had threatened to revoke his will but as he had presumably not done so, his death left the will still operative. In short, everything pointed to the guilt of our client, Robert Fletcher.

I had just reached this not very gratifying conclusion when a statement of Thorndyke's shattered my elaborate summing up into impalpable fragments.

"I suppose, sir," said the inspector, "there isn't anything that you would care to tell us, as you are for the defence. But we are not hostile to Fletcher. In fact, he hasn't been charged. He is only being detained in custody until we have heard what turns up at the inquest. I know you have examined that blood that Mr. Foxley took, and Fletcher's blood, too, and you've seen the premises. We have given all the facilities that we could, and if you could give us any sort of hint that might be useful, I should be very much obliged."

Thorndyke reflected for a few moments. Then he replied, "There is no reason for secrecy in regard to you, Inspector, who have been so helpful and friendly, so I will be quite frank. I have examined both samples of blood and Fletcher's, and I have inspected the premises, and what I am able to say definitely is this – the blood in the hall is *not* the blood of the deceased – "

"Ah!" exclaimed the inspector, "I was afraid it wasn't."

"And it is not the blood of Robert Fletcher."

"Isn't it now! Well, I am glad to hear that."

"Moreover," continued Thorndyke, "it was shed well after nine o'clock at night, probably not earlier than midnight."

"There, now!" the inspector exclaimed, with an admiring glance at Thorndyke, "just think of that. See what it is to be a man of science! I suppose, sir, you couldn't give us any sort of description of the person who dropped that blood in the hall?"

Staggered as I had been by Thorndyke's astonishing statements, I could not repress a grin at the inspector's artless question. But the grin faded rather abruptly as Thorndyke replied in matter-of-fact tones, "A detailed description is, of course, impossible. I can only sketch out the probabilities. But if you should happen to meet with a black man – a tall black man with a bandaged head or a contused wound of the scalp and a swollen leg – you had better keep your eye on him. The leg which is swollen is probably the left."

The inspector was thrilled, and so was I, for that matter. The thing was incredible, but yet I knew that Thorndyke's amazing deductions were the products of perfectly orthodox scientific methods. Only I could form no sort of guess as to how they had been arrived at. A black man's blood is no different from any other person's, and certainly affords no clue to his height or the condition of his legs. I could make nothing of it, and as the dialogue and the inspector's note-takings brought us to the little town hall in which the inquest was to be held, I dismissed the puzzle until such time as Thorndyke chose to solve it.

When we entered the town hall, we found everything in readiness for the opening of the proceedings. The jury were already in their places and the coroner was just about to take his seat at the head of the long table. We accordingly slipped on to the two chairs that were found for us by the inspector, and the latter took his place behind the jury and facing us. Near to him Mr. Foxley and Miss Markham were seated, and evidently hailed our arrival with profound relief, each of them smiling us a silent greeting. A professional-looking man sitting next to Thorndyke I assumed to be the medical witness, and a rather good young man who sat apart with a police constable I identified as Robert Fletcher.

The evidence of the "common" witnesses, who deposed to the general facts, told us nothing that we did not already know, excepting that it was made clear that Fletcher had left his uncle's house not later than seven o'clock, and that thereafter until the following morning his whereabouts were known. The medical witness was cautious, and kept an uneasy eye on Thorndyke. The wound which caused the death of deceased might have been inflicted by himself or by some other person. He had originally given the probable time of death as six or seven o'clock on Wednesday evening. He now admitted in reply to a question from Thorndyke that he had not taken the temperature of the body, and that the rigidity and other conditions were not absolutely inconsistent with a considerable later time of death. Death might even have occurred after midnight.

514

In spite of this admission, however, the sum of the evidence tended strongly to implicate Fletcher, and one or two questions from jurymen suggested a growing belief in his guilt. I had no doubt whatever that if the case had been put to the jury at this stage, a unanimous verdict of "Wilful Murder" would have been the result. But, as the medical witness returned to his seat, the coroner fixed an inquisitive eye on Thorndyke.

"You have not been summoned as a witness, Dr. Thorndyke," said he, "but I understand that you have made certain investigations in this case. Are you able to throw any fresh light on the circumstances of the death of the deceased, Joseph Riggs?"

"Yes," Thorndyke replied. "I am in a position to give important and material evidence."

Thereupon he was sworn, and the coroner, still watching him curiously, said, "I am informed that you have examined samples of the blood of deceased and the blood which was found in the hall of deceased's house. Did you examine them, and if so, what was the object of the examination?"

"I examined both samples and also samples of the blood of Robert Fletcher. The object was to ascertain whether the blood on the hall floor was the blood of the deceased or of Robert Fletcher."

The coroner glanced at the medical witness, and a faint smile appeared on the face of each.

"And did you," the former asked in a slightly ironical tone, "form any opinion on the subject?"

"I ascertained definitely that the blood in the hall was neither that of the deceased nor that of Robert Fletcher."

The coroner's eyebrows went up, and once more he glanced significantly at the doctor.

"But," he demanded incredulously, "is it possible to distinguish the blood of one person from that of another?"

"Usually it is not, but in certain exceptional cases it is. This happened to be an exceptional case."

"In what respect?"

"It happened," Thorndyke replied, "that the person whose blood was found in the hall suffered from the parasitic disease known as *filariasis*. His blood was infested with swarms of a minute worm named *Filaria nocturna*. I have here," he continued, taking out of his research-case the two bottles and the three boxes, "thirty-six mounted specimens of this blood, and in every one of them, one or more of the parasites is to be seen. I have also thirty-six mounted specimens each of the blood of the deceased and the blood of Robert Fletcher. In not one of these specimens is a single parasite to be found. Moreover, I have examined Robert

515

Fletcher and the body of the deceased, and can testify that no sign of *filarial* disease was to be discovered in either. Hence it is certain, that the blood found in the halt was not the blood of either of these two persons."

The ironic smile had faded from the coroner's face. He was evidently deeply impressed, and his manner was quite deferential as he asked, "Do these very remarkable observations of yours lead to any further inferences?"

"Yes," replied Thorndyke. "They render it certain that this blood was shed no earlier than nine o'clock and probably nearer midnight."

"Really!" the astonished coroner exclaimed. "Now, how is it possible to fix the time in that exact manner?"

"By inference from the habits of the parasite," Thorndyke explained. "This particular *filaria* is distributed by the mosquito, and its habits are adapted to the habits of the mosquito. During the day, the worms are not found in the blood, they remain hidden in the tissues of the body. But about nine o'clock at night they begin to migrate from the tissues into the blood, and remain in the blood during the hours when the mosquitoes are active. Then about six o'clock in the morning, they leave the blood and migrate back into the tissues.

"There is another very similar species – *Filaria diurna* – which has exactly opposite habits, adapted to day-flying suctorial insects. It appears in the blood about eleven in the forenoon and goes back into the tissues at about six o'clock in the evening."

"Astonishing!" exclaimed the coroner. "Wonderful! By the way, the parasites that you found could not, I suppose, have been *Filaria diurna*?"

"No," Thorndyke replied. "The time excludes that possibility. The blood was certainly shed after six. They were undoubtedly *nocturna*, and the large numbers found suggest a late hour. The parasites come out of the tissues very gradually, and it is only about midnight that they appear in the blood in really large numbers."

"That is very important," said the coroner. "But does this disease affect any particular class of persons?"

"Yes," Thorndyke replied. "As the disease is confined to tropical countries, the sufferers are naturally residents of the tropics, and nearly always natives. In West Africa, for instance, it is common among the black natives but practically unknown among the white residents."

"Should you say that there is a distinct probability that this unknown person was a black man?"

"Yes. But apart from the *filarial*, there is direct evidence that he was. Searching for some cause of the bleeding, I noticed a lamp-hook screwed into the ceiling, and low enough to strike a tall man's head. I examined it closely, and observed on it a dark, shiny mark, like a blood-smear, and one or two short coiled hairs which I recognised as the scalp-hairs of a black man. I have no doubt that the unknown man is a black man, and that he has a wound of the scalp."

"Does *filarial* disease produce any effects that can be recognised?

"Frequently it does. One of the commonest effects produced by *Filaria nocturna*, especially among black manes, is the condition known as *elephantiasis*. This consists of an enormous swelling of the extremities, most usually of one leg, including the foot – whence the name. The leg and foot look like those of an elephant. As a matter of fact, the black man who was in the hall suffered from elephantiasis of the left leg. I observed prints of the characteristically deformed foot on the oil-cloth covering the floor."

Thorndyke's evidence was listened to with intense interest by everyone present, including myself. Indeed, so spell-bound was his audience that one could have heard a pin drop, and the breathless silence continued for some seconds after he had ceased speaking. Then, in the midst of the stillness, I heard the door creak softly behind me.

There was nothing particularly significant in the sound. But its effects were amazing. Glancing at the inspector, who faced the door, I saw his eyes open and his jaw drop until his face was a very mask of astonishment. And as this expression was reflected on the faces of the jurymen, the coroner and everyone present, excepting Thorndyke, whose back was towards the door, I turned to see what had happened. And then I was as astonished as the others.

The door had been pushed open a few inches and a head thrust in – a black man's head, covered with a soiled and blood rag forming a rough bandage. As I gazed at the inquisitive face, the man pushed the door farther open and shuffled into the room, and instantly there arose on all sides a soft rustle and an inarticulate murmur followed by breathless silence, while every eye was riveted on the man's left leg.

It certainly was a strange, repulsive-looking member, its monstrous bulk exposed to view through the slit trouser and its great shapeless foot – shoeless, since no shoe could have contained it – rough and horny like the foot of an elephant. But it was tragic and pitiable too, for the man, apart from this horrible excrescence, was a fine, big, athletic-looking fellow.

The coroner was the first to recover. Addressing Thorndyke, but keeping an eye on the black man, he said, "Your evidence, then, amounts to this, On the night of Joseph Riggs' death, there was a stranger in the house. That stranger was a black man, who seems to have wounded his head and who, you say, had a swelled left leg."

"Yes," Thorndyke admitted, "that is the substance of my evidence."

517

Once more a hush fell on the room. The black man stood near the door, looking over the assembly as if uneasily conscious that everyone was looking at him. Suddenly, he shuffled up to the foot of the table and addressed the coroner in deep, buzzing, resonant tones. "You think I kill that ole man! I no kill him. He kill himself. I look him."

Having made this statement, he turned his eyes defiantly round the court, and then expectantly towards the coroner, who said, "You say you know that Mr. Riggs killed himself?"

"Yes. I look him. He shoot himself. You think I shoot him. I tell you I no shoot him. Why I fit kill this man? I no sabby him."

"Then," said the coroner, "if you know that he killed himself, you must tell us all that you know, and you must swear to tell us the truth."

"Yes," the black man agreed, "I tell you everyt'ing one time. I tell you the truth. That ol' man kill himself."

When the coroner had explained to him that he was not bound to make any statement that would incriminate him, as he still elected to give evidence, he was sworn and proceeded to make his statement with curious fluency and self-possession.

"My name is Robert Bruce. That's my English name. My country name Kwaku Mensah. I live for Winnebah on the Gold Coast. This time I cook's mate for that steamer *Leckie*. On Wednesday night I lay in my bunk. I no fit sleep. My leg he chook me. I look out of the porthole. Plenty moon live. In my country when the moon big, peoples walk about. So I get up. I go ashore to walk about the town. Then the rain come. Plenty rain. Rain no good for my sickness. So I try for open house doors. No fit. All doors locked. Then I come to this ol' man's house. I turn the handle. The door open. I go in. I look in one room. All dark. Nobody live. Then I look another room. The door open a little. Light live inside. I no like that. I think, suppose somebody come out and see me, be think I come for thief something. So I slink I go away.

"Then something make 'Ping!' same like gun. I hear something fall down in that room. I go to the door and I sing out, 'Who live in there?' Nobody say nothing. So I open the door and look in. The room full of smoke. I look that ol' man on de floor. I look that pistol. I sabby that ol' man kill himself. Then I frighten too much. I run out. The place all dark. Something knock my head. He make blood come plenty. I go back for ship. I no say nothing to nobody. This day I hear peoples talk 'bout this inquest to find out who kill that ol' man. So I come to hear what peoples say. I hear that gentleman say I kill that ol' man. So I tell you everything. I tell you the truth. Finish."

"Do you know what time it was when you came ashore?" the coroner asked.

518

"Yes. When I come down the ladder I hear eight bells ring. I get back to the ship jus' before they ring two bells in the middle watch."

"Then you came ashore at midnight and got back just before one o'clock?"

"Yes. That is what I say."

A few more questions put by the coroner having elicited nothing fresh, the case was put briefly to the jury.

"You have heard the evidence, gentlemen, and most remarkable evidence it was. Like myself, you must have been deeply impressed by the amazing skill with which Dr. Thorndyke reconstructed the personality of the unknown visitor to that house, and even indicated correctly the very time of the visit, from an examination of a mere chance blood-stain. As to the statement of Kwaku Mensab, I can only say that I see no reason to doubt its truth. You will note that it is in complete agreement with Dr. Thorndyke's evidence, and it presents no inconsistencies or improbabilities. Possibly the police may wish to make some further inquiries, but for our purposes it is the evidence of an eyewitness, and as such must be given full weight. With these remarks, I leave you to consider your verdict."

The jury took but a minute or two to deliberate. Indeed, only one verdict was possible if the evidence was to be accepted, and that was agreed on unanimously – suicide whilst temporarily insane. As soon as it was announced, the inspector, formally and with congratulations, released Fletcher from custody, and presently retired in company with the black man to make a few inquiries on board the ship.

The rising of the court was the signal for a wild demonstration of enthusiasm and gratitude to Thorndyke. To play his part efficiently in that scene he would have needed to be furnished, like certain repulsive Indian deities, with an unlimited outfit of arms, for everyone wanted to shake his hand, and two of them – Mr. Foxley and Miss Markham – did so with such pertinacity as entirely to exclude the other candidates.

"I can never thank you enough," Miss Markham exclaimed, with swimming eyes, "if I should live to be a hundred. But I shall think of you with gratitude every day of my life. Whenever I look at Robert, I shall remember that his liberty, and even his life, are your gifts."

Here she was so overcome by grateful emotion that she again seized and pressed his hand. I think she was within an ace of kissing him, but being, perhaps, doubtful how he would take it, compromised by kissing Robert instead. And, no doubt, it was just as well.

Gleanings from the Wreckage

There was a time, and not so very long ago, when even the main streets of London, after midnight, were as silent as – not the grave, that is an unpleasant simile. Besides, who has any experience of conditions in the grave? But they were nearly as silent as the streets of a village. Then the nocturnal pedestrian could go his way encompassed and soothed by quiet, which was hardly disturbed by the rumble of a country wagon wending to market or the musical tinkle of the little bells on the collar of the hansom-cab horse sedately drawing some late reveller homeward.

Very different is the state of those streets nowadays. Long after the hour when the electric trams have ceased from troubling and the motor omnibuses are at rest, the heavy road transport from the country thunders through the streets, the air is rent by the howls of the electric hooter, and belated motor-cyclists fly past, stuttering explosively like perambulant Lewis guns with an inexhaustible charge.

"Let us get into the by-streets," said Thorndyke, as a car sped past us uttering sounds suggestive of a dyspeptic dinosaur. "We don't want our conversation seasoned with mechanical objurgations. In the back-streets, it is still possible to hear oneself speak and forget the march of progress."

We turned into a narrow by-way with the confidence of the born-and-bred Londoner in the impossibility of losing our direction, and began to thread the intricate web of streets in the neighbourhood of a canal.

"It is a remarkable thing," Thorndyke resumed *anon*, "that every new application of science seems to be designed to render the environment of civilised man more and more disagreeable. If the process goes much farther, as it undoubtedly will, we shall presently find ourselves looking back wistfully at the Stone-Age as the golden age of human comfort."

At this point his moralising was cut short by a loud, sharp explosion. We both stopped and looked about from the parapet of the bridge that we were crossing.

"Quite like old times," Thorndyke remarked. "Carries one back to 1915, when friend Fritz used to call on us. Ah! There is the place, the top story of that tall building across the canal." He pointed as he spoke to a factory-like structure, from the upper windows of which a lurid light shone and rapidly grew brighter.

"It must be down the next turning," said I, quickening my pace.

But he restrained me, remarking, "There is no hurry. That was the sound of high explosive, and those flames suggest nitro compounds burning. *Festina lente*. There may be some other packets of high explosives."

He had hardly finished speaking when a flash of dazzling violet light burst from the burning building. The windows flew out bodily, the roof opened in places, and almost at the same moment the clang of a violent explosion shook the ground under our feet, a puff of wind stirred our hair, and then came a clatter of falling glass and slates.

We made our way at a leisurely pace towards the scene of the explosion, through streets lighted up by the ruddy glare from the burning factory. But others were less cautious. In a few minutes the street was filled by one of those crowds which, in London, seem mysteriously to spring up in an instant where but a moment before not a person was to be seen. Before we had reached the building, a fire-engine had rumbled past us, and already a sprinkling of policemen had appeared as if, like the traditional frogs, they had dropped from the clouds.

In spite of the ferocity of its outbreak, the fire seemed to be no great matter, for even as we looked and before the fire-hose was fully run out, the flames began to die down. Evidently, they had been dealt with by means of extinguishers within the building, and the services of the engine would not be required after all. Noting this flat ending to what had seemed so promising a start, we were about to move off and resume our homeward journey when I observed a uniformed inspector who was known to us, and who, observing us at the same instant, made his way towards us through the crowd.

"You remind me, sir," said be, when he had wished us good-evening, "of the stories of the vultures that make their way in the sky from nowhere when a camel drops dead in the desert. I don't mean anything uncomplimentary," he hastened to add. "I was only thinking of the wonderful instinct that has brought you to this very spot at this identical moment, as if you had smelt a case afar off."

"Then your imagination has misled you," said Thorndyke, "for I haven't smelt a case, and I don't smell one now. Fires are not in my province."

"No, sir," replied the inspector, "but bodies are, and the fireman tells me that there is a dead man up there – or at least the remains of one. I am going up to inspect. Do you care to come up with me?"

Thorndyke considered for a moment, but I knew what his answer would be, and I was not mistaken.

"As a matter of professional interest, I should," he replied, "but I don't want to be summoned as a witness at the inquest."

"Of course you don't, sir," the inspector agreed, "and I will see that you are not summoned, unless an expert witness is wanted. I need not mention that you have been here, but I should be glad of your opinion for my own guidance in investigating the case."

He led us through the crowd to the door of the building, where we were joined by a fireman – whose helmet I should have liked to borrow – by whom we were piloted up the stairs. Half up we met the night-watchman, carrying an exhausted extinguisher and a big electric lantern, and he joined our procession, giving us the news as we ascended.

"It's all safe up above," said he, "excepting the roof, and that isn't so very much damaged. The big windows saved it. They blew out and let off the force of the explosion. The floor isn't damaged at all. It's girder and concrete. But poor Mr. Manford caught it properly. He was fairly blown to bits."

"Do you know how it happened?" the inspector asked.

"I don't," was the reply. "When I came on duty Mr. Manford was up there in his private laboratory. Soon afterwards a friend of his – a foreign gentleman of the name of Bilsky – came to see him. I took him up, and then Mr. Manford said he had some business to do, and after that he had got a longish job to do and would be working late. So he said I might turn in and he would let me know when he had finished. And he did let me know with a vengeance, poor chap. I lay down in my clothes, and I hadn't been asleep above a couple of hours when some noise woke me up. Then there came a most almighty bang. I rushed for an extinguisher and ran upstairs, and there I found the big laboratory all ablaze, the windows blown out, and the ceiling down. But it wasn't so bad as it looked. There wasn't very much stuff up there, only the experimental stuff, and that burned out almost at once. I got the rest of the fire out in a few minutes."

"What stuff is it that you are speaking of?" the inspector asked.

"Celluloid, mostly, I think," replied the watchman. "They make films and other celluloid goods in the works. But Mr. Manford used to do experiments in the material up in his laboratory. This time he was working with alloys, melting them on the gas furnace. Dangerous thing to do with all that inflammable stuff about. I don't know what there was up there, exactly. Some of it was celluloid, I could see by the way it burned, but the Lord knows what it was that exploded. Some of the raw stuff, perhaps."

At this point we reached the top floor, where a door blown off its hinges and a litter of charred wood fragments filled the landing. Passing through the yawning doorway, we entered the laboratory and looked on a hideous scene of devastation. The windows were mere holes, the ceiling a gaping space fringed with black and ragged lathing, through which the damaged roof was visible by the light of the watchman's powerful lantern. The floor was covered with the fallen plaster and fragments of blackened woodwork, but its own boards were only slightly burnt in places – owing, no doubt, to their being fastened directly to the concrete which formed the actual floor.

"You spoke of some human remains," said the inspector.

"Ah!" said the watchman, "you may well say 'remains'. Just come here." He led the way over the rubbish to a corner of the laboratory, where he halted and threw the light of his lantern down on a brownish, dusty, globular object that lay on the floor half buried in plaster. "That's all that's left of poor Mr. Manford – that and a few other odd pieces. I saw a hand over the other side."

Thorndyke picked up the head and placed it on the blackened remnant of a bench, where, with the aid of the watchman's lantern and the inspection lamp which I produced from our research-case, he examined it curiously. It was extremely, but unequally, scorched. One ear was completely shrivelled, and most of the face was charred to the bone. But the other ear was almost intact, and though most of the hair was burned away to the scalp, a tuft above the less damaged ear was only singed, so that it was possible to see that the hair had been black, with here and there a stray white hair.

Thorndyke made no comments, but I noticed that he examined the gruesome object minutely, taking nothing for granted. The inspector noticed this, too, and when the examination was finished, looked at him inquiringly.

"Anything abnormal, sir?" he asked.

"No," replied Thorndyke, "nothing that is not accounted for by fire and the explosion. I see he had no natural teeth, so he must have worn a complete set of false teeth. That should help in the formal identification, if the plates are not completely destroyed."

"There isn't much need for identification," said the watchman, "seeing that there was nobody in the building but him and me. His friend went away about half-past twelve. I heard Mr. Manford let him out."

"The doctor means at the inquest," the inspector explained. "Somebody has got to recognise the body if possible."

He took the watchman's lantern, and throwing its light on the floor, began to search among the rubbish. Very soon he disinterred from under a heap of plaster the headless trunk. Both legs were attached, though the right was charred below the knee and the foot blown off, and one complete arm. The other arm – the right – was intact only to the elbow. Here, again, the burning was very unequal. In some parts the clothing had been burnt off or blown away completely. In others, enough was left to enable the watchman to recognise it with certainty. One leg was much more burnt than the other, and whereas the complete arm was only scorched, the dismembered one was charred almost to the bone. When the trunk had been carried to the bench and laid there beside the head, the lights were turned on it for Thorndyke to make his inspection.

"It almost seems," said the police officer, as the hand was being examined, "as if one could guess how he was standing when the explosion occurred. I think I can make out finger-marks – pretty dirty ones, too – on the back of the hand, as if he had been standing with his hands clasped together behind him while he watched something that he was experimenting with." The inspector glanced for confirmation at Thorndyke, who nodded approvingly.

"Yes," he said, "I think you are right. They are very indistinct, but the marks are grouped like fingers. The small mark near the wrist suggests a little finger and the separate one near the knuckle looks like a fore-finger, while the remaining two marks are close together." He turned the hand over and continued "And there, in the palm, just between the roots of the third and fourth fingers, seems to be the trace of a thumb. But they are all very faint. You have a quick eye, Inspector."

The gratified officer, thus encouraged, resumed his explorations among the debris in company with the watchman – the fireman had retired after a professional look round – leaving Thorndyke to continue his examination of the mutilated corpse, at which I looked on unsympathetically, for we had had a long day and I was tired and longing to get home. At length I drew out my watch, and with a portentous yawn, entered a mild protest.

"It is nearly two o'clock," said I. "Don't you think we had better be getting on? This really isn't any concern of ours, and there doesn't seem to be anything in it, from our point of view."

"Only that we are keeping our intellectual joints supple," Thorndyke replied with a smile. "But it is getting late. Perhaps we had better adjourn the inquiry."

At this moment, however, the inspector discovered the missing forearm – completely charred – with the fingerless remains of the hand, and almost immediately afterwards the watchman picked up a dental plate of some white metal, which seemed to be practically uninjured. But our brief inspection of these objects elicited nothing of interest, and having glanced at them, we took our departure, avoiding on the stairs an eager reporter, all agog for "copy".

A few days later we received a visit, by appointment, from a Mr. Herdman, a solicitor who was unknown to us, and who was accompanied by the widow of Mr. James Manford, the victim of the explosion. In the interval, the inquest had been opened, but had been adjourned for further examination of the premises and the remains. No mention had been made of our visit to the building, and so far as I knew nothing had been said to anybody on the subject.

Mr. Herdman came to the point with business directness.

"I have called," he said, "to secure your services, if possible, in regard to the matter of which I spoke in my letter. You have probably seen an account of the disaster in the papers?"

"Yes," replied Thorndyke. "I read the report of the inquest."

"Then you know the principal facts. The inquest, as you know, was adjourned for three weeks. When it is resumed, I should like to retain you to attend on behalf of Mrs. Manford."

"To watch the case on her behalf?" Thorndyke suggested.

"Well, not exactly," replied Herdman. "I should ask you to inspect the premises and the remains of poor Mr. Manford, so that, at the adjourned inquest, you could give evidence to the effect that the explosion and the death of Mr. Manford were entirely due to accident."

"Does anyone say that they were not?" Thorndyke asked.

"No, certainly not," Mr. Herdman replied hastily. "Not at all. But I happened, quite by chance, to see the manager of the Pilot Insurance Society on another matter, and I mentioned the case of Mr. Manford. He then let drop a remark which made me slightly uneasy. He observed that there was a suicide clause in the policy, and that the possibility of suicide would have to be ruled out before the claim could be settled, which suggested a possible intention to contest the claim."

"But," said Thorndyke, "I need not point out to you that if he sets up the theory of suicide, it is for him to prove it, not for you to disprove it. Has anything transpired which would lend colour to such a suggestion?"

"Nothing material," was the reply. "But we should feel more happy if you could be present and give positive evidence that the death was accidental."

"That," said Thorndyke, "would be hardly possible. But my feeling is that the suicide question is negligible. There is nothing to suggest it, so far as I know. Is there anything known to you?"

The solicitor glanced at his client and replied somewhat evasively, "We are anxious to secure ourselves. Mrs. Manford is left very badly off, unless there is some personal property that we don't know about. If the insurance is not paid, she will be absolutely ruined. There isn't enough to pay the debts. And I think the suicide question might be raised – even successfully – on several points. Manford had been rather queer lately, jumpy and rather worried. Then, he was under notice to terminate his

525

engagement at the works. His finances were in a confused state, goodness knows why, for he had a liberal salary. And then there was some domestic trouble. Mrs. Manford had actually consulted me about getting a separation. Some other woman, you know."

"I should like to forget that," said Mrs. Manford, "and it wasn't that which worried him. Quite the contrary. Since it began he had been quite changed. So smart in his dress and so particular in his appearance. He even took to dyeing his hair. I remember that he opened a fresh bottle of dye the very morning before his death and took no end of trouble putting it on. It wasn't that entanglement that made him jumpy. It was his money affairs. He had too many irons in the fire."

Thorndyke listened with patient attention to these rather irrelevant details and inquired, "What sort of irons?"

"I will tell you," said Herdman. "About three months ago, he had need for two-thousand pounds, for what purpose, I can't say, but Mrs. Manford thinks it was to invest in certain valuables that he used to purchase from time to time from a Russian dealer named Bilsky. At any rate, he got this sum on short loan from a Mr. Clines, but meanwhile arranged for a longer loan with a Mr. Elliott on a note of hand and an agreement to insure his life for the amount.

"As a matter of fact, the policy was made out in Elliott's name, he having proved an insurable interest. So if the insurance is paid, Elliott is settled with. Otherwise the debt falls on the estate, which would be disastrous – and to make it worse, the day before his death, he drew out five-hundred pounds – nearly the whole balance – as he was expecting to see Mr. Bilsky, who liked to be paid in bank-notes. He did see him, in fact, at the laboratory, but they couldn't have done any business, as no jewels were found."

"And the bank-notes?"

"Burned with the body, presumably. He must have had them with him."

"You mentioned," said Thorndyke, "that he occasionally bought jewels from this Russian. What became of them?"

"Ah!" replied Herdman, "there is a gleam of hope there. He had a safe deposit somewhere. We haven't located it yet, but we shall. There may be quite a nice little nest-egg in it. But meanwhile there is the debt to Elliott. He wrote to Manford about it a day or two ago. You have the letter, I think," he added, addressing Mrs. Manford, who thereupon produced two envelopes from her handbag and laid them on the table.

"This is Mr. Elliott's letter," she said. "Merely a friendly reminder, you see, telling him that he is just off to the Continent and that he has given his wife a power of attorney to act in his absence."

Thorndyke glanced through the letter and made a few notes of its contents. Then he looked inquiringly at the other envelope.

"That," said Mrs. Manford, "'is a photograph of my husband. I thought it might help you if you were going to examine the body."

As Thorndyke drew the portrait out and regarded it thoughtfully, I recalled the shapeless, blackened fragments of its subject, and when he passed it to me, I inspected it with a certain grim interest, and mentally compared it with those grisly remains. It was a commonplace face, rather unsymmetrical – the nose was deflected markedly to the left, and the left eye had a pronounced divergent squint. The bald head, with an abundant black fringe and an irregular scar on the the side of the forehead, sought compensation in a full beard and moustache, both apparently jet-black. It was not an attractive countenance, and it was not improved by a rather odd-shaped ear – long, lobeless, and pointed above, like the ear of a satyr.

"I realise your position," said Thorndyke, "but I don't quite see what you want of me. If," he continued, addressing the solicitor, "you had thought of my giving *ex parte* evidence, dismiss the idea. I am not a witness-advocate. All I can undertake to do is to investigate the case and try to discover what really happened. But in that case, whatever I may discover I shall disclose to the coroner. Would that suit you?"

The lawyer looked doubtful and rather glum, but Mrs. Manford interposed, firmly, "Why not? We are not proposing any deception, but I am certain that he did not commit suicide. I agree unreservedly to what you propose."

With this understanding – which the lawyer was disposed to boggle at – our visitors took their leave. As soon as they were gone, I gave utterance to the surprise with which I had listened to Thorndyke's proposal.

"I am astonished at your undertaking this case. Of course, you have given them fair warning, but still, it will be unpleasant if you have to give evidence unfavourable to your client."

"Very," he agreed. "But what makes you think I may have to?"

"Well, you seem to reject the probability of suicide, but have you forgotten the evidence at the inquest?"

"Perhaps I have," he replied blandly. "Let us go over it again."

I fetched the report from the office, and spreading it out on the table began to read it aloud. Passing over the evidence of the inspector and the fireman, I came to that of the night-watchman:

"Shortly after I came on duty at ten o'clock, a foreign, gentleman named Bilsky called to see Mr. Manford. I knew

527

him by sight, because he had called once or twice before at about the same time. I took him up to the laboratory, where Mr. Manford was doing something with a big crucible on the gas furnace. He told me that he had some business to transact with Mr. Bilsky and when he had finished he would let him out. Then he was going to do some experiments in making alloys, and as they would probably take up most of the night, he said I might as well turn in. He said he would call me when he was ready to go. So I told him to be careful with the furnace and not set the place on fire and burn me in my bed, and then I went downstairs. I had a look round to see that everything was in order, and then I took off my boots and laid down. About half-past-twelve I heard Mr. Manford and Bilsky come down. I recognised Mr. Bilsky by a peculiar cough that he had and by the sound of his stick and his limping tread – he had something the matter with his right foot and walked quite lame."

"You say that the deceased came down with him," said the coroner. "Are you quite sure of that?"

"Well, I suppose Mr. Manford came down with him, but I can't say I actually heard him."

"You did not hear him go up again?"

"No, I didn't. But I was rather sleepy and I wasn't listening very particular. Well, then I went to sleep and slept till about half-past one, when some noise woke me. I was just getting up to see what it was when I heard a tremendous bang, right overhead. I ran down and turned the gas off at the main and then I got a fire extinguisher and ran up to the laboratory. The place seemed to be all in a blaze, but it wasn't much of a fire after all, for by the time the fire engines arrived I had got it practically out."

The witness then described the state of the laboratory and the finding of the body, but as this was already known to us, I passed on to the evidence of the next witness, the superintendent of the fire brigade, who had made a preliminary inspection of the premises. It was a cautious statement and subject to the results of a further examination, but clearly the officer was not satisfied as to the cause of the outbreak. There seemed to have been two separate explosions, one near a cupboard and another – apparently the second – in the cupboard itself, and there seemed to be a burned track connecting the two spots. This might have been accidental or it might have been arranged. Witness did not think that the explosive was celluloid. It seemed to be a high explosive of some kind. But further investigations were being made.

The superintendent was followed by Mrs. Manford, whose evidence was substantially similar to what she and Mr. Herdman had told us, and by the police surgeon, whose description of the remains conveyed nothing new to us. Finally, the inquest was adjourned for three weeks to allow of further examination of the premises and the remains.

"Now," I said, as I folded up the report, "I don't see how you are able to exclude suicide. If the explosion was arranged to occur when Manford was in the laboratory. What object, other than suicide, can be imagined?"

Thorndyke looked at me with an expression that I knew only too well. "Is it impossible," he asked, "to imagine that the object might have been homicide?"

"But," I objected, "there was no one there but Manford – after Bilsky left."

"Exactly," he agreed, dryly, "*after* Bilsky left. But up to that time there were *two* persons there."

I must confess that I was startled, but as I rapidly reviewed the circumstances, I percieved the cogency of Thorndyke's suggestion. Bilsky had been present when Manford dismissed the night-watchman. He knew that there would be no interruption. The inflammable and explosive materials were there, ready to his hand. Then Bilsky had gone down to the door alone instead of being conducted down and let out – a very striking circumstance, this. Again, no jewels had been found, though the meeting had been ostensibly for the purpose of a deal, and the bank-notes had vanished utterly. This was very remarkable. In view of the large sum, it was nearly certain that the notes would be in a close bundle, and we all know how difficult it is to burn tightly-folded paper. Yet they had vanished without leaving a trace. Finally, there was Bilsky himself. Who was he? Apparently a dealer in stolen property – a hawker of the products of robbery and murder committed during the revolution.

"Yes," I admitted, "the theory of homicide is certainly tenable. But unless some new facts can be produced, it must remain a matter of speculation."

"I think, Jervis," he rejoined, "you must be overlooking the facts that are known to us. We were there. We saw the place within a few minutes of the explosion and we examined the body. What we saw established a clear presumption of homicide, and what we have heard this morning confirms it. I may say that I communicated my suspicions the very next day to the coroner and to Superintendent Miller."

"Then you must have seen more than I did," I began, but he shook his head and cut short my protestations.

"You saw what I saw, Jervis, but you did not interpret its meaning. However, it is not too late. Try to recall the details of our adventure and what our visitors have told us. I don't think you will then entertain the idea of suicide."

I was about to put one or two leading questions, but at this moment footsteps became audible ascending our stairs. The knock which followed informed me that our visitor was Superintendent Miller, and I rose to admit him.

"Just looked in to report progress," he announced as he subsided into an arm-chair. "Not much to report, but what there is supports your view of the case. Bilsky has made a clean bolt. Never went home to his hotel. Evidently meant to skedaddle, as he has left nothing of any value behind. But it was a stupid move, for it would have raised suspicion in any case. The notes were a consecutive batch. All the numbers are known, but, of course, none of them have turned up yet. We have made inquiries about Bilsky, and gather that he is a shady character, practically a fence who deals in the jewellery stolen from those unfortunate Russian aristocrats. But we shall have him all right. His description has been circulated at all the seaports and he is an easy man to spot with his lame foot and his stick and a finger missing from his right hand."

Thorndyke nodded, and seemed to reflect for a moment. Then he asked, "Have you made any other inquiries?"

"No, there is nothing more to find out until we get hold of our man, and when we do, we shall look to you to secure the conviction. I suppose you are quite certain as to your facts?"

Thorndyke shook his head with a smile.

"I am never certain until after the event. We can only act on probabilities."

"I understand," said the superintendent, casting a sly look at me, "but your probabilities are good enough for me."

With this, he picked up his hat and departed, leaving us to return to the occupations that our visitors had interrupted.

I heard no more of the Manford case for about a week, and assumed that Thorndyke's interest in it had ceased. But I was mistaken, as I discovered when he remarked casually one evening, "No news of Bilsky, so far, and time is running on. I am proposing to make a tentative move in a new direction." I looked at him inquiringly, and he continued, "It appears, 'from information received', that Elliott had some dealings with him, so I propose to call at his house to-morrow and see if we can glean any news of the lost sheep."

"But Elliott is abroad," I objected.

"True, but his wife isn't, and she evidently knows all about his affairs. I have invited Miller to come with me in case he would like to put any questions, and you may as well come, too, if you are free."

It did not sound like a very thrilling adventure, but one never knew with Thorndyke. I decided to go with him, and at that the matter dropped, though I speculated a little curiously on the source of the information. So, apparently, had the superintendent, for when he arrived on the following morning he proceeded to throw out a few cautious feelers, but got nothing for his pains beyond vague generalities.

"It is a purely tentative proceeding," said Thorndyke, "and you mustn't be disappointed if nothing comes of it."

"I shall be, all the same," replied Miller, with a sly glance at my senior, and with this we set forth on our quest.

The Elliotts' house was, as I knew, in some part of Wimbledon, and thither we made our way by train. From the station we started along a wide, straight main street from which numbers of smaller streets branched off. At the corner of one of these I noticed a man standing, apparently watching our approach, and something in his appearance seemed to me familiar. Suddenly he took off his hat, looked curiously into its interior, and put it on again. Then he turned about and walked quickly down the side street. I looked at his retreating figure as we crossed the street, wondering who he could be. And then it flashed upon me that the resemblance was to a certain ex-sergeant Barber whom Thorndyke occasionally employed for observation duties. Just as I reached this conclusion, Thorndyke halted and looked about him doubtfully.

"I am afraid we have come too far," said he. "I fancy we ought to have gone down that last turning." We accordingly faced about and walked back to the corner, where Thorndyke read out the name, Mendoza Avenue.

"Yes," he said, "this is the way," and we thereupon turned down the Avenue, following it to the bottom, where it ended in a cross-road, the name of which, Berners Park, I recognised as that which I had seen on Elliott's letter.

"Sixty-four is the number," said Thorndyke, "so as this corner house is Forty-six, and the next is Forty-eight, it will be a little way along on this side, just about where you can see that smoke – which, by the way, seems to be coming out of a window."

"Yes, by Jove!" I exclaimed. "The staircase window, apparently. Not our house, I hope!"

But it was. We read the number and the name, "*Green Bushes*", on the gate as we came up to it, and we hurried up the short path to the door. There was no knocker, but when Miller fixed his thumb on the bell-push, we heard a loud ringing within. But there was no response, and meanwhile the smoke poured more and more densely out of the open window above.

"Rum!" exclaimed Miller, sticking to the bell-push like a limpet. "House seems to be empty."

"I don't think it is." Thorndyke replied calmly.

The superintendent looked at him with quick suspicion, and then glanced at the ground-floor window.

"That window is unfastened," said he, "and here comes a constable."

Sure enough, a policeman was approaching quickly, looking up at the houses. Suddenly he perceived the smoke and quickened his pace, arriving just as Thorndyke had pulled down the upper window-sash and was preparing to climb over into the room. The constable hailed him sternly, but a brief explanation from Miller reduced the officer to a state of respectful subservience, and we all followed Thorndyke through the open window, from which smoke now began to filter.

"Send the constable upstairs to give the alarm," Thorndyke instructed Miller in a low tone. The order was given without question, and the next moment the officer was bounding up the stairs, roaring like a whole fire brigade. Meanwhile, the superintendent browsed along the hall through the dense smoke, sniffing inquisitively, and at length approached the street door. Suddenly, from the heart of the reek, his voice issued in tones of amazement.

"Well, I'm hanged! It's a plumber's smoke-rocket. Some fool has stuck it through into the letter-cage!"

In the silence which followed this announcement I heard an angry voice from above demand, "What is all this infernal row about? And what are you doing here?"

"Can't you see that the house is on fire?" was the constable's, stern rejoinder. "You'd better come down and help to put it out."

The command was followed by the sound of descending footsteps, on which Thorndyke ran quickly up the stairs, followed by the superintendent and me. We met the descending party on the landing, opposite a window, and here we all stopped, gazing at one another with mutual curiosity. The man who accompanied the constable looked distinctly alarmed – as well he might – and somewhat hostile.

"Who put that smoke in the hall?" Miller demanded fiercely. "And why didn't you come down when you heard us ringing the bell?"

"I don't know what you a talking about." the man replied sulkily, "or what business this is of yours. Who are you? And what are you doing in my house?"

"In your house?" repeated Thorndyke. "Then you will be Mr. Elliott?"

The man turned a startled glance on him and replied angrily, "Never you mind who I am. Get out of this house."

"But I do mind who *you* are," Thorndyke rejoined mildly. "I came here to see Mr. Elliott. Are you Mr. Elliott?

"No, I am not. Mr. Elliott is abroad. If you like to send a letter here for him, I will forward it when I get his address."

While this conversation had been going on, I had been examining the stranger, not without curiosity. For his appearance was somewhat unusual. In the first place, he wore an unmistakable wig, and his shaven face bore an abundance of cuts and scratches, suggesting a recently and unskilfully mown beard. His spectacles did not disguise a pronounced divergent squint of the left eye, but what specially caught my attention was the ear – large ear, lobeless and pointed at the tip like the ear of a satyr. As I looked at this, and at the scraped face, the squint and the wig, a strange suspicion flashed into my mind, and then, as I noted that the nose was markedly deflected to the left, I turned to glance at Thorndyke.

"Would you mind telling us your name?" the latter asked blandly.

"My name is – is – Johnson. Frederick Johnson."

"Ah," said Thorndyke. "I thought it was Manford – James Manford – and I think so still. I suggest that you have a scar on the right side of your forehead, just under the wig. May we see?"

As Thorndyke spoke the name, the man turned a horrible livid grey and started back as if to retreat up the stairs. But the constable blocked the way, and as the man was struggling to push past, Miller adroitly snatched off the wig, and there, on the forehead, was the tell-tale scar.

For an appreciable time we all stood stock-still like the figures of a tableau. Then Thorndyke turned to the superintendent.

"I charge this man, James Manford, with the murder of Stephan Bilsky."

Again there was a brief interval of intolerable silence. In the midst of it, we heard the street door open and shut, and a woman's voice called up the stairs, "Whatever is all this smoke? Are you up there, Jim?"

I pass over the harrowing details of the double arrest. I am not a policeman, and to me such scenes are intensely repugnant. But we must needs stay until two taxis and four constables had conveyed the prisoners away from the still reeking house to the *caravanserai* of the law. Then, at last, we went forth with relief into the fresh air and bent our steps towards the station.

"I take it," Miller said reflectively, "that you never suspected Bilsky?"

"I did at first. But when Mrs. Manford and the solicitor told their tale, I realised that he was the victim and that Manford must be the murderer."

"Let us have the argument," said I. "It is obvious that I have been a blockhead, but I don't mind our old friend here knowing it."

"Not a blockhead, Jervis," he corrected. "You were half asleep that night and wholly uninterested. If you had been attending to the matter, you would have observed several curious and anomalous appearances. For instance, you would have noticed that the body was, in parts, completely charred and brittle. Now we saw the outbreak of the fire and we found it extinguished when we reached the building. Its duration was a matter of minutes, quite insufficient to reduce a body to that state. For, as you know, a human body is an extremely incombustible thing. The appearance suggested the destruction of a body which had been already burnt, and this suggestion was emphasised by the curiously unequal distribution of the charring. The right hand was burnt to a cinder and blown to pieces. The left hand was only scorched. The right foot was utterly destroyed, but the left foot was nearly intact. The face was burned away completely, and yet there were parts of the head where the hair was only singed.

"Naturally, with these facts in mind, I scrutinised those remains narrowly. And presently something much more definite and sinister came to light. On the left hand, there was a faint impression of another hand – very indistinct and blurred, but still unmistakably a hand."

"I remember," said I. "The inspector pointed it out as evidence that the deceased had been standing with his hands clasped before or behind him, and I must admit that it seemed a reasonable inference."

"So it did, because you were both assuming that the man had been alone and that it must therefore have been the impression of his own hand. For that reason, neither of you looked at it critically. If you had, you would have seen at once that it was the impression of a left hand."

"You are quite right," I confessed ruefully. "As the man was stated to have been alone, the hand impression did not interest me. And it was a mere group of smudges, after all. You are sure that it was a left hand?"

"Quite," he replied. "Blurred as the smudges were, one could make out the relative lengths of the fingers. And there was the thumb mark at the distal end of the palm, but pointing to the outer side of the hand. Try how you may, you can't get a right hand into that position.

"Well, then, here was a crucial fact. The mark of a left hand *on* a left hand proved the presence of a second person, and at once raised a strong presumption of homicide – especially when considered in conjunction with the unaccountable state of the body. During the evening, a visitor had come and gone, and on him – Bilsky – the suspicion naturally fell. But Mrs. Manford unwittingly threw an entirely new light on the case. You remember she told us that her husband had opened a new bottle of hair dye on the very morning before the explosion and had applied it with unusual care. Then his hair was dyed. But the hair of the corpse was *not* dyed. Therefore, the corpse was not the corpse of Manford! Further, the presumption of murder applied now to *Manford*, and the body almost certainly was that of *Bilsky*."

"How did you deduce that the hair of the corpse was not dyed?" I asked.

"I didn't deduce it at all. I observed it. You remember a little patch of hair above the right ear, very much singed but still recognisable as hair? Well, in that patch I made out distinctly two or three white hairs. Naturally, when Mrs. Manford spoke of the dye, I recalled those white hairs, for though you may find silver hairs among the gold, you don't find them among the dyed. So the corpse could not be Manford's, and was presumably that of Bilsky.

"But the instant that this presumption was made, a quantity of fresh evidence arose to support it. The destruction of the body was now understandable. Its purpose was to prevent identification. The parts destroyed were the parts that had to be destroyed for that purpose – the face was totally unrecognisable, and the right hand and right foot were burnt and shattered to fragments. But these were *Bilsky's* personal marks. His right hand was mutilated and his right foot deformed. And the fact that the false teeth found were undoubtedly *Manford's* was conclusive evidence of the intended deception.

"Then there were those very queer financial transactions, of which my interpretation was this: Manford borrowed two-thousand pounds from Clines. With this he opened an account in the name of Elliott. As Elliott, he lent himself two-thousand pounds which he repaid Clines – subject to an insurance of his life for that amount, taken out in Elliott's name."

"Then he would have gained nothing," I objected.

"On the contrary, he would have stood to gain two-thousand pounds on proof of his own death. That, I assumed, was his scheme: To murder Bilsky, to arrange for Bilsky's corpse to personate his own, and then, when the insurance was paid, to abscond the company of some woman this sum, with the valuables that he had taken from Bilsky, and the five-hundred pounds that he had withdrawn from the bank.

"But this was only theory. It had to be tested, and as we had Elliott's address, I did the only thing that was possible. I employed our friend, ex-Sergeant Barber, to watch the house. He took lodgings in a house nearly opposite and kept up continuous observation, which soon convinced him that there was someone on the premises besides Mrs. Elliott. Then, late one night, he saw a man come out and walk away quickly. He followed the man for some distance, until the stranger turned back and began to retrace his steps. Then Barber accosted him, asking for a direction, and carefully inspecting him. The man's appearance tallied exactly with the description that I had given – I had assumed that he would probably shave off his beard – and with the photograph, so Barber, having seen him home, reported to me. And that is the whole story."

"Not quite the whole," said Miller, with a sly grin. "There is that smoke-rocket. If it hadn't been for the practical joker who slipped that through the letter-slit, we could never have got into that house. I call it a most remarkable coincidence."

"So do I," Thorndyke agreed, without moving a muscle, "but there is a special providence that watches over medical jurists."

We were silent for a few moments. Then I remarked, "This will come as a terrible shock to Mrs. Manford."

"I am afraid it will," Thorndyke agreed. "But it will be better for her than if Manford had absconded with this woman, taking practically every penny that he possessed with him. She stood to lose a worthless husband in either event. At least we have saved her from poverty. And, knowing the facts, we were morally and legally bound to further the execution of justice."

"A very proper sentiment," said the superintendent, "though I am not quite clear as to the legal aspects of that smoke-rocket."

About the Author

Richard Austin Freeman was born on April 11th, 1862 in the Soho district of London. He was the son of a skilled tailor and the youngest of five children. As he grew, it was expected that he would become a tailor as well, but instead he had an interest in natural history and medicine, and so he obtained employment in a pharmacist's shop. While there, he qualified as an apothecary and could have gone on to manage the shop, but instead he began to study medicine at Middlesex Hospital.

Austin Freeman qualified as a physician in 1887, and in that same year he married. Faced with the twin facts of his new marital responsibilities and his very limited resources as a young doctor, he made the unusual decision to join the Colonial Service, spending the next seven years in Africa as an Assistant Colonial Surgeon. This continued until the early 1890's, when he contracted Blackwater Fever, an illness that eventually forced him to leave the service and return permanently to England.

For several years, he served as a *locum tenens* for various physicians, a bleak time in his life as he moved from job to job, his income low, and his health never quite recovered. However, he supplemented his meager income and exercised his creativity during these years by beginning to write. His early publications included *Travels and Live in Ashanti and Jaman* (1898), recounting some of his African sojourns.

In 1900, Freeman obtained work as an assistant to Dr. John James Pitcairn (1860-1936) at Holloway Prison. Although he wasn't there for very long, the association between the two men was enough to turn Freeman's attention toward writing mysteries. Over the next few years, they co-wrote several under the pseudonym *Clifford Ashdown*, including *The Adventures of Romney Pringle* (1902), *The Further Adventures of Romney Pringle* (1903), *From a Surgeon's Diary* (1904-1905), and *The Queen's Treasure* (written around 1905-1906, and published posthumously in 1975.)

In approximately 1904, Freeman began developing a mystery novella based on a short job that he had held at the Western Ophthalmic Hospital. This effort, "31 New Inn", was published in 1905, and it is the true first Dr. Thorndyke story. In 1907, the first Thorndyke novel, *The Red Thumb Mark*, was published.

From Thorndyke's creation until 1914, Freeman wrote four novels and two volumes of short stories. Then, with the commencement of the

First World War, he entered military service. In February 1915, at the age of fifty-two, he joined the Royal Army Medical Corps. Due to his health, which had never entirely recovered from his time in Africa, he spent the duration of the war involved with various aspects of the ambulance corps, having been promoted very early to the rank of Captain. He wrote nothing about Thorndyke during this period, but he did publish one book concerning the adventures of a scoundrel, *The Exploits of Danby Croker* (1916).

Following the war, he resumed his previous life, writing approximately one Thorndyke novel per year, as well as three more volumes of Thorndyke short stories and a number of other unrelated items, until his death on September 28th, 1943 – likely related to Parkinson's Disease, which had plagued him in later years. He is buried in Gravesend.

If you enjoy Dr. Thorndyke, then you'll love
The MX Book of New Sherlock Holmes Stories
Edited by David Marcum
(MX Publishing, 2015-   )

"This is the finest volume of Sherlockian fiction I have ever read, and I have read, literally, thousands." – Philip K. Jones

"Beyond Impressive . . . This is a splendid venture for a great cause!
– Roger Johnson, Editor, *The Sherlock Holmes Journal,*
The Sherlock Holmes Society of London

The MX Book of New Sherlock Holmes Stories
Edited by David Marcum
(MX Publishing, 2015-   )

Publishers Weekly says:

Part VI: *The traditional pastiche is alive and well . . . .*

Part VII: *Sherlockians eager for faithful-to-the-canon plots and characters will be delighted.*

Part VIII: *The imagination of the contributors in coming up with variations on the volume's theme is matched by their ingenious resolutions.*

Part IX: *The 18 stories . . . will satisfy fans of Conan Doyle's originals. Sherlockians will rejoice that more volumes are on the way.*

Part X: *. . . new Sherlock Holmes adventures of consistently high quality.*

Part XI: *. . . an essential volume for Sherlock Holmes fans.*

Part XII: *. . . continues to amaze with the number of high-quality pastiches . . .*

Part XIII: *. . . Amazingly, Marcum has found 22 superb pastiches . . . This is more catnip for fans of stories faithful to Conan Doyle's original*

Part XIV: *. . . this standout anthology of 21 short stories written in the spirit of Conan Doyle's originals.*

Part XV: *Stories pitting Sherlock Holmes against seemingly supernatural phenomena highlight Marcum's 15th anthology of superior short pastiches.*

The MX Book of New Sherlock Holmes Stories
Edited by David Marcum
(MX Publishing, 2015-   )

Also From MX Publishing

Sherlock Holmes in Montague Street
by Arthur Morrison
Edited, Holmes-ed, and with Original Material
by David Marcum

Separate Paperback Editions

Combined Hardcover Edition

*"It's been suggested that Hewitt was the young Mycroft Holmes,
but David Marcum has a more plausible and attractive theory
– that he was Sherlock, early in his career as an investigator
... these are remarkably convincing in their new guise."*
– Roger Johnson, Editor, *The Sherlock Holmes Journal,*
The Sherlock Holmes Society of London

MX Publishing

MX Publishing is the world's largest specialist Sherlock Holmes publisher, with several hundred titles and over a hundred authors creating the latest in Sherlock Holmes fiction and non-fiction.

From traditional short stories and novels to travel guides and quiz books, MX Publishing caters to all Holmes fans.

The collection includes leading titles such as *Benedict Cumberbatch In Transition* and *The Norwood Author*, which won the 2011 *Tony Howlett Award* (Sherlock Holmes Book of the Year).

MX Publishing also has one of the largest communities of Holmes fans on *Facebook*, with regular contributions from dozens of authors.

www.mxpublishing.co.uk (UK) and *www.mxpublishing.com* (USA)